SEED TO HARVEST

SEED TO HARVEST

Wild Seed      *Clay's Ark*
Mind of My Mind   *Patternmaster*

OCTAVIA E. BUTLER

GRAND CENTRAL
PUBLISHING

NEW YORK   BOSTON

Grand Central Publishing Edition

Compilation copyright © 2007 by Octavia E. Butler
Wild Seed copyright © 1980 by Octavia E. Butler
Mind of My Mind copyright © 1977 by Octavia E. Butler
Clay's Ark copyright © 1984 by Octavia E. Butler
Patternmaster © 1976 by Octavia E. Butler

Grand Central Publishing
Hachette Book Group
237 Park Avenue
New York, NY 10017
www.HachetteBookGroup.com

This Grand Central Publishing edition is published by arrangement with the author.

Printed in the United States of America

First Hachette Book Group Edition: January 2007

10 9 8 7 6 5 4

Grand Central Publishing is a division of Hachette Book Group, Inc. The Grand Central Publishing name and logo is a trademark of Hachette Book Group, Inc.

LCCN: 2006928319

ISBN 978-0-446-69890-0

Book design by Stratford Publishing Services, Inc.
Cover design by Don Puckey/Julie Metz
Cover illustration by Herman Estevez

CONTENTS

Wild Seed   1

Mind of My Mind   255

Clay's Ark   453

Patternmaster   625

SEED TO HARVEST

WILD SEED

To Arthur Guy

To Ernestine Walker

To Phyllis White for listening.

BOOK ONE

Covenant
1690

Chapter One

Doro discovered the woman by accident when he went to see what was left of one of his seed villages. The village was a comfortable mud-walled place surrounded by grasslands and scattered trees. But Doro realized even before he reached it that its people were gone. Slavers had been to it before him. With their guns and their greed, they had undone in a few hours the work of a thousand years. Those villagers they had not herded away, they had slaughtered. Doro found human bones, hair, bits of desiccated flesh missed by scavengers. He stood over a very small skeleton—the bones of a child—and wondered where the survivors had been taken. Which country or New World colony? How far would he have to travel to find the remnants of what had been a healthy, vigorous people?

Finally, he stumbled away from the ruins bitterly angry, not knowing or caring where he went. It was a matter of pride with him that he protected his own. Not the individuals, perhaps, but the groups. They gave him their loyalty, their obedience, and he protected them.

He had failed.

He wandered southwest toward the forest, leaving as he had arrived—alone, unarmed, without supplies, accepting the savanna and later the forest as easily as he accepted any terrain. He was killed several times—by disease, by animals, by hostile people. This was a harsh land. Yet he continued to move southwest, unthinkingly veering away from the section of the coast where his ship awaited him. After a while, he realized it was no longer his anger at the loss of his seed village that drove him. It was something new—an impulse, a feeling, a kind of mental undertow pulling at him. He could have resisted it easily, but he did not. He felt there was something for him farther on, a little farther, just ahead. He trusted such feelings.

He had not been this far west for several hundred years, thus he could be certain that whatever, whoever he found would be new to him—new and potentially valuable. He moved on eagerly.

The feeling became sharper and finer, resolving itself into a kind of signal he would normally have expected to receive only from people he knew—people like his lost villagers whom he should be tracking now before they were forced to mix their seed with foreigners and breed away all the special qualities he valued in them. But he continued on southwest, closing slowly on his quarry.

Anyanwu's ears and eyes were far sharper than those of other people. She had increased their sensitivity deliberately after the first time men came stalking her, their machetes ready, their intentions clear. She had had to kill seven times on that terrible day—seven frightened men who could have been spared—and she had nearly died herself, all because she let people come upon her unnoticed. Never again.

Now, for instance, she was very much aware of the lone intruder who prowled the bush near her. He kept himself hidden, moved toward her like smoke, but she heard him, followed him with her ears.

Giving no outward sign, she went on tending her garden. As long as she knew where the intruder was, she had no fear of him. Perhaps he would lose his courage and go away. Meanwhile, there were weeds among her coco yams and her herbs. The herbs were not the traditional ones grown or gathered by her people. Only she grew them as medicines for healing, used them when people brought their sick to her. Often she needed no medicines, but she kept that to herself. She served her people by giving them relief from pain and sickness. Also, she enriched them by allowing them to spread word of her abilities to neighboring people. She was an oracle. A woman through whom a god spoke. Strangers paid heavily for her services. They paid her people, then they paid her. That was as it should have been. Her people could see that they benefited from her presence, and that they had reason to fear her abilities. Thus was she protected from them—and they from her—most of the time. But now and then one of them overcame his fear and found reason to try to end her long life.

The intruder was moving close, still not allowing her to see him. No person of honest intentions would approach so stealthily. Who was he then? A thief? A murderer? Someone who blamed her for the death of a kinsman or some other misfortune? During her various youths, she had been blamed several times for causing misfortune. She had been fed poison in the test for witchcraft. Each time, she had taken the test willingly, knowing that she had bewitched no one—and knowing that no ordinary man with his scanty knowledge of poisons could harm her. She knew more about poisons, had ingested more poisons in her long life than any of her people could imagine. Each time she passed the test, her accusers had been ridiculed and fined for their false charges. In each of her lives as she grew older, people ceased to accuse her—though not all ceased to believe she was a witch. Some sought to take matters into their own hands and kill her regardless of the tests.

The intruder finally moved onto the narrow path to approach her openly—now that he had had enough of spying on her. She looked up as though becoming aware of him for the first time.

He was a stranger, a fine man taller than most and broader at the shoulders. His skin was as dark as her own, and his face was broad and handsome, the mouth slightly smiling. He was young—not yet thirty, she thought. Surely too young to be any threat to her. Yet something about him worried her. His sudden openness after so much stealth, perhaps. Who was he? What did he want?

When he was near enough, he spoke to her, and his words made her frown in confusion. They were foreign words, completely incomprehensible to her, but there was a strange familiarity to them—as though she should have understood. She stood up, concealing uncharacteristic nervousness. "Who are you?" she asked.

He lifted his head slightly as she spoke, seemed to listen.

"How can we speak?" she asked. "You must be from very far away if your speech is so different."

"Very far," he said in her own language. His words were clear to her now, though he had an accent that reminded her of the way people spoke long ago when she was truly young. She did not like it. Everything about him made her uneasy.

"So you can speak," she said.

"I am remembering. It has been a long time since I spoke your language." He came closer, peering at her. Finally, he smiled and shook his head. "You are something more than an old woman," he said. "Perhaps you are not an old woman at all."

She drew back in confusion. How could he know anything of what she was? How could he even guess with nothing more than her appearance and a few words as evidence? "I am old," she said, masking her fear with anger. "I could be your mother's mother!" She could have been an ancestor of his mother's mother. But she kept that to herself. "Who are you?" she demanded.

"I could be your mother's father," he said.

She took another step backward, somehow controlling her growing fear. This man was not what he seemed to be. His words should have come to her as mocking nonsense, but instead, they seemed to reveal as much and as little as her own.

"Be still," he told her. "I mean you no harm."

"Who are you?" she repeated.

"Doro."

"Doro?" She said the strange word twice more. "Is that a name?"

"It is my name. Among my people, it means the east—the direction from which the sun comes."

She put one hand to her face. "This is a trick," she said. "Someone is laughing."

"You know better. When were you last frightened by a trick?"

Not for more years than she could remember; he was right. But the names... The coincidence was like a sign. "Do you know who I am?" she asked. "Did you come here knowing, or...?"

"I came here because of you. I knew nothing about you except that you were unusual and you were here. Awareness of you has pulled me a great distance out of my way."

"Awareness?"

"I had a feeling.... People as different as you attract me somehow, call me, even over great distances."

"I did not call you."

"You exist and you are different. That was enough to attract me. Now tell me who you are."

"You must be the only man in this country who has not heard of me. I am Anyanwu."

He repeated her name and glanced upward, understanding. Sun, her name meant. Anyanwu: the sun. He nodded. "Our peoples missed each other by many years and a great distance, Anyanwu, and yet somehow they named us well."

"As though we were intended to meet. Doro, who are your people?"

"They were called Kush in my time. Their land is far to the east of here. I was born to them, but they have not been my people for many years. I have not seen them for perhaps twelve times as long as you have been alive. When I was thirteen years old, I was separated from them. Now my people are those who give me their loyalty."

"And now you think you know my age," she said. "That is something my own people do not know."

"No doubt you have moved from town to town to help them forget." He looked around, saw a fallen tree nearby. He went to sit on it. Anyanwu followed almost against her will. As much as this man confused and frightened her, he also intrigued her. It had been so long since something had happened to her that had not happened before—many times before. He spoke again.

"I do nothing to conceal my age," he said, "yet some of my people have found it more comfortable to forget—since they can neither kill me nor become what I am."

She went closer to him and peered down at him. He was clearly proclaiming himself like her—long-lived and powerful. In all her years, she had not known even one other person like herself. She had long ago given up, accepted her solitude. But now...

"Go on talking," she said. "You have much to tell me."

He had been watching her, looking at her eyes with a curiosity that most people tried to hide from her. People said her eyes were like babies' eyes—the whites too white, the browns too deep and clear. No adult, and certainly no old woman should have such eyes, they said. And they avoided her gaze. Doro's eyes were very ordinary, but he could stare at her as children stared. He had no fear, and probably no shame.

He startled her by taking her hand and pulling her down beside him on the tree trunk. She could have broken his grip easily, but she did not. "I've come a long way today," he told her. "This body needs rest if it is to continue to serve me."

She thought about that. *This body needs rest.* What a strange way he had of speaking.

"I came to this territory last about three hundred years ago," he said. "I was looking for a group of my people who had strayed, but they were killed before I found them. Your people were not here then, and you had not been born. I know that because your difference did not call me. I think you are the fruit of my people's passing by yours, though."

"Do you mean that your people may be my kinsmen?"

"Yes." He was examining her face very carefully, perhaps seeking some resemblance. He would not find it. The face she was wearing was not her true face.

"Your people have crossed the Niger"—he hesitated, frowning, then gave the river its proper name—"the Orumili. When I saw them last, they lived on the other side in Benin."

"We crossed long ago," she said. "Children born in that time have grown old and died. We were Ado and Idu, subject to Benin before the crossing. Then we fought with Benin and crossed the river to Onitsha to become free people, our own masters."

"What happened to the Oze people who were here before you?"

"Some ran away. Others became our slaves."

"So you were driven from Benin, then you drove others from here—or enslaved them."

Anyanwu looked away, spoke woodenly. "It is better to be a master than to be a slave." Her husband at the time of the migration had said that. He had seen himself becoming a great man—master of a large household with many wives, children, and slaves. Anyanwu, on the other hand, had been a slave twice in her life and had escaped only by changing her identity completely and finding a husband in a different town. She knew some people were masters and some were slaves. That was the way it had always been. But her own experience had taught her to hate slavery. She had even found it difficult to be a good wife in her most recent years because of the way a woman must bow her head and be subject to her husband. It was better to be as she was—a priestess who spoke with the voice of a god and was feared and obeyed. But what was that? She had become a kind of master herself. "Sometimes, one must become a master to avoid becoming a slave," she said softly.

"Yes," he agreed.

She deliberately turned her attention to the new things he had given her to think about. Her age, for instance. He was right. She was about three hundred years old—something none of her people would have believed. And he had said something else—something that brought alive one of her oldest memories. There had been whispers when she was a girl that her father could not beget children, that she was the daughter not only of another man, but of a visiting stranger. She had asked her mother about this, and for the first and only time in her life, her mother had struck her. From then on, she had accepted the story as true. But she had never been able to learn anything about the stranger. She would not have cared—her mother's husband claimed her as his daughter and he was a good man—but she had always wondered whether the stranger's people were more like her.

"Are they all dead?" she asked Doro. "These... kinsmen of mine?"

"Yes."

"Then they were not like me."

"They might have been after many more generations. You are not only their child. Your Onitsha kinsmen must have been unusual in their own right."

Anyanwu nodded slowly. She could think of several unusual things about her mother. The woman had stature and influence in spite of the gossip about her. Her husband was a member of a highly respected clan, well known for its magical abilities, but in his household, it was Anyanwu's mother who made magic. She had highly accurate prophetic dreams. She made medicine to cure disease and to protect the people from evil. At market, no woman was a better trader. She seemed to know just how to bargain—as though she could read the thoughts in the other women's minds. She became very wealthy.

It was said that Anyanwu's clan, the clan of her mother's husband, had members who could change their shapes, take animal forms at will, but Anyanwu had seen no such strangeness in them. It was her mother in whom she found strangeness, closeness, empathy that went beyond what could be expected between mother and daughter. She and her mother had shared a unity of spirit that actually did involve some exchange of thoughts and feelings, though they were careful not to flaunt this before others. If Anyanwu felt pain, her mother, busy trading at some distant market, knew of the pain and came home. Anyanwu had no more than ghosts of that early closeness with her own children and with three of her husbands. And she had sought for years through her clan, her mother's clan, and others for even a ghost of her greatest difference, the shape changing. She had collected many frightening stories, but had met no other person who, like herself, could demonstrate this ability. Not until now, perhaps. She looked at Doro. What was it she felt about him—what strangeness? She had shared no thoughts with him, but something about him reminded her of her mother. Another ghost.

"Are you my kinsman?" she asked.

"No," he said. "But your kinsmen had given me their loyalty. That is no small thing."

"Is that why you came when... when my difference attracted you?"

He shook his head. "I came to see what you were."

She frowned, suddenly cautious. "I am myself. You see me."

"As you see me. Do you imagine you see everything?"

She did not answer.

"A lie offends me, Anyanwu, and what I see of you is a lie. Show me what you really are."

"You see what you will see!"

"Are you afraid to show me?"

"... No." It was not fear. What was it? A lifetime of concealment, of commanding herself never to play with her abilities before others, never to show them off as mere tricks, never to let her people or any people know the full extent of her power unless she were fighting for her life. Should she break her tradition now simply because this stranger asked her to? He had done much talking, but what had he actually shown her about himself? Nothing.

"Can my concealment be a lie if yours is not?" she asked.

"Mine is," he admitted.

"Then show me what you are. Give me the trust you ask me to give you."

"You have my trust, Anyanwu, but knowing what I am would only frighten you."

"Am I a child then?" she asked angrily. "Are you my mother who must shield me from adult truths?"

He refused to be insulted. "Most of my people are grateful to me for shielding them from my particular truth," he said.

"So you say. I have seen nothing."

He stood up, and she stood to face him, her small withered body fully in the shadow of his. She was little more than half his size, but it was no new thing for her to face larger people and either bend them to her will with words or beat them into submission physically. In fact, she could have made herself as large as any man, but she chose to let her smallness go on deceiving people. Most often, it put strangers at their ease because she seemed harmless. Also, it caused would-be attackers to underestimate her.

Doro stared down at her. "Sometimes only a burn will teach a child to respect fire," he said. "Come with me to one of the villages of your town, Anyanwu. There I will show you what you think you want to see."

"What will you do?" she asked warily.

"I will let you choose someone—an enemy or only some useless person that your people would be better without. Then I will kill him."

"Kill!"

"I kill, Anyanwu. That is how I keep my youth, my strength. I can do only one thing to show you what I am, and that is kill a man and wear his body like a cloth." He breathed deeply. "This is not the body I was born into. It's not the tenth I've worn, nor the hundredth, nor the thousandth. Your gift seems to be a gentle one. Mine is not."

"You are a spirit," she cried in alarm.

"I told you you were a child," he said. "See how you frighten yourself?"

He was like an ogbanje, an evil child spirit born to one woman again and again, only to die and give the mother pain. A woman tormented by an ogbanje could give birth many times and still have no living child. But Doro was an adult. He did not enter and re-enter his mother's womb. He did not want the bodies of children. He preferred to steal the bodies of men.

"You are a spirit!" she insisted, her voice shrill with fear. All the while part of her mind wondered why she was believing him so easily. She knew many tricks herself, many frightening lies. Why should she react now like the most ignorant stranger brought before her believing that a god spoke through her? Yet she did believe, and she was afraid. This man was far more unusual than she was. This man was not a man.

When he touched her arm lightly, unexpectedly, she screamed.

He made a sound of disgust. "Woman, if you bring your people here with your noise, I will have no choice but to kill some of them."

She stood still, believing this also. "Did you kill anyone as you came here?" she whispered.

"No. I went to great trouble to avoid killing for your sake. I thought you might have kinsmen here."

"Generations of kinsmen. Sons and their sons and even their sons."

"I would not want to kill one of your sons."

"Why?" She was relieved but curious. "What are they to you?"

"How would you receive me if I came to you clothed in the flesh of one of your sons?"

She drew back, not knowing how to imagine such a thing.

"You see? Your children should not be wasted anyway. They may be good—" He spoke a word in another language. She heard it clearly, but it meant nothing to her. The word was *seed*.

"What is seed?" she asked.

"People too valuable to be casually killed," he said. Then more softly, "You must show me what you are."

"How can my sons be of value to you?"

He gave her a long silent look, then spoke with that same softness. "I may have to go to them, Anyanwu. They may be more tractable than their mother."

She could not recall ever having been threatened so gently—or so effectively. Her sons... "Come," she whispered. "It is too open for me to show you here."

With concealed excitement, Doro followed the small, wizened woman to her tiny compound. The compound wall—made of red clay and over six feet high—would give them the privacy Anyanwu wanted.

"My sons would do you no good," she told him as they walked. "They are good men, but they know very little."

"They are not like you—any of them?"

"None."

"And your daughters?"

"Nor them. I watched them carefully until they went away to their husbands' towns. They are like my mother. They exert great influence on their husbands and on other women, but nothing beyond that. They live their lives and they die."

"They die...?"

She opened the wooden door and led him through the wall, then barred the door after him.

"They die," she said sadly. "Like their fathers."

"Perhaps if your sons and daughters married each other..."

"Abomination!" she said with alarm. "We are not animals here, Doro!"

He shrugged. He had spent most of his life ignoring such protests and causing the protestors to change their minds. People's morals rarely survived confrontations with him. For now, though, gentleness. This woman was valuable. If she were only half as old as he thought, she would be the oldest person he had ever met—and she was still spry. She was descended from people whose abnormally long lives, resistance to disease, and budding special abilities made them very important to him. People who, like so many others, had fallen victim to slavers or tribal enemies. There had been so few of

them. Nothing must happen to this one survivor, this fortunate little hybrid. Above all, she must be protected from Doro himself. He
must not kill her out of anger or by accident—and accidents could
happen so easily in this country. He must take her away with him
to one of his more secure seed towns. Perhaps in her strangeness,
she could still bear young, and perhaps with the powerful mates he
could get her, this time her children would be worthy of her. If not,
there were always her existing children.

"Will you watch, Doro?" she asked. "This is what you demanded
to see."

He focused his attention on her, and she began to rub her hands.
The hands were bird claws, long-fingered, withered, and bony. As he
watched, they began to fill out, to grow smooth and young-looking.
Her arms and shoulders began to fill out and her sagging breasts
drew themselves up round and high. Her hips grew round beneath
her cloth, causing him to want to strip the cloth from her. Lastly,
she touched her face and molded away her wrinkles. An old scar
beneath one eye vanished. The flesh became smooth and firm, and
the woman startlingly beautiful.

Finally, she stood before him looking not yet twenty. She cleared
her throat and spoke to him in a soft, young woman's voice. "Is this
enough?"

For a moment he could only stare at her. "Is this truly you,
Anyanwu?"

"As I am. As I would always be if I did not age or change myself
for others. This shape flows back to me very easily. Others are harder
to take."

"Others!"

"Did you think I could take only one?" She began molding
her malleable body into another shape. "I took animal shapes
to frighten my people when they wanted to kill me," she said.
"I became a leopard and spat at them. They believe in such things,
but they do not like to see them proved. Then I became a sacred
python, and no one dared to harm me. The python shape brought
me luck. We were needing rain then to save the yam crop, and while
I was a python, the rains came. The people decided my magic was
good and it took them a long time to want to kill me again." She
was becoming a small, well-muscled man as she spoke.

Now Doro did try to strip away her cloth, moving slowly so that she would understand. He felt her strength for a moment when she caught his hand and, with no special effort, almost broke it. Then, as he controlled his surprise, prevented himself from reacting to the pain, she untied her cloth herself and took it off. For several seconds, he was more impressed with that casual grip than with her body, but he could not help noticing that she had become thoroughly male.

"Could you father a child?" he asked.

"In time. Not now."

"Have you?"

"Yes. But only girl children."

He shook his head, laughing. The woman was far beyond anything he had imagined. "I'm surprised your people have let you live," he said.

"Do you think I would let them kill me?" she asked.

He laughed again. "What will you do then, Anyanwu? Stay here with them, convincing each new generation that you are best let alone—or will you come with me?"

She tied her cloth around her again, then stared at him, her large too-clear eyes looking deceptively gentle in her young man's face. "Is that what you want?" she asked. "For me to go with you?"

"Yes."

"That is your true reason for coming here then."

He thought he heard fear in her voice, and his throbbing hand convinced him that she must not be unduly frightened. She was too powerful. She might force him to kill her. He spoke honestly.

"I let myself be drawn here because people who had pledged loyalty to me had been taken away in slavery," he said. "I went to their village to get them, take them to a safer home, and I found... only what the slavers had left. I went away, not caring where my feet took me. When they brought me here, I was surprised, and for the first time in many days, I was pleased."

"It seems your people are often taken from you."

"It does not seem so, it is so. That is why I am gathering them all closer together in a new place. It will be easier for me to protect them there."

"I have always protected myself."

"I can see that. You will be very valuable to me. I think you could protect others as well as yourself."

"Shall I leave my people to help you protect yours?"

"You should leave so that finally you can be with your own kind."

"With one who kills men and shrouds himself in their skins? We are not alike, Doro."

Doro sighed, looked over at her house—a small, rectangular building whose steeply sloping thatched roof dipped to within a few feet of the ground. Its walls were made of the same red earth as the compound wall. He wondered obscurely whether the red earth was the same clay he had seen in Indian dwellings in southwestern parts of the North American continent. But more immediately, he wondered whether there were couches in Anyanwu's house, and food and water. He was almost too tired and hungry to go on arguing with the woman.

"Give me food, Anyanwu," he said. "Then I will have the strength to entice you away from this place."

She looked startled, then laughed almost reluctantly. It occurred to him that she did not want him to stay and eat, did not want him to stay at all. She believed the things he had told her, and she feared that he could entice her away. She wanted him to leave—or part of her did. Surely there was another part that was intrigued, that wondered what would happen if she left her home, walked away with this stranger. She was too alert, too alive not to have the kind of mind that probed and reached and got her into trouble now and then.

"A bit of yam, at least, Anyanwu," he said smiling. "I have eaten nothing today." He knew she would feed him.

Without a word, she walked away to another smaller building and returned with two large yams. Then she led him into her kitchen and gave him a deerskin to sit on since he carried nothing other than the cloth around his loins. Still in her male guise, she courteously shared a kola nut and a little palm wine with him. Then she began to prepare food. Besides the yams, she had vegetables, smoked fish, and palm oil. She built up a fire from the live coals in the tripod of stones that formed her hearth, then put a clay pot of water on to boil. She began to peel the yams. She would cut them up and boil the pieces until they were tender enough to be pounded as her people liked them. Perhaps she would make soup of the vegetables, oil, and fish, but that would take time.

"What do you do?" she asked him as she worked. "Steal food when you are hungry?"

"Yes," he said. He stole more than food. If there were no people he knew near him, or if he went to people he knew and they did not welcome him, he simply took a new strong, young body. No person, no group could stop him from doing this. No one could stop him from doing anything at all.

"A thief," said Anyanwu with disgust that he did not think was quite real. "You steal, you kill. What else do you do?"

"I build," he said quietly. "I search the land for people who are a little different—or very different. I search them out, I bring them together in groups, I begin to build them into a strong new people."

She stared at him in surprise. "They let you do this—let you take them from their people, their families?"

"Some bring their families with them. Many do not have families. Their differences have made them outcasts. They are glad to follow me."

"Always?"

"Often enough," he said.

"What happens when people will not follow you? What happens if they say, 'It seems too many of your people are dying, Doro. We will stay where we are and live.'"

He got up and went to the doorway of the next room where two hard but inviting clay couches had been built out from the walls. He had to sleep. In spite of the youth and strength of the body he was wearing, it was only an ordinary body. If he were careful with it—gave it proper rest and food, did not allow it to be injured—it would last him a few more weeks. If he drove it, though, as he had been driving it to reach Anyanwu, he would use it up much sooner. He held his hands before him, palms down, and was not surprised to see that they were shaking.

"Anyanwu, I must sleep. Wake me when the food is ready."

"Wait!"

The sharpness of her voice stopped him, made him look back.

"Answer," she said. "What happens when people will not follow you?"

Was that all? He ignored her, climbed onto one of the couches, lay down on the mat that covered it, and closed his eyes. He thought he heard her come into the room and go out again before he drifted off to sleep, but he paid no attention. He had long ago discovered that people were much more cooperative if he made them answer questions like hers for themselves. Only the stupid actually needed to hear his answer, and this woman was not stupid.

When she woke him, the house was full of the odor of food and he got up alert and ravenous. He sat with her, washed his hands absently in the bowl of water she gave him, then used his fingers to scoop up a bit of pounded yam from his platter and dip it into the common pot of peppery soup. The food was good and filling, and for some time he concentrated on it, ignoring Anyanwu except to notice that she was also eating and did not seem inclined to talk. He recalled distantly that there had been some small religious ceremony between the washing of hands and the eating when he had last been with her people. An offering of food and palm wine to the gods. He asked about it once he had taken the edge off his hunger.

She glanced at him. "What gods do you respect?"

"None."

"And why not?"

"I help myself," he said.

She nodded. "In at least two ways, you do. I help myself too."

He smiled a little, but could not help wondering how hard it might be to tame even partially a wild seed woman who had been helping herself for three hundred years. It would not be hard to make her follow him. She had sons and she cared for them, thus she was vulnerable. But she might very well make him regret taking her—especially since she was too valuable to kill if he could possibly spare her.

"For my people," she said, "I respect the gods. I speak as the voice of a god. For myself... In my years, I have seen that people must be their own gods and make their own good fortune. The bad will come or not come anyway."

"You are very much out of place here."

She sighed. "Everything comes back to that. I am content here, Doro. I have already had ten husbands to tell me what to do. Why should I make you the eleventh? Because you will kill me if I refuse? Is that how men get wives in your homeland—by threatening murder? Well, perhaps you cannot kill me. Perhaps we should find out!"

He ignored her outburst, noticed instead that she had automatically assumed that he wanted her as his wife. That was a natural assumption for her to make, perhaps a correct assumption. He had been asking himself which of his people she should be mated with first, but now he knew he would take her himself—for a while, at least. He often kept the most powerful of his people with him for a few months, perhaps a year. If they were children, they learned to accept him as father. If they were men, they learned to obey him as master. If they were women, they accepted him best as lover or husband. Anyanwu was one of the handsomest women he had ever seen. He had intended to take her to bed this night, and many more nights until he got her to the seed village he was assembling in the British-ruled Colony of New York. But why should that be enough? The woman was a rare find. He spoke softly.

"Shall I try to kill you then, Anyanwu? Why? Would you kill me if you could?"

"Perhaps I can!"

"Here I am." He looked at her with eyes that ignored the male form she still wore. Eyes that spoke to the woman inside—or he hoped they did. It would be much more pleasant to have her come to him because she wanted to rather than because she was afraid.

She said nothing—as though his mildness confused her. He had intended it to.

"We would be right together, Anyanwu. Have you never wanted a husband who was worthy of you?"

"You think very much of yourself."

"And of you—or why would I be here?"

"I have had husbands who were great men," she said. "Titled men of proven courage even though they had no special ability such as yours. I have sons who are priests, wealthy sons, men of standing. Why should I want a husband who must prey on other men like a wild beast?"

He touched his chest. "This man came to prey on me. He attacked me with a machete."

That stopped her for a moment. She shuddered. "I have been cut that way—cut almost in half."

"What did you do?"

"I... I healed myself. I would not have thought I could heal so quickly."

"I mean what did you do to the man who cut you?"

"Men. Seven of them came to kill me."

"What did you do, Anyanwu?"

She seemed to shrink into herself at the memory. "I killed them," she whispered. "To warn others and because... because I was angry."

Doro sat watching her, seeing remembered pain in her eyes. He could not recall the last time he had felt pain at killing a man. Anger, perhaps, when a man of power and potential became arrogant and had to be destroyed—anger at the waste. But not pain.

"You see?" he said softly. "How did you kill them?"

"With my hands." She spread them before her, ordinary hands now, not even remarkably ugly as they had been when she was an old woman. "I was angry," she repeated. "I have been careful not to get too angry since then."

"But what did you do?"

"Why do you want to know all the shameful details!" she demanded. "I killed them. They are dead. They were my people and I killed them!"

"How can it be shameful to kill those who would have killed you?"

She said nothing.

"Surely those seven are not the only ones you've killed."

She sighed, stared into the fire. "I frighten them when I can, kill only when they make me. Most often, they are already afraid and easy to drive away. I am making the ones here rich so that none of them have wanted me dead for years."

"Tell me how you killed the seven."

She got up and went outside. It was dark out now—deep, moonless darkness, but Doro did not doubt that Anyanwu could see with those eyes of hers. Where had she gone, though, and why?

She came back, sat down again, and handed him a rock. "Break it," she said tonelessly.

It was a rock, not hardened mud, and though he might have broken it with another rock or metal tool, he could make no impression on it with his hands. He returned it to her whole.

And she crushed it in one hand.

He had to have the woman. She was wild seed of the best kind. She would strengthen any line he bred her into, strengthen it immeasurably.

"Come with me, Anyanwu. You belong with me, with the people I'm gathering. We are people you can be part of—people you need not frighten or bribe into letting you live."

"I was born among these people," she said. "I belong with them." And she insisted, "You and I are not alike."

"We are more like each other than like other people. We need not hide from each other." He looked at her muscular young man's body. "Become a woman again, Anyanwu, and I will show you that we should be together."

She managed a wan smile. "I have borne forty-seven children to ten husbands," she said. "What do you think you can show me?"

"If you come with me, I think someday, I can show you children you will never have to bury." He paused, saw that he now had her full attention. "A mother should not have to watch her children grow old and die," he continued. "If you live, they should live. It is the fault of their fathers that they die. Let me give you children who will live!"

She put her hands to her face, and for a moment he thought she was crying. But her eyes were dry when she looked at him. "Children from your stolen loins?" she whispered.

"Not these loins." He gestured toward his body. "This man was only a man. But I promise you, if you come with me, I will give you children of your own kind."

There was a long silence. She sat staring into the fire again, perhaps making up her mind. Finally, she looked at him, studied him with such intensity he began to feel uncomfortable. His discomfort amazed him. He was more accustomed to making other people uncomfortable. And he did not like her appraising stare—as though she were deciding whether or not to buy him. If he could win her alive, he would teach her manners someday!

It was not until she began to grow breasts that he knew for certain he had won. He got up then, and when the change was complete, he took her to the couch.

Chapter Two

They arose before dawn the next day. Anyanwu gave Doro a machete and took one for herself. She seemed content as she put a few of her belongings into a long basket to be carried with her. Now that she had made her decision, she expressed no more doubts about leaving with him, though she was concerned for her people.

"You must let me guide you past the villages," she told him. She again wore the guise of a young man, and had twisted her cloth around her and between her legs in the way of a man. "There are villages all around me here so that no stranger can reach me without paying. You were fortunate to reach me without being stopped. Or perhaps my people were fortunate. I must see that they are fortunate again."

He nodded. As long as she kept him going in the right direction, she could lead as long as she wanted to. She had given him pounded yam from the night before to break his fast, and during the night, she had managed to exhaust his strong young body with lovemaking. "You are a good man," she had observed contentedly. "And it has been too long since I had this."

He was surprised to realize how much her small compliment pleased him—how much the woman herself pleased him. She was a worthwhile find in many ways. He watched her take a last look at her house, left swept and neat; at her compound, airy and pleasant in spite of its smallness. He wondered how many years this had been her home.

"My sons helped me build this place," she told him softly. "I told them I needed a place apart where I could be free to make my medicines. All but one of them came to help me. That one was my oldest living son, who said I must live in his compound. He was surprised when I ignored him. He is wealthy and arrogant and used to being listened to even when what he says is nonsense—as it often is. He did not understand anything about me, so I showed him a little of what I have shown you. Only a little. It closed his mouth."

"It would," laughed Doro.

"He is a very old man now. I think he is the only one of my sons who will not miss me. He will be glad to find me gone—like some others of my people, even though I have made them rich. Few of them living now are old enough to remember my great changes here—from woman to leopard to python. They have only their legends and their fear." She got two yams and put them into her basket, then got several more and threw them to her goats, who scrambled first to escape them, then to get them. "They have never eaten so well," she said laughing. Then she sobered, went to a small shelter where clay figurines representing gods sat.

"This is for my people to see," she told Doro. "This and the ones inside." She gestured toward her house.

"I did not see any inside."

Her eyes seemed to smile through her somber expression. "You almost sat on them."

Startled, he thought back. He usually tried not to outrage people's religious beliefs too quickly, though Anyanwu did not seem to have many religious beliefs. But to think he had come near sitting on religious objects without recognizing them . . .

"Do you mean those clay lumps in the corner?"

"Those," she said simply. "My mothers."

Symbols of ancestral spirits. He remembered now. He shook his head. "I am getting careless," he said in English.

"What are you saying?"

"That I am sorry. I've been away from your people too long."

"It does not matter. As I said, these things are for others to see. I must lie a little, even here."

"No more," he said.

"This town will think I am finally dead," she said staring at the figurines. "Perhaps they will make a shrine and give it my name.

Other towns have done that. Then at night when they see shadows and branches blowing in the wind they can tell each other they have seen my spirit."

"A shrine with spirits will frighten them less than the living woman, I think," Doro said.

Not quite smiling, Anyanwu led him through the compound door, and they began the long trek over a maze of footpaths so narrow that they could walk only in single file between the tall trees. Anyanwu carried her basket on her head and her machete sheathed at her side. Her bare feet and Doro's made almost no sound on the path—nothing to confuse Anyanwu's sensitive ears. Several times as they moved along at the pace she set—a swift walk—she turned aside and slipped silently into the bush. Doro followed with equal skill and always shortly afterward people passed by. There were women and children bearing water pots or firewood on their heads. There were men carrying hoes and machetes. It was as Anyanwu had said. They were in the middle of her town, surrounded by villages. No European would have recognized a town, however, since most of the time there were no dwellings in sight. But on his way to her, Doro had stumbled across the villages, across one large compound after another and either slipped past them or walked past boldly as though he had legitimate business. Fortunately, no one had challenged him. People often hesitated to challenge a man who seemed important and purposeful. They would not, however, have hesitated to challenge strangers who hid themselves, who appeared to be spying. As Doro followed Anyanwu now, he worried that he still might wind up wearing the body of one of her kinsmen—and having great trouble with her. He was relieved when she told him they had left her people's territory behind.

At first, Anyanwu was able to lead Doro along already cleared paths through territory she knew either because she had once lived in it or because her daughters lived in it now. Once, as they walked, she was telling him about a daughter who had married a handsome, strong, lazy young man, then run away to a much less imposing man who had some ambition. He listened for a while, then asked: "How many of your children lived to adulthood, Anyanwu?"

"Every one," she said proudly. "They were all strong and well and had no forbidden things wrong with them."

Children with "forbidden" things wrong with them—twins, for instance, and children born feet first, children with almost any deformity, children born with teeth—these children were thrown away. Doro had gotten some of his best stock from earlier cultures who, for one reason or another, put infants out to die.

"You had forty-seven children," he said in disbelief, "and all of them lived and were perfect?"

"Perfect in their bodies, at least. They all survived."

"They are my people's children! Perhaps some of them and their descendants should come with us after all."

Anyanwu stopped so suddenly that he almost ran into her. "You will not trouble my children," she said quietly.

He stared down at her—she had still not bothered to make herself taller though she told him she could—and tried to swallow sudden anger. She spoke to him as though he were one of her children. She did not yet understand his power!

"I am here," she said in the same quiet voice. "You have me."

"Do I?"

"As much as any man could."

That stopped him. There was no challenge in her voice, but he realized at once she was not telling him she was all his—his property. She was saying only that he had whatever small part of herself she reserved for her men. She was not used to men who could demand more. Though she came from a culture in which wives literally belonged to their husbands, she had power and her power had made her independent, accustomed to being her own person. She did not yet realize that she had walked away from that independence when she walked away from her people with him.

"Let's go on," he said.

But she did not move. "You have something to tell me," she said. He sighed. "Your children are safe, Anyanwu." For the moment.

She turned and led on. Doro followed, thinking that he had better get her with a new child as quickly as he could. Her independence would vanish without a struggle. She would do whatever he asked then to keep her child safe. She was too valuable to kill, and if he abducted any of her descendants, she would no doubt goad him into killing her. But once she was isolated in America with an infant to care for, she would learn submissiveness.

* * *

Paths became occasional luxuries as they moved into country Anyanwu did not know. More and more, they had to use their machetes
to clear the way. Streams became a problem. They flowed swiftly
through deep gorges that had to be crossed somehow. Where the
streams interrupted footpaths, local people had placed log bridges.
But where Doro and Anyanwu found neither paths nor bridges, they
had to cut their own logs. Travel became slower and more dangerous.
A fall would not have killed either of them directly, but Doro knew
that if he fell, he would not be able to stop himself from taking over
Anyanwu's body. She was too close to him. On his way north, he had
crossed several rivers by simply abandoning his body and taking over
the body nearest to him on the far side. And since he was leading
now, allowing his tracking sense to draw him to the crew aboard his
ship, he could not send her ahead or leave her behind. He would
not have wanted to anyway. They were in the country of people who
waged war to get slaves to sell to the Europeans. These were people
who would cut her to pieces if she began reshaping herself before
them. Some of them even had European guns and powder.

Their slow progress was not a complete waste of time, though. It
gave him a chance to learn more about Anyanwu—and there was
more to learn. He discovered that he would not have to steal food
while she was with him. Once the two yams were roasted and eaten,
she found food everywhere. Each day as they traveled, she filled her
basket with fruit, nuts, roots, whatever she could find that was edible. She threw stones with the speed and force of a sling and brought
down birds and small animals. At day's end, there was always a
hearty meal. If a plant was unfamiliar to her she tasted it and sensed
within herself whether or not it was poison. She ate several things she
said were poison, though none of them seemed to harm her. But she
never gave him anything other than good food. He ate whatever she
gave him, trusting her abilities. And when a small cut on his hand
became infected, she gave him even more reason to trust her.

The infected hand had begun to swell by the time she noticed
it, and it was beginning to make him sick. He was already deciding
how he would get a new body without endangering her. Then, to
his surprise, she offered to help him heal.

"You should have told me," she said. "You let yourself suffer needlessly."

He looked at her doubtfully. "Can you get the herbs you need out here?"

She met his eyes. "Sometimes the herbs were for my people—like the gods in my compound. If you will let me, I can help you without them."

"All right." He gave her his swollen, inflamed hand.

"There will be pain," she warned.

"All right," he repeated.

She bit his hand.

He bore it, holding himself rigid against his own deadly reaction to sudden pain. She had done well to warn him. This was the second time she had been nearer to death than she could imagine.

For a time after biting him, she did nothing. Her attention seemed to turn inward, and she did not answer when he spoke to her. Finally, she brought his hand to her mouth again and there was more pain and pressure, but no more biting. She spat three times, each time returning to his hand, then she seemed to caress the wound with her tongue. Her saliva burned like fire. After that she kept a watch on the hand, attending it twice more with that startling, burning pain. Almost at once, the swelling and sickness went away and the wound began to heal.

"There were things in your hand that should not have been there," she told him. "Living things too small to see. I have no name for them, but I can feel them and know them when I take them into my body. As soon as I know them, I can kill them within myself. I gave you a little of my body's weapon against them."

Tiny living things too small to see, but large enough to make him sick. If his wound had not begun to heal so quickly and cleanly, he would not have believed a word she said. As it was, though, his trust in her grew. She was a witch, surely. In any culture she would be feared. She would have to fight to keep her life. Even sensible people who did not believe in witches would turn against her. And Doro, breeder of witches that he was, realized all over again what a treasure she was. Nothing, no one, must prevent his keeping her.

It was not until he reached one of his contacts near the coast that someone decided to try.

Anyanwu never told Doro that she could jump all but the widest of the rivers they had to cross. She thought at first that he might guess because he had seen the strength of her hands. Her legs and thighs were just as powerful. But Doro was not used to thinking as she did about her abilities, not used to taking her strength or metamorphosing ability for granted. He never guessed, never asked what she could do.

She kept silent because she feared that he too could leap the gorges—though in doing so, he might leave his body behind. She did not want to see him kill for so small a reason. She had listened to the stories he told as they traveled, and it seemed to her that he killed too easily. Far too easily—unless the stories were lies. She did not think they were. She did not know whether he would take a life just to get across a river quickly, but she feared he might. This made her begin to think of escaping from him. It made her think long-ingly of her people, her compound, her home....

Yet she made herself womanly for him at night. He never had to ask her to do this. She did it because she wanted to, because in spite of her doubts and fears, he pleased her very much. She went to him as she had gone to her first husband, a man for whom she had cared deeply, and to her surprise, Doro treated her much as her first husband had. He listened with respect to her opinions and spoke with respect and friendship as though to another man. Her first husband had taken much secret ridicule for treating her this way. Her second husband had been arrogant, contemptuous, and brutal, yet he had been considered a great man. She had run away from him as she now wished to run away from Doro. Doro could not have known what dissimilar men he brought alive in her memory.

He had still given her no proof of the power he claimed, no proof that her children would be in danger from other than an ordinary man if she managed to escape. Yet she continued to believe him. She could not bring herself to get up while he slept and vanish into the forest. For her children's sake she had to stay with him, at least until she had proof one way or the other.

She followed him almost grimly, wondering what it would be like

finally to be married to a man she could neither escape nor outlive.
The prospect made her cautious and gentle. Her earlier husbands
would not have known her. She sought to make him value her and
care for her. Thus she might have some leverage with him, some
control over him later when she needed it. Much married as she
was, she knew she would eventually need it.

They were in the lowlands now, passing through wetter country.
There was more rain, more heat, many more mosquitoes. Doro got
some disease and coughed and coughed. Anyanwu got a fever, but
drove it out of herself as soon as she sensed it. There was enough
misery to be had without sickness.

"When do we pass through this land!" she asked in disgust. It was
raining now. They were on someone's pathway laboring through
sucking ankle-deep mud.

"There is a river not far ahead of us," he told her. He stopped for
a moment to cough. "I have an arrangement with people at a river-
side town. They will take us the rest of the way by canoe."

"Strangers," she said with alarm. They had managed to avoid
contact with most of the people whose lands they had crossed.

"You will be the stranger here," Doro told her. "But you need not
worry. These people know me. I have given them gifts—dash, they
call it—and promised them more if they rowed my people down
the river."

"Do they know you in this body?" she asked, using the question
as an excuse to touch the hard flat muscle of his shoulder. She liked
to touch him.

"They know me," he said. "I am not the body I wear, Anyanwu.
You will understand that when I change—soon, I think." He paused
for another fit of coughing. "You will know me in another body as
soon as you hear me speak."

"How?" She did not want to talk about his changing, his killing.
She had tried to cure his sickness so that he would not change, but
though she had eased his coughing, prevented him from growing
sicker, she had not made him well. That meant she might soon be
finding out more about his changing whether she wanted to or not.
"How will I know you?" she asked.

"There are no words for me to tell you—as with your tiny living
things. When you hear my voice, you will know me. That's all."

"Will it be the same voice?"

"No."

"Then how...?"

"Anyanwu..." He glanced around at her. "I am telling you, you will know!"

Startled, she kept silent. She believed him. How was it she always believed him?

The village he took her to was a small place that seemed not much different from waterside communities she had known nearer home. Here some of the people stared at her and at Doro, but no one molested them. She heard speech here and there and sometimes it had a familiar sound to it. She thought she might understand a little if she could go closer to the speakers and listen. As it was, she understood nothing. She felt exposed, strangely helpless among people so alien. She walked closely behind Doro.

He led her to a large compound and into that compound as though it belonged to him. A tall, lean young man confronted him at once. The young man spoke to Doro and when Doro answered, the young man's eyes widened. He took a step backward.

Doro continued to speak in the strange language, and Anyanwu discovered that she could understand a few words—but not enough to follow the conversation. This language was at least more like her own than the new speech, the *English*, Doro was teaching her. English was one of the languages spoken in his homeland, he had told her. She had to learn it. Now, though, she gathered what she could from the unspoken language of the two men, from their faces and voices. It was obvious that instead of the courteous greeting Doro had expected, he was getting an argument from the young man. Finally, Doro turned away in disgust. He spoke to Anyanwu.

"The man I dealt with before has died," he told her. "This fool is his son." He stopped to cough. "The son was present when his father and I bargained. He saw the gifts I brought. But now that his father has died, he feels no obligation to me."

"I think he fears you," Anyanwu said. The young man was blustering and arrogant; that she could see despite the different languages. He was trying hard to seem important. As he spoke, though, his eyes shifted and darted and looked at Doro only in brief glances. His hands shook.

"He knows he is doing a dangerous thing," Doro said. But he is young. His father was a king. Now the son thinks he will use me to prove himself. He has chosen a poor target."

"Have you promised him more gifts?"

"Yes. But he sees only my empty hands. Move away from me, Anyanwu, I have no more patience."

She wanted to protest, but her mouth was suddenly dry. Frightened and silent, she stumbled backward away from him. She did not know what to expect, but she was certain the young man would be killed. How would he die? Exactly what would Doro do?

Doro stepped past the young man and toward a boy-child of about seven years who had been watching the men talk. Before the young man or the child could react, Doro collapsed.

His body fell almost on top of the boy, but the child jumped out of the way in time. Then he knelt on the ground and took Doro's machete. People were beginning to react as the boy stood up and leaned on the machete. The sounds of their questioning voices and their gathering around almost drowned out the child's voice when he spoke to the young man. Almost.

The child spoke calmly, quietly in his own language, but as Anyanwu heard him, she thought she would scream aloud. The child was Doro. There was no doubt of it. Doro's spirit had entered the child's body. And what had happened to the child's spirit? She looked at the body lying on the ground, then she went to it, turned it over. It was dead.

"What have you done?" she said to the child.

"This man knew what his arrogance could cost," Doro said. And his voice was high and childlike. There was no sound of the man Doro had been. Anyanwu did not understand what she was hearing, what she was recognizing in the boy's voice.

"Keep away from me," Doro told her. "Stay there with the body until I know how many others of his household this fool will sacrifice to his arrogance."

She wanted nothing more than to keep away from him. She wanted to run home and try to forget she had ever seen him. She lowered her head and closed her eyes, fighting panic. There was shouting around her, but she hardly heard it. Intent on her own fear, she paid no attention to anything else until someone knocked her down.

Then someone seized her roughly, and she realized she was to pay for the death of the child. She thrust her attacker away from her and leaped to her feet ready to fight.

"That is enough!" Doro shouted. And then more quietly, "Do not kill him!"

She saw that the person she had thrust away was the young man—and that she had pushed him harder than she thought. Now he was sprawled against the compound wall, half conscious.

Doro went to him and the man raised his hands as though to deflect a blow. Doro spoke to him in quiet, chilling tones that should never have issued from the mouth of a child. The man cringed, and Doro spoke again more sharply.

The man stood up, looked at the people of the household he had inherited from his father. They were clearly alarmed and confused. Most had not seen enough to know what was going on, and they seemed to be questioning each other. They stared at the new head of their household. There were several young children, women, some of whom must have been wives or sisters of the young man, men who were probably brothers and slaves. Everyone had come to see.

Perhaps the young man felt that he had shamed himself before his people. Perhaps he was thinking about how he had cringed and whimpered before a child. Or perhaps he was merely the fool Doro took him to be. Whatever his reasoning, he made a fatal error.

With shouted words that had to be curses, the man seized the machete from Doro's hand, raised it, and brought it slashing down through the neck of the unresisting child-body.

Anyanwu looked away, absolutely certain of what would happen. There had been ample time for the child to avoid the machete. The young man, perhaps still groggy from Anyanwu's blow, had not moved very quickly. But the child had stood still and awaited the blow with a shrug of adult weariness. Now she heard the young man speaking to the crowd, and she could hear Doro in his voice. Of course.

The people fled. Several of them ran out of the compound door or scrambled over the wall. Doro ignored them, went to Anyanwu.

"We will leave now," he said. "We will take a canoe and row ourselves."

"Why did you kill the child?" she whispered.

"To warn this young fool," he said hitting the chest of his lean, new body. "The boy was the son of a slave and no great loss to the household. I wanted to leave a man here who had authority and who knew me, but this man would not learn. Come, Anyanwu."

She followed him dumbly. He could turn from two casual murders and speak to her as though nothing had happened. He was clearly annoyed that he had had to kill the young man, but annoyance seemed to be all he felt.

Beyond the walls of the compound, armed men waited. Anyanwu slowed, allowed Doro to move well ahead of her as he approached them. She was certain there would be more killing. But Doro spoke to the men—said only a few words to them—and they drew back out of his path. Then Doro made a short speech to everyone, and the people drew even farther away from him. Finally, he led Anyanwu down the river, where they stole a canoe and paddles.

"You must row," she told him as they put the craft into the water. "I will try to help you when we are beyond sight of this place."

"Have you never rowed a canoe?"

"Not perhaps three times as long as this new body of yours has been alive."

He nodded and paddled the craft alone.

"You should not have killed the child," she said sadly. "It was wrong no matter why you did it."

"Your own people kill children."

"Only the ones who must be killed—the abominations. And even with them... sometimes when the thing wrong with the child was small, I was able to stop the killing. I spoke with the voice of the god, and as long as I did not violate tradition too much, the people listened."

"Killing children is wasteful," he agreed. "Who knows what useful adults they might have grown into? But still, sometimes a child must be sacrificed."

She thought of her sons and their children, and knew positively that she had been right to get Doro away from them. Doro would not have hesitated to kill some of them to intimidate others. Her descendants were ordinarily well able to take care of themselves. But they could not have stopped Doro from killing them, from walking about obscenely clothed in their flesh. What could stop such a being—a spirit. He was a spirit, no matter what he said. He had no flesh of his own.

Not for the first time in her three hundred years, Anyanwu wished she had gods to pray to, gods who would help her. But she had only herself and the magic she could perform with her own body. What good was that against a being who could steal her body away from her? And what would he feel if he decided to "sacrifice" her? Annoyance? Regret? She looked at him and was surprised to see that he was smiling.

He took a deep breath and let it out with apparent pleasure. "You need not row for a while," he told her. "Rest. This body is strong and healthy. It is so good not to be coughing."

Chapter Three

Doro was always in a good mood after changing bodies—especially when he changed more than once in quick succession or when he changed to one of the special bodies that he bred for his use. This time, his pleasurable feelings were still with him when he reached the coast. He noticed that Anyanwu had been very quiet, but she had her quiet times. And she had just seen a thing that was new to her. Doro knew people took time to get used to his changes. Only his children seemed to accept them naturally. He was willing to give Anyanwu all the time she needed.

There were slavers on the coast. An English factor lived there, an employee of the Royal African Company, and incidentally, Doro's man. Bernard Daly was his name. He had three black wives, several half-breed children, and apparently, strong resistance to the numerous local diseases. He also had only one hand. Years before, Doro had cut off the other.

Daly was supervising the branding of new slaves when Doro and Anyanwu pulled their canoe onto the beach. There was a smell of cooking flesh in the air and the sound of a slave boy screaming.

"Doro, this is an evil place," Anyanwu whispered. She kept very close to him.

"No one will harm you," he said. He looked down at her. She always spent her days as a small, muscular man, but somehow, he could never think of her as masculine. He had asked her once why she insisted on going about as a man. "I have not seen you going about in women's bodies," she retorted. "People will think before they attack a man—even a small man. And they will not become as angry if a man gives them a beating."

He had laughed, but he knew she was right. She was somewhat safer as a man, although here, among African and European slavers, no one was truly safe. He himself might be forced out of his new body before he could reach Daly. But Anyanwu would not be touched. He would see to it.

"Why do we stop here?" she asked.

"I have a man here who might know what happened to my people—the people I came to get. This is the nearest seaport to them."

"Seaport..." She repeated the word as he had said it—in English. He did not know the word in her language for sea. He had described to her the wide, seemingly endless water that they had to cross, but in spite of his description, she stared at it in silent awe. The sound of the surf seemed to frighten her as it mixed with the screaming of slaves being branded. For the first time, she looked as though the many strange new things around her would overwhelm her. She looked as though she would turn and run back into the forest as slaves often tried to do. Completely out of character, she looked terrified.

He stopped, faced her, took her firmly by the shoulders. "Nothing will harm you, Anyanwu." He spoke with utter conviction. "Not these slavers, not the sea, not anything at all. I have not brought you all this way only to lose you. You know my power." He felt her shudder. "That power will not harm you either. I have accepted you as my wife. You have only to obey me."

She stared at him as he spoke, as though these eyes of hers could read his expression and discern truth. Ordinary people could not do that with him, but she was far from ordinary. She had had time enough in her long life to learn to read people well—as Doro himself had learned. Some of his people believed he could read their unspoken thoughts, so transparent were their lies to him. Half-truths, though, could be another matter.

Anyanwu seemed to relax, reassured. Then something off to one side caught her eye and she stiffened. "Is that one of your white men?" she whispered. He had told her about Europeans, explaining that in spite of their pale skins, they were neither albinos nor lepers. She had heard of such people but had not seen any until now.

Doro glanced at the approaching European, then spoke to Anyanwu. "Yes," he said, "but he is only a man. He can die as easily as a black man. Move away from me."

She obeyed quickly.

Doro did not intend to kill the white man if he could avoid it. He had killed enough of Daly's people back at their first meeting to put the Englishman out of business. Daly had proved tractable, however, and Doro had helped him to survive.

"Welcome," the white man said in English. "Have you more slaves to sell us?" Clearly, Doro's new body was no stranger here. Doro glanced at Anyanwu, saw how she was staring at the slaver. The man was bearded and dirty and thin as though wasted by disease—which was likely. This land swallowed white men. The slaver was a poor example of his kind, but Anyanwu did not know that. She was having a good look. Her curiosity now seemed stronger than her fear.

"Are you sure you know me?" Doro asked the man quietly. And his voice had the expected effect.

The man stopped, frowned in confusion and surprise. "Who are you?" he demanded. "Who... what do you want here?" He was not afraid. He did not know Doro. He merely assumed he had made a mistake. He stood peering up at the tall black man and projecting hostility.

"I'm a friend of Bernard Daly," Doro said. "I have business with him." Doro spoke in English as did the slaver and there was no doubt that the man understood him. Thus, when the slaver continued to stare, Doro started past him, walked toward the branding where he could see Daly talking with someone else.

But the slaver was not finished. He drew his sword. "You want to see the captain?" he said. Daly had not been master of a ship for fifteen years, but he still favored the title. The slaver grinned at

Doro, showing a scattering of yellow teeth. "You'll see him soon enough!"

Doro glanced at the sword, annoyed. In a single movement almost too swift to follow, he raised his heavy machete and knocked the lighter weapon from the slaver's hand.

Then the machete was at the man's throat. "That could have been your hand," Doro said softly. "It could have been your head."

"My people would kill you where you stand."

"What good would that do you—in hell?"

Silence.

"Turn, and we'll go to see Daly."

The slaver obeyed hesitantly, muttering some obscenity about Doro's ancestry.

"Another word will cost you your head," Doro said.

Again, there was silence.

The three marched single file past the chained slaves, past the fire where the branding had stopped, past Daly's men who stared at them. They went to the tree-shaded, three-sided shelter where Daly sat on a wooden crate, drinking from an earthen jug. He lowered the jug, though, to stare at Doro and Anyanwu.

"I see business is good," Doro said.

Daly stood up. He was short and square and sunburned and unshaven. "Speak again," he growled. "Who are you?" He was a little hard of hearing, but Doro thought he had heard enough. Doro could see in him the strange combination of apprehension and anticipation that Doro had come to expect from his people. He knew when they greeted him this way that they were still his servants, loyal and tame.

"You know me," he said.

The slaver took a step back.

"I've left your man alive," Doro said. "Teach him manners."

"I will." He waved the confused, angry man away. The man glared at Doro and at the now lowered machete. Finally, he stalked away.

When he was gone, Doro asked Daly, "Has my crew been here?"

"More than once," the slaver said. "Just yesterday, your son Lale chose two men and three women. Strong young blacks they were— worth much more than I charged."

"I'll soon see," Doro said.

Suddenly Anyanwu screamed.

Doro glanced at her quickly to see that she was not being molested. Then he kept his eyes on Daly and on his men. "Woman, you will cause me to make a mistake!" he muttered.

"It is Okoye," she whispered. "The son of my youngest daughter. These men must have raided her village."

"Where is he?"

"There!" She gestured toward a young man who had just been branded. He lay on the ground dirty, winded, and bruised from his struggles to escape the hot iron.

"I will go to him," Anyanwu said softly, "though he will not know me."

"Go," Doro told her. Then he switched back to English. "I may have more business for you, Daly. That boy."

"But... that one is taken. A company ship—"

"A pity," Doro said. "The profit will not be yours then."

The man raised his stump to rub his hairy chin. "What are you offering?" It was his habit to supplement his meager salary by trading with interlopers—non-Company men—like Doro. Especially Doro. It was a dangerous business, but England was far away and he was not likely to be caught.

"One moment," Doro told him, then switched language. "Anyanwu, is the boy alone or are there other members of your family here?"

"He is alone. The others have been taken away."

"When?"

She spoke briefly with her grandson, then faced Doro again. "The last ones were sold to white men many days ago."

Doro sighed. That was that, then. The boy's relatives, strangers to him, were even more completely lost than the people of his seed village. He turned and made Daly an offer for the boy—an offer that caused the slaver to lick his lips. He would give up the boy without coercion and find some replacement for whoever had bought him. The blackened, cooked gouge on the boy's breast had become meaningless. "Unchain him," Doro ordered.

Daly gestured to one of his men, and that man removed the chains.

"I'll send one of my men back with the money," Doro promised.

Daly shook his head and stepped out of the shelter. "I'll walk with you," he said. "It isn't far. One of your people might shoot you if they see you looking that way with only two more blacks as companions."

Doro laughed and accepted the man's company. He wanted to talk to Daly about the seed village anyway. "Do you think I'll cheat you?" he asked. "After all this time?"

Daly smiled, glanced back at the boy who walked with Anyanwu. "You could cheat me," he said. "You could rob me whenever you choose, and yet you pay well. Why?"

"Perhaps because you are wise enough to accept what you cannot understand."

"You?"

"Me. What do you tell yourself I am?"

"I used to think you were the devil himself."

Doro laughed again. He had always permitted his people the freedom to say what they thought—as long as they stopped when he silenced them and obeyed when he commanded them. Daly had belonged to him long enough to know this. "Who are you, then?" he asked the slaver. "Job?"

"No." Daly shook his head sadly. "Job was a stronger man."

Doro stopped, turned, and looked at him. "You are content with your life," he said.

Daly looked away, refusing to meet whatever looked through the very ordinary eyes of the body Doro wore. But when Doro began to walk again, Daly followed. He would follow Doro to his ship, and if Doro himself offered payment for the young slave, Daly would refuse to take it. The boy would become a gift. Daly had never taken money from Doro's hand. And always, he had sought Doro's company.

"Why does the white animal follow?" asked Anyanwu's grandson loudly enough for Doro to hear. "What has he to do with us now?"

"My master must pay him for you," said Anyanwu's grandson loudly enough for Doro to hear. "What has he to do with us now?"

"My master must pay him for you," said Anyanwu. She had presented herself to the boy as a distant kinsman of his mother. "And also," she added, "I think this man serves him somehow."

"If the white man is a slave, why should he be paid?"

Doro answered this himself. "Because I choose to pay him, Okoye. A man may choose what he will do with his slaves."

"Do you send your slaves to kill our kinsmen and steal us away?"

"No," Doro said. "My people only buy and sell slaves." And only certain slaves at that if Daly was obeying him. He would know soon.

"Then they send others to prey on us. It is the same thing!"

"What I permit my people to do is my affair," Doro said.

"But they—!"

Doro stopped abruptly, turned to face the young man who was himself forced to come to an awkward stop. "What I permit them to do is my affair, Okoye. That is all."

Perhaps the boy's enslavement had taught him caution. He said nothing. Anyanwu stared at Doro, but she too kept silent.

"What were they saying?" Daly asked.

"They disapprove of your profession," Doro told him.

"Heathen savages," Daly muttered. "They're like animals. They're all cannibals."

"These aren't," Doro said, "though some of their neighbors are."

"All of them," Daly insisted. "Just give them the chance."

Doro smiled. "Well, no doubt the missionaries will reach them eventually and teach them to practice only symbolic cannibalism."

Daly jumped. He considered himself a pious man in spite of his work. "You shouldn't say such things," he whispered. "Not even you are beyond the reach of God."

"Spare me your mythology," Doro said, "and your righteous indignation." Daly had been Doro's man too long to be pampered in such matters. "At least we cannibals are honest about what we do," Doro continued. "We don't pretend as your slavers do to be acting for the benefit of our victims' souls. We don't tell ourselves we've caught them to teach them civilized religion."

Daly's eyes grew round. "But... I did not mean you were a... a... I did not mean..."

"Why not?" Doro looked down at him, enjoying his confusion. "I assure you, I'm the most efficient cannibal you will ever meet."

Daly said nothing. He wiped his brow and stared seaward. Doro followed his gaze and saw that there was a ship in sight now, lying at anchor in a little cove—Doro's own ship, the *Silver Star,* small and hardy and more able than any of his larger vessels to go where it was not legally welcome and take on slave cargo the Royal African Company had reserved for itself. Doro could see some of his men a short distance away loading yams onto a longboat. He would be on his way home soon.

Doro invited Daly out to the ship. There, he first settled Anyanwu and her grandson in his own cabin. Then he ate and drank with Daly and questioned the slaver about the seed village.

"Not a coastal people," Doro said. "An inland tribe from the grasslands beyond the forests. I showed you a few of them years ago when we met."

"These blacks are all alike," Daly said. "It's hard to tell." He took a swallow of brandy.

Doro reached across the small table and grasped Daly's wrist just above the man's sole remaining hand. "If you can't do better than that," he said, "you're no good to me."

Daly froze, terrified, arresting a sudden effort to jerk his hand away. He sat still, perhaps remembering how his men had died years before whether Doro touched them or not. "It was a joke," he whispered hoarsely.

Doro said nothing, only looked at him.

"Your people have Arab blood," Daly said quickly. "I remember their looks and the words of their language that you taught me and their vile tempers. Not an easy people to enslave and keep alive. None like them have gone through my hands without being tested."

"Speak the words I taught you."

Daly spoke them—words in the seed people's own language asking them whether they were followers of Doro, whether they were "Doro's seed"—and Doro released Daly's wrist. The slaver had said the words perfectly and none of Doro's seed villagers had failed to respond. They were, as Daly had said, difficult people—bad-tempered, more suspicious than most of strangers, more willing than most to murder each other or attack their far-flung neighbors, more willing to satisfy their customs and their meat-hunger with human flesh. Doro had

isolated them on their sparsely populated savanna for just that reason. Had they been any closer to the larger, stronger tribes around
them, they would have been wiped out as a nuisance.

They were also a highly intuitive people who involuntarily saw
into each other's thoughts and fought with each other over evil
intentions rather than evil deeds. This without ever realizing that
they were doing anything unusual. Doro had been their god since
he had assembled them generations before and commanded them
to marry only each other and the strangers he brought to them. They
had obeyed him, throwing away clearly defective children born of
their inbreeding, and strengthening the gifts that made them so
valuable to him. If those same gifts made them abnormally quick
to anger, vicious, and savagely intolerant of people unlike themselves, it did not matter. Doro had been very pleased with them,
and they had long ago accepted the idea that pleasing him was the
most important thing they could do.

"Your people are surely dead if they have been taken," Daly said.
"The few that you brought here with you years ago made enemies
wherever they went."

Doro had brought five of the villagers out to cross-breed them
with certain others he had collected. They had insulted everyone
with their arrogance and hostility, but they had also bred as Doro
commanded them and gotten fine children—children with ever
greater, more controllable sensitivity.

"Some of them are alive," Doro said. "I can feel their lives drawing me when I think of them. I'm going to have to track as many of
them as I can before someone does kill them though."

"I'm sorry," Daly said. "I wish they had been brought to me. As
bad as they are, I would have held them for you."

Doro nodded, sighed. "Yes, I know you would have."

And the last of the slaver's tension melted away. He knew Doro
did not blame him for the seed people's demise, knew he would not
be punished. "What is the little Igbo you have brought aboard?" he
asked curiously. There was room for curiosity now.

"Wild seed," Doro said. "Carrier of a bloodline I believed was
lost—and, I think, of another that I did not know existed. I have
some exploring to do in her homeland once she is safely away."

"She! But... that black is a man."

"Sometimes. But she was born a woman. She is a woman most of the time."

Daly shook his head, unbelieving. "The monstrosities you collect! I suppose now you will breed creatures who don't know whether to piss standing or squatting."

"They will know—if I can breed them. They will know, but it won't matter."

"Such things should be burned. They are against God!"

Doro laughed and said nothing. He knew as well as Daly how the slaver longed to be one of Doro's monstrosities. Daly was still alive because of that desire. Ten years before, he had confronted what he considered to be just another black savage leading five other less black but equally savage-looking men. All six men appeared to be young, healthy—fine potential slaves. Daly had sent his own black employees to capture them. He had lost thirteen men that day. He had seen them swept down as grain before a scythe. Then, terrified, confronted by Doro in the body of the last man killed, he had drawn his own sword. The move cost him his right hand. He never understood why it had not cost him his life. He did not know of Doro's habit of leaving properly disciplined men of authority scattered around the world ready to serve whenever Doro needed them. All Daly understood was that he had been spared—that Doro had cauterized his wound and cared for him until he recovered.

And by the time he recovered, he had realized that he was no longer a free man—that Doro was capable of taking the life he had spared at any time. Daly was able to accept this as others had accepted it before him. "Let me work for you," he had said. "Take me aboard one of your ships or even back to your homeland. I'm still strong. Even with one hand, I can work. I can handle blacks."

"I want you here," Doro had told him. "I've made arrangements with some of the local kings while you were recovering. They'll trade with you exclusively from now on."

Daly had stared at him in amazement. "Why would you do such a thing for me?"

"So that you can do a few things for me," Doro had answered.

And Daly had been back in business. Doro sent him black traders who sold him slaves and his company sent him white traders who bought them. "Someone else would set up a factory here if you left," Doro told him. "I can't stop the trade even where it might touch my people, but I can control it." So much for his control. Neither his support of Daly nor his spies left along the coast—people who should have reported to Daly—had been enough. Now they were useless. If they had been special stock, people with unusual abilities, Doro would have resettled them in America, where they could be useful. But they were only ordinary people bought by wealth or fear or belief that Doro was a god. He would forget them. He might forget Daly also once he had returned to Anyanwu's homeland and sought out as many of her descendants as he could find. At the moment, though, Daly could still be useful—and he could still be trusted; Doro knew that now. Perhaps the seed people had been taken to Bonny or New Calabar or some other slave port, but they had not passed near Daly. The most talented and deceptive of Doro's own children could not have lied to him successfully while he was on guard. Also, Daly had discovered he enjoyed being an arm of Doro's power.

"Now that your people are gone," Daly said, "why not take me to Virginia or New York where you have blacks working. I'm sick to death of this country."

"Stay here," Doro ordered. "You can still be useful. I'll be coming back."

Daly sighed. "I almost wish I was one of those strange beings you call your people," he admitted.

Doro smiled and had the ship's captain, John Woodley, pay for the boy, Okoye, and send Daly ashore.

"Slimy little bastard," Woodley muttered when Daly was gone.

Doro said nothing. Woodley, one of Doro's ordinary, ungifted sons, had always disliked Daly. This amused Doro since he considered the two men much alike. Woodley was the child of a casual liaison Doro had had forty-five years before with a London merchant's daughter. Doro had married the woman and provided for her when he learned she would bear his child, but he quickly left her a widow, well off, but alone except for her infant son. Doro had seen John Woodley twice as the boy grew toward adulthood. When on the second visit, Woodley expressed a desire to go to sea, Doro had him apprenticed to one of Doro's shipmasters. Woodley had worked his own way up. He could have become wealthy, could be commanding a great ship instead of one of Doro's smallest. But he had chosen to stay near Doro. Like Daly, he enjoyed being an arm of Doro's power. And like Daly, he was envious of others who might outrank him in Doro's esteem.

"That little heathen would sail with you today if you'd let him," Woodley told Doro. "He's no better than one of his blacks. I don't see what good he is to you."

"He works for me," Doro said. "Just as you do."

"It's not the same!"

Doro shrugged and let the contradiction stand. Woodley knew better than Daly ever could just how much it was the same. He'd worked too closely with Doro's most gifted children to overestimate his own value. And he knew the living generations of Doro's sons and daughters would populate a city. He knew how easily both he and Daly could be replaced. After a moment he sighed as Daly had sighed. "I suppose the new blacks you brought aboard have some special talent," he said.

"That's right," Doro answered. "Something new."

"Godless animals!" Woodley muttered bitterly. He turned and walked away.

Chapter Four

The ship frightened Anyanwu, but it frightened Okoye more. He had seen that the men aboard were mostly white men, and in his life, he had had no good experiences with white men. Also, fellow slaves had told him the whites were cannibals.

"We will be taken to their land and fattened and eaten," he told Anyanwu.

"No," Anyanwu assured him. "It is not their custom to eat men. And if it were, our master would not permit us to be eaten. He is a powerful man."

Okoye shuddered. "He is not a man."

Anyanwu stared at him. How had he discovered Doro's strangeness so quickly?

"It was he who bought me, then sold me to the whites. I remember him; he beat me. It is the same face, the same skin. But something different is living inside. Some spirit."

"Okoye." Anyanwu spoke very softly and waited until he turned from his terrified gazing into space and looked at her. "If Doro is a spirit," she said, "then he has done you a service. He has killed your enemy for you. Is that reason to fear him?"

"You fear him yourself. I have seen it in your eyes."

Anyanwu gave him a sad smile. "Not as much as I should, perhaps."

"He is a spirit!"

"You know I am your mother's kinsman, Okoye."

He stared at her for a time without answering. Finally he asked, "Have her people also been enslaved?"

"Not when I last saw them."

"Then how were you taken?"

"Do you remember your mother's mother?"

"She is the oracle. The god speaks through her."

"She is Anyanwu, your mother's mother," Anyanwu said. "She fed you pounded yam and healed the sickness that threatened to take your life. She told you stories of the tortoise, the monkey, the birds. . . . And sometimes when you looked at her in the shadows of the fire and the lamp, it seemed to you that she became these creatures. You were frightened at first. Then you were pleased. You asked for the stories and the changes. You wanted to change too."

"I was a child," Okoye said. "I was dreaming."

"You were awake."

"You cannot know!"

"I know."

"I never told anyone!"

"I never thought you would," Anyanwu said. "Even as a child, you seemed to know when to talk and when to keep quiet." She smiled, remembering the small, stoic boy who had refused to cry with the pain of his sickness, who had refused to smile when she told him the old fables her mother had told her. Only when she startled him with her changes did he begin to pay attention.

She spoke softly. "Do you remember, Okoye, your mother's mother had a mark here?" She drew with her finger the jagged old scar that she had once carried beneath her left eye. As she drew it, she aged and furrowed the flesh so that the scar appeared.

Okoye bolted toward the door.

Anyanwu caught him, held him easily in spite of his greater size and his desperate strength. "What am I that I was not before?" she asked when the violence had gone out of his struggles.

"You are a man!" he gasped. "Or a spirit."

"I am no spirit," she said. "And should it be so difficult for a woman who can become a tortoise or a monkey to become a man?"

He began to struggle again. He was a young man now, not a child. The easy childhood acceptance of the impossible was gone, and she dared not let him go. In his present state, he might jump into the water and drown.

"If you will be still, Okoye, I will become the old woman you remember.

Still he struggled.

"*Nwadiani*—daughter's child—do you remember that even the pain of sickness could not make you weep when your mother brought you to me, but you wept because you could not change as I could?"

He stopped his struggles, stood gasping in her grip.

"You are my daughter's son," she said. "I would not harm you." He was still now, so she released him. The bond between a man and his mother's kin was strong and gentle. But for the boy's own safety, she kept her body between his and the door.

"Shall I become as I was?" she asked.

"Yes," the boy whispered.

She became an old woman for him. The shape was familiar and easy to slip into. She had been an old woman for so long.

"It is you," Okoye said wonderingly.

She smiled. "You see? Why should you fear an old woman?"

To her surprise, he laughed. "You always had too many teeth to be an old woman, and strange eyes. People said the god looked out of your eyes."

"What do you think?"

He stared at her with great curiosity, walked around her to look at her. "I cannot think at all. Why are you here? How did you become this Doro's slave?"

"I am not his slave."

"I cannot see how any man would hold you in slavery. What are you?"

"His wife."

The boy stared speechless at her long breasts.

"I am not this wrinkled woman, Okoye. I allowed myself to become her when my last husband, the father of your mother, died. I thought I had had enough husbands and enough children; I am older than you can imagine. I wanted to rest. When I had rested for many years as the people's oracle, Doro found me. In his way, he is as different as I am. He wanted me to be his wife."

"But he is not merely different. He is something other than a man!"

"And I am something other than a woman."

"You are not like him!"

"No, but I have accepted him as my husband. It was what I wanted—to have a man who was as different from other men as I am from other women." If this was not entirely true, Okoye did not need to know.

"Show me..." Okoye paused as though not certain of what he wanted to say. "Show me what you are."

Obligingly, she let her true shape flow back to her, became the young woman whose body had ceased to age when she was about twenty years old. At twenty, she had a violent, terrible sickness during which she had heard voices, felt pain in one part of her body after another, screamed and babbled in foreign dialects. Her young husband had feared she would die. She was *Anasi*, his first wife, and though she was in disfavor with his family because after five years of marriage, she had produced no children, he fought hard against losing her. He sought help for her,

frantically paying borrowed money to the old man who was then the
oracle, making sacrifices of valuable animals. No man ever cared more
for her than he did. And it seemed that the medicine worked. Her body
ceased its thrashing and struggling, and her senses returned, but she
found herself vastly changed. She had a control over her body that was
clearly beyond anything other people could manage. She could look
inside herself and control or alter what she saw there. She could finally
be worthy of her husband and of her own womanhood; she could
become pregnant. She bore her husband ten strong children. In the
centuries that followed, she never did more for any man.

When she realized the years had ceased to mark her body, she
experimented and learned to age herself as her husband aged.
She learned quickly that it was not good to be too different. Great
differences caused envy, suspicion, fear, charges of witchcraft. But
while her first husband lived, she never entirely gave up her beauty.
And sometimes when he came to her at night, she allowed her body
to return to the youthful shape that came so easily, so naturally—
the true shape. In that way, her husband had a young senior wife
for as long as he lived. And now Okoye had a mother's mother who
appeared to be younger than he was.

"*Nneochie?*" the boy said doubtfully. "Mother's mother?"

"Still," Anyanwu said. "This is the way I look when I do nothing.
And this is the way I look when I marry a new husband."

"But... you are old."

"The years do not touch me."

"Nor him...? Your new husband?"

"Nor him."

Okoye shook his head. "I should not be here. I am only a man.
What will you do with me?"

"You belong to Doro. He will say what is to be done with you—
but you need not worry. He wants me as his wife. He will not harm
you."

The water harmed him.

Soon after Anyanwu had revealed herself, he began to grow ill.
He became dizzy. His head hurt him. He said he thought he would
vomit if he did not leave the confinement of the small room.

Anyanwu took him out on deck where the air was fresh and cooler. But even there, the gentle rocking of the ship seemed to bother him—and began to bother her. She began to feel ill. She seized on the feeling at once, examining it. There was drowsiness, dizziness, and a sudden cold sweat. She closed her eyes, and while Okoye vomited into the water, she went over her body carefully. She discovered that there was a wrongness, a kind of imbalance deep within her ears. It was a tiny disturbance, but she knew her body well enough to notice the smallest change. For a moment, she observed this change with interest. Clearly, if she did nothing to correct it, her sickness would grow worse; she would join Okoye, vomiting over the rail. But no. She focused on her inner ears and remembered perfection there, remembered organs and fluids and pressures in balance, their wrongness righted. Remembering and correcting were one gesture; balance was restored. It had taken her much practice—and much pain—to learn such ease of control. Every change she made in her body had to be understood and visualized. If she was sick or injured, she could not simply wish to be well. She could be killed as easily as anyone else if her body was damaged in some way she could not understand quickly enough to repair. Thus, she had spent much of her long life learning the diseases, disorders, and injuries that she could suffer—learning them often by inflicting mild versions of them on herself, then slowly, painfully, by trial and error, coming to understand exactly what was wrong and how to impress healing. Thus, when her enemies came to kill her, she knew more about surviving than they did about killing.

And now she knew how to set right this new disturbance that could have caused her considerable misery. But her knowledge was of no help to Okoye—yet. She searched through her memory for some substance that would help him. Within her long memory was a catalogue of cures and poisons—often the same substances given in different quantities, with different preparation, or in different combinations. Many of them she could manufacture within her body as she had manufactured a healing balm for Doro's hand.

This time, though, before she thought of anything that might be useful, a white man came to her, bringing a small metal container full of some liquid. The man looked at Okoye, then nodded and put the container into Anyanwu's hands. He made signs to indicate that she should get Okoye to drink.

Anyanwu looked at the container, then sipped from it herself. She would not give anyone medicine she did not understand.

The liquid was startlingly strong stuff that first choked her, then slowly, pleasantly warmed her, pleased her. It was like palm wine, but much stronger. A little of it might make Okoye forget his misery. A little more might make him sleep. It was no cure, but it would not hurt him and it might help.

Anyanwu thanked the white man in her own language and saw that he was looking at her breasts. He was a beardless, yellow-haired young man—a physical type completely strange to Anyanwu. Another time, her curiosity would have driven her to learn more about him, try to communicate with him. She found herself wondering obscurely whether the hair between his legs was as yellow as that on his head. She laughed aloud at herself, and the young man, unknowing, watched her breasts jiggle.

Enough of that!

She took Okoye back into the cabin, and when the yellow-haired man followed, she stepped in front of him and gestured unmistakably for him to leave. He hesitated, and she decided that if he touched her uninvited, she would throw him into the sea. *Sea,* yes. That was the English word for water. If she said it, would he understand?

But the man left without coercion.

Anyanwu coaxed Okoye to swallow some of the liquid. It made him cough and choke at first, but he got it down. By the time Doro came to the cabin, Okoye was asleep.

Doro opened the door without warning and came in. He looked at her with obvious pleasure and said, "You are well, Anyanwu. I thought you would be."

"I am always well."

He laughed. "You will bring me luck on this voyage. Come and see whether my men have bought any more of your relatives."

She followed him deeper into the vessel through large rooms containing only a few people segregated by sex. The people lounged on mats or gathered in pairs or small groups to talk—those who had found others who spoke their language.

No one was chained as the slaves on shore had been. No one seemed to be hurt or frightened. Two women sat nursing their babies. Anyanwu heard many languages, including, finally, her own. She stopped at the mat of a young woman who had been singing softly to her.

"Who are you?" she asked the woman in surprise.

The woman jumped to her feet, took Anyanwu's hands. "You can speak," she said joyfully. "I thought I would never again hear words I could understand. I am Udenkwo."

The woman's own speech was somewhat strange to Anyanwu. She pronounced some of her words differently or used different words so that Anyanwu had to replay everything in her mind to be certain what had been said. "How did you get here, Udenkwo?" she asked. "Did these whites steal you from your home?" From the corner of her eye, she saw Doro turn to look at her indignantly. But he allowed Udenkwo to answer for herself.

"Not these," she said. "Strangers who spoke much as you do. They sold me to others. I was sold four times—finally to these." She looked around as though dazed, surprised. "No one has beaten me here or tied me."

"How were you taken?"

"I went to the river with friends to get water. We were all taken and our children with us. My son..."

"Where is he?"

"They took him from me. When I was sold for the second time, he was not sold with me." The woman's strange accent did nothing to mask her pain. She looked from Anyanwu to Doro. "What will be done with me now?"

This time Doro answered. "You will go to my country. You belong to me now."

"I am a freeborn woman! My father and my husband are great men!"

"That is past."

"Let me go back to my people!"

"My people will be your people. You will obey me as they obey."

Udenkwo sat still, but somehow seemed to shrink from him. "Will I be tied again? Will I be beaten?"

"Not if you obey."

"Will I be sold?"

"No."

She hesitated, examining him as though deciding whether or not to believe him. Finally, tentatively, she asked: "Will you buy my son?"

"I would," Doro said, "but who knows where he may have been taken—one boy. How old was he?"

"About five years old."

Doro shrugged. "I would not know how to find him."

Anyanwu had been looking at Udenkwo uncertainly. Now, as the woman seemed to sink into depression at the news that her son was forever lost to her, Anyanwu asked: "Udenkwo, who is your father and his father?"

The woman did not answer.

"Your father," Anyanwu repeated, "his people."

Listlessly, Udenkwo gave the name of her clan, then went on to name several of her male ancestors. Anyanwu listened until the names and their order began to sound familiar—until one of them was the name of her eighth son, then her third husband.

Anyanwu stopped the recitation with a gesture. "I have known some of your people," she said. "You are safe here. You will be well treated." She began to move away. "I will see you again." She drew Doro with her and when they were beyond the woman's hearing, she asked: "Could you not look for her son?"

"No," Doro said. "I told her the truth. I would not know where to begin—or even whether the boy is still alive."

"She is one of my descendants."

"As you said, she will be well treated. I can offer no more than that." Doro glanced at her. "The land must be full of your descendants."

Anyanwu looked somber. "You are right. They are so numerous, so well scattered, and so far from me in their generations that they do not know me or each other. Sometimes they marry one another and I hear of it. It is abomination, but I cannot speak of it without focusing the wrong kind of attention on the young ones. They cannot defend themselves as I can."

"You are right to keep silent," Doro said. "Sometimes ways must be different for people as different as ourselves."

"We," she said thoughtfully. "Did you have children of... of a body born to your mother?"

He shook his head. "I died too young," he said. "I was thirteen years old."

"That is a sad thing, even for you."

"Yes." They were on deck now, and he stared out at the sea. "I have lived for more than thirty-seven hundred years and fathered thousands of children. I have become a woman and borne children. And still, I long to know that my body could have produced. Another being like myself? A companion?"

"Perhaps not," said Anyanwu. "You might have been like me, having one ordinary child after another."

Doro shrugged and changed the subject. "You must take your daughter's son to meet that girl when he is feeling better. The girl's age is wrong, but she is still a little younger than Okoye. Perhaps they will comfort each other."

"They are kinsmen!"

"They will not know that unless you tell them, and you should be silent once more. They have only each other, Anyanwu. If they wish, they can marry after the customs of their new land."

"And how is that?"

"There is a ceremony. They pledge themselves to each other before a"—he said an English word, then translated—"a priest."

"They have no family but me, and the girl does not know me."

"It does not matter."

"It will be a poor marriage."

"No. I will give them land and seed. Others will teach them to live in their new country. It is a good place. People need not stay poor there if they will work."

"Children of mine will work."

"Then all will be well."

He left her and she wandered around the deck looking at the ship and the sea and the dark line of trees on shore. The shore seemed very far away. She watched it with the beginnings of fear, of longing. Everything she knew was back there deep within those trees through strange forests. She was leaving all her people in a way that seemed far more permanent than simply walking away.

She turned away from the shore, frightened of the sudden emotion that threatened to overwhelm her. She looked at the men, some black, some white, as they moved about the deck doing work she did not understand. The yellow-haired white man came to smile at her and stare at her breasts until she wondered whether he had ever seen a woman before. He spoke to her slowly, very distinctly.

"Isaac," he said pointing to his chest. "Isaac." Then he jabbed a finger toward her, but did not touch her. He raised his bushy pale eyebrows questioningly.

"Isaac?" she said stumbling over the word.

"Isaac." He slapped his chest. Then he pointed again. "You?"

"Anyanwu!" she said understanding. "Anyanwu." She smiled.

And he smiled and mispronounced her name and walked her around the deck naming things for her in English. The new language, so different from anything she had ever heard, had fascinated her since Doro began teaching it to her. Now she repeated the words very carefully and strove to remember them. The yellow-haired Isaac seemed delighted. When finally, someone called him away, he left her reluctantly.

The loneliness returned as soon as he was gone. There were people all around her, but she felt completely alone on this huge vessel at the edge of endless water. Loneliness. Why should she feel it so strongly now? She had been lonely since she realized she would not die like other people. They would always leave her—friends, husbands, children.... She could not remember the face of her mother or her father.

But now, the solitude seemed to close in on her as the waters of the sea would close over her head if she leaped into them.

She stared down into the constantly moving water, then away at the distant shore. The shore seemed even farther away now, though Doro had said the ship was not yet under way. Anyanwu felt that she had moved farther from her home, that already perhaps she was too far away ever to return.

She gripped the rail, eyes on the shore. What was she doing, she wondered. How could she leave her homeland, even for Doro? How could she live among these strangers? White skins, yellow hairs—what were they to her? Worse than strangers. Different ones, people who could be all around her working and shouting, and still leave her feeling alone.

She pulled herself up onto the rail.

"Anyanwu!"

She did not quite hesitate. It was as though a mosquito had whined past her ear. A tiny distraction.

"Anyanwu!"

She would leap into the sea. Its waters would take her home, or they would swallow her. Either way, she would find peace. Her loneliness hurt her like some sickness of the body, some pain that her special ability could not find and heal. The sea...

Hands grasped her, pulled her backward and down onto the deck. Hands kept her from the sea.

"Anyanwu!"

The yellow hair loomed above her. The white skin. What right had he to lay hands on her?

"Stop, Anyanwu!" he shouted.

She understood the English word "stop," but she ignored it. She brushed him aside and went back to the rail.

"Anyanwu!"

A new voice. New hands.

"Anyanwu, you are not alone here."

Perhaps no other words could have stopped her. Perhaps no other voice could have driven away her need to end the terrible solitude so quickly. Perhaps only her own language could have overwhelmed the call of the distant shore.

"Doro?"

She found herself in his arms, held fast. She realized that she had been on the verge of breaking those arms, if necessary, to get free, and she was appalled.

"Doro, something happened to me."

"I know."

Her fury was spent. She looked around dazedly. The yellow hair—what had happened to him? "Isaac?" she said fearfully. Had she thrown the young man into the sea?

There was a burst of foreign speech behind her, frightened and defensive in tone. Isaac. She turned and saw him alive and dry and was too relieved to wonder at his tone. He and Doro exchanged words in their English, then Doro spoke to her.

"He did not hurt you, Anyanwu?"

"No." She looked at the young man who was holding a red place on his right arm. "I think I have hurt him." She turned away in shame, appealed to Doro. "He helped me. I would not have hurt him, but... some spirit possessed me."

"Shall I apologize for you?" Doro seemed amused.

"Yes." She went over to Isaac, said his name softly, touched the injured arm. Not for the first time, she wished she could mute the pain of others as easily as she could mute her own. She heard Doro speak for her, saw the anger leave the young man's face. He smiled at her, showing bad teeth, but good humor. Apparently he forgave her.

"He says you are as strong as a man," Doro told her.

She smiled. "I can be as strong as many men, but he need not know that."

"He can know," Doro said. "He has strengths of his own. He is my son."

"Your..."

"The son of an American body." Doro smiled as though he had made a joke. "A mixed body, white and black and Indian. Indians are a brown people."

"But he is white."

"His mother was white. German and yellow-haired. He is more her son than mine—in appearance, at least."

Anyanwu shook her head, looking longingly at the distant coast.

"There is nothing for you to fear," Doro said softly. "You are not alone. Your children's children are here. I am here."

"How can you know what I feel?"

"I would have to be blind not to know, not to see."

"But..."

"Do you think you are the first woman I have taken from her people? I have been watching you since we left your village, knowing that this time would come for you. Our kind have a special need to be with either our kinsmen or others who are like us."

"You are not like me!"

He said nothing. He had answered this once, she remembered. Apparently, he did not intend to answer it again.

She looked at him—at the tall young body, well made and handsome. "Will I see, someday, what you are like when you are not hiding in another man's skin?"

For an instant, it seemed that a leopard looked at her through his eyes. A thing looked at her, and that thing feral and cold—a spirit thing that spoke softly.

"Pray to your gods that you never do, Anyanwu. Let me be a man. Be content with me as a man." He put his hand out to touch her and it amazed her that she did not flinch away, that she trembled, but stood where she was.

He drew her to him and to her surprise, she found comfort in his arms. The longing for home, for her people, which had threatened to possess her again receded—as though Doro, whatever he was, was enough.

When Doro had sent Anyanwu to look after her grandson, he turned to find his own son watching her go—watching the sway of her hips. "I just told her how easy she was to read," Doro said.

The boy glanced downward, knowing what was coming.

"You're fairly easy to read yourself," Doro continued.

"I can't help it," Isaac muttered. "You ought to put more clothes on her."

"I will, eventually. For now, just restrain yourself. She's one of the few people aboard who could probably kill you—just as you're one of the few who could kill her. And I'd rather not lose either of you."

"I wouldn't hurt her. I like her."

"Obviously."

"I mean..."

"I know, I know. She seems to like you too."

The boy hesitated, stared out at the blue water for a moment, then faced Doro almost defiantly. "Do you mean to keep her for yourself?"

Doro smiled inwardly. "For a while," he said. This was a favorite son, a rare, rare young one whose talent and temperament had matured exactly as Doro had intended. Doro had controlled the breeding of Isaac's ancestors for millennia, occasionally producing near successes that could be used in breeding, and dangerous, destructive failures that had to be destroyed. Then, finally, true success. Isaac. A healthy, sane son no more rebellious than was wise for a son of Doro, but powerful enough to propel a ship safely through a hurricane.

Isaac stared off in the direction Anyanwu had gone. He shook his head slowly.

"I can't imagine how your ability and hers would combine," Doro said, watching him.

Isaac swung around in sudden hope.

"It seems to me the small, complex things she does within her body would require some of the same ability you use to move large objects outside your body."

Isaac frowned. "How can she tell what she's doing down inside herself?"

"Apparently, she's also a little like one of my Virginia families. They can tell what's going on in closed places or in places miles from them. I've been planning to get you together with a couple of them."

"I can see why. I'd be better myself if I could see that way. Wouldn't have run the *Mary Magdalene* onto those rocks last year."

"You did well enough—kept us afloat until we made port."

"If I got a child by Anyanwu, maybe he'd have that other kind of sight. I'd rather have her than your Virginians."

Doro laughed aloud. It pleased him to indulge Isaac, and Isaac knew it. Doro was surprised sometimes at how close he felt to the best of his children. And, damn his curiosity, he did want to know what sort of child Isaac and Anyanwu could produce. "You'll have the Virginians," he said. "You'll have Anyanwu too. I'll share her with you. Later."

"When?" Isaac did nothing to conceal his eagerness.

"Later, I said. This is a dangerous time for her. She's leaving behind everything she's ever known, and she has no clear idea what she's exchanging it for. If we force too much on her now, she could kill herself before she's been of any use to us."

Chapter Five

Okoye stayed in Doro's cabin where Anyanwu could care for him until his sickness abated. Then Doro sent him below with the rest of the slaves. Once the ship was under way and beyond sight of the African coast, the slaves were permitted to roam where they pleased above or below deck. In fact, since they had little or no work to do, they had more freedom than the crew. Thus, there was no reason for Okoye to find the change restrictive. Doro watched him carefully at first to see that he was intelligent enough—or frightened enough—not to start trouble. But Anyanwu had introduced him to Udenkwo, and the young woman seemed to occupy much of his time from then on. Rebellion seemed not to occur to him at all.

"They may not please each other as much as they seem to," Anyanwu told Doro. "Who knows what is in their minds?"

Doro only smiled. What was in the young people's minds was apparent to everyone. Anyanwu was still bothered by their blood relationship. She was more a captive of her people's beliefs than she realized. She seemed to feel especially guilty about this union since she could have stopped it so easily. But it was clear even to her that Okoye and Udenkwo needed each other now as she needed Doro. Like her, they were feeling very vulnerable, very much alone.

Several days into the voyage, Doro brought Okoye on deck away from Udenkwo and told him that the ship's captain had the authority to perform a marriage ceremony.

"The white man, Woodley?" Okoye asked. "What has he to do with us?"

"In your new country, if you wish to marry, you must pledge yourselves before a priest or a man of authority like Woodley."

The boy shook his head doubtfully. "Everything is different here. I do not know. My father had chosen a wife for me, and I was pleased with her. Overtures had already been made to her family."

"You will never see her again." Doro spoke with utter conviction. He met the boy's angry glare calmly. "The world is not a gentle place, Okoye."

"Shall I marry because you say so?"

For a moment, Doro said nothing. Let the boy think about his stupid words for a moment. Finally, Doro said: "When I speak to be obeyed, young one, you will know, and you will obey."

Now it was Okoye who kept silent thoughtfully, and though he tried to conceal it, fearfully. "Must I marry?" he said at last.

"No."

"She had a husband."

Doro shrugged.

"What will you do with us in this homeland of yours?"

"Perhaps nothing. I will give you land and seed and some of my people will help you learn the ways of your new home. You will continue to learn English and perhaps Dutch. You will live. But in exchange for what I give, you will obey me whether I come to you tomorrow or forty years from now."

"What must I do?"

"I don't know yet. Perhaps I will give you a homeless child to care for or a series of children. Perhaps you will give shelter to adults who need it. Perhaps you will carry messages or deliver goods or hold property for me. Perhaps anything. Anything at all."

"Wrong things as well as right?"

"Yes."

"Perhaps I will not obey then. Even a slave must follow his own thoughts sometimes."

"That is your decision," Doro agreed.

"What will you do? Kill me?"

"Yes."

Okoye looked away, rubbed his breast where the branding iron had gouged. "I will obey," he whispered. He was silent for a moment, then spoke again wearily. "I wish to marry. But must the white man make the ceremony?"

"Shall I do it?"

"Yes." Okoye seemed relieved.

So it was. Doro had no legal authority. He simply ordered John Woodley to take credit for performing the ceremony. It was the ceremony Doro wanted the slaves to accept, not the ship's captain. As they had begun to accept unfamiliar foods and strange companions, they must accept new customs.

There was no palm wine as Okoye's family would have provided had Okoye taken a wife at home in his village, but Doro offered rum and there were the familiar yams and other foods, less familiar; there was a small feast. There were no relatives except Doro and Anyanwu, but by now the slaves and some members of the crew were familiar and welcome as guests. Doro told them in their own languages what was happening and they gathered around with laughter and gestures and comments in their own languages and in fragmentary English. Sometimes their meaning was unmistakably clear, and Okoye and Udenkwo were caught between embarrassment and laughter. In the benign atmosphere of the ship, all the slaves were recovering from their invariably harsh homeland experiences. Some of them had been kidnapped from their villages. Some had been sold for witchcraft or for other crimes of which they were usually not guilty. Some had been born slaves. Some had been enslaved during war. All had been treated harshly at some time during their captivity. All had lived through pain—more pain than they cared to remember. All had left kinsmen behind—husbands, wives, parents, children... people they realized by now that they would not see again.

But there was kindness on the ship. There was enough food—too much, since the slaves were so few. There were no chains. There were blankets to warm them and the sea air on deck to cool them. There were no whips, no guns. No woman was raped. People wanted to go home, but like Okoye, they feared Doro too much to complain or revolt. Most of them could not have said why they feared him, but he was the one man they all knew—the one who could speak, at least in limited fashion, with all of them. And once he had spoken with them, they shied away from attacking him, from doing anything that might bring his anger down on them.

"What have you done to them to make them so afraid?" Anyanwu asked him on the night of the wedding.

"Nothing," Doro said honestly. "You have seen me with them. I've harmed no one." He could see that she was not satisfied with this, but that did not matter. "You do not know what this ship could be," he told her. And he began to describe to her a slave ship—people packed together so that they could hardly move and chained in place so that they had to lie in their own filth, beatings, the women routinely raped, torture... large numbers of slaves dying. All suffering.

"Waste!" Doro finished with disgust. "But those ships carry slaves for sale. My people are only for my own use."

Anyanwu stared at him in silence for a moment. "Shall I be glad that your slaves will not be wasted?" she asked. "Or shall I fear the uses you will find for them?"

He laughed at her seriousness and gave her a little brandy to drink in celebration of her grandchildren's wedding. He would put her off for as long as he could. She did not want answers to her questions. She could have answered them herself. Why did *she* fear him? To what use did *she* expect to be put? She understood. She was simply sparing herself. He would spare her too. She was his most valuable cargo, and he was inclined to treat her gently.

Okoye and Udenkwo had been married for only two days when the great storm hit. Anyanwu, sleeping beside Doro in his too-soft bed, was awakened by the drumming of rain and running feet above. The ship lurched and rolled sickeningly, and Anyanwu resigned herself to enduring another storm. Her first storm at sea had been brief and violent and terrifying, but at least experiencing it gave her some idea what to expect now. The crew would be on deck, shouting, struggling with the sails, rushing about in controlled confusion. The slaves would be sick and frightened in their quarters, and Doro would gather with Isaac and a few other members of the crew whose duties seemed to involve nothing more than standing together, watching the trouble, and waiting for it to end.

"What do you do when you gather with them?" she had asked him once, thinking that perhaps even he had gods he turned to in times of danger.

"Nothing," he told her.

"Then... why do you gather?"

"We might be needed," he answered. "The men I gather with are my sons. They have special abilities that could be useful."

He would tell her nothing more—would not speak of these newly acknowledged sons except in warning. "Leave them alone," he said. "Isaac is the best of them, safe and stable. The others are not safe—not even for you."

Now he went up to his sons again, throwing on the white man's clothing he had taken to wearing as he ran. Anyanwu followed him, depending on her strength and agility to keep her safe.

On deck, she found wind and rain more violent than she had imagined. There were blue-white flares of lightning followed by absolute blackness. Great waves swept the deck and would surely have washed her overboard, but for her speed and strength. She held on, adjusting her eyes as quickly as she could. There was always a little light, even when ordinary vision perceived nothing. Finally, she could see—and she could hear above the wind and rain and waves. Fragments of desperate English reached her and she longed to understand. But if the words were meaningless, there was no mistaking the tone. These people thought they might die soon.

Someone slammed into her, knocking her down, then fell on her. She could see that it was only a crewman, battered by wind and waves. Most men had lashed themselves securely to whatever well-anchored objects they could find, and now, strove only to endure.

The wind picked up suddenly, and with it came a great mountain of water—a wave that rolled the ship over almost onto its side. Anyanwu caught the crewman's arm and, with her other hand, held onto the rail. If she had not, both she and the man would have been swept overboard. She dragged the man closer to her so that she could get an arm around him. Then for several seconds she simply held on. Back past the third of the great treelike masts, on what Isaac had called the poop deck, Doro stood with Isaac and three other men—the sons, waiting to see whether they could be useful. Surely it was time for them to do whatever they could.

She could distinguish Isaac easily from the others. He stood apart, his arms raised, his face turned down and to one side to escape some of the wind and rain, his clothing and yellow hair whipping about. For an instant, she thought he looked at her—or in her direction—but he could not have seen her through the darkness and rain. She watched him, fascinated. He had not tied himself to anything as the others had, yet he stood holding his strange pose while the ship rolled beneath him.

The wind blew harder. Waves swept high over the deck and there were moments when Anyanwu found even her great strength strained, moments when it would have been so easy to let the half-drowned crewman go. But she had not saved the man's life only to throw it away. She could see that other crewmen were holding on with fingers and line. She saw no one washed overboard. But still, Isaac stood alone, not even holding on with his hands, and utterly indifferent to wind and waves.

The ship seemed to be moving faster. Anyanwu felt increased pressure from the wind, felt her body lashed so hard by the rain that she tried to curl away from it against the crewman's body. It seemed that the ship was sailing against the wind, moving like a spirit-thing, raising waves of its own. Terrified, Anyanwu could only hold on.

Then, gradually, the cloud cover broke, and there were stars. There was a full moon reflecting fragmented light off calm waters. The waves had become gentle and lapped harmlessly at the ship, and the wind became no more than a cold breeze against Anyanwu's wet, nearly naked body.

Anyanwu released the crewman and stood up. Around the ship, people were suddenly shouting, freeing themselves, rushing to Isaac. Anyanwu's crewman picked himself up slowly, looked at Isaac, then at Anyanwu. Dazed, he looked up at the clear sky, the moon. Then with a hoarse cry and no backward glance at Anyanwu, he rushed toward Isaac.

Anyanwu watched the cheering for a moment—knew it to be cheering now—then stumbled below, and back to her cabin. There, she found water everywhere. It sloshed on the floor and the bed was sodden. She stood in it staring helplessly until Doro came to her, saw the condition of the cabin, and took her away to another, somewhat drier one.

"Were you on deck?" he asked her.

She nodded.

"Then you saw."

She turned to stare at him, uncomprehending. "What did I see?"

"The very best of my sons," he said proudly. "Isaac doing what he was born to do. He brought us through the storm—faster than any ship was ever intended to move."

"How?"

"How!" Doro mocked, laughing. "How do you change your shape, woman? How have you lived for three hundred years?"

She blinked, went to lie down on the bed. Finally, she looked around at the cabin he had brought her to. "Whose place is this?"

"The captain's," said Doro. "He'll have to make do with less for a while. You stay here. Rest."

"Are all your sons so powerful?"

He laughed again. "Your mind is leaping around tonight. But that's not surprising, I suppose. My other sons do other things. None of them manage their abilities as well as Isaac, though."

Anyanwu lay down wearily. She was not especially tired—her body was not tired. The strain she had endured was of a kind that should not have bothered her at all once it was over. It was her spirit that was weary. She needed time to sleep. Then she needed to go and find Isaac and look at him and see what she could see beyond the smiling, yellow-haired young man.

She closed her eyes and slept, not knowing whether Doro would lie down beside her or not. It was not until later, when she awoke alone that she realized he had not. Someone was pounding on her door.

She shook off sleep easily and got up to open the door. The moment she did, a very tall, thin crewman thrust a semiconscious Isaac through it into her arms.

She staggered for a moment, more from surprise than from the boy's weight. She had caught him reflexively. Now she felt the cold waxiness of his skin. He did not seem to know her, or even to see her. His eyes were half open and staring. Without her arms around him, he would have fallen.

She lifted him as though he were a child, laid him on the bed, and covered him with a blanket. Then she looked up and saw that the thin crewman was still there. He was a green-eyed man with a head that was too long and bones that seemed about to break through his splotchy, unshaven brown skin. He was a white man, but the sun had parched him unevenly and he looked diseased. He was one of the ugliest men Anyanwu had ever seen. And he was one of those who had stood beside Doro during the storm— another son. A much lesser son, if looks mattered. This was one of the sons Doro had ordered her to avoid. Well, she would will- ingly avoid him if he would only leave. He had brought her Isaac. Now, he should go away and let her give the boy what care she could. In the back of her mind, she wondered over and over what could be wrong with a boy who could speed great ships through the water. What had happened? Why had Doro not told her Isaac was sick?

Her thought of Doro repeated itself strangely as a kind of echo within her mind. She could see Doro suddenly—or an image of him. She saw him as a white man, yellow-haired like Isaac, and green-eyed like the ugly crewman. She had never seen Doro as white, had never heard him describe one of his white bodies, but she knew absolutely that she was seeing him as he had appeared in one of them. She saw the image giving Isaac to her—placing the half-conscious boy into her arms. Then abruptly, wrenchingly, she saw herself engaged in wild frantic sexual intercourse, first with Isaac, then with this ugly green-eyed man whose name was Lale. Lale Sachs.

How did she know that?

What was happening!

The green-eyed man laughed, and somehow his grating laughter echoed within her as had the thought of Doro. Somehow, this man was within her very thoughts!

She lunged at him and thrust him back through the door, her push hard enough to move a much heavier man. He flew backward out of control, and she slammed the door shut the instant he was through it. Even so, the terrible link she had with him was not broken. She felt pain as he fell and struck his head—stunning pain that dropped her to her knees where she crouched dizzily holding her head.

Then the pain was gone. He was gone from her thoughts. But he was coming through the door again, shouting words that she knew were curses. He seized her by the throat, literally lifted her to her feet by her neck. He was no weak man, but his strength was nothing compared to her own. She struck him randomly, as she broke away, and heard him cry out with pain.

She looked at him, and for an instant, she saw him clearly, the too-long face twisted with pain and anger, its mouth open and gasping, its nose smashed flat and spurting blood. She had hurt him more than she intended, but she did not care. No one had the right to go tampering with the very thoughts in her mind. Then the bloody face was gone.

A thing stood before her—a being more terrible than any spirit she could imagine. A great, horned, scaly lizard-thing of vaguely human shape, but with a thick lashing tail and a scaly dog head with huge teeth set in jaws that could surely break a man's arm.

In terror, Anyanwu transformed herself.

It was painful to change so quickly. It was agonizing. She bore the pain with a whimper that came out as a snarl. She had become a leopard, lithe and strong, fast and razor-clawed. She sprang.

The spirit screamed, collapsed, and became a man again.

Anyanwu hesitated, stood on his chest staring down at him. He was unconscious. He was a vicious, deadly being. Best to kill him now before he could come to and control her thoughts again. It seemed wrong to kill a helpless man, but if this man came to, he might well kill her.

"Anyanwu!"

Doro. She closed her ears to him. With a snarl, she tore out the throat of the being under her feet. In one way, that was a mistake. She tasted blood.

The speed of her change had depleted her as nothing else could. She had to feed soon. Now! She slashed her victim's shirt out of the way and tore flesh from his breast. She fed desperately, mindlessly until something struck her hard across the face.

She spat in pain and anger, realized dimly that Doro had kicked her. Her muscles tensed. She could kill him. She could kill anyone who interfered with her now.

He stood inches from her, head back, as though offering her his throat. Which was exactly what he was doing, of course.

"Come," he challenged. "Kill again. It has been a long time since I was a woman."

She turned from him, hunger driven, and tore more flesh from the body of his son.

He lifted her bodily and threw her off the corpse. When she tried to return to it, he kicked her, beat her.

"Control yourself," he ordered. "Become a woman!"

She did not know how she made the change. She did not know what held her from tearing him to pieces. Fear? She would not have thought that even fear could hold her at such a time. Doro had not seen the carnage she wrought on her own people so long ago when they attacked her and forced her to change too quickly. She had almost forgotten that part of the killing herself—the shame! Her people did not eat human flesh—but she had eaten it then. She had terrorized them into forgiving her, they outlived all but the legend of what she had done—or her mother had done, or her grandmother. People died. Their children ceased to be certain of exactly what had happened. The story became interwoven with spirits and gods. But what would she do now? She could not terrorize Doro into forgetting the grisly corpse on the floor.

Human again, she lay on the floor, face down and averted from the corpse. She was surprised that Doro did not go on beating her, that he did not kill her. She had no doubt that he could.

He lifted her, ignoring the blood that covered much of her body, and placed her on the bed beside Isaac. She lay there, limp, not looking at him. Oh, but the meat was warm inside her. Sustenance. She needed more!

"Why is Isaac here?" asked Doro. There was nothing in his voice. Not even anger.

"The other one brought him. Lale Sachs. He said you sent Isaac to me...." She stopped, confused. "No. He did not say it, he... he was in my thoughts, he..."

"I know."

She turned finally to look at him. He looked tired, haggard. He looked like a man in pain, and she wanted to touch him, comfort him. But her hands were covered with blood.

"What else did he tell you?"

She shook her head back and forth against the bed. "I do not know. He showed an image of me lying with Isaac, then lying with him. He made me see it—almost made me want it." She turned away again. "When I tried to send him away without... harming him, he did another thing.... Doro, I must have food!" This last was a cry of pain.

He heard. "Stay here," he said softly. "I'll bring you something."

He went away. When he was gone, it seemed that she could smell the meat on the floor. It beckoned to her. She moaned and turned her face down to the mattress. Beside her, Isaac made a small sound and moved closer to her. Surprised, she raised her head to look at him.

He was still semiconscious. His eyes were closed now, but she could see that they moved under the lids. And his lips moved, formed silent words. He had almost a black man's mouth, the lips fuller than those of the other whites she had seen. Stiff yellow hairs grew from his face, showing that he had not shaved for a while. He had a broad, square face not unattractive to Anyanwu, and the sun had burned him a good, even brown. She wondered what white women thought of him. She wondered how white women looked.

"Food, Anyanwu," Doro said softly.

She jumped, startled. She was becoming a deaf woman! Doro had never been able to approach her unheard before. But that did not matter. Not now.

She seized the bread and meat from his hands. Both were hard and dry—the kind of food the crew ate all the time, but they were no challenge to her teeth and jaws. Doro gave her wine and she gulped it down. The fresh meat on the floor would have been better, but now that she was in control of herself, nothing would make her touch that again.

"Tell me all that happened," said Doro when she had eaten what he had given her.

She told him. She needed sleep now, but not as badly as she had needed food. And he deserved to know why his son had died.

She expected some comment or action from him when she finished, but he only shook his head and sighed. "Sleep now, Anyanwu. I will take Lale away, and Isaac."

"But..."

"Sleep. You are almost asleep now, almost talking in your sleep." He reached over her and lifted Isaac from the bed.

"What happened to him?" she whispered.

"He overextended himself just as you did. He will heal."

"He is cold... so cold."

"You would warm him if I left him here. You would warm him as Lale intended. Even your strength would not be enough to stop him once he began to awaken."

And before her slow, drowsy mind could question this, Doro and Isaac were gone. She never heard him come back for Lale, never knew whether he returned to sleep beside her that night, never cared.

* * *

Lale Sachs was dropped into the sea the next day. Anyanwu was present at the small ceremony Captain Woodley made. She had not wanted to be, but Doro commanded it. He told everyone what she had done, then made her appear before them. She thought he did it to shame her, and she was ashamed. But later, he explained.

"It was for your protection," he told her. "Everyone aboard has been warned against molesting you. My sons have been doubly warned. Lale chose to ignore me. I cannot seem to breed stupidity out of some of my people. He thought it would be interesting to watch when Isaac came to as hungry for a woman as you were for food. He thought perhaps he would have you too when Isaac had finished."

"But how could he reach out and change the thoughts in my mind?"

"It was his special ability. I've had men who were better at it—good enough to control you absolutely, even control your changes. You would be no more than clay for such a man to mold. But Lale was the best of his generation to survive. His kind often don't survive long."

"I can understand that!" Anyanwu said.

"No, you can't," Doro told her. "But you will."

She turned away. They were on deck, so she stared out at the sea where several large fish were leaping into the air and arcing down again into the water. She had watched such creatures before, watched them longingly. She thought she could do what they did, thought she could become one of them. She could almost feel the sensation of wetness, of strength, of moving through the water as swiftly as a bird through the air. She longed to try, and she feared to try. Now, though, she did not think of trying. She thought only of the body of Lale Sachs, wrapped in cloth, its gaping wounds hidden. Would the leaping fish finish what she had begun? Consume the rest of the foolish, ugly, evil man?

She closed her eyes. "What shall we do now, Doro? What will you do with me?"

"What shall I do with you?" he mocked. He put his hands around her waist and pulled her against him.

Startled, she moved away. "I have killed your son."

"Do you think I blame you for that?"

She said nothing, only stared at him.

"I wanted him to live," Doro said. "His kind are so troublesome and so short-lived.... He has fathered only three children. I wanted more from him, but, Anyanwu, if you had not killed him, if he had succeeded in what he meant to do, I would have killed him myself."

She lowered her head, somehow not really surprised. "Could you have done it? Your son?"

"Anyone," he said.

She looked up at him, questioning, yet not wanting answers.

"I control powerful people," he said. "My people. The destruction they can cause if they disobey me is beyond your imagining. Any one of them, any group of them who refuse to obey is useless to me and dangerous to the rest of my people."

She moved uncomfortably, understanding what he was telling her. She remembered his voice when he spoke to her the night before. *"Come. Kill again. It has been a long time since I was a woman!"* He would have consumed her spirit as she had consumed his son's flesh. He would be wearing her body today.

She turned to look out at the leaping fish again, and when he drew her to his side this time, she did not move away. She was not afraid; she was relieved. Some part of her mind wondered how this could be, but she had no answer. People did not react rationally to Doro. When he did nothing, they feared him. When he threatened them, they believed him, but did not hate him or flee.

"Isaac is well," he told her.

"Is he? What did he do for his hunger?"

"Endured it until it went away."

To her surprise, his words sparked guilt in her. She had the foolish urge to find the young man and apologize for not keeping him with her. He would think she had lost her senses. "You should get him a wife," she told Doro.

Doro nodded absently. "Soon," he said.

There came a time when Doro said land was near—a time when the strange food was rotten and full of worms and the drinking water stank and the ship stank and the slaves fought among themselves and the crewmen fished desperately to vary their disgusting diet and the sun's heat intensified and the wind did not blow. In the

midst of all this discomfort, there were events that Anyanwu would
recall with pleasure for the rest of her life. This was when she came
to understand clearly just what Isaac's special ability was, and he
came to understand her own.

After Lale's death, she avoided the boy as best she could in the
confined space of the ship, thinking that he might not be as indifferent to the death of a brother as Doro was to the death of a son.
But Isaac came to her.

He joined her at the rail one day as she stood watching the leaping fish. He watched them himself for a moment, then laughed. She
glanced up at him questioningly, and he pointed out to sea. When
she looked there again, she saw one of the great fish hanging high
above the water, struggling in midair.

It was as though the creature had been caught in some invisible
net. But there was no net. There was nothing.

She looked at Isaac in amazement. "You?" she asked in her uncertain English. "You do this?"

Isaac only smiled. The fish, struggling wildly, drifted closer to
the ship. Several crewmen noticed it and began shouting at Isaac.
Anyanwu could not understand most of what they said, but she
knew they wanted the fish. Isaac made a gesture presenting it to
Anyanwu, though it still hung over the water. She looked around at
the eager crewmen, then grinned. She beckoned for the fish to be
brought aboard.

Isaac dropped it at her feet.

Everyone ate well that night. Anyanwu ate better than anyone,
because for her, the flesh of the fish told her all she needed to know
about the creature's physical structure—all she needed to know to take
its shape and live as it did. Just a small amount of raw flesh told her
more than she had words to say. Within each bite, the creature told
her its story clearly thousands of times. That night in their cabin, Doro
caught her experimentally turning one of her arms into a flipper.

"What are you doing!" he demanded, with what sounded like
revulsion.

She laughed like a child and stood up to meet him, her arm flowing easily back to its human shape. "Tomorrow," she said, "you will
tell Isaac how to help me, and I will swim with the fish! I will be a
fish! I can do it now! I have wanted to for so long."

"How do you know you can?" Curiosity quickly drove any negative feelings from him, as usual. She told him of the messages she had read within the flesh of the fish. "Messages as clear and fine as those in your books," she told him. Privately she thought her flesh-messages even more specific than the books he had introduced her to, read to her from. But the books were the only example she could think of that he might understand. "It seems that you could misunderstand your books," she said. "Other men made them. Other men can lie or make mistakes. But the flesh can only tell me what it is. It has no other story."

"But how do you read it?" he asked. *Read.* If he used that English word, he too saw the similarity.

"My body reads it—reads everything. Did you know that fish breathes air as we do? I thought it would breathe water like the ones we caught and dried at home."

"It was a dolphin," Doro murmured.

"But it was more like a land thing than a fish. Inside, it is much like a land animal. The changes I make will not be as great as I thought."

"Did you have to eat leopard flesh to learn to become a leopard?"

She shook her head. "No, I could see what the leopard was like. I could mold myself into what I saw. I was not a true leopard, though, until I killed one and ate a little of it. At first, I was a woman pretending to be a leopard—clay molded into leopard shape. Now when I change, I am a leopard."

"And now you will be a dolphin." He gazed at her. "You cannot know how valuable you are to me. Shall I let you do this?"

That startled her. It had not occurred to her that he would disapprove. "It is a harmless thing," she said.

"A dangerous thing. What do you know of the sea?"

"Nothing. But tomorrow I will begin to learn. Have Isaac watch me; I will stay near the surface. If he sees that I'm in trouble, he can lift me out of the water and let me change back on deck."

"Why do you want to do this?"

She cast about for a reason she could put into words, a reason other than the wrenching longing she had felt when she watched the dolphins leaping and diving. It was like the days at home when she had watched eagles fly until she could no longer stand to only watch. She had killed an eagle and eaten and learned and flown as no human was ever meant to fly. She had flown away, escaping her town, her duties, her kinsmen. But after a while, she had flown back to her people. Where else could she go? Afterward, though, when the seasons with them grew long and the duties tiresome, when the kinsmen by themselves became a great tribe, she would escape again. She would fly. There was danger. Men hunted her and once had nearly killed her. She made an exceptionally large, handsome eagle. But fear never kept her out of the sky. Nor would it keep her out of the water.

"I want this," she told Doro. "I will do it without Isaac if you keep him from helping me."

Doro shook his head. "Were you this way with your other husbands—telling them what you would do in spite of their wishes?"

"Yes," she said seriously, and was very much relieved when he laughed aloud. Better to amuse him than to anger him.

The next day she stood by the rail, watching Doro and Isaac argue in English. It was Isaac who did most of the arguing. Doro said only a few words, and then later repeated them exactly. Anyanwu could find only one word in what Isaac said that was repeated. The word was "shark," and Isaac said it with vehemence. But he stopped when he saw how little attention Doro was paying to him. And Doro turned to face her.

"Isaac fears for you," he told her.

"Will he help?"

"Yes—though I told him he didn't have to."

"I thought you were speaking for me!"

"In this, I am only translating."

His attitude puzzled her. He was not angry, not even annoyed. He did not even seem to be as concerned for her as Isaac was, and yet he said he valued her. "What is a shark?" she asked.

"A fish," Doro said. "A large flesh eater, a killer at least as deadly in the sea as your leopards are on land."

"You did not say there were such things."

He looked at the water. "It is as dangerous down there as in your forests," he told her. "You need not go."

"You didn't try hard to stop me from going."

"No."

"Why?"

"I want to see whether you can do it or not."

He reminded her of one of her sons who, when he was very young, had thrown several fowls into the river to see whether they could swim.

"Stay near the dolphins if they let you," Doro said. "Dolphins know how to deal with sharks."

Anyanwu tore off her cloth and dived into the sea before her confidence deserted her entirely. There, she transformed herself as quickly as was comfortable. She became the dolphin whose flesh she had eaten.

And she was moving through the water alongside the ship, propelling her long, sleek body forward with easy beats of her tail. She was seeing differently, her eyes now on the sides of her head instead of in front. Her head had extended itself into a hard beak. She was breathing differently—or rather, she was not breathing at all until she felt the need and found herself surfacing in a slow forward roll that exposed her blowhole-nose briefly and allowed her to expel her breath and take new air into her lungs. She observed herself minutely, saw that her dolphin body used the air it breathed much more efficiently than an ordinary human body. The dolphin body knew tricks her own human body had taken time and pain to learn. How to expel and renew a much larger portion of the air in its lungs with each breath. How to leach more of the usable portion of that air from the rest, the waste, and use it to fuel the body. Other things. None of it was new to her, but she thought she would have learned it all much sooner and more easily with the help of a bit of dolphin flesh. Instead, she had had only men who attempted to drown her.

She reveled in the strength and speed of her new body, and in its keen hearing. In her human shape, she kept her hearing abnormally keen—kept all her senses keen. But dolphin hearing was superior to anything she had ever created in herself. As a dolphin, she could close her eyes and perceive an only slightly diminished world around her with her ears. She could make sounds and they would come back to her as echoes bearing with them the story of all that lay before her. She had never imagined such hearing.

Finally, she directed her attention from herself to the other dolphins. She had heard them too, chattering not far from her, keeping alongside the ship as she did. Strangely, their chatter sounded more human now—more like speech, like a foreign speech. She swam toward them slowly, uncertainly. How did they greet strangers? How would they greet one small, ignorant female? If they were speaking among themselves somehow, they would think her mute—or mad.

A dolphin swam to meet her, paralleled her, observing her out of one lively eye. This was a male, she realized, and she watched him with interest. After a moment, he swam closer and rubbed his body against hers. Dolphin skin, she discovered, was pleasantly sensitive. It was not scaly as was the skin of true fish which she had never imitated, but whose bodies she understood. The male brushed her again, chattering in a way she felt was questioning, then swam away. She turned, checking the position of the ship, and saw that by keeping up with the dolphins, she was also keeping up with it. She swam after the male.

There were advantages, she thought, to being a female animal. The males of some species fought each other, mindlessly possessive of territory or females. She could remember being bullied as a female animal, being pursued by persistent males, but only in her true woman-shape could she remember being seriously hurt by males—men. It was only accident that made her a female dolphin; she had eaten the flesh of a female. But it was a fortunate accident.

A very small dolphin, a baby, she assumed, came to make her acquaintance, and she swam slowly, allowing it to investigate her. Eventually, its mother called it away, and she was alone again. Alone, but surrounded by creatures like herself—creatures she was finding it harder to think of as animals. Swimming with them was like being with another people. A friendly people. No slavers with brands and chains here. No Doro with gentle, terrible threats to her children, to her.

As time passed, several dolphins approached to touch her, rub themselves against her, get acquainted. When the male who had touched her first returned, she was startled to realize that she recognized him. His touch was his touch—not quite like that of any of the others as they were not quite like each other.

Suddenly, he leaped high out of the water and arced back, landing some distance ahead of her. She wondered why she had not tried this herself and leaped a short distance. Her dolphin body was wonderfully agile. She seemed to fly through the air, plunging back smoothly and leaping again without strain or weariness. This was the best body she had ever shaped for herself. If only dolphin speech came as easily as dolphin movement. Some part of her mind wondered why it did not, wondered whether Doro was superior to her in this. Did he gain a new language, new knowledge when he took a new body—since he actually did possess the body, not merely duplicate it?

Her male dolphin came to touch her again and drove all thoughts of Doro from her mind. She understood that the dolphin's interest had become more than casual. He stayed close to her now, touching her, matching his movements with her own. She realized that she did not mind his attention. She had avoided animal matings in the past. She was a woman. Intercourse with an animal was abomination. She would feel unclean reverting to her human form with the seed of a male animal inside her.

But now... it was as though the dolphins were not animals.

She performed a kind of dance with the male, moving and touching, certain that no human ceremony had ever drawn her in so quickly. She felt both eager and restrained, both willing and hesitant. She would accept him, had already accepted him. He was surely no more strange than the ogbanje, Doro. Now seemed to be a time for strange matings.

She continued the dance, wishing she had a song to go with it. The male seemed to have a song. She wondered whether he would leave her after the mating, and thought he probably would. But his would not be the greatest leave-taking. He would not leave the group as she would, deserting everyone. But that was something to think about in the future. It did not matter. Only what was happening now mattered.

Then, suddenly, there was a man in the water. Startled, both Anyanwu and her male swam a short distance away, their dance interrupted. The group of dolphins shied away from the man, but he pursued them, sometimes in the water, sometimes above it. He did not swim or leap or dive, but somehow arrowed through water and air holding his body still, apparently not using his muscles.

Finally, Anyanwu separated herself from the school and approached the man. It was Isaac, she knew. He looked very different to her now—a clumsy thing, stiff and strange, but not remarkably ugly or frightening. He was a threat, though. He had had no reason to lose his taste for dolphin flesh, but she had. He might make another kill if she did not distract him. She turned and swam to him, approaching very slowly so that he would see her and understand that she meant no harm. She was certain that he could not distinguish her from any other dolphin. She swam in a small circle around where he hovered now, just above the water.

He spoke in low, strange tones, said her name several times before she recognized it. Then, without stopping to wonder how she did it, she brought herself upright on her tail for a moment and managed a kind of nod. She swam to him, and he lowered himself into the water. She swam past his side, near enough to be touched. He caught her dorsal fin and said something else. She listened closely.

"Doro wants you back at the ship."

That was that. She looked back at the dolphins regretfully, trying to pick out her male. She found him surprisingly nearby—dangerously nearby. It would have been so good to return to him, stay with him, just for a while. The mating would have been good. She wondered whether Doro had known or suspected what she was doing when he sent Isaac out to get her.

It did not matter. Isaac was here, and he had to be taken away before he noticed the other dolphin so temptingly near. She swam back toward the ship, allowing him to keep his hold on her fin. She did not mind towing him.

"I'll go up first," he said when they reached the ship. "Then I'll lift you."

He rose straight out of the water and drifted onto the ship. He could fly without wings as easily as he could direct the ship out of a storm. She wondered whether he could be sick and need a woman after this too. Then something touched her, gripped her firmly but not painfully, lifted her out of the water. It was not, as she had thought, like being lifted by a net or by the arms of men. There was no special feeling of pressure on any part of her body. It was like being held and supported by the air itself—softness that seemed to envelop her entire body, firmness that all her strength could not free her from.

But she did not use her strength, did not struggle. She had seen the futility of the dolphin's struggles the day before, and she had felt the speed of the great ship as it plunged through the storm, propelled by isaac's power. No strength of her muscles could resist such power. Besides, she trusted the boy. He handled her more carefully than he had the other dolphin, gestured crewmen back out of his way before he set her down gently on deck. Then the crewmen, Doro, and Isaac watched, fascinated, as she began to grow legs. She had had to absorb her legs almost completely, leaving only the useless detached hip bones natural to her dolphin body—as though the dolphin itself were slowly developing legs—or losing them. Now, she began with this large change. And her flippers began to look more like arms. Her neck, her entire body, grew slender again and her tiny excellent dolphin ears enlarged to become less efficient human ears. Her nose migrated back to her face and she absorbed her beak, her tail, and her fin. There were internal changes that those watching could not be aware of. And her gray skin changed color and texture. That change caused her to begin thinking about what she might have to do to herself if someday she decided to vanish into this land of white people that she was approaching. She would have to do some experimenting later. It was always useful to be able to camouflage oneself to hide or to learn the things people either would not or could not deliberately teach her about themselves. This when she could speak English well, of course. She would have to work harder at the language.

When the transformation was complete, she stood up, and Doro handed her her cloth. Before the staring men, she wrapped it around her waist and tied it. It had been centuries since she had gone naked in the way of unmarried young girls. She felt ashamed now to be seen by so many men, but she understood that again, Doro wanted his people to see her power. If he could not breed stupidity out of them, he would frighten it out.

She looked around at them, allowing no hint of her shame to reach her expression. Why should they know what she felt? She read awe in their expressions, and two who were near her actually stepped back when she looked at them. Then Doro hugged her wet body to him and she was able to relax. Isaac laughed aloud, breaking the tension, and said something to Doro. Doro smiled.

In her language, he said: "What children you will give me!" She was caught by the intensity she could sense behind his words. It reminded her that his was more than an ordinary man's desire for children. She could not help thinking of her own children, strong and healthy, but as short-lived and powerless as the children of any other woman. Could she give Doro what he wanted—what she herself had wanted for so long—children who would not die?

"What children you will give me, husband," she whispered, but the words were more questioning than his had been.

And strangely, Doro also seemed to become uncertain. She looked at him and caught a troubled expression on his face. He was staring out at the dolphins who were leaping again, some of them just ahead of the ship. He shook his head slowly.

"What is it?" she asked.

He looked away from the dolphins, and for a moment, his expression was so intense, so feral that she wondered if he hated the animals, or envied her because she could join them.

"What is it?" she repeated.

He seemed to force himself to smile. "Nothing," he said. He pulled her head to his shoulder reassuringly, and stroked her glossy, newly grown skullcap of hair. Unreassured, she accepted the caress and wondered why he was lying.

Chapter Six

Anyanwu had too much power.

In spite of Doro's fascination with her, his first inclination was to kill her. He was not in the habit of keeping alive people he could not control absolutely. But if he killed her and took over her body, he would get only one or two children from her before he had to take a new body. Her longevity would not help him keep her body alive. He did not acquire the use of his victims' special abilities with his transmigrations. He inhabited bodies. He consumed lives. That was all. Had he killed Lale, he would not have acquired the man's thought-transfer ability. He would only have been able to pass on that ability to children of Lale's body. And if he killed Anyanwu, he would not acquire her malleability, longevity, or healing. He would have only his own special ability lodged within her small, durable body until he began to hunger—hunger in a way Anyanwu and Isaac could never understand. He would hunger, and he would have to feed. Another life. A new body. Anyanwu would last him no longer than any other good kill.

Therefore, Anyanwu must live and bear her valuable young. But she had too much power. In her dolphin form, and before that, in her leopard form, Doro had discovered that his mind could not find her. Even when he could see her, his mind, his tracking sense, told him she was not there. It was as though she had died, as though he confronted a true animal—a creature beyond his reach. And if he could not reach her, he could not kill her and take her body while she was in animal form. In her human shape, she was as vulnerable to him as anyone else, but as an animal, she was beyond him as animals had always been beyond him. He longed now for one of the animal sensitives his controlled breeding occasionally produced. These were people whose abilities extended to touching animal minds, receiving sensation and emotion from them, people who suffered every time someone wrung a chicken's neck or gelded a horse or slaughtered a pig. They led short, unenviable lives. Sometimes Doro killed them before they could waste their valuable bodies in suicide. But now, he could have used a living one. Without one, his control of Anyanwu was dangerously limited.

And if Anyanwu ever discoverd that limitation, she might run away from him whenever she chose. She might go the moment he demanded more of her than she was willing to give. Or she might go if she discovered that he meant to have both her and the children she had left behind in Africa. She believed her cooperation had bought their freedom—believed he would give up such potentially valuable people. If she found out the truth, she would surely run, and he would lose her. He had never before lost anyone in that way.

He lost people to disease, accident, war, causes beyond his control. People were stolen from him or killed as had been his people of the savanna. This was bad enough. It was waste, and he intended to end much of it by bringing his people to less widely scattered communities in the Americas. But no individual had ever succeeded in escaping him. Individuals who ran from him were caught and most often killed. His own people knew better than to run from him.

But Anyanwu, wild seed that she was, did not know. Yet.

He would have to teach her, instruct her quickly and begin using her at once. He wanted as many children as he could get from her before it became necessary to kill her. Wild seed always had to be destroyed eventually. It could never conform as children born among his people conformed. But like no other wild seed, Anyanwu would learn to fear him and bend herself to his will. He would use her for breeding and healing. He would use her children, present and future, to create more acceptable long-lived types. The troublesome shape-changing ability could probably be bred out of her line if it appeared. The fact that it had not appeared so far told him he might be able to extinguish it entirely. But then, none of her special abilities had appeared among her children. They had inherited nothing more than potential—good blood that might produce special abilities after a few generations of inbreeding. Perhaps he would fail with them. Perhaps he would discover that Anyanwu could not be duplicated, or that there could be no longevity without shape-changing. Perhaps. But any finding, positive or negative, was generations away.

Meanwhile, Anyanwu must never learn of his limitation, must never know it was possible for her to escape him, avoid him, live free of him even as an animal. This meant he must not restrict her transformations any more strenuously than he restricted his children in the use of their abilities. She would not be permitted to show what she could do among ordinary people or harm his people except in self-defense. That was all. She would fear him, obey him, consider him almost omnipotent, but she would notice nothing in his attitude that might start her wondering. There would be nothing for her to notice.

Thus, as the journey neared its end, he allowed Anyanwu and Isaac to indulge in wild, impossible play, using their abilities freely, behaving like the witch-children they were. They went into the water together several times when there was enough wind and Isaac was not needed to propel the ship. The boy was not fighting a storm now. He was able to handle the ship without overextending himself, able to expend energy cavorting in the water with a dolphin-shaped Anyanwu. Then Anyanwu took to the air as a great bird, and Isaac followed, doing acrobatics that Doro would never have permitted over land. Here, there was no one to shoot the boy out of the sky, no mob to chase him down and try to burn him as a witch. He had to restrain himself so much on land that Doro placed no restraints on him now.

Doro worried about Anyanwu when she ventured under water alone—worried that he would lose her to sharks or other predators. But when she was finally attacked by a shark, it was near the surface. She suffered only a single wound which she sealed at once. Then she managed to ram her beak hard into the shark's gills. She must also have managed to take an undolphinlike bite out of the shark, since she immediately shifted to the sleek, deadly shark form. As it happened, the change was unnecessary. The shark was crippled, perhaps dying. But the change had been made, and made too quickly. Anyanwu had to feed. With strength and speed she tore the true shark to pieces and gorged herself on it. When she became a woman again, Doro could find no sign of the wound she had suffered. He found her drowsy and content, not at all the shaking, tormented creature who had killed Lale. This time, her drive to feed had been quickly satisfied. Apparently, that was important.

She adopted the dolphins, refusing to let Isaac bring any more aboard to be killed. "They are like people," she insisted in her fast-improving English. "They are not fish!" She swore she would have nothing more to do with Isaac if he killed another of them.

And Isaac, who loved dolphin flesh, brought no more dolphins aboard. Doro listened to the boy's muttered complaints, smiled, and said nothing. Isaac listened to the crewmen's complaints, shrugged, and gave them other fish. He continued to spend his spare time with Anyanwu, teaching her English, flying or swimming with her, merely being with her whenever he could. Doro neither encouraged nor discouraged this, though he did approve. He had been thinking a great deal about Isaac and Anyanwu—how well they got along in spite of their communication problems, in spite of their potentially dangerous abilities, in spite of their racial differences. Isaac would marry Anyanwu if Doro ordered it. The boy might even like the idea. And once Anyanwu accepted the marriage, Doro's hold on her would be secure. The children would come—desirable, potentially multi-talented children—and Doro could travel as he pleased to look after his other peoples. When he returned to his New York village of Wheatley, Anyanwu would still be there. Her children would hold her if her husband did not. She could become an animal or alter herself enough to travel freely among whites or Indians, but several children would surely slow her down. And she would not abandon them. She was too much a mother for that. She would stay—and if Doro found another man he wished to breed her with he could come to her wearing that man's body. It would be a simple matter.

What would not be simple would be giving Anyanwu her first hard lesson in obedience. She would not want to go to Isaac. Among her people, a woman could divorce her husband by running away from him and seeing that the bride-wealth he had given for her was returned. Or her husband could divorce her by driving her away. If her husband was impotent, he could, with her consent, give her to another man so that she could bear children in her husband's name. If her husband died, she could marry his successor, usually his oldest son as long as this was not also her own son. But there was no provision for what Doro planned to do—give her to his son while he, Doro, was still alive. She considered Doro her husband now. No ceremony had taken place, but none was necessary. She was not a young girl passing from the hands of her father to those of her first husband. It was enough that she and Doro had chosen each other. She would think it wrong to go to Isaac. But her thinking would change as had the thinking of other powerful, self-willed people whom Doro had recruited. She would learn that right and wrong were what he said they were.

At the place Doro had called "New York Harbor," everyone except the crew was to change ships, move to a pair of smaller "river sloops" to travel up the "Hudson River" to Doro's village of "Wheatley."

With less experience at absorbing change and learning new dialects if not new languages, Anyanwu thought she would have been utterly confused. She would have been frightened into huddling together with the slaves and looking around with suspicion and dread. Instead, she stood on deck with Doro, waiting calmly for the transfer to the new ships. Isaac and several others had gone ashore to make arrangements.

"When will we change?" she had asked Doro in English. She often tried to speak English now.

"That depends on how soon Isaac can hire the sloops," he said. Which meant he did not know. That was good. Anyanwu hoped the wait would be long. Even she needed time to absorb the many differences of this new world. From where she stood she could see a few other large, square-rigged ships lying at anchor in the harbor. And there were smaller boats either moving under billowing, usually triangular sails or tied up at the long piers Doro had pointed out to her. But ships and boats seemed familiar to her now. She was eager to see how these new people lived on land. She had asked to go ashore with Isaac, but Doro had refused. He had chosen to keep her with him. She stared ashore longingly at the rows and rows of buildings, most two, three, even four stories high, and side against side as though like ants in a hill, the people could not bear to be far apart. In much of her own country, one could stand in the middle of a town and see little more than forest. The villages of the towns were well-organized, often long-established, but they were more a part of the land they occupied, less of an intrusion upon it.

"Where does one compound end and another begin?" she asked, staring at the straight rows of pointed roofs.

"Some of those buildings are used for storage and other things," Doro said. "Of the others, consider each one a separate compound. Each one houses a family."

She looked around, startled. "Where are the farms to feed so many?"

"Beyond the city. We will see farms on our way upriver. Also, many of the houses have their own gardens. And look there." He pointed to a place where the great concentration of buildings tapered off and ended. "That is farmland."

"It seems empty."

"It is sown with barley now, I think. And perhaps a few oats."

These English names were familiar to her because he and Isaac had told her about them. Barley for making the beer that the crew drank so much of, oats for feeding the horses the people of this country rode, wheat for bread, maize for bread and for eating in other ways, tobacco for smoking, fruits and vegetables, nuts and herbs. Some of these things were only foreign versions of foods already known to her, but many were as new to her as the anthill city.

"Doro, let me go to see these things," she pleaded. "Let me walk on land again. I have almost forgotten how it feels to stand on a surface that does not move."

Doro rested one arm comfortably around her. He liked to touch her before others more than any man she had ever known, but it did not seem that any of his people were amused or contemptuous of his behavior. Even the slaves seemed to accept whatever he did as the proper thing for him to do. And Anyanwu enjoyed his touches even now when she thought they were more imprisoning than caressing. "I will take you to see the city another time," he said. "When you know more of the ways of its people, when you can dress as they do and behave as one of them. And when I get myself a white body. I am not interested in trying to prove to one suspicious white man after another that I own myself."

"Are all black men slaves, then?"

"Most are. It is the responsibility of blacks to prove that they are free—if they are. A black without proof is taken to be a slave."

She frowned. "How is Isaac seen?"

"As a white man. He knows what he is but he was raised white. This is not an easy place to be black. Soon it will not be an easy place to be Indian."

She was silent for a moment, then asked fearfully, "Must I become white?"

"Do you want to?" He looked down at her.

"No! I thought with you I could be myself."

He seemed pleased. "With me, and with my people, you can. Wheatley is a long way upriver from here. Only my people live there, and they do not enslave each other."

"All belonging, as they do, to you," she said.

He shrugged.

"Are blacks there as well as whites?"

"Yes."

"I will live there then. I could not live in a place where being myself would mean being thought a slave."

"Nonsense," Doro said. "You are a powerful woman. You could live in any place I chose."

She looked at him quickly to see whether he was laughing at her—speaking of her power and at the same time reminding her of his own power to control her. But he was watching the approach of a small, fast-moving boat. As the boat came alongside, its one passenger and his several bundles rose straight up and drifted onto the ship. Isaac, of course. Anyanwu realized suddenly that the boy had used neither oars nor sails to propel the boat.

"You're among strangers!" Doro told him sharply, and the boy dropped, startled, to the deck.

"No one saw me," he said. "But look, speaking of being among strangers..." He unrolled one of the bundles that had drifted aboard with him, and Anyanwu saw that it was a long, full, bright blue petticoat of the kind given to slave women when they grew cold as the ship traveled north. Anyanwu could protect herself from the cold without such coverings though she had cut a petticoat apart to make new cloths from it. She disliked the idea of covering her body so completely, smothering herself, she called it. She thought the slave women looked foolish so covered.

"You've come to civilization," Isaac was telling her.

"You've got to learn to wear clothes now, do as the people here do."

"What is civilization?" she asked.

Isaac glanced at Doro uncomfortably, and Doro smiled. "Never mind," Isaac said after a moment. "Just get dressed. Let's see how you look with clothes on."

Anyanwu touched the petticoat. The material felt smooth and cool beneath her fingers—not like the drab, coarse cloth of the slave women's petticoats. And the color pleased her—a brilliant blue that went well with her dark skin.

"Silk," Isaac said. "The best."

"Who did you steal it from?" Doro asked.

Isaac blushed dark beneath his tan and glared at his father.

"Did you steal it, Isaac?" Anyanwu demanded, alarmed.

"I left money," he said defensively. "I found someone your size, and I left twice the money these things are worth."

Anyanwu glanced at Doro uncertainly, then stepped away from him as she saw how he was looking at Isaac.

"If you're ever caught and pulled down in the middle of a stunt like that," Doro said, "I'll let them burn you."

Isaac licked his lips, put the petticoat into Anyanwu's arms. "Fair enough," he said softly. "If they can."

Doro shook his head, said something harshly in a language other than English. Isaac jumped. He glanced at Anyanwu as though to see whether she had understood. She stared back at him blankly, and he managed a weak smile of what she supposed to be relief at her ignorance. Doro gathered Isaac's bundles and spoke in English to Anyanwu. "Come on. Let's get you dressed."

"It would be easier to become an animal and wear nothing," she muttered, and was startled when he pushed her toward the hatchway.

In their cabin, Doro seemed to relax and let go of his anger. He carefully unwrapped the other bundles. A second petticoat, a woman's waistcoat, a cap, underclothing, stockings, shoes, some simple gold jewelry...

"Another woman's things," Anyanwu said, lapsing into her own language.

"Your things now," Doro said. "Isaac was telling the truth. He paid for them."

"Even though he did not ask first whether the woman wished to sell them."

"Even so. He took a foolish, unnecessary risk. He could have been shot out of the air or trapped, jailed, and eventually executed for witchcraft."

"He could have gotten away."

"Perhaps. But he would probably have had to kill a few people. And for what?" Doro held up the petticoat.

"You care about such things?" she asked. "Even though you kill so easily?"

"I care about my people," he said. "Every witch-scare one person's foolishness creates can hurt many. We are all witches in the eyes of ordinary people, and I am the only witch they cannot eventually kill. Also, I care about my son. I would not want Isaac making a marked man of himself—marked in his own eyes as well as the eyes of others. I know him. He is like you. He would kill, then suffer over it, wallowing in shame."

She smiled, laid one hand on his arm. "It is only his youth making him foolish. He is good. He gives me hope for our children."

"He is not a child," Doro said. "He is twenty-five years old. Think of him as a man."

She shrugged. "To me, he is a boy. And to you, both he and I are children. I have seen you watching us like an all-knowing father."

Doro smiled, denying nothing. "Take off your cloth," he said. "Get dressed."

She stripped, eyeing the new clothing with distaste.

"Accustom your body to these things," he told her as he began helping her dress. "I have been a woman often enough to know how uncomfortable woman's clothing can be, but at least this is Dutch, and not as confining as the English."

"What is Dutch?"

"A people, like the English. They speak a different language."

"White people?"

"Oh yes. Just a different nationality—a different tribe. If I had to be a woman, though, I think I'd rather pass as Dutch than as English. I would here, anyway."

She looked at his tall, straight black man's body. "It is hard to think of you ever being a woman."

He shrugged. "It would be hard for me to imagine you as a man if I hadn't seen you that way."

"But..." She shook her head. "You would make a bad woman, however you looked. I would not want to see you as a woman."

"You will, though, sooner or later. Let me show you how to fasten that."

It became almost possible to forget that he was not a woman now. He dressed her carefully in the stifling layers of clothing, stepped back to give her a quick critical glance, then commented that Isaac had a good eye. The clothing fit almost perfectly. Anyanwu suspected that Isaac had used more than his eyes to learn the dimensions of her body. The boy had lifted her, even tossed her into the air many times without his hand coming near her. But who knew what he could measure and remember with his strange ability? She felt her face go hot. Who knew, indeed. She decided not to allow the boy to use his ability on her so freely any longer.

Doro cut off some of her hair and combed the rest with a wooden comb clearly purchased somewhere near her own country. She had seen Doro's smaller white man's comb made of bone. She found herself giggling like the young girl she appeared to be at the thought of Doro combing her hair.

"Can you braid it for me?" she asked him. "Surely you should be able to do that, too."

"Of course I can," he said. He took her face between his hands, looked at her, tilted her head to see her from a slightly different angle. "But I will not," he decided. "You look better with it loose and combed this way. I used to live with an island tribe who wore their hair this way." He hesitated. "What do you do with your hair when you change? Does it change, too?"

"No, I take it into myself. Other creatures have other kinds of hair. I feed on my hair, nails, any other parts of my body that I cannot use. Then later, I re-create them. You have seen me growing hair."

"I did not know whether you were growing it or it was ... somehow the same hair." He handed her his small mirror. "Here, look at yourself."

She took it eagerly, lovingly. Since the first time he had shown it to her, she had wanted such a glass of her own. He had promised to buy her one.

Now she saw that he had cut and combed her hair into a softly rounded black cloud around her head. "It would be better braided," she said. "A woman of the age I seem to be would braid her hair."

"Another time." He glanced at two small bits of gold jewelry. "Either Isaac has not looked at your ears, or he thinks it would be no trouble for you to create small holes to attach these earrings. Can you?"

She looked at the earrings, at the pins meant to fasten them to her ears. Already she wore a necklace of gold and small jewels. It was the only thing she had on that she liked. Now she liked the earrings as well. "Touch where the holes should be," she said.

He clasped each of her earlobes in the proper places—then jerked his hands away in surprise.

"What is the matter?" she asked, surprised herself.

"Nothing. I . . . I suppose it's just that I've never touched you before while you were changing. The texture of your flesh is . . . different."

"Is not the texture of clay different when it is pliable and when it has set?"

". . . yes."

She laughed. "Touch me now. The strangeness is gone."

He obeyed hesitantly and seemed to find what he felt more familiar this time. "It was not unpleasant before," he said. "Only unexpected."

"But not truly unfamiliar," she said. She looked off to one side, not meeting his eyes, smiling.

"But it is. I've never . . ." He stopped and began to interpret the look on her face. "What are you saying, woman? What have you been doing?"

She laughed again. "Only giving you pleasure. You have told me how well I please you." She lifted her head. "Once I married a man who had seven wives. When he had married me, though, he did not go as often to the others."

Slowly, his expression of disbelief dissolved into amusement. He stepped closer to her with the earrings and began to attach them through the small new holes in her earlobes. "Someday," he murmured, vaguely preoccupied, "we will both change. I will become a woman and find out whether you make an especially talented man."

"*No!*" She jerked away from him, then cried out in pain and surprise when her sudden movement caused him to hurt her ear. She doused the pain quickly and repaired the slight injury. "We will *not* do such a thing!"

He gave her a smile of gentle condescension, picked up the earring from where it had fallen, and put it on her ear.

"Doro, we will not do it!"

"All right," he said agreeably. "It was only a suggestion. You might enjoy it."

"No!"

He shrugged.

"It would be a vile thing," she whispered. "Surely an abomination."

"All right," he repeated.

She looked to see whether he was still smiling, and he was. For an instant, she wondered herself what such a switch might be like. She knew she could become an adequate man, but could this strange being ever be truly womanly? What if...? No!

"I will show Isaac the clothing," she said coldly.

He nodded. "Go." And the smile never left his face.

There was, in Isaac's eyes when Anyanwu stepped before him in the strange clothing, a look that warned her of another kind of abomination. The boy was open and easy to accept as a young stepson. Anyanwu was aware, however, that he would have preferred another relationship. In a less confined environment, she would have avoided him. On the ship, she had done the easy thing, the pleasurable thing, and accepted his company. Doro often had no time for her, and the slaves, who knew her power now, were afraid of her. All of them, even Okoye and Udenkwo, treated her with great formality and respect, and they avoided her as best they could. Doro's other sons were forbidden to her and it would not have been proper for her to spend time with other members of the crew. She had few wifely duties aboard. She did not cook or clean. She had no baby to tend. There were no markets to go to—she missed the crowding and the companionship of the markets very much. During several of her marriages, she had been a great trader. The produce of her garden and the pottery and tools she created were always very fine. Her goats and fowls were always fat.

Now there was nothing. Not even sickness to heal or gods to call upon. Both the slaves and the crew seemed remarkably healthy. She had seen no diseases but what Doro called seasickness among the slaves, and that was nothing. In her boredom, Anyanwu accepted Isaac's companionship. But now she could see that it was time to stop. It was wrong to torment the boy. She was pleased, though, to realize that he saw beauty in her even now, smothered as she was in so much cloth. She had feared that to eyes other than Doro's she would look ridiculous.

"Thank you for these things," she said softly in English.

"They make you even more beautiful," he told her.

"I am like a prisoner. All bound."

"You'll get used to it. Now you can be a real lady."

Anyanwu turned that over in her mind. "Real lady?" she said, frowning. "What was I before?"

Isaac's face went red. "I mean you look like a New York lady."

His embarrassment told her that he had said something wrong, something insulting. She had thought she was misunderstanding his English. Now she realized she had understood all too well.

"Tell me what I was before, Isaac," she insisted. "And tell me the word you used before: Civilization. What is civilization?"

He sighed, met her eyes after a moment of gazing past her at the main mast. "Before, you were Anyanwu," he said, "mother of I-don't-know-how-many children, priestess to your people, respected and valued woman of your town. But to the people here, you would be a savage, almost an animal if they saw you wearing only your cloth. Civilization is the way one's own people live. Savagery is the way foreigners live." He smiled tentatively. "You're already a chameleon, Anyanwu. You understand what I'm saying."

"Yes." She did not return his smile. "But in a land where most of the people are white, and of the few blacks, most are slaves, can only a few pieces of cloth make me a 'real lady.'"

"In Wheatley I can!" he said quickly. "I'm white and black and Indian, and I live there without trouble."

"But you look like a 'real man.'"

He winced. "I'm not like you," he said. "I can't help the way I look."

"No," she admitted.

"And it doesn't matter anyway. Wheatley is Doro's 'American' village. He dumps all the people he can't find places for in his pure families on us. Mix and stir. No one can afford to worry about what anyone else looks like. They don't know who Doro might mate them with—or what their own children might look like."

Anyanwu allowed herself to be diverted. "Do people even marry as he says?" she asked. "Does no one resist him?"

Isaac gave her a long, solemn look. "Wild seed resists sometimes," he said softly. "But he always wins. Always."

She said nothing. She did not need to be reminded of how dangerous and how demanding Doro could be. Reminders awakened her fear of him, her fear of a future with him. Reminders made her want to forget the welfare of her children whose freedom she had bought with her servitude. Forget and run!

"People run away sometimes," Isaac said, as though reading her thoughts. "But he always catches them and usually wears their bodies back to their hometowns so that their people can see and be warned. The only sure way to escape him and cheat him out of the satisfaction of wearing your body, I guess, is my mother's way." He paused. "She hanged herself."

Anyanwu stared at him. He had said the words with no particular feeling—as though he cared no more for his mother than he had for his brother Lale. And he had told her he could not remember a time when he and Lale had not hated each other.

"Your mother died because of Doro?" she asked, watching him carefully.

He shrugged. "I don't know, really. I was only four. But I don't think so. She was like Lale—able to send and receive thoughts. But she was better at it than he was, especially better at receiving. From Wheatley, sometimes she could hear people in New York City over a hundred and fifty miles away." He glanced at Anyanwu. "A long way. A damned long way for that kind of thing. She could hear anything. But sometimes she couldn't shut things out. I remember I was afraid of her. She used to crouch in a corner and hold her head or scratch her face bloody and scream and scream and scream." He shuddered. "That's all I remember of her. That's the only image that comes when I think of her."

Anyanwu laid a hand on his arm in sympathy for both mother and son. How could he have come from such a family and remained sane himself, she wondered. What was Doro doing to his people, to his own children, in his attempt to make them more as the children of his own lost body might have been. For each one like Isaac, how many were there like Lale and his mother?

"Isaac, has there been nothing good in your life?" she asked softly.

He blinked. "There's been a lot. Doro, the foster parents he found me when I was little, the travel, this." He rose several inches above the deck. "It's been good. I used to worry that I'd be crazy like my mother or mad-dog vicious like Lale, but Doro always said I wouldn't."

"How could he know?"

"He used a different body to father me. He wanted a different ability in me, and sometimes he knows exactly which families to breed together to get what he wants. I'm glad he knew for me."

She nodded. "I would not want to know you if you were like Lale."

He looked down at her in that intense disturbing way he had developed over the voyage, and she took her hand away from his arm. No son should look at his father's wife that way. How stupid of Doro not to find a good girl for him. He should marry and begin fathering yellow-haired sons. He should be working his own farm. What good was sailing back and forth across the sea, taking slaves, and becoming wealthy when he had no children?

In spite of slight faltering winds, the trip upriver to Wheatley took only five days. The Dutch sloop captains and their Dutch-speaking, black-slave crews peered at the sagging sails, then at each other, clearly frightened. Doro complimented them in pretended ignorance on the fine time they were making. Then in English, he warned Isaac, "Don't frighten them too badly, boy. Home isn't that far away."

Isaac grinned at him and continued to propel the sloops along at exactly the same speed.

Cliffs, hills, mountains, farmland and forests, creeks and landings, other sloops and smaller craft, fishermen, Indians... Doro and Isaac, having little to do as passengers on other men's vessels, entertained Anyanwu by identifying and pronouncing in English whatever caught her interest. She had an excellent memory, and by the time they reached Wheatley, she was even exchanging a few words with the Afro-Dutch crew. She was beautiful and they taught her eagerly until Doro or Isaac or their duties took her from them.

Finally, they reached "Gilpin" as the captains and crews called the village of Wheatley. Gilpin was the name given to the settlement sixty years before by its first European settlers, a small group of families led by Pieter Willem Gilpin. But the English settlers whom Doro had begun bringing in well before the 1664 British takeover had renamed the village Wheatley, wheat being its main crop, and Wheatley being the name of the English family whose leadership Doro had supported. The Wheatleys had been Doro's people for generations. They had vague, not-too-troublesome, mind-reading abilities that complemented their good business sense. With a little help from Doro, old Jonathan Wheatley now owned slightly less land than the Van Rensselaers. Doro's people had room to spread and grow. Without the grassland village, they would not grow as quickly as Doro had hoped, but there would be others, odd ones, witches. Dutch, German, English, various African and Indian peoples. All were either good breeding stock or, like the Wheatleys, served other useful purposes. In all its diversity, Wheatley pleased Doro more than any of his other New World settlements. In America, Wheatley was his home.

Now, welcomed with quiet pleasure by his people, he dispersed the new slaves to several separate households. Some were fortunate enough to go to houses where their native languages were spoken. Others had no fellow tribesmen in or around the village and they had to be content with a more alien household. Relatives were kept together. Doro explained to each individual or group exactly what was happening. All knew they would be able to see each other again. Friendships begun during the voyage did not have to end now. They were apprehensive, uncertain, reluctant to leave what had become a surprisingly tight-knit group, but they obeyed Doro. Lale had chosen them well—had hand-picked every one of them, searching out small strangenesses, buddings, beginnings of talents like his own. He had gone through every group of new slaves brought out of the forest to Bernard Daly while Doro was away—gone through picking and choosing and doubtless terrifying people more than was necessary. No doubt he had missed several who could have been useful. Lale's ability had been limited and his erratic temperament had often gotten in his way. But he had not included anyone who did not deserve to be included. Only Doro himself could have done a better job. And now, until some of his other potentially strong young thought readers matured, Doro would have to do the job himself. He did not seek people out as Lale did, deliberately, painstakingly. He found them almost as effortlessly as he had found Anyanwu—though not from as great a distance. He became aware of them as easily as a wolf became aware of a rabbit when the wind was right—and in the beginning he had gone after them for exactly the same reason wolves went after rabbits. In the beginning, he had bred them for exactly the same reason people bred rabbits. These strange ones, his witches, were good kills. They offered him the most satisfying durable food and shelter. He still preyed on them. Soon he would take one from Wheatley. The people of Wheatley expected it, accepted it, treated it as a kind of religious sacrifice. All his towns and villages fed him willingly now. And the breeding projects he carried on among them entertained him as nothing else could. He had brought them so far—from tiny, blind, latent talents to Lale, to Isaac, and even, in a roundabout way, to Anyanwu. He was building a people for himself, and he was feeding well. If he was sometimes lonely as his people lived out their brief lives, he was at least not bored. Short-lived people, people who could die, did not know what enemies loneliness and boredom could be.

There was a large, low yellow-brick farmhouse at the ledge of town for Doro—an ex-Dutch farmhouse that was more comfortable than handsome. Jonathan Wheatley's manor house was much finer, as was his mansion in New York City, but Doro was content with his farmhouse. In a good year, he might visit it twice.

An English couple lived in Doro's house, caring for it and serving Doro when he was at home. They were a farmer, Robert Cutler, and his wife, youngest of the nine Wheatley daughters, Sarah. These were sturdy, resilient people who had raised Isaac through his worst years. The boy had been difficult and dangerous during his adolescent years as his abilities matured. Doro had been surprised that the couple survived. Lale's foster parents had not—but then, Lale had been actively malevolent. Isaac had done harm only by accident. Also, neither of Lale's foster parents had been Wheatleys. Sarah's work with Isaac had proved again the worth of her kind—people with too little ability to be good breeding stock or food. It occurred to Doro that if his breeding projects were successful, there might come a time—in the far future—when he had to make certain such people continued to exist. Able people, but not so powerful that their ability might turn on them and cripple or kill them.

For now, though, it was his witches who had to be protected—even protected from him. Anyanwu, for instance. He would tell her tonight that she was to marry Isaac. In telling her, he would have to treat her not as ordinary recalcitrant wild seed, but as one of his daughters—difficult, but worth taking time with. Worth molding and coercing with more gentleness and patience than he would bother to use on less valuable people. He would talk to her after one of Sarah's good meals when they were alone in his room, warm and comfortable before a fire. He would do all he could to make her obey and live.

He thought about her, worried about her stubbornness as he walked toward home where she waited. He had just placed Okoye and Udenkwo in a home with a middle-aged pair of their countrymen— people from whom the young couple could learn a great deal. He walked slowly, answering the greetings of people who recognized his current body and worrying about the pride of one small forest peasant. People sat outside, men and women, Dutch fashion, gossiping on the stoops. The women's hands were busy with sewing or knitting while the men smoked pipes. Isaac got up from a bench where he had been sitting with an older woman and fell into step with Doro.

"Anneke is near her transition," the boy said worriedly. "Mrs. Waemans says she's been having a lot of trouble."

"That's to be expected," Doro answered. Anneke Strycker was one of his daughters—a potentially good daughter. With luck, she would replace Lale when her transition was complete and her abilities mature. She lived now with her foster mother, Margaret Waemans, a big, physically powerful, mentally stable widow of fifty. No doubt, the woman needed all her resources to handle the young girl now.

Isaac cleared his throat. "Mrs. Waemans is afraid she'll... do something to herself. She's been talking about dying."

Doro nodded. Power came the way a child came—with agony. People in transition were open to every thought, every emotion, every pleasure, every pain from the minds of others. Their heads were filled with a continuous screaming jumble of mental "noise." There was no peace, little sleep, many nightmares—everyone's nightmares. Some of Doro's best people—too many of them—stopped at this stage. They could pass their potential on to their children if they lived long enough to have any, but they could not benefit from it themselves. They could never control it. They became hosts for Doro, or they became breeders. Doro brought them mates from distant unrelated settlements because that kind of cross-breeding most often produced children like Lale. Only great care and fantastic good luck produced a child like Isaac. Doro glanced at the boy fondly. "I'll see Anneke first thing tomorrow," he told him.

"Good," Isaac said with relief. "That will help. Mrs. Waemans says she calls for you sometimes when the nightmares come." He hesitated. "How bad will it get for her?"

"As bad as it was for you and for Lale."

"My God!" Isaac said. "She's only a girl. She'll die."

"She has as much of a chance as you and Lale did."

Isaac glared at Doro in sudden anger. "You don't care what happens to her, do you? If she does die, there will always be someone else."

Doro turned to look at him, and after a moment, Isaac looked away.

"Be a child out here if you like," Doro told him. "But act your age when we go in. I'm going to settle things between you and Anyanwu tonight."

"Settle... you're finally going to give her to me?"

"Think of it another way. I want you to marry her."

The boy's eyes widened. He stopped walking, leaned against a tall maple tree. "You... you've made up your mind, I suppose. I mean... you're sure that's what you want."

"Of course." Doro stopped beside him.

"Have you told her?"

"Not yet. I'll tell her after dinner."

"Doro, she's wild seed. She might refuse."

"I know."

"You might not be able to change her mind."

Doro shrugged. Worried as he was, it did not occur to him to share his concern with Isaac. Anyanwu would obey him or she wouldn't. He longed to be able to control her with some refinement of Lale's power, but he could not—nor could Isaac.

"If you can't reach her," Isaac said, "if she just won't understand, let me try. Before you... do anything else, let me try."

"All right."

"And... don't make her hate me."

"I don't think I could. She might come to hate me for a while, but not you."

"Don't hurt her."

"Not if I can help it." Doro smiled a little, pleased by the boy's concern. "You like the idea," he observed. "You want to marry her."

"Yes. But I never thought you'd let me."

"She'll be happier with a husband who does more than visit her once or twice a year."

"You're going to leave me here to be a farmer?"

"Farm if you want to—or open a store or go back to smithing. No one could handle that better than you. Do whatever you like, but I am going to leave you here, at least for a while. She'll need someone to help her fit in here when I'm gone."

"God," Isaac said. "Married." He shook his head, then began to smile.

"Come on." Doro started toward the house.

"No."

Doro looked back at him.

"I can't see her until you tell her... now that I know. I can't. I'll eat with Anneke. She could use the company anyway."

"Sarah won't think much of that."

"I know." Isaac glanced homeward guiltily. "Apologize for me, will you?"

Doro nodded, turned, and went in to Sarah Cutler's linen-clothed, heavily laden table.

Anyanwu watched carefully as the white woman placed first a clean cloth, then dishes and utensils on the long, narrow table at which the household was to eat. Anyanwu was glad that some of the food and the white people's ways of eating it were familiar to her from the ship. She could sit down and have a meal without seeming utterly ignorant. She could not have cooked the meal, but that would come, too, in time. She would learn. For now, she merely observed and allowed the interesting smells to intensify her hunger. Hunger was familiar and good. It kept her from staring too much at the white woman, kept her from concentrating on her own nervousness and uncertainty in the new surroundings, kept her attention on the soup, thick with meat and vegetables, and the roast deer flesh—venison, the white woman had called it—and a huge fowl—a turkey. Anyanwu repeated the words to herself, reassured that they had become part of her vocabulary. New words, new ways, new foods, new clothing... She was glad of the cumbersome clothing, though, finally. It made her look more like the other women, black and white, whom she had seen in the village, and that was important. She had lived in enough different towns through her various marriages to know the necessity of learning to behave as others did. What was common in one place could be ridiculous in another and abomination in a third. Ignorance could be costly.

"How shall I call you?" she asked the white woman. Doro had said the woman's name once, very quickly, in introduction, then hurried off on business of his own. Anyanwu remembered the name—Sarahcutler—but was not certain she could say it correctly without hearing it again.

"Sarah Cutler," the woman said very distinctly. "Mrs. Cutler."

Anyanwu frowned, confused. Which was right. "Mrs. Cutler?"

"Yes. You say it well."

"I am trying to learn." Anyanwu shrugged. "I must learn."

"How do you say your name?"

"Anyanwu." She said it very slowly, but still the woman asked: "Is that all one name?"

"Only one. I have had others, but Anyanwu is best. I come back to it."

"Are the others shorter?"

"Mbgafo. That is the name my mother gave me. And once I was called Atagbusi, and honored by that name. I have been called—"

"Never mind." The woman sighed, and Anyanwu smiled to herself. She had had to give five of her former names to Isaac before he shrugged and decided Anyanwu was a good name after all.

"Can I help to do these things?" she asked. Sarah Cutler was beginning to put food on the table now.

"No," the woman said. "Just watch now. You'll be doing this soon enough." She glanced at Anyanwu curiously. She did not stare, but allowed herself these quick curious glances. Anyanwu thought they each probably had an equal number of questions about the other.

Sarah Cutler asked: "Why did Doro call you 'Sun Woman'?"

Doro had taken to doing that affectionately when he spoke to her in English, though Isaac complained that it made her sound like an Indian.

"Your word for my name is 'Sun,'" she answered. "Doro said he would find an English name for me, but I did not want one. Now he makes English of my name."

The white woman shook her head and laughed. "You're more fortunate than you know. With him taking such an interest in you, I'm surprised you're not already Jane or Alice or some such."

Anyanwu shrugged. "He has not changed his own name. Why should he change mine?"

The woman gave her what seemed to be a look of pity.

"What is Cutler?" Anyanwu asked.

"What it means?"

"Yes."

"A cutler is a knifemaker. I suppose my husband had ancestors who were knifemakers. Here, taste this." She gave Anyanwu a bit of something sweet and oily, fruit-filled, and delicious.

"It is very good!" Anyanwu said. The sweet was unlike anything she had tasted before. She did not know what to say about it except the words of courtesy Doro had taught her. "Thank you. What is this called?"

The woman smiled, pleased. "It's a kind of cake I haven't made before—special for Isaac and Doro's homecoming."

"You said..." Anyanwu thought for a moment. "You said your husband's people were knifemakers. Cutler is his name?"

"Yes. Here, a woman takes the name of her husband after marriage. I was Sarah Wheatley before I married."

"Then Sarah is the name you keep for yourself."

"Yes."

"Shall I call you Sarah—your own name?"

The woman glanced at her sidelong. "Shall I call you... Mbgafo?" She mispronounced it horribly.

"If you like. But there are very many Mbgafos. That name only tells the day of my birth."

"Like... Monday or Tuesday?"

"Yes. You have seven. We have only four: Eke, Oye, Afo, Nkwo. People are often named for the day they were born."

"Your country must be overflowing with people of the same name."

Anyanwu nodded. "But many have other names as well."

"I suppose Anyanwu really is better."

"Yes." Anyanwu smiled. "Sarah is good too. A woman should have something of her own."

Doro came in then, and Anyanwu noted how the woman bright-
ened. She had not been sad or grim before, but now, years seemed
to drop from her. She only smiled at him and said dinner was ready,
but there was a warmth in her voice that had not been there before
in spite of all her friendliness. At some time, this woman had been
wife or lover to Doro. Probably lover. There was still much fondness
between them, though the woman was no longer young. Where was
her husband, Anyanwu wondered. How was it that a woman here
could cook for a man neither her kinsman nor in-law while her
husband probably sat with others in front of one of the houses and
blew smoke out of his mouth?

Then the husband came in, bringing two grown sons and a
daughter, along with the very young, shy wife of one of the sons.
The girl was slender and olive-skinned, black-haired and dark-eyed,
and even to Anyanwu's eyes, very beautiful. When Doro spoke to her
courteously, her answer was a mere moving of the lips. She would
not look at him at all except once when his back was turned. But
the look she gave him then spoke as loudly as had Sarah Cutler's
sudden brightening. Anyanwu blinked and began to wonder what
kind of man she had. The women aboard the ship had not found
Doro so desirable. They had been terrified of him. But these women
of his people... Was he like a cock among them, going from one
hen to another? They were not, after all, his kinsmen or his friends.
They were people who had pledged loyalty to him or people he had
bought as slaves. In a sense, they were more his property than his
people. The men laughed and talked with him, but none presumed
as much as Isaac had. All were respectful. And if their wives or sisters or daughters looked at Doro, they did not notice. Anyanwu
strongly suspected that if Doro looked back, if he did more than
look, they would make an effort not to notice that either. Or perhaps they would be honored. Who knew what strange ways they
practiced?

But now, Doro gave his attention to Anyanwu. She was shy in this
company—men and women together eating strange food and talking in a language she felt she spoke poorly and understood imper-
fectly. Doro kept making her talk, speaking to her of trivial things.

"Do you miss the yams? There are none quite like yours here."

"It does not matter." Her voice was like the young girl's—no more than a moving of the lips. She felt ashamed to speak before all these strangers—yet she had always spoken before strangers, and spoken well. One had to speak well and firmly when people came for medicine and healing. What faith could they have in someone who whispered or bowed her head?

Determinedly, she raised her head and ceased concentrating so intently on her soup. She did miss the yams. Even the strange soup made her long for an accompanying mound of pounded yam. But that did not matter. She looked around, meeting the eyes first of Sarah Cutler, then of one of Sarah's sons and finding only friendliness and curiosity in both. The young man, thin and brown-haired, seemed to be about Isaac's age. Thought of Isaac made Anyanwu look around.

"Where is Isaac?" she asked Doro. "You said this was his home."

"He's with a friend," Doro told her. "He'll be in later."

"He'd better!" Sarah said. "His first night back and he can't come home to supper."

"He had reason," Doro told her. And she said nothing more.

But Anyanwu found other things to say. And she no longer whispered. She paid some attention to spooning up the soup as the others did and to eating the other meats and breads and sweets correctly with her fingers. People here ate more carefully than had the men aboard the ship; thus, she ate more carefully. She spoke to the shy young girl and discovered that the girl was an Indian—a Mohawk. Doro had matched her with Blake Cutler because both had just a little of the sensitivity Doro valued. Both seemed pleased with the match. Anyanwu thought she would have been happier with her own match with Doro had her people been nearby. It would be good for the children of their marriage to know her world as well as Doro's—to be aware of a place where blackness was not a mark of slavery. She resolved to make her homeland live for them whether Doro permitted her to show it to them or not. She resolved not to let them forget who they were.

Then she found herself wondering whether the Mohawk girl would have preferred to forget who she was as the conversation turned to talk of war with Indians. The white people at the table were eager to tell Doro how, earlier in the year, "Praying Indians" and a group of whites called French had stolen through the gates of a town west of Wheatley—a town with the unpronounceable name of Schenectady—and butchered some of the people there and carried off others. There was much discussion of this, much fear expressed until Doro promised to leave Isaac in the village, and leave one of his daughters, Anneke, who would soon be very powerful. This seemed to calm everyone somewhat. Anyanwu felt that she had only half understood the dispute between so many foreign people, but she did ask whether Wheatley had ever been attacked.

Doro smiled unpleasantly. "Twice by Indians," he said. "I happened to be here both times. We've had peace since that second attack thirty years ago."

"That's time enough for them to forget anything," Sarah said. "Anyway, this is a new war. French and Praying Indians!" She shook her head in disgust.

"Papists!" her husband muttered. "Bastards!"

"My people could tell them what powerful spirits live here," whispered the Mohawk girl, smiling.

Doro looked at her as though not certain whether she were serious, but she ducked her head.

Anyanwu touched Doro's hand. "You see?" she said. "I told you you were a spirit!"

Everyone laughed, and Anyanwu felt more comfortable among them. She would find out another time exactly what Papists and Praying Indians were and what their quarrel was with the English. She had had enough new things for one day. She relaxed and enjoyed her meal.

She enjoyed it too much. After much eating and drinking, after everyone had gathered around the tall, blue-tiled parlor hearth for talking and smoking and knitting, she began to feel pain in her stomach. By the time the gathering broke up, she was controlling herself very closely lest she vomit up all the food she had eaten and humiliate herself before all these people. When Doro showed her her room with its fireplace and its deep soft down mattresses covering a great bed, she undressed and lay down at once. There she discovered that her body had reacted badly to one specific food—a rich sweet that she knew no name for, but that she had loved. This on top of the huge amount of meat she had eaten had finally been too much for her stomach. Now, though, she controlled her digestion, soothed the sickness from her body. The food did not have to be brought up. Only gotten used to. She analyzed slowly, so intent on her inner awareness that she appeared to be asleep. If someone had spoken to her, she would not have heard. Her eyes were closed. This was why she had waited, had not healed herself downstairs in the presence of others. Here, though, it did not matter what she did. Only Doro was present—across the large room sitting at a great wooden desk much finer than the one he had had on the ship. He was writing, and she knew from experience that he would be making marks unlike those in any of his books. "It's a very old language," he had told her once. "So old that no one living can read it."

"No one but you," she had said.

And he had nodded and smiled. "The people I learned it from stole me away into slavery when I was only a boy. Now they're all dead. Their descendants have forgotten the old wisdom, the old writing, the old gods. Only I remember."

She had not known whether she heard bitterness or satisfaction in his voice then. He was very strange when he talked about his youth. He made Anyanwu want to touch him and tell him that he was not alone in outliving so many things. But he also roused her fear of him, reminded her of his deadly difference. Thus, she said nothing.

Now, as she lay still, analyzing, learning not only which food had made her ill, but which ingredient in that food, she was comfortably aware of Doro nearby. If he had left the room in complete silence, she would have known, would have missed him. The room would have become colder.

It was milk that had sickened her. Animal milk! These people cooked many things with animal milk! She covered her mouth with her hand. Did Doro know? But of course he did. How could he not? These were his people!

Again it required all her control to prevent herself from vomiting—this time from sheer revulsion.

"Anyanwu?"

She realized that Doro was standing over her between the long cloths that could be closed to conceal the bed. And she realized that this was not the first time he had said her name. Still, it surprised her that she had heard him without his shouting or touching her. He had only spoken quietly.

She opened her eyes, looked up at him. He was beautiful standing there with the light of candles behind him. He had stripped to
the cloth he still wore sometimes when they were alone together.
But she noticed this with only part of her mind. Her main thoughts
were still of the loathsome thing she had been tricked into doing—
the consumption of animal milk.

"Why didn't you tell me!" she demanded.

"What?" He frowned, confused. "Tell you what?"

"That these people were feeding me animal milk!"

He burst into laughter.

She drew back as though he had hit her. "Is it a joke then? Are the
others laughing too now that I cannot hear?"

"Anyanwu..." He managed to stop his laughter. "I'm sorry,"
he told her. "I was thinking of something else or I wouldn't have
laughed. But, Anyanwu, we all ate the same food."

"But why was some of it cooked with—"

"Listen. I know the custom among your people not to drink animal milk. I should have warned you—would have, if I had been
thinking. No one else who ate with us knew the milk would offend
you. I assure you, they're not laughing."

She hesitated. He was sincere; she was certain of that. It was a mistake
then. But still..."These people cook with animal milk all the time?"

"All the time," Doro said. "And they drink milk. It's their custom.
They keep some cattle especially for milking."

"Abomination!" Anyanwu said with disgust.

"Not to them," Doro told her. "And you will not insult them by
telling them they are committing abomination."

She looked at him. He did not seem to give many orders but she
had no doubt that this was one. She said nothing.

"You can become an animal whenever you wish," he said. "You
know there's nothing evil about animal milk."

"It is for animals!" she said. "I am not an animal now! I did not
just eat a meal with animals!"

He sighed. "You know you must change to suit the customs here.
You have not lived three hundred years without learning to accept
new customs."

"I will not have any more milk!"

"You need not. But let others have theirs in peace."

She turned away from him. She had never in her long life lived among people who violated this prohibition.

"Anyanwu!"

"I will obey," she muttered, then faced him defiantly. "When will I have my own house? My own cooking fire?"

"When you've learned what to do with them. What kind of meal could you cook now with foods you've never seen before? Sarah Cutler will teach you what you need to know. Tell her milk makes you sick and she'll leave it out of what she teaches you." His voice softened a little, and he sat down beside her on the bed. "It did make you sick, didn't it?"

"It did. Even my flesh knows abomination."

"It didn't make anyone else sick."

She only glared at him.

He reached under the blanket, rubbed her stomach gently. Her body was almost buried in the too-soft feather mattress. "Have you healed yourself?" he asked.

"Yes. But with so much food, it took me a long time to learn what was making me sick."

"Do you have to know?"

"Of course. How can I know what to do for healing until I know what healing is needed and why? I think I knew all the diseases and poisons of my people. I must learn the ones here."

"Does it hurt you—the learning?"

"Oh yes. But only at first. Once I learn it, it does not hurt again." Her voice became bantering. "Now, give me your hand again. You can touch me even though I am well."

He smiled and there was no more tension between them. His touches became more intimate.

"That is good," she whispered. "I healed myself just in time. Now lie down here and show me why all those women were looking at you."

He laughed quietly, untied his cloth, and joined her in the too-soft bed.

"We must talk tonight," he said later when both were satiated and lying side by side.

"Do you still have strength for talking, husband?" she said drowsily. "I thought you would go to sleep and not awaken until sunrise."

"No." There was no humor in his voice now. She had laid her head on his shoulder because he had shown her in the past that he wanted her near him, touching him until he fell asleep. Now, though, she lifted her head and looked at him.

"You've come to your new home, Anyanwu."

"I know that." She did not like the flat strangeness of his tone. This was the voice he used to frighten people—the voice that reminded her to think of him as something other than a man.

"You are home, but I will be leaving again in a few weeks."

"But—"

"I will be leaving. I have other people who need me to rid them of enemies or who need to see me to know they still belong to me. I have a fragmented people to hunt and reassemble. I have women in three different towns who could bear powerful children if I give them the right mates. And more. Much more."

She sighed and burrowed deeper into the mattress. He was going to leave her here among strangers. He had made up his mind. "When you come back," she said resignedly, "there will be a son for you here."

"Are you pregnant now?"

"I can be now. Your seed still lives inside me."

"No!"

She jumped, startled at his vehemence.

"This is not the body I want to beget your first children here," he said.

She made herself shrug, speak casually. "All right. I'll wait until you have... become another man."

"You need not. I have another plan for you."

The hairs at the back of her neck began to prickle and itch. "What plan?"

"I want you to marry," he said. "You'll do it in the way of the people here with a license and a wedding."

"It makes no difference. I will follow your custom."

"Yes. But not with me."

She stared at him, speechless. He lay on his back staring at one of the great beams that held up the ceiling.

"You'll marry Isaac," he said. "I want children from the two of you. And I want you to have a husband who does more than visit you now and then. Living here, you could go for a year, two years, without seeing me. I don't want you to be that alone."

"Isaac?" she whispered. "Your son?"

"My son. He's a good man. He wants you, and I want you with him."

"He's a boy! He's..."

"What man is not a boy to you, except me? Isaac is more a man than you think."

"But... he's your son! How can I have the son when his father, my husband, still lives? That is abomination!"

"Not if I command it."

"You cannot! It is abomination!"

"You have left your village, Anyanwu, and your town and your land and your people. You are here where I rule. Here, there is only one abomination: disobedience. You will obey."

"I will not! Wrong is wrong! Some things change from place to place, but not this. If your people wish to debase themselves by drinking the milk of animals, I will turn my head. Their shame is their own. But now you want me to shame myself, make myself even worse than they. How can you ask it of me, Doro? The land itself will be offended! Your crops will wither and die!"

He made a sound of disgust. "That's foolishness! I thought I had found a woman too wise to believe such nonsense."

"You have found a woman who will not soil herself! How is it here? Do sons lie with their mothers also? Do sisters and brothers lie down together?"

"Woman, if I command it, they lie down together gladly."

Anyanwu moved away from him so that no part of her body touched his. He had spoken of this before. Of incest, of mating her own children together with doglike disregard for kinship. And in revulsion, she had led him quickly from her land. She had saved her children, but now... who would save her?

"I want children of your body and his," Doro repeated. He stopped, raised himself to his elbow so that he leaned over her. "Sun woman, would I tell you to do something that would hurt my people? The land is different here. *It is my land!* Most of the people here exist because I caused their ancestors to marry in ways your people would not accept. Yet everyone lives well here. No angry god punishes them. Their crops grow and their harvests are rich every year."

"And some of them hear so much of the thoughts of others that they cannot think their own thoughts. Some of them hang themselves."

"Some of your own people hang themselves."

"Not for such terrible reasons."

"Nevertheless, they die. Anyanwu, obey me. Life can be very good for you here. And you will not find a better husband than my son."

She closed her eyes, dismissed his pleading as she had his commands. She strove to dismiss her budding fear also, but she could not. She knew that when both commanding and pleading failed, he would begin to threaten.

Within her body, she killed his seed. She disconnected the two small tubes through which her own seed traveled to her womb. She had done this many times when she thought she had given a man enough children. Now she did it to avoid giving any children at all, to avoid being used. When it was done, she sat up and looked down at him. "You have been telling me lies from the day we met," she said softly.

He shook his head against the pillow. "I have not lied to you."

"'Let me give you children who will live,' you said. 'I promise that if you come with me, I will give you children of your own kind,' you said. And now, you send me away to another man. You give me nothing at all."

"You will bear my children as well as Isaac's."

She cried out as though with pain, and climbed out of his bed. "Get me another room!" she hissed. "I will not lie there with you. I would rather sleep on the bare floor. I would rather sleep on the ground!"

He lay still, as though he had not heard her. "Sleep wherever you wish," he said after a while.

She stared at him, her body shaking with fear and anger. "What is it you would make of me, Doro? Your dog? I cared for you. It has been lifetimes since I cared as much for a man."

He said nothing.

She stepped nearer to the bed, looked down into his expressionless face, pleading herself now. She did not think it was possible to move him by pleading once he had made up his mind, but so much was at stake. She had to try.

"I came here to be a wife to you," she said. "But there were always others to cook for you, others to serve you in nearly all the ways of a wife. And if there had not been others, I know so little of this place that I would have performed my duties poorly. You knew it would be this way for me, but still you wanted me—and I wanted you enough to begin again like a child, completely ignorant." She sighed and looked around the room, feeling as though she were hunting for the words that would reach him. There was only the alien furniture: the desk, the bed, the great wooden cabinet beside the door—a *kas*, it was called, a Dutch thing for storing clothing. There were two chairs and several mats—rugs—of heavy, colorful cloth. It was all as alien as Doro himself. It gave her a feeling of hopelessness—as though she had come to this strange place only to die. She stared into the fire in the fireplace—the only familiar thing in the room—and spoke softly:

"Husband, it may be a good thing that you're going away. A year is not so long, or two years. Not to us. I have been alone before for many times that long. When you come back, I will know how to be a wife to you here. I will give you strong sons." She turned her eyes back to him, saw that he was watching her. "Do not cast me aside before I show you what a good wife I can be."

He sat up, put his feet on the floor. "You don't understand," he said softly. He pulled her down to sit beside him on the bed. "Haven't I told you what I'm building? Over the years, I've taken people with so little power they were almost ordinary, and bred them together again and again until in their descendants, small abilities grew large, and a man like Isaac could be born."

"And a man like Lale."

"Lale wasn't as bad as he seemed. He handled what ability he had very well. And I've created others of his kind who had more ability and a better temperament."

"Did you create him, then? From what? Mounds of clay?"

"Anyanwu!"

"Isaac tells me the whites believe their god made the first people of clay. You talk as though you think you were that god!"

He drew a deep breath, looked at her sadly. "What I am or think I am need not concern you at all. I've told you what you must do— no, be quiet. Hear me."

She closed her mouth, swallowed a new protest.

"I said you didn't understand," he continued. "Now I think you're deliberately misunderstanding. Do you truly believe I mean to cast you aside because you've been a poor wife?"

She looked away. No, of course she did not believe that. She had only hoped to reach him, make him stop his impossible demands. No, he was not casting her aside for any reason at all. He was merely breeding her as one bred cattle and goats. He had said it: "I want children of your body and his." What she wanted meant nothing. Did one ask a cow or a nanny goat whether it wished to be bred?

"I am giving you the very best of my sons," he told her. "I expect you to be a good wife to him. I would never send you to him if I thought you couldn't."

She shook her head slowly. "It is you who have not understood me." She gazed at him—at his very ordinary eyes, at his long, hand-some face. Until now, she had managed to avoid a confrontation like this by giving in a little, obeying. Now she could not obey.

"You are my husband," she said quietly, "or I have no husband. If I need another man, I will find one. My father and all my other husbands are long dead. You gave no gifts for me. You can send me away, but you cannot tell me where I must go."

"Of course I can." His quiet calm matched her own, but in him it was clearly resignation. "You know you must obey, Anyanwu. Must I take your body and get the children I want from it myself?"

"You cannot." Within herself, she altered her reproductive organs further, made herself literally no longer a woman, but not quite a man—just to be certain. "You may be able to push my spirit from my body," she said. "I think you can, though I have never felt your power. But my body will give you no satisfaction. It would take too long for you to learn to repair all the things I have done to it—if you can learn. It will not conceive a child now. It will not live much longer itself without me to keep watch on it."

She could not have missed the anger in his voice when he spoke again. "You know I will collect your children if I cannot have you."

She turned her back on him, not wanting him to see her fear and pain, not wanting her own eyes to see him. He was a loathsome thing.

He came to stand behind her, put his hands on her shoulders. She struck them away violently. "Kill me!" she hissed. "Kill me now, but never touch me that way again!"

"And your children?" he said unmoved.

"No child of mine would commit the abominations you want," she whispered.

"Now who's lying?" he said. "You know your children don't have your strength. I'll get what I want from them, and their children will be as much mine as the people here."

She said nothing. He was right, of course. Even her own strength was mere bravado, a façade covering utter terror. It was only her anger that kept her neck straight. And what good was anger or defiance? He would consume her very spirit; there would be no next life for her. Then he would use and pervert her children. She felt near to weeping.

"You'll get over your anger," he said. "Life will be rich and good for you here. You'll be surprised to see how easily you blend with these people."

"I will not marry your son, Doro! No matter what threats you make, no matter what promises, I will not marry your son!"

He sighed, tied his cloth around him, and started for the door. "Stay here," he told her. "Put something on and wait."

"For what!" she demanded bitterly.

"For Isaac," he answered.

And when she turned to face him, mouth open to curse both him and his son, he stepped close to her and struck her across the face with all his strength.

There was an instant before the blow landed when she could have caught his arm and broken the bones within it like dry sticks. There was an instant before the blow landed when she could have torn out his throat.

But she absorbed the blow, moved with it, made no sound. It had been a long time since she had wanted so powerfully to kill a man.

"I see you know how to be quiet," he said. "I see you're not as willing to die as you thought. Good. My son asked for a chance to talk to you if you refused to obey. Wait here."

"What can he say to me that you have not said?" she demanded harshly.

Doro paused at the door to give her a look of contempt. His blow had had less power to hurt her than that look.

When the door closed behind him, she went to the bed and sat down to stare, unseeing, into the fire. By the time Isaac knocked on the door, her face was wet with tears she did not remember shedding.

She made him wait until she had wrapped a cloth around herself and dried her face. Then with leaden, hopeless weariness, she opened the door and let the boy in.

He looked as depleted as she felt. The yellow hair hung limp into his eyes and the eyes themselves were red. His sun-browned skin looked as pale as Anyanwu had ever seen it. He seemed not only tired, but sick.

He stood gazing at her, saying nothing, making her want to go to him as though to Okoye, and try to give him comfort. Instead, she sat down in one of the room's chairs so that he could not sit close to her.

Obligingly, he sat opposite her in the other chair. "Did he threaten you?" he asked softly.

"Of course. That is all he knows how to do."

"And promise you a good life if you obey?"

" . . . yes."

"He'll keep his word, you know. Either way."

"I have seen how he keeps his word."

There was a long, uncomfortable silence. Finally, Isaac whispered, "Don't make him do it, Anyanwu. Don't throw away your life!"

"Do you think I want to die?" she said. "My life has been good, and very long. It could be even longer and better. The world is a much wider place than I thought; there is so much for me to see and know. But I will not be his dog! Let him commit his abominations with other people!"

"With your children?"

"Do you threaten me too, Isaac?"

"No!" he cried. "You know better, Anyanwu."

She turned her face away from him. If only he would go away. She did not want to say things to hurt him. He spoke softly:

"When he told me I would marry you, I was surprised and a little afraid. You've been married many times, and I not even once. I know Okoye is your grandson—one of your younger grandsons—and he's at least my age. I didn't see how I could measure up against all your experience. But I wanted to try! You don't know how I wanted to try."

"Will you be bred, Isaac? Does it mean nothing to you?"

"Don't you know I wanted you long before he decided we should marry?"

"I knew." She glanced at him. "But wrong is wrong!"

"It isn't wrong here. It..." He shrugged. "People from outside always have trouble understanding us. Not very many things are forbidden here. Most of us don't believe in gods and spirits and devils who must be pleased or feared. We have Doro, and he's enough. He tells us what to do, and if it isn't what other people do, it doesn't matter—because we won't last long if we don't do it, no matter what outsiders think of us."

He got up, went to stand beside the fireplace. The low flame seemed to comfort him too. "Doro's ways aren't strange to me," he said. "I've lived with them all my life. I've shared women with him. My first woman..." He hesitated, glanced at her as though to see how she was receiving such talk, whether she was offended. She was almost indifferent. She had made up her mind. Nothing the boy said would change it.

"My first woman," he continued, "was one he sent to me. The women here are glad to go to him. They didn't mind coming to me either when they saw how he favored me."

"Go to them then," Anyanwu said quietly.

"I would," he said, matching her tone. "But I don't want to. I'd rather stay with you—for the rest of my life."

She wanted to run out of the room. "Leave me alone, Isaac!"

He shook his head slowly. "If I leave this room tonight, you'll die tonight. Don't ask me to hurry your death."

She said nothing.

"Besides, I want you to have the night to think." He frowned at her. "How can you sacrifice your children?"

"Which children, Isaac? The ones I have had or the ones he will make me have with you and with him?"

He blinked. "Oh."

"I cannot kill him—or even understand what there is to kill. I have bitten him when he was in another body, and he seemed no more than flesh, no more than a man."

"You never touched him," Isaac said. "Lale did once—he reached out in that way of his to change Doro's thoughts. He almost died. I think he would have died if Doro hadn't struggled hard not to kill him. Doro wears flesh, but he isn't flesh himself—nor spirit, he says."

"I cannot understand that," she said. "But it does not matter. I cannot save my children from him. I cannot save myself. But I will not give him more people to defile."

He turned from the fire, went back to his chair and pulled it close to her. "You could save generations unborn if you wished, Anyanwu. You could have a good life for yourself, and you could stop him from killing so many others."

"How can I stop him?" she said in disgust. "Can one stop a leopard from doing what it was born to do?"

"He's not a leopard! He's not any sort of mindless animal!"

She could not help hearing the anger in his voice. She sighed. "He is your father."

"Oh God," muttered Isaac. "How can I make you see... I wasn't resenting an insult to my father, Anyanwu, I was saying that in his own way, he can be a reasonable being. You're right about his killing; he can't help doing it. When he needs a new body, he takes one whether he wants to or not. But most of the time, he transfers because he wants to, not because he has to; and there are a few people—four or five—who can influence him enough sometimes to stop him from killing, save a few of his victims. I'm one of them. You could be another."

"You do not mean stop him," she said wearily. "You mean"—she hunted through her memory for the right word—"you mean delay him."

"I mean what I said! There are people he listens to, people he values beyond their worth as breeders or servants. People who can give him... just a little of the companionship he needs. They're among the few people in the world that he can still love—or at least care for. Although compared to what the rest of us feel when we love or hate or envy or whatever, I don't think he feels very much. I don't think he can. I'm afraid the time will come when he won't feel anything. If it does—there's no end to the harm he could do. I'm glad I won't have to live to see it. You, though, you could live to see it— or live to prevent it. You could stay with him, keep him at least as human as he is now. I'll grow old; I'll die like all the others, but you won't—or, you needn't. You are treasure to him. I don't think he's really understood that yet."

"He knows."

"He knows, of course, but he doesn't... doesn't feel it yet. It's not yet real to him. Don't you see? He's lived for more than thirty-seven hundred years. When Christ, the Son of God of most white people in these colonies, was born, Doro was already impossibly old. Everyone has always been temporary for him—wives, children, friends, even tribes and nations, gods and devils. Everything dies but him. And maybe you, Sun Woman, and maybe you. Make him know you're not like everyone else—make him feel it. Prove it to him, even if for a while, you have to do some things you don't like. Reach out to him; keep reaching. Make him know he's not alone anymore!"

There was a long period of silence. Only the log in the fire-place slipped, then spat and crackled as new wood began to burn. Anyanwu covered her face, shook her head slowly. "I wish I knew you to be a liar," she whispered. "I am afraid and angry and desper-ate, yet you heap burdens on me."

He said nothing.

"What is forbidden here, Isaac? What is so evil that a man could be taken out and killed?"

"Murder," Isaac said. "Theft sometimes, some other things. And of course, defying Doro."

"If a man killed someone and Doro said he must not be pun-ished, what would happen?"

Isaac frowned. "If the man had to be kept alive—maybe for breeding, Doro would probably take him. Or if it was too soon, if he was being saved for a girl still too young, Doro would send him away from the colony. He wouldn't ask us to tolerate him here."

"And when the man was no longer needed, he would die?"

"Yes."

Anyanwu took a deep breath. "Perhaps you try to keep some decency then. Perhaps he has not made animals of you yet."

"Submit to him now, Anyanwu, and later, you can keep him from ever making animals of us."

Submit to him. The words brought a vile taste to her mouth, but she looked at Isaac's haggard face, and his obvious misery and his fear for her calmed her somehow. She spoke softly. "When I hear you speak of him, I think you love him more than he loves you."

"What does that matter?"

"It does not matter. You are a man to whom it need not matter. I thought he could be a good husband. On the ship, I worried that I could not be the wife he needed. I wanted to please him. Now I can only think that he will never let me go."

"Never?" Isaac repeated with gentle irony. "That's a long time, even for you and him."

She turned away. Another time she might have been amused to hear Isaac counseling patience. He was not a patient young man. But now, for her sake, he was desperate.

"You'll get freedom, Anyanwu," he said, "but first you'll have to reach him. He's like a tortoise encased in a shell that gets thicker every year. It will take a long time for you to reach the man inside, but you have a long time, and there is a man inside who must be reached. He was born as we were. He's warped because he can't die, but he's still a man." Isaac paused for breath. "Take the time, Anyanwu. Break the shell; go in. He might turn out to be what you need, just as I think you're what he needs."

She shook her head. She knew now how the slaves had felt as they lay chained on the bench, the slaver's hot iron burning into their flesh. In her pride, she had denied that she was a slave. She could no longer deny it. Doro's mark had been on her from the day they met. She could break free of him only by dying and sacrificing her children and leaving him loose upon the world to become even more of an animal. So much of what Isaac said seemed to be right. Or was it her cowardice, her fear of Doro's terrible way of killing that made his words seem so reasonable? How could she know? Whatever she did would result in evil.

Isaac got up, came to her, took her hands, and drew her to her feet. "I don't know what kind of husband I could be to... to someone like you," he said. "But if wanting to please you counts for anything..."

Wearily, hopelessly, she allowed him to draw her closer. Had she been an ordinary woman, he could have crushed the breath from her. After a moment, she said, "If Doro had done this differently, Isaac, if he had told me when we met that he wanted a wife for his son and not for himself, I would not have shamed you by refusing you."

"I'm not ashamed," he whispered. "Just as long as you're not going to make him kill you..."

"If I had the courage of your mother, I would kill myself."

He stared at her in alarm.

"No, I will live," she said reassuringly. "I have not the courage to die. I had never thought before that I was a coward, but I am. Living has become too precious a habit."

"You're no more a coward than the rest of us," he said.

"The rest of you, at least, are not doing evil in your own eyes."

"Anyanwu..."

"No." She rested her head against him. "I have decided. I will not tell any more brave lies, even to myself." She looked up at his young face, his boy face. "We will marry. You are a good man, Isaac. I am the wrong wife for you, but perhaps, somehow, in this place, among these people, it will not matter."

He lifted her with the strength of his arms alone and carried her to the great soft bed, there to make the children who would prolong her slavery.

BOOK TWO

Lot's Children
1741

Chapter Seven

Doro had come to Wheatley to see to the welfare of one of his daughters. He had a feeling something was wrong with her, and as usual, he allowed such feelings to guide him.

As he rode into town from the landing, he could hear a loud dispute in progress—something about one man's cow ruining another's garden.

Doro approached the disputants slowly, watching them. They stood before Isaac, who sat on a bench in front of the house he and Anyanwu had built over fifty years before. Isaac, slender and youthful-looking in spite of his age and his thick gray hair, had no official authority to settle disputes. He had been a farmer, then a merchant—never a magistrate. But even when he was younger, people brought their disagreements to him. He was one of Doro's favorite sons. That made him powerful and influential. Also, he was known for his honesty and fairness. People liked him as they could not quite like Doro. They could worship Doro as a god, they could give him their love, their fear, their respect, but most found him too intimidating to like. One of the reasons Doro came back to a son like Isaac, old and past most of his usefulness, was that Isaac was a friend as well as a son. Isaac was one of the few people who could enjoy Doro's company without fear or falseness. And Isaac was an old man, soon to die. They all died so quickly. . . .

Doro reached the house and sat slouched for a moment on his black mare—a handsome animal who had come with his latest less-than-handsome body. The two men arguing over the cow had calmed down by now. Isaac had a way of calming unreasonable people. Another man could say and do exactly what Isaac said and did and be knocked down for his trouble. But people listened to Isaac.

"Pelham," Isaac was saying to the older of the two men—a gaunt, large-boned farmer whom Doro remembered as poor breeding stock. "Pelham, if you need help repairing that fence, I'll send one of my sons over."

"My boy can handle it," Pelham answered. "Anything to do with wood, he can handle."

Pelham's son, Doro recalled, had just about enough sense not to wet himself. He was a huge, powerful man with the mind of a child—a timid, gentle child, fortunately. Doro was glad to hear that he could handle something.

Isaac looked up, noticed for the first time the small sharp-featured stranger Doro was just then, and did what he had always done. With none of the talents of his brother Lale to warn him, Isaac inevitably recognized Doro. "Well," he said, "it's about time you got back to us." Then he turned toward the house and called, "Peter, come out here."

He stood up spryly and took the reins of Doro's horse, handing them to his son Peter as the boy came out of the house.

"Someday, I'm going to get you to tell me how you always know me," Doro said. "It can't be anything you see."

Isaac laughed. "I'd tell you if I understood it myself. You're you, that's all."

Now that Doro had spoken, Pelham and the other man recognized him and spoke together in a confused babble of welcome.

Doro held up his hand. "I'm here to see my children," he said.

The welcomes subsided. The two men shook his hand, wished him a good evening, and hurried off to spread the news of his return. In his few words, he had told him that his visit was unofficial. He had not come to take a new body, and thus would not hold court to settle serious grievances or offer needed financial or other aid in the way that had become customary in Wheatley and some of his other settlements. This visit, he was only a man come to see his children—of whom there were forty-two here, ranging from infants to Isaac. It was rare for him to come to town for no other purpose than to see them, but when he did, other people left him alone. If anyone was in desperate need, they approached one of his children.

"Come on in," Isaac said. "Have some beer, some food." He did not have an old man's voice, high and cracking. His voice had become deeper and fuller—it contributed to his authority. But all Doro could hear in it now was honest pleasure.

"No food yet," Doro said. "Where's Anyanwu?"

"Helping with the Sloane baby. Mrs. Sloane let it get sick and almost die before she asked for help. Anyanwu says it has pneumonia." Isaac poured two tankards of beer.

"Is it going to be all right?"

"Anyanwu says so—although she was ready to strangle the Sloanes. Even they've been here long enough to know better than to let a child suffer that way with her only a few doors away." Isaac paused. "They're afraid of her blackness and her power. They think she's a witch, and the mold-medicine she made some poison."

Doro frowned, took a swallow of beer. The Sloanes were his newest wild seed—a couple who had found each other before Doro found them. They were dangerous, unstable, painfully sensitive people who heard the thoughts of others in intermittent bursts. When one received a burst of pain, anger, fear, any intense emotion, it was immediately transmitted to the other, and both suffered. None of this was deliberate or controlled. It simply happened. Helplessly, the Sloanes did a great deal of fighting and drinking and crying and praying for it to stop happening, but it would not. Not ever. That was why Doro had brought them to Wheatley. They were amazingly good breeding stock to be wild seed. He suspected that in one way or another, they were each descended from his people. Certainly, they were enough like his people to make excellent prey. And as soon as they had produced a few more children, Doro intended to take them both. It would be almost a kindness.

But for now, they would go on being abysmal parents, neglecting and abusing their children not out of cruelty, but because they hurt too badly themselves to notice their children's pain. In fact, they were likely to notice that pain only as a new addition to their own. Thus, sometimes their kind murdered children. Doro had not believed the Sloanes were dangerous in that way. Now, he was less certain.

"Isaac...?"

Isaac looked at him, understood the unspoken question. "I assume you mean to keep the parents alive for a while."

"Yes."

"Then you'd better find another home for the child—and for every other child they have. Anyanwu says they should never have had any."

"Which means, of course, that they should have as many as possible."

"From your point of view, yes. Good useful people. I've already begun talking to them about giving up the child."

"Good. And?"

"They're worried about what people might think. I got the impression they'd be glad to get rid of the child if not for that—and one other thing."

"What?"

Isaac looked away. "They're worried about who'll care for them when they're old. I told them you'd talk to them about that."

Doro smiled thinly. Isaac refused to lie to the people he thought Doro had selected as prey. Most often, he refused to tell them anything at all. Sometimes such people guessed what was being kept from them, and they ran. Doro took pleasure in hunting them down. Lann Sloane, Doro thought, would be especially good game. The man had a kind of animal awareness about him.

"Anyanwu would say you have on your leopard face now," Isaac commented.

Doro shrugged. He knew what Anyanwu would say, and that she meant it when she compared him to one kind of animal or another. Once she had said such things out of fear or anger. Now she said them out of grim hatred. She had made herself the nearest thing he had to an enemy. She obeyed. She was civil. But she could hold a grudge as no one Doro had ever known. She was alive because of Isaac. Doro had no doubt that if he had tried to give her to any of his other sons, she would have refused and died. He had asked her what Isaac said to change her mind, and when she refused to tell him, he had asked Isaac. To his surprise, Isaac refused to tell him, too. His son refused him very little, angered him very rarely. But this time...

"You've given her to me," Isaac had said. "Now she and I have to have things of our own." His face and his voice told Doro he would not say any more. Doro had left Wheatley the next day, confident that Isaac would take care of the details—marry the woman, build himself a house, help her learn to live in the settlement, decide on work for himself, start the children coming. Even at twenty-five, Isaac had been very capable. And Doro had not trusted himself to stay near either Isaac or Anyanwu. The depth of his own anger amazed him. Normally, people had only to annoy him to die for their error. He had to think to remember how long it had been since he had felt real anger and left those who caused it alive. But his son and this tiresome little forest peasant who was, fortunately for her, the best wild seed he had ever found, had lived. There was no forgiveness in Anyanwu, though. If she had learned to love her husband, she had not learned to forgive her husband's father. Now and then, Doro tried to penetrate her polite, aloof hostility, tried to break her, bring her back to what she was when he took her from her people. He was not accustomed to people resisting him, not accustomed to their hating him. The woman was a puzzle he had not yet solved—which was why now, after she had given him eight children, given Isaac five children, she was still alive. She would come to him again, without the coldness. She would make herself young without being told to do so, and she would come to him. Then, satisfied, he would kill her.

He licked his lips thinking about it, and Isaac coughed. Doro looked at his son with the old fondness and amended his thought. Anyanwu would live until Isaac died. She was keeping Isaac healthy, perhaps keeping him alive. She was doing it for herself, of course. Isaac had captured her long ago as he captured everyone, and she did not want to lose him any sooner than she had to. But her reasons did not matter. Inadvertently, she was doing Doro a service. He did not want to lose Isaac any sooner than he had to either. He shook his head, spoke to divert himself from the thought of his son's dying.

"I was down in the city on business," he said. "Then about a week ago when I was supposed to leave for England, I found myself thinking about Nweke." This was Anyanwu's youngest daughter. Doro claimed her as his daughter too, though Anyanwu disputed this. Doro had worn the body that fathered the girl, but he had not worn it at the time of the fathering. He had taken it afterward.

"Nweke's all right," Isaac said. "As all right as she can be, I suppose. Her transition is coming soon and she has her bad days, but Anyanwu seems to be able to comfort her."

"You haven't noticed her having any special trouble in the past few days?"

Isaac thought for a moment. "No, not that I recall. I haven't seen too much of her. She's been helping to sew for a friend who's getting married—the Van Ness girl, you know."

Doro nodded.

"And I've been helping with the Boyden house. I guess you could say I've been building the Boyden house. I have to use what I've got now and then, no matter how Anyanwu nags me to slow down. Otherwise, I find myself walking a foot or so off the ground or throwing things. The ability doesn't seem to weaken with age."

"So I've noticed. Do you still enjoy it?"

"You couldn't know how much," Isaac said, smiling. He looked away, remembered pleasure flickering across his face, causing him to look years younger than he was. "Do you know we still fly sometimes—Anyanwu and I? You should see her as a bird of her own design. Color you wouldn't believe."

"I'm afraid I'll see you as a corpse if you go on doing such things. Firearms are improving slowly. Flying is a stupid risk."

"It's what I do," Isaac said quietly. "You know better than to ask me to give it up entirely."

Doro sighed. "I suppose I do."

"Anyway, Anyanwu always goes along with me—and she always flies slightly lower."

Anyanwu the protector, Doro thought with bitterness that surprised him. Anyanwu the defender of anyone who needed her. Doro wondered what she would do if he told her he needed her. Laugh? Very likely. She would be right, of course. Over the years it had become almost as difficult for him to get a lie past her as it was for her to lie successfully to him. The only reason she did not know of his colony of her African descendants in South Carolina was that he had never given her reason to ask. Even Isaac did not know.

"Does it bother you?" he asked Isaac. "Having her protecting you that way?"

"It did, at first," Isaac said. "I would outdistance her. I'm faster than any bird if I want to be. I would leave her behind and ignore her. But she was always there, laboring to catch up, hampered by winds that didn't bother me at all. She never gave up. After a while, I began expecting her to be there. Now, I think I'd be more bothered if she didn't come along."

"Has she been shot?"

Isaac hesitated. "That's what the bright colors are for, I guess," he said finally. "To distract attention from me. Yes, she's been shot a couple of times. She falls a few yards, flops about to give me time to get away. Then she recovers and follows.

Doro looked up at the portrait of Anyanwu on the wall opposite the high, shallow fireplace. The style of the house was English here, Dutch there, Igbo somewhere else. Anyanwu had made earthen pots, variations of those she had once sold in the marketplaces of her homeland, and stout handsome baskets. People bought them from her and placed them around their houses as she had. Her work was both decorative and utilitarian, and here in her house with its Dutch fireplace and kas, its English settle and thronelike wainscot chairs, it evoked memories of a land she would not see again. Anyanwu had never sanded the floor as Dutch women did. Dirt was for sweeping out, she said contemptuously, not for scattering on the floor. She was more house proud than most English women Doro knew, but Dutch women shook their heads and gossiped about her "slovenly" housekeeping and pretended to pity Isaac. In fact, in the easy atmosphere of Wheatley, nearly every woman pitied Isaac so much that had he wished, he could have spread his valuable seed everywhere. Only Doro drew female attention more strongly—and only Doro took advantage of it. But then, Doro did not have to worry about outraged husbands—or an outraged wife.

The portrait of Anyanwu was extraordinary. Clearly, the Dutch artist had been captured by her beauty. He had draped her in a brilliant blue that set off her dark skin beautifully as blue always had.

Even her hair had been hidden in blue cloth. She was holding a child—her first son by Isaac. The child, too, only a few months old, was partly covered by the blue. He looked out of the painting, large-eyed and handsomer than any infant should have been. Did Anyanwu deliberately conceive only handsome children? Every one of them was beautiful, even though Doro had fathered some with hideous bodies.

The portrait was a black madonna and child right down to Anyanwu's too-clear, innocent-seeming eyes. Strangers were moved to comment on the likeness. Some were appreciative, looking at the still handsome Anyanwu—she kept herself looking well for Isaac even as she aged herself along with him. Others were deeply offended, believing that someone actually had tried to portray the Virgin and Child as "black savages." Race prejudice was growing in the colonies—even in this formerly Dutch colony where things had once been so casual. Earlier in the year, there had been mass executions at New York City. Someone had been setting fires and the whites decided it must be the blacks. On little or no evidence, thirty-one blacks were killed—thirteen of them burned at the stake. Doro was beginning to worry about this upriver town. Of all his English colonial settlements, only in this one did his blacks not have the protection of powerful white owners. How soon before whites from elsewhere began to see them as fair game.

Doro shook his head. The woman in the portrait seemed to look down at him as he looked up. He should have had too much on his mind to think about her or about her daughter Ruth, called Nweke. He should not have allowed himself to be drawn back to Wheatley. It was good to see Isaac... but that woman!

"She was the right wife for me after all," Isaac was saying. "I remember her telling me she wasn't once before we married, but that was one of the few times I've known her to be wrong."

"I want to see her," Doro said abruptly. "And I want to see Nweke. I think the girl's a lot closer to her change than you realize."

"You think that's why you were pulled back here?"

Doro did not like the word "pulled," but he nodded without comment.

Isaac stood up. "Nweke first, while you're still in a fairly good mood." He went out of the house without waiting for Doro to answer. He loved Doro and he loved Anyanwu and it bothered him that the two got along so badly together.

"I don't see how you can be such a fool with her," he told Doro once—to Doro's surprise. "The woman is not temporary. She can be everything you need if you let her—mate, companion, business partner, her abilities complement yours so well. Yet all you do is humiliate her."

"I've never hurt her," Doro had told him. "Never hurt one of her children. You show me one other wild-seed woman I've allowed to live as long as she has after childbearing." He had not touched her children because from the first, she promised him that if any one of them was harmed, she would bear no more. No matter what he did to her, she would bear no more. Her sincerity was unmistakable; thus he refrained from preying on her least success-ful children, refrained from breeding her daughters to her sons—or bedding those daughters himself. She did not know what care he had taken to keep her content. She did not know, but Isaac should have.

"You treat her a little better than the others because she's a little more useful," Isaac had said. "But you still humiliate her."

"If she chooses to be humiliated by what I have her do, she's creating her own problem."

Isaac had looked at him steadily, almost angrily, for several seconds. "I know about Nweke's father," he had said. He had said it without fear. Over the years, he had come to learn that he was one of the few people who did not have to be afraid.

Doro had gone away from him feeling ashamed. He had not thought it was still possible for him to feel shame, but Anyanwu's presence seemed to be slowly awakening several long dormant emo-tions in him. How many women had he sent Isaac to without feeling a thing. Isaac had done as he was told and come home. Home from Pennsylvania, home from Maryland, home from Georgia, home from Spanish Florida... Isaac didn't mind either. He didn't like being away from Anyanwu and the children for long periods, but he didn't mind the women. And they certainly didn't mind him. He didn't mind that Doro had begotten eight of Anyanwu's children. Or seven. Only Anyanwu minded that. Only she felt humiliated. But Nweke's father was, perhaps, another matter.

The girl, eighteen years old, small and dark like her mother, came through the door, Isaac's arm around her shoulders. She was red-eyed as though she had been crying or as though she hadn't been sleeping. Probably both. This was a bad time for her.

"Is it you?" she whispered, seeing the sharp-featured stranger.

"Of course," Doro said, smiling.

His voice, the knowledge that he was indeed Doro, triggered tears. She went to him crying softly, looking for comfort in his arms. He held her and looked over her shoulder at Isaac.

"Whatever you've got to say to me, I deserve it," Isaac said. "I didn't notice and I should have. After all these years, I surely should have."

Doro said nothing, motioned Isaac back out the door.

Isaac obeyed silently, probably feeling more guilt than he should have. This was no ordinary girl. None of her brothers or sisters had reached Doro miles away with their desperation as their transitions neared. What had he felt about her? Anxiety, worry, more. Some indefinable feeling not only that she was near transition, but that she was on the verge of becoming something he had not known before. Something new. It was as though from New York City he had sensed another Anyanwu—new, different, attracting him, pulling him. He had never followed a feeling more willingly.

The girl moved in his arms and he took her to the high-backed settle near the fireplace. The narrow bench was nearly as uncomfortable as the wainscot chairs. Not for the first time, Doro wondered why Isaac and Anyanwu did not buy or have made some comfortable modern furniture. Surely they could afford it.

"What am I going to do?" the girl whispered. She had put her head against his shoulder, but even that close, Doro could hardly hear her. "It hurts so much."

"Endure it," he said simply. "It will end."

"*When!*" From a whisper to almost a scream. Then back to the whisper. "When?"

"Soon." He held her away from him a little so that he could see the small face, swollen and weary. The girl's coloring was gray rather than its usual rich dark brown. "You haven't been sleeping?"

"A little. Sometimes. The nightmares... only they aren't nightmares, are they?"

"You know what they are."

She shrank against the back of the bench. "You know David Whitten, two houses over?"

Doro nodded. The Whitten boy was twenty. Fairly good breeding stock. His family would be worth more in generations to come. They had a sensitivity that puzzled Doro. He did not know quite what they were becoming, but the feeling he got from them was good. They were a pleasant mystery that careful inbreeding would solve.

"Almost every night," Nweke said, "David... he goes to his sister's bed."

Startled, Doro laughed aloud. "Does he?"

"Just like married people. Why is that funny? They could get into trouble—brother and sister. They could..."

"They'll be all right."

She looked at him closely. "Did you know about it?"

"No." Doro was still smiling. "How old is the girl? Around sixteen?"

"Seventeen." Nweke hesitated. "She likes it."

"So do you," Doro observed.

Nweke twisted away, embarrassed. There was no coyness to her; her embarrassment was real. "I didn't want to know about it. I didn't try to know!"

"Do you imagine I'm criticizing you for knowing? Me?"

She blinked, licked her lips. "Not you, I guess. Were you going to... to put them together anyway?"

"Yes."

"Here?"

"No. I was going to move them down to Pennsylvania. I see now that I'd better prepare a place for them quickly."

"They were almost a relief," Nweke said. "It was so easy to get caught up in what they were doing that sometimes I didn't have to feel other things. Last night, though... last night there were some Indians. They caught a white man. He had done something—killed one of their women or something. I was in his thoughts and they were all blurred at first. They tortured him. It took him so long... so long to die." Her hands were clinched tight around each other, her eyes wide with remembering. "They tore out his fingernails, then they cut him and burned him and the women bit him—bit pieces away like wolves at their kill. Then . . ." She stopped, choked. "Oh, God!"

"You were with him the whole time?" Doro asked.

"The whole time—through . . . everything." She was crying silently, not sobbing, only staring straight ahead as tears ran down her face and her nails dug themselves into her palms. "I don't understand how I can be alive after all that," she whispered.

"None of it happened to you," Doro said.

"All of it happened to me, every bit of it!"

Doro took her hands and unclinched the long, slender fingers. There were bloody marks on her palms where the nails had punctured. Doro ran a finger across the hard, neatly cut nails. "All ten," he said, "right where they should be. *None of it happened to you.*"

"You don't understand."

"I've been through transition, girl. In fact, I may have been the first person ever to go through it—back more years than you can imagine. I understand, all right."

"Then you've forgotten! Maybe what happens doesn't leave marks on your body, but it leaves marks. It's real. Oh God, it's so real!" She began sobbing now. "If someone whips a slave or a criminal, I feel it, and it's as real to me as to the person under the lash!"

"But no matter how many times others die," Doro said, "you won't die."

"Why not? People die in transition. You died!"

He grinned. "Not entirely." Then he sobered. "Listen, the one thing you don't have to worry about is becoming what I am. You're going to be something special, all right, but nothing like me."

She looked at him timidly. "I would like to be like you."

Only the youngest of his children said such things. He pushed her head back to his shoulder. "No," he said, "that wouldn't be safe. I know what you're supposed to be. It wouldn't be a good idea for you to surprise me."

She understood and said nothing. Like most of his people, she did not try to move away from him when he warned or threatened. "What will I be?" she asked.

"I hope, someone who will be able to do for others what your mother can do for herself. A healer. The next step in healers.

But even if you inherit talent from only one of your parents, you'll be formidable, and nothing like me. Your father, before I took him, could not only read thoughts but could see into closed places—mentally 'see.'"

"You're my father," she said against him. "I don't want to hear about anyone else."

"Hear it!" he said harshly. "When your transition is over, you'll see it in Isaac's mind and Anyanwu's. You should know from Anneke that a mind reader can't delude herself for long." Anneke Strycker Croon. She was the one who should have been having this talk with Nweke. She had been his best mind reader in a half-dozen generations—beautifully controlled. Once her transition was ended, she never entered another person's mind unless she wanted to. Her only flaw was that she was barren. Anyanwu tried to help her. Doro brought her one male body after another, all in vain. Thus, finally, Anneke had half adopted Nweke. The young girl and the old woman had found a similarity in each other that pleased Doro. It was rare for someone with Anneke's ability to take any pleasure at all in children. Doro saw the friendship as a good omen for Nweke's immature talents. But now, Anneke was three years dead, and Nweke was alone. No doubt her next words came at least partially out of her loneliness.

"Do you love us?" she asked.

"All of you?" Doro asked, knowing very well that she did not mean everyone—all his people.

"The ones of us who change," she said, not looking at him. "The different ones."

"You're all different. It's only a matter of degree."

She seemed to force herself to meet his eyes. "You're laughing at me. We endure so much pain... because of you, and you're laughing."

"Not at your pain, girl." He took a deep breath and stilled his amusement. "Not at your pain."

"You don't love us."

"No." He felt her start against him. "Not all of you."

"Me?" she whispered timidly, finally. "Do you love me?"

The favorite question of his daughters—only his daughters. His sons hoped he loved them, but they did not ask. Perhaps they did not dare to. Ah, but this girl...

When she was healthy, her eyes were like her mother's—clear whites and browns, baby's eyes. She had finer bones than Anyanwu—slenderer wrists and ankles, more prominent cheekbones. She was the daughter of one of Isaac's older sons—a son he had had by a wild-seed Indian woman who read thoughts and saw into distant closed places. The Indians were rich in untrapped wild seed that they tended to tolerate or even revere rather than destroy. Eventually, they would learn to be civilized and to understand as the whites understood that the hearing of voices, the seeing of visions, the moving of inanimate objects when no hand touched them, all the strange feelings, sensitivities, and abilities were evil or dangerous, or at the very least, imaginary. Then they too would weed out or grind down their different ones, thus freezing themselves in time, depriving their kind of any senses but those already familiar, depriving their children and their children's children of any weapons with which to confront Doro's people. And surely, in some future time, the day of confrontation would come. This girl, as rare and valuable for her father's blood as for her mother's, might well live to see that day. If ever he was to breed a long-lived descendant from Anyanwu, it would be this girl. He felt utterly certain of her. Over the years, he had taught himself not to assume that any new breed would be successful until transition ended and he saw the success before him. But the feelings that came to him from this girl were too powerful to doubt. He had no more certain urge than the urge that directed him toward the very best prey. Now it spoke to him as it had never spoken before, even for Isaac or Anyanwu. The girl's talent teased and enticed him. He would not kill her, of course. He did not kill the best of his children. But he would have what he could of her now. And she would have what she wanted of him.

"I came back because of you," he said, smiling. "Not because of any of the others, but because I could feel how near you were to your change. I wanted to see for myself that you were all right."

That was apparently enough for her. She caught him in a joyful stranglehold and kissed him not at all as a daughter should kiss her father.

"I do like it," she said shyly. "What David and Melanie do. Sometimes I try to know when they're doing it. I try to share it. But I can't. It comes to me of itself or not at all." And she echoed her stepfather—her grandfather. "I have to have something of my own!" Her voice had taken on a fierceness, as though Doro owed her what she was demanding.

"Why tell me?" he said, playing with her. "I'm not even handsome right now. Why not choose one of the town boys?"

She clutched at his arms, her hard little nails now digging into his flesh. "You're laughing again!" she hissed. "Am I so ridiculous? Please...?"

To his disgust, Doro found himself thinking about Anyanwu. He had always resisted the advances of her daughters before. It had become a habit. Nweke was the last child Doro had coerced Anyanwu into bearing, but Doro had gone on respecting Anyanwu's superstitions—not that Anyanwu appreciated the kindness. Well, Anyanwu was about to lose her place with him to this young daughter. Whatever he had been reaching for, trying to bribe from the mother, the daughter would supply. The daughter was not wild seed with years of freedom to make her stubborn. The daughter had been his from the moment of her conception—his property as surely as though his brand were burned into her flesh. She even thought of herself as his property. His children, young and old, male and female, most often made the matter of ownership very simple for him. They accepted his authority and seemed to need his assurance that strange as they were, they still belonged to someone.

"Doro?" the girl said softly.

She had a red kerchief tied over her hair. He pushed it back to reveal her thick dark hair, straighter than her mother's but not as straight as her father's. She had combed it back and pinned it in a large knot. Only a single heavy curl hung free to her smooth brown shoulder. He resisted the impulse to remove the pins, let the other curls free. He and the girl would not have much time together. He did not want her wasting what they had pinning up her hair. Nor did he want her appearance to announce at once to Anyanwu what had happened. Anyanwu would find out—probably very quickly—but she would not find out through any apparent brazenness on the part of her daughter. She would find out in such a way as to cause her to blame Doro. Her daughter still needed her too badly to alienate her. No one in any of Doro's settlements was as good at helping people through transition as Anyanwu. Her body could absorb the physical punishment of restraining a violent, usually very strong young person. She did not hurt her charges or allow them to hurt themselves. They did not frighten or disgust her. She was their companion, their sister, their mother, their lover through their agony. If they could survive their own mental upheaval, they would come through to find that she had taken good care of their physical bodies. Nweke would need that looking after—whatever she needed right now.

He lifted the girl, carried her to an alcove bed in one of the children's bedrooms. He did not know whether it was her bed, did not care. He undressed her, brushing away her hands when she tried to help, laughing softly when she commented that he seemed to know pretty well how to get a woman out of her clothes. She did not know much about undressing a man, but she fumbled and tried to help him.

And she was as lovely as he had expected. A virgin of course. Even in Wheatley, young girls usually saved themselves for husbands, or for Doro. She was ready for him. She had some pain, but it didn't seem to matter to her.

"Better than with David and Melanie," she whispered once, and held onto him as though fearing he might leave her.

Nweke and Doro were in the kitchen popping corn and drinking beer when Isaac and Anyanwu came in. The bed had been remade and Nweke had been properly dressed and cautioned against even the appearance of brazenness. "Let her be angry at me," Doro had said, "not at you. Say nothing."

"I don't know how to think about her now," Nweke said. "My sisters whispered that we could never have you because of her. Sometimes I hated her. I thought she kept you for herself."

"Did she?"

"... no." She glanced at him uncertainly. "I think she tried to protect us from you. She thought we needed it." Nweke shuddered. "What will she feel for me now?"

Doro did not know, and he did not intend to leave until he found out. Until he could see that any anger Anyanwu felt would do her daughter no harm.

"Maybe she won't find out," the girl said hopefully.

That was when Doro took her into the kitchen to investigate the stew Anyanwu had left simmering and the bread untended in its bake kettle, hot and tender, unburned in the coals. They set the table, then Nweke suggested beer and popcorn. Doro agreed, humoring her, hoping she would relax and not worry about facing her mother. She seemed peaceful and content when Isaac and Anyanwu came in, yet she avoided her mother's eyes. She stared down into her beer.

Doro saw Anyanwu frown, saw her go to Nweke and take the small chin in her fingers and raise it so that she could see Nweke's frightened eyes.

"Are you well?" she asked Nweke in her own language. She spoke perfect English now, along with Dutch and a few words of some Indian and foreign African dialects, but at home with her children, she often spoke as though she had never left home. She would not adopt a European name or call her children by their European names—though she had condescended to give them European names at Doro's insistence. Her children could speak and understand as well as she could. Even Isaac, after all the years, could understand and speak fairly well. No doubt, he heard as clearly as Doro and Nweke the wariness and tension in Anyanwu's soft question.

Nweke did not answer. Frightened, she glanced at Doro. Anyanwu followed the glance and her infant-clear, bright eyes took on a look of incongruous ferocity. She said nothing. She only stared with growing comprehension. Doro met her gaze levelly until she turned back to look at her daughter.

"Nweke, little one, are you well?" she whispered urgently.

Something happened within Nweke. She took Anyanwu's hands between her own, held them for a moment, smiling. Finally she laughed aloud—delighted child's laughter with no hint of falseness or gloating. "I'm well," she said. "I didn't know how well until this moment. It has been so long since there were no voices, nothing pulling at me or hurting me." Relief made her forget her fear. She met Anyanwu's eyes, her own eyes full of the wonder of her new-found peace.

Anyanwu closed her eyes for a moment, drew a long, shuddering breath.

"She's all right," Isaac said from where he sat at the table. "That's enough."

Anyanwu looked at him. Doro could not read what passed between them, but after a moment, Isaac repeated, "That's enough."

And it seemed to be. At that moment, the twenty-two-year-old son Peter, incongruously called Chukwuka—God is Supreme— arrived, and dinner was served.

Doro ate slowly, recalling how he had laughed at the boy's Igbo name. He had asked Anyanwu where she had found her sudden devotion to God—any god. Chukwuka was a common enough name in her homeland, but it was not a name he would have expected from a woman who claimed she helped herself. Predictably, Anyanwu had been silent and unamused at his question. It took him a surprisingly long time to begin to wonder whether the name was supposed to be a charm—her pathetic attempt to protect the boy from him. Where had Anyanwu found her sudden devotion to God? Where else but in her fear of Doro? Doro smiled to himself.

Then he stopped smiling as Nweke's brief peace ended. The girl screamed—a long, ragged, terrible sound that reminded Doro of cloth tearing. Then she dropped the dish of corn she had been bringing to the table and collapsed to the floor unconscious.

Chapter Eight

Nweke lay twitching, still unconscious in the middle of Isaac and Anyanwu's bed. Anyanwu said it was easier to care for her here in a bed merely enclosed within curtains than in one of the alcove beds. Oblivious to Doro's presence, Anyanwu had stripped Nweke to her shift and removed the pins from her hair. The girl looked even smaller than she was now, looked lost in the deep, soft feather mattress. She looked like a child. Doro felt a moment of unease, even fear for her. He remembered her laughter minutes earlier and wondered whether he would hear it again.

"This is transition," Anyanwu said to him, neutral-voiced.

He glanced at her. She stood beside the bed looking weary and concerned. Her earlier hostility had been set aside—and only set aside. Doro knew her too well to think it had been forgotten.

"Are you sure?" he asked. "She's passed out before, hasn't she?"

"Oh yes. But this is transition. I know it."

He thought she was probably right. He sensed the girl very strongly now. If his body had been a lesser one or one had given long use, he would not have dared to stay so near her.

"Will you stay?" Anyanwu asked, as though hearing his thoughts.

"For a while."

"Why? You have never stayed before when my children changed."

"This one is special."

"So I have seen." She gave him another of her venomous looks. "Why, Doro?"

He did not pretend to misunderstand. "Do you know what she has been receiving? What thoughts she has been picking up?"

"She told me about the man last night—the torture."

"Not that. She's been picking up people making love—picking it up often."

"And you thought that was not enough for an unmarried girl!"

"She's eighteen years old. It wasn't enough."

Nweke made a small sound as though she were having a bad dream. No doubt she was. The worst of dreams. And she would not be permitted to wake fully until it was over.

"You have not molested my children before," she said.

"I wondered whether you had noticed."

"Is that it?" She turned to face him. "Were you punishing me for my... my ingratitude?"

"... no." His eyes looked past her for a moment though he did not move. "I'm not interested in punishing you any longer."

She turned a little too quickly and sat down beside the bed. She sat on a chair Isaac had made for her—a taller-than-normal chair so that in spite of her small size and the height of the bed, she could see and reach Nweke easily. Eventually she would move onto the bed with the girl. People in transition needed close physical contact to give them some hold on reality.

But for now, Anyanwu's move to the chair was to conceal emotion. Fear, Doro wondered, or shame or anger or hatred.... His last serious attempt to punish her had involved Nweke's father. That attempt had stood between them all Nweke's life. Of all the things she considered that he had done to her, that was the worst. Yet it was a struggle she had come very near winning. Perhaps she had won. Perhaps that was why the incident could still make him uneasy.

Doro shook his head, turned his attention to the girl. "Do you think she'll come through all right?" he asked.

"I have never had any of them die in my care."

He ignored the sarcasm in her voice. "What do you feel, Anyanwu? How can you help them so well when you cannot reach their minds in even the shadowy way that I can?"

"I bit her a little. She is strong and healthy. There is nothing, no feeling of death about her." He had opened his mouth, but she held up a hand to stop him. "If I could tell you more clearly, I would. Perhaps I will find a way—on the day you find a way to tell me how you move from body to body."

"Touché," he said, and shrugged. He took a chair from beside the fireplace and brought it to the foot of the bed. There, he waited. When Nweke came to, shaking and crying wildly, he spoke to her, but she did not seem to hear him. Anyanwu went onto the bed silent, grim-faced, and held the girl until her tears had slowed, until she had stopped shaking.

"You are in transition," Doro heard Anyanwu whisper. "Stay with us until tomorrow and you will have the powers of a goddess." That was all she had time to say. Nweke's body stiffened. She made retching sounds and Anyanwu drew back from her slightly. But instead of vomiting, she went limp again, her consciousness gone to join someone else's.

Eventually, she seemed to come to again, but her open eyes were glazed and she made the kind of gibbering sounds Doro had heard in madhouses—especially in the madhouses to which his people had been consigned when their transitions caught them outside their settlements. Nweke's face was like something out of a madhouse, too—twisted and unrecognizable, covered with sweat, eyes, nose, and mouth streaming. Wearily, sadly, Doro got up to leave.

There had been a time when he had to watch transitions—when no one else could be trusted not to run away or murder his writhing charge or perform some dangerous, stupid ritual of exorcism. But that was long ago. He was not only building a people now; they were building themselves. It was no longer necessary for him to do everything, see everything.

He looked back once as he reached the door and saw that Anyanwu was watching him.

"It is easier to doom a child to this than to stay and watch it happen, isn't it?" she said.

"I watched it happen to your ancestors!" he said angrily. "And I'll watch it happen to your descendants when even you are dust!" He turned and left her.

When Doro had gone, Anyanwu clambered off the featherbed and went to the washstand. There she poured water from the pitcher to the basin and wet a towel. Nweke was having a difficult time already, poor girl. That meant a long, terrible night. There was no duty Anyanwu hated more than this—especially with her own children. But no one else could handle it as well as she could.

She bathed the girl's face, thinking, praying: *Oh, Nweke, little one, stay until tomorrow. The pain will go away tomorrow.*

Nweke quieted as though she could hear the desperate thoughts. Perhaps she could. Her face was gray and still now. Anyanwu caressed it, seeing traces of the girl's father in it as she always did. There was a man damned from the day of his birth—all because of Doro. He was fine breeding stock, oh yes. He was a forest animal unable to endure the company of other people, unable to get any peace from their thoughts. He had not been as Nweke was now, receiving only large emotions, great stress. He received everything. And also, he saw visions of things far from him, beyond the range of even her eyes, of things closed away from any eyes. In a city, even in a small town, he would have gone mad. And his vulnerability was not a passing thing, not a transition from powerlessness to godlike power. It was a condition he had had to endure to the day of his death. He had loved Doro pathetically because Doro was the one person whose thoughts could not entangle him. His mind would not reach into Doro's. Doro said this was a matter of self-preservation; the mind that reached into his became his. It was consumed, extinguished, and Doro took over the body it had animated. Doro said even people like this man—Thomas, his name was—even people whose mind-reading ability seemed completely out of control somehow never reached into Doro's thoughts. People with control could force themselves to try—as they could force their hands into fire—but they could not make the attempt without first feeling the "heat" and knowing they were doing a dangerous thing.

Thomas could not force his "hands" into anything at all. He lived alone in a filthy cabin well hidden within a dark, awesome Virginia woods. When Doro brought her to him, he cursed her. He told her she should not mind the way he lived, since she was from Africa where people swung through the trees and went naked like animals. He asked Doro what wrong he had done to be given a nigger woman. But it was not his wrong that had won him Anyanwu. It was hers.

Now and then, Doro courted her in his own way. He arrived with a new body—sometimes an appealing one. He paid attention to her, treated her as something more than only a breeding animal. Then, courting done, he took her from Isaac's bed to his own and kept her there until he was certain she was pregnant. Still, Isaac urged her to use these times to tie Doro to her and strengthen whatever influence she had with him. But Anyanwu never learned to forgive Doro's unnecessary killings, his casual abuse when he was not courting her, his open contempt for any belief of hers that did not concur with his, the blows for which she could not retaliate and from which she could not flee, the acts she must perform for him no matter what her beliefs. She had lain with him as a man while he wore the body of a woman. She had not been able to become erect naturally. He was a beautiful woman, but he repelled her. Nothing he did gave her pleasure. Nothing.

No...

She sighed and stared down at her daughter's still face. No, her children gave her pleasure. She loved them, but she also feared for them. Who knew what Doro might decide to do to them? What would he do to this one?

She lay down close to Nweke, so that the girl would not awake alone. Perhaps even now, some part of Nweke's spirit knew that Anyanwu was nearby. Anyanwu had seen that people in transition thrashed around less if she lay close to them and sometimes held them. If her nearness, her touch, gave them any peace, she was willing to stay close. Her thoughts returned to Thomas.

Doro had been angry with her. He never seemed to get truly angry with anyone else—but then, his other people loved him. He could not tell her that he was angry because she did not love him. Even he could not utter such foolishness. Certainly, he did not love her. He did not love anyone except perhaps Isaac and a very few of his other children. Yet he wanted Anyanwu to be like his many other women and treat him like a god in human form, competing for his attention no matter how repugnant his latest body nor even whether he might be looking for a new body. They knew he took women almost as readily as he took men. Especially, he took women who had already given him what he wanted of them—usually several children. They served him and never thought they might be his next victims. Someone else. Not them. More than once, Anyanwu wondered how much time she might have left. Had Doro merely been waiting for her to help this last daughter through transition? If so, he might be in for a surprise. Once Nweke had power and could care for herself, Anyanwu did not plan to stay in Wheatley. She had had enough of Doro and everything to do with him; and no person was better fitted to escape him than she was.

If only Thomas had been able to escape...

But Thomas had not had power—only potential, unrealized, unrealizable. He had had a long sparse beard when Doro took her to him, and long black hair clotted together with the grease and dirt of years of neglect. His clothing might have stood alone, starched as it was with layers of dirt and sweat, but it was too ragged to stand. In some places, it seemed to be held together by the dirt. There were sores on his body, ignored and filthy—as though he were rotting away while still alive. He was a young man, but his teeth were almost gone. His breath, his entire body, stank unbelievably.

And he did not care. He did not care about anything—beyond his next drink. He looked, except for the sparse beard, like an Indian, but he thought of himself as a white man. And he thought of Anyanwu as a nigger.

Doro had known what he was doing when in exasperation, he had said to her, "You think I ask too much of you? You think I abuse you? I'm going to show you how fortunate you've been!"

And he gave her to Thomas. And he stayed to see that she did not run away or kill the grotesque ruin of a man instead of sharing his vermin-infested bed.

But Anyanwu had never killed anyone except in self-defense. It was not her business to kill. She was a healer.

At first, Thomas cursed her and reviled her blackness. She ignored this. "Doro has put us together," she told him calmly. "If I were green, it would make no difference."

"Shut your mouth!" he said. "You're a black bitch brought here for breeding and nothing more. I don't have to listen to your yapping!"

She had not struck back. After the first moments, she had not even been angry. Nor had she been pitying or repelled. She knew Doro expected her to be repelled, but that proved nothing more than that he could know her for decades without really knowing her at all. This was a man sick in a dozen ways—the remnants of a man. Healer that she was, creator of medicines and poisons, binder of broken bones, comforter—could she take the remnants here and build them into a man again?

Doro looked at people, healthy or ill, and wondered what kind of young they could produce. Anyanwu looked at the sick—especially those with problems she had not seen before—and wondered whether she could defeat their disease.

Helplessly, Thomas caught her thoughts. "Stay away from me!" he muttered alarmed. "You heathen! Go rattle your bones at someone else!"

Heathen, yes. He was a god-fearing man himself. Anyanwu went to his god and said, "Find a town and buy us food. That man won't sire any children as he is now, living mostly on beer and cider and rum—which he probably steals."

Doro stared at her as though he could not think of anything to say. He was wearing a big burly body and had been using it to chop wood while Anyanwu and Thomas got acquainted.

"There's food enough here," he protested finally. "There are deer and bear and game birds and fish. Thomas grows a few things. He has what he needs."

"If he has it, he is not eating it!"

"Then he'll starve. But not before he gets you with a child."

In anger that night, Anyanwu took her leopard form for the first time in years. She hunted deer, stalking them as she had at home so long ago, moving with the old stealth, using her eyes and her ears even more efficiently than a true leopard might. The result was as it had been at home. Deer were deer. She brought down a sleek doe, then took her human form again, threw her prize across her shoulders, and carried it to Thomas' cabin. By morning, when the two men awoke, the doe had been skinned, cleaned, and butchered. The cabin was filled with the smell of roasting venison.

Doro ate heartily and went out. He didn't ask where the fresh meat had come from or thank Anyanwu for it. He simply accepted it. Thomas was less trusting. He drank a little rum, sniffed at the meat Anyanwu gave him, nibbled at a little of it.

"Where'd this come from?" he demanded.

"I hunted last night," Anyanwu said. "You have nothing here."

"Hunted with what? My musket? Who allowed you to..."

"I did not hunt with your musket! It's there, you see?" She gestured toward where the gun, the cleanest thing in the cabin, hung from a peg by the door. "I don't hunt with guns," she added.

He got up and checked the musket anyway. When he was satisfied, he came to stand over her, reeking and forcing her to breathe very shallowly. "What did you hunt with, then?" he demanded. He wasn't a big man, but sometimes, like now, he spoke in a deep rumbling voice. "What did you use?" he repeated. "Your nails and teeth?"

"Yes," Anyanwu said softly.

He stared at her for a moment, his eyes suddenly wide. "A cat!" he whispered. "From woman to cat to woman again. But how...?" Doro had explained that since this man had never completed transition, he had no control over his ability. He could not deliberately look into Anyanwu's thoughts, but he could not refrain from looking into them either. Anyanwu was near him and her thoughts, unlike Doro's, were open and unprotected.

"I was a cat," she said simply. "I can be anything. Shall I show you?"

"No!"

"It's like what you do," she reassured him. "You can see what I'm thinking. I can change my shape. Why not eat the meat? It is very good." She would wash him, she decided. This day, she would wash him and start on the sores. The stink was unendurable.

He snatched up his portion of food and threw it into the fire. "Witch food!" he muttered, and turned his jug up to his mouth.

Anyanwu stifled an impulse to throw the rum into the fire. Instead, she stood up and took it from his hands as he lowered it. He did not try to keep it from her. She set it aside and faced him.

"We are all witches," she said. "All Doro's people. Why would he notice us if we were ordinary?" She shrugged. "He wants a child from us because it will not be ordinary."

He said nothing. Only stared at her with unmistakable suspicion and dislike.

"I have seen what you can do," she continued. "You keep speaking my thoughts, knowing what you should not know. I will show you what I can do."

"I don't want to—"

"Seeing it will make it more real to you. It isn't a hard thing to watch. I don't become ugly. Most of the changes happen inside me." She was undressing as she spoke. It was not necessary. She could shrug out of the clothing as she changed, shed it as a snake sheds its skin, but she wanted to move very slowly for this man. She did not expect her nudity to excite him. He had seen her unclothed the night before and he had turned away and gone to sleep—leaving her to go hunting. She suspected that he was impotent. She had made her body slender and young for him, hoping to get his seed in her and escape quickly, but last night had convinced her that she had more work to do here than she had thought. And if the man was impotent, all that she did might not be enough. What would Doro do then?

She changed very slowly, took the leopard form, all the while keeping her body between Thomas and the door. Between Thomas and the gun. That was wise because when she had finished, when she stretched her small powerful cat-body and spread her claws, leaving marks in the packed earth floor, he dived for his gun.

Claws sheathed, Anyanwu batted him aside. He screamed and shrank back from her. By his manner, arm thrown up to protect his throat, eyes wide, he seemed to expect her to leap upon him. He was waiting to die. Instead, she approached him slowly, her body relaxed. Purring, she rubbed her head against his knee. She looked up at him, saw that the protective arm had come down from the throat. She rubbed her fur against his leg and went on purring. Finally, almost unwillingly, his hand touched her head, caressed tentatively. When she had him scratching her neck—which did not itch—and muttering to himself, "My God!" she broke away, went over and picked up a piece of venison and brought it back to him.

"I don't want that!" he said.

She began to growl low in her throat. He took a step back but that put him against the rough log wall. When Anyanwu followed, there was nowhere for him to go. She tried to put the meat into his hand, but he snatched the hand away. Finally, around the meat, she gave a loud, coughing roar.

Thomas sank to the floor terrified, staring at her. She dropped the meat into his lap and roared again.

He picked it up and ate—for the first time in how long, she wondered. If he wanted to kill himself, why was he doing it in this slow terrible way, letting himself rot alive? Oh, this day she would wash him and begin his healing. If he truly wanted to die, let him hang himself and be done with it.

When he had finished the venison, she became a woman again and calmly put on her clothing as he watched.

"I could see it," he whispered after a long silence. "I could see your body changing inside. Everything changing..." He shook his head uncomprehending, then asked: "Could you turn white?"

The question startled her. Was he really so concerned about her color? Usually Doro's people were not. Most of them had backgrounds too thoroughly mixed for them to sneer at anyone. Anyanwu did not know this man's ancestry but she was certain he was not as white as he seemed to think. The Indian appearance was too strong.

"I have never made myself white," she said. "In Wheatley, everyone knows me. Who would I deceive—and why should I try?"

"I don't believe you," he said. "If you could become white, you would!"

"Why?"

He stared at her hostilely.

"I'm content," she said finally. "If I have to be white some day to survive, I will be white. If I have to be a leopard to hunt and kill, I will be a leopard. If I have to travel quickly across land, I'll become a large bird. If I have to cross the sea, I'll become a fish." She smiled a little. "A dolphin, perhaps."

"Will you become white for me?" he asked. His hostility had died as she spoke. He seemed to believe her. Perhaps he was hearing her thoughts. If so, he was not hearing them clearly enough.

"I think you will have to endure it somehow that I am black," she said with hostility of her own. "This is the way I look. No one has ever told me I was ugly!"

He sighed. "No, you're not. Not by some distance. It's just that..." He stopped, wet his lips. "It's just that I thought you could make yourself look like my wife... just a little."

"You have a wife?"

He rubbed at a scabbed over sore on his arm. Anyanwu could see it through a hole in his sleeve and it did not look as though it was healing properly. The flesh around the scab was very red and swollen.

"I had a wife," he said. "Big, handsome girl with hair yellow as gold. I thought it would be all right if we didn't live in a town or have neighbors too nearby. She wasn't one of Doro's people, but he let me have her. He gave me enough money to buy some land, get a start in tobacco. I thought things would be fine."

"Did she know you could hear her thoughts?"

He gave her a look of contempt. "Would she have married me if she had? Would anyone?"

"One of Doro's people, perhaps. One who could also hear thoughts."

"You don't know what you're talking about," he said bitterly.

His tone made her think, made her remember that some of the most terrible of Doro's people were like Thomas. They weren't as sensitive, perhaps. Living in towns didn't seem to bother them. But they drank too much and fought and abused or neglected their children and occasionally murdered each other before Doro could get around to taking them. Thomas was probably right to marry a more ordinary woman.

"Why did your wife leave?" she asked.

"Why do you think! I couldn't keep out of her thoughts any more than I can keep out of yours. I tried not to let her know, but sometimes things came to me so clearly... I'd answer, thinking she had spoken aloud and she hadn't and she didn't understand and..."

"And she was afraid."

"God, yes. After a while, she was terrified. She went home to her parents and wouldn't even see me when I went after her. I guess I don't blame her. After that there were only... women like you that Doro brings me."

"We're not such bad women. I'm not."

"You can't wait to get away from me!"

"What would you feel for a woman who was covered with filth and sores?"

He blinked, looked at himself. "And I guess you're used to better!"

"Of course I am! Let me help you and you will be better. You could not have been this way for your wife."

"You're not her!"

"No. She could not help you. I can."

"I didn't ask for your—"

"Listen! She ran away from you because you are Doro's. You are a witch and she was afraid and disgusted. I am not afraid or disgusted."

"You'd have no right to be," he muttered sullenly. "You're more witch than I'll ever be. I still don't believe what I saw you do."

"If my thoughts are reaching you even some of the time, you should believe what I do and what I say. I have not been telling you lies. I am a healer. I have lived for over three hundred and fifty years. I have seen leprosy and huge growths that bring agony and babies born with great holes where their faces should be and other things. You are far from being the worst thing I have seen."

He stared at her, frowned intently as though reaching for a thought that eluded her. It occurred to her that he was trying to hear her thoughts. Finally, though, he seemed to give up. He shrugged and sighed. "Could you help any of those others?"

"Sometimes I could help. Sometimes I can dissolve away dangerous growths or open blind eyes or heal sores that will not heal themselves...."

"You can't take away the voices or the visions, can you?"

"The thoughts you hear from other people?"

"Yes, and what I 'see.' Sometimes I can't tell reality from vision."

She shook her head sadly. "I wish I could. I have seen others tormented as you are. I'm better than what your people call a doctor.

Much better. But I am not as good as I long to be. I think I am flawed like you."

"All Doro's children are flawed—godlings with feet of clay."

Anyanwu understood the reference. She had read the sacred book of her new land, the Bible, in the hope of improving her understanding of the people around her. In Wheatley, Isaac told people she was becoming a Christian. Some of them did not realize he was joking.

"I was not born to Doro," she told Thomas. "I am what he calls wild seed. But it makes no difference. I am flawed anyway."

He glanced at her, then down at the floor. "Well I'm not as flawed as you think." He spoke very softly. "I'm not impotent."

"Good. If you were and Doro found out... he might decide you could not be useful to him any longer."

It was as though she had said something startling. He jumped, peered at her in a way that made her draw back in alarm, then demanded: "What's the matter with you! How can you care what happens to me? How can you let Doro breed you like a goddamn cow—and to me! You're not like the others."

"You said I was a dog. A black bitch."

Even through the dirt, she could see him redden. "I'm sorry," he said after several seconds.

"Good. I almost hit you when you said it—and I am very strong."

"I don't doubt it."

"I care what Doro does to me. He knows I care. I tell him."

"People don't, normally."

"Yes. That's why I'm here. Things are not right to me merely because he says they are. He is not my god. He brought me to you as punishment for my sacrilege." She smiled. "But he does not understand that I would rather lie with you than with him."

Thomas said nothing for so long that she reached out and touched his hand, concerned.

He looked at her, smiled without showing his bad teeth. She had not seen him smile before. "Be careful," he said. "Doro should never find out how thoroughly you hate him."

"He has known for years."

"And you're still alive? You must be very valuable."

"I must be," she agreed bitterly.

He sighed. "I should hate him myself. I don't somehow. I can't. But... I think I'm glad you do. I never met anyone who did before." He hesitated again, raised his night-black eyes to hers. "Just be careful."

She nodded, thinking that he reminded her of Isaac. Isaac too was always cautioning her. Then Thomas got up and went to the door.

"Where are you going?" she asked.

"To the stream out back to wash." The smile again, tentatively. "Do you really think you can take care of these sores? I've had some of them for a long time."

"I can heal them. They will come back, though, if you don't stay clean and stop drinking so much. Eat food!"

"I don't know whether you're here to conceive a child or turn me into one," he muttered, and closed the door behind him.

Anyanwu went out and fashioned a crude broom of twigs. She swept the mounds of litter out of the cabin, then washed what could be washed. She did not know what to do about the vermin. The fleas alone were terrible. Left to herself, she would have burned the cabin and built another. But Thomas would not be likely to go along with that.

She cleaned and cleaned and cleaned and the terrible little cabin still did not suit her. There were no clean blankets, there was no clean clothing for Thomas. Eventually, he came in wearing the same filthy rags over skin scrubbed pale and nearly raw. He seemed acutely embarrassed when Anyanwu began stripping the rags from him.

"Don't be foolish," she told him. "When I start on those sores, you won't have time for shame—or for any other thing."

He became erect. Scrawny and sick as his body was, he was, as he had said, not impotent.

"All right," murmured Anyanwu with gentle amusement. "Have your pleasure now and your pain later."

His clumsy fingers had begun fumbling with her clothing, but they stopped suddenly. "No!" he said as though the pain had to come first after all. "No." He turned his back to her.

"But... why?" Anyanwu laid a hand on his shoulder. "You want to, and it's all right. Why else am I here?"

He spoke through his teeth as though every word was hurting him. "Are you still so eager to get away from me? Can't you stay a little while?"

"Ah." She rubbed the shoulder, feeling the bones sharply through their thin covering of flesh. "The women take your seed and leave you as quickly as possible."

He said nothing.

She stepped closer to him. He was smaller than Isaac, smaller than most of the male bodies Doro brought her. It was strange to be able to meet a man's eyes without looking up. "It will be that way for me too," she said. "I have a husband. I have children. And also... Doro knows how quickly I can conceive. I am always deliberately quick with him. I must take your seed and leave you. But I will not leave you today."

He stared at her for a moment, the black eyes intent as though again he was trying to control his ability, hear her thoughts now when he wanted to hear them. She found herself hoping her child— his child—would have those eyes. They were the only things about him that had never needed cleaning or healing to show their beauty. That was surprising considering how much he drank.

He seized her suddenly, as though it had just occurred to him that he could, and held her tightly for long moments before leading her to his splintery shelf bed.

Doro came in hours later, bringing flour, sugar, coffee, corn meal, salt, eggs, butter, dry peas, fresh fruit and vegetables, blankets, cloth that could be sewn into clothing, and, incidentally, a new body. He had bought or stolen someone's small crudely made wagon to carry his things.

"Thank you," Anyanwu told him gravely, wanting him to see that her gratitude was real. It was rare these days for him to do what she asked. She wondered why he had bothered this time. Certainly he had not planned to the day before.

Then she saw him looking at Thomas. The bath had made the most visible difference in Thomas' appearance, and Anyanwu had shaved him, cut off much of his hair, and combed the rest. But there were other more subtle changes. Thomas was smiling, was helping to carry the supplies into the cabin instead of standing aside apathetically, instead of muttering at Anyanwu when she passed him, her arms full.

"Now," he said, happily oblivious to Doro's eyes on him. "Now we'll see how well you can cook, Sun Woman."

That stupid name, she thought desperately. Why had he called her that? He must have read it in her thoughts. She had not told him it was Doro's name for her.

Doro smiled. "I never thought you could do this so well," he said to her. "I would have brought you my sick ones before."

"I am a healer," she said. His smile terrified her for Thomas' sake. It was a smile full of teeth and utterly without humor. "I have conceived," she said, though she had not meant to tell him that for days—perhaps weeks. Suddenly, though, she wanted him away from Thomas. She knew Doro. Over the years, she had come to know him very well. He had given her to a man he hoped would repel her, make her know how well off she had been. Instead, she had immediately begun helping the man, healing him so that eventually he would not repel anyone. Clearly, she had not been punished.

"Already," Doro said in mock surprise. "Shall we leave then?"

"Yes."

He glanced toward the cabin where Thomas was.

Anyanwu came around the wagon and caught Doro's arms. He was wearing the body of a round-faced very young-looking white man. "Why did you bring the supplies?" she demanded.

"You wanted them," he said reasonably.

"For him. So he could heal."

"And now you want to leave him before that healing is finished."

Thomas came out of the cabin and saw them standing together. "Is something wrong?" he asked. Anyanwu realized later that it was probably her expression or her thoughts that alerted him. If only he could have read Doro's thoughts.

"Anyanwu wants to go home," said Doro blandly.

Thomas stared at her with disbelief and pain. "Anyanwu...?"

She did not know what to do—what would make Doro feel that he had extracted enough pain, punished her enough. What would stop him now that he had decided to kill?

She looked at Doro. "I will leave with you today," she whispered. "Please, I will leave with you now."

"Not quite yet," Doro said.

She shook her head, pleaded desperately: "Doro, what do you want of me? Tell me and I will give it."

Thomas had come closer to them, looking at Anyanwu, his expression caught between anger and pain. Anyanwu wanted to shout at him to stay away.

"I want you to remember," Doro said to her. "You've come to think I couldn't touch you. That kind of thinking is foolish and dangerous."

She was in the midst of a healing. She had endured abuse from Thomas. She had endured part of a night beside his filthy body. Finally, she had been able to reach him and begin to heal. It was not only the sores on his body she was reaching for. Never had Doro taken a patient from her in the midst of healing, never! Somehow, she had not thought he would do such a thing. It was as though he had threatened one of her children. And, of course, he was threatening her children. He was threatening everything dear to her. He was not finished with her, apparently, and thus would not kill her. But since she had made it clear that she did not love him, that she obeyed him only because he had power, he felt some need to remind her of that power. If he could not do it by giving her to an evil man because that man obstinately ceased to be evil, then he would take that man from her now while her interest in him was strongest. And also, perhaps Doro had realized the thing she had told Thomas—that she would rather share Thomas' bed than Doro's. For a man accustomed to adoration, that realization must have been a heavy blow. But what could she do?

"Doro," she pleaded, "it's enough. I understand. I have been wrong. I will remember and behave better toward you."

She was clinging to both his arms now, and lowering her head before the smooth young face. Inside, she screamed with rage and fear and loathing. Outside, her face was as smooth as his.

But out of stubbornness or hunger or a desire to hurt her, he would not stop. He turned toward Thomas. And by now, Thomas understood.

Thomas backed away, his disbelief again clear in his expression. "Why?" he said. "What have I done?"

"Nothing!" shouted Anyanwu suddenly, and her hands on Doro's arms locked suddenly in a grip Doro would not break in any normal way. "You've done nothing, Thomas, but serve him all your life. Now he thinks nothing of throwing away your life in the hope of hurting me. Run!"

For an instant, Thomas stood frozen.

"Run!" screamed Anyanwu. Doro had actually begun struggling against her—no doubt a reflex of anger. He knew he could not break her grip or overcome her by physical strength alone. And he would not use his other weapon. He was not finished with her yet. There was a potentially valuable child in her womb.

Thomas ran off toward the woods.

"I'll kill her," shouted Doro. "Your life or hers."

Thomas stopped, looked back.

"He's lying," Anyanwu said almost gleefully. Man or devil, he could not get a lie past her. Not any longer. "Run, Thomas. He is telling lies!"

Doro tried to hit her, but she tripped him, and as he fell, she changed her grip on his arms so that he would not move again except in pain. Very much pain.

"I would have submitted," she hissed into his ear. "I would have done anything!"

"Let me go," he said, "or you won't live, even to submit. It's truth now, Anyanwu. Get up."

There was death frighteningly close to the surface in his voice. This was the way he sounded when he truly meant to kill—his voice went flat and strange and Anyanwu felt that the thing he was, the spirit, the feral hungry demon, the twisted ogbanje was ready to leap out of his young man's body and into hers. She had pushed him too far.

Then Thomas was there. "Let him go, Anyanwu," he said. She jerked her head up to stare at him. She had risked everything to give him a chance to escape—at least a chance—and he had come back.

He tried to pull her off Doro. "Let him go, I said. He'd go through you and take me two seconds later. There's nobody else out here to confuse him."

Anyanwu looked around and realized that he was right. When Doro transferred, he took the person nearest to him. That was why he sometimes touched people. In a crowd, the contact assured his taking the one person he had chosen. If he decided to transfer, though, and the person nearest to him was a hundred miles away, he would take that person. Distance meant nothing. If he was willing to go through Anyanwu, he could reach Thomas.

"I've got nothing," Thomas was saying. "This cabin is my future—staying here, getting older, drunker, crazier. I'm nothing to die for, Sun Woman, even if your dying could save me."

With far less strength than Doro had in his current body, he pulled her to her feet, freeing Doro. Then he pushed her behind him so that he stood nearest to Doro.

Doro stood up slowly, watching them as though daring them to run—or encouraging them to panic and run hopelessly. Nothing human looked out of his eyes.

Seeing him, Anyanwu thought she would die anyway. Both she and Thomas would die.

"I was loyal," Thomas said to him as though to a reasonable man.

Doro's eyes focused on him.

"I gave you loyalty," Thomas repeated. "I never disobeyed." He shook his head slowly from side to side. "I loved you—even though I knew this day might come." He held out a remarkably steady right hand. "Let her go home to her husband and children," he said.

Without a word, Doro grasped the hand. At his touch, the smooth young body he had worn collapsed and Thomas' body, thin and full of sores, stood a little straighter. Anyanwu stared at him wide-eyed, terrified in spite of herself. In an instant, the eyes of a friend had become demon's eyes. Would she be killed now? Doro had promised nothing. Had not even given his worshiper a word of kindness.

"Bury that," Doro said to her from Thomas' mouth. He gestured toward his own former body.

She began to cry. Shame and relief made her turn away from him. He was going to let her live. Thomas had bought her life.

Thomas' hand caught her by the shoulder and shoved her toward the body. She hated her tears. Why was she so weak? Thomas had been strong. He had lived no more than thirty-five years, yet he had found the strength to face Doro and save her. She had lived many times thirty-five years and she wept and cowered. This was what Doro had made of her—and he could not understand why she hated him.

He came to stand over her and somehow she kept herself from cringing away. He seemed taller in Thomas' body than Thomas had.

"I have nothing to dig with," she whispered. She had not intended to whisper.

"Use your hands!" he said.

She found a shovel in the cabin, and an adz that she could swing to break up the earth—probably the same tool Thomas had used to dress the timbers of his cabin. As she dug the grave, Doro stood watching her. He never moved to help, never spoke, never looked away. By the time she had finished a suitable hole—rough and oblong rather than rectangular, but large and deep enough—she was trembling. The gravedigging had tired her more than it should have. It was hard work and she had done it too quickly. A man half again her size would not have finished so soon—or perhaps he would have, with Doro watching over him.

What was Doro thinking? Did he mean to kill her after all? Would he bury Thomas' body with the earlier nameless one and walk away clothed in her flesh?

She went to the young man's body, straightened it, and wrapped it in some of the linen Doro had brought. Then, somehow, she struggled it into the grave. She was tempted to ask Doro to help, but one look at his face changed her mind. He would not help. He would curse her. She shuddered. She had not seen him make a kill since their trip from her homeland. He did kill, of course, often. But he was private about it. He arrived in Wheatley wearing one body and left wearing another, but he did not make the change in public. Also, he usually left as soon as he had changed. If he meant to stay in town for a while, he stayed wearing the body of a stranger. He did not let his people forget what he was, but his reminders were discreet and surprisingly gentle. If they had not been, Anyanwu thought as she filled in the grave, if Doro flaunted his power before others as he was flaunting it now before her, even his most faithful worshipers would have fled from him. His way of killing would terrify anyone. She looked at him and saw Thomas' thin face recently shaved by her own hand, recently taught a small, thin-lipped smile. She looked away, trembling.

Somehow, she finished filling in the grave. She tried to think of a white man's prayer to say for the nameless corpse, and for Thomas. But with Doro watching her, her mind refused to work. She stood empty and weary and frightened over the grave.

"Now you'll do something about these sores," Doro said. "I mean to keep this body for a while."

Thus she would live—for a while. He telling her she would live. She met his eyes. "I have already begun with them. Do they hurt?"

"Not much."

"I put medicine into them."

"Will they heal?"

"Yes, if you keep very clean and eat well and... don't drink the way he did."

Doro laughed. "Tend these things again," he said. "I want them healed as soon as possible."

"But there is medicine in them now. It has not had time to work." She did not want to touch him, even in healing. She had not minded touching Thomas, had quickly come to like the man in spite of his wretchedness. Without his uncontrolled ability hurting him, he would have been a good man. In the end, he was a good man. She would willingly bury his body when Doro left it, but she did not want to touch it while Doro wore it. Perhaps Doro knew that.

"I said tend the sores!" he ordered. "What will I have to do next to teach you to obey?"

She took him into the cabin, stripped him, and went over the sick, scrawny body again. When she finished, he made her undress and lie with him. She did not weep because she thought that would please him. But afterward, for the first time in centuries, she was uncontrollably sick.

Chapter Nine

Nweke had begun to scream. Doro listened calmly, accepting the fact that the girl's fate was temporarily out of his hands. There was nothing for him to do except wait and remind himself of what Anyanwu had said. She had never lost anyone to transition. She would not be likely to tarnish that record with the death of one of her own children.

And Nweke was strong. All Anyanwu's children were strong. That was important. Doro's personal experience with transition had taught him the danger of weakness. He let his thoughts go back to the time of his own transition and away from worry over Nweke. He could remember his transition very clearly. There were long years following it that he could not remember, but his childhood and the transition that ended that childhood were still clear to him.

He had been a sickly, stunted boy, the last of his mother's twelve children and the only one to survive—just right for the name Anyanwu sometimes called him: Ogbanje. People said his brothers and sisters had been robust healthy-looking babies, and they had died. He had been scrawny and tiny and strange, and only his parents seemed to think it right that he had lived. People whispered about him. They said he was something other than a child—some spirit. They whispered that he was not the son of his mother's husband. His mother shielded him as best she could while he was very young, and his father—if the man was his father—claimed him and was pleased to have a son. He was a poor man and had little else.

His parents were all he could recall that had been good about his youth. Both had loved and valued him extravagantly after eleven dead babies. Other people avoided him when they could. His were a tall, stately people—Nubians, they came to be called much later. It soon became clear to them that Doro would never be tall or stately. Eventually, it also became clear that he was possessed. He heard voices. He fell to the ground writhing with fits. Several people, fearful that he might loose his devils on them, wanted to kill him, but somehow, his parents protected him. Even then, he had not known how. But there was little, perhaps nothing, they would not have done to save him.

He was thirteen when the full agony of transition hit him. He knew now that was too young. He had never known one of his witches to live when transition came that early. He had not lived himself. But unlike anyone he had managed to breed so far, he had not quite died either. His body had died, and for the first time, he had transferred to the living human body nearest to him. This was the body of his mother in whose lap his head had rested.

He found himself looking down at himself—at his own body— and he did not understand. He screamed. Terrified, he tried to run away. His father stopped him, held him, demanded to know what had happened. He could not answer. He looked down, saw his woman's breasts, his woman's body, and he panicked. Without knowing how or what he did, he transferred again—this time to his father.

In his once quiet Nile River village, he killed and killed and killed. Finally, his people's enemies inadvertently rescued them. Raiding Egyptians captured him as they attacked the village. By then, he was wearing the body of a young girl—one of his cousins. Perhaps he killed some of the Egyptians too. He hoped so. His people had lived without the interference of Egypt for nearly two centuries while Egypt wallowed in feudal chaos. But now Egypt was back, wanting land, mineral wealth, slaves. Doro hoped he had killed many of them. He would never know. His memory stopped with the arrival of the Egyptians. There was a gap of what he later calculated to be about fifty years before he came to himself again and discovered that he had been thrown into an Egyptian prison, discovered that he now possessed the body of some middle-aged stranger, discovered that he was both more and less than a man, discovered that he could have and do absolutely anything.

It had taken him years to decide even approximately how long he had been out of his mind. It took more time to learn exactly where his village had been and that it was no longer there. He never found any of his kinsmen, anyone from his village. He was utterly alone.

Eventually, he began to realize that some of his kills gave him more pleasure than others. Some bodies sustained him longer. Observing his own reactions, he learned that age, race, sex, physical appearance, and except in extreme cases, health, did not affect his enjoyment of victims. He could and did take anyone. But what gave the greatest pleasure was something he came to think of as witchcraft or a potential for witchcraft. He was seeking out his spiritual kin—people possessed or mad or just a little strange. They heard voices, saw visions, other things. He did none of those things any longer—not since his transition ended. But he fed on those who did. He learned to sense them effortlessly—like following an aroma of food. Then he learned to gather reserves of them, breed them, see that they were protected and cared for. They, in turn, learned to worship him. After a single generation, they were his. He had not understood this, but he had accepted it. A few of them seemed to sense him as clearly as he sensed them. Their witch-power warned them but never seemed to make them flee sensibly. Instead, they came to him, competed for his attention, loved him as god, parent, mate, friend.

He learned to prefer their company to that of more normal people. He chose his companions from among them and restricted his killing to the others. Slowly, he created the Isaacs, the Annekes, the best of his children. These he loved as they loved him. They accepted him as ordinary people could not, enjoyed him, felt little or no fear of him. In one way, it was as though he repeated his own history with each generation. His best children loved him without qualification as his parents had. The others, like the other people of his village, viewed him through their various superstitions—though at least this time the superstitions were favorable. And this time, it was not his loved ones who fed his hunger. He plucked the others from their various settlements like ripe, sweet fruit and kept his special ones safe from all but sickness, old age, war, and sometimes, the dangerous effects of their own abilities. Occasionally, this last forced him to kill one of his special ones. One of them, drunk with his own power, displayed his abilities, drew attention to himself, and endangered his people. One of them refused to obey. One of them simply went mad. It happened.

These were the kills he should have enjoyed most. Certainly, on a sensory level, they were the most pleasurable. But in Doro's mind, these killings were too much like what he had done accidentally to his parents. He never kept these bodies long. He consciously avoided mirrors until he could change again. At these times more than any others, he felt again utterly alone, forever alone, longing to die and be finished. What was he, he wondered, that he could have anything at all but an end?

People like Isaac and soon Nweke did not know how safe they were from him. People like Anyanwu—good, stable wild seed—did not know how safe they could be—though for Anyanwu herself, it was too late. Years too late, in spite of Isaac's occasional pleas for her. Doro did not want the woman any longer—did not want her condemning stare, her silent, palpable hatred, her long-lived, grudge-holding presence. As soon as she was of no more use to Isaac, she would die.

* * *

Isaac paced around the kitchen, restless and frightened, unable to shut out the sound of Nweke's screams. It was difficult for him not to go to her. He knew there was nothing he could do, no help he could give. People in transition did not respond well to him. Anyanwu could hold them and pet them and become their mother whether she actually was or not. And in their pain, they clung to her. If Isaac tried to comfort them, they struggled against him. He had never understood that. They always seemed to like him well enough before and after transition.

Nweke loved him. She had grown up calling him father, knowing he was not her father, and never caring. She was not Doro's daughter either, but Isaac loved her too much to tell her that. He longed to be with her now to still the screaming and take away the pain. He sat down heavily and stared toward the bedroom.

"She'll be all right," Doro said from the table, where he was eating a sweet cake Isaac had found for him.

"How can even you know that?" Isaac challenged.

"Her blood is good. She'll be fine."

"My blood is good too, but I nearly died."

"You're here," Doro said reasonably.

Isaac rubbed a hand across his forehead. "I don't think I would feel this nervous if she were giving birth. She's such a little thing— so like Anyanwu."

"Even smaller," Doro said. He looked at Isaac, smiled as though at some secret joke.

"She's to be your next Anyanwu, isn't she?" Isaac asked.

"Yes." Doro's expression did not change. The smile remained in place.

"She's not enough," Isaac said. "She's a beautiful, lively young girl. After tonight, she'll be a powerful young girl. But you've said she'd keep some of the mind-listening ability."

"I believe she will."

"It kills." Isaac stared at the bedroom door, imagining the favored young stepdaughter turning vicious and bitter like his long-dead half-brother Lale, like his mother who had hanged herself. "That ability kills," he repeated sadly. "It may not kill quickly, but it kills."

Poor Nweke. Even transition would not mean an end to her pain. Should he wish her life or death? And what should he wish for her mother?

"I've had people as good at mental communication as you are at moving things," Doro said. "Anneke, for instance."

"Do you think she'll be like Anneke?"

"She'll complete her transition. She'll have some control."

"Is she related to Anneke?"

"No." Doro's tone indicated that he did not wish to discuss Nweke's ancestry. Isaac changed his approach.

"Anyanwu has perfect control over what she does," he said.

"Yes, within the limits of her ability. But she's wild seed. I'm tired of the effort it takes to control her."

"Are you?" Nweke had stopped screaming. The room was suddenly still and silent except for Isaac's two words.

Doro swallowed the last of his sweet. "You have something to say?"

"That it would be stupid to kill her. That it would be waste."

Doro looked at him—a look Isaac had come to recognize, a look that gave him permission to say what Doro would not hear from others. Over the years, Isaac's usefulness and loyalty had won him the right to say what he felt and be heard—though not necessarily heeded.

"I won't take her from you," Doro said quietly.

Isaac nodded. "If you did, I wouldn't last long." He rubbed his chest. "There's something wrong with my heart. She makes a medicine for it."

"With your heart!"

"She takes care of it. She says she doesn't like being a widow."

"I . . . thought she might be helping you a little."

"She was helping me 'a little' twenty years ago. How many children have I gotten for you in the past twenty years?"

Doro said nothing. He watched Isaac without expression.

"She's helped both of us," Isaac said.

"What do you want?" Doro asked.

"Her life." Isaac paused, but Doro said nothing. "Let her live. She'll marry again after a while. She always has. Then you'll have more of her children. She's a breed unto herself, after all. Something even you've never seen before."

"I had another healer once."

"Did she live to be three hundred? Did she bear dozens of children? Was she able to change her shape at will?"

"He. And no to all three questions. No."

"Then keep her. If she annoys you, ignore her for a while. Ignore her for twenty years or thirty. What difference would it make to you—or to her? When you go back to her, she'll have changed in one way or another. But, Doro, don't kill her. Don't make the mistake of killing her."

"I don't want or need her any longer."

"You're wrong. You do. Because left alone, she won't die or allow herself to be killed. She isn't temporary. You haven't accepted that yet. When you do, and when you take the trouble to win her back, you'll never be alone again."

"You don't know what you're talking about!"

Isaac stood up, went to the table to look down on Doro. "If I don't know the two of you and your needs, who does? She's exactly right for you—not so powerful that you would have to worry about her, yet powerful enough to take care of herself and of others on her own. You might not see each other for years at a time, but as long as both of you are alive, neither of you will be alone."

Doro had begun to watch Isaac with greater interest, causing Isaac to wonder whether he had really been too set in his ways to see the woman's value.

"You said you knew about Nweke's father," Doro said.

Isaac nodded. "Anyanwu told me. She was so angry and frustrated—I think she had to tell someone."

"How do you feel about it?"

"What difference does that make?" Isaac demanded. "Why bring it up now?"

"Answer."

"All right." Isaac shrugged. "I said I knew you—and her—so I wasn't surprised at what you'd done. You're both stubborn, vengeful people at times. She's kept you angry and frustrated for years. You tried to get even. You do that now and then, and it only fuels her anger. The only person I pity is the man, Thomas."

Doro lifted an eyebrow. "He ran. He sided with her. He had outlived his usefulness."

Isaac heard the implied threat and faced Doro with annoyance. "Do you really think you have to do that?" he asked quietly. "I'm your son, not wild seed, not sick, not stranded halfway through transition. I could never hate you or run from you no matter what you did, and I'm one of the few of your children who could have made a successful escape. Did you think I didn't know that? I'm here because I want to be." Deliberately, Isaac extended his hand to Doro. Doro stared at him for a moment, then gave a long sigh and clasped the large, calloused hand in his own briefly, harmlessly.

For a time, they sat together in relaxed silence, Doro getting up once to put another log on the fire. Isaac let his thoughts go back to Anyanwu, and it occurred to him that what he had said of himself might also be true of her. She might be another of the very few people who could escape Doro—the way she could change her form and travel anywhere... Perhaps that was one of the things that bothered Doro about her. Though it shouldn't have.

Doro should have let her go wherever she chose, do whatever she chose. He should only see her now and then when he was feeling lonely, when people died and left him, as everyone but her had to leave him. She was a healer in more ways than Doro seemed to understand. Nweke's father had probably understood. And now, in her pain, no doubt Nweke understood. Ironically, Anyanwu herself often seemed not to understand. She thought the sick came to her only for her medicines and her knowledge. Within herself, she had something she did not know she had.

"Nweke will be a better healer than Anyanwu could ever be," Doro said as though responding to Isaac's thoughts. "I don't think her mind reading will cripple her."

"Let Nweke become whatever she can," Isaac said wearily. "If she's as good as you think she'll be, then you'll have two very valuable women. You'd be a damned fool to waste either of them."

Nweke began screaming again—hoarse, terrible sounds.

"Oh God," Isaac whispered.

"Her voice will soon be gone at that rate," Doro said. Then, offhandedly, "Do you have any more of those cakes?"

Isaac knew him too well to be surprised. He got up to get the plate of fruit-filled Dutch *olijkoecks* that Anyanwu had made earlier. It was rare for another person's pain to disturb Doro. If the girl seemed to be dying, he would be concerned that good seed was about to be lost. But if she were merely in agony, it did not matter. Isaac forced his thoughts back to Anyanwu.

"Doro?" He spoke so softly that the girl's screams almost drowned his single word. But Doro looked up. He held Isaac's gaze, not questioningly or challengingly, not with any reassurance or compassion. He only looked back. Isaac had seen cats stare at people that way. Cats. That was apt. More and more often, nothing human looked out of Doro's eyes. When Anyanwu was angry, she said Doro was only a man pretending to be a god. But she knew better. No man could frighten her—and Doro, whatever he had failed to accomplish with her, had taught her to fear him. He had taught Isaac to fear for him.

"What will you lose," Isaac said, "if you leave Anyanwu her life?"

"I'm tired of her. That's all. That's enough. I'm just tired of her." He sounded tired—good, honest, human weariness, annoyance, and frustration.

"Then let her go. Send her away and let her make her own life."

Doro frowned, looked as harassed as Isaac had ever seen him. Surely that was a good sign. "Think about it," he said. "Finally to have someone who isn't temporary—and wild seed that she is, you'll have lifetimes to tame her. Surely she can feel loneliness too. She should be a challenge to you, not an annoyance."

He said nothing more. It was not good to try to get promises from Doro. Isaac had learned that long ago. It was best to push him almost to agreement, then leave him alone. Sometimes that worked. Sometimes Isaac did it well enough to save lives. And sometimes he failed.

They sat together, Doro slowly eating olijkoecks and Isaac listening to the sounds of pain from the bedroom—until those sounds ceased, Nweke's voice all but gone. The hours passed. Isaac made coffee.

"You should sleep," Doro told him. "Take one of the children's beds. It will be over when you wake."

Isaac shook his head wearily. "How could I sleep not knowing?"

"All right, then, don't sleep, but at least lie down. You look terrible." Doro took Isaac by the shoulder and steered him into one of the bedrooms. The room was dark and cold, but Doro made a fire and lit a single candle.

"Shall I wait with you here?" he asked.

"Yes," Isaac said gratefully. Doro brought a chair.

The screaming began again, and for a moment it confused Isaac. The girl's voice had become only a hoarse whisper long ago, and except for an occasional jarring or creaking of the bed and the harsh, ragged breathing of the two women, the house had been silent. Now there was screaming.

Isaac sat up suddenly and put his feet on the floor.

"What's the matter?" Doro asked.

Isaac barely heard him. Suddenly he was up and running toward the other bedroom. Doro tried to stop him but Isaac brushed the restraining hands away. "Can't you hear?" he shouted. "It's not Nweke. It's Anyanwu!"

It seemed to Doro that Nweke's transition was ending. The time was right—early morning, a few hours before dawn. The girl had survived the usual ten to twelve hours of agony. For some time now, she had been silent, not screaming, or groaning or even moving around enough to shake the bed. That was not to say, though, that she could not move. Actually, the final hours of transition were the most dangerous. They were the hours in which people lost control of their bodies, not only feeling what others felt, but moving as others moved. This was the time when someone like Anyanwu, physically strong, unafraid, and comforting was essential. Anyanwu herself was perfect because she could not be hurt—or at least, not in any permanent way.

Doro's people had told him this was the time they suffered most, too. This was the time when the madness of absorbing everyone else's feelings seemed endless—when, in desperation, they would do anything to stop the pain. Yet this was also the time when they began to feel there was a way just beyond their reach—a way of controlling the madness, shutting themselves away from it. A way of finding peace.

But instead of peace for Nweke, there was more screaming, and there was Isaac springing up like a boy, running for the door, shouting that the screams were not Nweke's, but Anyanwu's.

And Isaac was right. What had happened? Had Anyanwu been unable to keep the girl alive in spite of her healing ability? Or was it something else, some other trouble with transition? What could make the formidable Anyanwu scream that way?

"Oh my God," Isaac cried from within the bedroom. "What have you done? My God!"

Doro ran into the room, stood near the door staring. Anyanwu lay on the floor, bleeding from her nose and mouth. Her eyes were closed and she made no sound now at all. She seemed only barely alive.

On the bed, Nweke sat up, her body half concealed by the feather mattress. She was staring down at Anyanwu. Isaac had stopped for a moment beside Anyanwu. He shook her as though to rouse her and her head lolled over bonelessly.

He looked up and saw Nweke's face over a bulge of feather-filled cloth. Before Doro could guess what he meant to do Isaac seized the girl, slapped her hard across the face.

"Stop what you're doing!" he shouted. "Stop it! She's your mother!"

Nweke put a hand to her face, her expression startled, uncomprehending. Doro realized that before Isaac's blow, her face had held no expression at all. She had looked at Anyanwu, fallen and bleeding, with no more interest than she might have expressed in a stone. She had looked, but she had almost certainly not seen—did not see now. Perhaps she felt the pain of Isaac's blow. Perhaps she heard him shouting—though Doro doubted that she was able to distinguish words. All that reached her was pain, noise, confusion. And she had had enough of all three.

Her small, pretty, empty face contorted, and Isaac screamed. It had happened before. Doro had seen it happen. Some people's bodies survived transition well enough, but their minds did not. They gained power and control of that power, but they lost all that would have made that power meaningful or useful. Why had Doro been so slow to understand? What if the damage to Isaac could not be repaired? What if both Isaac and Nweke were lost?

Doro stepped over Anyanwu and around Isaac, who was now writhing on the floor, and to the girl.

He seized her, slapped her as Isaac had done. *"That's enough!"* he said, not shouting at all. If his voice reached her, she would live.

If it did not, she would die. Gods, let it reach her. Let her have her chance to come back to her senses—if she had any left.

She drew back from Doro like a cornered animal. Whatever she had done to hurt Isaac and perhaps kill Anyanwu, she did nothing to Doro. His voice had reached her—after a fashion.

She half leaped and half fell from the bed to get away from him and somehow she landed on Isaac. Anyanwu was farther away, as though she had been trying to escape when Nweke struck her down. Also, Anyanwu was unconscious. She would probably never have known it if the girl had landed on her. But Isaac knew, and he reacted instantly to this new pain.

He gripped Nweke, threw her upward away from his pain-racked body—threw her upward with all the power he had used so many times to propel great ships out of storms. He did not know what he was doing any more than she did. He never saw her hit the ceiling, never saw her body flatten into it, distorted, crushed, never saw her head slam into one of the great beams and break and send down a grisly rain of blood and bits of bone and brain.

Her body fell toward Doro, rag-limp and ruined. Somehow he caught it, kept it from landing on Isaac again. The girl was lost. She would have been lost with such wounds had she been twice the healer Doro had hoped for. He put her body on the bed hastily and bent to see whether Isaac was also lost. Later, he would feel this. Later, perhaps he would leave Wheatley—leave it for several years.

Isaac's face was pale—a gray, ugly color. He was still now, very still though not quite unconscious. Doro could hear him panting, trying to catch his breath. Trouble with his heart, he had said. Could Nweke have aggravated that somehow? Why not? Who was more suited to causing illness than one born to cure it?

Desperately, Doro turned to Anyanwu. The moment his attention was focused on her, he knew she was still alive. He could sense it. She felt like prey, not like a useless corpse. Doro took her hand, then released it because it felt limp and dead. He touched her face, leaned down close to her ear. "Can you hear me, Anyanwu?"

She gave no sign.

"Anyanwu, Isaac needs you. He'll die without your help."

Her eyes opened. She stared up at him for a second, perhaps reading his desperation on his face. "Am I on a rug?" she whispered finally.

He frowned wondering whether she too had gone out of her mind. But she was Isaac's only hope. "Yes," he said.

"Then use it to pull me close to him. As close as you can. Don't touch me otherwise." She took a deep breath. "Please don't touch me."

He moved back from her and drew her toward Isaac with the rug.

"She went mad," Anyanwu whispered. "Her mind broke somehow."

"I know," Doro said.

"Then she tried to break everything inside me. Like being cut and torn from the inside. Heart, lungs, veins, stomach, bladder... She was like me, like Isaac, like... maybe like Thomas too—reaching into minds, seeing into my body. She must have been able to see."

Yes. Nweke had been all Doro had hoped for and more. But she was dead. "Help Isaac, Anyanwu!"

"Go get me food," she said. "Is there some stew left?"

"Can you reach Isaac?"

"Yes. Go!"

Trying to trust her, Doro left the room.

Somehow, Anyanwu healed herself enough so that moving would not start her bleeding inside again. There was so much damage, and it had all been done so quickly, so savagely. When she changed her shape, she transformed organs that already existed and formed any necessary new organs while sustained by old ones. She was still partly human in most changes long after she had ceased to look human. But Nweke had all but destroyed organ after organ. If the girl had gone to work on her brain, Anyanwu knew she would have died before she could heal herself. Even now, there were massive repairs to be made and massive illnesses to be avoided. Even not touching her brain at all, Nweke had nearly killed her.

How could she make herself fit now to help Isaac? But she had to. She had known in the first year of their marriage that she had been wrong about him. He had been the best possible husband. With his power and hers, they had built this house. People came to watch them and watch *for* them so that no strangers happened by to see the witchcraft. Her strength had fascinated Isaac, but it had never disturbed him. His power she trusted absolutely. She had seen him carry great logs from the forest and strip them of bark. She had seen him kill wolves without touching them. In a fight once, she had seen him kill a man—a fool who had drunk too much and chosen to take offense at Isaac's quiet, easy refusal to be insulted. The fool had a gun and Isaac did not. Isaac never went armed. There was no need. The man died as the wolves had died—instantly, his head broken and bloodied as though he had been bludgeoned. Afterward, Isaac himself was sickened by the killing.

Anyanwu had seen these things, but none of them had made her fear her husband as she had feared Doro. Sometimes Isaac tossed her about and she screamed or laughed or swore at him—whichever seemed right for the occasion—but she never feared him. And she never held him in contempt. "He has more sense than men two and three times his age," she had told Doro when Isaac was young and she and Doro were on slightly better terms. In some ways, Isaac had more sense than Doro. And Isaac understood even better than she did that he would have to share her, at least with Doro. And she would have to share him with the women Doro gave to him. She was used to sharing a man, but she had had no experience in being shared. She did not like it. She grew to hate the sound of Doro's voice identifying him, warning her that she must give him another child. Isaac accepted each of her children as though they were his own. He accepted her without bitterness or anger when she came to him from Doro's bed. And somehow, he helped her to endure even when Doro strove to break and reshape her when her increasingly silent obedience ceased to be enough for him. Strangely, though she could not forgive Doro any longer even for small things, she felt no resentment when Isaac forgave him. The bond between Isaac and Doro was at least as firm as that between an ordinary father and a son of his body. If Isaac had not loved Doro, and if that love had not been returned strongly in Doro's own way, Doro would have seemed totally inhuman.

She did not want to think what her life would be like without Isaac—how she would endure Doro without Isaac. Not since her first husband had she allowed herself to become so dependent on anyone, husband or child. Other people were temporary. They died—except for Doro. Why, *why* could it not be Isaac who lived and lived, and Doro who died?

She kissed Isaac. She had given him many such kisses as he grew old. They were of more than love. Within her body, she synthesized medicine for him. She had studied him very carefully, had aged herself, her own organs to study the effects of age. It had been dangerous work. A miscalculation could have killed her before she understood it enough to counter it. She listened closely as Isaac described the pain he felt—the fearful tightening, the squeezing within his chest, the dizziness, the too-rapid beating of his heart, the way the pain spread from his chest to his left shoulder and arm.

The first time he felt the pain—twenty years before—he had thought he was dying. The first time she managed to induce such pain in her body, she too had feared she was dying. It was terrible, but she lived as Isaac had lived, and she came to understand how old age and too much good, rich food could combine to steal away the youthful flexibility of his blood vessels—especially, if her simulations had led her aright, the blood vessels that nourished his heart.

What needed doing, then? How could aging, fat-narrowed blood vessels be restored? She could restore her own, of course. Since the pain had not killed her, and since she understood what she had done to produce the disorder, she could simply, carefully replace the damaged vessels, then dissolve away the useless hardened tissue, become the physiologically young woman she had been since the time of her transition. But transition had not frozen Isaac in youth. It had paid him other wages, good wages, but was useless in prolonging his life. If only she could give him some of her power...

That was pointless dreaming. If she could not heal the damage age and bad habits had caused, she could at least try to prevent further damage. He must not eat so much any longer, must not eat some foods at all. He must not smoke or work so hard—not with his muscles nor with his witch-power. Both took a physical toll. He would save no more ships from storms. Lighter tasks were all right as long as they did not bring on pain, but she told Doro very firmly that unless he wanted to kill Isaac, he would have to find a younger man for his heavy lifting and towing.

That done, Anyanwu spent long painful hours trying to discover or create a medicine that would ease Isaac's pain when it did come. In the end, she so tired and weakened herself that even Isaac begged her to stop. She did not stop. She poisoned herself several times trying plant and animal substances she had not used before, noting minutely her every reaction. She rechecked familiar substances, found that as simple a thing as garlic had some ability to help, but not enough. She worked on, gained knowledge that helped others later. For Isaac, she at last, almost accidentally created a potentially dangerous medicine that would open wide the healthy blood vessels he had left, thus relieving the pressure on his undernourished heart and easing the pain. When his pain came again, she gave him the medicine. The pain vanished and he was amazed. He took her into New York City and made her choose the finest cloth. Then he took her to a dressmaker—a black freedwoman who stared at her with open curiosity. Anyanwu began telling the woman what she wanted, but when she paused for breath, the dressmaker spoke up.

"You are the Onitsha woman," she said in Anyanwu's native language. And she smiled at Anyanwu's surprise. "Are you well?"

Anyanwu found herself greeting a countrywoman, perhaps a kinswoman. This was another gift Isaac was giving her. A new friend. He was good, Isaac. He could not die now and leave her.

But this time, the medicine that had always worked seemed to be failing. Isaac gave no sign that his pain was ending.

He lay ashen, sweating and gasping for breath. When she lifted her head from him, he opened his eyes. She did not know what to do. She wanted to look away from him, but could not. In her experimenting, she had found conditions of the heart that could kill very easily—and that could grow out of the problem he already had. She had almost killed herself learning about them. She had been so careful in her efforts to keep Isaac alive, and now, somehow, poor Nweke had undone all her work.

"Nweke?" Isaac whispered as though he had heard her thought.

"I don't know," Anyanwu said. She looked around, saw how the feather mattress billowed. "She is asleep."

"Good," he gasped. "I thought I had hurt her. I dreamed..."

He was dying! Nweke had killed him. In her madness, she had killed him and he was worried that he might have hurt her! Anyanwu shook her head, thought desperately. What could she do? With all her vast knowledge, there must be something...

He managed to touch her hand. "You have lost other husbands," he said.

She began to cry.

"Anyanwu, I'm old. My life has been long and full—by ordinary standards, at least." His face twisted with pain. It was as though the pain knifed through Anyanwu's own chest.

"Lie by me," he said. "Lie here beside me."

She obeyed still weeping silently.

"You cannot know how I've loved you," he said.

Somehow, she controlled her voice. "With you it has been as though I never had another husband."

"You must live," he said. "You must make your peace with Doro."

The thought sickened her. She said nothing.

With an effort, he spoke in her language. "He will be your husband now. Bow your head, Anyanwu. Live!"

He said nothing more. There were only long moments of pain before he slipped into unconsciousness, then to death.

Chapter Ten

Anyanwu had gotten shakily to her feet when Doro arrived with a tray of food. She was standing beside the bed staring at the ruin of Nweke's body. She did not seem to hear Doro when he put the tray down on a small table near her. He opened his mouth to ask her why she was not caring for Isaac, but the moment he thought of Isaac, his awareness told him Isaac was dead.

His awareness had never failed him. In past years, he had prevented a number of people from being buried alive by the certainty of his ability. Yet now he knelt beside Isaac and felt at the neck for a pulse. Of course, there was none.

Anyanwu turned and stared at him bleakly. She was young. In restoring her nearly destroyed body, she had returned to her true form. She looked like a girl mourning her grandfather and sister rather than a woman mourning her husband and daughter.

"He did not know," she whispered. "He thought it was only a dream that he had hurt her."

Doro glanced upward where Nweke's body had left bloody smears on the ceiling. Anyanwu followed his gaze, then looked down again quickly. "He was out of his mind with pain," Doro said. "Then, by accident, she hurt him again. It was too much."

"One terrible accident after another." She shook her head dazed. "Everything is gone."

Surprisingly, she went to the food, took the tray out to the kitchen where she sat down and began to eat. He followed and watched her wonderingly. The damage Nweke had done her must have been even greater than he had thought if she could eat this way, tearing at the food like a starving woman while the bodies of those she loved most lay cooling in the next room.

After a while, she said, "Doro, they should have funerals."

She was eating a sweet cake from the plate Isaac had put on the table for Doro. Doro felt hungry too, but could not bring himself to touch food. Especially, not those cakes. He realized that it was not food he hungered for.

He had only recently taken the body he was wearing. It was a good, strong body taken from his settlement in the colony of Pennsylvania. Ordinarily, it would have lasted him several months. He could have used it to sire Nweke's first child. That would have been a fine match. There was stability and solid strength in his Pennsylvania settlers. Good stock. But stress, physical or emotional, took its toll, made him hunger when he should not have, made him long for the comfort of another change. He did not *have* to change. His present body would sustain him for a while longer. But he would feel hungry and uncomfortable until he changed. But he had no pressing reason to bear the discomfort. Nweke was dead; Isaac was dead. He looked at Anyanwu.

"We must give them a funeral," she repeated.

Doro nodded. Let her have the ritual. She had been good to Isaac. Then afterward...

"He said we should make our peace," she said.

"What?"

"Isaac. It was the last thing he said—that we should have peace between us."

Doro shrugged. "We'll have peace."

She said nothing more. Arrangements were made for the funeral, the numerous married children notified. It did not matter whether they were Isaac's children or Doro's, they had grown up accepting Isaac as their father. And there were several foster children—those Anyanwu had taken in because their parents were unfit or dead. And there was everyone else. Everyone in town had known Isaac and liked him. Everyone would come now to show their respect.

But on the day of the funeral, Anyanwu was nowhere to be found. To Doro's tracking sense, it was as though she had ceased to exist.

She flew as a large bird for a while. Then, far out at sea, she drifted down wearily to the water and took the long-remembered dolphin form. She had come down near where she saw a school of dolphins leaping through the water. They would accept her, surely, and she would become one of them. She would cause herself to grow until she was as large as most of them. She would learn to live in their world. It could be no more alien to her than the world she had just left. And perhaps when she learned their ways of communication, she would find them too honorable or too innocent to tell lies and plot murder over the still warm corpses of their children.

Briefly, she wondered how long she could endure being away from kinsmen, from friends, from any human beings. How long would she have to hide in the sea before Doro stopped hunting her—or before he found her. She remembered her sudden panic when Doro took her from her people. She remembered the loneliness that Doro and Isaac and her two now-dead grandchildren had eased. How would she stand it alone among the dolphins? How was it that she wanted to live so badly that even a life under the sea seemed precious?

Doro had reshaped her. She had submitted and submitted and submitted to keep him from killing her even though she had long ago ceased to believe what Isaac had told her—that her longevity made her the right mate for Doro. That she could somehow prevent him from becoming an animal. He was already an animal. But she had formed the habit of submission. In her love for Isaac and for her children, and in her fear of death—especially of the kind of death Doro would inflict—she had given in to him again and again. Habits were difficult to break. The habit of living, the habit of fear... even the habit of love.

Well. Her children were men and women now, able to care for themselves. She would miss them. No feeling was better than that of being surrounded by her own. Her children and grandchildren and great-grandchildren. She could never have been content moving constantly as Doro moved. It was her way to settle and make a tribe around her and stay within that tribe for as long as she could.

Would it be possible, she wondered, to make a tribe of dolphins? Would Doro give her the time she needed to try? She had committed what was considered a great sin among his people: She had run away from him. It would not matter that she had done so to save her life—that she could see he meant to kill her. After all her submission, he still meant to kill her. He believed it was his right to slaughter among his people as he chose. A great many of his people also believed this, and they did not run when he came for them. They were frightened, but he was their god. Running from him was useless. He invariably caught the runner and killed him or, very rarely, brought him home alive and chastened as proof to others that there was no escape. Also, to many, running was heretical. They believed that since he was their god, it was his right to do whatever he chose with them. "Jobs" she called them in her thoughts. Like the Job of the Bible, they had made the best of their situation. They could not escape Doro, so they found virtue in submitting to him.

Anyanwu found virtue in nothing that had to do with him. He had never been her god, and if she had to run for a century, never stopping long enough to build the tribes that brought her to much comfort, she would do it. He would not have her life. The people of Wheatley would see that he was not all-powerful. He would never show himself to them wearing her flesh. Perhaps others would notice his failure and see that he was no god. Perhaps they would run too— and how many could Doro chase? Surely some would escape and be able to live their lives in peace with only ordinary human fears. The powerful ones like Isaac could escape. Perhaps even a few of her children...

She put away from her the memory that Isaac had never wanted to escape. Isaac was Isaac, set apart from other people and not to be judged. He had been the best of all her husbands, and she could not even attend his funeral rites. Thinking of him, longing for him, she wished she had kept her bird form longer, wished she had found some solitary place, some rocky island perhaps where she could mourn her husband and her daughter without fearing for her own life. Where she could think and remember and be alone. She needed time alone before she could be a fit companion for other creatures.

But the dolphins had reached her. Several approached, chattering incomprehensibly, and for a moment, she thought they might attack her. But they only came to rub themselves against her and become acquainted. She swam with them and none of them molested her. She fed with them, snatching passing fish as hungrily as she had eaten the finest foods of Wheatley and of her homeland. She was a dolphin. If Doro had not found her an adequate mate, he would find her an adequate adversary. He would not enslave her again. And she would never be his prey.

BOOK THREE

Canaan
1840

Chapter Eleven

The old man had lived in Avoyelles Parish in the state of Louisiana for years, his neighbors told Doro. He had married daughters, but no sons. His wife was long dead and he lived alone on his plantation with his slaves—a number of whom were reputed to be his children. He kept to himself. He had never cared much for socializing, even when his wife was alive—nor had she.

Warrick, the old man's name was, Edward Warrick. Within the past century, he was the third human Doro had found himself drawn toward with the feeling that he was near Anyanwu.

Anyanwu.

He had not even said her name aloud for years. There was no one alive in the state of New York who had known her. Her children were dead. The grandchildren who had been born before she fled had also died. Wars had taken some of them. The War of Independence. The stupid 1812 War. The first had killed many of his people and sent others fleeing to Canada because they were too insular and apolitical for anyone's taste. British soldiers considered them rebels and colonists considered them Tories. Many lost all their possessions as they fled to Canada, where Doro found them months later. Now Doro had a Canadian settlement as well as a reconstructed

Wheatley in New York. Now, also, he had settlements in Brazil, in Mexico, in Kentucky, and elsewhere, scattered over the two large, empty continents. Most of his best people were now in the New World where there was room for them to grow and increase their power—where there was room for their strangeness.

None of that was compensation for the near destruction of Wheatley, though, just as there could be no compensation for the loss in 1812 of several of his best people in Maryland. These Marylanders were the descendants of the people he had lost when he found Anyanwu. He had reassembled them painstakingly and got them breeding again. They had begun to show promise. Then suddenly the most promising ones were dead. He had had to bring in new blood to rebuild them for a third time—people as much like them as possible. That caused trouble because the people who proved to be most like them in ability were white. There was resentment and hatred on both sides and Doro had had to kill publicly a pair of the worst troublemakers to terrify the others back into their habit of obedience. More valuable breeders wasted. Trouble to settle with the surrounding whites who did not know quite what they had in their midst...

So much time wasted. There were years when he almost forgot Anyanwu. He would have killed her had he stumbled across her, of course. Occasionally, he had forgiven people who ran from him, people who were bright enough, strong enough to keep ahead of him for several days and give him a good hunt. But he forgave them only because once caught, they submitted. Not that they begged for their lives. Most did not. They simply ceased to struggle against him. They finally came to understand and acknowledge his power. They had first given him good entertainment, then, fully aware, they gave him themselves. When pardoned, they gave him a kind of loyalty, even friendship, equal to what he received from the best of his children. As with his children, after all, he had given them their lives.

There had been times when he thought he might spare Anyanwu. There had even been moments when, to his amazement and disgust, he simply missed her, wished to see her again. Most often, however, he thought of her when he bred together her African and American descendants. He was striving to create a more stable, controlled Nweke, and he had had some success—people who could perceive and to some degree control the inner workings not only of their own bodies, but the bodies of others. But their abilities were not dependable. They brought agony as often as they brought relief. They killed as often as they healed. They could perform what ordinary doctors saw as miracles—or, as easily, as accidentally, what the most brutal slaveholder would see as atrocities. Also, they did not live long. Sometimes they made lethal mistakes within their own bodies and could not correct them in time. Sometimes relatives of their dead patients killed them. Sometimes they committed suicide. The better ones committed suicide—often after an especially ghastly failure. They needed Anyanwu's control. Even now, if he could, Doro would have liked to breed her with some of them—let her give birth to superior human children for a change instead of the animal young she must have borne over her years of freedom. But it was too late for that. She was spoiled. She had known too much freedom. Like most wild seed, she had been spoiled long before he met her.

Now, finally, he went to complete the unfinished business of killing her and gathering up any new human descendants.

He located her home—her plantation—by tracking her while she was in human form. It was not easy. She kept changing even though she did not seem to travel far. For days, he would have nothing to track. Then she turned human again and he could sense that she had not moved geographically. He closed in, constantly fearing that she would take bird or fish form and vanish for more years. But she stayed, drawing him across country to Mississippi, to Louisiana, to the parish of Avoyelles, then through pine woods and wide fields of cotton.

When he reached the house that his senses told him concealed Anyanwu, he sat still on his horse for several minutes, staring at it from a distance. It was a large white frame house with tall, unnecessary columns and a porch with upper and lower galleries—a solid, permanent-looking place. He could see slave cabins extending out away from the house, almost hidden by trees. And there was a barn, a kitchen, and other buildings that Doro could not identify from a distance. He could see blacks moving around the grounds—children playing, a man chopping wood, a woman gathering something in the kitchen garden, another woman sweating over a steaming caldron of dirty clothes which she occasionally lifted on her stick. A boy with arms no longer than his forearms should have been was bending low here and there collecting trash with tiny hands. Doro looked long at this last slave. Was his deformity a result of some breeding project of Anyanwu's?

Without quite knowing why he did it, Doro rode on. He had planned to take Anyanwu as soon as he found her—take her while she was off guard, still human and vulnerable. Instead, he went away, found lodging for the night at the cabin of one of Anyanwu's poorer neighbors. That neighbor was a man, his wife, their four younger children, and several thousand fleas. Doro spent a miserable, sleepless night, but over both supper and breakfast, he found the family a good source of information about its wealthy neighbor. It was from this man and woman that Doro learned of the married daughters, the bastard slave children, Mr. Warrick's unneighborly behavior—a great sin in the eyes of these people. And there was the dead wife, the frequent trips Warrick made to who knew where, and most strangely, that the Warrick property was haunted by what the local Acadians called a *loup-garou*—a werewolf. The creature appeared to be only a large black dog, but the man of the family, born and raised within a few miles of where he now lived, swore the same dog had been roaming that property since he was a boy. It had been known to disarm grown men, then stand over their rifles growling and daring them to take back what was theirs. Rumor had it that the dog had been shot several times—shot point-blank—but never felled. Never. Bullets passed through it as though through smoke.

That was enough for Doro. For how many years had Anyanwu spent much of her time either away from home or in the form of a large dog. How long had it taken her to realize that he could not find her while she was an animal? Most important, what would happen now if she had spotted him somehow, if she took animal form and escaped. He should have killed her at once! Perhaps he could use hostages again—let his senses seek out those of her slaves who would make good prey. Perhaps he could force her back by threatening them. They would almost certainly be the best of her children.

The next morning Doro headed his black gelding up the pathway to Anyanwu's mansion. As he reached it an adolescent boy came to take his horse. It was the boy with the deformed arms.

"Is your master at home?" Doro asked.

"Yes, sir," said the boy softly.

Doro laid a hand on the boy's shoulder. "Leave the horse here. He'll be all right. Take me to your master." He had not expected to make such a quick decision, but the boy was perfect for what he wanted. Despite his deformity, he was highly desirable prey. No doubt Anyanwu treasured him—a beloved son.

The boy looked at Doro, unafraid, then started toward the house. Doro kept a grip on his shoulder, though he did not doubt that the boy could have gotten away easily. Doro was wearing the body of a short, slight Frenchman while the boy was well-muscled, powerful-looking in spite of his own short stature. All Anyanwu's children tended to be short.

"What happened to your arms?" Doro asked.

The boy glanced at him, then at the foreshortened arms. "Accident, massa," he said softly. "I tried to bring horses out of a stable fire. 'Fore I could get 'em out, de beam fell on me." Doro did not like his slave patois. It sounded false.

"But..." Doro frowned at the tiny child's arms on the young man's body. No accident could cause such a deformity. "I mean were you born with your arms that way?"

"No, sir. I was born with two good arms—long as yours."

"Then why do you have deformed arms now!" Doro demanded exasperated.

"'Cause of de beam, massa. Old arms broken up and burnt. Had to grow new ones. Couple more weeks and dese be long enough."

Doro jerked the boy around to face him, and the boy smiled. For a moment, Doro wondered whether he was demented—as warped of mind as he was of body. But the eyes were intelligent—even mocking now. It seemed that the boy was perfectly intelligent, and laughing at him.

"Do you always tell people you can do such things—grow new arms?"

The boy shook his head, straightened so that he met Doro's eyes levelly. There was nothing of the slave in his gaze. When he spoke again, he ceased to make even his minimal effort to sound like a slave.

"I've never told any outsider before," he said. "But I'm told that if I let you know what I can do and that I'm the only one who can do it, I'll stand a better chance of living out the day."

There was no point in asking who had told him. Somehow, Anyanwu had spotted him. "How old are you?" he asked the boy.

"Nineteen."

"How old were you at transition?"

"Seventeen."

"What can you do?"

"Heal myself. I'm slower at it than she is, though, and I can't change my shape."

"Why not?"

"I don't know. I suppose because my father couldn't."

"What could he do?"

"I never knew him. He died. But she says he could hear what people were thinking."

"Can you?"

"Sometimes."

Doro shook his head. Anyanwu had come almost as near to success as he had—and with far less raw material. "Take me to her!" he said.

"She's here," the boy said.

Startled, Doro looked around, searching for Anyanwu, knowing she must be in animal form since he had not sensed her. She stood perhaps ten paces behind him near a yellow pine sapling. She was a large, sharp-faced black dog, standing statue-still, watching him. He spoke to her impatiently.

"I can't talk to you while you're like that!"

She began to change. She took her time about it, but he did not complain. He had waited too long for a few minutes to matter.

Finally, human, female, and unself-consciously naked, she walked past him onto the porch. In that moment, he meant to kill her. If she had taken any other form, become anyone other than her true self, she would have died. But she was now as she had been over a hundred and fifty years—a century and a half—before. She was the same woman he had shared a clay couch with thousands of miles away, lifetimes ago. He raised his hand toward her. She did not see it. He could have taken her then and there without further trouble.

But he lowered the hand before it touched her smooth, dark shoulder. He stared at her, angry with himself, frowning.

"Come into the house, Doro," she said.

Her voice was the same, soft and young. He followed her in feeling oddly confused, suspended in time, with only the watchful, protective young son to jar him to reality.

He looked at the son, ragged and shoeless and dusty. The boy should have seemed out of place inside the handsomely furnished home, but somehow, he did not.

"Come into the parlor," he said, catching Doro's arm in his child-sized hands. "Let her put her clothes on. She'll be back."

Doro did not doubt that she would. Apparently, the boy understood his role as hostage.

Doro sat down in an upholstered armchair and the boy sat opposite him on a sofa. Between them was a small wooden table and a fireplace of carved black stone. There was a large oriental rug on the floor and several other chairs and tables scattered around the room. A maid in a plain clean blue dress and white apron brought brandy and looked at the boy as though daring him to have any. He smiled and did not.

The maid would have been good prey too. A daughter? "What can she do?" Doro asked when she was gone.

"Nothing but have babies," the boy said.

"Did she have a transition?"

"No. She won't either. Not as old as she is."

A latent then. One who could pass her heritage on to her children, but could not use it herself. She should be bred to a near relative. Doro wondered whether Anyanwu had overcome her squeamishness enough to do this. Was that where this boy who was growing arms had come from? Inbreeding? Was his father, perhaps, one of Anyanwu's older sons?

"What do you know about me?" he asked the boy.

"That you're no more what you appear to be than she is." The boy shrugged. "She talked about you sometimes—how you took her from Africa, how she was your slave in New York back when they had slaves in New York."

"She was never my slave."

"She thinks she was. She doesn't think she will be again though."

*   *   *

In her bedroom, Anyanwu dressed quickly and casually as a man. She kept her body womanly—she wanted to be herself when she faced Doro—but after the easy unclothed freedom of the dog body, she could not have stood the layers of tight clothing women were expected to wear. The male clothing accented her womanliness anyway. No one had ever seen her this way and mistaken her for a man or boy.

Abruptly, she threw her shirt to the floor and stood, head in hands, before her dressing table. Doro would break Stephen into pieces if she ran now. He would probably not kill him, but he would make him a slave. There were people here in Louisiana and in the other Southern states who bred people as Doro did. They gave a man one woman after another and when the children came, the man had no authority over what was done to them, no responsibility to them or to their mothers. Authority and responsibility were the prerogatives of the masters. Doro would do that to her son, make him no more than a breeding animal. She thought of the sons and daughters she had left behind in Doro's hands. It was not likely that any of them were alive now, but she had no doubt of the way Doro had used them while they did live. She could not have helped them. It was all she had been able to do to get Doro to give his word not to harm them during her marriage to Isaac. Beyond that, she could have stayed with them and died, but she could not have helped them. And growing up as they had in Wheatley, they would not have wanted her help. Doro seduced people. He made them want to please him, made them strive for his approval. He terrified them into submission only when he could not seduce them.

And when he could not terrify them...

What could she do? She could not run again and leave him Stephen and the others. But she was no more able to help them by staying than she had been able to help her children in Wheatley. She could not even help herself. What would he do to her when she went downstairs? She had run away from him, and he murdered runaways. Had he allowed her to dress herself merely so that he would not have the inconvenience of taking over a naked body?

What could she do?

Doro and Stephen were talking like old friends when Anyanwu walked into the parlor. To her surprise, Doro stood up. He had always seemed lazily unconcerned with such courtesies before. She sat with Stephen on the sofa, noticing automatically that the boy's arms seemed to be forming well. He had been so good, so controlled on that terrible day when he lost them.

"Go back to your work now," she told him softly.

He looked at her, surprised.

"Go," she repeated. "I'm here now."

Clearly, that was what was concerning him. She had told him a great deal about Doro. He did not want to leave her, but finally, he obeyed.

"Good boy," Doro commented, sipping brandy.

"Yes," she agreed.

He shook his head. "What shall I do with him, Anyanwu? What shall I do with you?"

She said nothing. When had it ever mattered what she said to him? He did as he pleased.

"You've had more success than I have," he said. "Your son seems controlled—very sure of himself."

"I taught him to lift his head," she said.

"I meant his ability."

"Yes."

"Who was his father?"

She hesitated. He would ask, of course. He would inquire after the ancestry of her children as though after the bloodline of a horse. "His father was brought illegally from Africa," she said. "He was a good man, but... much like Thomas. He could see and hear and feel too much."

"And he survived a crossing on a slave ship?"

"Only part of him survived. He was mad most of the time, but he was docile. He was like a child. The slavers pretended that it was because he had not yet learned English that he seemed strange. They showed me how strong his muscles were—I had the form of a white man, you see."

"I know."

"They showed me his teeth and his hands and his penis and they said what a good breeder he would be. They would have pleased you, Doro. They thought very much as you do."

"I doubt it," he said amiably. He was being surprisingly amiable. He was at his first stage—seeking to seduce her as he had when he took her from her people. No doubt by his own reasoning he was being extremely generous. She had run from him, done what no one else could do, kept out of his hands for more than a lifetime; yet instead of killing her at once, he seemed to be beginning again with her—giving her a chance to accept him as though nothing had happened. That meant he wanted her alive, if she would submit.

Her own sense of relief at this realization startled her. She had come down the stairs to him expecting to die, ready to die, and here he was courting her again. And here she was responding. . . .

No. Not again. No more Wheatleys.

What then?

"So you bought a slave you knew was insane because he had a sensitivity you liked," Doro said. "You couldn't imagine how many times I've done things like that myself."

"I bought him in New Orleans because as he walked past me in chains on his way to the slave pens, he called to me. He said, 'Anyanwu! Does that white skin cover your eyes too?'"

"He spoke English?"

"No. He was one of my people. Not a descendant, I think; he was too different. In the moment he spoke to me, he was sane and hearing my thoughts. Slaves were passing in front of me all chained, and I was thinking, 'I have to take more sunken gold from the sea, then see the banker about buying the land that adjoins mine. I have to buy some books—medical books, especially to see what doctors are doing now. . . .' I was not seeing the slaves in front of me. I would not have thought I could be oblivious to such a thing. I had been white for too long. I needed someone to say what he said to me."

"So you brought him home and bore him a son."

"I would have borne him many sons. It seemed that his spirit was healing from what they had done to him on the ship. At the end, he was sane nearly all the time. He was a good husband then. But he died."

"Of what sickness?"

"None that I could find. He saw his son and said in praise, 'Ifeyinwa!—what is like a child.' I made that Stephen's other name, Ifeyinwa. Then Mgbada died. I am a bad healer sometimes. I am no healer at all sometimes."

"No doubt the man lived much longer and better than he would have without you."

"He was a young man," she said. "If I were the healer I long to be, he would still be alive."

"What kind of healer is the boy?"

"Less than I am in some ways. Slower. But he has some of his father's sensitivity. Didn't you wonder how he knew you?"

"I thought you had seen me and warned him."

"I told him about you. Perhaps he knew your voice from hearing it in my thoughts. I don't ask him what he hears. But no, I did not see you before you arrived—not to know you, anyway." Did he really think she would have stayed to meet him, kept her children here so that he could threaten them? Did he think she had grown stupid with the years? "He can touch people sometimes and know what is wrong with them," she continued. "When he says a thing is wrong, it is. But sometimes he misses things—things I wouldn't miss."

"He's young," Doro said.

She shrugged.

"Will he ever grow old, Anyanwu?"

"I don't know." She hesitated, spoke her hope in a whisper. "Perhaps I have finally borne a son I will not have to bury." She looked up, saw that Doro was watching her intently. There was a kind of hunger in his expression—hunger that he masked quickly.

"Can he control his thought reading?" he asked, neutral-voiced.

"In that, he is his father's opposite. Mgbada could not control what he heard—like Thomas. That was why his people sold him into slavery. He was a sorcerer to them. But Stephen must make an effort to hear other people's thoughts. It has not happened by accident since his transition. But sometimes when he tries, nothing happens. He says it is like never knowing when he will be struck deaf."

"That is a tolerable defect," Doro said. "He might be frustrated sometimes, but he will never go mad with the weight of other people's thoughts pressing in on him."

"I have told him that."

There was a long silence. Something was coming, and it had to do with Stephen, Anyanwu knew. She wanted to ask what it was, but then Doro would tell her and she would have to find some way to defy him. When she did... when she did, she would fail, and he would kill her.

"He is to me what Isaac was to you," she whispered. Would he hear that as what it was—a plea for mercy?

He stared at her as though she had said something incomprehensible, as though he was trying to understand. Finally, he smiled a small, uncharacteristically tentative smile. "Did you ever think, Anyanwu, how long a hundred years is to an ordinary person—or a hundred and fifty years?"

She shrugged. Nonsense. He was talking nonsense while she waited to hear what he meant to do to her son!

"How do the years seem to you?" he asked. "Like days? Like months? What do you feel when good companions are suddenly old and gray and addled?"

Again, she shrugged. "People grow old. They die."

"All of them," he agreed. "All but you and I."

"You die constantly," she said.

He got up and went to sit beside her on the sofa. Somehow, she kept still, subdued her impulse to get up, move away from him. "I have never died," he said.

She stared past him at one of the candlesticks on the mantel. "Yes," she said. "I should have said you kill constantly."

He was silenced. She faced him, looked into eyes that were large and wide-set and brown. He had the eyes of a larger man—or his current body did. They gave him a false expression of gentleness.

"Did you come here to kill?" she asked. "Am I to die? Are my children to become mares and studs? Is that why you could not leave me alone!"

"Why do you want to be alone?" he asked.

She closed her eyes. "Doro, tell me what is to happen."

"Perhaps nothing. Perhaps eventually, I will bring your son a wife."

"One wife?" she said, disbelieving.

"One wife here, as with you and Isaac. I never brought women to Wheatley for him."

That was so. From time to time, he took Isaac away with him, but he never brought women to Isaac. Anyanwu knew that the husband she had loved most had sired dozens of children with other women.

"Don't you care about them?" she had asked once, trying to understand. She cared about each one of her children, raised each one she bore and loved it.

"I never see them," he had answered. "They are his children. I sire them in his name. He sees that they and their mothers are well cared for."

"So he says!" She had been bitter that day, angry at Doro for making her pregnant when her most recent child by Isaac was less than a year old, angry at him for afterward killing a tall, handsome girl whom Anyanwu had known and liked. The girl, understanding what was to happen to her, had still somehow treated him as a lover. It was obscene.

"Have you ever known him to neglect the needs of the children he claims?" Isaac had asked. "Have you ever seen his people left landless or hungry? He takes care of his own."

She had gone away from Isaac to fly for hours as a bird and look down at the great, empty land below and wonder if there was nowhere in all the forests and rivers and mountains and lakes, nowhere in that endless land for her to escape and find peace and cleanness.

"Stephen is nineteen years old," she said. "He is a man. Your children and mine grow up very quickly, I think. He has been a man since his transition. But he's still young. You'll make him an animal if you use him as you used Isaac."

"Isaac was fifteen when I gave him his first woman," Doro said.

"Then he had been yours for fifteen years. For you, Stephen will be as much wild seed as I was."

Doro nodded agreeably. "It is better for me to get them before they reach their transitions—if they're going to have transitions. What will you give me then, Anyanwu?"

She turned to look at him in surprise. Was he offering to bargain with her? He had never bargained before. He had told her what he wanted and let her know what he would do to her or to her children if she did not obey.

Was he bargaining now, then, or was he playing with her? What could she lose by assuming that he was serious? "Bring Stephen the woman," she said. "One woman. When he is older, perhaps there can be others."

"Do you imagine there are none now?"

"Of course not. But he chooses his own. I don't tell him to breed. I don't send him women."

"Do women seem to like him?"

She surprised herself by smiling a little. "Some do. Not enough to suit him, of course. There is a widow paying a lot of attention to him now. She knows what she is doing. Left alone, he will find a good wife here when he is tired of wandering around."

"Perhaps I shouldn't let him get tired of it."

"I tell you, you will make an animal of him if you don't!" she said. "Haven't you seen the men slaves in this country who are used for breeding? They are never permitted to learn what it means to be a man. They are not permitted to care for their children. Among my people, children are wealth, they are better than money, better than anything. But to these men, warped and twisted by their masters, children are almost nothing. They are to boast of to other men. One thinks he is greater than another because he has more children. Both exaggerate the number of women who have borne them children, neither is doing anything a father should for his children, and the master who is indifferently selling off his own brown children is laughing and saying, 'You see? Niggers are just like animals!' Slavery down here opens one's eyes, Doro. How could I want such a life for my son?"

There was silence. He got up, wandered around the large room examining the vases, lamps, the portrait of a slender white woman with dark hair and solemn expression. "Was this your wife?" he asked.

She wanted to shake him. She wanted to use her strength, make him tell her what he meant to do. "Yes," she whispered.

"How did you like it—being a man, having a wife?"

"Doro . . . !"

"How did you like it?" He would not be rushed. He was enjoying himself.

"She was a good woman. We pleased each other."

"Did she know what you were?"

"Yes. She was not ordinary herself. She saw ghosts."

"Anyanwu!" he said with disgust and disappointment.

She ignored his tone, stared up at the picture. "She was only sixteen when I married her. If I hadn't married her, I think she would have been put in an asylum eventually. People spoke about her in the way you just said my name."

"I don't blame them."

"You should. Most people believe in a life that goes on after their bodies die. There are always tales of ghosts. Even people who think they are too sophisticated to be frightened are not immune. Talk to five people and at least three will have seen what they believe was a ghost, or they will know another person who has seen. But Denice really did see. She was very sensitive; she could see when no one else could—and since no one else could, people said she was mad. I think she had had a kind of transition."

"And it gave her a private view into the hereafter."

Anyanwu shook her head. "You should be less skeptical. You are a kind of ghost yourself, after all. What is there of you that can be touched?"

"I've heard that before."

"Of course." She paused. "Doro, I will talk to you about Denice. I will talk to you about anyone, anything. But first, please, tell me what you plan for my son."

"I'm thinking about it. I'm thinking about you and your potential value to me." He looked again at the portrait. "You were right, you know. I came here to finish old business—kill you and take your children to one of my settlements. No one has ever done what you did to me."

"I ran from you and lived. Other people have done that."

"Only because I chose to let them live. They had their freedom for only a few days before I caught them. You know that."

"Yes," she said reluctantly.

"Now, a century after I lost you, I find you young and well—greeting me as though we had just seen each other yesterday. I find you in competition with me, raising witches of your own."

"There is no competition."

"Then why have you surrounded yourself with the kinds of people I seek out? Why do you have children by them?"

"They need me...those people." She swallowed, thinking of some of the things done to her people before she found them. "They need someone who can help them, and I can help. You don't want to help them, you want to use them. But I can help."

"Why should you?"

"I'm a healer, Doro."

"That's no answer. You chose to be a healer. What you really are is what's called in this part of the country loup-garou—a werewolf."

"I see you've been talking to my neighbors."

"I have. They're right, you know."

"The legends say werewolves kill. I have never killed except to save myself. I am a healer."

"Most... healers don't have children by their patients."

"Most healers do as they please. My patients are more like me than any other people. Why shouldn't I find mates among them?"

Doro smiled. "There is always an answer, isn't there? But it doesn't matter. Tell me about Denice and her ghosts."

She drew a deep breath and let it out slowly, calming herself. "Denice saw what people left behind. She went into houses and saw the people who had preceded her there. If someone had suffered or died there, she saw that very clearly. It terrified her. She would go into a house and see a child running, clothing afire, and there would be no child. But two, ten, twenty years before, a child would have burned to death there. She saw people stealing things days or years before. She saw slaves beaten and tortured, slave women raped, people shaking with ague or covered with smallpox. She did not feel things as people do in transition. She only saw them. But she could not tell whether what she was seeing was actually happening as she saw it or whether it was history. She was slowly going mad. Then her parents gave a party and I was invited because I seemed young and rich and handsome—perhaps a good prospect for a family with five daughters. I remember, I was standing with Denice's father telling lies about my origins, and Denice brushed past. She touched me, you see. She could see people's past lives when she touched them just as she could see the past of wood and brick. She saw something of what I am even in that brief touch, and she fainted. I didn't know what had happened until she came to me days later. I was the only person she had ever found to be stranger than herself. She knew all that I was before we married."

"Why did she marry you?"

"Because I believed her when she told me what she could do. Because I was not afraid or ridiculing. And because after a while, we started to want each other."

"Even though she knew you were a woman and black?"

"Even so." Anyanwu stared up at the solemn young woman, remembering that lovely, fearful courting. They had been as fearful of marrying as they had been of losing each other. "She thought at first that there could be no children, and that saddened her because she had always wanted children. Then she realized that I could give her girls. It took her a long time to understand all that I could do. But she thought the children would be black and people would say she had been with a slave. White men leave brown children all about, but a white woman who does this becomes almost an animal in the eyes of other whites."

"White women must be protected," Doro said, "whether they want to be or not."

"As property is protected." Anyanwu shook her head. "Preserved for the use of owners alone. Denice said she felt like property—like a slave plotting escape. I told her I could give her children who were not related to me at all if she wished. Her fear made me angry even though I knew the situation was not her fault. I told her my Warrick shape was not a copy of anyone. I had molded myself freely to create it, but if she wished, I could take the exact shape of one of the white men I had treated in Wheatley. Then as with the dolphins, I could have young who inherited nothing at all from me. Even male young. She did not understand that."

"Neither do I," Doro said. "This is something new."

"Only for me. You do it all the time—fathering or giving birth to children who are no blood kin to you. They are the children of the bodies you wear, even though you call them your own."

"But... you only wear one body."

"And you have not understood how completely that one body can change. I cannot leave it as you can, but I can make it over. I can make it over so completely in the image of someone else that I am no longer truly related to my parents. It makes me wonder what I am—that I can do this and still know myself, still return to my true shape."

"You could not do this before in Wheatley."

"I have always done it. Each time I learned a new animal shape, I did it. But I did not understand it very well until I began running from you. Until I began to hide. I bore dolphin young—and they were dolphins. Not human at all. They were the young of the dolphin Isaac caught and fed to us so long ago. My body was a copy of hers down to the smallest living part. There are no words for me to tell you how deep and complete such a change is."

"So you could become another person so completely that the children you gave Denice were not really yours."

"I could have. But when she understood, she did not want that. She said she would rather have no children at all. But that sacrifice was not necessary. I could give her girl children of my own body. Girl children who would have her coloring. It was hard work arranging all that. There are so many tiny things within even one cell of a human body. I could have given her a monstrosity if I had been careless."

"I made you study these things by driving you away?"

"You did. You made me learn very much. Much of the time, I had nothing to do but study myself, try things I had not thought of before."

"If you duplicated another man's shape then, you could father sons."

"The other man's sons."

Slowly, Doro drew his mouth into a smile. "That's the answer then, Anyanwu. You'll take your son's place. You'll take the place of a great many people."

"You mean ... for me to go here and there getting children and then forgetting about them?"

"Either you go or I'll bring women to you here."

She got up wearily, without even outrage to make her stiff and hostile. "You are a complete fool," she told him quietly, and she walked into the hall, through the house, and out the back door. From there, through the trees she could see the bayou with its slow water. Nearer were the dependencies and the slave cabins that were not inhabited by slaves. She owned no slaves. She had brought some of the people who worked for her and recruited the others among freedmen, but those she bought, she freed. They always stayed to work for her, feeling more comfortable with her and with each other than they had ever been elsewhere. That always surprised the new ones. They were not used to being comfortable with other people. They were misfits, malcontents, troublemakers—though they did not make trouble for Anyanwu. They treated her as mother, older sister, teacher, and, when she invited it, lover. Somehow, even this last intimacy did nothing to diminish her authority. They knew her power. She was who she was, no matter what role she chose.

And yet, she did not threaten them, did not slaughter among them as Doro did among his people. The worse she did was occasionally fire someone. Firing meant eviction. It meant leaving the safety and comfort of the plantation and becoming a misfit again in the world outside. It meant exile.

Few of them knew how difficult it was for Anyanwu to turn one of them out—or worse, turn a family out. Few of them knew how their presence comforted her. She was not Doro, breeding people as though they were cattle, though perhaps her gathering of all these special ones, these slightly strange ones would accomplish the same purpose as his breeding. She was herself, gathering family. No doubt some of these people were of her family, her descendants. They felt like her children. Perhaps, there had been intermarriage, her descendants drawn together by a comforting but indefinable similarity and not knowing of their common origins. And there were other people probably not related to her, who had rudimentary sensitivity that could become true thought reading in a few generations. Mgbada had told her this—that she was gathering people who were like his grandparents. He had told her she was breeding witches.

An old woman came up to her—a white woman, withered and gray, Luisa, who did what sewing she could for her keep. She was one of five white people on the place. There could have been many more whites, fitting in very comfortably, but the race-conscious culture made that dangerous. The four younger whites tried to lessen the danger by telling people they were octoroons. Luisa was a Creole—a French-Spanish mixture—and too old to care who knew it.

"Is there trouble?" Luisa asked.

Anyanwu nodded.

"Stephen said he was here—Doro, the one you told me about."

"Go and tell the others not to come in from the fields until I call them in myself."

Luisa stared hard at her. "What if he calls—with your mouth?"

"Then they must decide whether to run or not. They know about him. If they want to run now, they can. Later, if the black dog is seen in the woods again, they can come back." If Doro killed her, he would not be able to use her healing or metamorphosing abilities. She had learned that from her stay in Wheatley. He could possess someone's body and use it to have children, but he could use only the body. When he possessed Thomas so long ago, he had not gained Thomas' thought-reading ability. She had never known him to use any extra ability from a body he possessed.

The old woman took Anyanwu by the shoulders and hugged her. "What will you do?" she asked.

"I don't know."

"I have never seen him and I hate him."

"Go," Anyanwu told her.

Luisa hurried across the grass. She moved well for her age. Like Anyanwu's children, she had lived a long, healthy life. Cholera, malaria, yellow fever, typhus, and other diseases swept acrosss the land and left Anyanwu's people almost untouched. If they caught a disease, they survived it and recovered quickly. If they hurt themselves, Anyanwu was there to care for them.

As Luisa disappeared into the trees, Doro came out of the house. "I could go after her," he said. "I know you sent her to warn your field hands."

Anyanwu turned to face him angrily. "You are many times as old as I am. You must have some inborn defect to keep you from getting wisdom to go with your years."

"Will you eventually condescend to tell me what wisdom you have gotten?" There was an edge to his voice finally. She was beginning to irritate him and end the seductive phase. That was good. How stupid of him to think she could be seduced again. It was possible, however, that she might seduce him.

"You were pleased to see me again, weren't you?" she said. "I think you were surprised to realize how pleased you were."

"Say what you have to say, Anyanwu!"

She shrugged. "Isaac was right."

Silence. She knew Isaac had spoken to him several times. Isaac had wanted them together so badly—the two people he loved best.

Did that mean anything at all to Doro? It had not years before, but now... Doro had been glad to see her. He had marveled over the fact that she seemed unchanged—as though he was only now beginning to realize that she was only slightly more likely to die than he was, and not likely at all to grow decrepit with age. As though her immortality had been emotionally unreal to him until now, a fact that he had accepted with only half his mind.

"Doro, I will go on living unless you kill me. There is no reason for me to die unless you kill me."

"Do you think you can take over work I've spent millennia at?"

"Do you think I want to?" she countered. "I was telling the truth. These people need me, and I need them. I never set out to build a settlement like one of yours. Why should I? I don't need new bodies as you do. All I need is my own kind around me. My family or people who feel like my family. To you, most of my people here wouldn't even be good breeding stock, I think."

"Forty years ago, that old woman would have."

"Does that make it competition for me to give her a home now?"

"You have others. Your maid..."

"My daughter!"

"I thought so."

"She is unmarried. Bring her a man. If she likes him, let her marry him and bear interesting children. If she doesn't like him, then find her someone else. But she needs only one husband, Doro, as my son needs only one wife."

"Is that what your own way of life tells them? Or shall I believe you sleep alone because your husbands are dead?"

"If my children show any signs of growing as old as I am, they may do as they please."

"They will anyway."

"But without you to guide them, Doro. Without you to make them animals. What would my son be in your hands? Another Thomas? You are going everywhere tending ten different settlements, twenty, and not giving enough of yourself to any of them. I am staying here looking after my family and offering to let your children marry mine. And if the offspring are strange and hard to handle, I will handle them. I will take care of them. They need not live alone in the woods and drink too much and neglect their bodies until they are nearly dead."

To her surprise, he hugged her very much as Luisa had, and he laughed. He took her arm and walked her over to the slave quarters, still laughing. He quieted though as he pushed open a random door and peered into one of the neat, sturdy cabins. There was a large brick fireplace with a bake kettle down amid the nearly dead coals. Someone's supper bread. There was a large bed in one corner and a trundle bed beneath. There were a table and four chairs all of which looked homemade, but adequate. There was a cradle that also looked homemade—and much used. There were a wood box and a water bucket with its gourd dipper. There were bunches of herbs and ears of corn hung from the ceiling to dry and cooking utensils over and alongside the fireplace. Overall, the cabin gave the impression of being a plain but comfortable place to live.

"Is it enough?" Anyanwu asked.

"I have several people, black and white, who don't live this well."

"I don't."

He tried to draw her into the cabin toward the chairs or the bed—she did not know which—but she held back.

"This is someone else's home," she said. "We can go back into the house if you like."

"No. Later, perhaps." He put an arm around her waist. "You must feed me again and find us another earthen couch to lie on."

And hear you threaten my children again, she thought.

As though in answer, he said: "And I must tell you why I laughed. It isn't because your offer doesn't please me, Anyanwu; it does. But you have no idea what kinds of creatures you are volunteering to care for."

Didn't she? Hadn't she seen them in Wheatley?

"I'm going to bring you some of your own descendants," Doro said. "I think they will surprise you. I've done a great deal of work with them since Nweke. I think you won't be wanting to care for them or their children for long."

"Why? What new thing is wrong with them?"

"Perhaps nothing. Perhaps your influence is just what they need. On the other hand, perhaps they will disrupt the family you've made for yourself here as nothing else could. Will you still have them?"

"Doro, how can I know? You haven't told me anything."

Her hair was loose and short and rounded as it had been when he first styled it for her. Now he put his hands on either side of it, pressing it to her head. "Sun Woman, either you will accept my people in this way that you have defined or you will come with me, taking mates when and where I command, or you will give me your children. One way or another, you will serve me. What is your choice?"

Yes, she thought bitterly. *Now the threats.* "Bring me my grandchildren," she said. "Even though they have never seen me, they will remember me. Their bodies will remember me down to the smallest structures of their flesh. You cannot know how well people's bodies remember their ancestors."

"You will teach me," he said. "You seem to have learned a great deal since I saw you last. I've been breeding people nearly all my life and I still don't know why some things work and others don't, or why a thing will work only some of the time even with the same couple. You will teach me."

"You will not harm my people?" she asked, watching him carefully.

"What do they know about me?"

"Everything. I thought if you ever found us, there wouldn't be time for me to explain the danger."

"Tell them to obey me."

She winced as though in pain and looked away. "You cannot always take everything," she said. "Or just take my life. What is the good of living on and on and having nothing?"

There was silence for a moment. "Did they obey Denice?" he asked finally. "Or Mgbada?"

"Sometimes. They are a very independent people."

"But they obey you."

"Yes."

"Then tell them to obey me. If you don't, I'll have to tell them myself—in whichever way they understand."

"Don't hurt them!"

He shrugged. "If they obey me, I won't."

He was making a new Wheatley. He had settlements everywhere, families everywhere. She had only one, and he was taking it. He had taken her from one people and driven her from another, and now, he was casually reaching out to strip her of a third. And she was wrong. She could live on and on and have nothing. She would. He would see to it.

Chapter Twelve

Anyanwu had never watched a group like her own break apart. She did not know whether there had ever before been a group like her own. Certainly, once Doro began to spend time at the plantation, exercising his authority as he chose while Anyanwu stood by and said nothing, the character of the group began to change. When he brought Joseph Toler as husband for one of Anyanwu's daughters, the young man changed the group more by refusing to do work of any kind. His foster parents had pampered him, allowed him to spend his time drinking and gambling and bedding young women. But he was a beautiful young man—honey-colored with curly black hair, tall and slender. Anyanwu's daughter Margaret Nneka was fascinated by him. She accepted him very quickly. Few other people on the plantation accepted him at all. He was not doing his share of the work, yet he could not be fired and sent away. He could, however, make a great deal of trouble. He had been on the plantation for only a few weeks when he went too far and lost a fist fight with Anyanwu's son Stephen.

Anyanwu was alone when Stephen came to tell her what had happened. She had just come from treating a four-year-old who had wandered down to the bayou and surprised a water moccasin. She had been able to manufacture within her own body a medicine to counter the poison easily, since one of the first things she had done on settling in Louisiana was allow herself to be bitten by such a snake. By now, countering the poison was almost second nature to her. She did like to have a meal afterward, though; thus Stephen, bruised and disheveled, found her in the dining room eating.

"You've got to get rid of that lazy, worthless bastard," he said.

Anyanwu sighed. There was no need to ask who the boy meant. "What has he done?"

"Tried to rape Helen."

Anyanwu dropped the piece of cornbread she had been about to bite. Helen was her youngest daughter—eleven years old. "He what!"

"I caught them in the Duran cabin. He was tearing her clothes off."

"Is she all right?"

"Yes. She's in her room."

Anyanwu stood up. "I'll see her in a little while, then. Where is he?"

"Lying in front of the Duran cabin."

She went out, not knowing whether she was going to give the young man another beating or help him if Stephen had hurt him seriously. But what kind of animal was he to try to rape a child? How could Anyanwu possibly tolerate him here after this? Doro would have to take him away, breeding be damned.

The young man was not beautiful when Anyanwu found him. He was half again as large as Stephen and strong in spite of his indolence, but Stephen had inherited much of Anyanwu's strength. And he knew how to administer a good beating, even with his tender, newly finished arms and hands.

The young man's face was a lumpy mass of bruised tissue. His nose was broken and bleeding. The flesh around his eyes was grotesquely swollen. The left ear was torn nearly off. He would lose it and look like one of the slaves marked and sold South for running away.

His body was so bruised beneath his shirt that Anyanwu was certain he had broken ribs. And he was lacking several of his front teeth. He would never be beautiful again. He began to come to as Anyanwu was probing at his ribs. He grunted, cursed, coughed, and with the cough, twisted in agony.

"Be still," Anyanwu said. "Breathe shallowly, and try not to cough anymore."

The young man whimpered.

"Be thankful Stephen caught you," she said. "If it had been me, you would take no more interest in women, I promise you. Not for the rest of your life."

In spite of his pain, the young man cringed away from her, clutching himself protectively.

"What can there be in you worth inflicting on descendants?" she asked in disgust. She made him stand up, ignoring his weakness, his moans of pain. "Now get into the house!" she said. "Or go lie in the barn with the other animals."

He made it into the house, did not pass out until he reached the stairs. Anyanwu carried him up to a small, hot attic bedroom, washed him, bandaged his ribs, and left him there with water, bread, and a little fruit. She could have given him something to ease his pain, but she did not.

The little girl, Helen, lay asleep on her bed still wearing her torn dress. Her face was swollen on one side as though from a heavy blow, and the sight of it made Anyanwu want to give the young man another beating. Instead, she woke the child gently.

In spite of her gentleness, Helen awoke with a start and cried out.

"You are safe," Anyanwu told her. "I'm here."

The child clung to her, not weeping, only holding tightly, holding with all her strength.

"Are you hurt?" Anyanwu asked. "Did he hurt you?"

The girl did not respond.

"Obiageli, are you hurt?"

The girl lay down again slowly and looked up at her. "He came into my thoughts," she said. "I could feel him come in."

"... into your thoughts?"

"I could feel it. I knew it was him. He wanted me to go to Tina Duran's house."

"He made you go?"

"I don't know." Finally, the child began to cry. She pulled her pillow around her swollen face and wept into it. Anyanwu rubbed her shoulders and her neck and let her cry. She did not think the girl was crying because she had nearly been raped.

"Obiageli," she whispered. Before the girl's birth, a childless white woman named Helen Matthews had asked Anyanwu to give a child her name. Anyanwu had never liked the name Helen, but the white woman had been a good friend—one of those who had overcome her own upbringing and her neighbors' noisy mouths and come to live on the plantation. She had never been able to have children, had been past the age of bearing when she met Anyanwu. Thus, Anyanwu's youngest daughter was named Helen. And Helen was the daughter Anyanwu most often called by her second name, Obiageli. Somehow, she had lost that custom with the others.

"Obiageli, tell me all that he did."

After a while, the girl sniffed, turned over, and wiped her face. She lay still, staring up at the ceiling, one small frown between her eyes.

"I was getting water," she said. "I wanted to help Rita." This was the os rouge cook—a woman of black and Indian ancestry and Spanish appearance. "She needed water, so I was at the well. He came to talk to me. He said I was pretty. He said he liked little girls. He said he had liked me for a long time."

"I should have thrown him into the pigsty," muttered Anyanwu. "Let his body wallow in shit so that it could be fit for his mind."

"I tried to go take the water to Rita," the girl continued. "But he told me to come with him. I went. I didn't like to go, but I could feel him in my thoughts. Then I was away from myself—someplace else watching myself walk with him. I tried to turn back, but I couldn't. My legs were walking without me." She stopped, looked at Anyanwu. "I never knew if Stephen was looking into my thoughts."

"But Stephen can only look," Anyanwu said. "He can't make you do anything."

"He wouldn't anyway."

"No."

Eyes downcast, the girl continued. "We went into Tina's cabin and he was closing the door when I found I could move my legs again. I ran out the door before he could get it shut. Then he took back my legs and I screamed and fell. I thought he would make me walk back, but he came out and grabbed me and dragged me back. I think that was when Stephen saw us." She looked up. "Did Stephen kill him?"

"No." Anyanwu shuddered, not wanting to think of what Doro might have done to Stephen if Stephen had killed the worthless

Joseph. If there had to be killing, she must do it. Probably no one on the plantation disliked killing more than she did, but she had to protect her people from both Doro's malicious strangers and Doro himself. Still, she hoped Joseph would behave himself until Doro returned and took him away.

"Stephen should have killed him," Helen said softly. "Now maybe he'll make my legs move again. Or maybe he'll do something worse." She shook her head, her child's face hard and old.

Anyanwu took her hand, remembering—remembering Lale, her Isaac's unlikely, unworthy brother. In all her time with Doro, she had not met another of his people as determinedly vicious as Lale. Until now, perhaps. Why had Doro given her such a man? And why had he not at least warned her?

"What will you do with him?" the girl asked.

"Have Doro take him away."

"Will Doro do that—just because you say so?"

Anyanwu winced. *Just because you say so...* How long had things been going on on the plantation just because she said so? People had been content with what she said. If they had problems they could not solve, they came to her. If they quarreled and could not settle matters themselves, they came to her. She had never invited them to come to her with their troubles, but she had never turned them away either. They had made her their final authority. Now her eleven-year-old daughter wanted to know if a thing would happen just because she said so. Her eleven-year-old! It had taken time, patience, and at least some wisdom to build the people's confidence in her. It took only a few weeks of Doro's presence to erode that confidence so badly that even her children doubted her.

"Will Doro take him away?" the girl persisted.

"Yes," Anyanwu said quietly. "I will see to it."

That night, Stephen walked in his sleep for the first time in his life. He walked out onto the upper gallery of the porch and fell or jumped off.

There was no disturbance; Stephen did not cry out. At dawn, old Luisa found him sprawled on the ground, his neck so twisted that Luisa was not surprised to find his body cold.

The old woman climbed the stairs herself to wake Anyanwu and take her to an upstairs sitting room away from the young daughter who was sleeping with her. The daughter, Helen, slept on, content, moving over a little into the warm place Anyanwu had left.

In the sitting room, Luisa stood hesitant, silent before Anyanwu, longing for a way to ease the terrible news. Anyanwu did not know how she was loved, Luisa thought. She gathered people to her and cared for them and helped them care for each other. Luisa had a sensitivity that had made closeness with other people a torture to her for most of her life. Somehow, she had endured a childhood and adolescence on a true plantation, where the ordinary accepted cruelties of slaveholder to slave drove her away into a marriage that she should not have made. People thought she was merely kind and womanishly unrealistic to be in such sympathy with slaves. They did not understand that far too much of the time, she literally felt what the slaves felt, shared fragments of their meager pleasure and far too many fragments of their pain. She had had none of Stephen's control, had never completed the agonizing change that she knew had come to the young man two years before. The man-thing called Doro had told her this was because her ancestry was wrong. He said she was descended from his people. It was his fault then that she had lived her life knowing of her husband's contempt and her children's indifference. It was his fault that she had been sixty years old before she found people whose presence she could endure without pain—people she could love and be loved by. She was "grandmother" to all the children here. Some of them actually lived in her cabin because their parents could not or would not care for them. Luisa thought some parents were too sensitive to any negative or rebellious feelings in their children. Anyanwu thought it was more than that—that some people did not want any children around them, rebellious or not. She said some of Doro's people were that way. Anyanwu took in stray children herself—as well as stray adults. Her son had shown signs of becoming much like her. Now, that son was dead.

"What is it?" Anyanwu asked her. "What has happened?"

"An accident," Luisa said, longing to spare her.

"Is it Joseph?"

"Joseph!" That son of a whore Doro had brought to marry one of Anyanwu's daughters. "Would I care if it were Joseph?"

"Who then? Tell me, Luisa."

The old woman took a deep breath. "Your son," she said. "Stephen is dead."

There was a long, terrible silence. Anyanwu sat frozen, stunned. Luisa wished she would wail with a mother's grief so that Luisa could comfort her. But Anyanwu never wailed.

"How could he die?" Anyanwu whispered. "He was nineteen. He was a healer. How could he die?"

"I don't know. He... fell."

"From where?"

"Upstairs. From the gallery."

"But how? Why?"

"How can I know, Anyanwu? It happened last night. It... must have. I only found him a few moments ago."

"Show me!"

She would have gone down in her gown, but Luisa seized a cloak from her bedroom and wrapped her in it. She noticed as she left with Anyanwu that the little girl was moving restlessly in her sleep, moaning softly. A nightmare?

Outside, others had discovered Stephen's body. Two children stood back, staring at him wide-eyed, and a woman knelt beside him wailing as Anyanwu would not.

The woman was Iye, a tall, handsome, solemn woman of utterly confused ancestry—French and African, Spanish and Indian. The mixture blended all too well in her. Luisa knew her to have thirty-six years, but she could have passed easily for a woman of twenty-six or even younger. The children were her son and daughter and the one in her belly would be Stephen's son or daughter. She had married a husband who loved wine better than he could love any woman, and wine had finally killed him. Anyanwu had found her destitute with her two babies, selling herself to get food for them, and considering very seriously whether she should take her husband's rusty knife and cut their throats and then her own.

Anyanwu had given her a home and hope. Stephen, when he was old enough, had given her something more. Luisa could remember Anyanwu shaking her head over the match, saying, "She is like a bitch in heat around him! You would never know from her behavior that she could be his mother."

And Luisa had laughed. "You should hear yourself, Anyanwu. Better yet, you should see yourself when you find a man that you want."

"I am not like that!" Anyanwu had been indignant.

"Of course not. You are very much better—and very much older."

And Anyanwu, being Anyanwu, had gone from angry silence to easy laughter. "No doubt he will be a better husband someday for having known her," she said.

"Or perhaps he will surprise you and marry her," Luisa countered. "Despite their ages, there is more than the ordinary pull between them. She is like him. She has some of what he has, some of the power. She cannot use it, but it is there. I can feel it in her sometimes—especially in those times when she is hottest after him."

Anyanwu had ignored this, preferring to believe that eventually her son would make a suitable marriage. Even now, Luisa did not know whether Anyanwu knew of the child coming. There was nothing showing yet, but Iye had told Luisa. She would not have told Anyanwu.

Now, Anyanwu went to the body, bent to touch the cold flesh of the throat. Iye saw her and started to move away, but Anyanwu caught her hand. "We both mourn," she said softly.

Iye hid her face and continued to weep. It was her youngest child, a boy of eight years, whose scream stopped both her crying and Anyanwu's more silent grief.

At the boy's cry, everyone looked at him, then upward at the gallery where he was looking. There, Helen was slowly climbing over the railing.

Instantly, Anyanwu moved. Luisa had never seen a human being move that quickly. When Helen jumped, Anyanwu was in position beneath her. Anyanwu caught her in careful, cushioning fashion, so that even though the girl had dived off the railing head first, her head did not strike the ground. Neither her head nor her neck were injured. She was almost as large as Anyanwu, but Anyanwu was clearly not troubled by her size or weight. By the time Luisa realized what was happening, it was over. Anyanwu was calming her weeping daughter.

"Why did she do it?" Luisa asked. "What is happening?"

Anyanwu shook her head, clearly frightened, bewildered.

"It was Joseph," Helen said at last. "He moved my legs again. I thought it was only a dream until..." She looked up at the gallery, then at her mother who still held her. She began to cry again.

"Obiageli," Anyanwu said. "Stay here with Luisa. Stay here. I'm going up to see him."

But the child clung to Anyanwu and screamed when Luisa tried to pry her loose. Anyanwu could have pried her loose easily, but she chose to spend a few moments more comforting her. When Helen was calmer, it was Iye, not Luisa, who took her.

"Keep her with you," Anyanwu said. "Don't let her go into the house. Don't let anyone in."

"What will you do?" Iye asked.

Anyanwu did not answer. Her body had already begun to change. She threw off her cloak and her gown. By the time she was naked, her body was clearly no longer human. She was changing very quickly, becoming a great cat this time instead of the familiar large dog. A great spotted cat.

When the change was complete, she went to the door, and Luisa opened it for her. Luisa started to follow her in. There would be at least one other door that needed opening, after all. But the cat turned and uttered a loud coughing cry. It barred Luisa's path until she turned and went outside again.

"My God," whispered Iye as Luisa returned. "I'm never afraid of her until she does something like that right in front of me."

Luisa ignored her, went to Stephen and straightened his neck and body, then covered him with Anyanwu's discarded cloak.

"What's she going to do?" Iye asked.

"Kill Joseph," Helen said gently.

"Kill?" Iye stared uncomprehending into the small solemn face.

"Yes," the child said. "And she ought to kill Doro too before he brings us somebody worse."

In leopard form, Anyanwu padded down the hall and up the main stairs, then up the narrower stairs to the attic. She was hungry. She had changed a little too quickly, and she knew she would have to eat soon. She would control herself, though; she would eat none of Joseph's disgusting flesh. Better to eat stinking meat crawling with maggots! How could even Doro have brought her human vermin like Joseph?

His door was shut, but Anyanwu opened it with a single blow of her paw. There was a hoarse sound of surprise from inside. Then, as she bounded into the room, something plucked at her forelegs, and she went sliding on chin and chest to jam her face against his washstand. It hurt, but she could ignore the pain. What she could not ignore was the fear. She had hoped to surprise him, catch him before he could use his ability. She had even hoped that he could not stop her while she was in a nonhuman form. Now, she gave her tearing, coughing roar of anger and of fear that she might fail.

For an instant, her legs were free. Perhaps she had frightened him into losing control. It did not matter. She leaped, claws extended, as though to the back of a running deer.

Joseph screamed and threw his arms up to shield his throat. At the same moment, he controlled her legs again. He was inhumanly quick in his desperation. Anyanwu knew that because she was inhumanly quick all the time.

Sensation left her legs, and she almost toppled off him. She seized a hold with her teeth, sinking them into one of his arms, tearing away flesh, meaning to get at the throat.

Feeling returned to her legs, but suddenly she could not breathe. Her throat felt closed, blocked somehow.

Instantly, she located the blockage, opened a place beneath it—a hole in her throat through which to breathe. And she got his throat between her teeth.

Utterly desperate, he jammed his fingers in the newly-made breathing hole.

At another time with other prey, she might have collapsed at the sudden, raw agony. But now the image of her dead son was before her, and her daughter nearly dead in the same way. What if he had merely closed their throats as he had just closed hers? She might never have known for sure. He might have gotten away with it.

She ripped his throat out.

He was dying when she gave way to her own pain. He was too far gone to hurt her any more. He died with soft bubbling noises and much bleeding as she lay across him reviving herself, mending herself. She was hungry. Great God, she was hungry. The smell of blood filled her nostrils as she restored her normal breathing ability, and the smell and the flesh beneath her tormented her.

She got up quickly and loped down the narrow stairs, down the main stairs. There, she hesitated. She wanted food before she changed again. She was sick with hunger now. She would be mad with it if she had to change to order food.

Luisa came into the house, saw her, and stopped. The old woman was not afraid of her. There was none of that teasing fear smell to make her change swiftly before she lost her head.

"Is he dead?" the old woman asked.

Anyanwu lowered her cat head in what she hoped would be taken for a nod.

"Good riddance," Luisa said. "Are you hungry?"

Two more quick nods.

"Go into the dining room. I'll bring food." She went through the house and out toward the kitchen. She was a good, steady, sensible friend. She did more than sewing for her keep. Anyanwu would have kept her if she had done nothing at all. But she was so old. Over seventy. Soon some frailty that Anyanwu could not make a medicine for would take her life and another friend would be gone. People were temporary. So temporary.

Disobeying orders, Iye and Helen came in through the front door and saw Anyanwu, still bloody from her kill, and not yet gone to the dining room. If not for the presence of the child, Anyanwu would have roared her anger and discomfort at Iye. She did not like having her children see her at such a time. She loped away down the hall to the dining room.

Iye stayed where she was, but allowed Helen to follow Anyanwu. Anyanwu, struggling with fear smell, blood smell, hunger, and anger, did not notice the child until they were both in the dining room. There, wearily, Anyanwu lay down on a rug before the cold fireplace. Fearlessly, the child came to sit on the rug beside her.

Anyanwu looked up, knowing that her face was smeared with blood and wishing she had cleaned herself before she came downstairs. Cleaned herself and left her daughter in the care of someone more reliable.

Helen stroked her, fingered her spots, caressed her as though she were a large house cat. Like most children born on the plantation, she had seen Anyanwu change her shape many times. She was as accepting of the leopard now as she had been of the black dog and the white man named Warrick who had to put in an occasional appearance for the sake of the neighbors. Somehow, under the child's hands, Anyanwu began to relax. After a while, she began to purr.

"*Agu*," the little girl said softly. This was one of the few words of Anyanwu's language Helen knew. It meant simply, "leopard." "*Agu*," she repeated. "Be this way for Doro. He wouldn't dare hurt us while you're this way."

Chapter Thirteen

Doro returned a month after Joseph Toler's grisly corpse had been buried in the weed patch that had once been a slaves' graveyard, and Stephen Ifeyinwa Mgbada had been buried in ground that had once been set aside for the master and his family. Joseph would be very lonely in his slave plot. No one else had been buried as a slave since Anyanwu bought the plantation.

Doro arrived knowing through his special senses that both Joseph and Stephen were dead. He arrived with replacements—two boy children no older than Helen. He arrived unannounced and walked through the front door as though he owned the house.

Anyanwu, unaware of his presence, was in the library writing out a list of supplies needed for the plantation. So much was purchased now instead of homemade. Soap, ordinary cloth, candles—even some medicines purchased ready-made could be trusted, though sometimes not for the purposes their makers intended. And of course, new tools were needed. Two mules had died and three others were old and would soon need replacing. Field hands needed shoes, hats. ... It was cheaper to have people working in the fields bringing in large harvests than it was to have them making things that could be bought cheaply elsewhere. That was especially important here, where there were no slaves, where people were paid for their work and supplied with decent housing and good food. It cost more to keep people decently. If Anyanwu had not been a good manager, she would have had to return to the sea much more often for the wearisome task of finding and robbing sunken vessels, then carrying away gold and precious stones—usually within her own body.

She was adding a long column of figures when Doro entered with the two little boys. She turned at the sound of his footsteps and saw a pale, lean, angular man with lank, black hair and two fingers missing from the hand he used to lower himself into the armchair near her desk.

"It's me," he said wearily. "Order us a meal, would you? We haven't had a decent one for some time."

How courteous of him to ask her to give the order, she thought bitterly. Just then, one of her daughters came to the door, stopped, and looked at Doro with alarm. Anyanwu was in her youthful female shape, after all. But Edward Warrick was known to have a handsome, educated black mistress.

"We'll be having supper early," Anyanwu told the girl. "Have Rita get whatever she can ready as quickly as possible."

The girl vanished obediently, playing her role as a maid, not knowing the white stranger was only Doro.

Anyanwu stared at Doro's latest body, wanting to scream at him, order him out of her house. It was because of him that her son was dead. He had let the snake loose among her children. And what had he brought with him this time? Young snakes? God, she longed to be rid of him!

"Did they kill each other?" Doro asked her, and the two little boys looked at him wide-eyed. If they were not young snakes, he would teach them to crawl. Clearly, he did not care what was said before them.

She ignored Doro. "Are you hungry now?" she asked the boys.

One nodded, a little shy. "I am!" the other said quickly.

"Come with me then," she said. "Rita will give you bread and peach preserve." She noticed that they did not look to Doro for permission to leave. They jumped up, followed her, and ran out to the kitchen when she pointed it out to them. Rita would not be pleased. It was enough, surely, to ask her to rush supper. But she would feed the children and perhaps send them to Luisa until Anyanwu called for them. Sighing, Anyanwu went back to Doro.

"You were always one to overprotect children," he commented.

"I only allow them to be children for as long as they will," she said. "They will grow up and learn of sorrow and evil quickly enough."

"Tell me about Stephen and Joseph."

She went to her desk, sat down, and wondered whether she could discuss this calmly with him. She had wept and cursed him so many times. But neither weeping nor cursing would move him.

"Why did you bring me a man without telling me what he could do?" she asked quietly.

"What did he do?"

Anyanwu told him, told him everything, and ended with the same falsely calm question. "Why did you bring me a man without telling me what he could do?"

"Call Margaret," Doro said, ignoring her question. Margaret was the daughter who had married Joseph.

"Why?"

"Because when I brought Joseph here, he couldn't do anything. Not anything. He was just good breeding stock with the potential to father useful children. He must have had a transition in spite of his age, and he must have had it here."

"I would have known. I'm called here whenever anyone is sick. And there were no signs that he was approaching transition."

"Get Margaret. Let's talk to her."

Anyanwu did not want to call the girl. Margaret had suffered more than anyone over the killings, had lost both the beautiful, worthless husband she had loved, and the younger brother she had adored. She had not even a child to console her. Joseph had not managed to make her pregnant. In the month since his and Stephen's death, the girl had become gaunt and solemn. She had always been a lively girl who talked too much and laughed and kept people around her amused. Now, she hardly spoke at all. She was literally sick with grief. Recently, Helen had taken to sleeping with her and following her around during the day, helping her with her work or merely keeping her company. Anyanwu had watched this warily at first, thinking that Margaret might resent Helen as the cause of Joseph's trouble—Margaret was not in the most rational of moods—but this was clearly not the case. "She's getting better," Helen told Anyanwu confidentially. "She was by herself too much before." The little girl possessed an interesting combination of ruthlessness, kindness, and keen perception. Anyanwu hoped desperately Doro would never notice her. But the older girl was painfully vulnerable. And now, Doro meant to tear open wounds that had only just begun to heal.

"Let her alone for a while, Doro. This has hurt her more than it's hurt anyone else."

"Call her, Anyanwu, or I will."

Loathing him, Anyanwu went to find Margaret. The girl did not work in the fields as some of Anyanwu's children did, thus she was nearby. She was in the washhouse sweating and ironing a dress. Helen was with her, sprinkling and rolling other clothing.

"Leave that for a while," Anyanwu told Margaret. "Come in with me."

"What is it?" Margaret asked. She put one iron down to heat and, without thinking, picked up another.

"Doro," Anyanwu said softly.

Margaret froze, holding the heavy iron motionless and upright in the air. Anyanwu took it from her hand and put it down on the bricks of the hearth far from the fire. She moved the other two irons away from where they were heating.

"Don't try to iron anything," she told Helen. "I have enough of a bill for cloth now."

Helen said nothing, only watched as Anyanwu led Margaret away.

Outside the washhouse, Margaret began to tremble. "What does he want with me? Why can't he leave us alone?"

"He will never leave us alone," Anyanwu said flatly.

Margaret blinked, looked at Anyanwu. "What shall I do?"

"Answer his questions—all of them, even if they are personal and offensive. Answer and tell him the truth."

"He scares me."

"Good. There is very much to fear. Answer him and obey him. Leave any criticizing or disagreeing with him to me."

There was silence until just before they reached the house. Then Margaret said, "We're your weakness, aren't we? You could outrun him for a hundred more years if not for us."

"I've never been content without my own around me," Anyanwu said. She met the girl's light brown eyes. "Why do you think I have all these children? I could have husbands and wives and lovers into the next century and never have a child. Why should I have so many except that I want them and love them? If they were burdens too heavy for me, they would not be here. You would not be here."

"But... he uses us to make you obey. I know he does."

"He does. That's his way." She touched the smooth, red-brown skin of the girl's face. "Nneka, none of this should concern you. Go and tell him what he wants to hear, then forget about him. I have endured him before. I will survive."

"You'll survive until the world ends," said the girl solemnly. "You and him." She shook her head.

They went into the house together and to the library where they found Doro sitting at Anyanwu's desk looking through her records.

"For God's sake!" Anyanwu said with disgust.

He looked up. "You're a better businesswoman than I thought with your views against slavery," he said.

To her amazement, the praise reached her. She was not pleased that he had gone snooping through her things, but she was abruptly less annoyed. She went to the desk and stood over him silently until he smiled, got up, and took his armchair again. Margaret took another chair and sat waiting.

"Did you tell her?" Doro asked Anyanwu.

Anyanwu shook her head.

He faced Margaret. "We think Joseph may have undergone transition while he was here. Did he show any signs of it?"

Margaret had been watching Doro's new face, but as he said the word *transition*, she looked away, studied the pattern of the oriental rug.

"Tell me about it," said Doro quietly.

"How could he have?" demanded Anyanwu. "There was no sign!"

"He knew what was happening," Margaret whispered. "I knew too because I saw it happen to... to Stephen. It took much longer with Stephen though. For Joe it came almost all at once. He was feeling bad for a week, maybe a little more, but nobody noticed except me. He made me promise not to tell anyone. Then one night when he'd been here for about a month, he went through the worst of it. I thought he would die, but he begged me not to leave him alone or tell anyone."

"Why?" Anyanwu demanded. "I could have helped you with him. You're not strong. He must have hurt you."

Margaret nodded. "He did. But... he was afraid of you. He thought you would tell Doro."

"It wouldn't have made much sense for her not to," Doro said.

Margaret continued to stare at the rug.

"Finish," Doro ordered.

She wet her lips. "He was afraid. He said you killed his brother when his brother's transition ended."

There was silence. Anyanwu looked from Margaret to Doro. "Did you do it?" she asked frowning.

"Yes. I thought that might be the trouble."

"But his brother! Why, Doro!"

"His brother went mad during transition. He was... like a lesser version of Nweke. In his pain and confusion he killed the man who was helping him. I reached him before he could accidentally kill himself, and I took him. I got five children by his body before I had to give it up."

"Couldn't you have helped him?" Anyanwu asked. "Wouldn't he have come back to his senses if you had given him time?"

"He attacked me, Anyanwu. Salvageable people don't do that."

"But..."

"He was mad. He would have attacked anyone who approached him. He would have wiped out his family if I hadn't been there." Doro leaned back and wet his lips, and Anyanwu remembered what he had done to his own family so long ago. He had told her that terrible story. "I'm not a healer," he said softly. "I save life in the only way I can."

"I had not thought you bothered to save it at all," Anyanwu said bitterly.

He looked at her. "Your son is dead," he said. "I'm sorry. He would have been a fine man. I would never have brought Joseph here if I had known they would be dangerous to each other."

He seemed utterly sincere. She could not recall the last time she had heard him apologize for anything. She stared at him, confused.

"Joe didn't say anything about his brother going crazy," Margaret said.

"Joseph didn't live with his family," Doro said. "He couldn't get along with them, so I found foster parents for him."

"Oh..." Margaret looked away, seeming to understand, to accept. No more than half the children on the plantation lived with their parents.

"Margaret?"

She looked up at him, then quickly looked down again. He was being remarkably gentle with her, but she was still afraid.

"Are you pregnant?" he asked.

"I wish I were," she whispered. She was beginning to cry.

"All right," Doro said, "All right, that's all."

She got up quickly and left the room. When she was gone, Anyanwu said, "Doro, Joseph was too old for a transition! Everything you taught me says he was too old."

"He was twenty-four. I haven't seen anyone change at that age before, but..." He hesitated, changed direction. "You never asked about his ancestry, Anyanwu."

"I never wanted to know."

"You do know. He's your descendant, of course."

She made herself shrug. "You said you would bring my grandchildren."

"He was the grandchild of your grandchildren. Both his parents trace their descent back to you."

"Why do you tell me that now? I don't want to know any more about it. He's dead!"

"He's Isaac's descendant too," Doro continued relentlessly. "People of Isaac's line are sometimes a little late going into transition, though Joseph is about as late as I've seen. The two children I've brought to you are sons of his brother's body."

"No!" Anyanwu stared at him. "Take them away! I want no more of that kind near me!"

"You have them. Teach them and guide them as you do your own children. I told you your descendants would not be easy to care for. You chose to care for them anyway."

She said nothing. He made it sound as though her choice had been free, as though he had not coerced her into choosing.

"If I had found you earlier, I would have brought them to you when' they were even younger," he said. "Since I didn't, you'll have to do what you can with them now. Teach them responsibility, pride, honor. Teach them whatever you taught Stephen. But don't be foolish enough to teach them you believe they'll grow up to be criminals. They'll be powerful men someday and they're liable to fulfill your expectations—either way."

Still she said nothing. What was there for her to say—or do? He would be obeyed, or he would make her life and her children's lives not worth living—if he did not kill them outright.

"You have five to ten years before the boys' transitions," he said. "They will have transitions; I'm as sure as I can be of that. Their ancestry is just right."

"Are they mine, or will you interfere with them?"

"Until their transitions, they're yours."

"And then?"

"I'll breed them, of course."

Of course. "Let them marry and stay here. If they fit here, they'll want to stay. How can they become responsible men if their only future is to be bred?"

Doro laughed aloud, opening his mouth wide to show the empty spaces of several missing teeth. "Do you hear yourself, woman? First you want no part of them, now you don't want to let go of them even when they're grown."

She waited silently until he stopped laughing, then asked: "Do you think I'm willing to throw away any child, Doro? If there is a chance for those boys to grow up better than Joseph, why shouldn't I try to give them that chance? If, when they grow up, they can be men instead of dogs who know nothing except how to climb onto one female after another, why shouldn't I try to help?"

He sobered. "I knew you would help—and not grudgingly. Don't you think I know you by now, Anyanwu?"

Oh, he knew her—knew how to use her. "Will you do it then? Let them marry and stay here if they fit?"

"Yes."

She looked down, examining the rug pattern that had held so much of Margaret's attention. "Will you take them away if they don't fit, can't fit, like Joseph?"

"Yes," he repeated. "Their seed is too valuable to be wasted."

He thought of nothing else. Nothing!

"Shall I stay with you for a while, Anyanwu?"

She stared at him in surprise, and he looked back neutral-faced, waiting for an answer. Was he asking a real question, then? "Will you go if I ask you to?"

"Yes."

Yes. He was saying that so often now, being so gentle and cooperative—for him. He had come courting again.

"Go," she said as gently as she could. "Your presence is disruptive here, Doro. You frighten my people." Now. Let him keep his word.

He shrugged, nodded. "Tomorrow morning," he said.

And the next morning, he was gone.

Perhaps an hour after his departure, Helen and Luisa came hand in hand to Anyanwu to tell her that Margaret had hanged herself from a beam in the washhouse.

For a time after Margaret's death, Anyanwu felt a sickness that she could not dispel. Grief. Two children lost so close together. Somehow, she never got used to losing children—especially young children, children it seemed had been with her for only a few moments. How many had she buried now?

At the funeral, the two little boys Doro had brought saw her crying and came to take her hands and stand with her solemnly. They seemed to be adopting her as mother and Luisa as grandmother. They were fitting in surprisingly well, but Anyanwu found herself wondering how long they would last.

"Go to the sea," Luisa told her when she would not eat, when she became more and more listless. "The sea cleanses you. I have seen it. Go and be a fish for a while."

"I'm all right," Anyanwu said automatically.

Luisa swept that aside with a sound of disgust. "You are not all right! You are acting like the child you appear to be! Get away from here for a while. Give yourself a rest and us a rest from you."

The words startled Anyanwu out of her listlessness. "A rest from me?"

"Those of us who can feel your pain as you feel it need a rest from you."

Anyanwu blinked. Her mind had been elsewhere. Of course the people who took comfort in her desire to protect them and keep them together, people who took pleasure in her pleasure, would also suffer pain when she suffered.

"I'll go," she told Luisa.

The old woman smiled. "It will be good for you."

Anyanwu sent for one of her white daughters to bring her husband and children for a visit. They were not needed or wanted to run the plantation, and they knew it. That was why Anyanwu trusted them to take her place for a while. They could fit in without taking over. They had their own strangenesses. The woman, Leah, was like Denice, her mother, taking impressions from houses and pieces of furniture, from rocks, trees, and human flesh, seeing ghosts of things that had happened in the past. Anyanwu warned her to keep out of the washhouse. The front of the main house where Stephen had died was hard enough on her. She learned quickly where she should not step, what she should not touch if she did not want to see her brother climbing the railing, diving off head-first.

The husband, Kane, was sensitive enough to see occasionally into Leah's thoughts and know that she was not insane—or at least no more insane than he. He was a quadroon whose white father had educated him, cared for him, and unfortunately, died without freeing him—leaving him in the hands of his father's wife. He had run away, escaped just ahead of the slave dealer and left Texas for Louisiana, where he calmly used all his father had taught him to pass as a well-bred young white man. He had said nothing about his background until he began to understand how strange his wife's family was. He still did not fully understand, but he loved Leah. He could be himself with her without alarming her in any way. He was comfortable with her. To keep that comfort, he accepted without understanding. He could come now and then to live on a plantation that would run itself without his supervision and enjoy the company of Anyanwu's strange collection of misfits. He felt right at home.

"What's this about your going to sea?" he asked Anyanwu. He got along well with her as long as she kept her Warrick identity. Otherwise, she made him nervous. He could not accept the idea that his wife's father could become a woman—in fact, had been born a woman. For him, Anyanwu wore the thin, elderly Warrick guise.

"I need to go away from here for a while," she said.

"Where will you go this time?"

"To find the nearest school of dolphins." She smiled at him. The thought of going to sea again had made her able to smile. During her years of hiding, she had not only spent a great deal of time as a large dog or a bird, but she had left home often to swim free as a dolphin. She had done it first to confuse and evade Doro, then to get wealth and buy land, and finally because she enjoyed it. The freedom of the sea eased worry, gave her time to think through confusion, took away boredom. She wondered what Doro did when he was bored. Kill?

"You'll fly to open water won't you?" Kane asked.

"Fly and run. Sometimes it's safer to run."

"Christ!" he muttered. "I thought I'd gotten over envying you."

She was eating as he spoke. Eating what would probably be her last cooked meal for some time. Rice and stew, baked yams, cornbread, strong coffee, wine, and fruit. Her children complained that she ate like a poor woman, but she ignored them. She was content. Now she looked up at Kane through her blue white-man's-eyes.

"If you're not afraid," she said, "when I come back, I'll try to share the experience with you."

He shook his head. "I don't have the control. Stephen used to be able to share things with me... both of us working together, but me alone..." He shrugged.

There was an uncomfortable silence, then Anyanwu pushed back from the table. "I'm leaving now," she said abruptly. She went upstairs to her bedroom where she undressed, opened her door to the upper gallery of the porch, took her bird shape, and flew away.

More than a month passed before she flew back, eagle-shaped but larger than any eagle, refreshed by the sea and the air, and ravenous because in her eagerness to see home again, she had not stopped often enought to hunt.

She circled first to see that there were no visitors—strangers to be startled, and perhaps to shoot her. She had been shot three times this trip. That was enough.

When she had satisfied herself that it was safe, she came down into the grassy open space three quarters enclosed by the house, its dependencies, and her people's cabins. Two little children saw her and ran into the kitchen. Seconds later, they were back, each tugging at one of Rita's hands.

Rita walked over to Anyanwu, looked at her, and said with no doubt at all in her voice, "I suppose you're hungry."

Anyanwu flapped her wings.

Rita laughed. "You make a fine, handsome bird. I wonder how you would look on the dining-room table."

Rita had always had a strange sense of humor. Anyanwu flapped her wings again impatiently, and Rita went back to the kitchen and brought her two rabbits, skinned, cleaned, ready for cooking. Anyanwu held them with her feet and tore into them, glad Rita had not gotten around to cooking them. As she ate, a black man came out of the house, Helen at his side. The man was a stranger. Some local freedman, perhaps, or even a runaway. Anyanwu always did what she could for runaways, either feeding and clothing them and sending them on their way better equipped to survive or, on those rare occasions when one seemed to fit into the house, buying him.

This was a compact, handsome little black man not much bigger than Anyanwu was in her true form. She raised her head and looked at him with interest. If this one had a mind to match his body, she might buy him even if he did not fit. It had been too long since she had had a husband. Occasional lovers ceased to satisfy her after a while.

She went back to tearing at the rabbits unself-consciously, as her daughter and the stranger watched. When she finished, she wiped her beak on the grass, gave the attractive stranger a final glance, and flew heavily around to the upper gallery outside her room. There, comfortably full, she dozed for a while, giving her body a chance to digest the meal. It was good to be able to take her time, do things at a pace her body found comfortable.

Eventually, she became herself, small and black, young and female. Kane would not like it, but that did not matter. The stranger would like it very much.

She put on one of her best dresses and a few pieces of good jewelry, brushed her glossy new crown of hair, and went downstairs.

Supper had just been finished without her. Her people never waited for her when they knew she was in one or another of her animal forms. They knew her leisurely habits. Now, several of her adult children, Kane and Leah, and the black stranger sat eating nuts and raisins, drinking wine, and talking quietly. They made room for her, breaking their conversation for greeting and welcome. One of her sons got her a glass and filled it with her favorite Madeira. She had taken only a single pleasant sip from it when the stranger said, "The sea has done you good. You were right to go."

Her shoulders drooped slightly, though she managed not to change expression. It was only Doro.

He caught her eye and smiled, and she knew he had seen her disappointment, had no doubt planned her disappointment. She contrived to ignore him, looked around the table to see exactly who was present. "Where is Luisa?" she asked. The old woman often took supper with the family, feeding her foster children first, then coming in, as she said, to relearn adult conversation.

But now, at the mention of Luisa's name, everyone fell silent. The son next to her, Julien, who had poured her wine, said softly, "She died, Mama."

Anyanwu turned to look at him, yellow-brown and plain except for his eyes, utterly clear like her own. Years before when a woman he wanted desperately would have nothing to do with him, he had gone to Luisa for comfort. Luisa had told Anyanwu and Anyanwu had been amazed to find that she felt no resentment toward the old woman, no anger at Julien for taking his pain to a stranger. With her sensitivity, Luisa had ceased to be a stranger the day she arrived on the plantation.

"How did she die?" Anyanwu whispered finally.

"In her sleep," Julien said. "She went to bed one night, and the next morning, the children couldn't wake her up."

"That was two weeks ago," Leah said. "We got the priest to come out because we knew she'd want it. We gave her a fine funeral." Leah hesitated. "She... she didn't have any pain. I lay down on her bed to see, and I saw her go out just as easy..."

Anyanwu got up and left the table. She had gone away to find some respite from loved ones who died and died, and others whose rapid aging reminded her that they too were temporary. Leah, only thirty-five, had far too much gray mixed with her straight black hair.

Anyanwu went into the library, closed the door—closed doors were respected in her house—and sat at her desk, head down. Luisa had been seventy... seventy-eight years old. It was time for her to die. How stupid to grieve over an old woman who had lived what, for her kind, was a long life.

Anyanwu sat up and shook her head. She had been watching friends and relatives grow old and die for as long as she could remember. Why was it biting so deeply into her now, hurting her as though it were a new thing? Stephen, Margaret, Luisa... There would be others. There would always be others, suddenly here, then suddenly gone. Only she would remain.

As though to contradict her thought, Doro opened the door and came in.

She glared at him angrily. Everyone else in her house respected her closed doors—but then, Doro respected nothing at all.

"What do you want?" she asked him.

"Nothing." He pulled a chair over to the side of her desk and sat down.

"What, no more children for me to raise?" she said bitterly. "No more unsuitable mates for my children? Nothing?"

"I brought a pregnant woman and her two children, and I brought an account at a New Orleans bank to help pay their way. I didn't come to you to talk about them, though."

Anyanwu turned away from him not caring why he had come. She wished he would leave.

"It goes on, you know," he said. "The dying."

"It doesn't hurt you."

"It does. When my children die—the best of my children."

"What do you do?"

"Endure it. What is there to do but endure it? Someday, we'll have others who won't die."

"Are you still dreaming that dream?"

"What could I do, Anyanwu, if I gave it up?"

She said nothing. She had no answer. "I used to believe in it too," she said. "When you took me from my people, I believed it. For fifty years, I made myself believe it. Perhaps... perhaps sometimes I still believe it."

"You never behaved as though you believed it."

"I did! I let you do all the things you did to me and to others, and I stayed with you until I could see you had decided to kill me."

He drew a deep breath. "That decision was a mistake," he said. "I made it out of habit as though you were just another not entirely controllable, wild-seed woman who had had her quota of children. Centuries-old habit said it was time to dispose of you."

"And what of your habit now?" she asked.

"It's broken now as far as you're concerned." He looked at her, looked past her. "I want you alive for as long as you can live. You cannot know how I have fought with myself over this."

She did not care how he had fought.

"I tried hard to make myself kill you," he said. "It would have been easier than trying to change you."

She shrugged.

He stood up and took her arms to raise her to her feet. She stood passively, knowing that if she let him have his way, they would wind up on the sofa together. He wanted her. He did not care that she had just suffered the loss of a friend, that she wanted to be alone.

"Do you like this body?" he asked. "It's my gift to you."

She wondered who had died so that he could give such a "gift."

"Anyanwu!" He shook her once, gently, and she looked at him. She did not have to look up. "You're still the little forest peasant, trying to climb the ship's railings and swim back to Africa," he said. "You still want what you can't have. The old woman is dead."

Again, she only shrugged.

"They'll all die, except me," he continued. "Because of me, you were not alone on the ship. Because of me, you will never be alone."

He took her to the sofa, finally, undressed her, made love to her. She found that she did not mind particularly. The lovemaking relaxed her, and when it was over, she escaped easily into sleep.

Not much time had passed when he woke her. The sunlight and the long shadows told her it was still evening. She wondered why he had not left her. He had what he wanted, and intentionally or not, he had given her peace. Now if only he would go away.

Anyanwu looked at him seated beside her half dressed, still shirtless. They were not crowded together on the large sofa as they would have been had he been wearing one of his usual large bodies.

Again, she wondered about the original owner of his beautiful, unlikely, new body, but she asked no questions. She did not want to learn that it had been one of her descendants.

He caressed her silently for a moment and she thought he meant to resume the lovemaking. She sighed and decided that it did not matter. So little seemed to matter now.

"I'm going to try something with you," he said. "I've wanted to do it for years. Before you ran away, I assumed I would do it someday. Now... now everything is changed, but I mean to have some of this anyway."

"Some of what?" she asked wearily. "What are you talking about?"

"I can't explain," he said. "But... Look at me, Anyanwu. Look!"

She turned onto her side, faced him.

"I won't hurt you," he said. "Hear and see whatever it is that helps you know I'm being honest with you. I won't hurt you. You'll be in danger only if you disobey me. This body of mine is strong and young and new to me. My control is excellent. Obey me, and you will be safe."

She lay flat again. "Tell me what you want, Doro. What shall I do for you now?"

To her surprise, he smiled and kissed her. "Just lie still and trust me. Believe that I mean you no harm."

She did believe, though at the moment, she barely cared. How ironic that now he was beginning to care, beginning to see her as more than only another of his breeding animals. She nodded and felt his hands grip her.

Abruptly, she was in darkness, falling through darkness toward distant light, falling. She felt herself twisting, writhing, grasping for some support. She screamed in reflexive terror, and could not hear her own voice. Instantly, the darkness around her vanished.

She was on the sofa again, with Doro gasping beside her. There were bloody nail marks on his chest and he was massaging his throat as though it hurt. She was concerned in spite of herself. "Doro, have I hurt your throat?"

He took a deep ragged breath. "Not much. I was ready for you— or I thought I was."

"What did you do? It was like the kind of dream children wake screaming from."

"Alter your hands," he said.

"What?"

"Obey me. Make claws of your hands."

With a shrug, she formed powerful leopard claws.

"Good," Doro said. "I didn't even weaken you. My control is as steady as I thought. Now change back." He fingered his throat lightly. "I wouldn't want you going at me with those."

Again she obeyed. She was behaving like one of his daughters, doing things she did not understand unquestioningly because he commanded it. That thought roused her to question.

"Doro, what are we doing?"

"Do you see," he said, "that the... the thing you felt has not harmed you in any way?"

"But what was it?"

"Wait, Anyanwu. Trust me. I'll explain all I can later, I promise you. For now, relax. I'm going to do it again."

"No!"

"It won't hurt you. It will be as though you were in midair under Isaac's control. He would never have hurt you, I won't either." He had begun stroking and caressing her again, trying to calm her—and succeeding. She had not really been hurt, after all. "Be still," he whispered. "Let me have this, Anyanwu."

"It will... please you somehow—as though we were making love?"

"Even more."

"All right." She wondered what she was saying all right to. It had nothing to do with Isaac's tossing her into the air and catching her with that gentle sure ability of his. This was nightmare stuff—helpless, endless falling. But it was not real. She had not fallen. She was not injured. Finally, Doro wanted something of her that would not hurt anyone. Perhaps if she gave it to him—and survived—she would gain leverage with him, be better able to protect her people from him. Let them live their brief lives in peace.

"Don't fight me this time," he said. "I'm no match for you in physical strength. You know that. Now that you know what to expect, you can be still and let it happen. Trust me."

She lay watching him, quiescent, waiting. "All right," she repeated. He moved closer to her, put his arm around her so that her head was pillowed on it.

"I like contact," he said, explaining nothing. "It's never as good without contact."

She glanced at him, then made herself comfortable with her body and his touching along their length.

"Now," he said softly.

There was the darkness again, the feeling of falling. But after a moment it seemed more like drifting slowly. Only drifting. She was not afraid. She felt warm and at ease and not alone. Yet it seemed that she was alone. There was a light far ahead of her, but nothing else, no one else.

She was drifting toward the light, watching it grow as she moved nearer. It was a distant star at first, faint and flickering. Eventually, it was the morning star, bright, dominating her otherwise empty sky.

Gradually, the light became a sun, filling her sky with brightness that should have blinded her. But she was not blinded, not uncomfortable in any way. She could feel Doro near her though she was no longer aware of his body or even her own body lying on the sofa. This was another kind of awareness, a kind she had no words to describe. It was good, pleasurable. He was with her. If he had not been, she would have been utterly alone. What had he said before the lovemaking, before the relaxed, easy sleep? That because of him, she would never be alone. The words had not comforted her then, but they comforted her now.

The sun's light enveloped her, and there was no darkness anywhere. In a sense now, she was blind. There was nothing to see except blazing light. But still, there was no discomfort. And there was Doro with her, touching her as no one had touched her before. It was as though he touched her spirit, enfolding it within himself, spreading the sensation of his touch through every part of her. She became aware slowly of his hunger for her—literal hunger—but instead of frightening her, it awakened a strange sympathy in her. She felt not only his hunger, but his restraint and his loneliness. The loneliness formed a kinship between them. He had been alone for so long. So impossibly long. Her own loneliness, her own long life seemed insignificant. She was like a child beside him. But child or not, he needed her. He needed her as he had never needed anyone else. She reached out to touch him, hold him, ease his long, long solitude. Or she seemed to reach.

She did not know what he did nor what she actually did but it was startlingly good. It was a blending that went on and on, a joining that it seemed to Anyanwu she controlled. Not until she rested, pleasantly weary, did she begin to realize she was losing herself. It seemed that his restraint had not held. The joining they had enjoyed was not enough for him. He was absorbing her, consuming her, making her part of his own substance. He was the great light, the fire that had englobed her. Now he was killing her, little by little, digesting her little by little.

In spite of all his talk he was betraying her. In spite of all the joy they had just given each other, he could not forego the kill. In spite of the new higher value he had tried to place on her, breeding and killing were still all that had meaning to him.

Well then, so be it. So be it; she was tired.

Chapter Fourteen

With meticulous care, Doro disentangled himself from Anyanwu. It was much easier than he had thought it would be—stopping in the middle of what could have been an intensely satisfying kill. But he had never intended to kill. He had gone further with her, though, than he did with the most powerful of his children. With them, he forced the potentially deadly contact to enable him to understand the limits of their power, understand whether that power could ever in any way threaten him. He did it soon after their transitions so that he found them physically depleted, emotionally weary, and too ignorant of their newly matured abilities to even begin to understand how to fight him—if they could fight him. Very rarely, he found someone who could, and that person died. He wanted allies, not rivals.

But he had not been testing Anyanwu. He knew she could not threaten him, knew he could kill her as long as she was in human form. He had never doubted it. She did not have the kinds of thought-reading and thought-controlling abilities that he considered potentially dangerous. He destroyed anyone who showed the potential, the strength to someday read or control his thoughts. Anyanwu had almost absolute control of every cell of her malleable body, but her mind was as open and defenseless as the mind of any ordinary person—which meant she would eventually have trouble with the people he was bringing her. They would marry into her large "family" and cause dissension. He had warned her of that. Eventually, she would have children and grandchildren here who were more like Joseph and Lale than like the congenial, weakly sensitive people she had collected around her. But that was another matter. He could think about it later. Now, all that was important was that she revive whole and well. Nothing must happen to her. No amount of anger or stupidity on her part or his must induce him to think again of killing her. She was too valuable in too many ways.

She awoke slowly, opening her eyes, looking around to find the library in darkness except for the fire he had made in the fireplace and a single lamp on the table at her head. He lay close beside her, warming himself by her warmth. He wanted her close to him.

"Doro?" she whispered.

He kissed her cheek and relaxed. She was all right. She had been so completely passive in her grief. He had been certain he could do this to her and not harm her. He had been certain that this once she would not resist and make him hurt or kill her.

"I was dying," she said.

"No you weren't."

"I was dying. You were—"

He put his hand over her mouth, then let her move it away when he saw that she would be still. "I had to know you that way at least once," he said. "I had to touch you that way."

"Why?" she asked.

"Because it's the closest I'll ever come to you."

She did not respond to that for a long while. Eventually, though, she moved her head to rest it on his chest. He could not remember when she had done that last on her own. He folded his arms over her, remembering that other more complete enfolding. How had he ever had the control to stop, he wondered.

"Is it that way, that easy for all the others?" she asked.

He hesitated, not wanting to lie to her, not wanting to talk about his kills at all. "Fear makes it worse for them," he said. "And they're always afraid. Also... I have no reason to be gentle with them."

"Do you hurt them? Is there pain?"

"No. I feel what they feel so I know. They don't feel pain any more than you did."

"It was... good," she said with wonder. "Until I thought you would kill me, it was so good."

He could only hold her and press his face into her hair.

"We should go upstairs," she said.

"Soon."

"What shall I do?" she asked. "I have fought you all these years. My reasons for fighting you still exist. What shall I do?"

"What Isaac wanted. What you want. Join with me. What's the good of fighting me? Especially now."

"Now..." She was still, perhaps, savoring their brief contact. He hoped she was. He was. He wondered what she would say if he told her no one had ever before enjoyed such contact with him. No one in nearly four thousand years. His people found contact with him terrifying. Thought readers and controllers who survived such contact quickly learned that they could not read or control him without sacrificing their lives. They learned to pay attention to the vague wariness they felt of him as soon as their transitions ended. Occasionally, he found a man or woman he cared for, enjoyed repeated contact with. These endured what he did since they could not prevent it, though their grim, long-suffering attitudes made him feel like a rapist. But Anyanwu had participated, had enjoyed, had even taken the initiative for a while, greatly intensifying his pleasure. He looked at her with wonder and delight. She looked back solemnly.

"Nothing is solved," she said, "except that now, I must fight myself as well as you."

"You're talking foolishness," he said.

She turned and kissed him. "Let it be foolishness for now," she said. "Let it be foolishness for this moment." She looked down at him in the dim light. "You don't want to go upstairs, do you?"

"No."

"We'll stay here then. My children will whisper about me."

"Do you care?"

"Now you are talking foolishness," she said, laughing. "Do I care! Whose house is this? I do as I please!" She covered them both with the wide skirt of her dress, blew out the lamp, and settled to sleep in his arms.

Anyanwu's children did whisper about her—and about Doro. They were careless—deliberately so, Doro thought—and he heard them. But after a while, they stopped. Perhaps Anyanwu spoke to them. For once, Doro did not care. He knew he was no longer fearsome to them; he was only another of Anyanwu's lovers. How long had it been since he was only someone's lover? He could not remember. He went away now and then to take care of his businesses, put in an appearance at one of his nearer settlements.

"Bring this body back to me as long as you can," Anyanwu would tell him. "There cannot be two as perfect as this."

He would laugh and promise her nothing. Who knew what punishment he might have to inflict, what madman he might have to subdue, what stupid, stubborn politician, businessman, planter, or other fool he might have to remove? Also, wearing a black body in country where blacks were under constant obligation to prove they had rights to even limited freedom was a hindrance. He traveled with one of his older white sons, Frank Winston, whose fine old Virginia family had belonged to Doro since Doro brought it from England 135 years before. The man could be as distinguished and aristocratic or as timid and naive as he chose to be, as Doro ordered him to be. He had no inborn strangeness great enough to qualify him as good breeding stock. He was simply the best actor, the best liar Doro knew. People believed what he told them even when he grew expansive and outrageous, when he said Doro was an African prince mistakenly enslaved, but now freed to return to his home-land and take the word of God back to his heathen people.

Though caught by surprise, Doro played his role with such a con-fusing mixture of arrogance and humility that slaveholders were first caught between bewilderment and anger, then convinced. Doro was like no nigger they had ever seen.

Later, Doro warned Frank to stick to more conventional lies—though he thought the man was probably laughing too hard to hear him.

He felt more at ease than he had for years—even at ease enough to laugh at himself—and his son enjoyed traveling with him. It was worth the inconvenience to keep Anyanwu happy. He knew that a kind of honeymoon phase of their relationship would end when he had to give up the body that pleased her so. She would not turn away from him again, he was certain, but their relationship would change. They would become occasional mates as they had been in Wheatley, but with better feelings. She would welcome him now, in whichever body he wore. She would have her men, and if she chose, her women—husbands, wives, lovers. He could not begrudge her these. There would be years, multiples of years, when he would not see her at all. A woman like her could not be alone. But there would always be room for him when he came back to her, and he would always go back to her. Because of her, he was no longer alone. Because of her, life was suddenly better than it had been for him in centuries, in millennia. It was as though she was the first of the race he was trying to create—except that he had not created her, had not been able to re-create her. In that way, she was only a promise unfulfilled. But someday...

Doro's woman Susan had her child a month after Iye bore Stephen's child. Both were boys, sturdy and healthy, promising to grow into handsome children. Iye accepted her son with love and gratitude that amazed Anyanwu. Anyanwu had delivered the child and all Iye could think of through her pain was that Stephen's child must live and be well. It had not been an easy birth, but the woman clearly did not care. The child was all right.

But Iye could not feed it. She had no milk. Anyanwu produced milk easily and during the day visited Iye's cabin regularly to nurse the child. At night, she kept the child with her.

"I'm glad you could do this," Iye told her. "I think it would be too hard for me to share him with anyone else." Anyanwu's prejudices against the woman were fast dissolving.

As were her prejudices against Doro—though this frightened and disturbed her. She could not look at him now with the loathing she had once felt, yet he continued to do loathsome things. He simply no longer did them to her. As she had predicted, she was at war with herself. But she showed him no signs of that war. For the time he wore the beautiful little body that had been his gift to her, it pleased her to please him. For that short time, she could refuse to think about what he did when he left her. She could treat him as the very special lover he appeared to be.

"What are you going to do now?" Doro asked her when he came home from a short trip to find her nursing the baby. "Push me away?"

They were alone in her upstairs sitting room so she gave him a look of mock annoyance. "Shall I do that? Yes, I think so. Go away."

He smiled, not believing her any more than she wished to be believed. He watched the nursing child.

"You will be father to one like this in seven months more," she said.

"You're pregnant now?"

"Yes. I wanted a child by this body of yours. I was afraid you would be getting rid of it soon."

"I will be," he admitted. "I'll have to. But eventually you'll have two children to nurse. Won't that be hard on you?"

"I can do it. Do you think I can't?"

"No." He smiled again. "If only I had more like you and Iye. That Susan..."

"I've found a home for her child," Anyanwu said. "It won't be fostered with the older ones, but it will have loving parents. And Susan is big and strong. She's a fine field hand."

"I didn't bring her here to be a field hand. I thought living with your people might help her—calm her and make her a little more useful."

"It has." She reached over and took his hand. "Here, if people fit in, I let them do whatever work they prefer. That helps to calm them. Susan prefers field work to anything indoors. She is willing to have as many more children as you want, but caring for them is beyond her. She seems especially sensitive to their thoughts. Their thoughts hurt her somehow. She is a good woman otherwise, Doro."

Doro shook his head as though dismissing Susan from his thoughts. He stared at the nursing child for a few seconds more, then met Anyanwu's eyes. "Give me some of the milk," he said softly.

She drew back in surprise. He had never asked such a thing, and this was certainly not the first child he had seen her nursing. But there were many new things between them now. "I had a man who used to do that," she said.

"Did you mind?"

"No."

He looked at her, waiting.

"Come here," she said softly.

The day after Anyanwu gave him milk, Doro awoke trembling, and he knew the comfortable time in the compact little body he had taken as a gift to her was over. It had not been a particularly power-ful body. It had little of the inborn strangeness he valued. Anyan-wu's child by it might be beautiful, but chances were, it would be very ordinary.

Now the body was used up. If he held onto it for much longer, he would become dangerous to those around him. Some simple excitement or pain that he would hardly notice normally might force transmigration. Someone whose life was important to him might die.

He looked over at Anyanwu, still asleep beside him and sighed. What had she said that night months before? That nothing had really changed. They had finally accepted each other. They would keep each other from loneliness now. But beyond that, she was right. Nothing had changed. She would not want him near her for a while after he had changed. She would still refuse to understand that whether he killed out of need, accident, or choice, he had to kill. There was no way for him to avoid it. An ordinary human might be able to starve himself to death, but Doro could not. Better, then, to make a controlled kill than to just let himself go until he did not know who he would take. How many lifetimes would pass before Anyanwu understood that?

She awoke beside him. "Are you getting up?" she asked.

"Yes. But there is no reason for you to. It's not even dawn."

"Are you going away? You've just come back."

He kissed her. "Perhaps I'll come back again in a few days." To see how she reacted. To be certain that nothing had changed—or perhaps in the hope that they were both wrong, that she had grown a little.

"Stay a little longer," she whispered.

She knew.

"I can't," he said.

She was silent for a moment, then she sighed. "You were asleep when I fed the child," she said. "But there is still milk for you if you want it."

At once, he lowered his head to her breast. Probably, there would not be any more of this either. Not for a long while. Her milk was rich and good and as sweet as this time with her had been. Now, for a while, they would begin the old tug of war again. She stroked his head and he sighed.

Afterward, he went out and took Susan. She was the kind of kill he needed now—very sensitive. As sweet and good to his mind as Anyanwu's milk had been to his former body.

He woke Frank and together they hauled his former body to the old slave graveyard. He did not want one of Anyanwu's people to find it and go running to Anyanwu. She would know what had happened without that. If it were possible, he wanted to make this time easy for her.

By the time he and Frank left, a hoe gang of field hands was trooping out toward the cotton fields.

"Are you going to be wearing that body long?" Frank asked him, looking at Susan's tall, stocky profile.

"No, I've already got what I need from it," Doro said. "It's a good body through. It could last a year, maybe two."

"But it wouldn't do Anyanwu much good."

"It might if it were anyone but Susan. Anyanwu's had wives, after all. But she knew Susan, liked her. Except in emergencies, I don't ask people to overcome feelings like that."

"You and Anyanwu," Frank muttered. "Changing sex, changing color, breeding like—"

"Shut your mouth," Doro said in annoyance, "or I'll tell you a few things you don't want to hear about your own family."

Startled, Frank fell silent. He was sensitive about his ancestry, his old Virginia family. For some foolish reason, it was important to him. Doro caught himself as he was about to destroy completely any illusions the man still had about his blue blood—or for that matter, his pure white skin. But there was no reason for Doro to do such a thing. No reason except that one of the best times he could remember was ending and he was not certain what would come next.

Two weeks later, when he went back to Anyanwu, home to Anyanwu, he was alone. He had sent Frank home to his family and put on the more convenient body of a lean, brown-haired white man. It was a good, strong body, but Doro knew better than to expect Anyanwu to appreciate it.

She said nothing when she saw him. She did not accuse him or curse him—did not seem hostile to him at all. On the other hand, she was hardly welcoming.

"You did take Susan, didn't you?" was all she said. When he said yes, she turned and walked away. He thought that if she had not been pregnant, she would have gone to sea and left him to deal with her not-quite-respectful children. She knew he would not harm them now.

Pregnancy kept her in human form, however. She was carrying a human child. She would almost certainly kill it by taking a nonhuman form. She had told him that during one of her early pregnancies by Isaac, and he had counted it a weakness. He had no doubt that she could abort any pregnancy without help or danger to herself. She could do anything with that body of hers that she wished. But she would not abort. Once a child was inside her, it would be born. During all the years he had known her, she had been as careful with her children before they were born as afterward. Doro decided to stay with her during this period of weakness. Once she accepted his two most recent changes, he did not think he would have trouble with her again.

It took him many long, uncommunicative days to find out how wrong he was. Finally, it was Anyanwu's young daughter Helen who made him understand. The girl sometimes seemed very much younger than her twelve years. She played with other children and fought with them and cried over trivial hurts. At other times, she was a woman wearing the body of a child. And she was very much her mother's daughter.

"She won't talk to me," the child told Doro. "She knows I know what she's going to do." She had come to sit beside him in the cool shade of a giant oak tree. For a time, they had watched in silence as Anyanwu weeded her herb garden. This garden was off limits to other gardeners and to helpful children, both of whom considered a great many of Anyanwu's plants nothing but weeds themselves. Now, though, Doro looked away from the garden and at Helen.

"What do you mean?" he asked her. "What is she going to do?"

She looked up at him, and he had no doubt that a woman looked out of those eyes. "She says Kane and Leah are going to come and live here. She says after the baby comes, she's going away."

"To sea?"

"No, Doro. Not to sea. Someday, she would have to come out of the sea. Then you would find her again, and she would have to watch you kill her friends, kill your own friends."

"What are you talking about?" He caught her by the arms, barely stopped himself from shaking her.

She glared at him, furious, clearly loathing him. Suddenly she lowered her head and bit his hand as hard as she could with her sharp little teeth.

Pain made Doro release her. She could not know how dangerous it was for her to cause him sudden unexpected pain. Had she done it just before he killed Susan, he would have taken her helplessly. But now, having fed recently, he had more control. He held his bloody hand and watched her run away.

Then, slowly, he got up and went over to Anyanwu. She had dug up several purple-stemmed, yellow-rooted weeds. He expected her to throw them away, but instead she cut the plants from their rootstocks, brushed the dirt from the stocks, and put the stocks in her gathering basket.

"What are those things?" he asked.

"A medicine," she said, "or a poison if people don't know what to do with it."

"What are you going to do with it?"

"Powder it, mix it with some other things, steep it in boiling water and give it to children who have worms."

Doro shook his head. "I'd think you could help them more easily by making the medicine within your own body."

"This will work just as well. I'm going to teach some of the women to make it."

"Why?"

"So that they can heal themselves and their families without depending on what they see as my magic."

He reached down and tipped her head up so that she faced him. "And why shouldn't they depend on your magic? Your medicines are more efficient than any ground weed."

She shrugged. "They should learn to help themselves."

He picked up her basket and drew her to her feet. "Come into the house and talk with me."

"There is nothing to say."

"Come in anyway. Humor me." He put his arm around her and walked her back to the house.

He started to take her into the library, but a group of the younger children were being taught to read there. They sat scattered in a half circle on the rug looking up at one of Anyanwu's daughters. As Doro guided Anyanwu away from them, he could hear the voice of one of his sons by Susan reading a verse from the Bible: "Be of the same mind one toward another. Mind not high things, but condescend to men of low estate. Be not wise in your own conceits."

Doro glanced back. "That sounds as though it would be an unpopular scripture in this part of the country," he said.

"I see to it that they learn some of the less popular ones," Anyanwu answered. "There is another: 'Thou shalt not deliver unto his master the servant which is escaped from his master unto thee.' They live in a world that does not want them to hear such things."

"You're raising them as Christians, then?"

She shrugged. "Most of their parents are Christian. They want their children to read so they can read the Bible. Besides"—she glanced at him, the corners of her mouth turned down—"besides, this is a Christian country."

He ignored her sarcasm, took her into the back parlor. "Christians consider it a great sin to take one's own life," he said.

"They consider it a sin to take any life, yet they kill and kill."

"Anyanwu, why have you decided to die?" He would not have thought he could say the words so calmly. What would she think? That he did not care? Could she think that?

"It's the only way I can leave you," she said simply.

He digested that for a moment. "I thought staying with you now would help you get used to ... to the things I have to do," he said.

"Do you think I'm not used to them?"

"You haven't accepted them. Why else should you want to die?"

"Because of what we have already said. Everything is temporary but you and me. You are all I have, perhaps all I would ever have." She shook her head slowly. "And you are an obscenity."

He frowned, staring at her. She had not said such things since their night together in the library. She had never said them this way, matter-of-factly, as though she were saying, "You are tall." He found that he could not even manufacture anger against her.

"Shall I go away?" he asked.

"No. Stay with me. I need you here."

"Even though I'm an obscenity."

"Even so."

She was as she had been after Luisa's death—uncharacteristically passive, ready to die. Then it was loneliness and grief pressing on her, weighing her down then. Now... what was it now, really?

"Is it Susan?" he asked. "I didn't think you had gotten that close to her."

"I hadn't. But you had. She gave you three children."

"But..."

"You did not need her life."

"There was no other way she could be of use to me. She had had enough children, and she could not care for them. What did you expect me to do with her?"

Anyanwu got up and walked out of the room.

Later, he tried to talk to her again. She would not listen. She would not argue with him or curse him. When he offered again to go, she asked him to stay. When he came to her room at night, she was strangely, quietly welcoming. And she was still planning to die. There was an obscenity. An immortal, a woman who could live through the millennia with him, yet she was intent on suicide—and he was not even certain why.

He became more desperate as her pregnancy advanced, because he could not reach her, he could not touch her. She admitted she needed him, said she loved him, but some part of her was closed away from him and nothing he said could reach it.

Finally, he did go away for a few weeks. He did not like what she was doing to him. He could not remember a time when his

thoughts had been so confused, when he had wanted so badly,
so painfully, something he could not have. He had done what
Anyanwu had apparently had done. He had allowed her to touch
him as though he were an ordinary man. He had allowed her to
awaken feelings in him that had been dormant for several times
as long as even she had been alive. He had all but stripped himself
before her. It amazed him that he could do such a thing—or that
she could see him do it, and not care. She, of all people!

He went down to Baton Rouge to a woman he had once known.
She was married now, but, as it happened, her husband was in
Boston and she welcomed Doro. He stayed with her for a few days,
always on the verge of telling her about Anyanwu, but never quite
getting around to it.

He took a new body—that of a free black who owned several
slaves and treated them brutally. Afterward, he wondered why he
had killed the man. It was no concern of his how a slaveholder
treated his chattels.

He shed the slaveholder body and took that of another free
black—one who could have been a lighter-skinned brother to the
one Anyanwu had liked, compact, handsome, red-brown. Perhaps
she would reject it because it was too like the other one without
being the other one. Perhaps she would reject it because it was
too unlike the other one. Who knew which way her mind would
turn. But perhaps she would accept it and talk to him and close
the distance between them before she shut herself off like used
machinery.

He went home to her.

Her belly got in the way when he hugged her in greeting. On any
other occasion, he would have laughed and stroked it, thinking of
his child inside. Now, he only looked at it, realized that she could
give birth any time. How stupid he had been to go away and leave
her, to give up any part of what might be their last days together.

She took his hand and led him into the house while her son
Julien took his horse. Julien gave Doro a long, frightened, pleading
look that Doro did not acknowledge. Clearly, the man knew.

Inside the house, he got the same kinds of looks from Leah and
Kane, whom Anyanwu had sent for. Nobody said anything except
in ordinary greeting, but the house was filled with tension. It was

as though everyone felt it but Anyanwu. She seemed to feel nothing except solemn pleasure in having Doro home again.

Supper was quiet, almost grim, and everyone seemed to have something to do to keep from lingering at the table. Everyone but Doro. He coaxed Anyanwu to share wine and fruit and nuts and talk with him in the smaller, cooler back parlor. As it turned out, they shared wine and fruit and nuts and silence, but it did not matter. It was enough that she was with him.

Anyanwu's child, a tiny, sturdy boy, was born two weeks after Doro's return, and Doro became almost sick with desperation. He did not know how to deal with his feelings, could not recall ever having had such an intense confusion of feelings before. Sometimes he caught himself observing his own behavior as though from a distance and noticing with even greater confusion that there was nothing outwardly visible in him to show what he was suffering. He spent as much time as he could with Anyanwu, watching her prepare and mix her herbs; instruct several of her people at a time in their cultivation, appearance and use; tend those few who could not wait for this or that herb.

"What will they do when they have only the herbs?" he asked her.

"Live or die as best they can," she said. "Everything truly alive dies sooner or later."

She found a woman to nurse her baby and she gave calm instructions to a frightened Leah. She considered Leah the strangest and the brightest of her white daughters and the one most competent to succeed her. Kane did not want this. He felt threatened, even frightened, by the thought of suddenly greater visibility. He would become more noticeable to people of his father's class—people who might have known his father. Doro thought this too unlikely to worry about. He found himself trying to explain to the man that if Kane played his role as well as Doro had always seen him play it, and if also he clearly possessed all the trappings of a wealthy planter, it would never occur to people to assume that he was anything but a wealthy planter. Doro told the story of Frank's passing him off as a Christianized African prince, and he and Kane laughed together over it. There had not been much laughter in the house recently, and even this ended abruptly.

"You have to stop her," Kane said as though they had been discussing Anyanwu all along. "You have to. You're the only one who can."

"I don't know what to do," Doro admitted bleakly. Kane would have no idea how unusual such an admission was from him.

"Talk to her! Does she want something? Give it to her!"

"I think she wants me not to kill," Doro said.

Kane blinked, then shook his head helplessly. Even he understood that it was impossible.

Leah came into the back parlor where they were talking and stood before Doro, hands on her hips. "I can't tell what you feel," she said. "I've never been able to somehow. But if you feel anything at all for her, go to her now!"

"Why?" Doro asked.

"Because she's going to do it. She's just about gotten herself to the brink. I don't think she plans to wake up tomorrow morning—like Luisa."

Doro stood up to go, but Kane stopped him with a question to Leah.

"Honey, what does she want? What does she really want from him?"

Leah looked from one man to another, saw that they were both awaiting her answer. "I asked her that myself," she said. "She just said she was tired. Tired to death."

She had seemed weary, Doro thought. But weary of what? Him? She had begged him not to go away again—not that he had planned to. "Tired of what?" he asked.

Leah held her hands in front of her and looked down at him. She opened and closed the fingers as though to grasp something, but she held only air. She gestured sometimes when receiving or remembering images and impressions no one else could see. In ordinary society, people would certainly have thought her demented.

"That's what I can feel," she said. "If I sit where she's recently sat or even more if I handle something she's worn. It's a reaching and reaching and grasping and then her hands are empty. There's nothing. She's so tired."

"Maybe it's just her age," Kane said. "Maybe it's finally caught up with her."

Leah shook her head. "I don't think so. She's not in any pain, hasn't slowed down at all. She's just..." Leah made a sound of frustration and distress—almost a sob. "I'm no good at this," she said. "Things either come to me clear and sharp without my working and worrying at them or they never come clear. Mother used to be able to take something cloudy and make it clear for herself and for me. I'm just not good enough."

Doro said nothing, stood still, trying to make sense of the strange grasping, the weariness.

"Go to her, damn you!" Leah screamed. And then more softly, "Help her. She's been a healer since she was back in Africa. Now she needs somebody to heal her. Who could do it but you?"

He left them and went looking for Anyanwu. He had not thought in terms of healing her before. Let the tables be turned, then. Let him do what he could to heal the healer.

He found her in her bedroom, gowned for bed and hanging her dress up to air. She had begun wearing dresses exclusively when her pregnancy began to show. She smiled warmly as Doro came in, as though she were glad to see him.

"It's early," he said.

She nodded. "I know, but I'm tired."

"Yes. Leah has just been telling me that you were... tired."

She faced him for a moment, sighed. "Sometimes I long for only ordinary children."

"You were planning... tonight..."

"I still am."

"No!" He stepped to her, caught her by the shoulders as though his holding her could keep life in her.

She thrust him away with strength he had not felt in her since before Isaac's death. He was thrown back against the wall and would have fallen if there had not been a wall to stop him.

"Don't say no to me anymore," she said softly. "I don't want to hear you telling me what to do anymore."

He doused a reflexive flare of anger, stared at her as he rubbed the shoulder that had struck the wall. "What is it?" he whispered. "Tell me what's wrong?"

"I've tried." She climbed onto the bed.

"Then try again!"

She did not get under her blanket, but sat on top of it, watching him. She said nothing, only watched. Finally he drew a deep, shuddering breath and sat down in the chair nearest her bed. He was shaking. His strong, perfectly good new body was shaking as though he had all but worn it out. He had to stop her. He had to.

He looked at her and thought he saw compassion in her eyes—as though in a moment, she could come to him, hold him not only as a lover, but as one of her children to be comforted. He would have permitted her to do this. He would have welcomed it.

She did not move.

"I've told you," she said softly, "that even when I hated you, I believed in what you were trying to do. I believed that we should have people more like ourselves, that we should not be alone. You had much less trouble with me than you could have because I believed that. I learned to turn my head and ignore the things you did to people. But, Doro, I could not ignore everything. You kill your best servants, people who obey you even when it means suffering for them. Killing gives you too much pleasure. Far too much."

"I would have to do it whether it gave me pleasure or not," he said. "You know what I am."

"You are less than you were."

"I..."

"The human part of you is dying, Doro. It is almost dead. Isaac saw that happening, and he told me. That is part of what he said to me on the night he persuaded me to marry him. He said someday you would not feel anything at all that was human, and he said he was glad he would not live to see that day. He said I must live so that I could save the human part of you. But he was wrong. I cannot save it. It's already dead."

"No." He closed his eyes, tried to still his trembling. Finally, he gave up, looked over at her. If he could only make her see. "It isn't dead, Anyanwu. I might have thought it was myself before I found you the second time, but it isn't. It will die, though, if you leave me." He wanted to touch her, but in his present state, he dared not risk being thrown across the room again. She must touch him. "I think my son was right," he said. "Parts of me can die little by little. What will I be when there is nothing left but hunger and feeding?"

"Someone will find a way to rid the world of you," she said tonelessly.

"How? The best people, the ones with the greatest potential power belong to me. I've been collecting them, protecting them, breeding them for nearly four millennia while ordinary people poisoned, tortured, hanged, or burned any that I missed."

"You are not infallible," she said. "For three centuries, you missed me." She sighed, shook her head. "It doesn't matter. I cannot say what will happen, but like Isaac, I'm glad I won't live to see it."

He stood up, furious with her, not knowing whether to curse or to plead. His legs were weak under him and he felt himself on the verge of obscene weeping. Why didn't she help him? She helped everyone else! He longed to get away from her—or kill her. Why should she be allowed to waste all her strength and power in suicide while he stood before her, his face wet with perspiration, his body trembling like a palsied old man.

But he could not leave or kill. It was impossible. "Anyanwu, you must not leave me!" He had control of his voice, at least. He did not have that half-in-and-half-out-of-his-body sound that frightened most people and that would have made Anyanwu think he was trying to frighten her.

Anyanwu pulled back the blanket and sheet and lay down. He knew suddenly that she would die now. Right in front of him, she would lie there and shut herself off.

"Anyanwu!" He was on the bed with her, pulling her up again. "Please," he said, not hearing himself any longer. "Please, Anyanwu. Listen." She was still alive. "Listen to me. There isn't anything I wouldn't give to be able to lie down beside you and die when you die. You can't know how I've longed..." He swallowed. "Sun Woman, please don't leave me." His voice caught and broke. He wept. He choked out great sobs that shook his already shaking body almost beyond bearing. He wept as though for all the past times when no tears would come, when there was no relief. He could not stop. He did not know when she pulled off his boots and pulled the blanket up over him, when she bathed his face in cool water. He did know the comfort of her arms, the warmth of her body next to him. He slept, finally, exhausted, his head on her breast, and at sunrise when he awoke, that breast was still warm, still rising and falling gently with her breathing.

Epilogue

There had to be changes.

Anyanwu could not have all she wanted, and Doro could no longer have all that he had once considered his by right. She stopped him from destroying his breeders after they had served him. She could not stop him from killing altogether, but she could extract a promise from him that there be no more Susans, no more Thomases. If anyone had earned the right to be safe from him, to have his protection, it was these people.

He did not command her any longer. She was no longer one of his breeders, nor even one of his people in the old proprietary way. He could ask her cooperation, her help, but he could no longer coerce her into giving it. There would be no more threats to her children.

He would not interfere with her children at all. There was disagreement here. She wanted him to promise that he would not interfere with any of her descendants, but he would not. "Do you have any idea how many descendants you have and how widely scattered they are?" he asked her. And, of course, she did not, though she thought by now they would no doubt make a fine nation. "I won't make you any promises I can't keep," he said. "And I won't wait to ask some stranger who interests me who his many-times-great-grandmother was."

Thus, uncomfortably, she settled for protecting her children and any grandchildren or even strangers who became members of her household. These were hers to protect, hers to teach, hers to move if she wished. When it became clear within a few years that there would be a war between the Northern and Southern states, she chose to move her people to California. The move displeased him. He thought she was leaving not only to get away from the coming war, but to make it more difficult for him to break his word regarding her children. Crossing the continent, sailing around the Horn, or crossing the Isthmus of Panama to reach her would not be quick or simple matters even for him.

He accused her of not trusting him, and she admitted it freely. "You are still the leopard," she said. "And we are still prey. Why should we tempt you?" Then she eased it all by kissing him and saying, "You will see me when you want to badly enough. You know that. When has distance ever really stopped you?"

It never had. He would see her. He stopped her cross-country plans by putting her and her people on one of his own clippers and returning to her one of the best of her descendants by Isaac to keep her safe from storms.

In California, she finally took a European name: Emma. She had heard that it meant grandmother or ancestress, and this amused her. She became Emma Anyanwu. "It will give people something to call me that they can pronounce," she told him on his first visit.

He laughed. He did not care what she called herself as long as she went on living. And she would do that. No matter where she went, she would live. She would not leave him.

MIND OF MY MIND

For Octavia, M., Harlan and Sid.

Prologue

Doro

Doro's widow in the southern California city of Forsyth had become a prostitute. Doro had left her alone for eighteen months. Too long. For the sake of the daughter she had borne him, he should have visited her more often. Now it was almost too late.

Doro watched her without letting her know that he was in town. He saw the men come and go from her new, wrong-side-of-the-tracks apartment. He saw that most of her time away from home was spent in the local bars.

Sometime during his eighteen-month absence, she had moved from the house he had bought her—an expensive house in a good neighborhood. And though he had made arrangements with a Forsyth bank for her to receive a liberal monthly allowance, she still needed the men. And the liquor. He was not surprised.

By the time he knocked at her door, the main thing he wanted to do was see whether his daughter was all right. When the woman opened the door, he pushed past her into the apartment without speaking.

She was half drunk and slurred her words a little as she called after him. "Hey, wait a minute. Who the hell do you think you—"

"Shut up, Rina."

She hadn't recognized him, of course. He was wearing a body that she had never seen before. But like all his people, she knew him the instant he spoke. She stared at him, round-eyed, silent.

There was a man sitting on her couch drinking directly from a bottle of Santa Fe Port. Doro glanced at him, then spoke to Rina. "Get rid of him."

The man started to protest immediately. Doro ignored him and went on to the bedroom, following his tracking sense to Mary, his daughter. The child was asleep, her breathing softly even. Doro turned on a light and looked at her more closely. She was three years old now, small and thin, not especially healthy-looking. Her nose was running.

Doro touched her forehead lightly but felt no trace of fever. The bedroom contained only a bed and a three-legged chest of drawers. There was a pile of dirty clothes in one corner on the floor. The rest of the floor was bare wood—no carpeting.

Doro took in all this without surprise, without changing his neutral expression. He uncovered the child, saw that she was sleeping nude, saw the bruises and welts on her back and legs. He shook his head and sighed, covered the little girl up carefully, and went back out to the living room. There the man and Rina were cursing at each other. Doro waited in silence until he was sure that Rina was honestly, in fact desperately, trying to get rid of her "guest" but that the man was refusing to budge. Then Doro walked over to the man.

The man was short and slight, not much more than a boy, really. Rina might have been able to throw him out physically, but she had not. Now it was too late. She stumbled back away from him, silent, abruptly terrified as Doro approached.

The man rose unsteadily to face Doro. Doro saw that he had put his bottle down and taken out a large pocket knife. Unlike Rina, he did not slur his words at all when he spoke. "Now, listen, you— Hold it! I said hold it!"

He broke off abruptly, slashing at Doro as Doro advanced on him. Doro made no effort to avoid the knife. It sliced easily through the flesh of his abdomen but he never felt the pain. He abandoned his body the instant the knife touched him.

Surprise and anger were the first emotions Doro tasted in the man's mind. Surprise, anger, then fear. There was always fear. Then yielding. Not all Doro's victims gave in so quickly, but this one was half anesthetized with wine. This one saw Doro as only Doro's victims ever saw him. Then, stunned, he gave up his life almost without a struggle. Doro consumed him, an easy if not especially satisfying meal.

Rina had gasped and begun to raise her hand to her mouth as the man slashed at Doro. When Doro finished his kill, Rina's hand was just touching her lips.

Doro stood uncomfortably disoriented, mildly sick to his stomach, the hand of his newly acquired body still clutching its bloody knife. On the floor lay the body that Doro had been wearing when he came in. It had been strong, healthy, in excellent physical condition. The one he had now was nothing beside it. He glanced at Rina in annoyance. Rina shrank back against the wall.

"What's the matter with you?" he asked. "Do you think you're safer over there?"

"Don't hurt me," she said. "Please."

"Why would you beat a three-year-old like that, Rina?"

"I didn't do it! I swear. It was a guy who brought me home a couple of nights ago. Mary woke up screaming from a nightmare or something, and he—"

"Hell," said Doro in disgust. "Is that supposed to be an excuse?"

Rina began to cry silently, tears streaming down her face. "You don't know," she said in a low voice. "You don't understand what it's like for me having that kid here." She was no longer slurring her words, in spite of her tears. Her fear had sobered her. She wiped her eyes. "I really didn't hit her. You know I wouldn't dare lie to you." She stared at Doro for a moment, then shook her head. "I've wanted to hit her though—so many times. I can hardly even stand to go near her sober anymore...." She looked at the body cooling on the floor and began to tremble.

Doro went to her. She stiffened with terror as he touched her. Then, after a moment, when she realized that he was doing nothing more than putting his arm around her, she let him lead her back to the couch.

She sat with him, beginning to relax, the tension going out of her body. When he spoke to her, his tone was gentle, without threat.

"I'll take Mary if you want me to, Rina. I'll find a home for her."

She said nothing for a long while. He did not hurry her. She looked at him, then closed her eyes, shook her head. Finally she put her head on his shoulder and spoke softly. "I'm sick," she said. "Tell me I'll be well if you take her."

"You'll be as well as you were before Mary was born."

"Then?" She shuddered against him. "No. I was sick then too. Sick and alone. If you take Mary away, you won't come back to me, will you?"

"No. I won't."

"You said, 'I want you to have a baby,' and I said, 'I hate kids, especially babies,' and you said, 'That doesn't matter.' And it didn't."

"Shall I take her, Rina?"

"No. Are you going to get rid of that corpse for me?" She nudged his former body with one foot.

"I'll have someone take care of it."

"I can't do anything," she said. "My hands shake and sometimes I hear voices. I sweat and my head hurts and I want to cry or I want to scream. Nothing helps but taking a drink—or maybe finding a guy."

"You won't drink so much from now on."

There was another long silence. "You always want so damn much. Shall I give up men, too?"

"If I come back and find Mary black and blue again, I'll take her. If anything worse happens to her, I'll kill you."

She looked at him without fear. "You mean I can keep my men if I keep them away from Mary. All right."

Doro sighed, started to speak, then shrugged.

"I can't help it," she said. "Something is wrong with me. I can't help it."

"I know."

"You made me what I am. I ought to hate your guts for what you made me."

"You don't hate me. And you don't have to defend yourself to me. I don't condemn you." He caressed her, wondering idly how she could want life badly enough to fight as hard as she had to fight to keep it. In producing her daughter, she had performed the function she had been born to perform. Doro had demanded that much of her as he had demanded it of others, her ancestors long before her. There had been a time when he disposed of people like her as soon as they had produced the number of offspring he desired. They were inevitably poor parents and their children grew up more comfortably with adoptive parents. Now, though, if such people wanted to live after having served him, he let them. He treated them kindly, as servants who had been faithful. Their gratitude often made them his best servants in spite of their seeming weakness. And the weakness didn't bother him. Rina was right. It was his fault—a result of his breeding program. Rina, in fact, was a minor favorite with him when she was sober.

"I'll be careful," she said. "No one will hurt Mary again. Will you stay with me for a while?"

"Only for a few days. Long enough to help you move out of here."

She looked alarmed. "I don't want to move. I can't stand it out there where I was, by myself."

"I'm not going to send you back to our old house. I'm just going to take you a few blocks over to Dell Street where one of your relatives lives. She has a duplex and you're going to live in one side of it."

"I don't have any relatives left alive around here."

He smiled. "Rina, this part of Forsyth is full of your relatives. Actually, that's why you came back to it. You don't know them, and you wouldn't like most of them if you met them, but you need to be close to them."

"Why?"

"Let's just say, so you won't be by yourself."

She shrugged, neither understanding nor really caring. "If people around here are my relatives, are they your people too?"

"Of course."

"And . . . this woman I'm going to live next door to—what is she to me?"

"Your grandmother several times removed."

Rina's terror returned full force. "You mean she's like you? Immortal?"

"No. Not like me. She doesn't kill—at least not the way I do. She's still wearing the same body she was born into. And she won't hurt you. But she might be able to help with Mary."

"All for Mary. She must be important, poor kid."

"She's very important."

Rina was suddenly the concerned mother, frowning at him worriedly. "She won't just be like me? Sick? Crazy?"

"She'll be like you at first, but she'll grow out of it. It isn't really a disease, you know."

"It is to me. But I'll keep her, and move, like you said, to this grandmother's house. What's the woman's name?"

"Emma. She started to call herself Emma about one hundred fifty years ago as a joke. It means grandmother or ancestress."

"It means she's somebody you can trust to watch me and see that I don't hurt Mary."

"Yes."

"I won't. I'll learn to be her mother at least... a little more. I can do that much—raise a child who'll be important to you."

He kissed her, believing her. If the child had not been such an important part of his breeding program, he would not have put a watch on her at all. After a while he got up and went to call one of his people to come and get his former body out of the apartment.

Emma

Emma was in the kitchen fixing her breakfast when she heard someone at her front door. She hobbled through the dining room toward the door, but before she could reach it, it opened and a slight young man stepped in.

Emma stopped where she was, straightened her usually bent body, and stared a question at the young man. She was not afraid. A couple of boys had broken in to rob her recently and she had given them quite a surprise.

"It's me, Em," said the young man, smiling.

Emma relaxed, smiled herself, but she did not let her body sink back into its stoop. "What are you doing here? You're supposed to be in New York."

"I suddenly realized that it had been too long since I checked on one of my people."

"You don't mean me."

"A relative of yours—a little girl."

Emma raised an eyebrow at him, then drew a deep breath. "Let's sit down, Doro. Ask me the favor you're going to ask me from a comfortable chair."

He actually looked a little sheepish. They sat down in the living room.

"Well?" said Emma.

"I see you have someone living in your other apartment," he said.

"Family," said Emma. "A great-grandson whose wife just died. He works and I keep an eye on the kids when they get home from school."

"How soon can you move him out?"

Emma stared at him expressionlessly. "The question is, will I move him out at all? Why should I?"

"I have a youngster who's going to be too much for her mother in a few years. Right now, though, her mother is too much for her."

"Doro, the kids next door really need my help. Even with guidance, you know they're going to have a hard time."

"But almost anyone could help those children, Em. On the other hand, you're just about the only one I'd trust to help the child I'm talking about."

Emma frowned. "Her mother abuses her?"

"So far, she only lets other people abuse her."

"Sounds as though the child would be better off adopted into another family."

"I don't want to do that if I can avoid it. She's probably going to have a strong need to be among her relatives. And you're the only relative she has that I'd care to trust her with. She's part of an experiment that's important to me, Em."

"Important to you. To you! And what shall I do with my great-grandson and his children?"

"Surely one of your apartment complexes has a vacancy. And you can pay a babysitter for the kids. You're already providing for God knows how many indigent relatives. This should be fairly easy."

"That's not the point."

He leaned back and sat looking at her. "Are you going to turn me down?"

"How old is the child?"

"Three."

"And just what is she going to grow up into?"

"A telepath. One with more control of her ability than any I've produced so far, I hope. And from the body I used to father her, I hope she'll have inherited a few other abilities."

"What other abilities?"

"Em, I can't tell you all of it. If I do, in a few years she'll read it in your mind."

"What difference would that make? Why shouldn't she know what she is?"

"Because she's an experiment. It will be better for her to learn the nature of her abilities slowly, from experience. If she's anything like her predecessors, the more slowly she learns the better it will be for the people around her."

"Who were her predecessors?"

"Failures. Dangerous failures."

Emma sighed. "Dead failures." She wondered what he would say if she refused to help. She didn't like having anything to do with his projects when she could help it. They always involved children, always had to do with his breeding programs. For all but the first few centuries of his four-thousand-year life, he had been struggling to build a race around himself. He existed apparently as a result of a mutation millennia past. His people existed as a result of less wildly divergent mutations and as a result of nearly four thousand years of controlled breeding. He now had several strong mutant strains, which he combined or kept separate, as he wished. And behind him he had an untold number of failures, dangerous or only pathetic, which he had destroyed as casually as other people slaughtered cattle.

"You must tell me *something* about your hopes for the girl," Emma said. "Just what kind of danger are you trying to expose me to?"

He laid a hand on her bony shoulder. "Very little, Em. If you have a hand in raising the girl, she should come out reasonably controllable. In fact, I was thinking of giving you the whole job of raising her."

"No! Absolutely not. I've raised enough children. More than enough."

"That's what I thought you'd say. All right. Just let me move her and her mother in next door, where you can keep an eye on them."

"What are you going to do with her after she's matured?—if she's a success, I mean."

He sighed. "Well, I guess I can tell you that. She's part of my latest attempt to bring my active telepaths together. I'm going to try to mate her with another telepath without killing either of them myself. And I'm hoping that she and the boy I have in mind are stable enough to stay together without killing each other. That will be a beginning."

Emma shook her head as he spoke. How many lives had he thrown away over the years in pursuit of that dream? "Doro, they've never been together. Why don't you leave them alone? Let them stay separate. They avoid each other naturally when you're not pushing them together."

"I want them together. Did you think I had given up?"

"I keep hoping you'll give up for the sake of your people."

"And settle for the string of warring tribes that I've got now? Not that most of them are even that united. Just families of people who don't like their own members much even though they usually need to be near them. Families who can't tolerate members of my other families at all. They all tolerate ordinary people well enough, though. They would have merged back into the general population long ago if I didn't police them."

"Perhaps they should. They would be happier."

"Would you be happier without your gifts, Emma? Would you like to be an ordinary human?"

"Of course not. But how many others are in full control of their abilities, as I am? And how many spend their lives in abject misery because they have 'gifts' that they can't control or even understand?" She sighed. "You can't take credit for me, anyway. I'm almost as much of an accident as you are. My people had been separated from one of your families for hundreds of years before I was born. They had merged with the people they took refuge among, and they still managed to produce me."

And Doro had been trying to duplicate the happy accident of her birth ever since. She had known him for three hundred years now, had borne him thirty-seven children through his various incarnations. None of her children had proved to be especially long-lived. Those who might have been were tortured, unstable people. They committed suicide. The rest lived normal spans and died natural deaths. Emma had seen to that last. She had not been able to keep track of her many grandchildren, but her children she had protected. From the beginning of her relationship with Doro, she had warned him that if he murdered even one of her children, she would bear him no more.

At first Doro had valued her and her new strain too much to punish her for her "arrogance." Later, as he became accustomed to her, to the idea of her immortality, he began to value her as more than just a breeder. She became a companion to him, a wife to whom he always returned. Both he and she married other people from time to time, but such matings were temporary.

For a while, Emma even believed in his race-building dream. But as he allowed her to know more of his methods of fulfilling that dream, her enthusiasm waned. No dream was worth the things he did to people.

It was his casually murderous attitude that finally caused her to tire of him, about two centuries into their relationship. She had turned away from him in disgust when he murdered a young woman who had borne him the three children he had demanded of her. For Emma, it had finally been too much.

But, by then, Doro had been a part of her life for too long, had become too important to her. She could not simply walk away from him, even if he had been willing to let her. She needed him, but she no longer wanted him. And she no longer wanted to be one of his people, supporting his butchery. There was only one escape, and she began preparing herself to take it. She began preparing herself to die.

And Doro, startled, alarmed, began to mend his ways somewhat. He gave her his word that he would no longer kill breeders who became useless to him. Then he asked her to live. He came to her, finally, as one human being to another, and asked her not to leave him. She hadn't left him. He had never commanded her again.

"Will you take the mother and child, Em?"

"Yes. You know I will. Poor things."

"Not so poor if I'm successful."

She made a sound of disgust.

He smiled. "I'll be seeing you more often, too, with the girl living next door."

"Well, that's something." She reached out and took one of Doro's hands between her own, observing the contrast. His was smooth and soft. The hand of a young man who had clearly never done any manual labor. Her hands were claws, hard, skinny, with veins and tendons prominent. She began to fill her hands out, smooth them, straighten the long fingers until the hands were those of a young woman, attractive in themselves but incongruous on the ends of withered, ancient arms.

"I wish the child were a boy instead of a girl," she said. "I'm afraid she isn't going to like me much for a while. At least not until she's old enough to see you clearly."

"I didn't want a boy," he said. "I've had trouble with boys in... in the special role I want her to fill."

"Oh." She wondered how many boy children he had slaughtered as a result of his trouble.

"I wanted a girl, and I wanted her to be one of the youngest of her generation of actives. Both those factors will help keep her in line. She'll be less likely to rebel against my plans for her."

"I think you underestimate young girls," said Emma. She had filled out her arms, rounding them, making them slender rather than skinny. Now she raised a hand to her face. She passed her fingers over her forehead and down her cheek. The flesh became smooth and flawless as she went on speaking. "Although, for this girl's own sake, I hope you're not underestimating her."

Doro watched her with the interest he had always shown when she reshaped herself. "I can't understand why you spend so much of your time as an old woman," he said.

She cleared her throat. "I am an old woman." She spoke now in a quiet, youthful contralto. "And most people are only too glad to leave an ugly old woman alone."

He touched the newly smooth skin of her face, his expression concerned. "You need this project, Em. Even though you don't want it. I've left you alone too long."

"Not really." She smiled. "I've finally written the trilogy of novels that I was planning when we lived together last. History. My story. The critics marveled at my realism. My work is powerful, compelling. I'm a born storyteller."

He laughed. "Hurry and finish reshaping yourself and I'll give you some more material."

PART ONE

Chapter One

Mary

I was in my bedroom reading a novel when somebody came banging on the door really loud, like the police. I thought it was the police until I got up, looked out the window, and saw one of Rina's johns standing there. I wouldn't have bothered to answer, but the fool was kicking at the door like he wanted to break it in. I went to the kitchen and got one of our small cast-iron skillets—the size just big enough to hold two eggs. Then I went to the door. The stupid bastard was drunk.

"Hey," he mumbled. "Where's Rina? Tell Rina I wanna see her."

"Rina's not here, man. Come back around five this evening."

He swayed a little, stared down at me. "I said tell Rina I wanna see her."

"And I said she's not here!" I would have shut the door in his face, but I knew he'd just start kicking it again unless he managed to understand what I was saying.

"Not here?"

"You got it."

"Well." He narrowed his eyes a little and sort of peered at me. "How about you?"

"Not me, man." I started to shut the door. I hate these scenes, really. The idiot shoved me and the door out of his way and came on in. That's what I get for being short and skinny. Ninety-eight pounds. At nineteen, I looked thirteen. Guys got the wrong idea.

"Man, you better get out of here," I warned him. "Come back at five. Rina's the whore, not me."

"Maybe it's time for you to learn." He stared at me. "What's that you got in your hand?"

I didn't say anything else. I had done my bit for nonviolence.

"I said what the hell you got in your—"

He lunged toward me. I side-stepped him and bashed his stupid head in. I left him lying where he fell, got my purse, and went out. Let Rina or Emma see to him.

I didn't know where I was going. I just wanted to get away from the house. I had a headache, and every now and then I would hear voices—a word, a scream, somebody crying. Hear them inside my head. Doro said that meant I was close to my change, my transition. Doro said that was good. I wished I could give him some of the pain and the craziness of it and let him see how good it was. I felt like hell all the time, and he came around grinning.

I walked over to Maple Avenue and there was a bus coming. A Los Angeles bus. On impulse, I got on. Not that there was anything for me in L.A. There wasn't anything for me anywhere except maybe wherever Doro was. If I was lucky, when Rina and Emma found that idiot lying in our living room, they would call Doro. They called him whenever they thought I was about to blow. The way things were now, I was always about to blow.

I got off the bus in downtown L.A. and went to a drugstore. I didn't remember until I was inside that the only money I had was bus fare. So I slipped a bottle of aspirin into my purse and walked out with it. Doro told me a few years ago that he'd beat the hell out of me if I ever got picked up for stealing. I had been stealing since I was seven years old, and I had never been caught. I used to steal presents for Rina back when I was still trying to pretend it meant something that she was my mother. Anyway, now I knew what I was going to do in L.A. I was going "shopping."

I didn't try very hard, but I got a few things. Got a nice little Sony portable radio—one of the tiny ones. I just walked out of a discount store with it while the salesman who had been showing it to me went to stop some kid from pulling down a display of plastic dishes. Got some perfume. I didn't like the way it smelled though, so I threw it away. I took four aspirins and my headache kind of dulled down a little. I got a blouse and a halter and some junky costume jewelry. I threw the jewelry away, too, after I got a better look at it. Trash. And I got a couple of paperbacks. Always some books. If I didn't have anything to read, I'd really go crazy.

On my way back to Forsyth, somebody screamed bloody murder inside my head. Along with that, I felt I was being hit in the face. Sometimes I got things mixed up, I couldn't tell what was really happening to me and what I was picking up accidentally from other people's minds. This time, I was getting onto a bus when it happened, and I just froze. I had enough control to hold myself there, to not scream or fall on the ground from the beating I felt like I was taking. But you don't stop half on and half off a bus at Seventh and Broadway at five in the evening. You could get killed.

I wasn't exactly trampled. I just kept getting shoved out of the way. Somebody shoved me away from the door of the bus. Other people pushed me out of their way. I couldn't react. All I could do was hang on, wait it out.

And then it was over. I was barely able to get on the bus before it pulled away. I had to stand up all the way to Forsyth. I did my best to knock a couple of people down when I got off.

I didn't want to go home. Even if Rina and Emma had called Doro, he couldn't have gotten there yet. I didn't want to hear Rina's mouth. But then I started to wonder about the john—how bad I had hurt him, if maybe he was dead. I decided to go home to see.

There was nothing else to do, anyway. Forsyth is a dead town. Rich people, old people, mostly white people. Even the southwest side, where we lived, wasn't a ghetto—or at least not a racial ghetto. It was full of poor bastards from any race you want to name—all working like hell to get out of there. Except us. Rina had been out, Doro told me, but she had come back. I never have thought my mother was very bright.

We lived in a corner house—Dell Street and Forsyth Avenue— so I walked home on the side of Dell Street opposite our house. I wanted to see if there were any police cars around the corner before I went in. If there had been any, I would have kept going. Doro would have gotten me out of any trouble I got into, I knew. But then he would have half killed me. It wasn't worth it.

Rina and Emma were waiting for me. I wasn't surprised. There was this little drama we had to go through.

Rina: Do you realize you could have killed that man! Do you want us to go to prison!

Emma: Can't you think for once in your life? Why'd you leave him here? Why didn't you at least—at least—come and get me? For God's sake, girl . . .

Rina: What did you hit him for? Will you tell us that?

They hadn't given me a chance to tell them anything.

Rina: He was just a harmless old guy. Hell, he wouldn't have hurt—

Emma: Doro is on his way here now, Mary, and you'd better have a good reason for what you did.

And, finally, I got a word in. "It was either hit him or screw him."

"Oh, Lord," muttered Rina. "Can't you talk decent even when Emma is here?"

"I talk as decent as you taught me, Momma! Besides, what do you want me to say? 'Make love to him?' I wouldn't have loved it. And if he had managed to do it, I would have made sure I killed him."

"You did enough," said Emma. She was calming down.

"What did you do with him, anyway?" I asked.

"Put him in the hospital." She shrugged. "Fractured skull."

"They didn't say anything at the hospital?"

"The way he smelled? I just shriveled myself up a little more and told them my grandson drank too much and fell on his head."

I laughed. She used that little-old-lady act to get sympathy from strangers, or at least to throw them off guard. Most of the time when Doro wasn't around, she was old and frail-looking. It was nothing but an act, though. I saw a guy try to snatch her purse once while she was hobbling down the street. She broke his arm.

"Was that guy really your grandson?" I asked.

"I'm afraid so."

I glanced at Rina with disgust. "You can't find anybody but relatives to screw? God!"

"It's none of your business."

"I wouldn't pretend to be so disgusted with the idea of incest if I were you, Mary." Emma sort of bared her teeth at me. It wasn't a smile. She and I didn't get along most of the time. She thought she knew everything. And she thought Doro was her private property. I got up and went to my room.

Doro arrived the next day.

I remember once when I was about six years old I was sitting on his lap frowning up into his latest face. "Shouldn't I call you 'Daddy'?" I asked. Until then, I had called him Doro, like everybody else did.

"I wouldn't if I were you," he said. And he smiled. "Later, you won't like it."

I didn't understand, and I was a stubborn kid anyway. I called him "Daddy." He didn't seem to mind. But, of course, later, I didn't like it. It still bothered me a little, and Doro and Emma both knew it. I had the feeling they laughed about it together.

Doro was a black man this time. That was a relief, because, the last couple of visits, he'd been white. He just walked into my bedroom early in the morning and sat down on my bed. That woke me up. All I saw was this big stranger sitting on the side of my bed.

"Say something," I said quickly.

"It's me," he said.

I let go of the steak knife I slept with and sat up. "Can I kiss you, or are you going to jump me, too?"

He pulled back my blankets and ran his hand down the side of the bed next to the wall. Of course he found the steak knife. I kept it sheathed in the tight little handle you're supposed to use to pick up the mattress. He threw it out the door. "Leave the knives and frying pans in the kitchen, where they belong," he said.

"That guy was going to rape me, Doro."

"You're going to kill somebody."

"Not unless I have to. If people leave me alone, I'll leave them alone."

He picked up a pair of jeans from the floor, where I had left them, and threw them in my face. "Get dressed," he said. "I want to show you something. I want to make a point in a way that even you might understand."

He got up and went out of the room.

I threw the jeans back on the floor and went to the closet for some clean ones. My head was aching already.

He drove me to the city jail. He parked outside the wall and just sat there.

"What now?" I asked.

"You tell me."

"Doro, why did you bring me here?"

"As I said,.to make a point."

"What point? That if I'm not a good little girl, this is where I'll wind up? God! Let's get away from here." Something was wrong with me. Or something was about to be wrong. Really wrong. I was picking up shadows of crazy emotions.

"Why should we go?" he asked.

"My head...!" I could feel myself losing control. "Doro, please...." I screamed. I tried to hang on. Tried to just shut down, the way I had the day before. Freeze. But I was caught in a nightmare. The kind of nightmare where the walls are coming together on you and you can't get out. The kind where you're locked in some dark, narrow place and you can't get out. The kind where you're at a zoo locked up like the animals, *and you can't get out!*

I had never been afraid of the dark. Not even when I was little. And I'd never been afraid of small, closed places. And the only place I had ever seen a room where the walls formed a vise was in a bad movie. But I screamed my head off outside that jail. I started flailing around, and Doro grabbed me to keep me from jumping out of the car. I almost made him have an accident, as he was trying to drive away.

Finally, when we were a good, long way from the jail, I calmed down. I sat bent over in the seat, holding my head.

"How long do you suppose you could stay even as sane as you are in the midst of a concentration of emotions like that?" he asked.

I didn't say anything.

"Most of the prisoners there aren't half as bothered by their thoughts and fears as you were," he said. "They don't like where they are, but they can live with it. You can't. Wouldn't you rather even be raped than wind up in a place like this even for a short time?"

"You got any aspirin?" I asked. My head was throbbing so that I could hardly hear him. And for some stupid reason, I had left my new bottle of aspirin at home on my night table.

"In the glove compartment," he said. "No water, though."

I fumbled open the glove compartment, found the aspirin, and swallowed four. He was stopped for a red light, watching me.

"You're going to get sick, doing that."

"Thanks to you, I'm already sick."

"You don't listen, girl. I talk to you and you don't listen. For your own good, I have to show you."

"From now on, I'll listen. Just tell me." I sat back and waited for the aspirin to work. Then I realized that he wasn't taking me home.

"Where are we going? You don't have another treat for me, do you?"

"Yes. But not the way you mean."

"What is it? Where are we going?"

"Here."

We were on South Ocean Avenue, in the good part of Forsyth's downtown shopping district. He was driving into the parking lot of Orman's, one of the best stores in town.

He parked, turned off the motor, and sat back. "I want you to step out of character for a while," he said. "Stop working so hard at your role as Rina's bitchy daughter."

I looked at him sidelong. "I usually do when you're around."

"Not enough, maybe. You think we can go into that store and buy—not steal—something other than blue jeans?"

"Like what?"

"Come on." He got out of the car. "Let's go see what you look good in."

I knew what I looked good in. Or at least acceptable in. But why bother when the only guy I was interested in was Doro and nothing I did seemed to reach him? He either had time for me or he didn't. And if he didn't, I could have walked around naked and he wouldn't have noticed.

But because he wanted it, I chose some dresses, some really nice pants, a few other things. I didn't steal anything. My headache sort of faded back to normal and my witchy reflection in the dressing-room mirror relaxed back to just strange-looking. Doro had said once that, except for my eyes and coloring, I look a lot like Emma—like the young version of Emma, I mean. My eyes—traffic-light green, Rina called them—and my skin, a kind of light coffee, were gifts from the white man's body that Doro was wearing when he got Rina pregnant. Some poor guy from a religious colony Doro controlled in Pennsylvania. Doro had people all over.

When he decided that I had bought enough, he paid for it with a check for more money than I had ever seen in my life. He had some kind of by-mail arrangement with the banks. A lot of banks. He ordered everything delivered to the hotel where he was staying. I waited until we were out of the store to ask him why he'd done that.

"I want you to stay with me for a few days," he told me.

I was surprised, but I just looked at him. "Okay."

"You have something to get used to. And for your own sake, I want you to take your time. Do all your yelling and screaming now, while it can't hurt you."

"Oh, Lord. What are you going to give me to yell and scream about?"

"You're getting married."

I looked at him. He'd said those words or others like them to Rina once. To Emma heaven knew how many times. Evidently, my time had come. "You mean to you, don't you?"

"No."

I wasn't afraid until he said that. "Who, then!"

"One of my sons. Not related to you at all, by the way."

"A stranger? Some total stranger and you want me to marry him?"

"You will marry him." He didn't use that tone much with me—or with anyone, I think. It was reserved for when he was telling you to do something he would kill you for not doing. A quiet, chilly tone of voice.

"Doro, why couldn't you be him? Take him and let me marry you."

"Kill him, you mean."

"You kill people all the time."

He shook his head. "I wonder if you're going to grow out of that."

"Out of what?"

"Your total disregard for human life—except for your own, of course."

"Oh, come on! Shit, the devil himself is going to preach me a sermon!"

"Maybe transition will change your thinking."

"If it does, I don't see how I'll be able to stand you."

He smiled. "You don't realize it, but that might really be a problem. You're an experimental model. Your predecessors have had trouble with me."

"Don't talk about me like I was a new car or something." I frowned and looked at him. "What kind of trouble?"

"Never mind. I won't talk about you like you were a new car."

"Wait a minute," I said more seriously. "I mean it, Doro. What kind of trouble?"

He didn't answer.

"Are any of them still alive?"

He still didn't answer.

I took a deep breath, stared out the window. "Okay, so how do I keep from having trouble with you?"

He put an arm around me, and for some reason, instead of flinching away, I moved over close to him. "I'm not threatening you," he said.

"Yes you are. Tell me about this son of yours."

He drove me over to Palo Verde Avenue, where the rich people lived. When he stopped, it was in front of a three-story white stucco mansion. Spanish tile roof, great arched doorway, clusters of palm trees and carefully trimmed shrubs, acres of front lawn, one square block of house and grounds.

"This is his house," said Doro.

"Damn," I muttered. "He owns it? The whole thing?"

"Free and clear."

"Oh, Lord." Something occurred to me suddenly. "Is he white?"

"Yes."

"Oh, Doro. Man, what are you trying to do to me?"

"Get you some help. You're going to need it."

"What the hell can he do for me that you can't? God, he'll take one look at me and... Doro, just the fact that he lives in this part of town tells me that he's the wrong guy. The first time he says something stupid to me, we'll kill each other."

"I wouldn't pick any fights with him if I were you. He's one of my actives."

An active: One of Doro's people who's already gone through transition and turned into whatever kind of monster Doro has bred him to be. Emma was one kind of active. Rina, in spite of her "good" family, was only a latent. She never quite made it to transition, so her ability was undeveloped. She couldn't control it or use it deliberately. All she could do was pass it on to me and put up with the mental garbage it exposed her to now and then. Doro said that was why she was crazy.

"What kind of active is he?" I asked.

"The most ordinary kind. A telepath. My best telepath—at least until you go through."

"You want him to read my mind?"

"He won't have much choice about that. If you and he are in the same house, sooner or later he will, as you'll read his eventually."

"You mean he doesn't have any more control over his ability than I do over mine?"

"He has a great deal more control than you. That's why he'll be able to help you during and after your transition. But none of my telepaths can shield out the rest of the world entirely. Sometimes things that they don't want to sense filter through to them. More often, though, they just get nosy and snoop through other people's thoughts."

"Is it because he's an active that you won't take him? No moralizing this time."

"Yes. He's too rare and too valuable to kill so carelessly. So are you. You and he aren't quite the same kind of creature, but I think you're alike enough to be complementary."

"Does he know about me?"

"Yes."

"And?"

"He feels just about the way you do."

"Great." I slumped back in the seat. "Doro... will you tell me, why marriage? I don't have to marry him for him to give me whatever help I'm supposed to need. Hell, I don't even have to marry him to have a baby by him, if that's what you want."

"That might be what I want once I've seen how you come through transition. All I want now is to get the two of you to realize that you might as well accept each other. I want you tied together in a way you'll both respect in spite of yourselves."

"You mean we'll be less likely to kill each other if we're married."

"Well... he'll be less likely to kill you. The match is going to be pretty uneven for a while. I'd keep low if I were you."

"Isn't there any way at all that I can get out of this?"

"No."

I felt like crying. I couldn't remember when I'd done that last. And the worst of it was, I knew that, as bad as I felt now, it was nothing to what I'd be feeling when I actually met this son. Somehow, I'd never thought of myself as just another of Doro's breeders—just another Goddamn brood mare. Rina was. Emma was for sure. But me, I was special. Sure. Doro had said it himself. An experiment. Apparently an experiment that had failed several times before. And Doro was trying to shore it up now by pairing me with this stranger.

"What's his name?"

"Karl. Karl Larkin."

"Yeah. When do I have to marry him?"

"In a week or two."

I would have put up more of a fight if I had known how to fight Doro. I never much wanted to fight him before. I remember, once when he was staying with Rina, an electronics company out in Carson—one of the businesses that he controlled—was losing money. Doro had the guy who ran the company for him come to our house to talk. Even then I knew that was a hell of a put-down to the guy. Our house was a shack compared to what he was used to. Anyway, Doro wanted to find out whether the guy was stealing, having real trouble, or was just plain incompetent. It turned out the guy was stealing. Big salary, pretty young wife, big house in Beverly Hills, and he was stealing from Doro. Stupid.

The guy was Doro's—born Doro's, just like me. And every dime of his original investment had been Doro's. Still, he cursed and complained and found reasons why, with all the work he'd done, he deserved more money. Then he ran.

Doro had shrugged. He had eaten dinner with us, got up, stretched, and finally gone out after the guy. The next day, he came back wearing the guy's body.

You didn't cheat him. You didn't steal from him or lie to him. You didn't disobey him. He'd find you out, then he'd kill you. How could you fight that? He wasn't telepathic, but I had never seen anyone get a lie past him. And I had never known anyone to escape him. He did have some kind of tracking sense. He locked in on people. Anybody he'd met once, he could find again. He thought about them, and he knew which way to go to get to them. Once he was close to them, they didn't have a chance.

I put my head against his shoulder and closed my eyes. "Let's get out of here."

He took me back to his hotel and bought me lunch. I hadn't had breakfast, so I was hungry. Then we went up to his room and made love. Really. I would call it screwing when I had to do it with his damn fool son. I had been in love with Doro since I was twelve. He had made me wait until I was eighteen. Now he was going to marry me off to somebody else. I probably loved him in self-defense. Hating him was too dangerous.

We had a week together. He decided to take me to Karl when I started passing out with the mental stuff I was picking up. It surprised him the first time it happened. Evidently I was closer to transition than he had thought.

Chapter Two

Doro

Actives were nearly always troublesome, Doro thought as he drove his car down Karl Larkin's long driveway. He already knew that Karl was not in his house, that he was somewhere in the backyard, probably in the pool. Doro let his tracking sense guide him. He had thought it would be safest to visit Karl once more before he placed Mary with him. Both Karl and Mary were too valuable to take chances with. Mary, if she survived transition, could prove invaluable. She would never have to know the whole reason for her existence—the thing Doro hoped to discover through her. It would be enough if she simply matured and paired successfully with Karl. Eventually the two of them could be told part of the truth—that they were a first, that Doro had never before been able to keep a pair of active telepaths together without killing one of them and taking that one's place. This would be explanation enough for them. Because by the time they had been together for a while they would know how hard it was for two actives to be together without losing themselves, merging into each other uncontrollably. They would understand why, always before, actives had been rigidly unwilling to permit such merging—why actives had defended their individuality, why they had killed each other.

Karl was in the pool. Doro could see him across a parklike expanse of grass and trees. Before Doro could reach him, though, the gardener, who had been mowing the lawn, drove up to Doro on his riding mower.

"Sir?" he said tentatively.

"It's me," said Doro.

The gardener smiled. "I thought it must be. Welcome back."

Doro nodded, went over to the pool. Karl owned his servants more thoroughly than even Doro usually owned people. Karl owned their minds. They were just ordinary people who had answered an ad in the Los Angeles *Times*. Karl did no entertaining—was almost a hermit except for the succession of women whom he lured in and kept until they bored him. The servants existed more to look after the house and grounds than to look after Karl himself. Still, he had chosen them less for their professional competence than for the fact that they had few if any living relatives. Few people to be pacified if he accidentally got too rough with them. He would not have hurt them deliberately. He had conditioned them, programmed them carefully to do their work and to obey him in every way. He had programmed them to be content with their jobs. He even paid them well. But his power made him dangerous to ordinary people—especially to those who worked near him every day. In an instant of uncontrolled anger, he could have killed them all.

Karl hauled himself out of the water when he saw Doro approaching. Then he leaned down and offered his hand to a second person, whom Doro had not noticed. Vivian, of course. A small, pretty, brown-haired woman whom Doro had prevented Karl from marrying.

Karl gave him a questioning look. "I was afraid you were bringing my prospective bride."

"Tomorrow," said Doro. He sat down on the dry end of the long, low diving board.

Karl shook his head, sat down on the concrete opposite him. "I never thought you'd do something like this to me."

"You seem to have accepted it."

"You didn't give me much of a choice." He glanced at Vivian, who had come to sit beside him. As he owned the servants, he owned her. Doro had been surprised to find him wanting to marry her. Karl usually had little but contempt for the women he owned.

"Do you intend to keep Vivian here?" Doro asked.

"You bet I do. Or are you going to stop me from doing that, too?"

"No. It will make things more difficult for you, but that's your problem."

"You seem to do all right handling harems."

Doro shrugged. "The girl will react badly to her." He looked at Vivian. "When's the last time you were in a fight?"

Vivian frowned. "A fight? A fistfight?"

"Knock-down, drag-out."

"God! Not since I was in third grade. Does she fight?"

"Fractured a man's skull last week with a frying pan. Of course, the man deserved it. He was trying to rape her. But she's been known to use violence on far less provocation."

Vivian looked at Karl wide-eyed. Karl shook his head. "You know I'm not going to let her get away with anything like that here."

"For a while, you might have to," said Doro.

"Oh, come on. Be reasonable. We have to protect ourselves."

"Sure you do. But not by tampering with her mind. She's too close to transition. I've seen potential actives pushed into transition prematurely that way. They usually die."

"What am I supposed to do with her, then?"

"I hope talking to her will be enough. I've done what I could to make her wary of you. And she's not stupid. But she's every bit as unstable as you were when you were near transition. Also, she comes from the kind of home where violence is pretty ordinary."

Karl stared down at the concrete for a moment. "You should have had her adopted. After all, I'd be in pretty bad shape myself if you had left me with my mother."

"You would never have lived to grow up if I had left you with your mother. Her mother wasn't quite as bad. And her family tends to cluster together more than yours. They need to be near each other more, and some of them get along together a little more peacefully than your family—not that they really like each other any better. They don't."

"What's the girl going to do about needing her family when you bring her here?"

"I'm hoping she'll transfer her need to you."

Karl groaned.

"I'm also hoping that you won't find that such a bad thing after a while. You should try to accept her, for the sake of your own comfort."

"What if talking to her doesn't quiet her down? You never answered that."

Doro shrugged. "Then use her methods. Beat the hell out of her. Don't let her near anything she can hit or cut you with for a while afterward, though."

Mary

I turned twenty just two days before Doro took me to Karl. Later, I decided Vivian must have been my birthday present. Somehow, Doro forgot to tell me about her until the last minute. Slipped his mind.

So I was not only going to marry a total stranger, a white man, a telepath who wouldn't even let me think in private, but I was going to marry a man who intended to keep his girlfriend right there in the same house with me. Son of a bitch!

I threw a fit. I finally did the yelling and screaming Doro had warned me I would do. I couldn't help it, I just went out of control. The whole thing was so Goddamn humiliating! Doro hit me and I bit a piece out of his hand. We sort of stood each other off. He knew that if I hurt him much worse, I would force him out of the body he was wearing—into my body. He'd take me, and all his efforts to get me this far would be wasted. I knew it myself, but I was past caring. I felt like a dog somebody was taking to be bred.

"Now, listen," he began. "This is stupid. You know you're going to—"

We both moved at the same time. He meant to hit me. I meant to dodge and kick him. But he moved a lot faster than I expected. He hit me with his fist—not hard enough to knock me unconscious, but hard enough to stop me from doing anything to him for a while.

He picked me up from where I had fallen, threw me onto the bed, and pinned me there. For a minute, he just glared down at me, his face for once looking like the mask it was. There's usually nothing frightening about the way he looks—nothing to give him away. Now, though, he looked like a corpse some undertaker had done a bad job on. Like whatever he really was had withdrawn way down inside the body and wasn't bothering to animate anything but the eyes. I had to force myself to stare back at him.

"The one thing I can't do," he said softly, "is prevent my people from committing suicide." Whatever there was about his voice that made it recognizable no matter what body it came from was much stronger. I felt the way I had once when I was ten years old and at a public swimming pool. I couldn't swim and some fool pushed me into twelve feet of water. I remember I just held my breath and waited. Somebody had told me to do that once, and, scared as I was, I did it. Sure enough, I floated to the surface, where I could breathe and where I could reach the edge of the pool. Now I lay still beneath Doro's body, waiting.

He reached out to the night table and picked up a switchblade knife. "This came with the body I'm wearing," he said. He rolled off me and lay on his back. He pressed a stud on the knife and about six inches of blade jumped out.

"As I recall, you like knives," he said. He took my hand and closed my fingers around the handle of the knife. "It doesn't really matter where you cut me. Just drive the knife in to the hilt anywhere in this body and the shock will force me to jump."

I threw the knife across the room. Broke the dresser mirror. "You could at least make him get rid of that damn woman!" I said bitterly.

He just lay there.

"Someday there's going to be a way for me to hurt you, Doro. Don't think I won't do it."

He shrugged. He didn't believe it. Neither did I, really. Who the hell could hurt him?

"I loved you. Why are you humiliating me like this?"

"Look," he said, "if he has the woman there to turn to, he's a lot less likely to let you goad him into hurting you."

"I'd be a lot less likely to goad him into anything if you'd get rid of Vivian."

"You underestimate yourself," he said grimly. "Besides, he's in love with Vivian. If I made him get rid of her, I guarantee you he'd take it out on you."

"I just wish I could find a way to take this out on you."

He got up and looked down at me. "Change your clothes," he said. "Then we'll go."

I looked at myself and saw that my pants and blouse were smeared with blood from his hand. I changed my clothes, then packed the rest of my things. Finally, we drove over to Palo Verde Avenue.

While Doro introduced us, Karl and Vivian stood together looking like sister and brother and staring at my eyes. Which gave them at least one thing in common with everybody else who meets me for the first time. There were times when I wished for a nice, bland pair of brown eyes. Like Karl's or Vivian's. Oh, well.

I watched Vivian, saw how pretty she was, how nervous she was. She was no bigger than me, thank God, and she looked scared, which was promising. Doro had told me Karl wouldn't let her really resent me or feel angry or humiliated. *Wouldn't let her!* She was a Goddamn robot and she didn't even know it. Or, rather, she did know it but she wasn't allowed to care.

Karl looked like one of the bright, ambitious, bookish white guys I remembered from high school. Intense, hair already thinning. Doro had said he was twenty-eight, but he looked older. And he sounded... well, he sounded just the way I would have expected a well-brought-up guy to sound when he's trying to be polite to somebody he can't stand. Strained.

After the short, stiff introductions, Doro took Vivian's hand as though this wasn't the first time he had taken it, and said, "Let's let them get acquainted. How about a swim?"

Vivian looked at Karl and Karl nodded. She and Doro went out together. I watched them go, wondering about things that weren't exactly any of my business. I looked at Karl but his face was closed and cold. Then I forgot about Vivian and Doro and wondered what the hell Karl and I were supposed to do now. We were in his tennis-court-sized living room, with its wood paneling and its big white fireplace. We were sitting near the fireplace and we both stared into it instead of at each other.

Then, finally, I decided to get things started. "Do you suppose there's any way we can do this and still have a little pride left?"

Karl looked surprised. I wondered what Doro had been telling him about me. "I was wondering if there was any way for us to manage it at all," he said.

I shrugged. "You know as well as I do that we don't have any choice about that. Do you know what kind of help you're supposed to give me?"

"I'm to shield you from the thoughts and emotions you receive when they get to be too much for you. Doro seems to think they will."

"Did they for you?"

"In a way. I passed out a few times."

"Shit, I'm already doing that. It hasn't killed me yet. Did anybody help you?"

"Not that way. All I had was someone to keep me from banging myself up too badly physically."

"Then, why the hell...? No offense, but why am I supposed to need you?"

"I don't know."

"Oh, well. I guess it doesn't matter. It's his decision and we're stuck with it. All we can do is try to find the least uncomfortable way of living with it."

"We'll work something out." He stood up. "Let me show you around the house."

He showed me his fantastic library first, and that helped me warm to him a little. A guy with a room like that in his house couldn't be all bad. Like the living room, it was huge, with that beautiful wood paneling. The fireplace and the windows were the only spots of wall not covered with books. Most of the floor was covered by the biggest oriental rug I had ever seen. There was a long, solid, heavy wooden reading table, a big desk, a lot of upholstered chairs. The high ceiling was wood carved in a regular octagonal pattern and hung with four small, simple chandeliers. While I was growing up, Forsyth Public Library was my second home. It was someplace I could go and be by myself. I could get away from Rina and her whining and her johns and away from Emma period. I actually liked the little old ladies who worked there, and they sort of adopted me. That was where I got into the habit of reading everything I could get my hands on. And now... well, old-fashioned libraries of wood and stone and books were still like home to me. The city tore down Forsyth Public a few years ago and built a new one of steel and glass and concrete and air-conditioning that was always turned too high. A cold box. I went to it two or three times, then gave up. But Karl's library was perfect. I had walked away from him to look at some of the book titles.

"You like books?"

I jumped. I hadn't heard him come up beside me. "I love them. I hope you don't care if I spend a lot of time in here."

Karl made a straight line of his mouth and glanced over at his desk. His desk, right. His work area.

"Okay, so I won't spend a lot of time in here. Show me my room, will you?"

"You can use the library whenever I'm not working in here," he said.

"Thanks." I could see there was going to be a certain coldness about this library, too.

He showed me the rest of the first floor before he took me up to what was going to be my bedroom. Large, businesslike kitchen. Large, businesslike cook. She was friendly, though, and she was a black woman. That helped. Formal dining room. Small, handsome study—why the hell couldn't Karl work there? Game room with billiard table. Large service porch. As big as the house was, though, it was smaller than it looked from the outside. I thought it might turn out to be a more comfortable home than I had expected.

Karl and I stood on the porch and looked out at his park of a backyard. Tennis court. Swimming pool and bath house. We could see Doro and Vivian splashing around in the pool. Grass. Trees. There was a multicar garage off to one side, and I got a glimpse of a cottage almost hidden by trees.

"The gardener and his wife live out there," Karl told me. "His wife is the maid. The cook helps with the housework, too, when she isn't busy in the kitchen. She lives upstairs, in the servants' quarters."

"Did you inherit all this or something?" I asked. I wouldn't have been surprised if he'd said, "None of your business."

"I had one of my people sign it over to me," he said. "He was going to put it up for sale anyway and he didn't need the money."

I looked at him. The expression on his thin, angular face hadn't changed at all. I hooted with laughter. I couldn't help it. "You stole it! Oh, God. Beautiful; you're human, after all. And here I have to make do with shoplifting."

He gave me a forced smile. "I'll show you where your room is now."

"Okay. Can I ask you another question?"

He shrugged.

"How do you feel about black people?"

He looked at me, one eyebrow raised. "You've seen my cook."

"Right. So how do you feel about black people?"

"I've known exactly two of them well before now. They were all right." Emphasis on the "they."

I frowned, looked at him. "What's that supposed to mean?"

"That you shouldn't get the idea that I dislike you because you're black."

"Oh."

"I wouldn't want you here no matter what color you were."

I sighed. "You're going to make this even harder than it has to be, aren't you?"

"You asked."

"Well... I'm no happier to be here than you are to have me, but we're either going to have to get used to each other or we're going to have to keep out of each other's way a lot. Which won't be easy even in a house as big as this."

"Why did you and Doro fight?"

"What?" My first thought was that he was reading my mind. Then I realized that even if he hadn't seen Doro's hand, I had a big bruise on my jaw.

"You know damn well why we fought."

"Tell me. I answered your questions."

"Why does a telepath bother to ask questions?"

"Out of courtesy. Shall I stop?"

"No! We fought... because Doro didn't tell me about Vivian until about two hours ago."

There was a long pause. Then, "I see. How did you feel about marrying me before you found out about Vivian?"

"My grandmother married Doro," I said. "And, of course, my mother married him. I've expected to marry him myself ever since I was old enough to know what was going on. I wanted to. I loved him."

"Past tense?"

I almost didn't answer. I realized that I was ashamed. "No."

"Not even after he decides to marry you off to a stranger?"

"I've loved him for years. I guess it takes me a while to turn my emotions around."

"You probably never will. I've met several of his people since my transition. He uses me to keep them in line without killing them. And he's done terrible things to some of them. But I've never met one who hates him. Those who don't kill themselves by attacking him as soon as he acts against them always seem to forgive him."

Somehow that didn't surprise me. "Do you hate him?"

"No."

"In spite of... everything?" I remembered Vivian going out hand in hand with Doro.

"In spite of everything," he said quietly.

"Can you read his mind?"

"No."

"But why not? He says he's not a telepath. How could he stop you?"

"You'll find out after your transition. This will be your room." We were on the second floor. He opened the door he had stopped in front of.

The bedroom was white, and I guess you could call it elegant. There was a small crystal chandelier. There was a huge bed and a large dresser with a beautiful mirror. I'd have to be careful how I threw things. There was a closet that was going to look empty even after I hung up the new clothes Doro had bought me. There were chairs, little tables....

It was just a really nice room. I peered into the mirror at my bruise. Then I sat down in a chair by the window and looked out at the front lawn as I spoke to Karl. "What do I do after my transition?"

"Do?"

"Well, I'll be able to read minds. I'll be able to steal better without getting caught—if I still want to. I'll be able to snoop through other people's secrets, even make robots of people. But...."

"But?"

"What am I supposed to do—except maybe have babies?" I turned to face him and saw by his expression that he wished I hadn't said that last. I didn't care.

"I'm sure Doro will find some work for you," he said. "He probably already has something in mind."

Just at that moment, someone was hit by a car. I sensed enough to know that it was nearby, within a few blocks of Karl's house. I felt the impact. I might have said something. Then I felt the pain. A slow-motion avalanche of pain. I know I screamed then. That hit me harder than anything I'd ever received. Finally the pain got to be too much for the accident victim. He passed out. I almost passed out with him. I found myself curled into a tight knot on the chair, my feet up and my head down and throbbing.

I looked up to see whether Karl was still there, and found him watching me. He looked interested but not concerned, not inclined to give me any of the help he was supposed to give. I had a feeling that, if I survived transition, I would do it on my own.

"There's aspirin in the bathroom," he said, nodding toward a closed door. Then he turned and left.

Five days later, we were married at city hall. For those five days, I might as well have been alone in that big house. Doro left the day he brought me, and didn't come back. I saw Karl and Vivian at meals or ran into them accidentally around the house. They were always polite. I wasn't.

I tried talking to the servants, but they were silent, contented slaves. They worked, or they sat in their quarters watching television and waiting for the master's voice.

I joined Karl and Vivian out by the pool one day and what looked like a really interesting conversation came to a dead halt.

The only times I ever felt comfortable was when I was in my room with the door shut, or in the library when Karl wasn't home. He spent a lot of time in Los Angeles keeping an eye on the businesses he controlled for Doro and the ones he had taken over for his own, personal profit. Evidently he did more for them than just steal part of their profits. For me, he did nothing at all.

Doro showed up to see us married. Not that there was any kind of ceremony beyond the bare essentials. He went home with us—or with Vivian and me. Karl dropped the three of us off, then headed for L.A. Doro challenged Vivian to a game of tennis. I walked three blocks to a bus stop, caught a bus, and rode.

I knew where I was going. I had to transfer to get there, so there was no way for me to pretend to myself that I wound up there by accident. I got off at Maple and Dell and walked straight to Rina's house.

Rina was home, but she had company. I could hear her and her company yelling at each other way out on the sidewalk. I walked around the corner and knocked on Emma's door. She opened it, looked at me, stood back from the door. I went in and sat down in the big overstuffed chair near the door. I closed my eyes for a while and the ugly old house seemed to go around me like a blanket, shutting out the cold. I took a deep breath, felt relief, release.

Emma laid a hand on my forehead and I looked up at her. She was young. That meant she had had Doro with her recently. I didn't look anything like her when she was young. Doro was crazy. I wished I did look that good.

"You were supposed to get married," she said.

"I did. Today."

She frowned. "Where's your husband?"

"I don't know. Or care."

She sort of half smiled in her know-it-all way that I had always resented before. Now I didn't care. She could throw all the sarcasm she wanted to at me if she just let me sit there for a while.

"Stay here for a while," she said.

I looked at her, surprised.

"Stay until someone comes to get you."

"They might not even know I've gone anywhere. I didn't say anything. I just left."

"Honey, you're talking about Doro and an active telepath. They know, believe me."

"I guess so. I came here on the bus, though. I don't mind going back that way." I never liked depending on other people and their cars, anyway. When I rode the bus, I went when I wanted, where I wanted.

"Stay put. Doro might not have heard you yet."

"What?"

"You've said something by coming here. Now the way to make sure that Doro's heard you is to inconvenience him a little. Just stay where you are. Are you hungry?"

"Yeah."

She brought me cold chicken, potato salad, and a Coke. Brought it to me like I was a guest. She'd never brought me anything she could send me after before in her life.

"Emma."

She had gone back to whatever she was doing at her desk in the dining room. The desk was half covered with official-looking papers. She looked around.

"Thanks," I said quietly.

She just nodded.

Karl came after me that night. I answered the door, saw him, and turned to say good-bye to Emma, but she was right there looking at Karl.

"You're too high, Karl," she said quietly. "You've forgotten where you came from."

He looked at her, then looked away. His expression didn't change, but his voice, when he spoke, was softer than normal. "That isn't it."

"It doesn't really matter. If you've got a problem, you know who to complain to about it—or who to take it out on."

He drew a deep breath, met her eyes again, smiled his thin smile. "I hear, Em."

I didn't say anything to him until we were in the car together. Then, "Is she one of the two?"

He gave me a kind of puzzled glance, then seemed to remember. He nodded.

"Where do you know her from?"

"She took care of me once when I was between foster homes. That was before Doro found a permanent home for me. She took care of me again when I was approaching transition. My adoptive parents couldn't handle me." He smiled again.

"What happened to your real parents—real mother, I mean?"

"She . . . died."

I turned to look at him. His expression had gone grim. "By herself," I asked, "or with help?"

"It's an ugly story."

I shrugged. "Okay." I looked out the window.

"But, then, you're no stranger to ugly stories." He paused. "She was an alcoholic, my mother. And she wasn't exactly normal—sane—during those rare times when she was sober. Doro says she was too sensitive. Anyway, when I was about three, I did something that made her mad. I don't remember what. But I remember very clearly what happened afterward. For punishment, she held my hand over the flame of our gas range. She held it there until it was completely charred. But I was lucky. Doro came to see her later that same day. I wasn't even aware of when he killed her. I remember, I wasn't aware of anything but alternating pain and exhaustion between the time she burned me and the time Doro's healer arrived. You might know the healer. She's one of Emma's granddaughters. Over a period of weeks, she regenerated the stump that I had left into a new hand. Even now, ten years after my transition, I don't understand how she did it. She does for other people the things Emma can only do for herself. When she had finished, Doro placed me with saner people."

I whistled. "So that's what Emma meant."

"Yes."

I moved uncomfortably in the seat. "As for the rest of what she said, Karl...."

"She was right."

"I don't want anything from you."

He shrugged.

He didn't say much more to me that night. Doro was still at the house, paying a lot of attention to Vivian. I had dinner with them all, then went to bed. I could put up with them until my transition, surely. Then maybe for a change I'd be one of the owners instead of one of the owned.

I was almost asleep when Karl came up to my room. Neither of us put a light on but there was light enough from one of the windows for me to see him. He took off his robe, threw it into a chair and climbed into bed with me.

I didn't say anything. I had plenty to say and all of it was pretty caustic. I didn't doubt that I could have gotten rid of him if I had wanted to. But I didn't bother. I didn't want him but I was stuck with him. Why play games?

He was all right, though. Gentle and, thank God, silent. I didn't know whether he had come to me out of charity, or curiosity, and I didn't want to know. I knew he still resented me—at least resented me. Maybe that was why, when we were finished, he got up and went to get his robe. He was going back to his own room.

"Karl."

I could see him turn to look in my direction.

"Stay the night."

"You want me to?" I didn't blame him for sounding surprised. I was surprised.

"Yes. Come on back." I didn't want to be alone. I couldn't have put into words how much I suddenly didn't want to be alone, couldn't stand to be alone, how much it scared me. I found myself remembering how Rina would pace the floor at night sometimes. I would see her crying and pacing and holding her head. After a while, she would go out and come back with some bum who usually looked a little like her—like us. She'd keep him with her the rest of the night even if he didn't have a dime in his pocket, even if he was too drunk to do anything. And sometimes even if he knocked her around and called her names that trash like him didn't have the right to call anybody. I used to wonder how Rina could live with herself. Now, apparently, I was going to find out.

Karl came back to my bed without another word. I didn't know what he was thinking, but he could have really hurt me with just a few words. He didn't. I tried to thank him for that.

Chapter Three

Karl

The warehouse was enormous. Whitten Coleman Service Building, serving thirty-three department stores over three states. Doro had begun the chain seventy years before, when he bought a store for a small, stable family of his people. The job of the family was simply to grow and prosper and eventually become one of Doro's sources of money. Descendants of the original family still held a controlling interest in the company. They were obedient and self-sufficient, and, for the most part, Doro let them alone. Through the years, their calls to him for help had become fewer. As they grew in size and experience, they became more able to handle their own problems. Doro still visited them from time to time, though. Sometimes he asked favors of them. Sometimes they asked favors of him. This was one of the latter times. Karl, Doro, the warehouse manager, and the chief of security walked through the warehouse toward the loading docks. Karl had never been inside the warehouse before, but now he led the way through the maze of dusty stock areas and busy marking rooms. In turn, he was led by the thoughts of several workers who were efficiently preparing to steal several thousand dollars' worth of Whitten Coleman merchandise. They had gotten away with several earlier thefts in spite of the security people who watched them, and the cameras trained on them.

Quietly, Karl pointed out the thieves—including two security men—and explained their methods to the security chief. And he told the chief where the group had hidden what they had left of the merchandise they had already stolen. He had almost finished when he realized that something was wrong with Mary.

He maintained a mental link with the girl now that he was married to her. And now that Doro had made clear what would happen to him if Mary died in transition.

Karl broke off what he was saying to the security chief. Suddenly he was caught up in the experience Mary was having. She was running, screaming. . . .

No. No, it wasn't Mary who was running. It was another woman—the woman Mary was receiving from. The two were one. One woman running down stark white corridors. A woman fleeing from men who were also dressed in white. She gibbered and babbled and wept. Suddenly she realized that her own body was covered with slimy yellow worms. She tore at the worms frantically to get them off. They changed their coloring from yellow to yellow streaked with red. They began to burrow into her flesh. The woman fell to the floor tearing at herself, vomiting, urinating.

She hardly felt the restraining hands of her pursuers, or the prick of the needle. She did not have even enough awareness of the world outside her own mind to be grateful for the eventual oblivion.

Karl snapped back to the reality of the warehouse with a jolt. He found himself holding on to the steel support of some overhead shelving. His hands hurt from grasping it so tightly. He shook his head, saw Doro and the two warehousemen staring at him. The warehousemen looked concerned. Doro looked expectant. Karl spoke to Doro. "I've got to get home. Now."

Doro nodded. "I'll drive you. Come on."

Karl followed him out of the building, then blindly, mechanically got in on the driver's side. Doro spoke to him sharply. Karl jumped, frowned, moved over. Doro was right. Karl was in no shape to drive. Karl was in no shape to do anything. It was as though he were plunging into his own transition again.

"You're too close to her," said Doro. "Pull back a little. See if you can sense what's happening to her without being caught up in it."

Pull back. How? How had he gotten so close, anyway? He had never been caught up in Mary's pretransition experiences.

"You know what to expect," Doro told him. "At this point she's going to be reaching for the worst possible stuff. That's what's familiar to her. That's what's going to attract her attention. She'll get an avalanche of it—violence, pain, fear, whatever. I don't want you caught up in it unless she obviously needs help."

Karl said nothing. He was already trying to separate himself from Mary. The mental link he had established with her had grown into something more than he had intended it to be. If two minds could be tangled together, his and Mary's were.

Then he realized that she had become aware of him, was watching him as he tried to untangle himself. He had never permitted her to be aware of his mental probing before. He stopped what he was doing now, concerned that he had frightened her. She would have enough fear to contend with within the next twelve hours without his adding to it.

But she was not afraid. She was glad to have him with her. She was relieved to discover that she was not facing the worst hours of her life alone.

Karl relaxed for a few minutes, less eager to leave her now. He could still remember how glad he had been to have Emma with him during his transition. Emma couldn't help mentally, but she was a human presence with him, drawing him back to sanity, reality. He could do at least that much for Mary.

"How is she?" Doro asked.

"All right. She understands what's happening."

"Something is liable to snatch her away again any minute."

"I know."

"When it happens, let it happen. Watch, but stay out of it. If you see a way to help her, don't."

"I thought that's what I was for. To help."

"You are, later, when she can't help herself. When she's ready to give up."

Karl glanced at Doro while keeping most of his attention on Mary. "Do you lose a lot of her kind?"

Doro smiled grimly. "She doesn't have a 'kind.' She's unique. So are you, though you aren't as unusual as I hope she'll be. I've been working toward both of you for a good many generations. But yes." The smile vanished. "Several of her unsuccessful predecessors have died in transition."

Karl nodded. "And I'll bet most of them took somebody with them. Somebody who was trying to help them."

Doro said nothing.

"I thought so," said Karl. "And I already know from Mary's thoughts that you killed the ones who managed to survive transition."

"If you know, why bring it up?"

Karl sighed. "I guess because it still surprises me that you can do things like that. Or maybe I'm just wondering whether she or I will still be alive this time tomorrow—even if we both survive her transition."

"Bring her through for me, Karl, and you'll be all right."

"And her?"

"She's a dangerous kind of experiment. Believe me, if she turns out to be another failure, you'll want her dead more than I will."

"I wish I knew what the hell you were doing. Aside from playing God, I mean."

"You know enough."

"I don't know anything."

"You know what I want of you. That's enough."

It never did any good to argue with Doro. Karl leaned back and finished disentangling himself from Mary. He would be with her in person soon. And even without Doro's warning he would not have wanted to go through much more of her transition with her.

Before he broke the connection, he let her know that he was on his way to her, that she wouldn't be alone long. It had been two weeks since their marriage, two weeks since she had called him back to her bed, he hadn't gone out of his way to hurt her since then.

He watched Doro maneuver the car into the right lane so that they could get on the Forsyth Freeway. Doro cut across the lanes, wove through the light traffic carelessly, speeding as usual. He had no more regard for traffic laws than he did for any other laws. Karl wondered how many accidents Doro had caused or been involved in. Not that it mattered to Doro. Had human life ever mattered to Doro beyond his interest in human husbandry? Could a creature who had to look upon ordinary people literally as food and shelter ever understand how strongly those people valued life? But yes, of course he could. He understood it well enough to use it to keep his people in line. He probably even understood it well enough to know how Karl and Mary both felt now. It just didn't make any difference. He didn't care.

Fifteen minutes later, Doro pulled into Karl's driveway. Karl was out of the car and heading for the house before Doro brought the car to a full stop. Karl knew that Mary was in the midst of another experience. He had felt it begin. He had kept her under carefully distant observation even after he had severed the link between them. Now, though, even without a deliberately established link, he was having trouble preventing himself from merging into her experience. Mary was trapped in the mind of a man who had to eventually burn to death. The man was trapped inside a burning house. Mary was experiencing his every sensation.

Karl went up the back stairs two at a time and ran through the servants' quarters toward the front of the house. He knew Mary was in her room, lying down, knew that, for some reason, Vivian was with her.

He walked into the room and looked first at Mary, who lay in the middle of her bed, her body rolled into a tight, fetal knot. She made small noises in her throat like choked screams or moans, but she did not move. Karl sat down on the bed next to her and looked at Vivian.

"Is she going to be all right?" Vivian asked.

"I think so."

"Are *you* going to be all right?"

"If she is, I will be."

She got up, came to rest one hand on his shoulder. "You mean, if she comes through all right, Doro won't kill you."

He looked at her, surprised. One of the things he liked about her was that she could still surprise him. He left her enough mental privacy for that. He had read his previous women more than he read her and they had quickly become boring. He had hardly read Vivian at all until she had asked him to condition her and let her stay with him, help her stay, in spite of Mary. He had not wanted to do it, but he had not wanted to lose her, either. The conditioning he had imposed on her kept her from feeling jealousy or hatred toward Mary. But it did not prevent her from seeing things clearly and drawing her own conclusions.

"Don't worry," he told her. "Both Mary and I are going to make it all right."

She looked at Mary, who still lay knotted in the agony of her experience. "Is there anything I can do to help?"

"Nothing."

"Can I ... can I stay. I'll keep out of the way. I just—"

"Vee, no."

"I just want to see what she has to go through. I want to see that the price she has to pay to ... to be like you is too high."

"You can't stay. You know you can't."

She closed her eyes for a moment, dropped her hand to her side. "Then, let me go. Let me leave you."

He stared at her, surprised, stricken. "You know you're free to go if that's really what you want. But I'm asking you not to."

"I'll become an outsider if I don't leave you now." She shrugged hopelessly. "I'll be alone. You and Mary will be alike, and I'll be alone." There was no anger or resentment in her, he could see. Her conditioning was holding well enough. But she had been much more aware of Mary's loneliness than Karl had realized. And when Karl began occasionally sleeping with Mary, Vivian had begun to see Mary's life as a preview of her own. "You won't need me," she said softly. "You'll only come to me now and then to be kind."

"Vee, will you stay until tomorrow?"

She said nothing.

"Stay at least until tomorrow. We've got to talk." He reinforced the request with a subtle mental command. She had no telepathic ability at all. She would not be consciously aware of the command, but she would respond to it. She would stay until the next day, as he had asked, and she would think her staying was her own decision. He promised himself that he would not coerce her further. Already it was getting too easy to treat her like just another pet.

She drew a deep breath. "I don't know what good it will do," she said. "But yes, I'll stay that long." She turned to go out of the room and ran into Doro. He caught her as she was stumbling blindly around him, and held her.

Doro looked at Mary, who had finally straightened herself out on the bed. She looked back at him wearily.

"Good luck," he said quietly.

She continued to watch him, not responding at all.

He turned and left with Vivian, still holding her as she cried.

Karl looked down at Mary.

She continued to stare after Doro and Vivian. She spoke softly. "Why is it Doro is always so kind to people after he messes up their lives?"

Karl took a tissue from the box on her night table and wiped her face. It was wet with perspiration.

She gave him a tired half smile. "You being 'kind' to me, man?"

"That wasn't my word," said Karl.

"No?"

"Look," he said, "you know how it's going to be from now on. One bad experience after another. Why don't you use this time to rest?"

"When it's over, if I'm still alive, I'll rest." And then explosively, "Shit!"

He felt her caught up in someone else's fear, stark terror. Then he was caught too. He was too close to her again.

For a moment, he let the alien terror roll over him, engulf him. He broke into an icy sweat. Abruptly he was elsewhere—standing outside in the backyard of a house built near the edge of one of the canyons. Coming up the slope from the canyon was the longest, thickest snake he had ever seen. It was coming toward him. He couldn't move. He was terrified of snakes. Abruptly he turned to run. He caught his foot on a lawn sprinkler, fell screaming, his body twisting, thrashing. He felt his own leg snap as he hit the ground. But the break registered less on him than the snake. And the snake was coming closer.

Karl had had enough. He drew back, screened out the man's terror. At that instant, Mary screamed.

As Karl watched, she turned on her side, curling up again, pressing her face into the pillow so that the sounds she made were muffled.

He watched her mentally as well, or watched the ophidiophobe whose mind held her. He thought he understood something now. Something he had wondered about. He knew how Mary's expanding talent, acting without control, was opening one pathway after another to other people's raw emotions. And now he realized that when he let himself be caught up in those emotions, he was standing in the middle of an open pathway. He was shielding her from the infant fumbling of her own ability by accepting the consequences of that fumbling himself. That was why Doro had told him to back off. When he was too close to Mary, he was helping her. He was preventing her from going through the suffering that was normal for a person in transition. And since the suffering was normal, perhaps it was in some way necessary. Perhaps an active could not mature without it. Perhaps that was why Doro had warned him to help Mary only when she could no longer help herself.

"Karl?"

He looked at her, realizing that he had let his attention wander. He didn't know what had finally happened to the frightened man. He didn't care.

"What did you do?" she asked. "I could feel myself getting caught up in something else. Then for a while it was gone."

He told her what he had learned, and what he had guessed. "So at least now I know how to help you," he finished. "That gives you a better chance."

"I thought Doro would tell you how to help me."

"No, I think half Doro's pleasure comes from watching us, running us through mazes like rats and seeing how well we figure things out."

"Sure," she said. "What are a few rat lives?" She took a deep breath. "And, speaking of lives, Karl, don't help me unless I'm about to lose mine. Let me try to get through this on my own."

"I'll do whatever seems necessary as you progress," he said. "You're going to have to trust my judgment. I've been through this already."

"Yeah, you've been through it," she said. He saw her hands tighten into fists as something clutched at her mind before she could finish. But she managed to get a few more words out. "And you went through it on your own. Alone."

She struggled all evening, all night, and well into the next morning. During her few lucid moments he tried to show her how to interpose her own mind shield between herself and the world outside, how to control her ability and regain the mental peace that she had not known for months. That was what he had had to learn to bring his own transition to an end. If she didn't want his protection, perhaps he could at least show her how to protect herself.

But she did not seem to be able to learn.

She was growing weaker and wearier. Dangerously weary. She seemed ready to sink into oblivion with the unfortunate people whose thoughts possessed her. She had passed out a few times, earlier. Now, though, he was afraid to let her go again. She was too weak. He was afraid she might never regain consciousness.

He lay beside her on the bed listening to her ragged breathing, knowing that she was with a fifteen-year-old boy somewhere in Los Angeles. The boy was being methodically beaten to death by three older boys—members of a rival gang.

Just watching the things she had to live through was sickening. Why couldn't she pick up the simple shielding technique?

She started to get up from the bed. Her self-control was all but gone. She was moving as the boy moved miles away. He was trying to get up from the ground. He didn't know what he was doing. Neither did she.

Karl caught her and held her down, thankful, not for the first time that night, that she was small. He managed to catch her hands before she could slash him again with her nails. The blood was hardly dry on his face where she had scratched him before. He held her, pinning her with his weight, waiting for it to end.

Then, abruptly, he was tired of waiting. He opened his mind to the experience and took the finish of the beating himself.

When it was over, he stayed with her, ready to take anything else that might sweep her away. Even now she was stubborn enough not to want him there, but he no longer cared what she wanted. He brushed aside her wordless protests and tried to show her again how to erect shielding of her own. Again he failed. She still couldn't do it.

But after a while, she seemed to be doing something.

Staying with her mentally, Karl opened his eyes and moved away from her body. Something was happening that he did not understand. She had not been able to learn from him, but she was using him somehow. She had ceased to protest his mental presence. In fact, her attention seemed to be on something else entirely. Her body was relaxed. Her thoughts were her own, but they were not coherent. He could make no sense of them. He sensed other people with her mentally, but he could not reach them even clearly enough to identify them.

"What are you doing?" he asked aloud. He didn't like having to ask.

She didn't seem to hear him.

I asked what you were doing! He gave her his annoyance with the thought.

Mary noticed him then, and somehow drew him closer to her. He seemed to see her arms reaching out, her hands grasping him, though her body did not move. Suddenly suspicious, he tried to break contact with her. Before he could complete the attempt, his universe exploded.

Mary

I couldn't have said what I was doing. I knew Karl was still with me. His mental voice was still reaching me. I didn't mean to grab him the way I did. I didn't realize until afterward that I had done it. And even then, it seemed a perfectly natural thing to do. It was what I had done to the others.

Others, yes. Five of them. They seemed to be far away from me, perhaps scattered around the country. Actives like Karl, like me. People I had noticed during the last minutes of my transition. People who had noticed me at the same time. Their thoughts told me what they were, but I became aware of them—"saw" them—as bright points of light, like stars. They formed a shifting pattern of light and color. I had brought them together somehow. Now I was holding them together—and they didn't want to be held.

Their pattern went through kaleidoscopic changes in design as they tried to break free of me. They were bright, darting fragments of fear and surprise, like insects beating themselves against glass. Then they were long strands of fire, stretching away from me, but somehow never stretching quite far enough to escape. They were writhing, shapeless things, merging into each other, breaking apart, rolling together again as a tidal wave of light, as a single clawing hand.

I was their target. They tore at me desperately with the hand they had formed. I didn't feel it. All I could feel was their emotions. Desperation, anger, fear, hatred.... They tore at me harmlessly, tore at each other in their confusion. Finally they wore themselves out.

They rested grouped around me, relaxed. They were threads of fire again, each thread touching me, linked with me. I was comfortable with them that way. I didn't understand how or why I was holding them, but I didn't mind doing it. It felt right. I didn't want them frightened or angry or hating me. I wanted them the way they were now, at ease, comfortable with me.

I realized that there was something really proprietary about my feelings toward them. As though I was supposed to have charge over them and they were supposed to accept me. But I also realized that I had no idea how dangerous it might be for me to hold a group of experienced active telepaths on mental leashes. Not that it would have mattered if I had known, though, since I couldn't find a way to let them go. At least they were peaceful now. And I was so tired. I drifted off to sleep.

It was light out when Karl woke me by sitting up in bed and pulling the blankets off me. Late morning. Ten o'clock by the clock on my night table. It was a strange awakening for me. My head didn't hurt. For the first time in months, I didn't have even a slight headache. I didn't realize until I moved, though, that several other parts of my body hurt like hell. I had strained muscles, bruises, scratches—most of them self-inflicted, I guess. At least, none of them were very serious; they were just going to leave me sore for a while.

I moved, gasped, then groaned and kept still. Karl looked down at me without saying anything. I could see a set of deep, ugly scratches down the left side of his face, and I knew I had put them there. I reached up to touch his face, ignoring the way my arm and shoulder muscles protested. "Hey, I'm sorry. I hope that's all I did."

"It isn't."

"Oh, boy. What else?"

"This." He did something—tugged at the mental strand of himself that still connected him to me. That brought me fully awake. I had forgotten about my captives, my pattern. Karl's sudden tug was startling, but it didn't hurt me, or him. And I noticed that it didn't seem to bother the five others. Karl could tug only his own strand. The other strands remained relaxed. I knew what Karl wanted. I spoke to him softly.

"I'd let you go if I knew how. This isn't something I did on purpose."

"You're shielded against me," he said. "Open and let me see if there's anything I can do."

I hadn't realized I was shielded at all. He had tried so hard to teach me to form my own shield, and I hadn't been able to do it. Apparently I had finally picked up the technique without even realizing it—picked it up when I couldn't stand any more of the mental garbage I was getting.

So now I had a shield. I examined it curiously. It was a mental wall, a mental globe with me inside. Nothing was reaching me through it except the strands of the pattern. I wondered how I was supposed to open it for him. As I wondered, it began to disintegrate.

It surprised me, scared me. I wanted it back.

And it was back.

Well, that wasn't hard to understand. The shield kept me secure as long as I wanted it to. And there were degrees of security.

I began the disintegration process again, felt the shield grow thinner. I let it become a kind of screen—something I could receive other people's thoughts through. I experimented until I could hold it just heavy enough to keep out the kind of mental noise I had been picking up before and during my transition. It kept out the noise, but it didn't keep me in. I could reach out and sense whatever there was to be sensed. I swept my perception through the house experimentally.

I sensed Vivian still asleep in Doro's bed. And, in another way, I sensed Doro beside her. Actually, I only sensed a human shape beside her—a body. I was aware of it in the way I was aware of the lamp on the night table beside it. I could read Vivian's thoughts with no effort at all. But somehow, without realizing it, I had drawn back from trying to read the mind of that other body. Now, cautiously, I started to reach into Doro's mind. It was like stepping off a cliff.

I jerked back instantly, thickening my screen to a shield and struggling to regain my balance. As fast as I had moved to draw away, I had the feeling I had almost fallen. Safe as I knew I was in my own bed, I had the feeling that I had just come very near death.

"You see?" said Karl as I lay gasping. "I told you you'd find out why actives don't read his mind. Now open again."

"But what was it? What happened?"

"You almost committed suicide."

I stared at him.

"Telepaths are the people he kills most easily," he said. "Normally he can only kill the person physically nearest to him. But he can kill telepaths no matter where they are. Or, rather, he can if they help him by trying to read his mind. It's like begging him to take you."

"And you let me do it?"

"I could hardly have stopped you."

"You could have warned me! You were watching me, reading me. I could feel you with me. You knew what I was going to do before I did it."

"Your own senses warned you. You chose to ignore them."

He was colder than he had been on the day I met him. He was sitting there beside me in bed acting like I was his enemy. "Karl, what's the matter with you? You just worked your ass off trying to save my life. Now, for heaven's sake, you'd let me blunder to my death without saying a word."

He took a deep breath. "Just open again. I won't hurt you. But I've got to find a way out of whatever it is you've caught me in."

I opened. Obviously, he wasn't going to act human again until I did. I felt him reach into my mind, watched him review my memories—all those that had anything to do with the patterns. There wasn't much.

So, in a couple of seconds he knew how little I knew. He had already found out he couldn't break away from the pattern. Now he knew for sure that I couldn't let him go either. He knew there wasn't even a way for him to force me to let him go. I wondered why he thought he'd have to force me—why he thought I wouldn't have let him go if I could have. He answered my thought aloud.

"I just didn't believe anyone could create and maintain a trap like that without knowing what they were doing," he said. "You're holding six powerful people captive. How can you do that by accident or instinct or whatever?"

"I don't know."

He withdrew from my thoughts in disgust. "You also have some very Dorolike ideas," he said. "I don't know how the others feel about it, Mary, but you don't own me."

It took me a minute to realize what he was talking about. Then I remembered. My proprietary feelings. "Are you going to blame me for thoughts I had while I was in transition?" I asked. "You know I was out of my head."

"You were when you first started to think that way. But you aren't now, and you're still thinking that way."

That was true. I couldn't help the feeling of rightness that I had about the pattern—about the people of the pattern being my people. I felt it even more strongly than I had felt Doro's mental keep-out sign. But that didn't matter. I sighed. "Look, Karl, no matter what I feel, you find me a way to break this thing, free you and the others, and I'll co-operate in any way I can."

He had gotten up. He was standing by the bed watching me with what looked like hatred. "You'd better," he said quietly. He turned and left the room.

PART TWO

Chapter Four

Seth Dana

There was water. That was the important thing. There was a well covered by a tall, silver-colored tank. And beside it there was an electric pump housed in a small wooden shed. The electricity was shut off, but the power poles were all sturdily upright, and the wire that had been run in from the main road looked all right. Seth decided to have the electricity turned on as soon as possible. Otherwise he and Clay would either have to haul water from town or get it from some of the nearer houses.

Seth looked over at Clay, saw that his brother was examining the pump. Clay looked calm, relaxed. That alone made Seth's decision to buy him this desert property worthwhile. There were few neighbors, and those widely scattered. The nearest town was twenty miles away. Adamsville. And it wasn't much of a town. About twelve hundred dull, peaceful people. Clay had been reasonably comfortable even while they were passing through it. Seth wiped the sweat from his forehead and stepped into the shadow cast by the well's tank. Just morning and it was hot already.

"Pump look all right, Clay?"

"Looks fine. Just waiting for some electricity."

"How about you?" He knew exactly how Clay was, but he wanted to hear his brother say it aloud.

"I'm all right too." Clay shook his head. "Man, I better be. If I can't make it out here, I can't make it anywhere. I'm not picking up anything now."

"You will, sooner or later," said Seth. "But probably not much. Not even as much as if you were in Adamsville."

Clay nodded, wiped his brow, and went to look at the shack that had served to house the land's former occupant. An old man had lived there pretty much as a hermit. He had built the shack just as, several years before, he had built a real house—a home for his wife and children. A home that they had lived in for only a few days when the wind blew down the power lines and they had to resort to candles. One of the children had invented a game to play with the candles. In the resulting fire, the man had lost his wife, his two sons, and most of his sanity. He had lived on the property as a recluse until his death, a few months back. Seth had bought the property from his surviving daughter, now an adult. He had bought it in the hope that his latent brother might finally find peace there.

Clay shouldn't have been a latent. He was thirty, a year older than Seth, and he should have gone through transition at least a decade before. Even Doro had expected him to. Doro was father to both of them. He had actually worn one body long enough to father two children on the same woman with it. Their mother had been annoyed. She liked variety.

Well, she had variety in Clay and Seth. One son was not only a failure but a helpless failure. Clay was abnormally sensitive even for a latent. But as a latent, he had no control. Without Seth he would be insane or dead by now. Doro had suggested privately to Seth that a quick, easy death might be kindest. Seth had been able to listen to such talk calmly only because he had been through his own agonizing latent period before his transition. He knew what Clay would have to put up with for the rest of his life. And he knew Doro was doing something he had never done before. He was allowing Seth to make an important decision.

"No," Seth had said. "I'll take care of him." And he had done it. He had been nineteen then to Clay's twenty. Clay had not cared much for the idea of being taken care of by anyone, least of all his younger brother. But pain had dulled his pride.

They had traveled around the country together, content with no one place for long. Sometimes Seth worked—when he wanted to. Sometimes he stole. Often he shielded his brother and accepted punishment in his stead. Clay never asked it. He saved what was left of his pride by not asking. He was too unstable to work. He got jobs, but inevitably he lost them. Some violent event caught his mind and afterward he had to lie, tell people he was an epileptic. Employers seemed to accept his explanation, but afterward they found reason to fire him. Seth could have stopped them, could have seen to it that they considered Clay their most valuable employee. But Clay didn't want it that way. "What's the point?" he had said more than once. "I can't do the work. The hell with it."

Clay was slowly deciding to kill himself. It was slow because, in spite of everything, Clay did not want to die. He was just becoming less and less able to tolerate the pain of living.

So now a lonely piece of land. A so-called ranch in the middle of the Arizona desert. Clay could have a few animals, a garden, whatever he wanted. Whatever he could take care of in view of the fact that he would be incapacitated part of the time. He would be receiving money from some income property Seth had insisted on stealing for him in Phoenix, but in more personal ways he would be self-sufficient. He would be able to bear his own pain—now that there would be less of it. He would be able to make his land productive. He would be able to take care of himself. If he was to live at all, he would have to be able to do that.

"Hey, come on in here," Clay was calling from within the hermit's shack. "Take a look at this thing."

Seth went into the shack. Clay was in what had been a combination kitchen-bedroom-living room. The only other room was piled high with bales of newspapers and magazines and stacked with tools. A storage room, apparently. What Clay was looking at was a large cast-iron wood-burning stove.

Seth laughed. "Maybe we can sell that thing as an antique and use the money to buy an electric stove. We'll need one."

"What we?" demanded Clay.

"Well, you, then. You don't want to have to fight with that thing every time you want to eat, do you?"

"Never mind the stove. You're starting to sound like you changed your mind about leaving."

"No I haven't. I'm going as soon as you're settled in here. And—" He stopped, looked away from Clay. There was something he had not mentioned to his brother yet.

"And what?"

"And as soon as you get somebody to help you."

Clay stared at him. "You've got to be kidding."

"Man, you need somebody."

"The hell I do! Some crazy old man lived out here by himself, but me, I need somebody. No! No way!"

"You want to try to drive the van into town yourself?" Suddenly Seth was shouting. "How many people you figure you'll kill along the way? Aside from yourself, I mean." Clay had not dared to drive since his last accident, in which he had nearly killed three people. But obviously he had not been thinking about that. Seth spoke again, softly this time. "Man, you know you're going to have to go into town sooner or later."

"I'd rather hitch in with somebody who lives around here," muttered Clay. "I could go to that place we passed—the one with the windmill."

"Clay, you need somebody. You know you do."

"Another Goddamn babysitter."

"How about a wife? Or at least a woman."

Now Clay looked outraged. "*You* want to find me a woman?"

"Hell no. Find your own woman. But I'm not leaving until you do."

Clay looked around the shack, looked out the open door. "No woman in her right mind would want to come out here and share this place with me."

"This place isn't bad. Hell, tell her what you're going to do with it. Tell her about the house you're going to build her. Tell her how good *you're* going to take care of *her*."

Clay stared at him.

"Well?"

"She's going to have to be some woman to look at these Godforsaken rocks and bushes and listen to me daydreaming."

"You'll do all right. I never knew you to have trouble finding a woman when you wanted one."

"Hell, that was different."

"I know. But you'll do all right." Seth would see that he did all right. When Clay found a woman he liked, Seth would fix things for him. Clay would never have to know. The woman would "fall in love" faster and harder and more permanently than she ever had before. Seth didn't usually manipulate Clay that way, but Clay really needed somebody around. What if something caught his mind while he was fixing food, and he fell across the stove? What if a lot of things! Best to get him a good woman and tie her to him tight. Best to tie Clay to her a little, too. Otherwise Clay might get mean enough to kick her out over nothing.

And it would be a good idea to see that a couple of Clay's nearest neighbors were friendly. Clay tended to make friends easily, then lose them just as easily because his violent "epileptic seizures" scared people. People decided that he was either crazy or going crazy, and they backed away. Seth would see that the neighbors here didn't back away.

"I think I'll go back to Adamsville and make one of the store owners open up," he told Clay. "You want to go along and start your hunt?" He could feel Clay cringe mentally at the thought.

"No thanks. I'm not in any hurry. Besides, I need a chance to look the place over myself before I think about bringing somebody else out here."

"Okay." Seth managed not to smile. He looked around the shack. There was an ancient electric refrigerator in one corner waiting for the electricity to be turned on. And in the storage room, he could see an old-fashioned icebox—the kind you had to put ice in. He decided to bring back some ice for it. The electricity couldn't be turned on until late tomorrow at the soonest, and he wanted to buy some food.

"Anything special you want me to bring back, Clay?"

Clay wiped his forehead on his sleeve and looked out into the bright sunlight. "Couple of six-packs."

Seth grunted. "Yeah. You didn't have to tell me that." He went out to the van and got in. The van was a big oven. He almost blistered his hand on the steering wheel. And he was getting a headache.

He hadn't had a headache since his transition. In fact, this one felt like the ones he used to get when he was approaching transition. But you only went through that once. The sun must have been affecting him. Best to get moving and let the wind cool him off.

He started down the winding dirt path that led to the edge of his property. The path crossed railroad tracks and met a gravel road. That road led to the main highway. The place was isolated, all right. It was a bad place to get sick. And Seth was getting sick. It wasn't the heat—or, if it was, the wind blowing through the van window wasn't helping. He felt worse than ever. He was just reaching the railroad tracks when he lost control of the van.

Something slammed into his thoughts as though his mental shield didn't exist. It was an explosion of mental static that blotted out everything else, left him able to do nothing other than endure it, and endure the fierce residue of pain and shock that followed it.

By some miracle, he did not wreck the van. He ran it into the sign that identified his property as the something-or-other ranch. But the dry wooden signpost snapped easily against the bumper and fell without damaging the van.

Seth lost consciousness for a moment. When he came to, he saw that he had managed to stop the van and that he had fallen across the horn. He sat up wondering whether he had made enough noise to alert Clay, back at the shack.

Several seconds later, he heard someone—it must have been Clay—running toward the van. Then all real sound was drowned by the "sound" within his head. Mental static welling up again agonizingly. It was not like transition. He received no individual violent incidents that he could distinguish. Instead he felt himself seized, held, and somehow divided against himself. When he tried to shield himself from whatever was attacking him, it was as though he had tried to close a door while his leg or arm was still in the doorway. He was being used against himself somehow.

He was vaguely aware of the van door opening, of Clay asking what had happened. He did not even try to answer. If he had opened his mouth, he would have screamed.

When he finally found the strength to try again to defend himself against whatever had attacked him, his defense was thrown back in his face. With it, he received his only comprehensible communication from his attacker. A one-word command that left him no opportunity for argument or disobedience.

Come.

He was being drawn westward, toward California, toward Los Angeles, toward Forsyth, one of the many suburbs of Los Angeles, toward...

He could see the house he was to go to, a white stucco mansion. But he could not see who called him there, or why he had been called, or how his caller was able to exert such influence over him. Because he would definitely go to Forsyth. He had no choice. The pull was too strong.

The intensity of the call lessened to a bearable din and the shock of the attack passed.

He and Clay would go to California. He couldn't leave Clay here alone in the desert. And he couldn't stay to see Clay settled in. He couldn't stay for anything at all. Clay's independence would have to wait. Everything would have to wait.

Rachel Davidson

Rachel had made herself sick by following Eli's suggestion. Thus it seemed only reasonable that Eli take her place and preach the sermon today. And it was only reasonable that she stay at the hotel, relaxed, semiconscious, so that her body did not shake from this one illness that she was helpless against.

And since everything was so reasonable, she thought, why had she brought herself to full consciousness despite her shaking? Why was she now in a cab on her way to the church, hastily dressed, her hair barely combed, without a prepared sermon? Returning, Eli would say, like an addict to her heroin.

Well, let Eli say whatever he wanted to. Let him do whatever he wanted to. But when she reached the church, let him not stand in that pulpit one minute longer than it took him to introduce her. But he would know that. He would take one look at her face and get out of her way.

He and his ideas of how a healing should be performed! He

had never performed one in his life. Never dared to try, because he knew that, even if he managed to succeed a time or two with great help from the sick person's own suggestibility, he would never equal Rachel. He could never perform one tenth of the healings she performed, because she never failed. What he would strain to do, what he would sweat over and call for divine assistance with, she could do easily. Easily, but not without cost. The power, the energy she used in a healing service had to come from somewhere. Eli had called her a parasite, a second Doro. He had talked her into forgoing her usual "price." She had tried, and that was why she was sick now. That was why the taxi driver, who was black too and who knew the church at the address she gave, asked her sympathetically whether she was going to see "that traveling faith healer."

"I'm going to see her, all right," said Rachel through her teeth. Her grimness must have surprised him. He asked no more questions. A few moments later, when he pulled up at the church, she threw him a few bills and ran in without waiting for her change.

She managed to remember her robe because wearing it had become such a habit with her. Eli, as much a showman as a minister, had insisted on it through all the six years that they had worked together. A flowing white robe.

The congregation was singing when she walked into the auditorium. Watery, pallid, uninspired singing. They were making uncoordinated noises with their throats. And their number! In her tours, Rachel was used to people sitting in the aisles, pushing in from outside when there was no more room for them. She had filled circus-type tents when she appeared in them. But there were empty seats out there now.

Had her last performance been so bad? Had following Eli's stupid advice hurt her so much?

She needed more people. She took a deep breath and walked into view from one of the choir doors. Today, of all days, she needed more people.

"Sister Davidson! Praise the Lord, she's here!" The cry went up in the middle of the song, and the song would have died away had she not joined in and kept it going. Her voice was a strong, full contralto that her audiences loved. She could have moved them with

her singing even if she had nothing else. But she had a great deal
more to offer than singing. If only there were more of them!

Eli Torrey gave her a long, bitter look. She knew the expression
on her own face as she looked back at him. She could see it as he
saw it. She could see it through his eyes. The hungry, drawn look
that so many mistook for religious fervor.

Eli started to step away from the pulpit as the song ended.

She stopped him with a thought. *Introduce me!*

Why? She had to pluck his thoughts from his mind. He was only
a latent. He could not project in any controlled way. *You think there's
one person out there who doesn't know who you are?*

*Introduce me, Eli, or I'll control you and do it myself. I'll run you like a
puppet!* She did not bother to take his reply.

Furious as he was, he was too much of a showman not to give her
the best introduction he could.

The service.

She could have preached to her people in Chinese and it literally
would not have mattered. All that mattered was that she was there
and she had them. From that first song, they were hers. Not one of
them could have gotten up and walked out of the church. Not one
of them would have wanted to. Her control of them was not usually
so rigid, but, then, she was not usually so desperate in her need of
them. Their minds were full of her. Their voices, the very swaying,
hand-clapping movements of their bodies were for her. When their
mouths said, "Yes, Jesus!" and "Preach it!" and "Amen!" they really
meant "Rachel, Rachel, Rachel!" She drank it in and loved them for
it. She demanded more and more.

By the time the service was half over, they would have cut their
own throats for her. They fed her, strengthened her, drove out her
sickness, which was, after all, no more than a need for them, for
their adoration.

Eli said she was playing God, perverting religion, turning good,
Christian people into pagans who worshiped only her. Eli was right,
of course. He should have been. He was one of her first and oldest worshipers. But his conscience bothered him, and, from time to
time, he managed to infect her with some of his guilt.

Behind her was a childhood spent in a home that was Christian before it was anything else. Eli's home. Eli was a distant cousin of hers. Doro had had her adopted by Eli's minister parents. Both his father and his mother were ministers. But in spite of the pressure they had put on Rachel she had rejected much of their religious teaching. All she retained was enough to make her nervous sometimes. Nervous and vulnerable to Eli. But not now.

Now she drew all she dared from the small crowd, forcing herself to stop before she was satisfied, to avoid doing them any real harm. Then she prepared to repay them. The candidates for healing had already formed a line in the main aisle.

And the healing began.

Eyes closed, she would mouth a prayer and lay her hands on the candidate. Sometimes she shouted, imploring God to hear and answer her. Sometimes she seemed to have trouble and have to try a second time.

Showmanship! Eli and his parents had taught her some of it. The rest she had learned from watching real faith healers. It meant nothing, as far as the actual healing was concerned.

In her years of healing, she had learned enough to diagnose quickly just by allowing her perception to travel over the candidate's body once. That was useful in that many of the people who came to her did not really know what was wrong with them. Even some who came with doctors' diagnoses were mistaken. Thus she saved a few seconds of looking for a nonexistent problem and went right to work on whatever was really wrong. The work?

Stimulating the growth of new tissues—even brain and nerve tissues that were not supposed to regenerate. Destroying tissue that was useless and dangerous—cancer, for instance. Strengthening weak organs, "reprogramming" organs that malfunctioned. More. Much more. Psychological problems, injuries, birth defects, etc. Rachel could have been even more spectacular than she was. The totally deaf child gained hearing, but the one-armed man— he had come to get help in his fight against alcoholism—did not grow a new arm. He could have. It would have taken weeks, but Rachel could have handled it. To do so, though, she would have had to show herself to be more than a faith healer. She was afraid of what people might decide she was. Whether or not she accepted the story of Christ as fact, she realized that anyone with abilities like his—and hers—would get into trouble if he really put them to work.

Eli knew what she could do. And he knew all that she could make him understand about how she did it. Because she had to tell someone. Eli was her family now that his parents were dead. And he filled other functions. Doro had said he would. Cousin, business manager, lover, slave. She was a little ashamed of that last sometimes, but never ashamed enough to let him go.

Now, though, she was almost content. She had fed. It was not enough, but it would hold her until the next night, when, no doubt, a bigger crowd would gather. Soon she would send this small crowd home tired, weak, spent, but eager to return and feed her again. And eager to bring their friends and families out to see her.

She accepted only a limited number of candidates—again as a matter of self-protection—and that number was almost exhausted when the interruption came. Interruption. . . .

It was a mental explosion that, for uncounted seconds, blotted out her every other sense. She had been standing, one hand on a woman in a wheelchair, the other raised in apparent supplication. Now she froze there, blind, deaf, mute with shock. The only thing that kept her on her feet was her habit of strictness with herself. Minor theatrics she had always used. They were part of her show. Uncontrolled hysterics—especially of the kind that she could have—were absolutely forbidden.

Somehow when the din inside her head lessened she finished with the woman in the wheelchair, sent her away walking slowly, pushing her own chair, and crying.

Then, without explanation, Rachel handed the service back to Eli and walked away from her bewildered congregation. She shut herself in an empty Sunday-school classroom to be alone to fight the thing that was happening to her.

Sometime later, she heard Eli in the hall calling her. By then the battle was ended, lost. By then Rachel knew she had to go to Forsyth. Someone had called her in a way that she could not ignore. Someone had made a puppet of her. There was justice in that, she supposed. She reached out to Eli, called him to her to tell him that she was leaving.

Jesse Bernarr

Jesse and the girl, this one's name was Tara, slept late, then got up and drove into Donaldton. It was Sunday and Jesse's twenty-sixth birthday. He was feeling generous enough to ask the girl what she wanted to do instead of telling her.

She wanted to get a lunch and go to the park. There, though she did not say it, she wanted to show Jesse off. She would be the envy of the female population of Donaldton and she knew it. Best to show him off while she had him. She knew she could only have him until someone else caught his eye. When that happened, he would send her home to her husband and her turn might not come again for months—might not ever come again.

Jesse smiled to himself as he read her thoughts. Donaldton girls, even shy, undemanding ones like Tara, thought that way when they were with him. They worked as hard as they could to keep him and flaunt him—which was understandable and all right as far as Jesse was concerned. But sometimes Jesse went after girls from the surrounding towns. Girls who didn't know him even by reputation, and who weren't quite so eager.

He and Tara went to a little cafe and had a lunch prepared. There was only one waitress on duty and there were two other customers waiting to be served when Jesse arrived. But they didn't mind waiting a little longer. They wished him a happy birthday.

Jesse wasn't carrying any cash. He rarely did. He never needed it in Donaldton. The waitress smiled at him as he and Tara took the lunch and went back to the car.

Tara drove to the lake as she had driven into Donaldton. Jesse had wrecked three cars and nearly killed himself before he gave up driving. There was just no future in it for someone who might at any time be hit by mental disturbances from other drivers, pedestrians, whatever. It wasn't as bad as it had been during his transition, but it still happened. Doro said his mental shielding was defective. Jesse didn't worry about it. The advantages of his sensitivity outweighed the disadvantages. And Tara was a good driver. All his girls were.

There were other Sunday picnickers in the park—old people sunning themselves and families with young children. And there was a scattering of young couples and teen-agers. Donaldton, Pennsylvania, was small and didn't offer much in the way of entertainment or recreation. People who would have preferred something more exciting wound up in the park.

The people were well spread out, though. There was plenty of room. There was so much room, in fact, that Tara was silently annoyed when Jesse chose a place only a few yards from another couple.

Jesse pretended not to notice her annoyance. "Want to go for a swim before we eat?"

"Oh, but... we don't have suits. I didn't know we were coming here when we left the house..."

Jesse glanced around, seemingly casually. "That girl over there has a new one that will fit you," he said, nodding toward the female half of the nearby fully clothed couple.

"Oh." He was in one of his moods again, she was thinking. She was going to be humiliated. This wasn't like taking food from the cafe. That had been more like a gift. But this girl had brought her bathing suit for her own use.

Jesse smiled, reading her every thought. "Go on. Go get it. And while you're at it, get the guy's trunks for me."

She cringed inside but got up to do as he said. He watched her walk toward the couple.

The distance was too great for him to hear what she said to them clearly, so he picked up the conversation mentally.

"Could I borrow... I mean... Jesse wants your bathing suits." She could not have felt more completely foolish, but she expected nothing more than that the couple would hand her the suits and let her escape back to Jesse.

The girl took one look at Tara and at the watching Jesse and started to get her suit out. The man didn't move. It was his reaction that Jesse was waiting for. He didn't have to wait long.

"You want to borrow our *what?*"

"Bathing suits." Tara looked at the girl. "You're from town, aren't you? Tell him."

"You tell him." The girl didn't particularly resent the loss of the suit. Donaldton people never resented giving Jesse what he wanted. The girl resented Tara.

Tara didn't want to be there. She didn't even want the damned suits. If the girl couldn't realize that... "Never mind. I'll have Jesse come over and tell him." She started away.

"All right, wait. Wait!" When Tara turned back to face the girl, the girl was holding out her own suit and the man's trunks. But before Tara could take them, the man snatched them away.

"What the hell are you doing?"

The girl was angry now, and the man was the only one she could take her anger out on safely. "He's Jesse Bernarr and he wants to borrow our suits. Will you please let me give them to him?"

"No! Why the hell should I?" He glanced at Tara. "Look, you go back and tell Jesse Bernarr, whoever he is...." He stopped as Jesse's shadow fell across him. He looked up, confused, and by now angry. He was a big man, Jesse noticed. He would be tall when he stood up. Massive shoulders and chest. He looked a little bigger than Jesse, in fact. And he did not like not knowing what was going on.

"You've got to be Jesse Bernarr," he said. He paused as though he expected confirmation from Jesse. He got only silence. "Look, I don't know what the joke is, mister, but it's not funny. Now, why don't you take your girl and go play your kid games somewhere else."

"I could." Jesse plucked the man's name from his mind. It was Tom. "I don't feel like swimming any more. But there are a couple of things I think you ought to learn."

And there was a simple, effortless way of teaching them to him. But sometimes Jesse liked to expend a little effort. Especially with characters like this Tom who took so much inner pride in their physical prowess. Sometimes Jesse liked to reassure himself that even without his extra abilities he would still be better than Tom's kind.

He said, "You visit a place for the first time, Tom, you ought to be more willing to listen when the natives try to warn you about local customs." He smiled at Tom's girl. She smiled back a little uncertainly. "It could save you a lot of trouble."

Tom got up, watching Jesse. "Man, you sure want to fight bad. I'd give a lot to know why." They faced each other, Tom looking down at Jesse from his slightly superior height.

Tom's girl stood up quickly and stepped between them, her back to Tom. "He'll listen to me, Jess. Let me talk to him."

Jesse pushed her out of the way gently, casually. If he hadn't, Tom would have. But Tom resented Jesse doing it for him. Resented it enough to take the first swing. Jesse, anticipating him, dodged easily.

A stray child saw them, yelled, and people began to take notice and gather around.

Only people from outside Donaldton who didn't know the odds against Tom came to watch a fight. Donaldton people came to see Jesse Bernarr having himself some fun. And they didn't mind. Even Tom's girl didn't mind Jesse having a little fun with Tom. What frightened her was that Tom didn't know what he was up against. He was liable to make Jesse angry enough to really hurt him. If she had been out with a Donaldton man, she wouldn't have worried.

As the two men fought, though, it was Tom whose anger grew, silently encouraged by Jesse. Jesse mentally goaded Tom to fight as though his life were at stake. Then an explosion went off in Jesse's head and Tom got his chance.

Jesse was only vaguely aware of the beating his body was taking as he struggled to close out the mental blast. But there was no way to close it out. No way to dull it as it screamed through him. Tom had a field day.

When the "noise" finally lessened, when it didn't fill every part of Jesse's mind, he realized that he was on the ground. He started groggily to get up, and the man whose anger he had mentally encouraged kicked him in the face.

His head snapped back—not as far as Tom would have liked— and he lost consciousness.

He didn't come to all at once. First he was aware only of the call drawing him, destroying any mental peace he might have had before he became aware of the condition of his body. He didn't seem to be hurt seriously, but he could feel a dozen places where his flesh was split and bruised. His face was lumpy and already swollen. Some of his teeth had been kicked in. And he hurt. He hurt all over. He spat out blood and broken teeth.

Damn that out-of-town bastard to hell!

The thought of Tom roused him to look around. Somebody from Donaldton was standing over him, thinking about moving him back into town to a bed.

Not far away, Tom struggled between two more Donaldton men and cursed steadily.

Jesse staggered to his feet. The crowd was still there. Probably some out-of-towner had gone for the police. Not that it mattered. The police were old friends of Jesse's.

Jesse refused to mute his own pain. It came as near as anything could to blocking out the call to Forsyth. And, although Jesse had not yet analyzed what had happened to him, the message of the call was clear—and clearly something he wanted no part of. Besides, he wanted to hurt. He wanted to look at Tom and hurt. He started to smile, had to spit more blood, then spoke softly. "Let him go."

Jesse moved in, anticipating Tom's swings, avoiding them. Tom couldn't surprise him. And as angry as Jesse was now, that meant Tom couldn't touch him. Slowly, methodically, he cut the bigger man to pieces.

Now Tom's strength betrayed him. It kept him on his feet when he should have fallen, kept him fighting, well after he was beaten. When he finally did collapse to the ground, it kept him conscious and aware—aware solely of pain.

Jesse walked away and left him lying there. Let his girl take care of him.

The townspeople drifted away, too. They had had a much better show than they had bargained for. To the out-of-towners, Tom seemed to have gotten no more than he deserved. They resumed their Sunday outing.

A few minutes later, Tara was shaking her head and wiping blood from Jesse's face with a cold, wet paper napkin. "Jess, why'd you let him beat you up like that? How are you going to go to your birthday party tonight, now?"

He glanced at her in annoyance and she fell silent. Party, hell! If he could just get rid of this damned buzzing in his head, he would be all right.

So, somewhere in California, there was a town called Forsyth, and there were other actives there—more of Doro's people. So what! Why should he run to them, come when they called? Nobody on the other end of that buzz could have anything to offer him that was better than what he had.

Ada Dragan

They were screaming at each other over some small thing—a party Ada would not attend. Yesterday the screaming had been over the neighbors whom Ada had interfered with. She had sensed them beating their six-year-old brutally, and she had stopped them. For once, she had accomplished something good with her ability. Foolish pride had made her tell Kenneth. Kenneth had decided that her interference had been wrong.

She could not tolerate large groups of people, and she could not tolerate child abuse. Kenneth called the first immature and the second none of her business. Everything she did either angered or humiliated him. Everything. Yet she stayed with him. Without him she would be totally alone.

She was an active. She had power. And all her power did, most of the time, was cut her off from other people, make it impossible for her ever to be one of them. Her power was more like a disease than a gift. Like a mental illness.

She had gone to a doctor once, secretly. A psychiatrist a few miles away, in Seattle. She had given him a false name and told him only a little. She had stopped when she realized that he was about to suggest a period of hospitalization. . . .

Now she wondered bitterly whether the doctor had been right. It was her "illness," after all, that had caused her to descend to this screaming. She said things to Kenneth that she had not thought herself capable of saying to anyone. He did not realize the degradation and despair this signified in her. Only one thought saved her from complete loss of control. The man was her husband.

She had married him out of desperation, not love. But he was her husband nonetheless, and he had served a purpose. If she had not married him, she might be saying these things to her parents—her stepparents—the only people besides Doro whom she could ever remember loving. It had been very important once—that she protect her parents from what she had become. She wondered if it was still important. If she still cared what she said, even to them.

Abruptly she was tired of the argument. Tired of the man's fury pounding at her mind and her ears. Tired of her own pointless anger. She turned and walked away.

Kenneth caught her shoulder and spun her around so quickly that she had no time to think. He slapped her hard, throwing all the weight of his big body against her. She fell back against the wall, then slipped silently to the floor to lie stunned, while, above her, he demanded that she learn to listen when he spoke. At that moment, violence, chaos convulsed her treacherous mind.

Ada was quick. She did not need time to wonder what was happening or to realize that there would finally be an end to her aloneness. She reacted immediately. She screamed.

Kenneth had hurt her, but suddenly the physical pain lost all meaning in the face of this new thing. This thing that brought her the pain of a hope roughly torn away.

Since her change, that terrible night three years before, when all the world had come flooding into her mind, she had treated her condition as a temporary thing. Something that would someday end and let her be as she had been. This was a belief that Doro had tried to talk her out of. But she had been able to convince herself that he was lying. He had refused to introduce her to others who were like her, though he claimed there were others. He had said that it would be painful to her to meet them, that her kind tolerated each other badly. But she had looked for herself, had sifted through thousands of minds without finding even one like her own. Thus she had decided that Doro was lying. She had believed what she wanted to believe. She was good at that; it kept her alive. She had decided that Doro had told only part of the truth. That there had been others like her. It was unthinkable that she had been the only person to undergo this change. And that the others had recovered, changed back.

This hope had sustained her, given her a reason to go on living. Now she had to see it for the fallacy it was.

She lay on the floor crying, as she rarely did, in noisy, gasping sobs. Others. How had she searched for so long without finding them? It seemed that they had no trouble finding her. And the strength of the first attack, and even of the call that now pulled at her insistently, was far greater than anything she felt herself able to generate. Such power gave the unknown caller a terrible air of permanence.

Unexpectedly, Kenneth was lifting her to her feet, reassuring her that she was all right.

Steadying herself enough to sample his thoughts, she learned that he was a little frightened by her screaming. He had hit her before and gotten no reaction other than quiet tears.

The selfishness of his thoughts stabilized her. He was wondering what would happen to him if he had hurt her. He had long before ceased worrying about her for her own sake. And she had never forced him to do anything more than stay with her. She pulled away from him tiredly and went into the bedroom.

She would never be well again, never be able to go among people without being bombarded by their thoughts. And facing this, she could not possibly continue her present living arrangement. She could no longer force Kenneth to stay with her when he hated her as he did. Nor would she exert more control over him, to force an obscene, artificial love.

She would follow the call. Even if it had been less insistent, she would have followed it. Because it was all she had.

She would quarantine herself with others who were afflicted as she was. If she was alone with them, she would be less likely to hurt people who were well. How would it be, though? How much worse than anything she had yet known? A life among outcasts.

Jan Sholto

The neighborhood had changed little in the three years since Jan had seen it. New cars, new children. Two small boys ran past her; one of them was black. That was new too. She was glad her mind had not been open and vulnerable when the boy ran past. She had problems enough without *that* alienness. She looked back at the boy with distaste, then shrugged. She planned only a short visit. She didn't have to live there.

It occurred to her, not for the first time, that even visiting was foolish, pointless. She had placed her own children in a comfortable home where they would be well cared for, have better lives than she had had. There was nothing more that she could do for them. Nothing she could accomplish by visiting them. Yet for days she had felt a need to make this visit. Need, urge, premonition?

Thinking about it made her uncomfortable. She deliberately turned her attention to the street around her instead. The newness of it disgusted her. The unimaginative modern houses, the sapling trees. Even if the complexion of the neighborhood had not been changing, Jan could never have lived there. The place had no depth in time. She could touch things, a fence, a light standard, a signpost. Nothing went back further than a decade. Nothing carried real historical memory. Everything was sterile and perilously unanchored to the past.

A little girl of no more than seven was standing in one of the yards watching Jan walk toward her. Jan examined the child curiously. Small, fine-boned and fair-haired, like Jan. Her eyes were blue, but not the pale, faded blue of Jan's eyes. The girl's eyes had the same deep, startling blue that had been one of her father's best features—or one of the best features of the body her father had been wearing.

Jan turned to walk down the pathway to the child's house.

As she came even with the girl, some sentimentality about the eyes made her stop and hold out her hand. "Will you walk to the house with me, Margaret?"

The child took the offered hand and walked solemnly beside Jan.

Jan automatically blocked any mental contact with her. She had learned painfully that children not only had no depth but that their unstable little animal minds could deliver one emotional outburst after another.

Margaret spoke as Jan opened the door. "Did you come to take me away?"

"No."

The child smiled at Jan in relief, then ran away, calling, "Mommy, Jan is here."

Jan raised an eyebrow at the irony of her daughter's words. Jan had once tried to condition the family here, the Westleys, to believe that they were the natural parents of Jan's children. She had had the power to do it, but she had not been skillful enough in her use of that power. She had failed. But time, combined with the simpler command that she had managed to instill in the Westleys—to care for the children and protect them—had turned her failure into success. Margaret knew that Jan was actually her mother. But it made no difference. Not to her; not to the Westleys.

In fact, the children were such a permanent part of the Westley household that Margaret's question seemed out of character. The question revived the feeling of foreboding that Jan had been trying to ignore.

Even the feel of the house was wrong. So wrong that she found herself being careful not to touch anything. Just being inside was uncomfortable.

The woman, Lea Westley, came in slowly, hesitantly, without Margaret or the boy, Vaughn. Jan resisted the temptation to reach into her thoughts and learn at once what was wrong. That part of her ability was still underdeveloped, because she did not like to use it. She enjoyed touching inanimate objects and winding back through the pasts of the people who had handled them before her. But she had never learned to enjoy direct mind-to-mind contact. Most people had vile minds anyway.

"I thought you might be coming, Jan." Lea Westley fumbled with her hands. "I was even afraid you might take Margaret."

Verbal confirmation of Jan's fears. Now she had to have the rest. "I don't know what's happened, Lea. Tell me."

Lea looked away for a moment, then spoke softly. "There was an accident. Vaughn is dead." Her voice broke on the last word and Jan had to wait until she could compose herself and go on.

"It was a hit-and-run. Vaughn was out with Hugh," her husband, "and someone ran a red light.... It happened last week. Hugh is still in the hospital."

The woman was genuinely upset. Even through layers of shielding, Jan could feel her suffering. But, more than anything else, Lea Westley was afraid. She was afraid of Jan, of what Jan might decide to do to the people who had failed in the responsibility she had given them.

Jan understood that fear, because she was feeling a slightly different version of it herself. Someday Doro would come back and ask to see his children. He had promised her he would, and he kept the few promises he made. He had also promised her what he would do to her if she was unable to produce two healthy children.

She shook her head thinking about it. "Oh, God."

Lea was instantly at her side, holding her, weeping over her, saying again and again, "I'm so sorry, Jan. So sorry."

Disgusted, Jan pushed her away. Sympathy and tears were the last things Jan needed. The boy was dead. That was that. He had been a burden to her before she placed him with the Westleys. Now, dead, he was again a burden in spite of all her efforts to see that he was safe. If only Doro had not insisted that she have children. She had been looking forward to his return for so long. Now, instead of waiting for it, she would have to flee from it. Another town, another state, another name—and the likelihood that none of it would do any good. Doro was a specialist at finding people who ran from him.

"Jan, please understand. . . . It wasn't our fault."

Stupid woman! Lea became an outlet for Jan's frustration. Jan seized control of her, spun her around, and propelled her puppet-like out of the living room.

Lea Westley's scream of terror when Jan finally released her was the last thing Jan was physically aware of for several minutes.

A mental explosion rocked her. Then came the forced mind-to-mind contact that she fought savagely and uselessly. Then the splitting away of part of herself, the call to Forsyth.

Jan regained consciousness on Lea Westley's sofa, with Lea herself sitting nearby, crying. The woman had come back despite Jan's heavy-handed treatment. She knew how foolish it would be to run from Jan even if she had known positively that Jan meant her harm. Perhaps, in that knowledge of her own limitations, she was more sensible than Jan herself. Lying still now with the call drawing her, Jan felt unusual pity for Lea.

"I don't care that he's dead, Lea." The words came out in a whisper even though Jan had intended to speak normally.

"Jan!" Lea was on her feet at once, probably not understanding, probably realizing only that Jan was again conscious.

"You don't have to worry, Lea. I'm not going to hurt you."

Lea heard this time, and she collapsed weeping with relief. Jan tried standing, and found herself weak but able to manage.

"Be good to Margaret for me, Lea. I might not be able to come to see her again."

She walked out, leaving Lea staring after her.

California.

Was it Doro calling her somehow with this thing in her mind? She knew he had other telepaths—better telepaths. He might be using one of them to reach her. It was possible that he had somehow learned of his son's death and struck at her through someone else. If he had, his efforts were paying off. She was going to California.

She felt all the terror that the controlled Lea must have known. She couldn't help herself. She had to go to Forsyth. And if Doro was there, she would be going to her death.

Chapter Five

Mary

When Karl left my room, I lay in bed thinking, remembering. Karl and I had sort of accepted each other over the past two weeks. He had gotten a lot easier to talk to—and I suppose I had too. He had stopped trying to pretend I wasn't there, and I had stopped resenting him. In fact, I had probably come to depend on him more than I should have. And he really had just worked damned hard to keep me alive. Yet, only a few hours later, he had done enough emotional backsliding to sit by and let me almost kill myself—all because of this pattern thing. I wondered how big a mental leap it would be for him to go from a willingness to let me be killed to a willingness to kill me himself.

Or maybe I was overreacting. Maybe I was just disappointed because I had expected my transition to bring me closer to him. I had expected just what I knew Vivian was afraid of: that, after my transition, she would become excess baggage. If I had to be Karl's wife, I meant to be his only wife.

But now. . . . I had never felt anyone's hostility the way I felt Karl's just before he went out. That was part of what it meant to be in full control of my telepathic ability. Not a very comfortable part. I knew he had gone to see Doro—had gone to roust Doro out of bed and ask him what the hell had gone wrong. I wondered if anything really had gone wrong.

Doro wanted an empire. He didn't call it that, but that was what he meant. Maybe I was just one more tool he was using to get it. He needed tools, because an empire of ordinary people wasn't quite what he had in mind. That, to him, would be like an ordinary person making himself emperor over a lot of cattle. Doro thought a lot of himself, all right. But he didn't think much of the families of half-crazy latents he had scattered across the country. They were just his breeders—if they were lucky. He didn't want an empire of them either. He and I had talked about it off and on since I was thirteen. That first conversation said most of it, though.

He had taken me to Disneyland. He did things like that for me now and then while I was growing up. They helped me survive Rina and Emma.

We were sitting at an outdoor table of a cafe having lunch when I asked the key question.

"What are we for, Doro?"

He looked at me through deep blue eyes. He was wearing the body of a tall, thin white man. I knew he knew what I meant, but still he said, "For?"

"Yeah, for. You have so many of us. Rina said your newest wife just had a kid." He laughed for some reason. I went on. "Are you just keeping us for a hobby—so you'll have something to do, or what?"

"No doubt that's part of it."

"What's the other part?"

"I'm not sure you'd understand."

"I'm mixed up in it. I want to know about it whether I understand or not. And I want to know about you."

He was still smiling. "What about me?"

"Enough about you so that I'll have a chance to understand why you want us."

"Why does anyone want a family?"

"Oh, come on, Doro. Families! Dozens of them. Tell me, really. You can start by telling me about your name. How come you only have one, and one I never heard of at that."

"It's the name my parents gave me. It's the only thing they gave me that I still have."

"Who were your parents?"

"Farmers. They lived in a village along the Nile."

"Egypt!"

He shook his head. "No, not quite. A little farther south. The Egyptians were our enemies when I was born. They were our former rulers, seeking to become our rulers again."

"Who were your people?"

"They had another name then, but you would call them Nubians."

"Black people!"

"Yes."

"God! You're white so much of the time, I never thought you might have been born black."

"It doesn't matter."

"What do you mean, 'It doesn't matter'? It matters to me."

"It doesn't matter because I haven't been any color at all for about four thousand years. Or you could say I've been every color. But either way, I don't have anything more in common with black people—Nubian or otherwise—than I do with whites or Asians."

"You mean you don't want to admit you have anything in common with us. But if you were born black, you *are* black. Still black, no matter what color you take on."

He crooked his mouth a little in something that wasn't quite a smile. "You can believe that if it makes you feel better."

"It's true!"

He shrugged.

"Well, what race do you think you are?"

"None that I have a name for."

"That doesn't make any sense."

"It does when you think about it. I'm not black or white or yellow, because I'm not human, Mary."

That stopped me cold. He was serious. He couldn't have been more serious. I stared at him, chilled, scared, believing him even though I didn't want to believe. I looked down at my plate, slowly finished my hamburger. Then, finally, I asked my question. "If you're not human, what are you?"

And his seriousness broke. "A ghost?"

"That's not funny!"

"No. It may even be true. I'm the closest thing to a ghost that I've run into in all my years. But that's not important. What are you looking so frightened for? I'm no more likely to hurt you now than I ever was."

"What are you?"

"A mutation. A kind of parasite. A god. A devil. You'd be surprised at some of the things people have decided I was."

I didn't say anything.

He reached over and took my hand for a moment. "Relax. There's nothing for you to be afraid of."

"Am I human?"

He laughed. "Of course you are. Different, but certainly human."

I wondered whether that was good or bad. Would he have loved me more if I had been more like him? "Am I descended from your... from the Nubians, too?"

"No. Emma was an Ibo woman." He ate a piece of french fry and watched a couple with about seven yelling little kids troop by. "I don't know of any of my people who are descended from Nubians. Certainly none of them were descended from my parents."

"You were an only child?"

"I was one of twelve. I survived, the others didn't. They all died in infancy or early childhood. I was the youngest and I only survived until I was your age—thirteen."

"And they were too old to have more kids."

"Not only that. I died while I was going through something a lot like transition. I had flashes of telepathy, got caught in other people's thoughts. But of course I didn't know what it was. I was afraid, hurt. I thrashed around on the ground and made a lot of noise. Unfortunately, both my mother and my father came running. I died then for the first time, and I took them. First my mother, then my father. I didn't know what I was doing. I took a lot of other people too, all in panic. Finally I ran away from the village, wearing the body of one of my cousins—a young girl. I ran straight into the arms of some Egyptians on a slave raid. They were just about to attack the village. I assume they did attack."

"You don't know?"

"Not for sure, but there was no reason for them not to. I couldn't hurt them—or at least not deliberately. I was already half out of my mind over what I had done. I snapped. After that I don't know what happened. Not then, not for about fifty years after. I figured out much later that the span I didn't remember, still don't remember, was about fifty years. I never saw any of the people of my village again." He paused for a moment. "I came to, wearing the body of a middle-aged man. I was lying on a pallet of filthy, vermin-infested straw in a prison. I was in Egypt, but I didn't know it. I didn't know anything. I was a thirteen-year-old boy who had suddenly come awake in someone else's forty-five-year-old body. I almost snapped again.

"Then the jailer came in and said something to me in a language that, as far as I knew, I had never heard before. When I just lay there staring at him, he kicked me, started to beat me with a small whip he was carrying. I took him, of course. Automatic. Then I got out of there in his body and wandered through the streets of a strange city trying to figure out what a lot of other people have been trying to figure out ever since: Just what in the name of all gods was I?"

"I never thought you might wonder that."

"I didn't for long. I came to the conclusion that I was cursed, that I had offended the gods and was being punished. But after I had used my ability a few times deliberately and seen that I could have absolutely anything I wanted, I changed my mind. Decided that the gods had favored me by giving me power."

"When did you decide that it was okay for you to use that power to make people...make them..."

"Breed them, you mean."

"Yeah," I muttered. *Breed* didn't sound like the kind of word that should be applied to people. The minute he said it, though, I realized it was the right word for what he was doing.

"It took time for me to get around to that," he said. "A century or two. I was busy first getting involved in Egyptian religion and politics, then traveling, trading with other peoples. I started to notice the way people bred animals. It stopped being just part of the background for me. I saw different breeds of dogs, of cattle, different ethnic groups of people—how they looked when they kept to themselves and were relatively pure, when there was crossbreeding."

"And you decided to experiment."

"In a way. I was able by then to recognize the people... the kinds of people that I would get the most pleasure from if I took them. I guess you could say, the kinds of people who tasted best."

I suddenly lost my appetite. "God! That's disgusting."

"It's also very basic. One kind of people gave me more pleasure than other kinds, so I tried to collect several of the kind I liked and keep them together. That way, they would breed and I would always have them available when I needed them."

"And that's how we began? As food?"

"That's right."

I was surprised, but I wasn't afraid. I didn't think for one minute that he was going to use me or anybody I knew for food. "What kind of people taste best?" I asked.

"People with a certain mental sensitivity. People who have the beginnings, at least, of some unusual abilities. I found them in every race I encountered, but I never found them in very large numbers."

I nodded. "Psis," I said. "There's the word you need. A word that sort of groups everybody's abilities together. I read it in a science-fiction magazine."

"I know about it."

"You know everything. So people with some psionic ability 'taste' better than others. But we're not still just food, are we?"

"Some of my latents are. But my actives and potential actives are part of another project. They have been for some time."

"What project?"

"To build a people, a race."

So that was it. I thought about it for a moment. "A race for you to be part of?" I asked. "Or a race for you to own?"

He smiled. "That's a good question."

"What's the answer?"

"Well... to get an active, I have to bring together people of two different latent families—people who repel each other so strongly that I have to take one of them to bring them together. That means all the actives of each generation are my children. So maybe the answer is... a little of both."

*   *   *

Maybe it was a lot of both. Maybe he hadn't told me just how experimental I was—just what different things I was supposed to do. And maybe he hadn't told Karl, either.

I got out of bed trying to ignore the parts of me that hurt. I took a long, hot bath, hoping to soak away some of the pain. It helped a little. By the time I finally dressed and went downstairs, nobody but Doro was still around.

"Tell me about it while you're having breakfast," he said.

"Hasn't Karl already told you?"

"Yes. Now I want to hear it from you."

I told him. I didn't add in any of my suspicions. I just told him and watched him. He didn't look happy.

"What can you tell me about the other actives you're holding?" he asked.

I almost said "nothing" before I realized it wasn't true. "I can tell where they are," I said. "And I can tell them apart. I know their names and I know—" I stopped, looked at him. "The more I concentrate on them, the more I find out about them. How much do you want to know?"

"Just tell me their names."

"A test? All right. Rachel Davidson, a healer. She's some relation to Emma. She works churches pretending to be a faith healer, but faith doesn't have anything to do with it. She—"

"Just their names, Mary."

"Okay. Jesse Bernarr, Jan Sholto, Ada Dragan, and Seth Dana. There's something strange about Seth."

"What?"

"Something wrong, painful. But no, wait a minute, it's not Seth who has something wrong with him. It's Seth's brother, Clay. I see. Clay's a latent and Seth is protecting him."

"Doesn't it bother you that most of these people are shielded?"

"I didn't realize they were." I checked quickly. "You're right. Everyone but Seth is shielded. Hell, I'm still shielded. I forgot the shield was there, but it is. Not even thinned a little."

"But you don't have any trouble reading them through it?"

"No. It's one-way communication, though. I can read them, but none of them have managed to find out who I am. And none of them realize when I'm reading them. A while ago, when Karl was reading me, I could feel it. I knew when he started, when he stopped, and what he got."

"Can you tell whether any of the others are closer to you, closer to Forsyth now than they were when you first became aware of them?"

I checked. It was like turning my head to read a wall chart. That easy. And I noticed what I hadn't noticed before. "Two of them are a lot closer. Rachel and Seth. They're approaching from slightly different directions, and Rachel's coming much faster, but, Doro, they're both on their way here."

"And the others?"

I checked again. "They'll be coming too. They can't help it. I see that now. My pattern is pulling them here."

Doro said something that I knew had to be a curse even though it was in a foreign language. He came over to me and put his hand on my shoulder. He looked worried. That was unusual for him. I sat there knowing damned well that he was thinking he was going to have to kill me. This pattern thing wasn't part of his plan, then. I was an experiment going bad before his eyes.

I looked up at him. I wasn't afraid. I realized that I should have been, but I wasn't. "Give it a chance," I said quietly. "Let the five of them get here, and let's see how they react."

"You don't know how badly my actives usually react to each other."

"Karl's reaction to me was bad enough. Why did you put us together if you didn't think we could get along?"

"You and Karl are more stable than the others; you come from four of my best lines. You were supposed to get along fairly well together."

"Another experiment. All right, it can still work. Just give it a chance. After all, what have you got to lose?"

"Some very valuable people."

I stood up and faced him. "You want to throw me away before you see how valuable I might be?"

"Girl, I don't *want* to throw you away at all."

"Give me a chance, then."

"A chance to do what?"

"To find out whether this group of actives is different—or whether I can make them different. To find out whether I or my pattern can keep them from killing each other, or me. That's what we're talking about, isn't it?"

"Yes."

"Well?"

He looked at me. After a moment, he nodded. I didn't even feel relieved. But, then, I had never really felt threatened. I smiled at him. "You're curious, aren't you?"

He looked surprised.

"I know you. You really want to see what will happen—if it will be different from what's happened before. Because this has happened before, hasn't it?"

"Not quite."

"What was different before? I might be able to learn from my predecessors' mistakes."

"Do you think anything you could have learned before your transition could have helped you avoid trapping my actives in your pattern?"

I took a deep breath. "No. But tell me anyway. I want to know."

"No you don't. But I'll tell you. Your predecessors were parasites, Mary. Not quite the way I am, but parasites nevertheless. And so are you."

I thought about that, then shook my head slowly. "But I haven't hurt anybody. Karl was right next to me and I didn't—"

"I said you weren't like me. I'm fairly sure you could have killed Karl, though. I suspect Karl realizes that."

I sat down. He had finally said something that really hit me. I had kind of built Karl up as a superman in my mind. I could see how he owned Vivian and the servants. His house and his life style were clear evidence of his power. He wasn't Doro, but he was a good second. "I could have *killed* him? How?"

"Why? Want to try it?"

"Oh, shit, Doro, come on. I want to know how to avoid trying it. Or is that going to be impossible too?"

"That's the question I want an answer to. That's what I'm curious about. More than curious. Your predecessors never trapped more than one active at a time. Their first was always the one who had helped them through transition. They always needed help to get through transition. If I didn't provide it, they died. On the other hand, if I did provide it, sooner or later they killed the person who had helped them. They never wanted to kill, and especially they didn't want to kill that person. But they couldn't help themselves. They got... hungry, and they killed. Then they latched onto another active, drew him to them, and went through the feeding process again. Unfortunately, they always killed other actives. I can't afford that."

"Did they... trade bodies the way you do?"

"No. They took what they needed and left the husk."

I winced.

"And their patterns gave them an access to their victims that their victims couldn't close off—as you already know."

"Oh." I felt almost guilty—as though he were telling me about things that I had already done. As though I had already killed the people in my pattern. People who hadn't done anything to me.

"So you can see why I'm worried," he said.

"Yes. But I can't see why you'd want somebody like me around at all—why you'd breed somebody like me if all my kind can do is feed on other actives."

"Not your kind, Mary. Your predecessors."

"Right. They killed one at a time. I kill several at once. Progress."

"But do you kill several at once?"

"I hope I don't kill any at all—at least not unintentionally. But you don't give me much to base that hope on. What am I for, Doro? What are you progressing toward?"

"You know the answer to that."

"Your race, your empire, yes, but what place is there in it for me?"

"I'll be able to tell you that after I've watched you for a while."

"But—"

"The thing for you to do now is rest so that you'll have a better chance of handling your people when they get here. Your transition was several hours longer than normal, so you're probably still tired."

I was tired. I had gotten only a couple of hours' sleep. I wanted answers, though, more than I wanted rest. But he'd made it pretty clear that I wasn't going to get them. Then I realized what he had just said. "My people?"

"Both you and Karl say you feel as though they're yours."

"And both Karl and I know that, if they really belong to anybody other than themselves, it's you."

"You belong to me," he said. "So I'm not giving up anything when I give you charge of them. They're yours as long as you can handle them without killing them."

I stared at him in surprise. "One of the owners," I muttered, remembering the bitter thoughts I'd had two weeks before. "How did I suddenly become one of the owners?"

"By surviving your transition. What you have to do now is to survive your new authority."

I leaned back in my chair. "Thanks. Any pointers?"

"A few."

"Speak up, then. I have the feeling I'm going to need all the help I can get."

"Very likely. First you should realize that I'm delegating authority to you only because you'll need it if you're to have any chance at all of staying alive among these people. You're going to have to accept your own proprietary feelings as legitimate and demand that your people accept you on your terms." He paused, looked hard at me. "Keep them out of your mind as much as you can. Use your advantage. Always know more about them than they know about you. Intimidate them quietly."

"The way you do?"

"If you can."

"I have a feeling you're rooting for me."

"I am."

"Well... I wouldn't ask why, on a bet. I'd rather think it was because you really gave a damn about me."

He just smiled.

Karl

Karl had never wanted quite as much as he did now to hurt something, to kill something, someone. He looked at Vivian sitting next to him, her mind ablaze with fear, her face carefully expressionless.

The blast of a horn behind him let him know that he was sitting through a green light. He restrained an impulse to lash back at the impatient driver. He could kill with his ability. He had, twice, accidentally, not long after his transition. He wondered why he refrained from doing it again. What difference would it make?

"Are we going back home?" Vivian asked.

Karl glanced at her, then looked around. He realized that he was heading back toward Palo Verde. He had left home heading nowhere in particular except away from Mary and Doro. Now he had made a large U and was heading back to them. And it wasn't just an ordinary unconscious impulse driving him. It was Mary's pattern.

He pulled over to the curb, stopped under a NO PARKING sign. He leaned back in the seat, his eyes closed.

"Will you tell me what's the matter with you?" Vivian asked.

"No."

She was doing all she could to keep calm. It was his silence that frightened her. His silence and his obvious anger.

He wondered why he had brought her with him. Then he remembered. "You're not leaving me," he said.

"But if Mary came through transition all right—"

"I said you're not leaving!"

"All right." She was almost crying with fear. "What are you going to do with me?"

He turned to glare at her in disgust.

"Karl, for heaven's sake! Tell me what's wrong." Now she was crying.

"Be quiet." Had he ever loved her, really? Had she ever been more than a pet—like all the rest of his women? "How was Doro last night?" he asked.

She looked startled. By mutual agreement, they did not discuss her nights with Doro. Or they hadn't until now. "Doro?" she said.

"Doro."

"Oh, now—" She sniffed, tried to compose herself. "Now, just a minute—"

"How was he?"

She frowned at him, disbelieving. "That can't be what's bothering you. Not after all this time. Not as though it was my fault, either!"

"That's a pretty good body he's wearing," said Karl. "And I could see from the way you were hanging on him this morning that he must have given you a pretty good—"

"That's enough!" Outrage was fast replacing her fear.

A pet, he thought. What difference did it make what you said or did to a pet?

"I'll defy Doro when you do," she said icily. "The moment you refuse to do what he tells you and stick to your refusal, I'll stand with you!"

A pet. In pets, free will was tolerated only as long as the pet owner found it amusing.

"You've got your nerve complaining about Doro and me," she muttered. "You'd climb into bed with him yourself if he told you to."

Karl hit her. He had never done such a thing before, but it was easy.

She screamed, then foolishly tried to get out of the car. He caught her arm, pulled her back, hit her again, and again.

He was panting when he stopped. She was bloody and only half conscious, crumpled down on the seat, crying. He hadn't controlled her. He had wanted to use his hands. Just his hands. And he wasn't satisfied. He could have hurt her more. He could have killed her.

Yes, and then what? How many of his problems would her death erase? He would have to get rid of her body, and then still go back to his master, and now, by God, his mistress. Once he was there, at least Mary's pattern would stop pulling at him, dragging at him, subverting his will as easily as he subverted Vivian's. Nothing would be changed, though, except that Vivian would be gone.

Only a pet?

Who was he thinking about? Vivian or himself? Now that Doro had tricked him into putting on a leash, it could be either, or both.

He took Vivian by the shoulders and made her sit up. He had split her lip. That was where the blood came from. He took out a handkerchief and wiped away as much of it as he could. She looked at him first, vacillating between fear and anger; then she looked away.

Without a word, he drove her to Monroe Memorial Hospital. There he parked, took out his checkbook, and wrote a check. He tore it out and put it in her hands. "Go. Get away from me while you can."

"I don't need a doctor."

"All right, don't see one. But go!"

"This is a lot of money," she said, looking at the check. "What's it supposed to pay me for?"

"Not pay you," he said. "God, you know better than that."

"I know you don't want me to go. Whatever you're angry about, you still need me. I didn't think you would, but you do."

"For your own good, Vee, go!"

"I'll decide what's good for me." Calmly she tore the check into small pieces. She looked at him. "If you really wanted me to go—if you want me to go now—you know how to make it happen. You do know."

He looked at her for a long moment. "You're making a mistake."

"And you're letting me make it."

"If you stay, this might be the last time you'll have the freedom to make your own mistakes."

"You're wrong to try so hard to frighten me away when you want me to stay so badly."

He said nothing.

"And I am staying, as long as you let me. Will you tell me what was wrong now?"

"No."

She sighed. "All right," she said, trying not to look hurt. "All right."

Chapter Six

Doro

It occurred to Doro when Rachel Davidson arrived that she was the most subtly dangerous of his seven actives. Mary was the most dangerous period, though he doubted that she understood this yet. But there was nothing subtle about Mary. Rachel was, as Mary had said, related to Emma. She was the daughter of Emma's most successful granddaughter, Catherine—a woman who could easily have out-lived Emma if she had had better control of her mental shielding. As it was, she had spent too much of her time and energy trying to keep the mental noise of the rest of humanity out of her mind—as though she were a latent. But a latent would have been less sensi-tive. Catherine Davidson had simply decided at thirty-nine that she couldn't stand any more. She had lain down and died. Every one of Doro's previous healers had made similar decisions. But Rachel was only twenty-five, and her shielding was much better. Doro hoped that her decision, if she made it at all, was several years away. At any rate, she was very much alive now, and she would be more trouble than Mary could be expected to handle so quickly. But Doro decided to watch for a while before he warned Rachel. Before he gave Mary the help Mary did not know she needed. He sat by the fireplace and watched the two women meet.

Rachel was a full head taller, several shades darker, and from the look on her face, very puzzled. "Whoever you are," she said, "you're the one I'm looking for—the one who called me here."

"Yes."

"Why? Who are you? What do you want?"

"My name is Mary Larkin. Come on in and sit down." Then, when Rachel was seated, "I'm an active, like you. Or not quite like you. I'm an experiment." She looked at Doro. "One of his experi-ments that got out of hand."

Rachel and Doro found themselves staring at each other, Doro almost as surprised as Rachel. Clearly, Mary was not going to let him be the observer that he had intended to be.

"Doro?" said Rachel tentatively.

"Yes."

"Thank goodness. If you're here, this must make sense somehow. I just walked out in the middle of a service in New York. I was so desperate to get here that I had to steal some poor person's place on a plane."

"What did you do with Eli?" Doro asked.

"Left him to handle the rest of the day's services. No one will be healed, I know, but no doubt he'll entertain them. Doro, what's going on?"

"An experiment, as Mary said."

"But it obviously isn't out of hand yet. She's still alive. Or is that temporary?"

"If it is, it's none of your business," said Mary quickly.

"It wouldn't be if you hadn't dragged me here," said Rachel. "But since you did—"

"Since I did, Rachel, and since I am still alive, you'd better plan on my being around for a while."

"Either plan on it or do something about it myself," muttered Rachel. Then she frowned. "How do you know my name? I didn't tell you."

"Yes you did. This morning, when this whole damn thing started. When it was supposed to be ending for me." Suddenly, Mary seemed to sag. She looked more than tired, Doro thought. She looked a little frightened. Doro had made her rest for a few hours before Rachel's arrival. But how much real rest could she get thinking about what was in store for her? Thinking about it but not really knowing?

"What are you talking about?" demanded Rachel.

"I finished my transition this morning," said Mary. "And then, as if that wasn't enough, this other thing, this pattern, just sort of snapped into existence. Suddenly I was holding six other actives in a way that I didn't understand. Holding them, and calling them here."

Rachel was watching her, still frowning. "I thought there were others, but this whole thing was so insane I didn't trust my own senses. Are the others coming here, then?"

"Yes. They're on their way now."

"Do you want us here?"

"No!" Mary's vehemence startled Doro. Had she already decided that being "one of the owners" was so bad?

"Then, why don't you let us go?" said Rachel.

"I've tried," said Mary. "Karl has tried. My husband. He's been an active for ten years and he couldn't find a way out. As far as I can see, the only person who might have any helpful ideas is Doro."

And both women looked at him. Mary's whole attitude had changed. Suddenly she was edging away from the chance she had all but begged for earlier. And she kept passing the buck to Doro— kept saying in one way or another, "It's his fault, not mine!" That was true enough, but it was going to hurt her if she didn't stop emphasizing it. Rachel had already all but dismissed her as having no real importance. She was an irritant. No more. And healers were very efficient at getting rid of irritants.

"What kind of call did you receive, Rae?" he asked. "Was it like a verbal command, or like—"

"It was like getting hit with a club at first," she said. "And the noise... mental static like the worst moments of transition. Maybe I was picking up the last of Mary's transition. Then I was drawn here. There may have been words. I was only aware of images that let me see where I was going. Images, and that terrible planted compulsion to go. So here I am. I had to come. I had no choice at all."

Doro nodded. "And now that you're here, do you think you could leave if you wanted to?"

"I want to."

"And you can't?"

"I could, yes. But I wouldn't be very comfortable. At the airport, I realized that I was only a few miles away from here. I wanted that to be enough. I wanted to get a hotel room and wait until whoever was calling me got tired and gave up. I went to a hotel and tried to register. My hand was shaking so much I couldn't write." She shrugged. "I had to come. Now that I'm here I have to stay—at least until someone figures out a way to make your little experiment let me go."

"You'll need a room here, then," said Doro. "Mary."

Mary looked at him, then at Rachel. "Upstairs," she said tonelessly. "Come on."

They were on their way out when Doro spoke again. "Just a moment, Rae." Both women stopped. "It's possible that in a few days you'll need my help more than Mary will, but right now she is just out of transition."

Rachel said nothing.

"She'd better not even catch a cold, healer."

"Are you going to warn the others away from her too when they get here?"

"Of course. But since you're here now, and since you've already made your feelings clear, I didn't think I should wait to speak to you."

She smiled a little in spite of herself. "All right, Doro, I won't hurt her. But get me out of this, please. I feel like I'm wearing a damned leash."

Doro said nothing to that. He spoke to Mary. "Come back when you've got Rachel settled. I want to talk to you."

"Okay." She must have read something of what he wanted to say in his tone. She looked apprehensive. It didn't matter. She was an adult now, and on the verge of being a success. The first success of her kind. He would push her. She could stand it, and right now she needed it.

She came back a few minutes later and he motioned her into a chair opposite him.

"Are you shielded?" he asked.

"Yes."

"Can you tell by your pattern whether anyone else is near here—about to arrive?" His own ability had told him that no one was.

"No one is," she said.

"Good. We won't be interrupted." He looked at her silently for a long moment. "What happened?"

Her eyes slid away from his. "I don't know. I was just nervous, I guess."

"Of course you were. The trick is not to tell everyone about it."

She looked at him again, frowning, her small, expressive face a mask of concern. "Doro, I saw them in my mind and they didn't scare me. I didn't feel a thing. I had to keep reminding myself that they were probably dangerous, that I should be careful. And even when I was reminding myself, I don't think I really believed it. But now ... just meeting one of them ..."

"You're afraid of Rachel?"

"I sure as hell am."

It was an unusual thing for her to admit. Rachel must have thoroughly shaken her. "What is it about her that frightens you?"

"I don't know."

"You should know."

She thought for a moment. "It was just a feeling at first—like the feeling I ignored when I tried to read you this morning. A feeling of danger. A feeling that she could carry out those threats she kept not quite making." She stopped, looked at Doro. He said nothing. She went on. "I guess the dangerous thing about her is the one you hinted at just before we went up. That if she can heal the sick, she can probably make people sick too."

"I didn't say you should guess," said Doro. "I said you should *know*. You can read her every thought, every memory, without her being aware of it. Use your ability."

"Yeah." She took a deep breath. "I'm not used to that yet. I guess I'll be doing it automatically after a while."

"You'd better. And when I'm finished with you here, I want you to read them all. Including Karl. I want you to learn their weaknesses and their strengths. I want you to know them better than they know themselves. I don't want you to be uncertain or afraid with even one more of them."

She looked a little surprised. "Well, I can find out about them, all right. But as for not being afraid... if a person like Rachel wants to kill me, I'm not going to be able to stop her just because I know her." She paused for a moment. "Now I know—I just found out—that Rachel can give me a heart attack or a cerebral hemorrhage or any other deadly thing she wants to. So I know. So what?"

"What else did you find out about Rachel?"

"Junk. Nothing that does me any good. Stuff about her personal life, her work. I see she's a kind of parasite too. It must run in my family."

"Of course it does. But she's got nothing like your power. And you've seen a thing you don't realize you've seen, girl."

"What?"

"That you're at least as dangerous to Rachel as she is to you. Since you can read her through her shield, she won't be able to surprise you—unless you're just careless. And if you see her coming, you should be able to stop her."

"I don't see how, unless I kill her. But it doesn't matter. I was reading her again as you spoke. She's not about to come after me, now that you've ordered her not to."

"No, she wouldn't. But I won't always be standing between you and her. I'm giving you time—not very much time—to learn to handle yourself among these people. You'd better use it."

She swallowed, nodded.

"Do you understand what Rachel does? Do you see that you are to her, and to the others, what she is to her congregations?"

"A kind of mental vampire draining strength ... or something from people. Strength? Life force? I don't know what to call it."

"It doesn't matter what you call it. She has to take it to do her healing, and healing is the only purpose she's found for her life. Can you see that what she sets up at each of her services is a kind of temporary pattern?"

"Yes. But at least she doesn't kill anybody."

"She could, very easily. Ordinarily people have no defense against what she does—the way she feeds. If she took too much from her crowds, she'd begin killing the very old, the very young, the weak, even the sick that she intended to heal."

"I see."

"See, too, that while you can take from her, she can't take from you."

"Because I can shield her out."

"You don't have to shield her out. Let her in if you like."

"What do you mean?" She looked at him in horror.

"Exactly what you think I mean."

She frowned. "Are you telling me it's all right for me to kill now when, just a few hours ago, you said—"

"I know what I said. And I still don't *want* anyone killed. But I'm gambling on you, Mary. If you survive among these people, I have a chance of winning."

"Winning your empire. Is there anybody whose life you wouldn't risk for your Goddamn empire?"

"No."

For a moment, she glared at him angrily. Then the anger faded as though she didn't have the energy to sustain it. Doro was accustomed to the look. All his people faced him with it at one time or another. It was a look of submission.

"What I've decided to do," said Doro, "is give you the life of one of the actives if you need it. If you have to make an example of someone, I'll let it pass as long as you keep control of yourself and don't go beyond that one."

She thought about that for a long moment. "Permission to kill," she said finally. "I don't know how I feel about that."

"I hope you won't have to use it. But I don't want you totally handicapped."

"Thanks. I think. God, I hope I'm like Rachel. I hope I don't have to kill."

"You won't find out until you get started on someone."

She sighed. "Since this is all your fault, will you stay around for a while? I won't have Karl. I'll need somebody."

"That's another thing."

"What?"

"Stop telling the actives that the one show of power you've given them, the one thing you've done that they can't resist or undo, is my fault."

"But it is. . . ."

"Of course it is. And the moment they realize I'm here, they'll know it is. They don't have to be told. Especially when your telling them sounds like whining for pity. There's no pity in them, girl. They're going to feel about as sorry for you as you do for Vivian, or for Rina."

That seemed to sober her.

"You're going to have to grow up, Mary," he said quietly. "You're going to have to grow up fast."

She studied her hands, large, frankly ugly, her worst feature. They lay locked together in her lap. "Just stay with me for a while, Doro. I'll do the best I can."

"I had intended to stay."

She didn't bother hiding her relief. He got up and went to her.

Mary

There were incidents as my actives straggled in. I had pried through their minds and gotten to know all of them except Rachel before I even met them—so that none of them surprised me much.

Doro beat the holy shit out of Jan almost as soon as she arrived, because she'd done something stupid. I don't think he would have touched her, otherwise. One of the two kids she'd had by him was dead and he wasn't happy about it. She said it was an accident. He knew she was telling the truth. But she panicked.

He was talking to her—not very gently—and he started toward her for some reason. She ran out the front door. That, he doesn't allow. Don't run from him. Never run. He called her back, warned her. But she kept going. He would have gone after her if I hadn't stopped him.

"She'll be back," I said quickly. "Give her a chance. The pattern will bring her back." I wondered why I bothered to try to help her. I shouldn't have cared what happened to her. She had taken one look at Rachel and me and thought, *Oh, God, niggers!* And she was the one Doro had chosen to have kids by. Surely Rachel and Ada would have been better parents.

Anyway, Doro waited—more out of curiosity than anything else, I think. Jan came back in about thirty minutes. She came back cursing herself for the coward she was and believing that Doro would surely kill her now. Instead, he took her up to his room and beat her. Beat her for God knows how long. We could hear her screaming at first. I read the others and found what I thought I'd find. That every one of them knew from personal experience how bad Doro's beatings could be. I knew myself, though, like the others, I hadn't had one for a few years.

Now we just sat around not looking at each other and waiting for it to be over. After a while things were quiet. Jan was in bed for three days. Doro ordered Rachel not to help her.

Rachel had enough to do helping Jesse when he came in. He was the last to arrive, because he wasted two days trying to fight the pattern. He came in mad and tired and still pretty cut up from a fight he'd gotten into on the day I called him. I had found out about that by reading his mind. And I knew about the little town he owned in Pennsylvania, and the things he did to the people there, and the way he made them love him for it. I was all ready to hate his guts. Meeting him in person didn't give me any reason to change my mind.

He said, "You green-eyed bitch, I don't know how you dragged me here, but you damned well better let me go. Fast."

I was in a bad mood. I had been hearing slightly different versions of that same song from everybody for two days. I said, "Man, if you don't find something better to call me, I'm going to knock the rest of your teeth out."

He stared at me as though he wasn't quite sure he'd heard right. I guess he wasn't very used to people talking back to him and making it stick. He started toward me. The two words he managed to get out were, "Listen, bitch—"

I picked up a heavy little stone horse statuette from the end table next to me and tried to break his jaw with it. My thoughts were shielded so that he couldn't anticipate what I was going to do the way he did with the guy he beat up back in Donaldton. I left him lying on the floor bleeding and went up to Rachel's room.

She answered my knock and stood in her doorway glaring down at me. "Well?"

"Come downstairs," I said. "I have a patient for you."

She frowned. "Someone is hurt?"

"Yeah, Jesse Bernarr. He's the last member of our 'family' to come in. He came in a little madder than the rest of you."

I could feel Rachel sweep the downstairs portion of the house with her perception. She found Jesse and focused in tight on him. "Oh, fine," she muttered after a moment. "And me with nothing to draw on."

But she went right down to him. I followed, because I wanted to see her heal him. I hadn't seen anything so far but her memories.

She knelt beside him and touched his face. Suddenly she was viewing the damage from the inside, first coming to understand it, then stimulating healing. I couldn't find words to describe how she did it. I could see. I could understand, I thought. I could even show somebody else mentally. But I couldn't have talked about it. I began wondering if I could do it.

Rachel was still busy over Jesse when I left. I went into the kitchen, sort of in a daze. I was mentally going over a lot of Rachel's other healings—the ones I'd gotten from her memory. What I had learned from her just now made everything clearer. I felt as though I had just begun to understand a foreign language—as though I had been hearing it and hearing it, and suddenly a little of it was getting through to me. And that little was opening more to me.

I pulled open a drawer and took out a paring knife. I put it to my left arm, pressed down, cut quickly. Not deep. Not too deep. It hurt like hell, anyway. I made a cut about three inches long, then threw the knife into the sink. I held my arm over the sink too, because it started to bleed. I stopped the pain, just to find out whether or not I could. It was easy. Then I let it hurt again. I wanted to feel everything I did in every way I could feel it. I stopped the bleeding. I closed my eyes and let the fingers of my right hand move over the wound. Somehow that was better. I could concentrate my perception on the wound, view it from the inside, without being distracted by what my eyes were seeing. My arm began to feel warm as I began the healing, and it grew warmer, hot. It wasn't really an uncomfortable feeling, though, and I didn't try to shut it out. After a while it cooled, and I could feel that my arm was completely healed.

I opened my eyes and looked at it. Part of the arm was still wet with blood, where it had run down. But where the cut had been, I couldn't see much more than a fine scar. I rinsed my arm under the faucet and looked again. Nothing. Just that little scar that nobody would even see unless they were looking for it.

"Well," said Rachel's voice behind me. "Doro said you were related to me."

I turned to face her, smiling, a little prouder of myself than I should have been in the presence of a woman who could all but raise the dead. "I just wanted to see if I could do it."

"It took you about five times longer than it should have for a little cut like that."

"Shit, how long did it take you the first time you tried it?" Then I thought I saw a chance to make peace with her. I had been in one argument after another with the actives since they arrived. It was time to stop. It really was. "Never mind," I said. "You're right. I did take a long time, compared to you. Maybe you could help me learn to speed it up. Maybe you could teach me a little more about healing, too."

"Either you learn on your own or you don't learn," she said. "No one taught me."

"Was there anybody around who could have?"

She didn't say anything.

"Look, you'd be a good teacher, and I'd like to learn."

"Good luck."

"The hell with you, then." I turned away from her, disgusted, and went to the refrigerator to make myself a ham-and-cheese sandwich. I was skinny at least partly because I didn't usually snack on things like that, but I felt hungry now. I figured Rachel would leave, but she didn't.

"Where's the cook?" she asked.

"In her room watching soap operas, I guess. That's usually where she is when she isn't in here."

"Would you call her down?"

"Why?"

"I made Jesse sleep when I finished with him, but I could feel then how hungry he was."

I froze with my sandwich halfway to my mouth. "Is he? And how do *you* feel?" I didn't have to ask. I could read it from her faster than she could say it.

"Fine. Not drained at all. I—" She looked at me, suddenly accusing. "You know how I should be feeling, don't you?"

"Yes."

"How do you know?"

I was surprised to realize how much I didn't want to tell her. None of them knew that I could read them through their shields, that nothing they could do would keep me out. They hated me enough already. But I had already decided not to hide my ability. Not to act as though I were ashamed of it or afraid of them. "I read it in your mind," I said.

"When?" She was beginning to look outraged.

"That doesn't matter. Hell, I don't even remember exactly when."

"I've been shielded most of the time. Unless you read it just now while I was healing... you were reading me then, weren't you?"

"Yes."

"You watched what I did, then came in here to try it on yourself."

"That's right. Doesn't it seem strange to you that you don't feel drained?"

"We'll get back to that. I want to find out more about your snooping. I didn't feel you reading me just now."

I took a deep breath. "I could say that was because you were so busy with Jesse, but I won't bother. Rachel, you'll never feel me reading you unless I want you to."

She looked at me silently for several seconds. "It's part of your special ability, then. You can read people without their being aware of it. And... you can read people without thinning your shield enough to have them read you. Because you weren't open just now. I would have noticed." She stopped as though waiting for me to say something. I didn't. She went on, "And you can read people right through their shields. Can't you!" It was a demand or an accusation. Like she was daring me to admit it.

"Yes," I said. "I can."

"So you've taken our mental privacy as well as our freedom."

"It looks like I've given you something, too."

"Given me what?"

"Freedom from the parasitic need you feel so guilty about sometimes."

"If you weren't hiding behind Doro, I'd show you how much I appreciate your gift."

"No doubt you'd try. But since Doro is on my side, shouldn't we at least try to get along?"

She turned and walked away from me.

Nothing was settled and I had one more strike against me. But at least I was starting to learn to heal. I had a feeling I should learn as much as I could about that as quickly as I could. In case Rachel tried something desperate.

Nobody tried anything for a while, though. There was only the usual arguing. Jesse promised me he was going to "get" me. He was a big, dumb, stocky guy, blond, good-looking, mean—a troublemaker. But, somehow, he was the one active that I was never afraid of. And he was wary of me. He told himself I was crazy, and he kept away from me in spite of his threat.

People began to get together in the house to do something besides argue.

Seth started sleeping in Ada's room, and Ada, our mouse, started to look a little more alive.

Jesse went to Rachel's room one night to thank her for healing him. His gratitude must have pleased her. He went back the next night to thank her again.

Karl said "Good morning" to me once. I think it just slipped out.

Rachel told Doro—not me—that I had been right. That she could heal now without taking strength from a crowd. In fact, she said she wasn't sure she still could draw strength from crowds. She said the pattern had changed her, limited her somehow. Now she seemed to be using her patients' own strength to heal them—which sounded as though it would be dangerous if her patient was in bad shape to start with. Jesse had merely eaten a couple of steaks when she let him wake up. Steaks, a lot of fries, salad, and about a quart of milk. But Jesse was such a big guy that I suspected that was the way he usually ate. I found out later that I was right. So, evidently, the healing hadn't weakened him that much.

I kept to myself during those first days. I watched everybody—read everybody, that is. I found that Rachel had spread the word about my abilities and everybody figured I was watching them. They didn't like it. They thought a lot of shit at me when I was in a room with them. But I almost never read them steadily when I was with them, talking to them. I had to keep my attention on what they were saying. So it took me a while to realize that I was being cursed out on two levels.

I was settling in, though. I was learning not to be afraid of any of them. Not even Karl. They were all older than I was and they were all physically bigger. For a while, I had to keep telling myself I couldn't afford to let that matter. If I went on letting them scare me, I'd never be able to handle them. After a while, I started to convince myself. Maybe I was influenced by the kind of thoughts I picked up from them when they were off guard. Sometimes, even while they were complaining or arguing or cursing at me, they were aware of being very comfortable within the pattern. Jesse wasn't getting any of the mental static that had used to prevent him from driving a car, and Jan didn't have to always be careful what she touched—bothered by the latent mental images she had used to absorb from everything. And, of course, Rachel didn't need her crowds. And Clay Dana didn't need as much help from Seth as he had before he came to us. Clay seemed to be getting some benefit from the pattern even though he wasn't a member of it. And that left Seth with more time for Ada.

Everybody was settling in. But the others didn't like it. It scared them that they were not only getting used to their leashes but starting to see benefits in them. It scared hell out of them that maybe they were giving in the way ordinary people gave in to them. That they were getting to be happy slaves like Karl's servants. Their fear made them fight harder than ever against me. I could understand their feelings, but that wasn't enough. I had to do something about them. I was fed up with hearing about them. I thought for a while, then went to talk to Doro.

I had come to depend on Doro more now than I ever had before. He was the only person in the house that I could talk to without getting blamed, cursed, or threatened. I had all but moved into his room. So, one night, about two weeks after my transition, I walked into his room, fell across his bed, and said, "Well, I guess this has gone on long enough."

"What?" he asked. He was at his desk scribbling something that looked like ancient Egyptian hieroglyphics in a notebook.

"Everybody sitting around waiting for something that isn't going to happen," I said. "Waiting for the pattern to just disappear."

"What are you going to do?"

"Get them all together and make them face a few facts. And then, after they stop screaming, get them thinking about what they can do with themselves in spite of the pattern." I sat up and looked at him. "Hell, they're all telepaths. They don't have to be able to go miles from home to get work done. And God knows they need something to do!"

"Work?"

"Right. Jobs, interests, goals." I had been thinking about it for days now. "They can make their own jobs. It will give them less time to bitch at me. Rachel can have a church if she wants one. The others can look around, find out what they want."

"If they're reasonable. They might not be, you know."

"Yeah."

"They might not stop screaming, as you put it, until they've tried to lynch you."

"Yeah," I repeated. I took a deep breath. "Want to sit in and see the blood?"

He smiled. "There might not be any blood if I'm there."

"Then, by all means, sit in."

"Oh, I will. But it will only be to let them know I'm acknowledging your authority over them. I'm going to turn them loose, Mary."

I swallowed. "Already, huh?"

"They're yours. It's time you jumped in among them."

"I guess so." I really wasn't surprised. I had seen him working up to this. He couldn't read my mind, but he watched me as closely as I watched everybody else. He questioned me. I didn't mind. He let the others complain to him about me, but he didn't question them about me or make them promises. That, I appreciated. So now it was time for me to be kicked out of the nest.

"You'll be leaving if this works, won't you?" I asked.

"For a while. I'll be back. I have a suggestion that might help you both before and after I leave, though."

"What?"

"Let Karl in on what you're going to do before you do it. Let him get over some of his anger with you and see the sense in what you're saying. Then, if I understand him as well as I think I do, he'll stand with you if any of the others threaten you."

"Isn't that just trading one protector for another? I'm supposed to be able to protect myself."

"Oh, you can. But, chances are, you'll have to do it by killing someone. I was trying to help you avoid that."

I nodded. I knew he was still worried that my killing might be a chain-reaction thing. That if I took one of the actives, then, sooner or later, I'd have to take another. And another. I had a feeling that, when he left, he wouldn't go any farther than Emma's house. And from there, he'd keep whatever special senses he had trained on me.

"Is Karl alone now?" he asked.

I checked. "Yes, for a change." Karl had been screwing around with Jan, of all people. He couldn't have found a better way to disgust me.

"Then, go to him now. Talk to him."

I gave Doro a dirty look. It was late, and I was in no mood to hear the things Karl would probably say to me. I just wanted to go to bed. But I got up and went to see Karl.

He was lying on his back interfering with the thoughts of some sleeping local politician. I hesitated for a moment to find out what he was doing. He was just making sure that a company he and Doro controlled got a zone variance it needed to erect a building. He had a job, anyway. I knocked at his door.

He listened silently to what I had to tell him, his face expressionless.

"So we're here, we belong to you, and that's that," he said quietly.

"That wasn't my point."

"Yes it was. Along with the fact that we might as well find some way to live our lives this way and make the best of it."

"All I want us to do is settle down and start acting like human beings again."

"If that's still what we are. What do you want from me?"

"Help, if you can give it. If you will."

"Me, help you?"

"You're my husband."

"That wasn't my idea."

I opened my mouth, then closed it again. This wasn't the time to fight with him.

"Doro will back you up," he said. "He's all you need."

"He's putting me on my own. He's putting *us* on *our* own."

"Why? What have you done?"

"Nothing, so far. It's not punishment. He just thinks it's time we found out whether we can survive without him—as a group."

"Whether *you* can survive."

"No, us, really. Because, if things go bad, I'm not about to let the others get me without taking as many of them as I can with me." I took a deep breath. "That's why I want your help. I'd like to get through this without killing anybody."

He looked a little surprised. "Are you so sure you can kill?"

"Positive."

"How can you know? You've never tried."

"You don't want to hear how I know, believe me."

"Don't be stupid. If you want my help at all, you'd better tell me everything."

I looked at him. I made myself just look at him until I could answer quietly. "I know the same way you know how to eat when you're hungry. I'm that kind of parasite, Karl. I suppose you and the others might as well face it the way I have."

"You... you're saying you're a female Doro?"

"Not exactly, but that's close enough."

"I don't believe you."

"Oh yes you do."

He stared at me silently for a moment. "I didn't want to believe you could read me through my shield either."

"I can. That's part of my ability, too."

"You have enough abilities not to need my help."

"I told you why I need you."

"Yes. You don't want to kill."

"Not unless somebody is stupid enough to attack me."

"But if hunger is what you feel, how can you avoid doing something about it eventually? You'll have to kill."

"It's more like having an appetite—like being able to eat but not really being hungry."

"But you will get hungry. It seems to me that's why we're here. We're your food supply. You're gathering people the way Doro does. It just isn't as much work for you as it is for him."

"Yeah," I said softly. "I've been thinking things like that myself. They might be all wrong. But even if they aren't, I don't know what to do about it."

He turned his head, stared at a bookcase. "Short of committing suicide, there's not much you can do."

"And I'm not about to do that. But I'll tell you, as mad as these people make me sometimes, it would be almost as hard for me to kill one of them as it would be for me to commit suicide. I don't want their lives."

"For now."

"And I don't want anybody forcing me to change my mind. Because, if I do, I'm not sure I'll be able to control myself. I might kill more of you than I mean to." I got up to leave. "Karl, I'm not asking you to make up your mind now, or promise me anything. I just wanted you to know there was a choice to make." I started for the door.

"Wait a minute."

I stopped, waited.

"You're closed, shielded all the time," he said. "I don't think you've unshielded once since you did it for me after your transition."

"Would you if you were living with people who wanted to kill you?"

"What if I asked you to open for me? Just for me. Now."

"Why?"

"Because you need me. And because I need to see the truth of what you're telling me."

"I thought that was settled."

"I've got to see it for myself, Mary. I've got to be certain. I can't... do what you're asking until I've seen for myself that it's necessary."

I read him, saw that he was telling the truth. He was angry and bitter and he didn't like himself much for even thinking about siding with me. But he knew it was his best chance for survival—for a while, at least.

I opened. I was more worried about accidentally taking him than I was about what he might find out. I was a little touchier about his rummaging through my memories than I had been before, but I put up with it. He didn't go after anything more than verification of what I had told him. That was all he cared about.

"All right," he said after a moment.

I shielded, looked at him.

"I'll do what I can to help you," he said. "And heaven help both of us."

Chapter Seven

Mary

Winning Karl over gave me the courage to get right to work on the others. I called everybody together in the living room at around ten the next morning. Karl came in with Vivian, and Seth Dana came with Ada and Clay. Vivian and Clay didn't really have to be there, of course, but it didn't matter to me that they were.

Karl had to go and get Jan. She said she wasn't about to take orders from me. I figured we'd have this meeting and then, if she still felt that way, I'd show her how gentle Doro had been with her.

And Doro had to get Jesse and Rachel. They were shacked up in Jesse's room now, like they meant to stay together for a while. They were sure as hell together in their opinion of me. In fact, they were so close together and they hated me so much that I knew if I had to take anybody, it would probably be one of them. And the way they had been acting for the past few days, I didn't see how I could get away with taking just one. Neither of them was going to sit by and watch the other killed.

That bothered me. I realized that their feelings for each other could be used against them—that, for a while at least, I could control one by threatening the other. But, somehow, I didn't want to do that. I'd try it if I had to, rather than kill them both and make myself a liability to Doro, but I hoped they wouldn't push me that far.

Once they were all in the room, with Doro sitting by himself off to one side, I made my speech. Doro told me later that I was too blunt, too eager to threaten and challenge. He was probably right.

I told everybody that the pattern was a permanent fixture binding them to me. It wasn't going anywhere, I wasn't going anywhere, and they weren't going to do anything to me. I told them I could kill them, would kill them if they pushed me, but that I didn't want to kill them if I could avoid it. I told them to follow the feelings I knew they were suppressing and accept the pattern. Get themselves some new interests or revive some old ones, get jobs if they wanted them, stop sitting around bitching like kids. I spoke quietly to them. I didn't rant and rave. But they still didn't like what I had to say.

And, of course, except for Karl, they didn't want to believe me. I had to open to them. I had thought that might be necessary. I hadn't been looking forward to it but I was ready to do it. First, though, I did what I could to throw a scare into them.

"Look," I said quietly. "You all know me. You know I'll do whatever I have to to defend myself. Try anything more than reading me now, and you've had it. That's all."

I opened. I could see that they were moving cautiously, trying to find out whether I had the power I claimed before they made any move against me—which was intelligent of them.

I had never opened my mind to anyone but Karl before. I had only the memories of the others to tell me what it was like to open to more than one person at a time. They had never done it deliberately. It was just that they couldn't stay shielded all the time, the way I could. Their shields cut off their mental perception totally. In a way, for them, shielding was like wandering around wearing a gag, a blindfold, and earplugs. None of them could put up with it for long. So sometimes they picked up things from each other. Sometimes two or three of them picked up something from one. They didn't like it, but they were learning to live with it. Doro had said that in itself was more than he had dared to hope for. Actives had never been able to live with it before. He said it seemed much easier for my actives to keep out of each other's minds than it had been for earlier generations. He gave my pattern the credit for that. Maybe my pattern deserved the credit for the way I was able to accept them all into my mind, too. Like them, I didn't enjoy it. But I wasn't nervous or afraid, because I knew I could defend myself if I had to, and I knew none of them meant to try anything—yet. I was just uncomfortable. Like I'd suddenly found myself stark naked in front of a lot of strangers, all of whom were taking a good look.

At least it was easy to keep track of them and know who was getting what. I hadn't been sure it would be with so many. But I spotted Jesse the moment he decided to do a little snooping into matters other than the truth of what I had told them.

I reached out and contracted the muscle of his lower leg into a tight, hard knot.

I had taken Rachel's advice and been working on my own to develop whatever healing ability I had. I was still a long way from being ready to call myself a healer, but I had learned a few things from viewing my body and other people's bodies from the inside. And I had read medical books and I had read Rachel. I found that I learned best, though, by watching people who had things wrong with them—seeing how their bodies healed, understanding what had gone wrong in the first place. If I could understand it, I could make it happen.

A few days before, I had gotten a bad cramp in my leg.

So now Jesse had a bad cramp in his leg. He yelled, more surprised than hurt—although it did hurt. And, of course, he snapped his attention away from me like a released rubber band.

It was a very quick, very easy thing, to cause a cramp. By the time the others realized I had done it, I was finished and paying attention to them again. They dropped away from me almost all at once. Almost. Rachel hung on, shaped her thoughts into words for me.

Don't think you can ever handle me that way!

Of course not, I sent back. *Unfortunately for you, the only way I can handle you is by killing you.*

She dropped away from me mad and scared and ashamed of herself for being scared.

As she broke contact, Jesse stood up. His cramp had faded away normally, since I hadn't done anything to prolong it or make it worse. I could have used his own muscle to break his leg. He didn't seem to realize that. He started toward me.

Karl got up quickly, stepped in front of Jesse. A distance runner facing a football player. They made a contrast. Karl spoke just as Jesse was about to knock him out of the way.

"A question, Jess," he said quietly. "Only a question. What do you imagine you'll do when you reach her—aside from letting her make an example of you, I mean." And he stepped out of Jesse's path and sat down again. Jesse stayed where he was, glaring first at Karl, then at me.

"One woman," he said bitterly. "A woman, for Godsake! The biggest damn thing about her is her mouth! And you're all going to let her tell you you're serving a life sentence in this place." He looked around the room, his eyes accusing. "She couldn't kill more than one or two of us if we all hit her at once. Don't you see? Her only hold on us is that the rest of you are so afraid of being the one she gets that you'd rather stay on her Goddamn leash than stand up to her!"

He looked around the room again, this time challengingly. "I'm willing to take a chance. Who'll stand with me? Who's as sick of being in jail as I am?"

I was watching Rachel. She looked at me and I glanced from her to Jesse, then back to her. The threat was delivered that simply, for what it was worth. Rachel understood. She kept quiet. Jesse was turning toward her when Seth spoke up.

"Jess, it seems to me you're forgetting about Doro."

Jesse looked over at Doro. Doro looked back expressionlessly. "I'm not forgetting." Jesse spoke to Seth, but kept his eyes on Doro. "I may have read a little more from Mary than you did—than any of the rest of you did. Maybe nobody but me noticed that Doro was about to dump her—put her on her own with us and let her sink or swim as best she could."

Nobody said anything.

"Well?" said Jesse to Doro. "Weren't you?"

"I was," said Doro. "But I hadn't done it yet."

"As long as you were going to, what difference does it make?"

Doro leaned back in his chair. "You tell me."

"You didn't say anything," said Jesse, frowning. "You weren't going to stop me."

"No."

"What were you going to do? Let me go through with it, and then kill me if she hadn't managed to?"

"Yes."

Jesse stared at him as though he was finally realizing that it was Doro he was talking to, not one of us. Without another word, he turned and went back to his chair.

Doro got up, came closer in to join the group. He sat down beside me, spoke to me softly.

"I warned you."

"I know," I said.

He looked around at the others. "You're all powerful people," he said. "I wish you weren't in such a hurry to kill yourselves. Alive, you could grow into something impressive and worthwhile."

"All seven of us," said Rachel bitterly.

"If you survive as a group, you won't be only seven long. Your numbers are small because I've deliberately kept them small. If you can work together now, you can begin to grow slowly through your own children and through the latents scattered around the country who are capable of producing telepathically active children. Latents who need only the right mates to produce actives. The seven of you can be the founders and the leaders of a new race." He paused, glanced at Jesse. "For any of you who don't realize it, that's what I want. That's what I've been trying to achieve for thousands of years. It's what I'll be on my way to achieving if the seven of you can stay together on your own without killing each other. I think you can. I think that, in spite of the way you've been acting, your own lives are still of some importance to you. Of course, if they aren't, I want to know that, too. So I'm withdrawing my protection from Mary. And, incidentally, I'm releasing her from the restriction put on her." He glanced at me. "The rest of you don't know about that. You don't have to. You're free now to behave as intelligently or as stupidly as you like."

"You want us to spend the rest of our lives here?" demanded Rachel.

"If that's what turns out to be necessary," said Doro. "I doubt that it will be, though. You're a very young group. If you survive to grow older, I think you'll work out a comfortable arrangement."

"What arrangement!"

"I don't know, Rae. You're also a new kind of group. You'll have to find your own way. Perhaps pairs of you will take over other houses in this neighborhood. Perhaps, in time, you'll even find a way to travel long distances from Mary without discomfort."

"I wish I could show you what it feels like to go just a few miles from her," muttered Jesse. "Compare it to straining against a choke chain."

Doro looked over at him. "It's easier to take now, though, than it was when you first got here, isn't it?" He knew it was. I had read Jesse and told him so days before.

Jesse opened his mouth, probably to lie. But he knew he had about as much chance of getting a lie past Doro as he did of getting one past me. He closed his mouth for a moment, then said, "Easier or not, I don't like it any more now than I ever did. None of us do!"

"That's at least partly because all of you are trying so hard not to."

"I'm not trying," said Jan. "I'm just slowly going out of my mind from being cooped up in this place. I can't stand it!"

"You'll find a way to stand it," said Doro coldly.

"But why should I? Why should any of us? Why should we all suffer because of *her?*"

There was loud agreement all around.

"You needn't suffer at all," he said. "You know better than I do how easily you could slip into your new roles here if you wanted to." That was something else I had told him—how they were fighting not only me but their own inclinations. He took a deep breath. "But you're on your own. It would be wise of you to look for ways to live with your new situation, but if you choose not to, go ahead and kill each other."

"What if we just kill Mary?" said Rachel. She was looking at me as she spoke.

Doro gave her a look of disgust. Then he got up and left me sitting alone, went back to his place. Rachel looked at Jesse. Jesse picked it right up.

"Who's with us?" he said. "Who wants out of this jail now? Jan?"

"You want to... to kill her?" asked Jan.

"You know any other way out?"

"No. All right. I'm with you."

"Seth?"

"How many people you figure you need to kill one woman, Jess?"

"As many as I can get, man, and you're a damned fool if you can't see why. You've read her. You've seen what kind of parasite she is. We either get together and kill her, or we wait, and maybe she kills us off one by one."

I sat there watching, listening to all this, wondering why I was waiting. Jesse was getting people together to kill me and I was waiting. The only intelligent thing I was doing was keeping part of my attention on Rachel. She was the only one of them who might try something on her own. She could damage my body, and she could do it very quickly, I knew. But she couldn't do it without thinking about it first, deciding to do it. She was dead when she made that decision.

Seth turned to face me, stared at me for several seconds. "You know," he said, "in the two weeks I've been here, I don't think you and I have done much more than pop off at each other a couple of times. I don't know you."

"You've been busy," I said. I glanced at Ada, who sat close to him, looking scared.

"You're not afraid," said Seth.

I shrugged.

"Or, if you are, you hide it pretty good."

And Jesse. "Are you in or out, Dana?"

"Out," said Seth quietly.

"You're with her?" Jesse gestured sharply at me. "You like being a Goddamn slave?"

"No, not with her. Not against her, either. She hasn't done anything to me, man. At least, not anything that was her fault."

"What the hell does 'fault' have to do with it? You're going to be stuck with her for the rest of your life unless we get rid of her now."

Seth looked at Ada, then at Clay on his other side. I knew already that Ada wanted no part of this. Jesse, Jan, and Rachel were confirming Ada's worst fears; were, in her opinion, acting like people who deserved to be quarantined. Clay had been bitter about being dragged away from the fresh start he was going to make in Arizona. And when he heard I was the one who had done the dragging, he decided I was the one to hate. Then, like Seth, he had started to see me as just another of Doro's creations, no more to blame for what I was than anyone else in the house. Ironically, he felt sorry for me. He didn't want Seth involved in killing me.

"Well?" demanded Jesse. He glared at Seth.

"I've said what I had to say," said Seth.

Jesse turned away from him in disgust. "Well, Karl, I don't suppose you want to change sides."

Karl smiled a little. "I would if you had a chance, Jess. You don't, you know."

"Karl, please." Jan. Sweet Jan. Maybe I could get her, too. "Karl, with you helping us, we would have a chance."

Karl ignored her, glanced at me. "You are going to try to talk them out of this, aren't you?"

I nodded, turned to face Jesse. "Man, with three people insisting that they're going to attack me, I won't have time to be gentle. No more little cramps. You jump me, and you and Rachel are dead. I might not be able to get Jan, but you two don't have a chance."

"Let's make it even stronger than that," said Karl. "I don't want fighting. There's a possibility that Mary might lose control and do a lot more damage than she intends to do. I've read her more thoroughly than you have. I think there's a real danger that, once she got started, she might take us all. If the three of you are foolish enough to attack her in spite of that possibility, you'd better attack me too."

The words were goads to Jesse. Abruptly, he dove at me through his strand of the pattern. I had no warning. He acted on impulse, without thinking. And using the pattern that way.... Until now, nobody had really used the pattern except me. His strand of the pattern struck at me snakelike. Fast. Blindingly fast.

I didn't have time to think about reacting. What happened, happened automatically. And it happened even faster than Jesse had moved.

He was mine. His strength was mine. His body was worthless to me, but the force that animated it was literally my ambrosia—power, sustenance, life itself.

By the time Jesse realized what was happening and tried to twist away, there was almost nothing left of him. His strand of the pattern thrashed feebly, uselessly.

I realized that I could leave him that way. I watched him with a kind of detached interest, and it occurred to me that if I let him go he would grow strong again. He was terrified now, and weak, but he wasn't getting any weaker on his own. He could live, if I let him, if I wasn't too greedy. He could live and grow strong and feed me again.

I opened my eyes, wondering when I had shut them. I felt higher than I ever had before. I held out my hand and looked at it. It was shaking. I was shaking all over, but, God, I felt good.

Everybody was looking at Jesse slumped in his chair. The surprise they were all radiating told me that he had just lost consciousness. They were not quite aware yet of what had happened. Rachel began to realize it first. She began turning toward me—in slow motion, it seemed—meaning to get her revenge. She thought Jesse was dead. She, a healer, thought he was dead, but I knew he was alive.

She finished turning. She was going to rupture a good-sized blood vessel in my brain.

I took her.

She didn't hand herself to me the way Jesse had. She fought me briefly. But somehow her struggles only helped me drain her strength. I was more conscious of what I was doing with her. I could see how my mental image of her shrank in proportion to the amount of strength I took. I took less from her than I had from Jesse. I didn't need anything at all from her—except peace. I wanted her to stop her useless struggling. I wanted her not to be able to do what she wanted to do to me. That was all. I let her know it.

Jesse! Her thought was full of bitterness and anger and grief. I tried to soothe her wordlessly the way I might have handled a frightened child. She struggled harder, terrified, hysterical, giving me more of her strength by her struggles.

Finally, she stopped, exhausted. *Jesse.* Grief now. Only grief.

He's alive, I sent.

He's dead! I saw him die.

I tell you he's alive. You took too quick a look. I pressed through her grief so that she could see that I was giving her truth. *He is alive. I didn't want his life. I don't want yours. Will you make me take yours anyway?*

You aren't going to kill me?

Not unless you make me.

Then, let me go. Let me see Jesse.

I let her go, opened my eyes again. Evidently, closing them was some kind of reflex. Now the others were looking at Rachel, were turning to look at me. I felt better than ever. But steadier now. No more shaking. I felt in control. Before, I'd felt ready to take off and fly across the room. Everybody was staring at me.

"They're both all right," I said. "Weak, I guess. Put them to bed. They'll regain their strength." Like Rachel's crowds going away to regain their strength. I remembered Jan suddenly and looked at her.

She stared back, round-eyed.

"How about you?" I said.

"No!" I thought she was going to get up and run out the door again. "No."

I laughed at her. I don't think I would have done that if I hadn't been so high. I might have had a lot more to say to her, but I wouldn't have laughed.

"What did you do?" asked Karl.

I looked at him, and I could have hugged him for no reason at all. No. There was a reason. A big one. "I found out something," I said. "I just found out that I don't have to kill."

"But what did you do to them?"

Abruptly I was annoyed, almost angry at him for wanting details now, when it was all so new, when I just wanted to sit back and savor what I was feeling. Doro came up behind me, put his hands on my shoulders, and massaged gently.

"Calm down a little," he said. "I know you feel good, but calm down."

"High," I said. I grinned at him. "I feel high. You know."

"Yes. See if you can rein yourself in enough to tell us what you did."

"You know."

"Tell us anyway."

"Took some of their strength." I leaned back, relaxed against the couch, pulling my thoughts together. "Only some. I'm not a monster. At least not the kind you made me think I was." Then, as an afterthought. "I took more from Jesse. I didn't know what I was doing when he jumped me."

"Seth, check Jesse," Doro ordered.

Apparently Seth did. I didn't pay any attention. "He's still breathing," Seth said after a moment.

"Rae," Doro said, "how do you feel?" Rachel was conscious then. But she didn't say anything. Curiosity reached me through my private haze. I looked at her.

She was crying. She wasn't making any noise at all, but her whole body shook. She made a sound of pain as we all turned to look at her, and hid her face in her hands. She was shielded to the others. But to me she radiated shame and defeat. Humiliation.

That reached me and cleared the nonsense out of my head. I stood up, half expecting to find myself staggering. I was steady enough, though. Good.

I went to her and took her arm. I knew she wanted to be away from us. Tears, especially tears of defeat, were private things. She looked up, saw that it was me, and tried to pull her arm away.

"Stop acting stupid," I told her. "Get up and come on."

She stared at me. I still had hold of her arm. She started to get up, then realized how weak she was. She was glad enough to lean on me then.

She swallowed, whispered, "What about Jesse?"

What in the name of heaven did she see in him? "The others will see that he gets upstairs," I said. I glanced back at Doro. "She'll be okay."

He nodded, went over and draped Jesse's big body over one shoulder, then followed Rachel and me upstairs.

Chapter Eight

Mary

The meeting just dissolved. Nobody made me any promises. Nobody bowed or scraped. Nobody even looked scared—or felt scared. I checked. Once they got over their surprise, they were even reassured. They could see that Jesse and Rachel were going to be all right. They could see that all I wanted from them was a little co-operation. And now they knew they would be better off if they co-operated. The atmosphere of the house was more relaxed than it had been since the day of my transition.

Seth Dana came up and grinned at me. "Don't you get the feeling you should have done this two weeks ago?"

I smiled back and shook my head. "I don't think so. Two weeks ago, I would have had to kill somebody."

He frowned. "I don't see why."

"Everything was too new. You were all on short fuses. You and Ada hadn't gotten together and mellowed each other, so one or both of you would have been against me. If you had, Karl probably would have, too. He was about ready to strangle me anyway, then." I shrugged. "This is better. People have had time to cool off."

He gave me an odd look. "What do you think might have happened if you'd waited a little longer than two weeks, then, let Jesse and Rachel do some mellowing?"

"Jesse and Rachel weren't mellowing. They were feeding on each other's hatred, building each other up to jump me."

"You know," he said, "I got the impression at first that you just threw this meeting together on the spur of the moment."

"I did."

"Yeah. After two weeks of watching everybody and making sure your timing was as right as you could make it."

Clay Dana came over to where Seth and I were talking. Close up, he looked sort of gray and sick. I thought he must have just had a bad bout of mental interference. "Congratulations," he said to me. "Now that we all know the new pecking order, do either of you have any aspirins?"

Seth looked at him with concern. "Another headache?"

"Another, hell. It's the same one I've had for three days."

"From mental interference?" I asked.

"What else?"

"I thought you weren't getting as much of that now as you used to."

"I wasn't," he said. "It stopped altogether for a few days. That never happened in the middle of a city before. Then, three days ago, it started to come back worse than ever."

That bothered me. I hadn't paid much attention to Clay since he arrived, but I knew that anything new and different that went wrong with him, with his out-of-control mental ability, would eventually get blamed on me, on my pattern.

Seth spoke up as though on cue. "Look, Mary, I've been meaning to ask you if you could figure out what was happening to Clay. He's been in really bad shape, and it just about has to have something to do with the pattern."

"First the aspirins," said Clay. "Find out what you want after—Hey!"

That "Hey!" was almost a shout. I had gotten rid of his headache for him fast—like switching off a light.

"Okay?" I asked, knowing it was.

"Sure." He looked at me as though he suddenly wanted to get away from me.

I stayed with him mentally for a few moments longer, trying to find out just what was wrong with him. I didn't really know what to look for. I just assumed that it had something to do with the pattern. I took a quick look through his memories, thinking that that uncontrolled ability of his might have tuned in on the pattern somehow. But it hadn't in any way that I could see.

I scanned all the way back to the day he and Seth had arrived at the house. It was quick work but frustrating. I couldn't find a damned thing. Nothing. I switched my attention to the pattern. I had no idea at all of what to look for there and I was getting mad. I checked the pattern strand that stretched from Seth to me. Seth was in mental contact with Clay sometimes to protect him. Maybe, without realizing it, he had done something more than protect.

He hadn't.

I had nowhere else to go. There was something especially galling about suffering a defeat now, just minutes after I had won my biggest victory. But what could I do?

I shifted my attention back to Clay. There was a glimmer of something just as I shifted—like the glimmer of a fine spider web that catches the light just for a second and then seems to vanish again. I froze. I shifted back to the pattern, bringing it into focus very slowly. At first there was nothing. Then, just before I would have had a strong, clear focus on the pattern strands of my six actives, there was that glimmer again. I managed to keep it, this time, by not trying to sharpen my focus on it. Like looking at something out of the corner of your eye.

It was a pattern strand. A slender, fragile-seeming thread, like a shadow of one of the comparatively substantial strands of my actives. But it was a pattern strand. Somehow, Clay had become a member of the pattern. How?

I could think of only one answer. The pattern was made up of actives. Just actives, no latents until now. No latents period. Clay was on his way to transition.

The moment the thought hit me, I knew it was right. After a ten-year delay, Clay was going to make it. I tried to tell myself that I wasn't sure. After all, I had never seen anyone who was about to go into transition before. But I couldn't even make myself doubt. Clay was going to come through. He would belong to me, like the others. I knew it.

I brought my attention back to Seth and Clay, who stood waiting.

"That took long enough," said Seth. "What did you find out?"

"That your brother's not a latent any more," I said. "That he's headed toward transition."

There was a moment of complete silence. Then came quick, bitter disappointment radiating from both men. They didn't believe me.

Seth spoke quietly. "Mary, Doro himself gave up on Clay years ago, said he wouldn't ever reach transition."

"I know it. But there was no pattern back then."

"But Doro explained that—"

"Damnit, Seth, I'm explaining that Doro was wrong. He might know a hell of a lot, but he can't foretell the future. And he can't use my pattern to see what I can see!"

Karl came up as I was talking. When I finished, he asked, "What are you shouting about now?"

I told him and he just shrugged.

"Doro wants to see us both in the library," he said. "Now."

"Wait a minute," said Seth. "She can't leave now." He looked at me. "You've got to tell us how you know... how after all these years this could happen." So they were beginning to believe me.

"I'll have to talk to you after I see what Doro wants," I said. "It probably won't take long."

I followed Karl away from them, hoping I could get back to them soon. I wanted to learn more about what was happening to Clay myself. I was excited about it. But now, Doro and the Dana brothers aside, there was something else I had to do.

"Karl."

We had almost reached the library door. He stopped, looked at me.

"Thanks for your help."

"You didn't need it."

"Yes I did. I might not have been able to stop myself from killing if they had pushed me harder."

Karl nodded disinterestedly, turned to go into the library.

"Wait a minute."

He gave me a look of annoyance.

"I have a feeling that, even though you sided with me, you're the only one in the house that I haven't really won over."

"You didn't win anyone over," he said. "You bludgeoned the others into submission. I had already submitted."

"The hell with that," I said. I lowered my gaze a little, stared at his chest instead of his face. He was wearing a blue shirt open at the neck so that a little of his mat of brown chest hair showed. "I did what I had to do," I said. "What I was evidently born to do. I'm not fighting it any more, for the same reason Jesse and Rachel probably won't fight me any more. It doesn't do any good."

"Don't you think I understand that?"

"If you understand it, why are you still holding it against me?"

"Because Jesse was right about one thing. It doesn't really matter whether what you're doing to us is your fault or not. You're doing it. I'm not fighting you, but you shouldn't expect me to thank you, either."

"I don't."

He looked a little wary. "Just what do you want from me?"

"You know damn well what I want."

"Do I?" He stared at me for a long moment. "I suppose I do. Doro must be leaving." He turned and walked away.

I let him go this time. I felt like throwing something at him, but I let him go. The son of a bitch had Jan and Vivian both, and he had the nerve to talk about Doro and me. Or, rather, he had the nerve to use Doro to try to hurt me. If he couldn't get away from me, he'd hurt me. He shouldn't have been able to hurt me. But he was.

In the library, Doro was sitting at the reading table leafing through a book, and probably reading it. He read fast. Karl and I sat opposite him with an empty chair between us.

"I'll be leaving tomorrow," said Doro.

I felt rather than saw Karl's glance at me. I ignored him. Doro went on.

"Mary, it looks as though you've established yourself fairly well. I don't think anyone will bother you again."

"No."

"You're just going to leave?" said Karl. "Don't you have any plans for us now that Mary has become what you seemed to want her to become?"

"Mary's plan sounded all right to me," said Doro. "It might be harder for the group of you to organize your lives, held together as you are. But I'd rather give you a chance to try it. Let you find out whether you can build something of your own."

"Or at least of Mary's own," said Karl bitterly.

Doro looked from one of us to the other.

"He's still holding the pattern against me," I said. "But he might be right, anyway. I might have something we can start working on together." I told him about Clay Dana. He sat there listening, and looking more and more as though he didn't believe me.

"Clay lost any chance he had for becoming an active over ten years ago," he said.

"Ten years ago he didn't have the pattern to help him along."

"I find it hard to believe the pattern is helping him now. How could it? What did you do?"

"I don't know, exactly. But it must be the pattern. What other new thing has there been in his life in the past two weeks? He was a latent before he came here. And if I can push one latent toward transition, why can't I push others?"

"Oh, my God," muttered Karl. I ignored him.

"Look," I said, "we actives were all latents once. We moved up. Why can't others?"

"The others weren't bred for it. Clay was, and I can see now that you were right about him. But that doesn't mean—"

"*You* can see?"

"Of course. How could I have raised generations of actives if I wasn't able to judge my people's potential?"

"Oh, yeah." The ones who *tasted good*, yes. "Doro, I want to try bringing other latents to transition."

"How?"

"By doing to them the only thing I'd ever done to Clay before today. By reading them. Just reading them."

Doro shook his head. "Go ahead. It won't work."

Yes, it would. I felt sure that it would. And I could try it without even leaving the room. I thought of two of my cousins, a brother and sister—Jamie and Christine Hanson. We used to get into trouble together when we were little. As we grew older and started to receive mental interference, we got more antisocial. We abandoned each other and started to get into trouble separately. Doro didn't pay any attention to Jamie and Christine, and their parents had given up on them years ago. No transition was supposed to come along and put them back in control of their lives, so, let alone, they'd probably wind up in prison or in the morgue before they were a lot older. But I wasn't going to let them alone.

I reached out to the old neighborhood, got a bird's-eye view of it all at once. Dell Street and Forsyth Avenue. Emma's house. I could have focused in tight and read Rina or Emma. Instead, I followed Forsyth Avenue south past Piedras Altas, where heaven knew how many of my relatives lived, and on to Cooper Street, where I had even more family. On Cooper I recognized the Hanson house and focused in on it.

Christine was inside screaming at her mother. I noticed that she had shaved her head—probably more to get on her mother's nerves than for any other reason. I didn't pay any attention to what they were fighting about. I read her the way you skim pages of a phone book looking for a number. Only, I wasn't looking for anything. I noticed that she'd been pregnant three times—one miscarriage and two abortions. And she was only nineteen. And she'd been with some idiot friends when they decided to rob a liquor store. Some other things. I didn't care. I just read her. Then I went after Jamie.

I found him sitting on an old sofa in the garage, fooling around with a guitar. I read him and learned, among other things, that he had just gotten out of jail a few days before. He had been driving drunk, smashed into a parked car, backed up, drove away. But somebody got his license number. Ninety days.

Now that he was out, he couldn't take the running battle that was usually going on inside the house. So he was living in the garage until some money came his way and he could get his own place.

I shifted my attention to the pattern. I knew what to look for now. My experience with Clay had taught me. Slender threads, fragile, tentative, soon to grow into the real thing. I found them stretching between me and both Hansons. Both of them. They were mine.

I snapped back to the library, excited, elated. "I did it!"

I'm not quite sure what expression I was wearing, but Doro frowned and drew back from me a little.

"I did it! I got two more! You're going to have your damn empire sooner than you thought."

"Which two?" He spoke very quietly.

"Hanson. Christine and Jamie. They live over on Cooper Street. You used to see them around Emma's house sometimes when I was little."

"I remember." He stared down at the table for several seconds, still frowning. I assumed he was doing his own checking.

Karl reached over and touched my arm. "Show me," he said.

Not tell him, show him. Just like that. And just minutes after our little conversation in the hall. If he had caught me in any other mood I would have told him to go to hell. But I felt good. I opened to him.

He looked at the way I had brought the Hansons in, and he looked at my memories on Clay. That was all.

"You want to build an empire, all right," he said when he was finished. "But Doro isn't the one you want to build it for."

"Does it matter?" I asked.

And Doro answered. "No, it doesn't. All that matters is that you obey me." There was something frightening, something too intense about the way he was looking at me.

It was my turn to draw back a little. "I've always obeyed you."

"More or less. It could get harder now, though. Sometimes it's harder for a leader to obey. And sometimes it's harder to be lenient with a disobedient leader."

"I understand."

"No you don't. Not yet. But I think you're capable of understanding. That's why I'm willing to let you go ahead with what you're planning."

"It isn't exactly a plan yet," I said. "I haven't had time to think.... I just want to start bringing in latents, letting the pattern push them through transition—you were satisfied that the Hansons were on their way, I guess."

"Yes."

"Good. The houses in this neighborhood have room for a lot more people. All our neighbors can be persuaded to take in house guests."

"All of them?" said Karl sarcastically. "How many latents are you planning to enslave?"

"None," I said. "But I mean to have as many of them brought through transition as I can."

"Why?" Doro asked. "I mean aside from the fact that you've suddenly discovered you enjoy power."

"You should talk."

"Is there a reason?"

I thought about it. I needed a few hours of solitude to think and nose around other people's heads and decide what I was doing myself. "They're latents," I said. "And if Rina and the Hanson family and just about all the rest of my relatives are any indication, latents live like dogs. They spend most of their lives sharing other people's pain and slowly going crazy. Why should they have to go through that if I can give them a better way?"

"Are you so sure it is better?" asked Karl.

"You're damn right I am. How many latents do you imagine burn the hands off their kids like your mother did—or worse? And you know Doro doesn't pay attention to those kids. How could he? God knows how many thousands of them there are. So they get shitted on, and if they live to grow up, they shit on their own kids."

"And you're going to save them all." Karl radiated sarcasm.

I turned to look at him.

"You're not exactly vicious, Mary," he said. "But you're not altruistic, either. Why pretend to be?"

"Wait a minute, Karl," said Doro. And then to me, "Mary, as angry as he's just made you, I think he's right. I think there's a reason for what you want to do that you haven't faced yet. Think about it."

I had been just about to explode at Karl. Somehow, though, when Doro said the same thing in different words, it didn't bother me as much. Well, why did I want to see as many latents as possible brought through transition? So I could be an empress? I wouldn't even say that out loud. It sounded too stupid. But, whatever I called myself, I was definitely going to wind up with a lot of people taking orders from me, and that really didn't sound like such a bad thing. And as for altruism, whether it was my real motive or not, every latent we brought into the pattern would benefit from being there. He would regain control of his life and be able to use his energy for something besides fighting to stay sane. But, honestly, as bad as it sounds, I had known that latents were suffering for most of my life. I grew up watching one of them suffer. Rina. Of course I couldn't have done anything about it until now, but I hadn't really wanted to do anything. I hadn't cared. Not even during the time, just before my transition, when I found out just how much latents suffered. After all, I knew I wasn't going to be one much longer.

Altruism, ambition—what else was there?

Need?

Did I need those latents, somehow? Was that why I was so enthusiastic, so happy that I was going to get them? I knew I wanted them in the pattern. They belonged to me and I wanted them. The only way to find out for sure whether or not I *needed* them was to leave them alone and see how I fared without them. I didn't want to do that.

"I'm not sure what you want me to say," I told him. "You're right. I want to bring latents through for my own satisfaction. I admit that. I want them here around me. But as for why...." I shook my head.

"You don't have to kill," said Doro quietly. "But you do have to feed. And six people aren't enough."

Karl looked startled. "Wait a minute, are you saying she's going to have to keep doing what she did to Jesse and Rachel? That she'll have to choose one or two of us regularly and—"

"I don't know," said Doro. "It's possible, of course. And if it turns out to be true, I would think you'd want her to fill the neighborhood with other actives. But, on the other hand, she didn't take Rachel and Jesse because she wanted them. She took them in self-defense." He looked at me. "You haven't been an active long enough for this to mean much, but in the two weeks since your transition, have you felt any need, any inclination to take anyone?"

"No," I said. "Never. The idea disgusted me until I did it. Then I felt... well, you probably know."

"He might know," said Karl. "But I don't."

I opened and projected the sensation.

He jumped, whispered, "Jesus Christ." From him it sounded more like praying than cursing. "If that's what you felt, I'm surprised you didn't go ahead and take the rest of us."

"It's possible that she was only saving the rest of you for another time," said Doro. "But I don't think so. Somehow, her ability reminds me more of Rachel's. Rachel could have left her congregations unconscious or dead, but she never did. Never felt inclined to. It was easy for her to be careful, easy for her not to really take anyone. But, to a lesser degree, she took everyone. She gained what she needed, and her congregations lost nothing more than they could afford. Nothing that they couldn't easily replace. Nothing that they even noticed was gone."

Karl sat frowning at Doro for several seconds after Doro had finished. Then he turned to look at me. "Open to me again."

I sighed and did it. He would be easier to live with if he knew whether Doro was right or wrong—or at least knew he couldn't find out. I watched him, not really caring what he found. I stopped him just as he was about to break contact.

You and I are going to have to talk later.

About what?

About making some kind of truce before you manage to goad me into hitting back at you.

He changed the subject. *Do you realize you're exactly the kind of parasite he's described? Except, of course, you prey on actives instead of ordinary people.*

I can see what you've found. I do seem to be taking a tiny amount of strength from you and from the others. But it's so small it's not bothering any of you.

That's not the point.

The point is, you don't want me taking anything. Do you have to be told that I don't know how to stop it any more than I know how it got started?

I know. The thought carried overtones of weary frustration. He broke contact, spoke to Doro. "You're right about her. She's like Rachel."

Doro nodded. "That's best for all of you. Are you going to help her with her cousins?"

"Help her?"

"I've never seen a person born to be a latent suddenly pushed into transition. I'm assuming they'll have their problems and need help."

Karl looked at me. "Do you want my help again?"

"Of course I do."

"You'll need at least one other person."

"Seth."

"Yes." He looked at Doro. "Are you finished with us?"

Doro nodded.

"All right." He got up. "Come on, Mary. We may as well have that talk before you get back to Seth and Clay."

Doro

Doro did not leave the Larkin house, as he had planned. Suddenly there was too much going on. Suddenly things were getting out of hand—or at least out of his hands.

Mary was doing very well. She was driven by her own need to enlarge the pattern and aided not only by Doro's advice but by the experience of the six other actives. From the probing Doro had made her do and the snooping she had done on her own, she now had detailed mental outlines of the other actives' lives. Knowing what they had done in the past helped her decide what she could reasonably ask them to do now. Knowing Seth, for instance, made her decide to take Clay from him, take charge of Clay herself.

"How necessary is the pain of transition?" she asked Doro before making her decision. "Karl said you told him to hold off helping me until I was desperate. Why?"

"Because, in earlier generations of actives, the more help the person in transition received, the longer it took him to form his own shield." Doro grimaced remembering. "Before I understood that, I had several potentially good people die of injuries that wouldn't have happened if their transitions had ended when they should have. And I had others who died of sheer exhaustion."

Mary shuddered. "Sounds like it would be best to leave them alone completely." She glanced at Doro. "Which is probably why I'm the only one out of the seven of us who had any help."

"You were also the only one of the seven to have a seventeen-hour transition. Ten to twelve hours is more normal. Seventeen isn't that bad, though, and since your predecessors died whenever I left them alone in transition, I decided that you needed someone. Actually, Karl did a good job."

"I think I'll pass on the favor," she said, "by doing a good job for Clay Dana before his brother helps him to death." She went to Seth, told him what Doro had just told her, then told him that she, not Seth, would attend Clay at Clay's transition. Later she repeated the conversation to Doro.

"You've got to be kidding," Seth had said. "No. No way."

"You're too close to Clay," she had told him. "You've spent more than ten years shielding him from pain."

"That doesn't make any difference."

"The hell it doesn't! What's your judgment going to be like when you have to hold off shielding him—when you have to decide whether he's in enough trouble for you to risk helping him? How objective do you think you're going to be when he's lying in front of you screaming?"

"Objective...!"

"His life is going to depend on what you decide to do, man—or decide not to do." She looked at Clay. "How objective do you think he can be? It's your life."

Clay looked uncomfortable, spoke to his brother. "Could she be right, Seth? Could this be something you should leave to somebody else?"

"No!" said Seth instantly. And then again, with a little less certainty, "No."

"Seth?"

"Look, I can handle it. Have I ever let you down?"

And Mary broke in. "You probably never have, Seth, and I'm not going to give you a chance to ruin your record."

Seth turned to look at her. "Are you saying you're going to force me to stand aside?" His tone made the words more a challenge than a question.

"Yes," said Mary.

Seth stared at her in surprise. Then, slowly, he relaxed. "You could do it," he said quietly. "You could knock me cold when the time came. But, Mary, if anything happens to my brother, you'd better not let me come to."

"Clay will be all right," she said. "I plan to see to it. And I'm really not interested in knocking you out. I hope you won't make me do it."

"Then, tell me why. Make me understand why you're interfering in something that shouldn't even be any of your business."

"I started it, man. I'm the reason for it. If it's anybody's business, it's mine. Now, Clay has a better chance with me than he has with you because I can see what's happening to him both mentally and physically. I'm going to know if he really needs help. I'm not going to have to guess."

"What can you do but guess? You're barely out of transition yourself."

"I've got seven transition experiences to draw on. And you can believe I've studied all of them. Now it's settled, Seth."

Seth took it. Doro watched him with interest after Mary reported the conversation. And Doro caught Seth watching Mary. Seth did not seem angry or vindictive. It was more as though he was waiting for something to happen. He had accepted Mary's authority as, years before, he had accepted Doro's. Now he watched to see how she handled it. He seemed surprised when, days later, she gave him charge of her cousin Jamie, but he accepted the responsibility. After that, he seemed to relax a little.

Rachel was on her feet again two days after her attack on Mary. Jesse, more severely weakened, was in bed a day longer. Both became quieter, more cautious people. They, too, watched Mary—warily.

Mary sent Rachel to kidnap the Hansons. Forsyth was a small

city; Rachel could go across town without much discomfort. She wouldn't be staying long, anyway.

"Make their parents believe they've left home for good," Mary told her. "Because, one way or another, they have. You shouldn't have much tampering to do, though. The parents aren't going to be sorry to lose them."

Rachel frowned. "Even so, it seems wrong to just go in and take them—people's children...."

"They're not children. Hell, Jamie's a year older than I am. And if we don't take them, they probably won't make it through transition. If they don't manage to kill themselves by losing control at a bad time, somebody else will kill them by taking them to a hospital. You can imagine what it would be like to be a mental sponge picking up everything in a hospital."

Rachel shuddered, nodded, turned to go. Then she stopped and faced Mary again. "I was talking to Karl about what you're trying to do—the community of actives that you want to put together."

"Yes?"

"Well, if I have to stay here, I'd rather live in a community of actives—if such a thing is possible. I'd like us to stop hiding so much and start finding out what we're really capable of."

"You've been thinking about it," said Mary.

"I had time," said Rachel dryly. "What I'm working up to is that I'm willing to help you. Help more than just going after these kids, I mean."

Mary smiled, looked pleased but not surprised. "I would have asked you," she said. "I'm glad I didn't have to. I didn't ask you to help anybody through transition because I wanted you standing by for all three transitions in case some medical problem comes up. Jan broke her arm during her transition and you probably know Jesse did some kind of damage to his back that could have been serious. It will be best if you're sort of on call."

"I will be," said Rachel. She left to get the Hansons.

Mary looked after her for a moment, then walked over to the sofa nearest to the fireplace, where Doro was sitting with a closed book on his lap.

"You're always around," she said. "My shadow."

"You don't mind."

"No. I'm used to you. In fact, I'm really going to miss you when you leave. But, then, you won't be leaving soon. You're hooked. You've got to see what happens here."

She couldn't have been more right. And it wasn't just the three coming transitions that he wanted to see. They were important, but Mary herself was more important. Her people were submitting now, all but Karl. And she would overcome Karl's resistance slowly.

Doro had wondered what Mary would do with her people once she had subdued them. Before she discovered Clay's potential, she had probably wondered herself. Now, though... Doro had reworded Karl's question. How many latents did she think she wanted to bring through? "All of them, of course," she had said.

Now Doro was waiting. He didn't want to put limits on her, yet. He was hoping that she would not like the responsibility she was creating for herself. He was hoping that, before too long, she would begin to limit herself. If she didn't, he would have to step in. Success—his and hers—was coming too quickly. Worse, all of it depended on her. If anything happened to her, the pattern would die with her. It was possible that her actives, new and old, would revert to their old, deadly incompatibility without it. Doro would lose a large percentage of his best breeding stock. This quick success could set him back several hundred years.

Mary gave Karl charge of her bald girl cousin, Christine, and then probably wished she hadn't. Surprisingly, Christine's shaved head did not make her ugly. And, unfortunately, her inferior position in the house did not make her cautious. Fortunately, Karl wasn't interested. Christine just didn't have the judgment yet to realize how totally vulnerable she was. Mary had a private talk with her.

Mary gave Christine and Jamie a single, intensive session of telepathic indoctrination. They learned what they were, learned their history, learned about Doro, who had neglected their branch of Emma's family for two generations. They learned what was going to happen to them, what they were becoming part of. They learned that every other active in the house had gone through what they were facing and that, while it wasn't pleasant, they could stand it. The double rewards of peace of mind and power made it worthwhile.

The Hansons learned, and they believed. It wouldn't have been easy for them to disbelieve information force-fed directly into their minds. Once the indoctrination was over, though, they were let alone mentally. They became part of the house, accepting Mary's authority and their own pain with uncharacteristic docility.

Jamie went into transition first, about a month after he moved to Larkin House. He was young, strong, and surprisingly healthy in spite of having tried every pill or powder he could get his hands on.

He came through. He had sprained his wrist, blackened one of Seth's eyes, and broken the bed he was lying on, but he came through. He became an active. Seth was as proud as though he had just become a father.

Clay, who should have been first, was next. He came through in a short, intense transition that almost killed him. He actually suffered heart failure, but Mary got his heart started again and kept it going until Rachel arrived. Clay's transition was over in only five hours. It left him with none of the usual bruises and strains, because Mary did not try to restrain him with her own body or tie him down. She simply paralyzed his voluntary muscles and he lay motionless while his mind writhed through chaos.

Clay became an active, but not a telepathic active. His budding telepathic ability vanished with the end of his transition. But he was compensated for it, as he soon learned.

When his transition ended and he was at peace, he saw that a tray of food had been left beside his bed. He could just see it out of the corner of his eye. He was still paralyzed and could not reach it, but in his confusion and hunger, he did not realize this. He reached for it anyway.

In particular, he reached for the bowl of soup that he could see steaming so near him. It was not until he lifted the soup and drew it to him that he realized that he was not using his hands. The soup hovered without visible support a few inches above his chest. Startled, Clay let it fall. At the same instant, he moved to get away from it. He shot about three feet to one side and into the air. And stayed suspended there, terrified.

Slowly, the terror in his eyes was replaced by understanding. He looked around his bedroom at Rachel, at Doro, and, finally, at Mary. Mary apparently released him then from his paralysis, because he began to move his arms and legs now like a human spider hanging in mid-air from an invisible web. Slowly, deliberately, Clay lowered himself to the bed. Then he drifted upward again, apparently finding it an easy thing to do. He looked at Mary, spoke apparently in answer to some thought she had projected to him.

"Are you kidding? I can fly! This is good enough for me."

"You're not a member of the pattern any more," she said. She seemed saddened, subdued.

"That means I'm free to go, doesn't it?"

"Yes. If you want to."

"And I won't be getting any more mental interference?"

"No. You can't pull it in any more. You're not even an out-of-control telepath. You're not a telepath at all."

"Lady, you read my mind. You'll see that's no tragedy to me. All that so-called power ever brought me was grief. Now that I'm free of it, I think I'll go back to Arizona—raise myself a few cows, maybe a few kids."

"Good luck," said Mary softly.

He drifted close to her, grinned at her. "You wouldn't believe how easy this is." He lifted her clear off the floor, brought her up to eye level with him. She gazed at him, unafraid. "What I've got is better than what you've got," he joked.

She smiled at him finally. "No it isn't, man. But I'm glad you think it is. Put me down."

He lowered both her and himself to the floor as though he had been doing it all his life. Then he looked at Doro. "Is this something brand-new, or have you seen it before?"

"Psychokinesis," said Doro. "I've seen it before. Seen it several times in your father's family, in fact, although I've never seen it come about this smoothly before."

"You call that transition smooth?" said Mary.

"Well, with the heart problem, no, I guess not. But it could have been worse. Believe me, this room could be a shambles, with everyone in it injured or dead. I've seen it happen."

"My kind throw things," guessed Clay.

"They throw everything," said Doro. "Including some things that are nailed down securely. Instead of doing that, I think you might have turned your ability inward a little and caused your own heart to stop."

Clay shook himself. "I could have. I didn't know what I was doing, most of the time."

"A psychokinetic always has a good chance of killing himself before he learns to control his ability."

"That may be the way it was," said Mary. "But it won't be that way any more."

Doro heard the determination in her voice and sighed to himself. She had just shared a good portion of Clay's agony as she worked to keep him alive, and immediately she was committing herself to do it again. She had found her work. She was some sort of mental queen bee, gathering her workers to her instead of giving birth to them. She would be totally dedicated, and difficult to reason with or limit. Difficult, or perhaps impossible.

Christine Hanson came through in an ordinary transition, perhaps a little easier than most. She made more noise than either of the men because pain, even slight pain, terrified her. She had had a harder time than the others during the pretransition period, too. Finally, hoarse but otherwise unhurt, Christine completed her transition. She remained a telepath, like her brother. It was possible that one or both of them might learn to heal, and it was possible that they, Rachel, and Mary might be very long-lived.

Whatever potential Jamie and Christine had, they accepted their places in the pattern easily. They were Mary's first grateful pattern members. And their membership brought an unexpected benefit that Jesse accidentally discovered. Now all the members could move farther from Mary without discomfort. Suddenly, more people meant more freedom.

Doro watched and worried silently. The day after Christine's transition, Mary began pulling in more of her cousins. And Ada, who knew a few of her relatives, began trying to reach them in Washington. Doro could have helped. He knew the locations of all his important latent families. But as far as he was concerned, things were moving too quickly even without his help. He said nothing.

He had decided to give Mary two years to make what she could of her people. That was enough time for her to begin building the society she envisioned—what she was already calling a Patternist society. But two years should still leave Doro time to cut his losses— if it became necessary—without sacrificing too large a percentage of his breeding stock.

He had admitted to himself that he didn't want to kill Mary. She was easily controllable in most matters, because she loved him; and she was a success. Or a partial success. She was giving him a united people, a group finally recognizable as the seeds of the race he had been working to create. They were a people who belonged to him, since Mary belonged to him. But they were not a people he could be part of. As Mary's pattern brought them together, it shut him out. Together, the "Patternists" were growing into something that he could observe, hamper, or destroy but not something he could join. They were his goal, half accomplished. He watched them with carefully concealed emotions of suspicion and envy.

PART THREE

Chapter Nine

Emma

Emma was at the typewriter in her dining room when Doro arrived. He had not called to say he was coming, but at least when he walked in without knocking, he was wearing a body she had seen him in before: the body of a small man, black-haired, green-eyed, like Mary. But the hair was straight and this body was white. He threw himself down on Emma's sofa and waited silently until she finished the page that she was working on.

"What is it?" he asked her when she got up. "Another book?"

She nodded. She was young. She was young most of the time now, because he was around so much. "I've discovered that I like writing," she said. "I should have tried it years earlier than I did." She sat down in a chair, because he was sprawled over the length of the sofa. He lay there frowning.

"What's the matter?" she asked.

"Mary's the matter."

Emma grimaced. "I'm not surprised. What's she done?"

"Nothing yet. It's what she's going to do after I talk to her. I'm going to put on the brakes, Em. The Patternist section of Forsyth is as big as a small town already. She has enough people."

"If you ask me, she had enough two years ago. But now that you're ready to stop her, what are you going to do with all those actives—all those Patternists—when she's not around any more to maintain the Pattern?"

"I'm not out to kill Mary, Em. The Pattern will still be there."

"Will it?"

He hesitated. "You think she'll make me kill her?"

"Yes. And if you're realistic about it, you'll think so too."

He sighed, sat up. "Yes. I don't expect to salvage many of her people, either. Most of them were animals before she found them. Without her, they'll revert."

"Animals... with such power, though."

"I'll have to destroy the worst of them."

Emma winced.

"I thought you'd be more concerned about Mary."

"I was concerned about her. But it's too late for her now. You helped her turn herself into something too dangerous to live."

He stared at her.

"She's got too much power, Doro. She terrifies me. She's doing exactly what you always said you wanted to do. But she's doing it, not you. All those people, those fifteen hundred people in the section, are hers, not yours."

"But she's mine."

"You wouldn't be thinking about killing her if you believed that was enough."

"Em...." He got up and went to sit on the arm of her chair. "What are you afraid of?"

"Your Mary." She leaned against him. "Your ruthless, egotistical, power-hungry little Mary."

"Your grandchild."

"Your creation! Fifteen hundred actives in two years. They bring each other through on an assembly line. And how many conscripted servants—ordinary people unfortunate enough to be taken over by those actives. People forced now to be servants in their own houses. Servants and worse!"

Her outburst seemed to startle him. He looked down at her silently.

"You're not in control," she said more softly. "You've let them run wild. How many years do you think it will take at this rate for them to take over the city? How long before they begin tampering with the state and federal government?"

"They're very provincial people, Em. They honestly don't care what's happening in Washington or Sacramento or anywhere else as long as they can prevent it from hurting them. They pay attention to what's going on, but they don't influence it very often."

"I wonder how long that will last."

"Quite a while, even if the Pattern survives. They honestly don't want the burden of running a whole country full of people. Not when those people can run themselves reasonably well and the Patternists can reap the benefits of their labor."

"That, they have to have learned from you."

"Of course."

"You mentioned Washington and Sacramento. What about here in Forsyth?"

"This is their home territory, Em. They're interfering too much here to avoid being noticed by Forsyth city government, half asleep as it is. To avoid trouble, they took over the city about a year and a half ago."

Emma stared at him, aghast.

"They've completely taken over the best section of town. They did it quietly, but still Mary thought it safest for them to control key mutes in city hall, in the police department, in—"

"Mutes!"

He looked annoyed, probably with himself. "It's a convenient term. People without telepathic voices. Ordinary people."

"I know what it means, Doro. I knew the first time I heard Mary use it. It means niggers!"

"Em—"

"I tell you, you're out of control, Doro. You're not one of them. You're not a telepath. And if you don't think they look down on us non-telepaths, us niggers, the whole rest of humanity, you're not paying attention."

"They don't look down on me."

"They don't look up to you, either. They used to. They used to respect you. Damnit, they used to love you, the originals. The 'First Family.'" Her tone ridiculed the name that the original seven actives had adopted.

"Obviously this has been bothering you for a long time," said Doro. "Why haven't you said anything about it before?"

"It wasn't necessary."

He frowned.

"You knew." Her tone became accusing. "I haven't told you a single thing that you haven't been aware of for at least as long as I have."

He moved uncomfortably. "Sometimes I wonder if you aren't a little telepathic yourself."

"I don't have to be. I know you. And I knew you'd reach a point when no matter how fascinated you were with what Mary was doing, no matter how much you loved the girl, she'd have to go. I just wish you'd made up your mind sooner."

"Back when she brought her first latents through, I decided to give her two years. I'd like to give her a good many more if she'll co-operate."

"She won't. How willing would you be to give up all that power?"

"I'm not asking her to give up anything but this recruitment drive of hers. She's got a good many of my best latents now. I don't dare let her go on as she has been."

"You want the section to grow now by births only?"

"By births, and through the five hundred or so children they've collected. Children who'll eventually go through transition. Have you seen the private school they've taken over for the children?"

"No. I keep away from the section as much as I can. I assume Mary knows how I feel about her already. I don't want to keep reminding her until she decides to change my mind for me."

Doro started to say something, then stopped.

"What is it?" asked Emma.

For a moment, she thought he wasn't going to answer. Then, "I mentioned you to her once. I said I didn't want you bothered by any of her people. She gave me a strange look and said she'd already taken care of that. She said, 'Don't worry about her. Bitchy old woman that she is, she's wearing my brand. If anybody even tries to read her, the first thing they'll see is that she's my private property.'"

"Her what!"

"She means you're under her protection, Em. It might not sound like much, but, with it, none of the others are going to touch you. And, apparently, she isn't interested in controlling you herself."

Emma shuddered. "How generous of her! She must feel awfully secure in her power. You trained her too well. She's too much like you."

"Yes," said Doro. "I know."

She looked at him sharply. "Did I hear pride in your voice?"

Doro smiled faintly. "She's shown me a lot, Em. She's shown me something I've been trying to find out for most of my life."

"All I can see that she's shown you is what you'd be like as a young woman. I recall warning you about underestimating young women."

"Not what I'd be like as a woman. I already know that. I've been a woman I-don't-know-how-many times. No. What I'd be like as a complete entity. What I'd be like if I hadn't died that first time—died before I was fully formed."

"Before you were...." Emma frowned. "I don't understand. How do you know you weren't fully formed when you died?"

"I know. I've seen enough almost-Doros, enough near successes to know. I should be telepathic, like Mary. If I were, I would have created a pattern and fed off live hosts instead of killing. As it is, the only time I can feel mind-to-mind contact with another person is when I kill. She and I kill in very much the same way."

"That's it?" said Emma. "That's all you've been reaching for, for so long—someone who kills in the same way you do?"

"All?" There was bitterness in his voice. "Does it seem such a small thing, Em, for me to want to know what I am—what I should have been?"

"Not a small thing, no. Not a wise thing, either. Your curiosity—and your loneliness, I think—have driven you to make a mistake."

"Perhaps. I've made mistakes before."

"And survived them. I hope you survive this one. I can see now why you kept your purpose secret for so long."

"Yes."

"Does Mary know?"

"Yes. I never told her, but she knows. She saw it herself after a while."

"No wonder you love her. No wonder she's still alive. She's you—the closest thing you've ever had to a true daughter."

"I never told her any of that, either."

"She knows. You can depend on it." She paused for a moment. "Doro, is there any way she could. . . . I mean, if she's complete and you're not, she might be able to. . . . "

"To take me?"

Emma nodded.

"No. If she could, she would never have lived past the morning of her transition. She tried to read me then. If she hadn't, I would have ordered her to try as soon as I saw her. I wanted to look at her in the only way that would tell me whether she could possibly become a danger to me. I looked, and what I saw told me she couldn't. She's like a scaled-down model of me. I could have taken her then, and I can now."

"It's been a long time since you've seen someone you thought could be dangerous. I hope your judgment is still as good as you think it is."

"It is. In my life, I've met only five people I considered potentially dangerous."

"And they all died young."

Doro shrugged.

"I assume you're not forgetting that Mary can increase her strength by robbing her people."

"No. It doesn't make any difference. I watched her very carefully back when she took Rachel and Jess. I could have taken her then. In fact, the extra strength she had acquired made her seem a more attractive victim. Strength alone isn't enough to beat me. And she has a weakness I don't have. She doesn't move. She has just that one body, and when it dies, she dies." He thought about that and shook his head sadly. "And she will almost certainly die."

"When?"

"When she—if she disobeys me. I'm going to tell her my decision when I go there today. No more latents. She'll decide what she wants to do after that."

Seth

Seth Dana came out the back door of Larkin House thinking about the assignment Mary had just given him. The same old thing. Recruit

more seconds—more people to help latents through transition. Patternists liked the way their numbers were increasing. Expansion was
exciting. It was their own kind growing up, coming of age at last.
But seconding was hard work. You were mother, father, friend, and,
if your charge needed it, lover to an erratic, frightened, dependent
person. People volunteered to be seconds when they were shamed
into it. They accepted it as their duty, but they evaded that duty as
long as they could. It was Seth's job to prompt them and then present them with sullen, frightened charges.

He was a kind of matchmaker, sensing easily and accurately
which seconds would be compatible with which latents. His worst
mistake had been his first, his decision to second Clay. Mary had
stopped him then. She had not had to stop him again. He had no
more close relatives to warp his judgment.

He got into his car, preoccupied, deciding which Patternists to
draft this time. He started the car automatically, then froze, his hand
poised halfway to the emergency brake. Someone had shoved the
cold steel barrel of a gun against the base of his skull.

Startled from his thoughts, Seth knew a moment of fear.

"Turn off the ignition, Dana," said a man's voice.

Reacting finally, Seth read the man. Then he turned off the ignition. With equal ease, he turned off the gunman. He gave the man
a mental command, then reached back and took the gun from his
suddenly limp hand. He shut the gun in the glove compartment and
looked around at the intruder. The man was a mute and a stranger,
but Seth had seen him before, in the thoughts of a woman Seth had
seconded. A woman named Barbara Landry, who had once been
this man's wife.

"Palmer Landry," said Seth quietly. "You've gone to a lot of trouble
for nothing."

The man stared at Seth, then at his own empty hand. "Why did
I give you...? How could you make me...? What's going on here?"

Seth shrugged. "Nothing now."

"How do you know who I am? Why did I hand you...?"

"You're a man who deserted his wife nearly a year ago," said
Seth. "Then suddenly decided he wanted her back. The gun wasn't
necessary."

"Where is she? Where's Barbara?"

"Probably at her house." Seth had personally brought Barbara Landry from New York two months before. A month and a half later, she had come through transition. Almost immediately, she had discovered that Bartholomew House—and Caleb Bartholomew—suited her perfectly. Seth hadn't bothered to erase her from the memories of the people she knew in New York. None of them had been friends. None of them had really cared what happened to her. But, apparently, she had told a couple of them where she was going, and with whom. And when Landry came back looking for her, he had found the information waiting. Seth had been careless. And Palmer Landry had been lucky. No one had noticed him watching Larkin House, and the person he had asked to point out Seth Dana had been an unsuspecting mute.

"You mean to tell me you've gotten rid of Barbara already?" Landry demanded.

"I never had her," said Seth. "Never wanted her, for that matter, nor she me. I just helped her when she happened to need help."

"Sure. You're Santa Claus. Just tell me where she's living."

"I'll take you there if you want." He had intended to draft Bartholomew into some seconding anyway. But later. Bartholomew House was right across the street.

"Who's she living with?" asked Landry.

"Her family," said Seth. "She found a house she fit into quicker than most of us do."

"House?" The man frowned. "Whorehouse?"

"Hell no!" Seth looked around at him. Landry had a justifiably low opinion of his wife. Latents were hard people to live with. But Seth had not realized that it was that low. "We live communally here, several of us to a house. So when we say house, we don't just mean the building. We mean household. We mean people."

"What the hell are you? Some kind of religious nuts or something?"

Seth was about to answer him when Barbara Landry herself came out the back door of Larkin House.

The sound of her footsteps caused Landry to turn. He saw her, shouted her name once, then was out of the car, running toward her.

Barbara Landry was weak, as Patternists went, and she was inexperienced at handling her new abilities. That last made her a possible danger to her husband. Seth reached out to warn her, but he was a second too late.

Recoiling in surprise from Landry's sudden rush, Barbara instinctively used her new defenses. Instead of controlling him gently, she stopped him solidly, suddenly, as though she had hit him, as though she had clubbed him down. He fell, unconscious, without ever having touched her.

"My God," Barbara whispered horrified. "I didn't mean to hurt him. I had come to see you. Then I sensed him out here threatening you. I came to ask you not to hurt him."

"He'll be all right," said Seth. "No thanks to you. You're going to kill somebody if you don't learn to be careful."

"I know. I'm sorry."

He lectured her as though she were still his charge. "I've warned you. No matter how weak you are as a Patternist, you're a powerhouse as far as any ordinary mute is concerned."

She nodded solemnly. "I'll be careful. But, Seth, would you help him for me? I mean, after he comes to. He probably needs money, and I know he needs even more to forget about me. I don't even like to think about what I put him through when we were together."

"He wants to be with you."

"No!"

"He could be programmed to live very comfortably here, Barbara. Matter of fact, he'd be happier here than anywhere else."

"I don't want him enslaved! I've done enough to him. Seth, please. Help him and let him go."

Seth smiled finally. "All right, honey, in exchange for a promise from you."

"What?"

"That you'll go back to Bart and make him give you a few more lessons on how to handle mutes without killing them."

She nodded, embarrassed.

"Oh, yeah, and tell him he's going to second a couple of people for me. I'm bringing the first one over tomorrow."

"Oh, but—"

"No excuses. Save me the trouble of arguing with him and I'll do a good job for you here." He gestured toward Landry.

She smiled at him. "You would anyway. But, all right, I'll do your dirty work for you." She turned and went down the driveway. She was a rare Patternist. Like Seth, she cared what happened to the people she had left behind in the mute world. Seth had always liked her. Now he would see that her husband got as good a start as Clay had gotten.

Rachel

Rachel's newest assignment had bothered her from the moment Mary gave it to her. It was still bothering her now, as she stood at the entrance of a long communal driveway that led back into a court of dilapidated, dirty, green stucco houses. The houses were small—no more than three or four rooms each. The yards were littered with beer cans and wine bottles, and they were overgrown with weeds and shrubs gone wild. The look of the place seemed to confirm Rachel's suspicions.

Farther up the driveway, a group of teen-age boys tossed around a pair of dice and a surprisingly large amount of money. Intent on their game, they paid no attention to Rachel. She let her perception sweep over them and found three that she would have to come back for. Three latents who lived in the court, but who were not as bad off as those Mary had sent Rachel after.

This was a pocket of Emma's descendants hidden away in a corner of Los Angeles, suffering without knowing why, without knowing who they were. The women in three of the houses were sisters. They hated each other, usually spoke only to trade obscenities. Yet they continued to live near each other, satisfying a need they did not realize they had. One of them still had a husband. All three had children. Rachel had come for the youngest sister—the one whose husband was still with her. This one lived in the third house back, with her husband and their two young children. Rachel looked at the house and realized that she had been unconsciously refraining from probing it. She was going entirely on what Mary had told her. That meant that there were surely things inside that she would not want to see. Mary swept the areas she checked so quickly that she received nothing more than a momentary feeling of anxiety from the latents who were in serious trouble. She was like a machine, sweeping, detecting latents here and there mixed in with the mute population. And the worst ones, she gave to Rachel.

"Come on, Rae," she would say. "You know they're going to die if I send anybody else."

And she was right. Only Rachel could handle the most pathetic of Doro's discards. Or only she had been able to until now. Now her students were beginning to come into their own. The one she had with her now was just about ready to work alone. Miguela Daniels. Her father had married a Mexican woman, a mute. But he traced his own lineage back to Emma through both his parents. And Miguela was turning out to be a very good healer. Miguela came up beside her.

"What are you waiting for?" she asked.

"You," Rachel told her. "All right, let's go in. You won't like it, though."

"I can already feel that."

As they went to the door, Rachel finally swept the house with her perception and moaned to herself. She did not knock. The door was locked, but the people inside were beyond answering her knock.

The top portion of the door had once been a window, but the glass had long ago been broken. The hole had been covered by an oversized piece of plywood.

"Keep your attention on the boys in the back," Rachel told Miguela. "They can't see us from here, but this might be noisy."

"You could get one of them to break in."

"No, I can do it. Just watch."

Miguela nodded.

Rachel took hold of the overhanging edge of plywood, braced herself, and pulled. The wood was dry and old and thin. Rachel had hardly begun to put pressure on it when it gave along its line of nails and part of it came away in her hands. She broke off more of it until she could push the rest in and unlock the door. The smell that greeted them made Rachel hold her breath for a few seconds. Miguela breathed it and gagged.

"What's that Goddamn stink!"

Rachel said nothing. She pushed the door open and went in. Miguela grimaced and followed.

Just inside the door lay a young man, the husband, half propped up against the wall. Around him were the many bottles he had already managed to empty. In his hand was one he had not quite emptied yet. He tried to get up as the two women came in, but he was too drunk or too sick or too weak from hunger. Probably all three. "Hey," he said, his voice slurred and low. "What you think you're doing? Get out of my house."

Rachel scanned him quickly while Miguela went through the kitchen, into the bedroom. The man was a latent, like his wife. That was why the two of them had so much trouble. They had not only the usual mental interference to contend with, but they unwittingly interfered with each other. They were both of Emma's family and they would make good Patternists, but, as latents, they were killing each other. The man on the floor was of no use to himself or anyone else as he was now.

He was filthy—not only unwashed but incontinent. He wallowed in his own feces and vomit, contributing his share to the strong evil smell of the place.

From the bedroom, Miguela cried out, "Mother of God! Rachel, come in here quickly."

Rachel turned from the man, intending to go to her. But, as she turned, there was a sound, a weak, thin cry from the sofa. Rachel realized abruptly that what she had thought were only bundles of rags were actually the two children she had sensed in the house. She went to them quickly.

They were skin and bones, both breathing shallowly, unevenly, making small sounds from time to time. Malnourished, dehydrated, bruised, beaten, and filthy, they lay unconscious. Mercifully unconscious.

"Rachel—" Miguela seemed to choke. "Rachel, come here. Please!"

Rachel left the children reluctantly, went to the bedroom. In the bedroom there was another child, an infant who was beyond even Rachel's ability. It had been dead for at least a few days. Neither Rachel nor Mary had sensed it before, because both had scanned for life, touching the living minds in the house and skimming over everything else.

The baby's starved body was crawling with maggots, but it still showed the marks of its parents' abuse. The head was a ruin. It had been hit with something or slammed into something. The legs were twisted as no infant's legs would have twisted normally. The child had been tortured to death. The man and the woman had fed on each other's insanity until they murdered one child and left the others dying. Rachel had stolen enough latents from prisons and insane asylums to know how often such things happened. Sometimes the best a latent could do was realize that the mental interference, the madness, was not going to stop, and then end their own lives before they killed others.

Staring down at the dead child in its ancient, peeling crib, Rachel wondered how even Doro had managed to keep so many latents alive for so long. How had he done it, and how had he been able to stand himself for doing it? But, then, Doro had nothing even faintly resembling a conscience.

The crib was at the foot of an old, steel-frame bed. On the bed lay the mother, semiconscious, muttering drunkenly from time to time. "Johnny, the baby's crying again." And then, "Johnny, make the baby stop crying! I can't stand to hear him crying all the time." She wept a little herself now, her eyes open, unseeing.

Miguela and Rachel looked at each other, Miguela in horror, Rachel in weariness and disgust.

"You were right," said Miguela. "I don't like this one damn bit. And this is the kind of thing you want me to handle?"

"There are too many of them for me," said Rachel. "The more help I get, the fewer of these bad ones will die."

"They deserve to die for what they did to that baby—" She choked again and Rachel saw that she was holding back tears.

"You're the last person I'd expect to hold latents responsible for what they do," Rachel told her. "Do I have to remind you what you did?" Miguela, unstable and violent, had set fire to the house of a woman whose testimony had caused her to spend some time in Juvenile Hall. The woman had burned to death.

Miguela closed her eyes, not crying but not casting any more stones, either. "You know," she said after a moment, "I was glad I turned out to be a healer, because I thought I could make up for that, somehow. And here I am bitching."

"Bitch all you want to," said Rachel. "As long as you do your work. You're going to handle these people."

"All of them? By myself?"

"I'll be standing by—not that you'll need me. You're ready. Why don't you back the van in and I'll draft a couple of the boys out back to help us carry bodies."

Miguela started to go, then stopped. "You know, sometimes I wish we could make Doro pay for scenes like this. He's the one who deserves all the blame."

"He's also the one who'll never pay. Only his victims pay."

Miguela shook her head and went out after the van.

Jesse

Jesse pulled his car up sharply in front of a handsome, redbrick, Georgian mansion. He got out, strode down the pathway and through the front door without bothering to knock. He went straight to the stairs and up them to the second floor. There, in a back bedroom, he found Stephen Gilroy, the Patternist owner of the house, sitting beside the bed of a young mute woman. The woman's face was covered with blood. It had been slashed and hacked to pieces. She was unconscious.

"My God," muttered Jesse as he crossed the room to the bed. "Did you send for a healer?"

Gilroy nodded. "Rachel wasn't around, so I—"

"I know. She's on an assignment."

"I called one of her kids. I just wish he'd get here."

One of her students, he meant. Even Jesse found himself referring to Rachel's students as "her kids."

There was the sound of the front door opening and slamming again. Someone else ran up the bare, wooden stairs, and, a moment later, a breathless young man hurried into the room. He was one of Rachel's relatives, of course, and as Rachel would have in a healing situation, he took over immediately.

"You'll have to leave me alone with her," he said. "I can handle the injuries, but I work best when I'm alone with my patient."

"Her eyes are hurt, too, I think," said Gilroy. "Are you sure you—"

The healer unshielded to show them that his self-confidence was real and based on experience. "Don't worry about her. She'll be all right."

Jesse and Stephen Gilroy left the room, went down to Gilroy's study.

Jesse spoke with quiet fury. "The main reason I got here so fast was so I could see the damage through my own eyes instead of somebody's memory. I want to remember it when I go after Hannibal."

"I should go after him," said Gilroy softly, bitterly. He was a slender, dark-haired man with very pale skin. "I would go after him if he hadn't already proved to me how little good that does." His voice was full of self-disgust.

"People who abuse mutes are my responsibility," said Jesse. "Because mutes are my responsibility. Hannibal is even a relative of mine. I'll take care of him."

Gilroy shrugged. "You gave her to me; he took her from me. You ordered him to send her back; he sent her back in pieces. Now you'll punish him. What will that inspire him to do to her?"

"Nothing," said Jesse. "I promise you. I've talked to Mary and Karl about him. This isn't the first time he's sliced somebody up. He's still the animal he was when he was a latent."

"That's what's bothering me. He'd think nothing of killing Arlene when you're finished with him. I'm surprised he hasn't killed her already. He knows I can't stop him."

"There's no sense beating yourself with that, Gil. Except for the members of the First Family, nobody can stop him. He's the strongest telepath we've ever brought through transition. And the first thing he did, once he was through, was to smash his way through the shielding of his second and nearly kill her. For no reason. He just discovered that he could do it, so he did it."

"Somebody should have smashed him then and there."

"That's what Doro said. He claims he used to cull out people like Hannibal as soon as he spotted them."

"Well, I hate to find myself agreeing with Doro but—"

"So do I. But he made us. He knows just how far wrong we can go. Hannibal is too strong for Rachel or her kids to help him. Especially since he doesn't really want help. And he's too dangerous for us to tolerate any longer."

Gilroy's eyes widened. "You are going to kill him, then?"

Jesse nodded. "That's why I had to talk to Karl and Mary. We don't like to give up on one of our own, but Hannibal is a God-damn cancer."

"You're going to do it yourself?"

"As soon as I leave here."

"With his strength... are you sure you can?"

"I'm First Family, Gil."

"But still—"

"Nobody who needed the Pattern to push him into transition can stand against one of us—not when we mean to kill." Jesse shrugged. "Doro had to breed us to be strong enough to come through without being prodded. After all, when the time came for us, there was nobody who could prod us without killing us." He stood up. "Look, contact me when that healer finishes with Arlene, will you? I just want to be sure she's all right."

Gilroy nodded, stood up. They walked to the door together and Jesse noticed that there were three Patternists in the living room. Two women and a man.

"Your house is growing," he said to Gilroy. "How many now?"

"Five. Five Patternists."

"The best of the people you've seconded, I'll bet."

Gilroy smiled, said nothing.

"You know," said Jesse as they reached the door. "That Hannibal... he even looks like me. Reminds me a little of myself a couple of years ago. There, but for the grace of Doro, go I. Shit."

Jan

Holding a smooth, rectangular block of wood between her hands, Jan Sholto closed her eyes and reached back in her disorderly memory. She reached back two years, to the creation of the Pattern. She had not only her own memories of that event but the memories of each of the original Patternists. They had unshielded and let her read them—not that they could have stopped her by refusing to open. Mary wasn't the only one who could read people through their shields. No one except Doro could come into physical contact with Jan without showing her some portion of his thoughts and memories. In this case, though, physical contact hadn't been necessary. The others had shown their approval of what she was doing by co-operating with her. She was creating another learning block—assembling their memories into a work that would not only tell the new Patternists of their beginnings but show them.

She was teacher to all the new Patternists as they came through. For over a year now, seconds had used her learning blocks to give their charges quick, complete knowledge of the section's rules and regulations. Other learning blocks offered them choices, showed them the opportunities available to them for making their own place within the section.

Abruptly, Jan reached Mary's memories. They jarred her with their raw intensity, overwhelmed her as other people's memories rarely did any more. They were good material, but Jan knew she would have to modify them. Left as they were they would dominate everything else Jan was trying to record.

Sighing, Jan put her block aside. Of course it would be Mary's thoughts that gave trouble. Mary was trouble. That small body of hers was deceptive. Yet it had been Mary who saw possible use for Jan's psychometry. A few months after Mary had begun drawing in latents, she had decided to learn as much as she could about the special abilities of the rest of the First Family. In investigating Jan's psychometry, she had discovered that she could read some objects herself in a fragmented, blurred way, but that she could read much more clearly anything that Jan had handled.

"You read impressions from the things you touch," she had said to Jan. "But I think you put impressions into things, too."

"Of course I do," Jan had said impatiently. "Everyone does every time they touch something."

"No, I mean . . . you kind of amplify what's already there."

"Not deliberately."

"Nobody ever noticed it before?"

"No one pays any attention to my psychometry. It's just something I do to amuse myself."

Mary was silent for a long moment, thinking. Then, "Have you ever liked the impressions that you got from something enough to keep them? Not just keep them in your memory but in the thing, the object itself—like keeping a film or a tape recording."

"I have some very old things that I've kept. They have ancient memories stored in them."

"Get them."

"*Please* get them," mimicked Jan. "May I see them, *please?*" Mary had taken to her new power too easily. She loved to order people around.

"The hell with you," said Mary. "Get them."

"They're my property!"

"Your property." The green eyes glittered. "I'll trade you last night for them."

Jan froze, staring at her. The night before, Jan had been with Karl. It was not the first time, but Mary had never mentioned it before. Jan had tried to convince herself that Mary did not know. Now, confronted with proof that she was wrong, she managed to control her fear. She wanted to ask what Mary traded Vivian for all the mute woman's nights with Karl, but she said nothing. She got up and went to get her collection of ancient artifacts stolen from various museums.

Mary handled one piece after another, first frowning, then slowly taking on a look of amazement. "This is fantastic," she said. She was holding just a fragment of what had been an intricately painted jar. A jar that held the story of the woman whose hands shaped it 6,500 years ago. A woman of a Neolithic village that had existed somewhere in what was now Iran. "Why is it so pure?" asked Mary. "God knows how many people have touched it since this woman owned it. But she's all I can sense."

"She was all I ever wanted to sense," said Jan. "The fragment has been buried for most of the time between our lives and hers. That's the only reason there was any of her left in it at all."

"Now there's nothing but her. How did you get rid of the others?"

Jan frowned. "There were archaeologists and some other people at first, but I didn't want them. I just didn't want them."

Mary handed her the fragment. "Am I in it now?"

"No, it's set. I had to learn to freeze them so that I didn't disturb them myself every time I handled them. I never tried letting another telepath handle them, but you haven't disturbed this one."

"Or the others, most likely. You like seconding, Jan?"

Jan looked at her through narrowed eyes. "You know I hate it. But what does that have to do with my artifacts?"

"Your artifacts just might stop you from ever having to second anybody else. If you can get to know your own abilities a little better and use them for more than your own amusement they can open another way for you to contribute to the Pattern."

"What way?"

"A new art. A new form of education and entertainment—better than the movies, because you really live it, and you absorb it quicker and more completely than you do books. Maybe." She snatched up the jar fragment and a small Sumerian clay tablet and ran out to try them on someone. Minutes later she was back, grinning.

"I tried them on Seth and Ada. All I told them to do was hold these things and unshield. They picked up everything. Look, you show me you can use what you've got for more than a toy and you're off seconding for good." The rush of words stopped for a moment, and when Mary spoke again, her tone had changed. "And, Jan, guess what else you're off of for good."

Jan had wanted to kill her. Instead, she had thrown her energy into refining her talent and finding uses for it. Instead, she had begun to create a new art.

Ada

Ada Dragan waited patiently in the principal's office of what was finally her school. A mute guardian who was programmed to notice such things had reported that one of her latent foster children—a fifteen-year-old girl—was having serious pretransition difficulties.

From the office, Ada looked out at the walled grounds of the school. It had been a private school, situated right there in the Palo Verde neighborhood. A school where people who were dissatisfied with the Forsyth Unified School District, and who could afford an alternative, sent their children. Now those people had been persuaded to send their children elsewhere.

This fall semester, only a month old, was the beginning of the first all-Patternist year. Ada welcomed it with relief. She had been working gradually toward the takeover, feeling her way for almost two years. Finally it was done. She had learned the needs of the children and overcome her own shyness enough to meet those needs. On paper, mutes still owned the school. But Ada and her Patternist assistants owned the mutes. And Ada herself was in full charge, responsible only to Mary.

It was a responsibility that had chosen Ada more than she had chosen it. She had discovered that she worked easily with children, enjoyed them, while most Patternists could not work with them at all. Only some of her relatives were able to assist her. Other Patternists found the emotional noise of children's minds intolerable. Children's emotional noise penetrated not only the general protection of the Pattern but the individual mental shields of the Patternists. It frayed their nerves, chipped away their tempers, and put the children in real danger. It made Patternists potentially even worse parents than latents.

Thus, no matter how much Patternists wanted to insure their future as a race—and they did want it now—they could not care for the children who were that future. They had to draft mutes to do it for them. First Doro, and now Mary, was creating a race that could not tolerate its own young.

Ada turned away from the window just as the mute guardian brought the girl in. The mute was Helen Dietrich, an elementary-school teacher who, with her husband, also cared for four latent children. Jan had moved the Dietrichs and several other teachers into the section, where they could do both jobs.

This girl, Ada recalled, had been a particularly unfortunate case— one of Rachel's assignments. Her life with the pair of latents who were her parents had left both her body and her mind a mass of scar tissue. Rachel had worked hard to right the damage. Now Ada wondered just how good a job she had done.

"Page," said Helen Dietrich nervously, "this is Ada Dragan. She's here to help you."

The girl stared at Ada through dark, sullen eyes. "I've already seen the school psychologist," she volunteered. "It didn't do any good."

Ada nodded. The school psychologist was a kind of experiment. He was completely ignorant of the fact that the Patternists now owned him. He was being allowed to learn as much as he could on his own. Nothing was hidden from him. But, on the other hand, nothing was handed to him. He, and a few others like him scattered around the section, were being used to calculate just how much information ordinary mutes needed to come to understand their situation.

"I'm not a psychologist," said Ada. "Nor a psychiatrist."

"Why not?" asked the girl. She extended her arms, which she had been holding behind her. Both wrists were bandaged. "I'm crazy, aren't I?"

Ada only glanced at the bandages. Helen Dietrich had told her about the suicide attempt. Ada spoke to the mute. "Helen, it might be easier on you if you left now."

The woman met Ada's eyes and realized that she was really being offered a choice. "I'd rather stay," she said. "I'll have to handle this again."

"All right." Ada faced the girl again. Very carefully, she read her. It was difficult here at the school, where so many other child minds intruded. This was one time when they became a nuisance. But, in spite of the nuisance, Ada had to handle the girl gently. At fifteen, Page was not too young to be nearing transition. Children who lived in the section, surrounded by Patternists and thus by the Pattern, did not need direct contact with Mary to push them into transition. The Pattern pushed them as soon as their bodies and minds could tolerate the shock. And this girl seemed ready—unless Rachel had just missed some mental problem and the girl was suffering needlessly. That was what Ada had to find out. She maintained contact with Page as she questioned her.

"Why did you try to kill yourself?"

The young mind made an effort to hold itself emotionless, but failed. The thought broke through, *To keep from killing others.* Aloud, the girl spoke harshly. "Because I wanted to die! It's my life. If I want to end it, it's my business."

She had not been told what she was. Children were told when they were about her age. They spent a few days with Ada or more likely, with one of Ada's assistants, and they learned a little of their history and got some idea what their future would be like. Ada had dubbed these sessions "orientation classes." Page was scheduled for one next month, but apparently, nature had decided to rush things.

"You won't be allowed to kill yourself, Page. You realize that, don't you?" Deftly, Ada planted the mental command as she spoke so that even as the girl opened her mouth to insist that she would try again, she realized that she could not—or, rather, realized that she no longer wanted to. That she had changed her mind.

Page stood still for a moment, her mouth open, then backed away from Ada in horror. "You did that! I felt it. It was you!"

Ada stared at her in surprise. No nontelepath, no latent should have known—

"You're one of them," the girl accused shrilly.

Mrs. Dietrich stood frowning at her. "I don't understand. What's wrong with the girl?"

Page faced her. "Nothing!" Then, more softly, "Oh, God, everything. Everything." She looked down at her arms. "I'm not sick. I'm not crazy, either. But if I tell you what... what *she* is," she gestured sharply toward Ada, "you'd let me be locked up. You wouldn't believe—"

"Tell her what I am, Page," said Ada quietly. She could feel the girl's terror bleating against her mind.

"You read people's minds! You make them do things they don't want to do. You're not human!" She raised a hand to her mouth, muffling her next words slightly. "Oh, God, you're not human... and neither am I!" She was crying now, working herself into hysterics. "Now go ahead and lock me up," she said. "At least then I won't be able to hurt anyone."

Ada looked over at Helen Dietrich. "That's it, really. She knows just enough about what's happening to her to be frightened by it. She thinks she's becoming something that will hurt you or your husband or one of the other children."

"Oh, Page." The mute woman tried to put her arms around the girl, but Page twisted away.

"You already knew! You brought me to her even though you knew what she was!"

"Be still, Page," said Ada quietly. And the girl lapsed into terrified silence. To the mute, Ada said, "Leave now, Helen. She'll be all right." This time, no choice was offered and Helen Dietrich left obediently. The girl, attempting to flee with her found herself seemingly rooted to the floor. Realizing that she was trapped, she collapsed, crying in helpless panic. Ada went to her, knelt beside her.

"Page..." She laid a hand on the girl's shoulder and felt the shoulder trembling. "Listen to me."

The girl continued to cry.

"You're not going to be hurt. You're certainly not going to be locked up. Now, listen."

After a moment the words seemed to penetrate. Page looked up at her. Clearly still frightened, she allowed Ada to help her from the floor onto one of the chairs. Her tears slowed, stopped, and she wiped her face with tissue from a box on the principal's desk.

"You should ask questions," said Ada softly. "You could have saved yourself a lot of needless worrying."

Page breathed deeply, trying to still her trembling. "I don't even know what to ask. Except... what's going to happen to me?"

"You're going to grow up. You're going to become the kind of adult your parents should have been but couldn't become alone."

"My parents," said Page with quiet loathing. "I hope you locked them up. They're animals."

"They were. They aren't now, though. We were able to help them—just as we've helped you, as we'll go on helping you." The girl should not have remembered enough about her parents to hate them. Rachel was always especially careful about that. But there was no mistaking the emotion behind the girl's words.

"You should have killed them," she said. "You should have cut their filthy throats!" She fell silent and stared down at her left arm. She touched the arm with her right hand, frowned at it. Ada knew then that the conditioning Rachel had imposed on the girl was still breaking down. From Page's mind Ada took the memory of a twisted, useless left arm permanently bent at the elbow, the hand hanging from it rag-limp, dead. The whole arm had been dead, thanks to an early violent beating that Page had received from her father. A beating and no medical attention. But Rachel had repaired the damage. Page's arm was normal now, but she was just remembering that it should not have been. And she was remembering more about her parents. Ada had to try to ease the knowledge.

"Our healers were able to do as much for your parents' minds as they were for your body," she said. "Your parents are different people now, living different lives. They're... sane people now. They aren't responsible for what they did when you knew them."

"You're afraid I'll try to get even."

"We can't let you do that."

"You can't make me forgive them, either." She stopped, frightened, suddenly realizing that Ada could probably do just that. "I hate them! I'd... I'd kill them myself if you sent me back to them." But she spoke without conviction.

"You won't be sent back to them," said Ada. "And I think, once you find out for yourself what made them the way they were, you'll know why we helped them instead of punishing them."

"They're... like you now?"

"They're both telepaths, yes." At thirty-seven, they were the oldest people to come through transition successfully. They had almost died in spite of everything Rachel could do. And they and three others who did die made Mary realize that most latents who hadn't been brought through by the time they were thirty-five shouldn't be brought through at all. To make their lives more comfortable, Mary had worked out a way of destroying their uncontrollable ability without harming them otherwise. At least then they could live the rest of their lives as normal mutes. But Page's parents had made it. They were strong Patternists, as Page would be strong.

"I'll be like you, too, then, won't I?" the girl asked.

"You will, yes. Soon."

"What will I be then to the Dietrichs?"

"You'll be the first of their foster children to grow up. They'll remember you."

"But... they're not like you. I can tell that much. I can feel a difference."

"They're not telepaths."

"They're slaves!" Her tone was accusing.

"Yes."

Page was silent for a moment, startled by Ada's willingness to admit such a thing. "Just like that? Yes, you make slaves of people? I'm going to be part of a group that makes slaves of people?"

"Page—"

"*Why do you think I tried to die?*"

"Because you didn't understand. You still don't."

"I know about being a slave! My parents taught me. My father used to strip me naked, tie me to the bed, and beat me, and then—"

"I know about that, Page."

"And I know about being a slave." The girl's voice was leaden. "I don't want to be a part of anything that makes people slaves."

"You have no choice. Neither do we."

"You could stop doing it."

"You'd still be with your parents if we didn't do it. We couldn't have cared for you." She took a deep breath. "We don't harm people like the Dietrichs in any way. In fact they're healthier and more comfortable now than they were before we found them. And the work they're doing for us is work they enjoy."

"If they didn't enjoy it, you'd change their minds for them."

"We might, but they wouldn't be aware of it. They would be content."

The girl stared at her. "Do you think that makes it better?"

"Not better. Kinder, in a frightening sort of way, I know. I'm not pretending that theirs is the best possible way of life, Page— although they think it is. They're slaves and I wouldn't trade places with them. But we, our kind, couldn't exist long without them."

"Then maybe we shouldn't exist! If our way is to enslave good people like the Dietrichs and let animals like my parents go free, the world would be better without us."

Ada looked away from her for a moment, then faced her sadly. "You haven't understood me. Perhaps you don't want to; I wouldn't blame you. The Dietrichs, Page, those good people who took you in, cared for you, loved you. Why, do you imagine, they did all that?"

And abruptly, Page understood. "No!" she shouted. "No. They wanted me. They told me so."

Ada said nothing.

"They might have been taking in foster children, anyway."

"You know better."

"No." The girl glared at Ada furiously, still trying to make herself believe the lie. Then something in her expression crumbled. How did it feel, after all, to learn that the foster parents you adored, the only parents who had ever shown you love, loved you only because they had been programmed to?

Ada watched her, fully aware of what she was going through, but choosing for a moment to ignore it. "We call ourselves Patternists," she said quietly. "This is our school. You and the others here are our children. We want the best for you even though we're not capable of giving it to you personally. It isn't possible for us to take you into our homes and give you the care you need. It just isn't possible. You'll understand why soon. So we make other arrangements."

The girl was crying silently, her head bowed, her face wet with tears and twisted with pain. Now Ada went to her, put an arm around her. She continued to speak, now offering comfort in her words. The girl was going to be too strong to be soothed with lies or partial amnesia. She had already proved that. Nothing would do for her but the truth. But that truth was not entirely disillusioning.

"The Dietrichs deserve the love and respect you feel for them, Page, because you're right about them. They are good people. They love children naturally. All we did was focus that love on you, on the others. In your case we didn't even have to focus it much. I didn't think we would. That's why I chose them for you—and you for them."

Finally Page looked up. "You did? You?"

"Yes."

She thought about that, then leaned her head to one side, against Ada's arm. "Then I guess it's only right that you be the one to take me away from them."

Ada said nothing.

Page lifted her head, met Ada's eyes. "You are going to take me away, aren't you?"

"Yes."

"I don't want to go."

"I know. But it's time."

Page nodded, lowered her head again to rest it against Ada's arm.

Chapter Ten

Mary

A few months into our first year, the original group of actives broke up. Rachel and Jesse moved out first—moved down the street to a house almost as big as ours. Then Jan moved alone. I had had a talk with her about using her psychometry as a kind of educational tool, or even as an art. At the same time, I told her to keep her hands off Karl. I didn't have that good a grip on him myself at the time, but I had already decided that, whether I got him or not, she wasn't going to. She left the next day.

Our new Patternists had been leaving us right along, taking over nearby houses, with Jesse preparing the way for them with the mutes who already lived there. They all had to learn to handle mutes— learn not to smash them and not to make robots of them. That was something Jesse had been able to do easily since his transition.

Seth and Ada moved to a house around the corner and across the street from us. Suddenly Karl and I were the only Patternists in Larkin House. We weren't back where we'd started or anything. Doro had finally left us, and we had a pair of latents with us. Everybody except Jan and Rachel was seconding somebody then. New Patternists too, as soon as they could be trusted to handle it. But Karl and I were more alone together than we had ever been before. Even Vivian didn't matter much anymore. She should have left Karl when he gave her the chance. Now she was a placid, bovine little pet. Karl controlled her without even thinking about it.

I was a predator and, frankly, not a very good one. But that was all right, because Karl wasn't as sure as he had once been that he minded being the prey. He was a little wary, a little amused. He had never really hated me, though. Hell, he and I would have gotten along fine together from back when he first climbed into my bed if it hadn't been for the Pattern and what the Pattern represented. It represented power. Power that I had and that he would never have. And while that wasn't something I threw at him, ever, it wasn't something I denied either.

The Pattern was growing because I searched out latents, had them brought in, and gave them their push toward transition. It was growing because of me. And nobody was better equipped to run it than I was. I hoped Karl could accept that and be comfortable enough with it to accept me. If he couldn't... well, I wanted him, but I wanted the thing I was building too. If I couldn't have both, Karl could go his way. I'd move out like the others and let him have his house back. Maybe he knew that.

"You know," he said one night, "for a while I thought you'd leave, like the others. There isn't really anything holding you here." We were in the study listening to the rain outside and not looking at a variety show on the television. Neither of us liked television. I don't know why we had bothered to turn it on that night.

"I didn't want to go," I said. "And since you weren't absolutely sure you wanted me to, I thought I'd hang around at least a while longer."

"I thought you might be afraid to leave—afraid that when Doro found out, he'd just order us back together."

"He might. But I doubt it. He's already gotten more than he bargained for from us."

"From you."

I shrugged.

"Why did you stay?"

"You know why. I wanted to be with you."

"The husband he chose for you."

"Yeah." I turned to face him. "Stupid me, falling in love with my own husband."

He didn't look away from me, didn't even change expression.

After a moment I grinned at him. "Not so stupid. We're a match."

He smiled thinly, almost grimly. "You're changing. I've been watching you change, wondering how far you would go."

"Changing how?"

"Growing up perhaps. I can remember when it was easier to intimidate you."

"Oh." I glanced at the television for a moment, listened as some woman tortured a song. "I'm a lot easier to get along with when I don't feel intimidated."

"So am I."

"Yeah." I listened to a few more bars of the woman's screaming, then shook my head. "You aren't paying any attention to this noise, are you?"

"No."

I got up and turned off the television. Now there was only the soft, rustling sound of the rain outside. "So, what are we going to do?" I asked him.

"We don't really have to do anything," he said. "Just let things progress as they have been."

I stared at him in silent frustration. That "silent" part was an effort. He laughed and moved over next to me.

"You don't read me very much anymore, do you?"

"I don't want to read you all the time," I said. "Talk to me."

He winced and drew back, muttering something I didn't quite catch.

"What?" I asked.

"I said how generous of you."

I frowned. "Generous, hell. You can say whatever you've got to say to me."

"I suppose so. After all, if you read me all the time, I'll begin to bore you very quickly."

So that was it! He was afraid he was going to get paid for some of the things he'd done to his women. He was afraid I was going to try to make a male Vivian of him. Not likely. "Keep that up," I said, "and I won't have to read you to be bored. You're not pitiful, Karl, so, coming from you, self-pity is kind of disgusting."

I thought he would hit me. I'm sure he thought about it. After a moment, though, he just sort of froze over. He stood up. "Find yourself a place tomorrow and get out of here."

"Better," I said. "There's nothing boring about you when you get mad."

He started to walk away from me in disgust. I got up quickly and caught him by the hand. He could have pulled away easily, but he didn't. I took that to be significant and moved closer to him.

"You ought to trust me," I said. "By now you ought to trust me."

"I'm not sure trust is an issue here."

"It is." I reached up and touched his face. "A very basic issue. You know it."

He began to look harassed, as though I was really getting on his nerves. Or maybe as though I was really getting to him in another way. I slipped my arms around him hopefully. It had been a long time. Too long.

"Come on, Karl, humor me. What's it going to cost you?" Plenty. And he knew it.

We stood together for a long moment, my head against his chest. Finally he sighed and steered us back to the sofa. We lay down together, just touching, holding each other.

"Will you unshield?" he asked.

I was surprised but I didn't mind. I unshielded. And he lowered his shield so that there were no mental barriers between us. We seemed to flow together—frighteningly at first. I felt as though I were losing myself, combining so thoroughly with him that I wouldn't be able to free myself again. If he hadn't been so calm, I would have tried to reshield after the first couple of seconds. But I could see that he wasn't afraid, that he wanted me to stay as I was, that nothing irreversible was happening. I realized that he had done this with Jan. I could see the experience in his memory. It was something like the blending that he did naturally with the shieldless, mute women he had had. Jan hadn't liked it. She didn't much like any kind of direct mind-to-mind contact. But she had been so lonely among us, and so without purpose, that she had endured this mental blending just to keep Karl interested in her. But the blending wasn't an act that one person could enjoy while the other grimly endured.

I closed my eyes and explored the thing that Karl and I had become. A unit. I was aware of the sensations of his body and my own. I could feel my own desire for him exciting him and his excitement circling back to me.

We lost control. The spiral of our own emotions got out of hand. We hurt each other a little. I wound up with bruises and he had nail marks and bites. Later I took one look at what was left of the dress I had been wearing and threw it away.

But, my God, it was worth it.

"We're going to have to be more careful when we do that again," he said, examining some of his scratches.

I laughed and moved his hands away. The wounds were small. I healed them quickly. I found others and healed them too. He watched me with interest.

"Very efficient," he said. He met my eyes. "It seems you've won."

"All by myself?"

He smiled. "What, then? We've won?"

"Sure. Want to go take a shower together?"

At the end of the Pattern's first year of existence, we all knew we had something that was working. Something new. We were learning to do everything as we went along. Soon after Karl and I got together, we found latents with latent children. That could have turned out really bad. We discovered we were "allergic" to children of our own kind. We were more dangerous to them than their latent parents were. That was when Ada discovered her specialty. She was the only one of us who could tolerate children and care for them. She began using mutes as foster parents, and she began to take over the small private school not far from us. And she and Seth moved back to Larkin House.

They had been the last to leave, and now they were the first to return. They had only left, they said, because the others were leaving. Not because they wanted to be out of Larkin House. They didn't. They were as comfortable with us as our new Patternists were with each other in their groups, their "families" of unrelated adults. We Patternists seemed to be more-social creatures than mutes were. Not one of our new Patternists chose to live alone. Even those who wanted to go out on their own waited until they could find at least one other person to join them. Then, slowly, the pair collected others. Their house grew.

Rachel and Jesse came back to us a few days after Seth and Ada. They were a little shamefaced, ready to admit that they wanted back into the comfort they had not realized they had found until they walked away from it.

Jan just reappeared. I read her. She had been lonely as hell in the house she had chosen, but she didn't say anything to us. She wanted to live with us, and she wanted to use her ability. She thought she would be content if she could do those two things. She was learning to paint, and even the worst of her paintings lived. You touched them and they catapulted you into another world. A world of her imagination. Some of the new Patternists who were related to her began coming to her to learn to use whatever psychometric ability they had. She taught them, took lovers from among them, and worked to improve her art. And she was happier than she had ever been before.

The seven of us became the First Family. It was a joke at first. Karl made some comparison between our position in the section and the position of the President's family in the nation. The name stuck. I think we all thought it was a little silly at first, but we got used to it. Karl did his bit to help me get used to it.

"We could do something about making it more of a family," he said. "We'd be the first ones to try it, too. That would give some validity to our title."

The Pattern was just over a year old then. I looked at him uncertainly, not quite sure he was saying what I thought he was saying.

"Try that again?"

"We could have a baby."

"Could *we?*"

"Seriously, Mary. I'd like us to have a child."

"Why?"

He gave me a look of disgust.

"I mean... we wouldn't be able to keep it with us."

"I know that."

I thought about it, surprised that I hadn't really thought about it before. But, then, I had never wanted children. With Doro around, though, I had assumed that sooner or later I would be ordered to produce some. Ordered. Somehow, being asked was better.

"We can have a child if you want," I said.

He thought for a moment. "I don't imagine you could arrange for it to be a boy?"

I arranged for it to be a boy. I was a healer by then. I could not only choose the child's sex but insure his good health and my own good health while I was pregnant. So being pregnant was no excuse for me to slow our expansion.

I was pulling in latents from all over the country. I could pick them out of the surrounding mute population without trouble. It didn't matter anymore that I had never met them or that they were three thousand miles away when I focused in on them. My range, like the distance the Patternists could travel from me, had increased as the Pattern had grown. Now I located latents by their bursts of telepathic activity and gave a general picture of their location to one of my Patternists. The Patternist could pinpoint them more closely when he was within a few miles of them.

So the Pattern grew. Karl and I had a son: Karl August Larkin. The name of the man whose body Doro had used to father me was Gerold August. I had never made any gesture in his memory before, and I probably never would again. But having the baby had made me sentimental.

Doro wasn't around to watch us much as we grew. He checked on us every few months, probably to remind us—remind me—where the final authority still rested. He showed up twice while I was pregnant. Then we didn't see him again until August was two months old. He showed up at a time when we weren't having any big problems. I was kind of glad to see him. Kind of proud that I was running things so smoothly. I didn't realize he'd come to put an end to that.

He came in and looked at my flat stomach and said, "Boy or girl?" I hadn't bothered to tell him I'd deliberately conceived a boy.

So Karl and I sat around and probably bored him with talk about the baby. I was surprised when he said he wanted to see it.

"Why?" I asked. "Babies his age all look pretty much alike. What is there to see?"

Both men frowned at me.

"Okay, okay," I said. "Let's go see the baby. Come on."

Doro got up, but Karl stayed where he was. "You two go ahead," he said. "I was out to see him this morning. My head won't take it again for a while."

No wonder he could afford to be indignant at my attitude! He was setting me up. I wished Ada was around to take Doro in. August wasn't at the school itself, but he was at one of the buffer houses surrounding the school. That was almost as bad. The static from the school and from children in general didn't hit me as hard as it did most of the others, but it still wasn't very pleasant.

We went in. Doro stared at August, and August stared back from the arms of Evelyn Winthrop, the mute woman who took care of him. Then we left.

"Drive somewhere far enough from the school for you to be comfortable, and park," said Doro when we got back to the car. "I want to talk to you."

"About the baby?"

"No. Something else. Although I suppose I should compliment you on your son."

I shrugged.

"You don't give a damn about him, do you?"

I turned onto a quiet, tree-lined street and parked. "He's got all his parts," I said. "Healthy mentally and physically. I saw to that. Watched him very carefully before he was born. Now I keep an eye on Evelyn and her husband to be sure they're giving him the care he needs. Beyond that, you're right."

"Jan all over again."

"Thanks."

"I'm not criticizing you. Telepaths are always the worst possible parents. I thought the Pattern might change that, but it hasn't. Most actives have to be bulldozed into even having children. You and Karl surprised me."

"Karl wanted a child."

"And you wanted Karl."

"I already had him by then. But the idea of having a child wasn't that repulsive. It still isn't. I'd do it again. Now, what did you want to talk to me about?"

"Your doing it again."

"What?"

"Or at least having your people do it. Because that's the only way I'm going to allow the Pattern to grow for a while."

I turned to look at him. "What are you talking about?"

"I'm suspending your latent-gathering as of today. You're to call your people in from their searches, and recruit no more new Patternists."

"But—but why? What have we done, Doro?"

"Nothing. Nothing but grow. And that's the problem. I'm not punishing you; I'm slowing you down a little. I'm being cautious."

"For what? Why should you be cautious about our growth? The mutes don't know anything about us, and they'd have a hard time hurting us if they did. We aren't hurting each other. I'm in control. There's been no unusual trouble."

"Mary... fifteen hundred adults and five hundred children in only two years! It's time you stopped devoting all your energy to growth and started figuring out just what it is you're growing. You're one woman holding everything together. Your only possible successor at this point is about two months old. There'd be a blood bath if anything happened to you. If you were hit by a car tomorrow, your people would disintegrate—all over each other."

"If I were hit by a car and there were anything at all of me left alive, I'd survive. If I couldn't put myself together again Rachel would do it."

"Mary, what I'm saying is that you're irreplaceable. You're all your people have got. Now, you can go on playing the part of their savior if you do as I've told you. Or you can destroy them by plunging on headlong as you are now."

"Are you saying I have to stop recruiting until August is old enough to replace me if anything happens to me?"

"Yes. And for safety's sake, I suggest that you not make August an only child."

"Wait twenty years?"

"It only sounds like a long time, Mary, believe me." He smiled a little. "Besides, not only are you a potential immortal as a descendant of Emma, but you have your own and Rachel's healing ability to keep you young if your potential for longevity doesn't work out."

"Twenty Goddamn years...!"

"You would have something firm and well established to bring your people into by then, too. You wouldn't be just spreading haphazardly over the city."

"We aren't doing that now! You know we aren't. We're growing deliberately into Santa Elena, because that's where the living room we need is. Jesse is working right now to prepare a new section of Santa Elena for us. We've got the school in the most protected part of our Palo Alto district. We didn't manage that by accident! The people don't just move wherever they want to. They go to Jesse and he shows them what's available."

"And all that's available is what you take from mutes. You don't build anything of your own."

"We build ourselves!"

"You will build yourselves more slowly now."

I knew that tone of voice. I used it myself from time to time. I knew he was letting me argue so that I'd have time to get used to the idea, not because there was any chance of changing his mind. But twenty years!

"Doro, do you know what kind of work I've had Rachel doing for most of the past two years?"

"I know."

"Have you seen the people she brings in—walking corpses most of them? That is if they can even walk."

"Yes."

"My people, so far gone they look like they've been through Dachau!"

"Mary—"

"They turn out to be my best telepaths when they're like that, you know? That's why they're in such bad shape as latents. They're so sensitive, they pick up everything."

"Mary, listen."

"How many of those people do you imagine will die, probably in agony, in twenty years?"

"It doesn't matter, Mary. It doesn't matter at all."

End of conversation. At least as far as he was concerned. But I just couldn't let go.

"You've been watching them die for thousands of years," I said. "You've learned not to care. I've just been saving them for two years, but I've already learned the opposite lesson. I care."

"I was afraid you would."

"Is it such a bad thing?"

"It's going to hurt you. It's already started to hurt you."

"You could let me go after just the worst ones. Just the ones who would die without me."

"No."

"Goddamnit, Doro, they'd die anyway. What could you lose?"

He looked at me silently for a long moment. "Do you remember what I told you on the day, two years ago, when you discovered Clay Dana's potential?"

The crap about obeying. I remembered, all right. "I wondered when you'd get to that."

"You know I meant it."

I slumped back in the seat, wondering what I was going to do. I took his hand almost absently. "What a pity we had to become competitors!"

"We haven't. There's enough for both of us."

I looked down at his hand, calloused, with fingers that were too long. It hit me how much like my own, big, ugly hands it was, and I took another look at the body he was wearing—green-eyed, black-haired.... "Who is this you're wearing?" I asked.

He raised an eyebrow. "A relative of your father—as you've probably already guessed."

"What relation?"

His expression hardened. "A son. Your older half brother." He wasn't just giving me information. He was challenging me with it.

"Right," I said. "Just the kind of person I would be looking for. A close relative, a potentially good Patternist, and a likely victim to ease your hunger. You know damn well we're competitors, Doro."

I had never spoken that bluntly to him before. He stared at me as though I'd surprised him—which was what I had set out to do.

"Hey," I said softly. "You know what I am. You made me what I am. Don't cut me off from the thing I was born to do. Just let me have the worst of the latents. Rachel's kind. Okay that, and I won't touch any of the others."

He shook his head slowly. "I'm sorry, Mary."

"But why?" I yelled. "Why?"

"Let's get back to the house. You can start calling your people in."

I got out of the car, slammed the door, and walked around to the sidewalk. I couldn't stay sitting there beside him for a minute longer. I would have done something stupid and useless—and probably suicidal. He called to me a couple of times, but, thank God, he had the sense not to come after me.

I walked home. Palo Alto wasn't far. I needed to burn off some of my anger before I got home, anyway.

Chapter Eleven

Mary

Karl was settling some kind of dispute when I got home. He was standing between two Patternist men who were trying to glare each other to death. Their communication was all mental and easy for me to ignore as I walked through the living room. I went to the library and began to call in my searchers. As usual, they were scattered around the country—around the continent. Doro had begun planting the best of his families from Africa, Europe, and Asia in various parts of North America hundreds of years before. He had decided then that the North American continent was big enough to give them room to avoid each other and that it would be racially diverse enough to absorb them all. Now I had people in three countries demanding to know why they should stop their searches before they had found all the latents they sensed—why they should abandon potential Patternists. I didn't blame them for being mad, but I wasn't about to tell them, one by one, what the problem was. I pulled a "Do it because I said so!" on them and broke contact before they could argue more.

Karl came into the library as I was finishing and said, "What are you doing sitting in here in the dark?"

I was in contact with a Patternist in Chicago who was crying in anger and frustration at my "stupid, arbitrary, dictatorial orders...." On and on.

Just get your ass on the next plane to L.A., I told her. I broke contact with her and blinked as Karl turned on the light. I hadn't realized it was so late.

"Uh-oh," he said, looking at me. "I'll listen if you want to talk about it."

I just opened and gave it all to him.

"Twenty years," he said, frowning. "But why? It doesn't make sense."

"Doro doesn't have to make sense," I said. "Although in this case I think he has his reasons. I think it's interesting that he first denied that he and I were competitors."

Karl looked hard at me. "I don't think that's a point you should emphasize to him."

"I wasn't emphasizing it. I was letting him know I understood it, and that because I understood it I was willing to accept a reasonable limitation—willing to settle for just the worst of the latents."

"But it didn't do any good."

"No."

"I wonder why. It sounds fairly harmless, and he would be able to check on you just by questioning you now and then."

"Maybe it was something I said—although he knew it already."

"What?"

"That the really bad latents turn out to be my best Patternists. They're probably the victims that give him the most pleasure too, when he can catch them before they kill themselves or get themselves locked up. I'll bet that half brother of mine was a mess before Doro took him."

"Competition again," said Karl. "Possible." He looked at me curiously. "Does it bother you that the body he's wearing was your brother?"

"No. I never knew the man. Doro's appetite in general bothers me. He warned me that it would. But I can keep quiet about it as long as he isn't taking my Patternists."

"For all we know, that could be next."

"God! No, he wouldn't do that while I'm still alive. The only Patternist he's likely to take right now is me." Something occurred to me suddenly. "Wait a minute! He may have left me more clues to whatever the hell he's doing than I thought."

"What?"

"I'll get back to you in a minute." I reached out to the old neighborhood, to Emma. I could reach her fast now, because she belonged to me. I had a kind of link with her that would let me know the minute some other Patternist touched her, and at the same time let the Patternist know she was mine. I had that kind of connection with Rina too, since she was too old for me to risk her life by trying to push her into transition.

I read Emma, saw that Doro had been to see her just a few hours before. And he'd talked a lot. Now since he knew Emma was mine, knew that anything he said to her I would eventually pick up, I assumed that he had been talking at least partly to me. Perhaps more to me than about me. I looked at Karl. "This morning, Doro told Emma he was afraid I'd disobey him in this and make him kill me."

"Obviously he was wrong," said Karl.

"But he seemed so sure about it—and Emma seemed so sure. I can discount Emma, I guess. She's frightened enough of me—and jealous enough of me—to want me dead. But Doro...."

"Do you have any intention of defying him?"

"None... now." I stared down at the table. "I wouldn't risk the people, the Pattern, even if I were willing to risk myself. I'm wondering, though...."

"Wondering what?"

"Well, remember when we started this—when I pulled in Christine and Jamie Hanson?"

"Yes."

"And you and Doro and I tried to figure out why I was so eager to bring in more people. Doro finally decided that I needed them for the same reasons he needed them. For sustenance."

Karl smiled faintly, which had to be a mark of how much he had relaxed and accepted his place in the Pattern. "Don't you think fifteen hundred people might be enough to sustain you?"

I looked at him. "You don't know how much I'd like to say yes to that."

His smile vanished. "For the sake of the fifteen hundred, you'd better say yes to it."

"Yeah. I just wish I could be sure that *saying* yes was enough."

"Why wouldn't it be?"

"I might be too much like Doro." I sighed. "I'm supposed to be like him. He finally admitted that to Emma this morning. Have you ever seen him when he needs a change really badly?"

"No. But I know that's not a safe time to be near him."

"Right. If he's really in trouble, he's liable to lose control—just take whoever's closest to him. Usually, though, he prevents himself from getting into that situation by changing often and keeping to healthy, young bodies. I seem to prefer young minds—not necessarily healthy."

"But with so many young minds already here, there's no reason for you to defy Doro and go after more."

"There are more of them out there, Karl. I'm afraid that might be reason enough. Now that I'm thinking about it. . . ." I glanced at him. "You've felt how eager I am when I go after new people—the first ones two years ago, and the last ones this morning. I don't like thinking about what my life will be like now that I can't go after any more of them."

He put one elbow on the table and rested his chin on his hand. "You know, in his way, I think Doro does love you."

I stared at him in surprise. "What's that got to do with anything?"

"Am I right?"

"He loves me. What passes for love with him."

"Don't belittle it. I think it's the only lever you have that might move him—make him change his mind."

"I've never in my life been able to change his mind once he's made it up. His love . . . it lasts as long as I do what he tells me."

"All right, then; you may not have any influence. But you'll find out for sure, won't you. You'll try."

I took a deep breath, nodded. "I'll try anything within reason. But I don't think anything less than my complete obedience will satisfy him. I've made him wary and uncomfortable. I've been moving too fast, and letting him see me too clearly."

"It sounds as though you're saying he's afraid of you. And if you believe that, you're deluding yourself. Dangerously."

"No, not afraid. Cautious. He's alive because he's cautious. And I'm too powerful. Fifteen hundred people aren't giving me any trouble at all. Whatever the Pattern is, I'm not likely to overload it soon. Doro isn't worried that I can't handle the thing I'm building. He's worried that I can."

Karl thought about that for a long moment. "If you're right, if he is worried, it might not only be because you're competing with him and taking his people."

I looked at him questioningly.

"It might be because you could use those people against him. You can't hurt him alone, but if you took strength from some of us—or all of us. . . ."

"He made a point of telling Emma that wouldn't work."

"Did he convince you?"

"He didn't have to. I already knew better than to try anything like that with him."

"You had no reason to risk trying it before now. Now... you might have to try something. Or let us try. There should be enough Patternists now for us to overwhelm him without your help."

"No way."

"It's never been tried. You don't know—"

"I know. You couldn't do it. Not even all fifteen hundred of you together, because, as far as he's concerned, you wouldn't really be together. He'd take you one at a time, but so fast you'd fall like dominoes. I know. Because that's something I could do myself."

He frowned. "That's out, then. But I don't understand why he's so convinced that you couldn't defeat him using our strength."

"He said, 'Strength alone isn't enough to defeat me.' And part of the reason he gave is that I can't change bodies. But that doesn't hold up. I can kill his body with a thought, and that same thought will force him to attack me on a mental level. My territory."

"That sounds promising."

"Yes, but he knows it as well as I do. That means he has some other reason for his confidence. The only thing I can think of is my own ignorance. I just don't know how to take him. He's not a Patternist, he's not a mute—he's bound to have some surprises for me. If I go after him, the chances are I'll be dead before I can figure out how to kill him. He knows so much more than I do."

"But he's never faced anyone like you before. You'd be as new to him as he is to you."

"But killing is a way of life to him, Karl. He's damned good at it. And he has killed people who he thought were dangerous to him before. He claims I don't even have the potential to be dangerous to him personally."

"Do you imagine he's never made a mistake?"

"He's still alive."

"No wonder. Look how good he is at scaring hell out of his opponents before he faces them. If you accept him as all-knowing and invulnerable, you'd better be able to live without recruiting for as long as he says. Because you'll be in no shape to face him. You'll have already beaten yourself!"

We stared at each other for a long moment, and I could see that he was as worried as he sounded. "You know I'm not going to give him my life," I said quietly. "Or the lives of my Patternists. If I have to fight him, it will be a battle, not a rout."

"You'll take strength from us."

I winced, looked away. "Some of you at least."

"The strongest of us. Beginning with me."

I nodded. To protect them, I had to risk them. They could be killed even if I wasn't. If I was desperate and rushed, as I probably would be, I might take too much of their strength. And I would be killing them. Not Doro. They were my people, and I would be killing them.

Doro stayed at Larkin House that night. We still kept his room ready for him though he didn't use it much anymore. He didn't intend to use it that night. Instead he came across the hall to my room. I was sitting in the middle of my bed in the dark, thinking. He walked in without knocking.

He and I hadn't made love for over a year, but he walked in as though there had been no break at all. Knowing him, I wasn't surprised. He sat on the side of my bed, took off his shoes, and lay down beside me fully clothed. I was stark naked myself.

"I checked on a few of your searchers," he said. "I see they're starting for home."

I didn't say anything. I had mixed emotions about his just being there. I had promised Karl that I'd use my "lever," try to change Doro's mind. Now looked like a good time for that. But, since he was Doro, I wouldn't get anything past him that I didn't mean. If I was going to be able to reach him at all, it had to be with truth.

"I'm glad you're co-operating," he said. "I was afraid you might not."

"I got the message you left with Emma," I said. "Although I think you laid it on kind of thick."

"I wasn't acting. I wasn't trying to scare you, either. I was honestly worried about you."

"Why make impossible demands of me and then worry about me?"

"Impossible?"

"Hard, then. Too hard."

He just looked at me—at what he could see of me in the light from the window.

"Hard on the others, too."

He shrugged.

"You've stayed away from us too long," I said. "It's easy for you to hurt us, because you don't really know us anymore."

"Oh, I know you, girl."

That didn't sound too good. "I mean you used to be one of us. You could be again, you know."

"Your people don't need me. Neither do you."

"You're our founder," I said. "Our father. We teach the new Patternists about you, but that isn't enough. They should get to know you."

"And me them."

"Yes."

"It won't work, Mary."

I frowned down at him. He was lying flat on his back now, looking up at the ceiling. "If you get to know us as we are now. Doro, you might find that we really are the people, the race, that you've been working for so long to build. We already belong to you, and you can be one of us. We haven't shut you out."

"It's surprising how eloquent you can become when you want something."

I hung on to my temper. "You know I'm not just talking. I mean what I'm saying."

"It doesn't matter. Because it's not going to change anything. The order I gave you is final. I'm not going to be talked out of it. Not by getting to know your people better. Not by renewing my relationship with you."

"What are you doing here, then?"

"Oh, I intend to renew our relationship. I just don't intend to let you charge me for it."

I kicked him out of the bed. We were positioned perfectly for it. I just let him have it in the side with both feet. He fell, cursing, and got up holding his side.

"What the hell was that supposed to prove?" he demanded. "I thought you had outgrown that kind of behavior."

"I have. I only give it to you because it's what you want."

He ignored that, sat down on the bed. "That was a stupid, dangerous thing to do."

"No it wasn't. You have some control. You can control your mouth too when you want to."

He sighed. "Well, at least you're back to normal."

"Shit!" I muttered and turned away from him. "Pleading for my people isn't normal. Acting like a latent is normal. Stay with us, Doro. Get to know us again, whether you think you'll change your mind or not."

"What is it you want me to see that you think I've missed?"

"The fact that your kids really have grown up, man. I know actives and latents didn't use to be able to do that. They had too many problems just surviving. Surviving alone. We weren't meant for solitude. But the Pattern has let us grow up."

"What makes you think I haven't noticed that?"

I looked at him sharply. Something really ugly had come into his voice just then. Something I would have expected to hear in Emma's voice but not his. "Yeah," I said softly. "Of course you know. You even said it yourself a couple of minutes ago. It must have come as kind of a shock to you that after four thousand years, your work, your children, were suddenly as finished as you could make them. That they... didn't need you anymore."

He gave me a look of pure hatred. I think he was as close to taking me at that moment as he had ever been. I touched his hand.

"Join us, Doro. If you destroy us, you'll be destroying part of yourself. All the time you spent creating us will be wasted. Your long life, wasted. Join us."

The hatred that had flared in his eyes was concealed again. I suspected it was more envy than hatred. If he had hated me, I would already have been dead. Envy was bad enough. He envied me for doing what he had bred me to do—because he was incomplete, and he would never be able to do it himself. He got up and walked out of my room.

Karl

In only ten days Karl knew without doubt that Mary's suspicions had been justified. She wasn't going to be able to obey Doro. She had begun sensing latents again without intending to, without searching for them. Sooner or later she was going to have to begin pulling them in again. And the day she did that would very likely be the day she died.

She and how many others?

Karl watched her with growing concern. She was like a latent now, trying to hold herself together, and no one knew it but she and Karl. She kept shielded, and she was actress enough to conceal it from the others—except possibly Doro. And Doro didn't care.

Mary had already talked to him and been refused. That tenth night, Karl went in to talk to him. He pleaded. Mary was in trouble. If she could even be given a small quota of the latents that Doro valued least—

"I'm sorry," said Doro. "I can't afford her unless she can obey me."

It was a dismissal. The subject was closed. Karl got up wearily and went to Mary's room.

She was lying on her back, staring up at the ceiling. Just staring. She did not move as he came to sit beside her, except to take his hand and hold it.

"What did he say?" she asked.

"You've been reading me," he said mildly.

"If I had, I'd know what he said. I was coming upstairs a few minutes ago. I saw you go into his room." She sat up and looked at him intently. "What did he say, Karl?"

"He said no."

"Oh." She lay down again. "I knew damned well he would. I just keep hoping."

"You're going to have to fight."

"I know."

"And you're going to win. You're going to kill him. You're going to do whatever you have to do to kill him!"

Like a latent, she turned onto her side, clutched her head between her hands, and curled her body into a tight knot.

The next day, Karl called the family together. Mary had gone to see August, and Karl wanted to talk to the others before she returned. She would find out what had been said. He planned to tell her himself, in fact. But he wanted to talk to them first without her.

They already knew why Mary had called in her searchers. They didn't like it. Mary's enthusiasm over the Pattern's growth had infected them long ago. Now Karl told them that Mary's submission could not last. That Mary's own needs would force her to disobey, and that when she disobeyed, Doro would kill her. Or try to.

"It's possible that with our numbers we can help her defeat him," Karl said. "I don't know how she'll handle things when the time comes, but I have a feeling she'll want to get as many of the people away from the section as she can. Doro has told us that actives couldn't handle themselves in groups before the Pattern. I know Mary's afraid of the chaos that might happen here if she's killed while we're all together. So I think she'll try to give the people some warning to get out of Forsyth, scatter. If any of you want to scatter with them, she'll almost certainly let you go. The idea of other Patternists dying either because she dies or because she takes too much strength from them is bothering her more than the thought of her own death."

"Sounds like you're telling us to cut and run," said Jesse.

"I'm offering you a choice," said Karl.

"Only because you know we won't take it," said Jesse.

Karl looked from him to the others, let his gaze pass over them slowly.

"He speaks for all of us," said Seth. "I didn't know Mary was in trouble. She hides things too well sometimes. But now that I do know, I'm not going to walk out on her."

"And how could I leave the school?" said Ada. "All the children...."

"I think Doro has made a mistake," said Rachel. "I think he's waited too long to do this. I don't see how any one person could resist so many of us. I don't even see why we have to risk Mary, since she's the only one of us who's irreplaceable. If the rest of us got together and—"

"Mary says that wouldn't work," said Karl. "She says it wouldn't even work against her."

"Then, we'll all have to give her our strength."

"To be honest, she's not sure that will work either. Doro says strength alone isn't enough to beat him. I suspect he's lying. But the only way to find out for sure is for her to tackle him. So she will gather strength from some or all of us when the time comes. We're the only weapons she has."

"If she's not careful," said Jesse, "she won't have time to try it—or time to warn the people to scatter. Doro knows she's in trouble, doesn't he?"

"Yes."

"He might decide there's no point in waiting for her to break."

"I've thought about that," said Karl. "I don't think she'll let him surprise her. But, to be sure, I'm going to start work on her tonight—talk her into going after him. Preparing herself, and going after him."

"Are you sure you can talk her into it?" asked Jan.

"Yes." Karl looked at her. "You haven't said anything. Are you with us?"

Jan looked offended. "I'm a member of this family, aren't I?"

Karl smiled. Jan had changed. Her art had given her the strength that she had always lacked. And it had given her a contentment with her life. She might even be a live woman now, instead of a corpse, in bed. Karl wondered briefly but not seriously. Mary was woman enough for him if he could find some way of keeping her alive.

"I think Doro has made more than one mistake," said Jan. "I think he's wrong to believe that Mary still belongs to him. With the responsibility she's taken on for all that she's built here, she belongs to us, the people. To all of us."

"I suspect she thinks it's the other way around," said Rachel. "But it wouldn't hurt if we went to some of the heads of houses and said it Jan's way. They're our best, our strongest. Mary will need them."

"I don't know whether I'll be able to get her to take them," said Karl. "I intend to try, though."

"When Doro starts chewing at her, she'll take anybody she can get," said Jesse.

"If she has time, as you said," said Karl. "I don't want it to come to that. That's why I'm going to work on her. And, look, don't say anything to the heads of houses. Word will spread too quickly. It might spread to Doro. God knows what he'd do if he realized his cattle had finally gotten the nerve to plot against him."

Chapter Twelve

Mary

When I woke up on the morning after Karl had talked to Doro, I found that my hands wouldn't stop shaking. I felt the way I had a few days before my transition. With Karl, I didn't even bother to hide it.

He said, "Open to me. Maybe I can help."

"You can't help," I muttered. "Not this time."

"Let me try."

I looked at him, saw the concern in his eyes, and felt almost guilty about doing as he asked. I opened to him not because I thought he could help me but because I wanted him to realize that he couldn't.

He stayed with me for several seconds, sharing my need, my hunger, my starvation. Sharing it but not diminishing it in any way. Finally he withdrew and stood staring at me bleakly. I went to him for the kind of comfort he could give, and he held me.

"You could take strength from me," he said. "It might ease your—"

"No!" I rested my head against his chest. "No, no, no. You think I haven't thought of that?"

"But you wouldn't have to take much. You could—"

"I said no, Karl. It's like you said last night. I'm going to have to fight him. I'll take from you then, and from the others. But not until then. I'm not the vampire he is. I give in return for my taking." I pulled away from him, looked at him. "God, I've got ethics all of a sudden."

"You've had them for some time, now, whether you were willing to admit to them or not."

I smiled. "I remember Doro wondering before my transition whether I would ever develop a conscience."

Karl made a sound of disgust. "I just wish Doro had developed one. Are you going out?"

"Yes. To see August."

He didn't say anything to that, and I wondered whether he realized this might be my last visit to our son. I finished dressing and left.

I saw August and spent some time strengthening Evelyn's programming, seeing to it that she would go on being a good mother to him even if Karl and I weren't around. And I planted some instructions that she wouldn't need or remember until August showed signs of approaching transition. I didn't want her panicking then, and taking him to a doctor or a hospital. Maybe I needn't have worried. Maybe Doro would see that he was taken care of. And maybe not.

I went home and managed to get through a fairly ordinary day. I passed a man and a woman to become heads of houses. They had been Patternists for over a year, and I read just about everything they had done during that year. Karl and I checked all prospective heads of houses. Back when we hadn't checked them, we'd gotten some bad ones. Some who had been too warped by their latent years to turn human again. We still got that kind, but they didn't become heads of houses anymore. If we couldn't straighten them out, or heal them—if healing was what they needed—we killed them. We had no prison, needed none. A rogue Patternist was too dangerous to be left alive.

That was probably the way Doro felt about me. It went with what he had told Karl. "I can't afford her unless she can obey me." We were too much alike, Doro and I. What ever gave him the idea that someone bred to be so similar to him would consent—could consent—to being controlled by him all her life?

I passed my two new heads of houses, but I told them not to do anything toward beginning their houses for a week. They didn't like that much, but they were so happy to be passed that they didn't argue. They were bright and capable. If, by some miracle, the Pattern still existed in a week, they would be a credit to it in their new positions.

I went with Jesse to see the houses he was opening up in Santa Elena. He asked me to go. I didn't have to see them. I only checked on the family now and then. And when I did, I could never find much to complain about. They cared about what we were building. They always did a good job.

In the car Jesse said, "Listen, you know we're all with you, don't you?"

I looked at him, not really surprised. Karl had told him. No one else could have.

"I just wish we could take him on for you," said Jesse.

"Thanks, Jess."

He glanced at me, then shook his head. "You don't look any more nervous over facing him than you did over facing me a couple of years ago."

I shrugged. "I don't think I can afford to broadcast my feelings."

"With all of us behind you, I think you can beat him."

"I intend to."

Big talk. I wondered why I bothered.

There were a few other routine duties. I welcomed them, because they kept my mind off how bad I felt. That night, I didn't feel like eating. I went to my room while everyone else was at dinner. Let them eat. It might be their last meal.

Karl came up about two hours later and found me looking out my window at nothing, waiting for him.

"I've got to talk to you," he said—just before I could say it to him.

"Okay." I sat down in the chair by the window. He sprawled on my bed.

"We had a meeting today—just the family. I told them what kind of trouble you were in, told them that you were going to fight. And I told them they could run if they wanted to."

"They won't run."

"I know that. I just wanted them to put it into words. I wanted them to hear themselves say it and know that they were committed."

"Everybody's committed. Every Patternist in the section. And all those who don't know it are about to find out."

He sat up straight. "What are you going to do?"

"First I'm going to clear the section."

"Clear it? Send everybody away?"

"Yes. Including the family, if they'll go. They won't be deserting me. I can use them just as effectively if they're a couple of states away."

"They won't go."

I shrugged. "I hope they don't wind up regretting that."

"I assume you're going after Doro in the morning."

"After everybody has had time to get out, yes. I want them to spread out, scatter as widely as possible, just in case."

"I know. I just hope Doro gives them time to go. If he notices that people are leaving—if he thinks of someone and that tracking sense of his tells him that that person is headed for Oregon, he's going to start checking around. He'll think you're sending out searchers again. Then, when he realizes everybody's going, he'll get the idea pretty quickly."

"We could see that he's distracted for the night."

He looked at me. I didn't say anything. Obviously this was no night to distract Doro with a Patternist. Karl gazed down at his hands for a moment, then looked up. "All right; it's done. Vivian will distract him. And she'll think it's her own idea."

We waited, our perception focused on Doro's room. Vivian knocked at his door, then went in. Her mind gave us Doro's words, and we knew we were safe. He was glad to see her. They hadn't been together for a long time.

"Now," said Karl.

"Now," I agreed. I went to the bed and lay down. It was best for me to be completely relaxed when I used the Pattern this way. I closed my eyes and brought it into focus. Now I was aware of the contented hum of my people. They were ending their day, resting or preparing to rest, and unconsciously giving each other calm.

I jerked the Pattern sharply, shattering their calm. It didn't hurt them, or me, but it startled them to attention. I felt Karl jump beside me, and he had been expecting it.

I could feel their attention on me as though I had walked onto the stage of a crowded auditorium. It was as easy to reach all 1,538 of them as it had been to reach just the family two years before. And there was no need for me to identify myself. Nobody else could have reached them through the Pattern as I did.

The Pattern is in danger, I sent bluntly. *It may be destroyed.*

I could feel their alarm at that. In the two short years of its existence the Pattern had given these people a new way of life. A way of life that they valued.

The Pattern may be destroyed, I repeated. *If it is, and if you're together when it happens, you will be in danger.* I gave them a short history lesson. A lesson they had already been exposed to once in orientation classes or through learning blocks. That, before the Pattern, active telepaths had not been able to survive together in groups. That they could not tolerate each other, could not accept the mental blending that occurred automatically without the control of the Pattern.

It might not be true any longer, I told them. *But it has been true for thousands of years. For safety's sake, we have to assume that it's still true. So you are all to get up tonight, now, and leave the section. Separate. Scatter.*

Their dismay was almost a physical force—that many people frightened, agreeing with each other and disagreeing with me. I put force of my own into my next thought, amplified it to a mental shout.

Be still!

A lot of them winced as though I had hit them.

I'm sending you away to save your lives, and you will go.

Some of them were upset enough to try to shut me out. But of course they couldn't. Not as long as I spoke through the Pattern.

You are all powerful people, I sent. *You will have no trouble making your ways alone. And if the Pattern survives, you know that I'll call you all back. I want you here as much as you want to be here. We're one people. But now, for your own sake, you must go. Leave tonight so that I can be sure you're safe.*

I let them feel the emotion I felt. Now was the time. I wanted them to see how important their safety was to me. I wanted them to know that I meant every word I gave them. But the words that I didn't give them were the ones they were concerned with. Most of the questions they threw at me were drowned in the confusion of their mental voices. I could have sorted them out and made sense of them, but I didn't bother. The one that I didn't have to sort out, though, was the one that was on everyone's mind. *What is the danger?* I couldn't miss reading it, but I could ignore it. My people knew Doro from classes and blocks. Most of them had had no personal contact with him at all. They were capable of shrugging off what they had learned—all their theoretical knowledge—and going after him for me. And getting themselves slaughtered. What they didn't know, in this case, could save them from committing suicide. I addressed them again.

You who are heads of houses—you know your responsibilities to your families. See that all the members of your families get out, and get out tonight. Help them get out. Take care of them.

There. I broke contact. Now the strongest people in the section, the most responsible people, had been charged with seeing that my commands were obeyed. I had faith in my heads of houses.

I opened my eyes—and knew at once that something was wrong. I turned my head and saw Karl standing beside the bed, his back to me, his body tense. Beyond him, at the door, stood Doro. It was Doro's expression that made me instantly re-establish contact with my Patternists. I jerked the Pattern again to get their attention. I felt their confusion, their fear. Then their surprise as they felt me with them again. I gave them my thoughts very clearly, but quickly.

Everybody, stop what you're doing. Be still.

They could see what I saw. My eyes were open now, and my mind was open to them. They could see Doro watching me past Karl. They could know that Doro was the danger. It was too late for them to make suicidal mistakes.

You won't have time to leave. You'll have to help me fight. Obey me, and we can kill him.

That thought cut through their confusion, as I had hoped it would. Here was a way to destroy what threatened them. Here was Doro, whom they had been warned against, but whom most of them did not really fear.

Sit down, or lie down. Wait. Do nothing. I'm going to need you.

Doro started toward Karl. I sat up, scrambled over close to Karl, and laid a hand on his shoulder. He glanced at me.

"It's okay," I said. "It's as okay as it's ever going to be. Get out of here."

He relaxed a little, but, instead of going, he sat down on the end of the bed. I didn't have time to argue with him. I began absorbing strength from my people. Not Karl. He would have collapsed and given me away. But the others. I had to collect from as many of them as I could before Doro attacked. Because I had no doubt that he was going to attack.

Doro

Doro stood still, gazing at the girl, wondering why he waited. "You have time to try again to get rid of Karl if you like," he said.

"Karl's made his decision." There was no fear in her voice. That pleased Doro somehow.

"Apparently you've made yours, too."

"There was no decision for me to make. I have to do what I was born to do."

Doro shrugged.

"What did you do with Vivian?"

"Nothing at all after I thought about it," he said. "Faithful little pet that she is now, Vivian hasn't looked at me for well over a year. Karl's women get like that when he stops trying to preserve their individuality—when he takes them over completely." He smiled. "Karl's mute women, I mean. So, when Vivian, who no longer had initiative enough to go looking for lovers other than Karl, suddenly came to me, I realized that she had almost certainly been sent. Why was she sent?"

"Does it matter?"

Doro gave her a sad smile. "No. Not really." In his shadowy way, Doro was aware of a great deal of psionic activity going on around her. He felt himself drawn to her as he had been two years before, when she took Jesse and Rachel. Now, he guessed, she would be taking a great many of her people. As many as he gave her time to take. She remained still as Doro sat down beside her. She looked at Karl, who sat on her other side.

"Move away from us," she said quietly.

Without a word, Karl got up and went to sit in the chair by the window. The instant he reached the chair he collapsed, seemed to pass out. Mary had finally taken him. An instant later, Doro took her.

At once, Doro was housed with her in her body. But she was no quick, easy kill. She would take a few moments.

She was power, strength concentrated as Doro had never felt it before—the strength of dozens, perhaps hundreds of Patternists. For a moment Doro was intoxicated with it. It filled him, blotted out all thought. The fiery threads of her Pattern surrounded him. And before him... before him was a slightly smaller replica of himself as he had perceived himself through the fading senses of his thousands of victims over the years. Before him, where all the threads of fire met in a wild tangle of brilliance, was a small sun.

Mary.

She was like a living creature of fire. Not human. No more human than he was. He had lied to her about that once—lied to calm her—when she was a child. And her major weakness, her vulnerable, irreplaceable human body, had made the lie seem true. But that body, like his own series of bodies, was only a mask, a shell. He saw her now as she really was, and she might have been his twin.

But, no, she was not his twin. She was a smaller, much younger being. A complete version of him. A mistake that he would not make again. But, ironically, her very completeness would help to destroy her. She was a symbiont, a being living in partnership with her people. She gave them unity, they fed her, and both thrived. She was not a parasite, though he had encouraged her to think of herself as one. And though she had great power, she was not naturally, instinctively, a killer. He was.

When he had had his look at her, he embraced her, enveloped her. On the physical level, the gesture would have seemed affectionate—until it was exposed as a strangle hold.

When Mary struggled to free herself, he drank in the strength she spent, consumed it ecstatically. Never had one person given him so much.

Alarmed, Mary struck at him, struggled harder, fed him more of herself. She fed him until her own strength and her borrowed strength were gone. Finally he tasted the familiar terror in her mind.

She knew she was about to die. She had nothing left, no time to draw strength from more of her people. She felt herself dying. Doro felt her dying.

Then he heard her voice.

No, he sensed it, disembodied, cursing. She was so much a part of him already that her thoughts were reaching him. He moved to finish her, consume the final fragments of her. But the final fragments were the Pattern.

She was still alive because she was still connected to all those people. The strength that Doro took now, the tiny amounts of strength that she had left, were replaced instantly. She could not die. New life flowed into her continually.

Furiously, Doro swept her into himself, where she should have died. For the fifth time, she did not die. She seemed to slither away from him, regaining substance apart from him as no victim of his should have been able to.

She was doing nothing on her own now. She was weak and exhausted. Her Pattern was doing its work automatically. Apparently it would go on doing that work as long as there were Patternists alive to support it.

Then Mary began to realize that Doro was having trouble. She began to wonder why she was still alive. Her thoughts came to him clearly. And apparently his thoughts reached her.

You can't kill me, she sent. *After all that, you can't kill me. You may as well let me go!*

He was surprised at first that she was still aware enough to communicate with him. Then he was angry. She was helpless. She should have been his long ago, yet she would not die.

If he could manage to leave her body—a thing he had never done before without finishing his kill—he would only have to try again. He couldn't possibly let her live to collect more of his latents, to search until she found a way to kill him.

He would jump to Karl, and perhaps from Karl to someone else. Karl would already be more dead than alive now that she had taken strength from him. Doro would move on, find himself an able body and come back to her in it. Then he would simply cut her throat—decapitate her if necessary. Not even a healer could survive that. She might be mentally strong, but physically she was still only a small woman. She would be easy prey.

Mary seemed to clutch at him. She was trying to hold him as he had held her, but she had neither the technique nor the strength. She had learned a little, but it was too late. She was barely an annoyance. Doro focused on Karl.

Abruptly Mary became more than an annoyance.

She tore strength from the rest of her people. Not one at a time now. This time she took them all at once, the way Rachel had used to take from her congregations. But Mary stripped her Patternists as Rachel had never stripped her mutes. Then, desperately, Mary tried again to grasp Doro.

For a moment, she seemed not to realize that she was strong again—that her act of desperation had gained her a second chance.

Then her new strength brought her to life. It became impossible for Doro to focus on anyone but her. Her power drew him.

Abruptly, she stopped clutching at him and threw herself on him. She embraced him.

Startled, Doro tried to shake her off. For a moment, his struggles fed her as hers had fed him earlier. She was a leech, riding, feeding orgiastically.

Doro caught himself, ceased his struggles. He smiled to himself grimly. Mary was learning, but there was still much that she didn't know. Now he taught her how difficult it was to get strength from an opponent who not only refused to give it away by struggling but who actively resisted her efforts to take it. And there was only one way to resist. As she sought to consume him, he countered by trying to consume her.

For long moments they strained against each other, neither of them gaining or losing power. They neutralized each other.

Disgusted, Doro tried again to focus on Karl. Best to get away from Mary mentally and get back to her physically.

Mary let him go.

Startled, Doro brought his attention back to her. For a moment, he could not focus on her. There was a roar of something like radio static in his mind—"noise" so intense that he tried to twist away from it. It cleared slowly.

Then he noticed that he had not drawn away from Mary completely. He was still joined to her. Joined by a single strand of fire. She had used her mental closeness with him to draw him into her web. Her Pattern.

He panicked.

He was a member of the Pattern. A Patternist. Property. Mary's property.

He strained against the seemingly fragile thread. It stretched easily. Then he realized that he was straining against himself. The thread was part of him. A mental limb. A limb that he could find no way to sever.

The Patternists had told him how it felt at first—that feeling of being trapped, of being on a leash. They had lived to get over their feelings. They had lived because Mary had wanted them to live. Doro himself had helped Mary understand how thoroughly their lives were in her hands.

Doro fought desperately, uselessly. He could feel Mary's amusement now. He had nearly killed her, had been about to kill the man she had attached herself to so firmly. Now she took her revenge. She consumed him slowly, drinking in his terror and his life, drawing out her own pleasure, and laughing through his soundless screams.

Epilogue

Mary

They cremated Doro's last body before I was able to get out of bed. I was in bed for two days. A lot of others were there even longer. The few who were on their feet ran things with the help of the mute servants. One hundred and fifty-four Patternists never got up again at all. They were my weakest, those least able to take the strain I put on them. They died because it took me so long to learn how to kill Doro. By the time Doro was dead and I began to try to give back the strength I had taken from my people, the 154 were already dead. I had never tried to give back strength before, but I had never taken so much before, either. I managed it, and probably saved the lives of others who would have died. So that I only had to get used to the idea that I had killed the 154....

Emma died. The day Rachel told her about Doro, she decided to die. It was just as well.

Karl lived. The family lived. If I had killed them, Emma's way out could have started to look good to me. Not that I would have taken it. I wouldn't have the freedom to consider a thing like that for about twenty years, no matter what happened. But that was all right. It wasn't a freedom I wanted. I had already won the only freedom I cared about. Doro was dead. Finally, thoroughly dead. Now we were free to grow again—we, his children.

CLAY'S ARK

In memory of Phyllis White

PART 1

Physician

Past 1

The ship had been destroyed five days before. He did not remember how. He knew he was alone now, knew he had returned home instead of to the station as planned or to the emergency base on Luna. He knew it was night. For long stretches of time, he knew nothing else.

He walked and climbed automatically, hardly seeing the sand, the rock, the mountains, noticing only those plants that could be useful to him. Hunger and thirst kept him moving. If he did not find water soon, he would die.

He had hidden for five days and two nights, had wandered for nearly three nights with no destination, no goal but food, water, and human companionship. During this time he killed jack rabbits, snakes, even a coyote, with his bare hands or with stones. These he ate raw, splashing their blood over his ragged coverall, drinking as much of it as he could. But he had found little water.

Now he could smell water the way a dog or a horse might. This was no longer a new sensation. He had become accustomed to using his senses in ways not normally thought human. In his own mind, his humanity had been in question for some time.

He walked. When he reached rocks at the base of a range of mountains, he began to climb, rousing to notice the change only because moving began to require more effort, more of his slowly fading strength.

For a few moments, he was alert, sensitive to the rough, eroded granite beneath his hands and feet, aware that there were people in the direction he had chosen. This was not surprising. On the desert, people would either congregate around water or bring water with them. On one level, he was eager to join them. He needed the company of other people almost as badly as he needed water. On another level, he hoped the people would be gone from the water when he reached it. He was able to distinguish the smell of women among them, and he began to sweat. He hoped at least that the women would be gone. If they stayed, if anyone stayed, they risked death. Some of them would surely die.

Present 2

The wind had begun to blow before Blake Maslin left Needles on his way west toward Palos Verdes Enclave and home. City man that he was, Blake did not worry about the weather. His daughter Keira warned him that desert winds could blow cars off the road and that wind-driven sand could blast paint off cars, but he reassured her. He had gotten into the habit of reassuring her without really listening to her fears; there were so many of them.

This time, however, Keira was right. She should have been. The desert had long been an interest of hers, and she knew it better than Blake did. This whole old-fashioned car trip had happened because she knew and loved the desert—and because she wanted to see her grandparents—Blake's parents—in Flagstaff, Arizona, one last time. She wanted to visit them in the flesh, not just see them on a phone screen. She wanted to be with them while she was still well enough to enjoy them.

Twenty minutes out of Needles, the wind became a gale. There were heavy, billowing clouds ahead, black and gray slashed by lightning, but there was no rain yet. Nothing to hold down the dust and sand.

For a while Blake tried to continue on. In the back seat, Keira slept, breathing deeply, almost snoring. It bothered him when he could no longer hear her over the buffeting of the wind.

His first-born daughter, Rane, sat beside him, smiling slightly, watching the storm. While he fought to control the car, she enjoyed herself. If Keira had too many fears, Rane had too few. She and Keira were fraternal twins, different in appearance and behavior. Somehow, Blake had slipped into the habit of thinking of the hardier, more impulsive Rane as his younger daughter.

A gust of wind slammed into the car broadside, almost blowing it off the road. For several seconds, Blake could see nothing ahead except a wall of pale dust and sand.

Frightened at last, he pulled off the road. His armored, high-suspension Jeep Wagoneer was a hobby, a carefully preserved relic of an earlier, oil-extravagant era. It had once run on one-hundred-percent gasoline, though now it used ethanol. It was bigger and heavier than the few other cars on the road, and Blake was a good driver. But enough was enough—especially with the girls in the car.

When he was safely stopped, he looked around, saw that other people were stopping too. On the other side of the highway, ghostly in the blowing dust and sand, were three large trucks—expensive private haulers, carrying God-knew-what: anything, from the household possessions of the wealthy, who could still afford the archaic luxury of moving across country, to the necessities of the few remaining desert enclaves and roadside stations, to illegal drugs, weapons, and worse. Several yards ahead, there was a battered Chevrolet and a new little electric something-or-other. Far behind, he could see another private hauler parked at such a strange angle that he knew it had come off the highway barely under control. Only a few thrill-seekers in aging tour buses continued on.

From out of the desert over a dirt road Blake had not previously noticed came another car, making its way toward the highway. Blake stared at it, wondering where it could have come from. This part of the highway was bordered on both sides by some of the bleakest desert Blake had ever seen—worn volcanic hills and emptiness.

Incongruously, the car was a beautiful, old, wine-red Mercedes—the last thing Blake would have expected to see coming out of the wilderness. It drove past him on the sand, traveling east, though the only lanes open to it carried westbound traffic. Blake wondered whether the driver would be foolish enough to try to cross the highway in the storm. He could see three people in the car as it passed but could not tell whether they were men or women. He watched them disappear into the dust behind him, then forgot them as Keira moaned in her sleep.

He looked at her, felt rather than saw that Rane also turned to look. Keira, thin and frail, slept on.

"Back in Needles," Rane said, "I heard a couple of guys talking about her. They thought she was so pretty and fragile."

Blake nodded. "I heard them too." He shook his head. Keira had been pretty once—when she was healthy, when she looked so much like her mother that it hurt him. Now she was ethereal, not quite of this world, people said. She was only sixteen, but she had acute myeloblastic leukemia—an adult disease—and she was not responding to treatment. She wore a wig because the epigenetic therapy that should have caused her AML cells to return to normal had not worked, and her doctor, in desperation, had resorted to old-fashioned chemotherapy. This had caused most of her hair to fall out. She had lost so much weight that none of her clothing fit her properly. She said she could see herself fading away. Blake could see her fading, too. As an internist, he could not help seeing more than he wanted to see.

He looked away from Keira and out of the corner of his eye he saw something bright green move at Rane's window. Before he could speak, a man who seemed to come from nowhere tore open her door, *which had been locked*, and moved to shove his way in beside Rane.

The man was quick, and stronger than any two men should have been, but he was also slightly built and off-balance. Before he could regain his balance, Rane screamed an obscenity, drew her legs back against her body, and spring-released them so that they slammed into his abdomen.

The man doubled and fell backward onto the ground, his green shirt flapping in the wind. Instantly another man took his place. The second man had a gun.

Frightened, Rane drew back against Blake, and Blake, who had reached for his own automatic rifle sheathed diagonally on the door next to him, froze, staring at the intruder's gun. It was not aimed at him. It was aimed at Rane.

Blake raised his hands, held them in midair, clearly empty. For a long moment, he couldn't speak. He could only stare at the short, dull black carbine leveled at his daughter.

"You can have my wallet," he said finally. "It's in my pocket."

The man seemed to ignore him.

The red Mercedes pulled up beside Blake's car and Blake could see that there was only one person inside now. A woman, he thought. He could see what looked like a great deal of long, dark hair.

The man in the green shirt picked himself up and drew a handgun. Now there were two guns, both aimed at Rane. Thug psychologists. The green-shirted one walked around the car toward Blake's side.

"Touch the lock," the remaining one ordered. "Just the lock. Let him in."

Blake obeyed, let Green Shirt open the door and take the rifle. Then, in an inhumanely swift move, the man reached across Blake and ripped out the phone. "City rich!" he muttered contemptuously as Blake realized what he had done. "City slow and stupid. Now take out the wallet and give it to me."

Blake handed his wallet to Green Shirt, moving slowly, watching the guns. Green Shirt snatched the wallet, slammed the door, and went back to the other side where the two cars together offered some protection from the wind. There, he opened the wallet. Surprisingly, he did not check the cash compartment, though Blake actually had over two thousand dollars. He liked to carry small amounts of cash when he traveled. Green Shirt flipped through Blake's computer cards, pulled out his Palos Verdes Enclave identification.

"Doctor," he said. "How about that. Blake Jason Maslin, M.D. Know anybody who needs a doctor, Eli?"

The other gunman gave a humorless laugh. He was a tall, thin black man with skin that had gone gray with more than desert dust. His health may have been better than Keira's, Blake thought, but not by much.

For that matter, Green Shirt, shorter and smaller-boned, did not look healthy himself. He was blond, tanned beneath his coating of dust, though his tan seemed oddly gray. He was balding. His gun shook slightly in his hand. A sick man. They were both sick—sick and dangerous.

Blake put his arm around Rane protectively. Thank God Keira had managed to sleep through everything so far.

"What is this, anyway?" Eli demanded, glancing back at Keira, then staring at Rane. "What kind of cradles have you been robbing, Doc?"

Blake stiffened, felt Rane stiffen against him. His wife Jorah had been black, and he and Rane and Keira had been through this routine before.

"These are my daughters," Blake said coldly. Without the guns, he would have said more. Without his hand gripping Rane's shoulder, she would have said much more.

Eli looked surprised, then nodded, accepting. Most people took longer to believe. "Okay," he said. "Get out here, girl."

Rane did not move, could not have if she had wanted to. Blake held her where she was. "Dad?" she whispered.

"You have my money," Blake told Eli. "You can have anything else you want. But let my daughters alone!"

Green Shirt glanced into the back seat at Keira. "I think that one's dead," he said casually. This was supposed to be a joke about Keira's sound sleeping, Blake knew, but he could not prevent himself from looking back at her quickly—just to be sure.

"Hey, Eli," Green Shirt said, "they really are his kids, you know."

"I can see," Eli said. "And that makes our lives easier. All we have to do is take one of them and he's ours."

It was beginning to rain—fat, dirty, wind-whipped drops. In the distance, thunder rumbled over the howl of the wind.

Eli spoke so softly to Rane that Blake was hardly able to hear. "Is he your father?"

"You just admitted he was," Rane said. "What the hell do you want?"

Eli frowned. "My mother always used to say 'Think before you speak.' Your mother ever say anything like that to you, girl?"

Rane looked away, silent.

"Is he your father?" Eli repeated.

"Yes."

"And you wouldn't want to see him get hurt, would you?"

Rane continued to look away, but could not conceal her fear. "What do you want?"

Ignoring her, Eli held his hand out to Green Shirt. After a moment, Green Shirt gave him the wallet. "Blake Jason Maslin," he read. "Born seven-four-seventy-seven. 'Oh say can you see.'" He looked at Rane. "What's your name, baby?"

Rane hesitated, no doubt repelled by the casual "baby." Normally she tore into people who seemed to be patronizing her. "Rane," she muttered finally. Thunder all but drowned her out.

"Rain? Like this dirty stuff falling on us now?"

"Not rain, Rah-ney. It's Norwegian."

"Is it now? Well, listen, Rane, you see that woman over there?" He pointed to the red Mercedes alongside them. "Her name is Meda Boyd. She's crazy as hell, but she won't hurt you. And if you do what we tell you and don't give us trouble, we won't hurt your father or your sister. You understand?"

Rane nodded, but Eli continued to look at her, waiting.

"I understand!" she said. "What do you want me to do?"

"Go get in that car with Meda. She'll drive you. I'll follow with your father."

Rane looked at Blake. He could feel her trembling. "Listen," he began, "you can't do this! You can't just—"

Green Shirt placed his gun against Rane's temple. "Why not?" he asked.

Blake jerked Rane away. It was a reflex, a chance he would never have taken if he had had time to think about it. He pulled her head down against his chest.

At the same moment, Eli pulled Green Shirt's gun hand away, twisting it so that if the gun had gone off, the bullet would have hit the windshield.

The gun did not go off. It should have, Blake realized later, considering Green Shirt's tremor and the suddenness of Eli's move. But all that happened was some sort of brief, wordless exchange between Eli and Green Shirt. They looked at each other—first with real anger, then with understanding and a certain amount of sheepishness.

"You'd better drive," Eli said. "Let Meda watch the kids."

"Yeah," Green Shirt agreed. "The past catches up with you sometimes."

"You okay?"

"Yeah."

"She's a strong girl. Good material."

"I know."

"Good material for what?" Blake demanded. He had released Rane, but she stayed close to him, watching Eli.

"Look, Doc," Eli said, "the last thing we want to have to do is kill one of you. But we don't have much time or patience."

"Let my daughters stay with me," Blake said. "I'll cooperate. I'll do anything you want. Just don't—"

"We're leaving you one. Don't make us take them both."

"But—"

"Ingraham, get the other kid out here. Get her up."

"No!" Blake shouted. "Please, she's sick. Let her alone!"

"What? Carsick?"

"My sister has leukemia," Rane said. "She's dying. What are you going to do? Help her along?"

"Rane, for God's sake!" Blake whispered.

Eli and the green-shirted Ingraham looked at each other, then back at Blake. "I thought they could cure that now," Eli said. "Don't they have some kind of protein medicine that reprograms the cells?"

Blake hesitated, wondering how much pity the details of Keira's illness might evoke in the gunmen. He was surprised that Eli knew as much as he did about epigenetic therapy. But Eli's knowledge did not matter. If he was not moved by Keira's imminent death, nothing else was likely to touch them. "She's receiving therapy," he said.

"And it isn't enough?" Ingraham asked.

Blake shrugged. It hurt to say the words. He could not recall ever having said them aloud.

"Shit," Ingraham muttered. "What are we supposed to do with a kid who's already—"

"Shut up," Eli said. "If we've made a mistake, it's too late to cry about it." He glanced back at Keira, then faced Blake. "Sorry, Doc. Her bad luck and ours." He sighed. "Well, you take the good with the bad. We won't hurt her—if you and Rane do as you're told."

"What are you going to do with us?" Blake asked.

"Don't worry about it. Come on, Rane. Meda's waiting."

Rane clung to Blake as she had not for years.

Eli gazed at her steadily, and she stared back but would not move. "Come on, kid," he said softly. "Do it the easy way."

Blake wanted to tell her to go—before these people hurt her. Yet the last thing he wanted her to do was leave him. He was terrified that if they took her, he would never get her back. He stared at the two men. If he had had his gun, he would have shot them without a thought.

"Use your head, Doc," Eli said. "Just slide over to the passenger side. I'll drive. You keep your eyes on Rane. It will make you feel better. Make you act better, too."

Abruptly, Blake gave in, moved over, pushing Rane. He wanted to believe the gray-skinned black man. It would have been easier to believe him if Blake had had some idea what these people wanted. They were not just one of the local car gangs, obscenely called car families. No one had looked at the money in his wallet. In fact, as he thought about the wallet, Eli tossed it onto the dashboard as though he were finished with it. Were they after more money? Ransom? They did not sound as though they were. And they seemed strangely resigned, as though they did not like what they were doing—almost as though they were under the gun themselves.

Blake hugged Rane. "Watch yourself," he said, trying to sound steadier than he felt. "Be more careful than you usually are—at least until we find out what's going on."

Blake watched Ingraham follow Rane through the muddy downpour, watched her get into the red Mercedes. Ingraham said a few words to the woman, Meda, then exchanged places with her.

When that was done, Eli relaxed. He thrust his gun into his jacket, walked around the Wagoneer as casually as an old friend, and got in. It never occurred to Blake to try anything. Part of himself had walked away with Rane. His stomach churned with anger, frustration, and worry.

After a moment of spinning its wheels, the Mercedes leaped forward, shot all the way across the highway, and onto another dirt road. The Wagoneer followed easily. Eli patted its dashboard as though it were alive. "Sweet-running car," he said. "Big. You don't find them this size anymore. Too bad."

"Too bad?"

"Strongest-looking car we saw parked along the highway. We didn't want some piece of junk that would stall or get stuck on us. One tank full and the other nearly full of ethanol. Damn good. We make ethanol."

"You mean it was my car you wanted?"

"We wanted a decent car with two or three healthy, fairly young people in it." He glanced back at Keira. "You can't win 'em all."

"But why?"

"Doc, what's the kid's name?" He jerked a thumb over his shoulder at Keira.

Blake stared at him.

"Tell her she can get up. She's been awake since Ingraham took your wallet."

Blake turned sharply, found himself looking into Keira's large, frightened eyes. He tried to calm himself for her sake. "Do you feel all right?" he asked.

She nodded, probably lying.

"Sit up," he said. "Do you know what's happened?"

Another nod. If Rane talked too much, Keira didn't talk enough. Even before her illness became apparent, she had been a timid girl, easily frightened, easily intimidated, apparently slow. Patience and observation revealed her intelligence, but most people wasted neither on her.

She sat up slowly, staring at Eli. His coloring was as bad as her own. She could not have helped noticing that, but she said nothing.

"You get an earful?" Eli asked her.

She drew as far away from him as she could get and did not answer.

"You know your sister's in that car up ahead with some friends of mine. You think about that."

"She's no danger to you," Blake said angrily.

"Have her give you whatever she's got in her left hand."

Blake frowned, looked toward Keira's left hand. She was wearing a long, multicolored, cotton caftan—a full, flowing garment with long, voluminous sleeves. It was intended to conceal her painfully thin body. At the moment, it also concealed her left hand.

Keira's expression froze into something ugly and determined.

"Kerry," Blake whispered.

She blinked, glanced at him, finally brought her left hand out of the folds of her dress and handed him the large manual screwdriver she had been concealing. Blake could remember misplacing the old screwdriver and not having time to look for it. It looked too large for Keira's thin fingers. Blake doubted that she had the strength to do any harm with it. With a smaller, sharper instrument, however, she might have been dangerous. Anyone who could look the way she did now could be dangerous, sick or well.

Blake took the screwdriver from her hand and held on to the hand for a moment. He wanted to reassure her, calm her, but he thought of Rane alone in the car ahead, and no words would come. There was no way everything was going to be all right. And he had always found it difficult to lie to his children.

After a moment, Keira seemed to relax—or at least to give up. She leaned back bonelessly, let her gaze flicker from Eli to the car ahead. Only her eyes seemed alive.

"What do you want with us?" she whispered. "Why are you doing this?" Blake did not think Eli had heard her over the buffeting of the wind and the hissing patter of the rain. Eli obviously had all he could do to keep the car on the dirt road and the Mercedes in sight. He ignored completely the long, potentially deadly screwdriver Blake gripped briefly, then dropped. He was a young man, Blake realized—in his early thirties, perhaps. He looked older—or had looked older before Blake got a close look at him. His face was thin and prematurely lined beneath its coating of dust. His air of weary resignation suggested an older man. He looked older, Blake thought, in much the same way Keira looked older. Her disease had aged her, as apparently his had aged him—whatever his was.

Eli glanced at Keira through the rearview mirror. "Girl," he said, "you won't believe me, but I wish to hell I could let you go."

"Why can't you?" she asked.

"Same reason you can't get rid of your leukemia just by wishing."

Blake frowned. That answer couldn't have made any more sense to Keira than it did to him, but she responded to it. She gave Eli a long thoughtful look and moved slowly toward the middle of the seat away from her place of retreat behind Blake.

"Do you hurt?" she asked.

He turned to look back at her—actually slowed down and lost sight of the Mercedes for a moment. Then he was occupied with catching up and there was only the sound of the rain as it was whipped against the car.

"In a way," Eli answered finally. "Sometimes. How about you?"

Keira hesitated, nodded.

Blake started to speak, then stopped himself. He did not like the understanding that seemed to be growing between his daughter and this man, but Eli, in his dispute with Ingraham, had already demonstrated his value.

"Keira," Eli muttered. "Where did you ever get a name like that?"

"Mom didn't want us to have names that sounded like everybody's."

"She saw to that. Your mother living?"

". . . no."

Eli gave Blake a surprisingly sympathetic look. "Didn't think so." There was another long pause. "How old are you?"

"Sixteen."

"That all? Are you the oldest or the youngest?"

"Rane and I are twins."

A startled glance. "Well, I guess you're not lying about it, but the two of you barely look like members of the same family—let alone twins."

"I know."

"You got a nickname?"

"Kerry."

"Oh yeah. That's better. Listen, Kerry, nobody at the ranch is going to hurt you; I promise you that. Anybody bothers you, you call me. Okay?"

"What about my father and sister?"

Eli shook his head. "I can't work no miracles, girl."

Blake stared at him, but for once, Eli refused to notice. He kept his eyes on the road.

Past 3

In a high valley surrounded by stark, naked granite weathered round and deceptively smooth-looking, he found a finished house of wood on a stone foundation and the skeletal beginnings of two other houses. There was also a well with a huge, upended metal tank. There were pigs in wood-fenced pens, chickens in coops, rabbits in hutches, a large fenced garden, and a solar still. The still and electricity produced by photovoltaic intensifiers appeared to be the only concessions to modernity the owners of the little homestead had made.

He went to the well, turned the faucet handle of the storage tank, caught the cold, sweet, clear water in his hands, and drank. He had not tasted such water in years. It restored thought, cleared the fog from his mind. Now the senses that had been totally focused on survival were freed to notice other things.

The women, for instance.

He had scented at least one man in the house, but there were several women. Their scents attracted him powerfully. Yet the moment he caught himself moving toward the house in response to that attraction, he began to resist.

For several minutes he stood frozen outside the window of one of the women. He was so close to her he could hear her soft, even breathing. She was asleep, but turning restlessly now and then. He literally could not move. His body demanded that he go to the woman. He understood the demand, the drive, but he refused to be just an animal governed by instinct. The woman was as near to being in heat as a female human could be. She had reached the most fertile period of her monthly cycle. It was no wonder she was sleeping so badly. And no wonder he could not move except to go to her.

He stood where he was, perspiring heavily in the cold night air and struggling to remember that he had resolved to be human plus, not human minus. He was not an animal, not a rapist, not a murderer. Yet he knew that if he let himself be drawn to the woman, he would rape her. If he raped her, if he touched her at all, she might die. He had watched it happen before, and it had driven him to want to die, to try to die himself. He had tried, but he could not deliberately kill himself. He had an unconscious will to survive that transcended any conscious desire, any guilt, any duty to those who had once been his fellow humans.

He tried furiously to convince himself that a break-in and rape would be stupidly self-destructive, but his body was locked into another reality, focused on a more fundamental form of survival. He did not move until the war within had exhausted him, until he had no strength left to take the woman.

Finally, triumphant, he dragged himself back to the well and drank again. The electric pump beside the well switched on suddenly, noisily, and in the distance, dogs began to bark. He looked around, knowing from the sound that the dogs were coming toward him. He had already discovered that dogs disliked him, and, rightly enough, feared him. Now, however, he had been weakened by days of hunger and thirst and by his own internal conflict. Two or three large dogs might be able to bring him down and tear him apart.

The dogs came bounding up—two big mongrels, barking and growling. They were put off by his strange scent at first, and they kept back out of his reach while putting on a show of ferocity. He thought by the time they found the courage to attack, he might be ready for at least one of them.

Present 4

Eventually, the Mercedes and the Jeep emerged from the storm into vast, flat, dry desert, still following their arrow-straight dirt road. They approached, then passed between ancient black and red volcanic mountains. Later, they turned sharply from their dirt road onto something that was little more than a poorly marked trail. This led to a range of earth and granite mountains. The two cars headed into the mountains and began winding their way upward.

By then they had been driving for nearly an hour. At first, Blake had seen a few signs of humanity. A small airport, a lonely ranch here and there, many steel towers carrying high voltage lines from the Hidalgo and Joshua Tree Solar Power Plants. (The water shortage had hurt desert settlement even as the desert sun began to be used to combat the fuel shortage. Over much of the desert, communities were dead or dying.) But for some time now, Blake had seen no sign at all that there were other people in the world. It was as though they had left 2021 and gone back in time to primordial desert. The Indians must have seen the land this way.

Blake wondered whether he and his daughters would die in this empty place. It occurred to him that his abductors might be more likely to feel they needed him if they thought of him as their doctor. They might even give him enough of an opening to take his daughters and escape.

"Look," he said to Eli, "you're obviously not well. Neither is your friend Ingraham. I have my bag with me. Maybe I can help."

"You can't help, Doc," Eli said.

"You don't know that."

"Assume that I do." Eli squeezed the car around another of a series of boulders that seemed to have been scattered deliberately along the narrow mountain road. "Assume that I'm at least as complex a man as you are."

Blake stared at him, noting with interest that Eli had dropped the easy, old-fashioned street rhythms that made his speech seem familiar and made him seem no more than another semieducated product of city sewers. If he wished, then, he could speak flat, standard, correct American English.

"What's the matter with you, then?" Blake asked. "Will you tell us?"

"Not yet."

"Why?"

Eli took his time answering. He smiled finally—a smile full of teeth and utterly without humor. "We got together and decided that for your sake and ours, people in your position should be protected from too much truth too soon. I was a minority of one, voting for honesty. I could have been a majority of one, but I've played the role long enough. The others thought people like you wouldn't believe the truth, that it would scare you more than necessary and you'd try harder to escape."

To the surprise of both men, Keira laughed. Blake looked back at her, and she fell silent, embarrassed. "I'm sorry," she whispered, "but not knowing is worse. Do they really think we wouldn't do just about anything to get away now?"

"Nothing to be sorry for, girl," Eli said. The accent was back. "I agree with you."

"Who are the others who disagreed?" Keira asked.

"People. Just people like you and your father. Meda's family owned the land we live on. Ingraham... well, he was with a gang of bikers that came calling one day and tried to rape Meda—among other things. And we have a private hauler and a music student from L.A., a couple of people from Victorville, one from Twenty-nine Palms, and a few others."

"Ingraham tried to rape someone, and you let him stay?" Blake demanded. He was suddenly glad Ingraham was driving the car ahead. At least he would not have time to try anything until they got where they were going—but what then?

"That was another life," Eli said. "We don't care what he did before. He's one of us now."

Blake thought of Ingraham's gun against Rane's head.

Eli seemed to read his thoughts. "Hey," he said, "I know how it looked, but Ingraham wouldn't have shot her. I was afraid you or she might make a dumb move and cause an accident, but there's no way he would have shot her."

"Was the gun empty?" Keira asked.

"Hell no," Eli said, surprised. He hesitated. "Listen, I'll be this straight with you. The safest person of the three of you is Rane. She's young, she's female, and she's healthy. If only one of you makes it, chances are it will be her." He slowed, looked at Blake, then at Keira. "What I'm trying to do is build a fire under you two. I want you to use your minds and your plain damn stubbornness to make a liar of me. I want you all to survive." He stopped the car. "We're here."

"Here" was a small high valley—a little space between the ancient rocks that formed the mountains. There was a large old house of wood and stone and three other wooden houses, less well built. A fifth house was under construction. Two men worked on it with hand tools, hammering and sawing as almost no one did these days.

"Population explosion," Eli said. "We've been lucky lately."

"You mean people have been surviving whatever it is you do to them here?" Blake asked.

"That's what I mean," Eli admitted. "We're learning to help them."

"Are you some kind of... well, some kind of religious group?" Keira asked. "I don't mean any offense, but I've heard there were... groups in the mountains."

"Cultists?" Eli said, smiling a real smile. "No, we didn't come up here to worship anybody, girl. There were some religious people up here once, though. Not cultists, just... What do you call them? People who never saw sweet reason around the turn of the century, and who decided to make a decent, moral, God-fearing place of their own to raise their kids and wait for the Second Coming."

"Leftovers," Blake said. "At least that's what we called such people when I was younger. But this place looks as though it hasn't been touched by this century or the last one. Looks more like a holdover from the nineteenth."

"Yeah," Eli said, and smiled again. "Get out, Doc. Let's see if I can talk Meda into cooking you folks a meal." He took the keys, then waited until Blake and Keira got out. Then he locked their doors and got out himself.

Blake looked around and decided that almost everything he saw reminded him of descriptions he'd read of subsistence farming more than a century before. Chickens running around loose, pecking at the sand, others in coops and in a large chicken house and yard. Hogs poking their snouts between the wooden planks of their pens, rabbits in wood-and-wire hutches, a couple of cows. But every building was topped by photovoltaic intensifiers. The well had an electric pump—clearly an antique—and on the front porch of one of the houses, a woman was using an ancient black Singer sewing machine. There was a large garden growing over perhaps half the valley floor. And near the two most distant houses were small structures that might have been, of all things, outhouses.

Blake had turned to ask Eli about it when suddenly, Rane was in his arms. He hugged her, startled that even this strange place had made him forget her danger for a moment. Now, flanked by both his daughters, he felt better, stronger. The feeling was irrational, he knew. The girls were no safer for their being with him. Their captors still had the guns. And they were all still trapped in this isolated, atavistic place. Worst of all, something was being planned for them—something they might not survive.

"What did you hear?" he asked Rane while Eli was busy talking to Meda.

"I think they're on some weird drugs or something," Rane whispered. "That guy Ingraham—his hands shake when he isn't using them, and when he is, he has other tics and twitches."

"That doesn't have to mean drugs," Blake said. "What about the woman?"

"Well... no twitches, but if you think I'm too outspoken, wait until you meet her."

"What did she say?"

Uncharacteristically, Rane looked away. "It wasn't anything that would help. I don't want to repeat it."

Keira touched Rane's arm to get her attention. "Was it about you being more likely to survive than the two of us? Because if it was, we got that too."

"Yes."

"Plus?"

"Kerry, I'm not going to tell you."

It must have been bad then. There was very little Rane would hesitate to say. Blake resolved to get it out of her later. Now, Eli was coming toward them, motioning them into the wood-and-stone house. The dark-haired woman, Meda, came with him, stopping abruptly in front of Blake so that he had to stop or collide with her. She was a tall bony woman with no attractiveness at all beyond the long, thick, dark brown hair. She may have been attractive once, but now she had no shape, poor coloring, and not even the sense to cover herself as Keira had. She wore jeans cut off at mid-thigh and a man's short-sleeved shirt, buttoned to her skinny midriff, then tied. Blake wondered whether Rane might be right about the drugs.

"For your own sake," Meda said quietly, "you ought to know that we can hear better than most people. I don't usually care who hears what I say, but you might. Now what I told your kid, what she was too embarrassed to repeat, was that I meant to ask Eli for you. I like your looks. It doesn't matter whether you like mine. Everybody here looks like me, sooner or later."

"Jesus Christ," Blake muttered disgustedly. He began to laugh, not meaning to, but not able to stop. "You *are* crazy," he said, still laughing. "All of you." The laughter died finally, and he could only stare at them. They stared back impassively.

"What are you going to do?" he asked Eli. "Give me to her?"

"How can I?" Eli asked. "I don't think I own you. Meda and your kid have a way with words, Doc. With more people like them, we never would have avoided World War Three."

Blake managed to stifle more laughter. He rubbed a hand across his forehead, and was surprised to find it wet. He was standing in the hot desert sun, but between his daughters and his captors, he had hardly noticed.

"What are you going to do with me?" he asked.

"Oh, you'll spend some time with her. That can't be helped. I wish it weren't necessary, but she's your jailer—which is what she was really asking to be. We're going to have to confine you pretty closely for a while, and things will work out better if your jailer is a woman."

"Why?"

"You'll know, Doc. Just give it a little more time. Meanwhile, for the record, what you and Meda do together is your business." He turned, faced Meda. "There are limits," he said softly. "You're getting to like this too goddamn much, you know?"

She glared at him for a moment. "You should talk," she said harshly, though somehow, not quite angrily. She turned and went inside, slamming the door behind her.

Eli sighed. "Lord, I hope you'll all make it—all three of you so we won't have to do this again soon." He glanced to where Ingraham stood watching, managed a crooked smile. "You figure she'll feed us?"

"She'll feed me," Ingraham said, smiling. "She invited me to dinner. Let's go in and see if she's set a place for you."

They herded Blake and the girls into the house, somehow communicating amusement, weariness, hunger, but no threat. It was almost as though the Maslin family had been invited to eat with new friends. Blake shook his head. On his own, he would have tried to break away from these people—whatever they were—long ago. Now... He wondered what his chances were of getting Eli alone, getting his gun and the car keys. If he didn't move soon, Rane or Keira might be separated from him again. These people were in such bad physical condition, they had to take precautions.

Abruptly, it occurred to him that a simple precaution might be to drug something they were to eat or drink.

"What are you planning, Doc?" Eli asked as he sat down in a big, leather wing chair.

The house was cool and dark, comfortably well-kept and old. Blake had to fight off the feeling of security it seemed to offer. He sat on a sofa with his daughters on either side of him.

"Doc?" Eli said.

Blake looked at him.

"I wonder if I can stop you from getting hurt."

"Forget it," Ingraham said. "He's going to have to try something. Just like you'd have to in his place."

"Yeah. Listen, you still have that knife?"

"Sure."

Eli nodded, gestured with one hand. "Come on."

"You mark the wall and Meda'll find some way to get you, man."

"I'm not going to mark the damn wall. Come on."

"Don't break my knife either." Ingraham reached toward his boot, then his hand seemed to blur. Something flashed toward Eli, Eli blurred, and the floorboards beneath Blake's feet vibrated. Blake looked down, saw that there was a large, heavy knife buried in the floor between his feet. It had hit the wood just short of the oriental rug. He gave Eli a single outraged glance, then seized the knife, meaning to pull it free. It remained rooted where it was. He pulled again, using all his strength. Still the knife did not move. It occurred to him that he was making a fool of himself. He sat up straight and glared at Eli.

Eli looked tired and unamused. "Just a trick, Doc." He got up, walked over, and tugged the knife free with little apparent effort. With one long arm, he handed it handle-first to Ingraham, while keeping his attention on Blake. "I know we look scrawny and sick," he said. "We look like one of us alone would equal nothing at all. But if you're going to survive, you have to understand that guns or no guns, you're no match for us. We're faster, better coordinated, stronger, and some other things you wouldn't believe yet."

"You think a circus trick is going to make us believe you're superhuman?" Rane demanded. Blake had felt her jump and cringe when the knife hit. She had been frightened, so now she had to attack. His first impulse was to shut her up, but he held back, remembering the value Eli had placed on her. Eli might tell her to shut up himself, but he would not hurt her just for talking. And she might get something out of him.

"We're not superhuman," Eli said quietly. "We're not anything you won't be eventually. We're just... different."

"And sometimes you hurt," Keira whispered.

Eli looked at her—looked until she stopped studying the pattern on the rug and looked back. "It isn't like your pain," he said. "It isn't as clean as your pain."

"Clean?"

"Mine is kind of like what an addict might feel when he tries to kick his habit."

"Drugs?"

"No drugs, I promise you. We don't even use aspirin here."

"I use things. I have to."

"We won't stop you."

"What are you?" she pleaded suddenly. "Please tell us."

Eli put his hands behind his back, though not before Blake noticed that they were trembling.

"Hey," Ingraham said softly. "You okay?"

Eli glanced at him angrily. "No, I'm not okay. Are you okay?"

Keira looked from one of them to the other, then spoke to Eli. "What is it you're keeping yourself from doing to me?"

"Kerry," Rane cautioned. That was a switch—Rane cautioning. Blake wanted to stop Keira himself, would have stopped her, had he not wanted an answer as badly as she did.

"Give me your hands," Eli said to her.

"No!" Blake said, suddenly wary.

But Keira was already extending her hands, palms up, toward Eli. Blake grabbed her hands and pulled them down.

"You made a promise!" he said to Eli. "You said you'd keep her safe!"

"Yes." Eli's coloring looked worse than ever in the cool dimness of the room. His voice was almost too soft to be heard. "I said that." He was perspiring heavily.

"What were you going to do?"

"Answer her question. Nothing else."

Blake did not believe him, but saw no point in saying so. Eli smiled as though Blake had spoken the thought aloud anyway. He unclasped his hands, and Blake noticed that even they were dripping wet. Diaphoresis, Blake thought. Excessive sweating—symptomatic of what? Emaciation, trembling, bad coloring, now sweating—plus surprising strength, speed, and coordination. God knew what else. *Symptomatic of what?*

"Want to hear something funny, Doc?" Eli said in an oddly distant voice. He held his wrist where Blake could see it and pointed to a small double scar that looked black against his gray-brown skin. "A couple of weeks ago while I was helping with the building, I got careless about where I put my hand. A rattlesnake bit me." Eli laughed hollowly. "You know, the damn thing died."

He turned stiffly and went to the door, no longer laughing.

"Eli?" Ingraham said.

"I got to get out of here for a while, man, I'm getting punchy. I'll be back." Eli stumbled out the door and away from the house. When Blake could no longer hear him, he spoke to Ingraham. "That did look like a snakebite scar," he said.

"What the hell do you think it was?" demanded Ingraham. "I was there. The rattler bit him, tried to crawl off, then doubled up a few times and died. We kept the tail. Fifteen-bead rattle."

Blake decided he was being lied to. He sighed and leaned back in silent rejection of whatever fantasy might come next.

"This whole thing is going to be hard on you, Doc," Ingraham said. "You're going to want to ignore just about everything we say because none of it makes any sense in the world you come from. You'll deny and Rane will try to deny and it won't make a damn bit of difference because one way or another, all three of you are here to stay."

Past 5

The dogs were winning.

They had attacked almost in unison, furiously, angered by his alien scent. Together, they managed to bring him down before he could hurt either of them. Then the smaller one, who appeared to be part Doberman, bit into the arm he had thrown up to protect his throat.

Pain was the trigger that threw him into his changed body's version of overdrive. Moving faster than the dogs could follow, he rolled, came to his feet, locked both hands together and battered the smaller dog down in midair. The dog gave a short shrieking cry, fell, and lay twitching on the ground.

The larger dog leaped for his throat. He threw himself to one side, avoiding its teeth, but hunger and weariness had taken their toll. He stumbled, fell. The dog lunged again. He knew he could not avoid it this time, knew he was about to die.

Then there was a thunderous sound—a shot, he realized. The dog landed awkwardly, unhurt, but startled by the sound. There was human shouting. Someone pulled the dog back before it could renew its attack.

He looked up and saw a man standing over him, holding an old shotgun. In that brief moment, he noted that the man was frightened both of him and for him, that the man did not want to do harm, but certainly would in self-defense, that this man, according to his body language, would not harm anything helpless.

That was enough.

He let his weariness, hunger, and pain take him. Leaving his abused body to the care of the stranger with the out-of-date conscience and the old-fashioned shotgun, he passed out.

When he came to, he was in a big, cool, blue-walled room, lying in a clean, comfortable bed. He smiled, lay still for a while, taking mental inventory of his already nearly healed injuries. His arm had been bitten and torn in three places. His hands and arms had been scratched and bruised. His legs were bruised. Some of this was from climbing the rocks to this house. Some was from climbing out of the red volcanic mountains where he had hidden when the ship was destroyed. His muscles ached and he was thirsty again. But more important, he was intensely hungry. Food was available now. He could smell it. Someone was cooking pork, roasting it, he thought, so that the savory meat smell drifted through the house and seemed almost edible itself. His body required more food than a normal person's and in spite of his desert kills, he had been hungry for days. The food smells now made him almost sick with hunger.

He found a pitcher of water and a glass on the night table next to his bed. He drank all the water directly from the pitcher, then sat up and looked himself over.

He had been bathed, and clothed in someone's gray pajamas. Whoever had removed his coverall and bathed him was probably ill. They would not realize it for about three weeks, but when the symptoms began to make themselves felt, chances were, his rescuer would go to a doctor and pass the infection on beyond this isolated place. And chances were, neither the rescuer nor the doctor would survive—though, of course, both would live long enough to infect others. Many others. Both would be infectious long before they began to exhibit symptoms. The doctor would not recognize the illness, would probably give it first to family and friends.

The ship had died, the three people he had come to love most had died with it to prevent the epidemic he had probably just begun. He should have died with them. But of the four, only his enhanced survival drive had saved him—much against his will. He had been a prisoner within his own skull, cut off from conscious control of his body. He had watched himself running for cover, saving himself, and thus nullifying the sacrifice of the others. To his sorrow, to his ultimate shame, he, and he alone, had brought the first extraterrestrial life to Earth.

What could he do now? Could he do anything? Was not the whole matter literally out of his hands? Had it ever been otherwise?

A woman came into the room. She was tall and rangy and about fifty—too old to attract his interest in any dangerous way.

"So," she said, "you're among the living again. I thought you might be. Are you hungry?"

"Yes," he croaked. He coughed and tried again. "Please, yes."

"Coming right up," the woman said. "By the way, what's your name?"

"Jake," he lied. "Jacob Moore." Jake Moore had been his maternal grandfather, a good man, an old-style, shouting Baptist preacher who had stepped in and taken the place of his father when his father died. It was a name he would not forget, no matter how his body distracted him. His own name would send this woman hurrying to the nearest phone or radio or whatever people in this desolate place used to communicate with the world outside. She would call the would-be rescuers he had hidden from for three days after the destruction of the ship, and she would feel that she had done him a great favor. Then how many people would he be driven to infect before someone realized what was happening?

Or was he wrong? Should he give himself up? Would he be able to tell everything he knew and dump the problem and himself into the laps of others?

The moment the thought came to him, he knew it was impossible. To give himself up would be an act of self-destruction. He would be confined, isolated. He would be prevented from doing the one thing he *must* do: seeking out new hosts for the alien microorganisms that had made themselves such fundamental parts of his body. Their purpose was now his purpose, and their only purpose was to survive and multiply. All his increased strength, speed, coordination, and sensory ability was to keep him alive and mobile, able to find new hosts or beget them. Many hosts. Perhaps three out of four of those found would die, but that magical fourth was worth any amount of trouble.

The organisms were not intelligent. They could not tell him how to keep himself alive, free, and able to find new hosts. But they became intensely uncomfortable if he did not, and their discomfort was his discomfort. He might interpret what they made him feel as pleasure when he did what was necessary, desirable, *essential*: or as pain when he tried to do what was terrifying, self-destructive, *impossible*. But what he was actually feeling were secondhand advance-retreat responses of millions of tiny symbionts.

The woman touched him to get his attention. She had brought him a tray. He took it on his lap, trying, and in the final, driven instant, failing to return the woman's kindness. He could not spare her. He scratched her wrist just hard enough to draw blood.

"I'm sorry," he said at once. "The rocks..." He displayed his jagged nails. "Sorry."

"It's nothing," the woman said. "I'd like to hear how you wound up out here so far from any other settlement. And here." She handed him a linen napkin—real linen. "Wipe your hands and face. Why are you perspiring so? It's cool in here."

Present 6

In surprisingly little time, Meda served a huge meal. There was a whole ham—Blake wondered whether it was homegrown—several chickens, more salad than Blake thought six people could possibly eat, corn on the cob, buttered carrots, green beans, baked potatoes, rolls... Blake suspected this was the first meal he had eaten that contained almost nothing from boxes, bags, or cans. Not even salt on most of the food, he realized unhappily. He wondered whether the food was clean and free of live parasites. Could some parasite, some worm, perhaps, be responsible for these people's weight loss? Parasitic worm infestations were almost unknown now, but these people had not chosen to live in the present. They had adopted a nineteenth-century lifestyle. Perhaps they had contracted a nineteenth-century disease. Yet they were strong and alert. If they were sharing their bodies with worms, the worms were damned unusual.

Blake picked at the barely seasoned food, eating little of it. He wasn't concerned about any possible worm infestation. That could be taken care of easily once he was free. And since everyone took food from the same serving dishes, selective drugging was impossible. He let the girls eat their fill. And he watched the abductors—especially Eli—eat prodigious amounts.

Keira tried to talk to him during the meal, but he gave the impression of being too busy eating to listen. Blake thought he tried a little too hard to give that impression. Eli was attracted to Keira; that was obvious. Blake hoped his ignoring her meant he was rejecting the attraction. The girl was sixteen, naïve, and sheltered. Like most enclave parents, Blake had done all he could to re-create the safe world of perhaps sixty years past for his children. Enclaves were islands surrounded by vast, crowded, vulnerable residential areas through which ran sewers of utter lawlessness connecting cesspools— economic ghettos that regularly chewed their inhabitants up and spat the pieces into surrounding communities. The girls knew about such things only superficially. Neither of them would know how to handle a grown man who saw them as fair game. Nothing had ever truly threatened them before.

Meda was staring at Blake.

She must have been doing it for some time now. She had eaten her meal—a whole, roasted chicken plus generous helpings of everything else. Now she nibbled at a thick slice of ham and stared.

"What is it?" he asked her.

She looked at Eli. "Why wait?" she asked.

"God knows I almost didn't," he said. "Do what you want to."

She got up, walked around the table, stood over Blake, staring down at him intently. Sweat ran down her thin, predatory face. "Come on, Doc," she whispered.

Blake was afraid of her. It was ridiculous, but he was afraid.

"Get up," she said. "Come on. Believe it or not, I don't like to humiliate people."

Sweat ran into her eyes, but she did not seem to notice. In a moment, she would take hold of him with her skinny claws. He stood up, stiff with fear of the woman and fear of showing it. He bumped the table, palmed a knife, secretly, he thought. The idea of threatening her with it, maybe using it on her, repelled him, but he gripped it tightly.

"Bring the knife if you want to," she said. "I don't care." She turned and walked to the hall door. There she stood, waiting.

"Dad," Keira said anxiously. "Please... do what they say."

He looked at her, saw that she was frightened too.

She looked from him to Eli, but Eli would not meet her eyes. She faced Blake again. "Dad, don't make them hurt you."

What was it about these people? How were they able to terrify when they did nothing? It was as though there were something other than human about them. Or was it only their several guns?

"Dad," Rane said, "do it. They're crazy."

He looked at Eli. If the girls were hurt in any way—any way at all—Eli would pay. Eli seemed to be in charge. He could permit harm or prevent it. If he did not prevent it, no circus trick would save him.

Eli stared back, and Blake felt that he understood. Eli had shown himself to be unusually perceptive. And now he looked almost as miserable as Blake felt.

Blake turned and followed Meda. He kept the knife. Everyone saw it now, and they let him keep it. That alone was almost enough to make him leave it. They managed to make him feel like a fool for wanting a weapon against armed people who had kidnapped him and his children at gunpoint. But he would have felt like a bigger fool if he had left the knife behind.

Meda led him into a back bedroom with blue walls, a solid, heavy door, and barred windows.

"My daughter is going to need her medication," he said, wondering why he had not spoken of it to Eli.

"Eli will take care of her," the woman said. Blake thought he heard bitterness in her voice, but her face was expressionless.

"He doesn't know what she needs."

"She knows, doesn't she?" In the instant before he could lie, Meda nodded. "I thought she did. Give me the knife, Blake." She said it quietly as she locked the door and turned to face him. She saw his refusal before he could voice it. "I didn't want to tear into you in front of your kids," she said. "Human nature being what it is, you probably wouldn't be able to forgive me for that as quickly as you'll forgive me for... other things. But in here, I'm not going to hold back. I don't have the patience."

"What are you talking about?"

She reached out so quickly that by the time he realized she had moved, she had him by the wrist in a grip just short of bone-cracking. As she forced the knife from his captive hand, he hit at her. He had never hit a woman with his fist before, but he had had enough from this one.

His fist met only air. Inhumanly fast, inhumanly strong, the woman dodged his blow. She caught his fist in her crushing grip.

He lurched against her to throw her off-balance. She fell, dragging him with her, cursing him as they hit the floor. The knife was still between them in one of his captive hands. He fought desperately to keep it, believing that at any moment the noise would draw one or both of the men into the room. What would they do to him for attacking her? He was committed. He had to keep the knife and, if necessary, threaten to use it on her. His daughters were not the only people who could be held as hostages.

The woman tried to get him off her. He had managed to fall on top and he weighed perhaps twice what she did. As strong as she was, she did not seem to know how to fight. She managed to take the knife and throw it off to one side so that it skittered under a chair. Angrily, he tried to punch her again. This time he connected. She went limp.

She was not unconscious; only stunned. She tried feebly to stop him when he went after the knife, but she no longer had the strength.

The knife was embedded in the wall behind the chair. Before he could pull it free, she was on him again. This time, she hit him. While he lay semiconscious, she retrieved the knife, opened a window, and threw it out between the bars. Then she staggered back to him, sat down on the floor next to him, hugging her knees, resting her forehead against them. She did not look as though she could see him. She was temptingly close, and as his vision cleared, he was tempted.

"You start that shit again, I'll break your jaw!" she muttered. She stretched out on the rug beside him, rubbing her jaw. "If I break your bones, you won't survive," she said. "You'll be like those damn bikers. We had to hurt them because there were too many of them for us to take it easy. All but two wound up with broken bones or other serious injuries. They died."

"They died of their injuries ... or of a disease?"

"It's a disease," she said.

"Have I been infected?"

She turned her head to look at him, smiled sadly. "Oh yes."

"The food?"

"No. The food was just food. Me."

"Contact?"

"No, inoculation." She lifted his right arm, exposing the bloody scratches she had made. They hurt now that she had drawn his attention to them.

"You would have done that even if I hadn't had the knife?" he asked.

"Yes."

"All right, you've done it. Get away from me."

"No, we'll talk now. You're our first doctor. We've wanted one for a long time."

Blake said nothing.

"It's something like a virus," she said. "Except that it can live and multiply on its own for a few hours if it has warmth and moisture."

Then it wasn't a virus, he thought. She didn't know what she was talking about.

"It likes to attach itself to cells the way a virus does," she continued. "It can multiply that way too. Don't tune me out yet, Blake," she said. "I'm no doctor, but I have information for you. Maybe you can use it to help yourself and your kids."

That got his attention. He sat up, climbed painfully into the antique wooden rocking chair that he had shoved aside when he tried to reach the knife. "I'll listen," he said.

"It's a virus-sized microbe," she said. "Filtrable. I hear that means damned small."

"Who told you?"

She looked surprised. "Eli. Who else?"

He could not quite bring himself to ask whether Eli was a doctor.

"He was a minister for a while," she said as though he had asked. "A boy minister at the turn of the century when the country was full of ministers. Then he went to college and became a geologist. He married a doctor."

Blake frowned at her. "What are you going to tell me now? That you're telepathic?"

She shook her head. "I wish we were. We read body language. We see things you wouldn't even notice—things we didn't notice before. We don't work at it; it isn't a conscious thing. Among ourselves, it's communication. With strangers, it's protection."

"Why haven't you gotten treatment?"

"What treatment?"

"You haven't tried to get any treatment, have you? What about Eli's wife? Hasn't she—"

"She's dead. The disease killed her."

Blake stared at her. "Good God. And you've deliberately given it to me?"

"Yes," she said. "I know it doesn't make sense to you. It wouldn't have to me before. But now... You'll understand eventually. And when you do, I hope you'll accept our way of living. It's so damn hard when people don't. Like having one of my kids go wrong."

Blake tried to make sense of this. Before he could give up on her again, she got up and went over to him.

"It isn't necessary for you to understand now," she said. "For now, just listen and ask questions if you want to. Pretend you believe me." She touched his face. Repelled, he caught her hand and pushed it away. His cheek hurt a little and he realized she had scratched him again. He touched his face and his hand came away bloody.

"What the hell are you going to do?" he demanded. "Keep scratching me as long as you can find a few inches of clear skin?"

"Not that bad," she said softly. "I don't understand why—maybe you will—but people with original infections at the neck or above get the disease faster. And infected people who get a lot of attention from us usually survive. The organism doesn't use cells up the way a virus does. It combines with them, lives with them, divides with them, changes them just a little. Eli says it's a symbiont, not a parasite."

"But it kills," Blake said.

"Sometimes." She sounded defensive. "Sometimes people work hard to die. Those bikers, for instance... I took care of Orel—Ingraham, I mean. His first name's Orel. He hates it. Anyway, I took care of him. He didn't like me much then, but he let me. He survived okay. But the other biker who had a chance was a real bastard. Lupe stuck with him, but he kept trying to kill her—strangling, smothering, beating... When he tried to burn her to death in her sleep, she got mad and hit him too hard. Broke his neck."

Blake put most of this aside for later consideration and focused on one implication. "Are you planning to sleep here?" he demanded.

She smiled. "Get used to the idea. After all, I can't very well rape you, can I?"

He did not answer. He was thinking about his daughters.

She drew a deep breath, touched his hand without scratching this time. "I'm sorry," she said. "I'm told I have the sensitivity of a hunk of granite sometimes. None of us are rapists here. No one is going to take your kids to bed against their wills."

"So you say!"

"It's true. Our men don't rape. They don't have to."

"You haven't had to do any of the things you've done."

"But we have. Like I said, you'll understand eventually. For now, you'll just have to accept what I tell you. We're changed, but we have ethics. We aren't animals."

Blake thought that was exactly what they were, but he kept quiet. There was no point in arguing with her. But Rane and Keira... What was happening to them?

Meda took a chair from the desk on the other side of the room and brought it over so that she could sit next to him. He watched her swing her thin body around. She moved like a man. She must have been a powerful-looking woman before her illness. Yet the illness had reduced her to wiry thinness. What would it do to Keira who had no weight to lose, who already had a disease that was slowly killing her?

Meda sat down and took his hands. "I wish you could believe me," she said. "This is the worst time for you. I wish I could help more."

"Help!" He snatched his hands away from her, disgusted. She was still perspiring heavily. In a cool room, she was soaking wet. And no doubt the perspiration was loaded with disease organisms. "You've 'helped' enough!"

She wiped her face and smiled grimly. "You still bring out the worst in me. You don't feel or smell like one of us—like an infected person—yet."

"Smell?"

"Oh yes. Part of your body language, part of your identity is your odor. And one of your earliest symptoms is going to be suddenly smelling things you never consciously noticed before. Eli found our place by following his nose. He was lost in the desert. We had water, and he smelled it."

"He came here? This was your home, then?"

"... yes."

He wondered about her sudden pensiveness, but took no time to question it. He had something more important to ask. "Where did Eli come from, Meda? Where did he catch the disease?"

She hesitated. "Look, I'll tell you if you want me to. It's my job to explain things to you. But there are some things you'll have to understand before I tell you about Eli. First, like I said, I scratched your face just now so you'd get sick sooner. Most people take about three weeks to start feeling symptoms. Sometimes a little longer. You'll feel yours a lot sooner—and you should be infectious in a few days."

"That could mean I'll die sooner," Blake said.

"I'm not going to give you up that easily," she said. "You're going to make it!"

"Why did you rush things for me?"

"We're afraid of you. We want you on our side because you might be able to help us save more converts—that's what Eli calls them. We... we care about the people we lose. But we have to be sure of you, and we can't until you're one of us. Right now, you're sort of in-between. You're not one of us yet, but you're... not normal either. If you escaped now and managed to reach other people, you'd eventually give them the disease. You'd spread it to everyone you could reach, and you wouldn't be able to stay and help them. Nobody can fight the compulsion alone. We need each other."

"Who did Eli have?" Blake asked. "His wife?"

"He had nobody. That was the problem. But before I get into that, I want to be sure you understand that there's no way to leave here without starting an epidemic. The compulsion quiets down a little after you've been sick. You should have enough control then to go into town and buy whatever you'll need that isn't in that computerized bag Eli says you have."

"Buy medical supplies?"

"Yes."

"You're going to trust me enough to let me go into town?"

"Yes, but nobody travels alone. There's too much temptation to do harm. Blake, you aren't ever going to be comfortable among ordinary people again."

He didn't know how he would have felt if he had believed her. But in fact, he meant to take any opportunity to escape that came his way. He did not intend to live his life as an emaciated carrier of a deadly disease. Yet he was afraid. Some of what Meda had said about the disease reminded him of another illness—one he had read about years before. He could not remember the name of it. It was something people did not get any longer—something old and deadly that people had once gotten from animals. And the animals had gone out of their way to spread it. The name came to him suddenly: rabies.

She watched him silently. "You don't believe me, but you're afraid," she said. "That's a start. There's a lot to be afraid of."

He stifled an impulse to deny his fear or explain it. "You were going to tell me about Eli," he said.

She nodded. "Remember that ship a few years ago—the *Clay's Ark?*"

"The *Ark?* You mean the starship?"

"Yeah. Brand-new technology, tested all to hell, and it still blew up when it got back from the Centauri system. People figured the scientists rushed things so they would have something flashy to keep them from losing their funding again. At least, that's what I read. The *Ark* came down about thirty miles from here. It was supposed to land at one of the space stations or on the moon, but it came all the way home. And before it blew up, Eli got out."

"Eli…? What are you telling me?"

"His name is Asa Elias Doyle. He was their geologist. In case you haven't noticed, he can drop that dumb accent of his whenever he wants to. The disease is from the second planet of Proxima Centauri. It killed ten of a crew of fourteen. I think more would have lived, but they began by isolating anyone who got sick. Then they found they had to restrain them to keep them isolated." She shuddered. "That amounted to slow death by torture.

"Anyway, four survived to come home. I think they had to come home. The compulsion drove them. But when they landed something went wrong. Maybe for once, someone managed to break the compulsion. The ship was destroyed. Only Eli managed to get out. But in one way, that didn't matter. He brought Proxi Two back to us as well as a crew of fourteen could have. And now… now it's as Terran as you or me."

Past 7

A few minutes of careful listening told him there were seven people sharing the isolated wood-and-stone house with him. There were the two adult sons and a twenty-year-old daughter, who had spent the night in Barstow. There was their mother, who had brought food and who had been kind, and the sons' new young wives, who were eager for the separate houses to be finished. There was the white-haired patriarch of the household—a stern man who believed in an outdated, angry God and who knew how to use a shotgun. He reminded himself of this last when he met the daughter. Meda, her name was.

Meda introduced herself by walking into the room he had been given just as he pulled on a borrowed pair of pants. And instead of retreating when she saw that he was dressing, she stayed to watch. He was so glad she was not the woman of the night before, the woman whose scent had frozen him outside her window, that her brazenness did not bother him. This one's scent was far more interesting than a man's would have been, but she had not yet reached that dangerous time in her cycle. She was big like her mother—perhaps six feet tall, and stocky where her mother was becoming old-woman thin. Meda was brown-haired, heavily tanned, and strong-looking—probably used to hard work.

She stared at him curiously and was unable to conceal her disappointment at his thin, wiry body. He did not blame her. He was disgusted with his appearance himself, though he knew how deceptive it was. He had been good-looking once. Women had never been a problem for him.

This woman, however, was a problem already. Her expression said she recognized him. That was completely unexpected—that someone in this isolated place would keep up with current events enough to know what one of fourteen astronauts looked like. Unfortunately, his face had changed less than the rest of him. It had always been thin. And with the *Ark* returning, there must have been a great rebroadcasting and republishing of old pictures. This woman had probably just seen several of them in Barstow.

"How have you lost so much weight?" she asked as he pulled on a shirt. The clothing belonged to Gabriel Boyd, the father of the family. He was thin, too, though not quite as tall. The pants were too short. "You look like you haven't eaten for weeks," Meda said.

"I am hungry," he admitted.

"My mother says you just ate enough for two people."

He shrugged. He was still hungry. He was going to have to do something about it soon.

"We don't have a videophone," she said, "or a telephone, or even a radio."

"That's okay. I don't want to call anyone."

"Why not?"

He did not answer.

"What do you want?" she asked.

"I want you to get out of here before your father or one of your brothers gets the wrong idea."

"This is my room."

That did not surprise him. The room did not look as though it belonged to a young woman. There was no clothing in sight, no perfume or makeup, no frills. But it smelled of her. The bed smelled of her.

"I was in Barstow with my brothers overnight," she said. "There are some supplies my brothers can't be trusted to buy, even with a list." She gave him a sad smile. "So I went to the big city."

"Barstow?" Like most desert towns, it had been water-short and shrinking for years—not that it had ever been big.

"Anything bigger would be too sinful. It might tempt me or contaminate me or something. You know, I've only been to L.A. twice in my life."

He wiped his wet face with dripping hands. She did not know how she tempted him to contaminate her. His compulsion was to touch her, take her hands perhaps, scratch or bite if she pulled away. Sex would have been very satisfying with her, too, though not as satisfying as when she reached her fertile time. She was not the kind of woman who would have attracted him in any way at all before. Now all a woman had to do to attract him was smell uncontaminated.

He looked away from her, sweat soaking into his borrowed clothing. "You're not missing anything by keeping away from cities," he said. He had been born in a so-called middle-class residential area of that same vast, deadly Los Angeles she wanted more of, and if not for his grandfather, he would probably already have died there. Many of the people he had grown up with had died of too much L.A. A girl like this one, not pretty, eager for attention and excitement, would not survive a year in L.A.

"We barely have running water here," she grumbled.

Fool. She had clean, sweet well water here, free for the taking. In stinking L.A., she would have a limited amount of flat, desalinized, purified, expensive ocean water. In L.A., you could tell how little money a man had by how bad he smelled. "You don't know when you're well off," he told her. "But if you're crazy enough to want to try city life, why don't you just move?"

She shrugged, looking surprisingly young and vulnerable. "I'm afraid," she admitted. "I guess I haven't cut the umbilical yet. But I'm working on it." She fell silent for a moment, then said, "Asa?"

He looked at her sidelong. "Girl, even my enemies have more sense than to call me that."

"Elias then," she said, smiling.

"Eli."

"Okay."

"You tell anybody?"

"No."

That was true. She was enjoying having the secret too much to give it away. Now he had to keep her quiet.

"Why are you here?" she asked. "Why aren't you being debriefed or paraded down some big city street or something?"

Why was he not in isolation, she meant. Why was he not waiting and contending with a misery no one but him could understand while a dozen doctors discovered what a dangerous man he was? Why was he not dead in an escape attempt? And considering the loss of the ship, its wealth of data, its frozen, dead crew, and its diseased, living crew, debriefing was a laughably mild name for what he would have been put through.

"What's the matter?" Meda asked softly. She had a big voice, not intended for speaking softly, but she managed. She had come closer. God help her, why didn't she go away? Why didn't he order her away or leave himself?

She touched his arm. "Are you all right?"

His body went on automatic. Helplessly, he grasped her hand. He managed not to scratch her, and tried to feel good about that until he saw that she had a small abrasion on the back of her hand. That was enough. His touch would probably have been enough anyway. Eventually she would have eaten something with that hand or scratched her lip or wiped her mouth or scratched or licked her hand to quiet the slight itching sensation contamination sometimes produced. And the disease organism could live on the skin for hours in spite of normal, haphazard hand-washing. Any person he touched was almost certainly doomed in one way or another.

"Why are your hands wet?" she asked. And when he did not answer, she examined his hands. He had expected her to drop them in disgust, but she did not seem disgusted. She was a big, strong girl. Maybe she could be saved. Maybe he could save her—if he stayed.

He remembered trying vainly to save his wife, Disa. She had been a short, slender woman with no weight to lose, barely big enough to qualify for the space program. The disease had eaten her alive. She had been one of the mission's two M.D.s, however, and before she died, she and Grove Kenyon, the other doctor, had discovered that the disease organism caused changes that could be beneficial— if the host survived its initial onslaught. Surviving hosts became utterly resistant to more conventional diseases and more efficient at performing certain specialized functions. Only the toxin excreted by the disease organism was life-threatening. Not surprisingly, the human body had no defense against it. But in time the organism changed, adapted, and chemically encouraged its host to adapt. Its by-products ceased to be toxic to its host and the host ceased to react as strongly to increased sexual needs and heightened sensory awareness—inevitable effects of the disease. The needed time was bought by new organisms of the same disease—new organisms introduced after significant adaptation had occurred. The new, unadapted organisms quickly spent themselves neutralizing the toxic wastes of the old. Thus, the new organisms had to be replaced frequently. The host body was a hostile environment for them—an environment already occupied, claimed, chemically marked by others of their kind. Their toxin-neutralization was merely their reflexive effort to survive in that hostile environment.

But the original invading organisms had too much of a start. Or, if they were not well started, if the new organisms were introduced too soon, those new organisms simply became part of the original invasion, and the host, the patient, was no better, no worse.

The meager statistics provided by the crew and the few experimental animals they managed to raise from frozen embryos seemed to support these findings. All four of the surviving crew members had been reinfected several times. There were no survivors among the first crew members stricken. These had been isolated and restrained. Their vital functions had been continually monitored and restored when they failed. But finally their brains had ceased to function.

Reinfection was the answer, then—or *an* answer. A partial answer. Without it, everyone died. With it, some lived. Disa had died. Meda was obviously stronger. Perhaps she could live.

Present 8

Meda brought Blake his bag when he asked for it and permitted him to examine her. She even permitted him to cleanse the scratches she had made on his arm and face, though she warned it would do no good. It had never done any good before when someone was infected, she said. The organisms were aggressive and fast. He had the disease.

She or someone else had found and sabotaged his panic button with one of the new permanent glues. With these, permanent meant permanent. He could not use the bag to call for help. Otherwise, the bag was intact. For Keira's sake in particular, it was one of the best. His scope would probably give him a look at the *Clay's Ark* organism, even if it was as small as Meda had said. He needed all the information he could get before he made his escape. It was not only a matter of his wanting to pass the information on. He also needed to know now of any weaknesses these people had. They were too good to be true in every way except appearance. He had to find something he could use against them.

"I could have used you when my children were born," Meda told him as he took her blood pressure.

"Didn't you have a doctor?" he asked. He checked her pulse.

"No. Just Eli and Lorene, my sister-in-law. We don't bring anyone here if we don't plan to keep them. And I didn't dare go to a hospital. Imagine how many people I'd infect there."

"Not if you told them the truth."

She watched as he drew blood from her left arm. It went directly into the analyzer as would all her other specimens. "They'd put me in a goddamn cage," she said. "They'd put my kids in one, too. They were born with the disease, you know."

"Did they have any special problems?"

She turned her head to stare directly at him. "Not a one," she said. She made no effort to conceal the fact that she was lying.

"What about you?" Blake asked gently. "Easy births?"

"Yeah," she said. Her defensiveness vanished. "The first one really surprised me. I mean, I was scared. I expected to be in agony, and I don't handle real pain that well. But the kid popped out with no trouble at all. Felt like cramps."

"You were lucky there was no emergency. May I see your children?"

"Not until you're safe, Blake."

"Safe?"

"When you've been sick and gotten well again, then we'll have nothing to worry about. We'll show you anything you want."

He frowned. "Do you imagine I'd hurt a child?"

"Probably not," she said. "But you're at the seeking-weakness stage, and Jacob and Joseph would be a hell of a weakness. If you used them, we'd have to kill you. We want you alive, Blake."

He looked away from her in growing desperation. They really were too good—always a step ahead. How many times had they done this—abducted people, made them vanish from the world outside. He had to beat them at a game they knew all too well. But how?

Meda rubbed his arm with a wet hand. "Look," she said, "it isn't so bad here. You can do a lot of good—maybe more good than you could do anywhere else. You can help us prevent an epidemic."

"It's only a matter of time before your disease gets out of hand," he said.

"We've kept that from happening for more than four years."

"Yet it could happen tomorrow."

"No!" She got up and began to pace. "I can't really make you understand until you've felt it, but we'd go crazy if we were caged. We'd probably kill ourselves trying to escape. The compulsion keeps us on a pretty thin edge as it is. Eli says we're holding on to our humanity by our fingernails. I'm not sure we're holding on to it at all. In some ways, I'm more realistic than he is. But maybe we need a little of his idealism. God knows how he's kept it." She glanced at Blake. "He's my kids' father, you know."

"I guessed," Blake said.

"He helps us hold on even if all we're holding on to is an illusion. Take away that illusion and what's left is something you wouldn't want to deal with. You'll see."

"If your veneer of humanity is that thin," Blake said, "it's only a matter of time before someone finds it too thin. And if what you've told me about the disease is true, one person could infect hundreds and those hundreds could infect thousands—all before the first victim began to show symptoms and realize they were sick."

"Your estimate is low," she said. "Now do you see why you have to stay here? *You* could become that one person."

He did not argue with her. He would escape and go to a hospital; that was all. "I'd like you to undress," he said. He had just collected a little of her sweat and taken—almost painlessly—a minute specimen of her flesh. The analyzer found something incomprehensible in both—probably the same something it had found in her blood and urine.

"Unidentifiable microbes," the small screen said. It was able to show him tiny, spiderlike organisms in her flesh, some of them caught in the act of reproducing along with her cells—*as part of her cells*. They were not viruses. According to the computer, they were more complete, independent organisms. Yet they had made themselves at home in human cells in a way that should not have been possible—like plasmids invading and making themselves at home in bacteria. But these were hardly plasmids—solitary rings of DNA. These were more complex organisms that had sought out higher game than bacteria and managed to combine with it without killing it. They had changed it, however, altered it slightly, subtly, cell by cell. In the most basic possible way, they had tampered with Meda's genetic blueprint. They had left her no longer human.

"The ones that live in the brain don't have little legs—cilia, I mean," Meda said over his shoulder.

"What?"

"Eli told me they get into the brain cells, too. It sounds frightening, but there isn't anything we can do about it. I guess they'd have to reach the brain to change us so."

She did not know how changed she was. Could there be any hope of reversing such elemental changes? There must be, for his daughters' sake.

"Eli and I used to talk about it a lot," she said. "He wanted me to know everything he knew—in case anything happened to him. He said his wife and the other doctor did autopsies on the crew members who died before them. They found little round organisms in the brains of every one of them."

"Rabies again," Blake muttered. But no. Rabies was only a virus, preventable and curable.

"Eli's wife tried to make antibodies," Meda said. "It didn't work. I don't remember what else she tried. I didn't understand, anyway. But nothing worked except reinfection. They found out about that by accident. And it works better person-to-person than person-to-syringe. Maybe that's just psychological, but we don't care. We'll use anything that works. That's why I'm here with you."

"You're here to try to make a good carrier of me," he said.

She shrugged. "You'll be that or die. I'd rather live myself."

There was another answer. There had to be. He could not find it with only his bag, but others, researchers with lab computers, would sooner or later come up with answers. First, though, they had to be made aware of the questions.

He turned to look at Meda and saw that she had stripped. Surprisingly, she looked less scrawny without her clothing. More like the human female she was not. What could her children be like?

She smiled. "All my clothes are too big," she said. "I put them on and I look like a collection of sticks, I know. Maybe now I'll buy a few new things next time I'm in town."

He ignored the obvious implication, but could not ignore the way she kept reading him. He became irrationally afraid that she was reading his mind, that he would never be able to keep an escape plan from her. He tried to shake off the feeling as he proceeded with the examination. She said nothing more. He got the impression she was sparing him, humoring him.

He asked to examine others in the community when he finished with her, but she was not ready to share him with anyone else.

"Start checking them tomorrow if they'll let you," she said. "You'll smell different then. Less seductive."

"Seductive?"

"I mean you'll smell more like one of us. Nobody will take any special pleasure in touching you then." She had dressed again in her loose, ugly clothing. "It's sexual," she said. "Or rather, it feels sexual. Touching you is almost as good as screwing. It would be good even if I didn't like you. If not for people like you—people we have to catch and keep, I could never control myself enough to go into town. With no outlet it gets—painful and crazy, sort of frenzied when there are a lot of unconverted people around. I have dreams about suddenly finding myself moving through a crowd—maybe on a big city street. Moving through a crowd where I have no choice but to keep touching people. I don't even know whether to call it a nightmare or not. I'm on automatic. It's just happening."

"You'd like it to happen," he said, watching her.

"Pigshit!" she replied, abruptly angry. "If I wanted it to happen, it would happen. I'd get in my car and I'd drive. I could infect people in towns from here to New York. And I'd do exactly that if I ever had to leave this place. There would be no one to help me, stop me." She hesitated, then sat down on the bed beside him. He managed not to recoil when she took his hand. He was getting information from her. Let her touch him as long as she kept talking.

"You've got to understand," she said. "It's really hard on us the way we limit our growth. We can only do it because we're so isolated. But if you escaped—with or without your kids—we'd have to escape too before you could send people here to corral us. I don't know where we'd go, but chances are, we'd have to split up. Now you imagine, for instance, Ingraham out there on his own. He was high-strung before, and damned undisciplined. He doesn't shake because there's more wrong with him than with the rest of us. He shakes because he's holding himself back almost all the time. He respects Eli and he loves Lupe. She's going to have his kid. But you force him out of here, and all by himself, he'll start an epidemic you won't believe."

"And you're saying that will be my fault," Blake said angrily. She was boxing him in. Everything she said was intended to close another exit.

"We'll do *anything* to avoid being locked up," she said. "I'll do *anything* to keep my sons from being taken from me."

"Nobody would take your—"

"Shut your mouth! They'd take them. They'd treat them like things. If they killed them—accidentally or deliberately, it would just be one of their problems solved."

"Meda, listen—"

"So if you're afraid of an epidemic, *Doctor*, don't even think about leaving us. Even if you spread the word, you can't possibly stop us." She switched tracks abruptly. "I'm starving. Do you want anything to eat?"

He was disoriented for a moment. "Food?"

"We eat a lot. You'll see."

"What if you didn't?" he asked, immediately alert. "I mean, I couldn't have put away the meal I saw you eat only a few hours ago. What if you just ate normally?"

"We do eat normally—for us."

"You know what I mean."

"Yeah, I know. You're still seeking weakness. Well, you've found one. We eat a lot. Now what are you going to do? Destroy our food supply?" She produced a key from somewhere, seemingly by magic. Her hands actually were quicker than his eyes. "Don't even think about doing anything to the food," she said. "Someday I'll tell you how people like you smell to my kids." She let herself out and slammed the door behind her.

She returned sometime later, bringing him a ham sandwich and a fruit salad.

"I'd like to see my daughters," he told her.

"I'll see," she said. "Maybe I can bring you one of them for a few minutes."

Her cooperativeness pleased but did not surprise him. She had children of her own and she could see that his concern was genuine; there was no reason for her to find that concern suspect.

He was lying down, tired and frightened, hanging on to the bare bones of an escape plan when Eli brought Keira in.

Keira seemed calm. Eli left her without saying a word. He locked her in and probably stood outside listening.

"Are you all right?" Blake asked.

She answered the question he intended rather than the one he had asked. "He hasn't touched me," she said. She did not sit down, but stood in the middle of the room and looked at Blake. He looked back, realizing that for her sake, he could not touch her either. Such a simple, terrible thing. He could not touch her.

"He said Meda scratched you," she whispered.

Blake nodded.

"He told me about the disease and... where he got it. I didn't know what to think. Do you believe him?"

"'Her' in my case." Blake stared through the bars of the window into the desert night. "I believe. Maybe I shouldn't, but I do."

"Rane always says I'll believe anything. At first, I was afraid to believe this. I do now, though."

"Have you seen Rane?"

"No. Daddy?"

He looked away from the bright full moon, met her eyes and saw that in a moment she would come to him, disease or no disease.

"No!" he said sharply.

"Why?" she demanded. "What difference does it make? Someone's going to touch me sooner or later, anyway. And even if they don't, I've probably already got the disease—from the salad or the bread or the furniture or the dishes... What's the difference?" she wiped away tears angrily. She tended to cry when she got upset, whether she wanted to or not.

"Why hasn't he touched you?"

She looked at Blake, looked away. "He likes me. He's afraid he'll kill me."

"I wonder how long that will stop him?"

"Not long. He obviously feels terrible. Sooner or later, he's going to just grab me."

Blake opened his bag again, turned it on, and keyed in a prescription form. "ARE YOU LOCKED UP?" he typed. "ARE YOUR WINDOWS BARRED?"

She shook her head, mouthed, "No bars."

"THEN YOU CAN ESCAPE!"

"Alone?" she mouthed. She shook her head.

"YOU MUST!" he typed. "AT TWO A.M., I'LL TRY. I WANT YOU WITH ME!" Aloud, he said, "I can't help you, Kerry."

"I know," she whispered. "Most of the time, I'm not even worried about myself. I'm worried about you and Rane. I don't even know where Rane is."

He began typing soundlessly again. "THEN BREAK FREE ALONE! THEY THINK YOU'RE HELPLESS. THEY'LL BE CARELESS WITH YOU."

She shook her head as she read the words. "I can't," she mouthed. "I can't!"

"Are you having any pain?" he asked aloud. "Did you take your medicine?"

"No pain," she said softly. "I had some, but I told Eli and he got my medicine from the car. He wore what he called his town gloves." She glanced at the door. "He said if he wasn't careful, he could transmit the disease just by paying for supplies. They all have to wear special gloves when they're in town."

"Yet they deliberately spread the disease to people like us," Blake said. He wiped everything he had typed and began again on a clean form. "YOU MUST ESCAPE! THERE'S AN EPIDEMIC BREWING HERE! WE MUST GIVE WARNING, GET TREATMENT!"

She was shaking her head again. God, why hadn't Meda sent Rane to him? Rane would be afraid, too, but that would not stop her.

"EVEN IF I FAIL," he typed, "YOU MUST TAKE THE CAR AND GO—OR WE COULD ALL DIE. DO YOU REMEMBER HOW TO START THE CAR WITHOUT THE KEY?"

She nodded.

"THEN GO! SEND BACK HELP. GIVE WARNING!"

Tears ran down her face, but she did not seem to notice them. He spoke aloud with painfully calculated brutality. "Meda told me people with serious injuries die of the disease. She's seen them die. She didn't say anything about people with serious illnesses, but Kerry, she didn't have to." He gave her a long look, trying to read her, reach her. She knew he was right. She wanted to please him. But she had to overcome her own fear.

He typed, "SOONER OR LATER, ELI WILL TOUCH YOU—AT LEAST."

She read the words without responding.

"BE NEAR THE WAGONEER TONIGHT," he typed. "AT TWO."

She swallowed, nodded once.

At that moment, there was a sound at the door. Instantly, Blake shut off the computer, automatically wiping the prescription form and everything he had typed. He closed the bag and turned to face the door just as Eli opened it.

Blake looked at Keira, aching to hug her. He felt he was about to lose her in one way or another, but he could not touch her.

Past 9

Within twenty-four hours, Eli had infected everyone on the mountaintop ranch. He had also talked the old man, Gabriel Boyd, into giving him a job as a handyman. Boyd was not willing to pay much more than room and board, but room and board was all Eli really wanted—a chance to stay and perhaps save some of these people.

He was given a cot in a back room that had been used for storage. He was given his meals with the family, and he worked alongside the men of the family. He knew nothing about ranching or building houses, but he was strong and willing and quick. Also, he knew his Bible. This in particular impressed both the old man and his wife. Few people read the Bible now, except as literature. Religion was about as far out of fashion as it had ever been in the United States—a reaction against the intense religious feeling at the turn of the century. But Eli had been a boy preacher during that strange, not entirely sane time. He had been precocious and sincere, had read the Bible from Genesis to Revelation, and could still talk about it knowledgeably. Also, Eli knew how to be easygoing and personable, a refugee from the city, grateful to be away from the city. He knew how to win people over even as he condemned them to illness and possible death.

He wanted them all to start showing symptoms at about the same time, and he wanted that time to be soon. Left to themselves, infected people feeling their symptoms tended to huddle together in an us-against-the-world attitude. If everyone became ill at the same time, he would have less trouble keeping individuals from trying to go for help. He had started what could become an epidemic. Now, if he were going to be able to live with himself at all, he had to contain it.

He worked hard on the house that was intended for the son named Christian—Chris to everyone but his father. Christian's wife Gwyn was going to have a baby and Christian had decided that the house would be finished before the baby arrived. Eli did not know or care whether this was possible, but he liked Christian and Gwyn. He worried about what the disease might do to a pregnant woman and her child. Whatever happened would be his fault.

Sometimes guilt and fear rode him very nearly into insanity, and only the exhausting hard work of building kept him connected to the world outside himself. He liked these people. They were decent, kind, and in spite of the angry God they worshipped, they were remarkably peaceful and uncorrupted by the cynicism and violence outside. They were good people. Yet it was inevitable that some of them would die.

The daughter Meda was doing her best to add to his burdens by seducing him. She had no subtlety, did not attempt any.

"I'd like to sleep with you," she told him when she got her courage up. He had known since he met her that she wanted to sleep with someone, and would settle for him. He fended her off gently.

"Girl, what are you trying to do? Get yourself in trouble and get me shot? Your people have been good to me."

"They wouldn't," she said, "if I told them who you are. They think heaven is only for God and his chosen."

He became serious. "Don't play games with me, Meda. I like your honesty and I like you, but don't threaten me."

She grinned. "You know I wouldn't tell."

"I know."

"And if I can keep one secret, I can keep two." She touched his face. "I'm not going to let you alone."

Her touch produced a interesting tingle. She was coming into her time. He had apparently arrived just after her time of fertility the month before. That had been a blessing. He had been able to avoid the other two young women, but Meda would not let him avoid her. Now, she had no idea the trouble she was courting. She probably imagined a romantic interlude. She did not imagine being thrown on the rocky ground and hurt—inevitably hurt.

"No," he said, pushing her away. She was still smiling when he turned from her and began hammering in siding nails. She watched for a while, and he discovered he enjoyed the attention. He had not believed women outside the crew would want to look at him with his body so changed. Meda was trouble, but he was sorry when she decided to leave. She looked as though she had lost a little weight, he noticed.

As she walked away, her brother Christian came out of the main house and stopped her. They were too far from Eli to worry about his hearing them, but he heard every word.

"That guy been talking to you, Mead?" Christian demanded. Eli could not recall having heard Christian refer to him as "that guy" before. For Christian this was damned unfriendly.

"Sure he has," Meda said. "I came out here to talk to him. Why shouldn't he talk to me?" Blast her honesty!

"What'd you say to him?"

"What did you do this morning, Chris? Look in the mirror and mistake yourself for Dad?"

"What did he say to you?"

Eli looked at them and saw even over the distance that she smiled sadly. "Relax," she told her brother. "He said no. He said the family had been good to him and he didn't want trouble."

Christian gave an oddly brittle laugh. "Anybody who recognizes you as trouble has the right idea," he said. "If that guy were white, I'd tell you to marry him."

Meda watched her brother with visibly growing confusion. Living in the house, Eli had heard enough to know Christian was her favorite brother. They had shared secrets since childhood. Christian knew how tired she was of being an isolated virgin, and she knew how nervous he was about becoming a father. Right now, she knew there was something wrong with him.

"Did you break down and buy some perfume?" he asked. "You smell good."

Eli put down his hammer and stood up. It was beginning. Meda had bathed and she smelled of soap, but she was not wearing

perfume. She was simply coming into her time. If she and her brothers lived, they would have to learn to avoid each other at these times.
Now, however, Eli might have to help them. He stood still, waiting to
see whether Christian could control himself. He realized Meda might
not be as much in control as she should be either. He would not let
them commit incest. They would be losing enough of their humanity
shortly.

Eli jumped down from the floor of the house and started toward
them. At that moment, Christian reached up and touched Meda's
face with one trembling hand. Then, with a strange, whining cry, he
folded slowly to the ground, out cold.

Present 10

When Eli and Keira were gone, Blake opened his bag and turned
it on again. He punched in his identity code, then the words "TIMED
SLEEP" and the number three. He hit the deliver button. Moments
later, he had a capsule that would put him to sleep for three hours
and let him awake fully alert. Next he ordered a much less precise
dosage for Meda. This he ordered in injectable form—a sleep tab.

He placed Meda's dosage under the pillow he intended to use,
then turned off the bag and closed it. He stripped to his shorts, and
got into bed. Remembering Keira, he doubted that he could have
slept at all without the capsule. And he had to sleep. If he did not,
Meda would look at him and realize he was up to something. She
might even figure out what it was. He did not underestimate her
any longer.

He thought he heard her come in before he dozed off, thought
she called his name. He may have muttered something before the
drug took full effect.

He awakened on time, clearheaded, aware of what he must do. The
room was full of moonlight and Meda lay snoring softly beside him. It
amused him that she snored. It seemed utterly right that she should.

He was surprised to find himself feeling sorry for her as he eased the sleep tab from beneath his pillow and pressed it to her thin, bare right arm. She repelled him, but she was not responsible for what she had become.

There was no pain involved, but at his touch, she jumped, came awake, found him leaning over her.

"What did you do?" she demanded, fully alert.

He touched her hair, thinking he would have to hit her again, not wanting to hit her, not wanting to hurt her at all. Perhaps that was what she saw in his expression—if she could see him well enough to read his expression. She smiled uncertainly, turned her face to meet his caressing hand.

Then the smile vanished. "Oh God," she said. "What have you done?" She reached for him, but her hands had no strength. She tried to get up and almost slid out of bed. Finally the drug stopped her. She moaned and slipped into unconsciousness.

Blake stared at her, feeling irrationally guilty. He straightened her body, placed her in a more comfortable-looking position, and covered her. She would awaken in three or four hours.

He dressed, looked around the room, noticed at once that his bag was gone. He looked through the closet and in the bathroom, searched the bedroom, but the bag was not to be found. Finally, desperately, he forgot the bag and began searching for the key that would let him out of the room. Since he already knew where it was not, he began by searching the one place he had ignored: the bed and Meda herself. He found it on a chain around her neck. It hung down inside her gown where he could not have touched it normally without awakening her.

Seconds later, he let himself out of the room. Feeling his way carefully, silently, he reached the front door. He wondered just before he let himself out whether these people posted a watch. If they did, he was probably finished. He hoped they had enough confidence in their ability to handle their prisoners not to bother with guards.

He slipped out and closed the door behind him. From where he stood on the porch, he could see no one. Things looked confusingly different in the moonlight. For several seconds, he could not find the car. It had been moved. He feared it had been hidden and he would have to risk stealing another. Then he saw it in the distance near one of the outhouses. Getting it started without his key would be no problem if he had time to disconnect the trap-alarm system. The alarm itself was sound and indelible dye sprayed over any would-be thief. If the thief persisted, he was sprayed with a nausea gas. The gas was utterly disabling whether it was breathed or merely came in contact with the skin. A car—even a fuel-gulper like this one—was a prestige item. The automobile age had peaked and passed. People who drove cars or rode motorcycles now were either professional drivers, the rich, law-enforcement people, or parasites. The pros, the rich, and the police usually went to even greater, dead-lier lengths than Blake had to protect their vehicles.

Hugging the shadows, Blake worked his way toward his car. He had reached it and used his own special catch to get past the hood lock when someone spoke to him.

"You don't have to do that. I have the keys."

He turned sharply, found himself facing Keira. Solemnly, she handed him the keys. He stared at them.

"I took them," she said. She shrugged. "Now you won't have to worry about touching me."

"You exposed yourself just to get the keys?" he demanded.

"No." She was in shadow. He could not see her well enough to be certain of her expression, but she sounded odd. He took the keys and her hand, held both for a moment, then hugged her tightly, probably painfully, though she did not complain. Then he held her by her shoulders and spoke what he strongly suspected was nonsense. "Meda says the disease is transmitted by inocula-tion, not contact. Don't touch your mouth or scratch your skin until you wash."

She did not seem to hear. "I hit him, Dad."

"Good. Get in the car."

"He had some books—made of paper, I mean—and an old book-end in the shape of an elephant. It was made of cast iron."

"Get in, Kerry!"

"I didn't want to hurt him. I didn't think I could hit him hard enough to do any real harm." She got in through the door he had opened.

He started to close the door, then instead squatted beside her. "Kerry, did you hear anything about Rane? Do you know where she is?"

"With Ingraham and Lupe. I don't know which house they're in."

She did not know. And how many people would he wake up if he tried to find out? One would be enough to recapture him. He had not even been bright enough to get himself another knife—not that the first one had done him any good. What he needed was a gun.

"Daddy, I heard something," Keira said.

He froze, listened, heard it himself—someone moving around carelessly in the house nearest to him. It may have been just someone going to the bathroom, but it frightened him. He rounded the car in a few long steps, got in, and heedless of noise, started the engine. At that moment, someone opened the door of the house from which the noise had come. It was a man, a stranger, who actually managed to catch the car as Blake swung it around toward the rocky trail that led down from the ranch. The stranger tried to tear Blake's door open as Ingraham had earlier. But with the car moving and his body inadequately braced, he failed to break the lock. He was dragged several yards as Blake picked up speed. As a final gesture, he managed to release his hold with one hand, raise his fist, and smash it into the window beside Blake's head. Like the lock, the glass held. It broke, cracks raying outward in all directions from the impact of the blow, but it did not shatter. Its breaking amazed Blake. The glass was special, expected to stop bullets with less damage. Blake realized again how powerful these people were. If they caught him, they could literally tear him limb from limb.

He drove on, praying that he would see Rane, that he would have a chance to pick her up. But he saw only stick people—menacing, utterly terrifying in their difference and their intensity. In the moonlight, they seemed other than human. One refused to move from the car's path, apparently trying to make Blake swerve and hit a house or a huge rock.

Blake did not swerve. No experienced city driver would have swerved or slowed. At the last possible instant, the "victim" leaped aside and clung to the rock like an insect.

Something that moved like a cat, but was too big to be a cat, ran alongside the car briefly, and Keira screamed.

"Don't hit him," she said. "Don't hurt him!"

The car accelerated, leaving the running thing behind.

"What the hell was that?" Blake asked.

"Be careful," she said. "Remember the rocks Eli had to dodge around."

He remembered. It was impossible to speed past those boulders. On the other hand, it was very possible that Meda's people in the mountains above could start rockslides that would close the narrow road entirely if he crept along slowly.

As though in answer to his thought, he heard a rumbling from above. Praying as he had not since childhood, he drove on, managed to swerve around one boulder just in time to see a rockslide beginning ahead.

He pushed the accelerator to the floor, sped past the slide area as the first rocks came down. Twice the car was hit by rocks big enough to shake it, but Blake managed to stay on the road. He did not slow down until he came to a sharp curve around which he thought he recalled a rock.

There was a rock. Many rocks. Another slide had blocked the road with a steep hill of loose rocks and dirt. Blake had no time to think. The car would climb the slide or it would not. It was a Jeep, after all, antique or no.

The car struggled for traction in the loose dirt and rock, then shuddered heavily as something landed on its roof. The something made an indentation they could see inside the car.

Suddenly Keira pushed her door open. Blake grabbed for her, not understanding. His hand just missed her as she leaned out. Then he saw what she had seen—a small, bloody face hanging upside down from the cartop.

"Rane!" he shouted. He leaned across Keira, indifferent for the moment to the way Keira bruised almost at a touch. He caught Rane's arm, pulled her down and into the car across Keira, then slammed the door and locked it as something else began tearing at it.

Blake hit the accelerator and the car leaped onto the loose dirt and rock. For an instant, the wheels spun uselessly, throwing out sand. Then they found traction and the car lunged up the slide. A rock bounced off the windshield, chipping it slightly. Another hit the top, doing no important damage.

Blake reached the crest of the slide, rolled down it, and sped on down the mountain. Minutes later, they were in open desert. Keira and Rane, still tangled together, both hurting, both silent with terror until they looked around and saw that they had left the mountains and their captivity behind. Then they hugged each other, Rane laughing and Keira crying. Rane's bare arms and her face had been cut and bruised somehow. If she had not been contaminated before, she was now. Blake worried, but said nothing. Contamination had probably been inevitable, however. The disease could be studied, understood, stopped, or at least controlled—and it had to be. The disease was only a disease. It was the willing human carriers intent on spreading it that made it so deadly.

Blake relaxed in his seat and surveyed the damage to the car. Nothing terminal. Nothing that would stop him from reaching civilization and getting medical care. He wondered why Eli's people had not shot him, or at least shot at him. Bullets would have been more effective than rocks. But then, it was like Eli to hold back. He had saved Rane from Ingraham, held off contaminating Keira—probably for as long as he could—even tried bloodlessly to avoid a fight with Blake, though he could probably have broken Blake's bones with no effort.

"How did you get free?" Keira was asking Rane. "Did you have to hurt someone?"

"I was tied up for the night," Rane said. "Jacob let me loose. He didn't like me, but he couldn't stand the thought of anything being tied up. Then you two broke away and everyone was too busy chasing you to watch me. I almost killed myself running and falling down that goddamn mountain."

"Jacob?" Blake said. "Isn't that one of Meda's sons?"

The girls looked at each other, then at him warily. "You know about Jacob?" Rane asked.

"Only that Meda has a son by that name."

"He's her son and Eli's." There was an odd pause. For the second time in twenty-four hours, Rane seemed unwilling to say what was on her mind. "Have you seen him?" she asked.

"No. But I don't imagine he would be normal. Not after what the bag told me about Meda."

"... he isn't."

"What's he like?"

"You saw him," Keira said softly. "He ran alongside the car for a few seconds. That was him."

Blake frowned, gave her a quick glance. "But that was... an animal."

"Disease-induced mutation. Every child born to them after they get the disease is mutated that way. Jacob is the oldest of eleven."

Blake glanced at Keira. She was not looking at him, would not look at him.

"Jacob's beautiful, really," she continued. "The way he moves—catlike, smooth, graceful, very fast. And he's as bright as or brighter than any other kid his age. He's—"

"Not human," Blake said flatly. "Jesus, what are they breeding back there?"

The girls looked at each other again, shifted uncomfortably, sharing some understanding that excluded him. Now neither would face him. Suddenly he wanted to be excluded. He drove on in silence, suspicion growing in his mind. He concentrated on putting distance between himself and those who would certainly follow—though he could not help wondering whether what followed was really worse than what they carried with them.

PART 2

P. O. W.

Past 11

Within a day of Christian's collapse, Eli had seven irrational people huddling around him. They had no idea what was happening to them, but they knew they were in trouble. They were combative, fearful, confused, lustful, driven, guilt-ridden, and utterly miserable.

They huddled together, not knowing what to do. They were fearful of going near outsiders with their painfully enhanced senses and their odd compulsions, but Eli was one of them. More, he was complete. He smelled *right* to them. And he could see their needs clearer than they could. He could respond to them as they required, offering comfort, sternness, advice, brute strength, whatever was necessary from moment to moment.

He found comfort in shepherding them. It was as though in a very real way, he was making them his family—a family with ugly problems.

Meda found both her brothers and her father after her, and she, like them, was alternately lustful and horrified. Her father suffered more than the others. He felt he had gone from patriarch and man of God to criminally depraved pervert unable to keep his hands off his own daughter. Nor could he accept these feelings as his own. They must be signs of either demonic possession or God's punishment for some terrible sin. He and his sons were badly frightened.

His wife and daughters-in-law were terrified. Not only were they unable to understand the behavior of their men, but they were confused and embarrassed by their own enhanced sensory awareness. They could smell the men and each other as they never had before. They kept trying to wash away normal scents that would not vanish. They spoke more softly as they realized the substantial walls no longer stopped sound as well as they had. They discovered they were able to see in the dark—whether they wanted to or not. Touching, even accidentally, became a startlingly intense sensual experience. The women ceased to touch each other. They also ceased to touch the men except for their own husbands. And Eli.

They all developed huge appetites as their bodies changed. Worse, they developed unusual tastes, and this frightened them.

"I'm so hungry," Gwyn told Eli on the day her symptoms became undeniable. She gestured toward a pair of chickens—part of the Boyd flock of thousands. This pair were scratching and pecking at the sand in the shade of the well tank. "Suddenly, those things smell good to me," she said. "Can you believe that? They smell edible."

"They are," Eli said softly. It had been necessary for him to supplement his diet with one or two of them or with several eggs every night when the family was asleep.

"But how could they smell good raw?" Gwyn said. "And alive?"

Living prey smelled wonderful, Eli knew. But Gwyn was not ready to face that yet. "Go raid the refrigerator," he told her. "Maybe Junior is hungry."

She looked down at her pregnant belly and tried to smile, but she was clearly frightened.

He did what he would never have done before this day. He took her arm and led her back to the house to the kitchen. There he saw to it that she ate. She seemed to appreciate the attention.

"Something feels wrong," she said once. "Not with the baby," she added quickly when Eli looked alarmed. "I don't know. The food tastes too sweet or too salty or too spicy or too something. It tasted okay yesterday, but now... When I started to eat, I thought I was going to be sick. But that's not right either. It's not really nauseating. It's just... I don't know."

"Bad?" he asked, knowing the answer.

"Not really. Just different." She shook her head, picked up a piece of cold fried chicken. "This is okay, but I'm not sure the ones running around outside wouldn't be better."

Eli said nothing. Since his return to Earth, he knew he preferred his food raw and unseasoned. It tasted better. Yet he would go on eating cooked food. It was a human thing that he clung to. His changed body seemed able to digest almost anything. It tempted him by making nonhuman behavior pleasurable, but most of the time, it let him decide, let him choose to cling to as much of his humanity as he could.

Though certain drives at certain times inevitably went out of control.

Meda brought him her symptoms and her suspicions not long after he left Gwyn.

"This is your doing," she said. "Everybody's crazy except you. You've done something to us."

"Yes," he admitted, breathing in the scent of her. She had some idea now what she was doing to him just by coming near.

"What have you done?" she demanded.

"What do you feel?" he asked, facing her.

She blinked, turned away frightened. "What have you done?" she repeated.

"It's a disease." He took a deep breath. He had never imagined that telling her would be easy. He had already decided to be as straightforward as possible. "It's an extraterrestrial disease. It will change you, but no more than I'm changed."

"A disease?" She frowned. "You came back sick and gave us a disease? Did you know you had it?"

"Yes."

"And you knew we could catch it?"

He nodded.

"Then you gave it to us deliberately!"

"No, not deliberately."

"But if you knew . . ."

"Meda . . ." He wanted to touch her, take her by the shoulders and reassure her. But if he began to touch her, he would not be able to stop. "Meda, you'll be all right. I'll take care of you. I stayed to take care of you."

"You came here to give us a disease!"

"No!" He turned his head toward the well tank. "No, I came... to get water and food."

"But you—"

"I couldn't die. I wanted to, but I couldn't. I can go out of my mind; I can become an animal; but I can't kill myself."

"What about the others, the crew?"

"All dead like I told you, like your Barstow news said. The disease took some of them—before we found out how to help them." A half-truth. A deletion. Disa and two others had died in spite of the help they got. "The others died here—with the ship. Someone—maybe more than one—apparently managed a little sabotage. I wish they'd done it in space, or back on Proxi Two."

"How do you know someone sabotaged the ship? Maybe it was an accident."

"I don't know. I don't remember. I blacked out."

"How did you get off the ship?"

"I don't know. I have off-and-on memories of running, hiding. I know I took shelter in mountains of volcanic rock, lived in a half-collapsed lava tunnel for three days and two nights. I nearly starved to death."

"People can't starve in just three days."

"We can. You and me, now."

She only stared at him.

"It was raining," he continued. "I remember we deliberately chose to land in a storm in the middle of nowhere so we could get away before anyone found out what we were. Even with speeded up reflexes, increased strength, and enhanced senses, we nearly disintegrated, then nearly crashed. We kept them from shooting us down by talking. God, we talked. The brave heroes giving all the information they could before they crashed. Before they died. We could no more imagine ourselves dying than we could imagine not coming straight in to Earth. It was a magnet for us in more ways than one. All those people... all those... billions of uninfected people."

"You came to infect... everybody?" she whispered.

"We *had* to come. We couldn't not come; it was impossible. But we thought we could control it once we were here. We thought we could take only a few people at a time. A few isolated people. That's why we chose such an empty place."

"Why would you think you could have any... any luck controlling yourselves here in the middle of all the billions if you couldn't control yourselves on Proxima Centauri Two?"

"We weren't sure," he said. "Maybe it was just something we told ourselves to keep from going completely crazy. On the other hand..." He looked at her, glad she was alive and well enough to be her questioning, demanding self. "On the other hand, maybe we were right. I don't want to leave this place to reach anyone else. Not now. Not yet."

"You've done enough damage here."

"Do you want to leave?"

"Eli, I live here!"

"Doesn't matter. Do you want to go to a hospital? See if somebody can figure out a cure?"

She looked uncomfortable, a little frightened. "I was wondering why you didn't do that."

"I can't. Can you?"

"What do you mean you can't?"

"Go if you can. I'll... try not to stop you. I'll try."

"This is my home! I don't have to go anywhere!"

"Meda—"

"Why don't *you* leave! You're the cause of all this! You're the problem!"

"Shall I go, Meda?"

Silence. He had frightened and confused her, touched a brand new tender spot that she might not have discovered on her own for a while. She wanted to stay with her own kind. Being alone was terrifying, mind-numbing, he knew.

"You went away," she said, reading him unconsciously. "You left the rest of the crew."

"Not deliberately."

"Do you ever do anything deliberately?" She came a little closer to him. "You got out. Only you."

He realized where she was headed and did not want to hear her, but she continued.

"The one sure way you could have known when to run is if you were the saboteur."

His hands gripped each other. If they had gripped anything else at that moment, they would have crushed it. "Do you think I haven't thought about that?" he said. "I've tried to remember."

"If I were you, I wouldn't want to remember."

"But I've tried. Not that it makes any difference in the end. The others died and I should have died. If I did it, I killed my friends then made their deaths meaningless. If someone else did it, my survival made the sacrifice meaningless anyway."

"The dogs died," she said. "Remember? One of them was hurt, but not bad. The other wasn't hurt at all, but they died. We couldn't understand it."

"I'm sorry."

"They *died!* Maybe we'll die!"

"You won't die. I'll take care of you."

She touched his face, finally, traced the few premature lines there. "You aren't sure," she said. "My touch hurts you, doesn't it?"

He said nothing. His body had gone rigid. Its center, its focus was where her fingers caressed.

"It must hurt you to hold back," she said. "Your holding back hurts me." There were agonizing seconds of silence. "You probably were the saboteur," she said. "You're strong enough to hurt yourself, so you thought you were strong enough to kill yourself. I want you. But I wish you had succeeded. I wish you had died."

He had no more strength of will at all. He seized her, dragged her behind the well, pushed her to the ground. She was not surprised, did not struggle. In fact, with her own drives compelling her, she helped him.

But it was not only passion or physical pain that caused her to scratch and tear at his body with her nails.

Present 12

When Orel Ingraham grasped Rane's arm and led her from Meda's house, she held her terror at bay by planning her escape. She would go either with her father and Keira or without them. If she had to leave them behind, she would send help back to them. She had no idea which law enforcement group policed this wilderness area, but she would find out. All that mattered now was escaping. Living long enough to escape, and escaping.

She was terrified of Ingraham, certain that he was crazy, that he would kill her if she were not careful. If she committed herself to a poorly planned escape attempt and he caught her, he would certainly kill her.

She noticed no trembling in the hand that held her arm. There were no facial tics now, no trembling anywhere. She did not know whether that was a good sign or not, but it comforted her. It made him seem more normal, less dangerous.

As they walked, she looked around, memorizing the placement of the animal pens, the houses, the large chicken house, and something that was probably a barn. The buildings and large rocks could be excellent hiding places.

The people were spooky; she saw only a few, all adults. They were busy feeding the animals, gardening, repairing tools. One woman sat in front of a house, cleaning a chicken. Rane watched with interest. She planned to be a doctor eventually, and was pleased that the sight did not repel her. What did repel her was the way people looked at her. Each person she passed paused for a moment to stare at her. They were all scrawny and their eyes seemed larger than normal in their gaunt faces. They looked at her with hunger or lust. They looked so intently she felt as though they had reached for her with their thin fingers. She could imagine them all grabbing her.

At one point, an animal whizzed past—something lean and brown and catlike, running at a startling speed. It was much bigger than a housecat. Rane stared after it, wondering what it had been.

"Show-off," Ingraham muttered. But he was smiling. The smile made him look years younger, less intense, saner. Rane dared to question him.

"What was that?" she asked.

"Jacob," Ingraham answered. "Stark naked as usual."

"Naked?" Rane said, frowning. "What was it?"

He led her onto the porch of an unpainted, but otherwise complete, wooden house. There he stopped her. "Not 'it,'" he said, "him. That was one of Meda's kids. Now, shut up and listen!"

Rane closed her mouth, swallowing her protests. But the running thing had definitely not been a child.

"Our kids look like that," he said. "You may as well get used to it because yours are going to look like that too. It's a disease that we have, and now you have it—or you'll soon get it. There isn't a damn thing you can do about it."

With no further explanation, he took her into the house and turned her over to a tall, pregnant woman whose hair was almost long enough for her to trip over.

Lupe, the woman's name was. She was sharp-featured with thin arms and legs. In spite of her pregnancy, she clearly belonged among these people. She wore a caftan much like Keira's. Her pregnant body looked like a balloon beneath it. She reached for Rane with thin, grasping hands.

Rane drew back, but Ingraham still held her. She could not escape. The woman caught Rane's other arm and held it in a grip just short of painful. The thinness was deceptive. These people were all abnormally strong.

"Don't be afraid," the woman said with a slight accent. "We have to touch you, but we won't hurt you." Her voice was the friendliest thing Rane had heard since her capture. Rane tried to relax, tried to trust the friendly voice.

"Why do you have to touch me?" she asked.

"Because you're not one of us yet," Lupe said. "You will be. Be still." She reached up so quickly that Rane had no chance to struggle, and made scratches across Rane's left cheek.

Rane squealed in surprise and pain, and, too late, jerked her head back. "What did you do that for?" she demanded.

They ignored her. "You're in a hurry," Ingraham said to Lupe.

"Eli says the sooner the better with this one and her father," Lupe told him.

"While he takes his time with his. Treats her like she'll break if he touches her."

"She might. We never had anybody who was already sick."

"Yeah. I got us a healthy one, though."

They talked about her as though she were not there, Rane thought. Or as though she were no more than an animal who could not understand.

She tried to pull free when Lupe took her away from Ingraham and sat her down on a long wooden bench. There, finally, she released Rane and stood before her studying Rane's angry, hostile posture. Lupe shook her head.

"I lied," she told Rane. "We are going to hurt you. You're going to fight us every chance you get, aren't you? You're going to make us hurt you." The corners of her mouth turned downward. "Too bad. I can tell you from experience, it won't help. It might kill you."

Rane glanced at the woman's claws and said nothing. Lupe was as crazy as Ingraham and even more unpredictable with her soft words and sharp nails. Rane was terrified of her—and furious at her for inspiring fear. Why should one thin-limbed, pregnant woman be so frightening? One thin-limbed, startlingly strong, pregnant woman who sat down beside Rane and caressed Rane's arm absently.

Rane looked at Ingraham—actually found herself looking for help from the man who had held a gun to her head. To her utter humiliation, he laughed. Rane's vision blurred and for an instant, she saw herself smashing his head with a rock.

Suddenly Lupe grasped her chin, turned her head until she could see only Lupe, hear only Lupe.

"*Chica*, nothing has ever truly hurt you before," Lupe said. "Nothing has even threatened you enough to make you believe you could die. Not even your sister's illness. So now you must learn a hard lesson very quickly. No, don't say anything yet. Just listen. You think I'm threatening you, but I'm not. At least, not in the way you believe. We have given you a disease that can kill you. That's what you need to understand. Some of our differences are signs of that disease. You must decide whether it's better to live with such signs or die. Listen."

Rane listened. She heard about Eli and the *Clay's Ark* and Proxima Centauri Two. She listened, but she believed almost nothing.

"You know," Lupe said when she had been talking for perhaps a half hour, "sometimes I look around and everything seems to be the wrong color. The sun is too bright and... not red. I feel surprised that it isn't red. I couldn't figure out what was going on when it first happened. It scared me. But when I told Eli, he said Proxi was red. A cool red star with its three planets hugging in close around it. He bought some red light bulbs in Needles and put

them in his den. They're not right either, really, but every now and
then I go over there. Every now and then, everyone goes over there
and stays for a while. It relaxes us. When things start to smell funny
to you and you feel like you want to eat a live rabbit or rape a man,
we'll take you over there. It helps. Keeps you from jumping out of
your skin."

"I've got a better solution for that last feeling," Ingraham said,
grinning. He had gone away and come back. Now he sat watching
Rane in a way that made her nervous. In spite of the huge meal Rane
had seen him eat, he was munching nuts from a dish on the coffee
table.

Lupe looked at him and smiled—all teeth. "You touch her like
that and I'll cut your thing off."

Ingraham laughed, got up and kissed her, then stood before her,
smiling. "You want me to get one of the kids for her to see?"

"Get Jacob if you can catch up with him."

"Okay." He went out.

Looking after him, Rane sorted out two impressions. First, that
Lupe meant her threat absolutely. She would kill him if she caught
him with Rane or any other woman. Second, he knew it. He enjoyed
her possessiveness. Thus Rane was probably safe from him in one
way at least. Thank God.

"You're bright," Lupe said to her softly. "Very bright, but stubborn. You think you can choose your realities. You can't."

Rane made herself meet the woman's eyes. "Reality," she said with
contempt. "My father is a doctor. He really could have gone out on
the *Ark*. He has valuable training, he was within the age range when
it left, and he was in good physical shape. Would you believe me if I
told you he was a fugitive astronaut?"

"Not if you're his kid, honey. Nobody with young kids went. No
white guy married to a black woman went either. Things never got
that loose."

"And no ignorant con artist who can barely speak English went,"
Rane snapped. "If Eli's convinced you he did, you're no smarter
than he is!"

Surprisingly, Lupe smiled. "You're a lot less tolerant than I would
have expected. A lot less observant too. But it doesn't matter. Here's
Jacob."

Ingraham came into the room carrying a small, large-eyed, brown boy. The boy was slender—without childish pudginess—but not bone-thin like the adults. He wore a pair of blue shorts, but no shirt. He was startlingly beautiful, Rane realized when he turned in Ingraham's arms and faced her. But there was something odd about him. He seemed nothing like the thing that had run past her outside, but he did appear to be built for speed. An odd, slender little boy.

"Come on, *niño*," Lupe said. "Let's show you off a little bit. Come sit with us."

The boy scrambled against Ingraham, braced, and leaped to the bench on which Rane and Lupe sat. He landed next to Rane, who started violently. Jacob had leaped like a cat and landed on all fours. His legs and arms were clearly intended to be used this way. He was a quadruped. He had hands, however, and fingers. He looked at them, following Rane's eyes.

"They work," he said in a clear, slightly deeper than average child's voice. "They work like yours." He grasped her arm with the small, startlingly strong, hard hands. Sharp little nails dug into her flesh, and she drew away. Squatting, the boy sniffed his hands, then wiped them on his shorts.

"You smell," he told Rane, and leaped off the bench and onto it again next to Lupe.

Lupe laughed. "Shame, Jacob. That's not nice to say."

"She does," the boy insisted.

"She's not one of us yet. She will be soon. Then she'll smell different."

Rane completely passed over the insult in her fascination with the boy—the whatever-it-was.

"Can he walk on his feet alone?" she asked Lupe.

"Not so well," Lupe answered. "He tries sometimes because we all do, but it's not natural to him. He gets tired, even sore if he keeps at it. And it's too slow for him. You like to move fast, don't you, *niño*?" She lifted the strange little body and placed it on her lap. Jacob immediately put his ear to her belly.

"I can hear it," he announced.

"Hear the baby?" Rane asked.

"Its heartbeat," Lupe said. "He can hear it without putting his ear to me. It's just a game he likes. He says this one's going to be a girl. He doesn't understand how he can tell, but he knows. Smell, maybe."

"Guessing, maybe," Rane said.

"Oh no, he does know. He's called it right four times so far. Now women come and ask him."

"But... but, Lupe—"

"Stop for a moment," Lupe said. Then to the boy, "Okay, *niño*. Back out to play. Take some nuts."

The boy leaped down from her lap, trotted on all fours to the china nut dish on the plain, homemade coffee table. He took a handful of nuts, stuffed them into the pocket of his shorts and zipped it shut. He seemed to have no trouble using his hands. They were smaller than Rane thought they should have been, but he was less clumsy with them than a normal child would have been. He was certainly much faster than any normal child, probably faster than most adults. All his movements were smooth and graceful. A graceful four-year-old.

He stopped in front of her—beautiful child head, sleek catlike body. A miniature sphinx. What would it be when it grew up? Not a man, certainly.

"I don't like you either," Jacob said. "You're fat and you smell and you're ugly!"

"Jacob!" Lupe stood up and started toward him. "*Vayase! Ahora mismo!* Outside!"

Jacob bounded out the door. No, human beings did not move that way. How had any disease made such a creature of a child?

"He's telling the truth, you know," Lupe said. "You do look fat and odd to him, though you're not. And you smell... different. Also, he couldn't miss how much you were repelled by him."

"I don't understand how such a thing could happen," Rane whispered.

"It's the disease, I told you. We don't even have a name for it—the disease of *Clay's Ark*. All our children are like Jacob."

"All...?" Rane swallowed. "All animals? All *things*?"

"Shit!" Lupe said. "You're worse than I was. You should be more tolerant. He's a little boy."

Rane stared at her pregnant belly.

"Oh yes," Lupe said. "This child will be like Jacob too, just as my son is. Beautiful and different. And, *chica*, your children will be like him too. The disease doesn't go away. It just settles in and stays with you and you pass it on to strangers and to your children."

"Or you get treatment!" Rane said. "What the hell are you doing sitting in the middle of the desert giving birth to monsters and kidnapping people?"

Lupe smiled. "Eli says we're preserving humanity. I agree with him. We are. Our own humanity and everyone else's because we let people alone. We isolate ourselves as much as we can, and the people outside stay alive and healthy—most of them."

"Most," Rane said with bitterness. "Most for now. But even now, not me. Not my father or sister. And what about you? You don't belong here either, do you?"

"I do now," Lupe said. "Before, I was a private hauler. You know. Good money if you survive. My truck broke down all the way over on I-Fifteen, and Eli caught me outside. When I realized what he had done to me, I thought I would bide my time and kill him. Now, I think I'd kill anyone who tried to hurt him. He's family."

"Why?" demanded Rane. "If you really believe he's the cause of this sickness—and you know he's the guy who kidnapped you..." Rane shook her head. "Didn't you have a husband or anything back in the real world? What about your business?"

"I was divorced," Lupe said. "I lived in the truck on the road." She paused. Her voice became wistful. "I miss the road. I almost got killed more times than I like to think about, but I miss it."

Rane listened without comprehension. A woman who could be nostalgic for work that kept nearly killing her could probably make any irrational adjustment.

"I didn't have anybody," Lupe said. "We lived in a cesspool. My parents' house got caught in a gang war, got bombed. One of the gangs wanted to make a no-man's-land, you know. They needed to put some space between their territory and their rivals'. So they bombed some houses, torched others. They got their no-man's-land. My parents, my brother, and a lot of other people got killed. My ex-husband, he's a wino somewhere. Who cares? So I was alone. I'm not alone here. I'm part of something, and it feels good. Even Orel. There was a time when I carried two guns plus the truck's usual defenses—and defensively, my truck was a goddamn tank—all to fight off people like him: bike packers, car bums, rogue truckers, every slimy maggot crawling over what's left of the highway system. But they're not all as bad as I thought. Orel isn't. Take away the gang and give him something better and he turns into a person. A man."

Rane listened with interest in spite of herself. She could not understand Lupe's interest in a man like Ingraham but she was beginning to respect Lupe. Rane liked to think of herself as tough, but she had an uncomfortable suspicion she could not have survived Lupe's life. She had never been alone, never been without someone who would help her if she could not help herself. Now none of the people who cared about her could help her. Her father, her sister, two sets of grandparents, and on her mother's side, a number of aunts, uncles, and cousins. Only a few of them were close to her, but every one of them could be counted on to come running if a member of the family needed help. Now, the only ones who knew of her need needed help as badly as she did.

Past 13

Gabriel Boyd died.

Death was a relief to him, an end to more than physical suffering. Alive, he was frightened, confused, full of self-loathing for feelings he could neither control nor understand.

He had had to be put to bed because he was no longer able to keep his balance. He overcompensated, first for walking up and down steps, then for negotiating the irregularities of the ground outside, finally for walking over a level surface. He could crawl, but nothing more.

As his sensitivity increased, he began to react with terror to slight sounds and cringe at the slightest touch. Most food—even the smell of food—nauseated him, though he was always hungry. Eli fed him ground, unseasoned raw meat, fresh vegetables, and fruit. He ate a little of this and kept it down.

His eyes had to be covered since any slight movement frightened him. His movements, even in bed, were either exaggerated and awkward or fine and incredibly controlled. He could no longer feed himself. Then he could no longer eat or drink even if fed. On the *Ark*, he would have been fed intravenously. But no member of the *Ark* crew who reached this stage had survived, reinfection or no. Eli and a weeping Meda cared for him, then for his wife, whose symptoms also worsened. He lost control of all his bodily functions. He urinated and defecated, spat and drooled. His body twitched and convulsed and sweated profusely. He probably shed enough disease organisms to contaminate a city.

On the fourth day following the onset of symptoms, he died— probably of dehydration and exhaustion. On life support, he would have lasted longer, but the end would have been the same. Eli was glad there were no facilities for prolonging the old man's suffering.

Meda's mother died a day later as did her two brothers and a tiny, perfectly formed nephew born three months too soon.

Meda herself never really sickened. She became more and more despondent as her family died, became almost suicidal, but her physical symptoms remained bearable. She was learning to use her enhanced senses or at least tolerate them. And in spite of all the horror, every night and sometimes during the day, she went to Eli or he came to her. Without discussion, he moved into her room. She did not understand how she could touch him with the disaster he had brought to her family happening all around her. Yet she found comfort with him. And, though she did not know it, she gave him comfort, eased his guilt by continuing to live. They leaned on each other desperately, and somehow held each other up.

Her father realized what they were doing before he died. He first cursed her, called her a harlot. Then he apologized and wept. He seized Eli's wrist with only a ghost of the great strength he should have possessed.

"Take care of her!" he whispered. It was more a command than a request. Even more softly, he said, "I know it might have been me or one of her brothers if not for you. Take care of her, please."

To Eli's own surprise, he wept. He was trapped in a vise of guilt and grief. He was alive because of the old man. Gabriel Boyd had given him a home and thus kept him from drifting into a town and spreading the disease. It was his grandfather all over again—a stern, godly old man who took in strays. A dangerous practice these days—taking in strays.

He worried about Meda. Worried that he might not be able to take care of her—that she might die in spite of her apparent adjustment. That would make him a complete failure. That would drive him away even if her sisters-in-law lived. In his mind, only her living would ease his questioning of his own humanity. He had stayed to save her. Now she must live or he was a monster, utterly evil, completely without control of the thing that made him monstrous.

She lived. He stayed with her constantly during the period when she might try to take her life. Later when the organism took firmer hold, suicide would be impossible. Now, he watched her.

Most of the time she hated him at least as much as she needed him. She lost weight and her clothing sagged on her. She gained strength, and when she hit him, it hurt. Guiltily, he did not strike back.

She helped him wash the corpses of her parents, her brothers, and her nephew. For him it was a penance he would not permit himself to avoid. For her it was a good-bye.

They wrapped the bodies in clean sheets, took them to a place she had chosen. There, together, they broke the ground, dug the graves. The sisters-in-law did not help, but they crept out to stand red-eyed over the graves as Eli read from Lamentations and from Job. They cried and Meda said a prayer and it was over.

Later, Meda tried to comfort her sisters-in-law. They were older than she, but she had a more dominant personality, and they tended to defer to her—except in one important way. They preferred to be comforted by Eli. Their drives were as much increased as Meda's and they had no men.

Meda understood their need, and resented it. Even when she hated Eli, she did not want to share him. Her possessiveness seemed to surprise her, but it did not surprise Eli. He would have been equally possessive of her if there had been another man on the ranch. He saw to it that Gwyn and Lorene were reinfected until he was certain they would live. Then he avoided temptation as best he could until Meda was comfortably pregnant—and her pregnancy did comfort her. She did not understand why. She had been isolated and sheltered by her parents, brought up to believe having a child outside marriage was a great sin. But her pregnancy relieved tension she had not recognized until it was gone. It also relieved tension she had recognized all too clearly.

"I'm going to sleep with Lorene," Eli told her one day. "It's her time."

Meda rubbed her stomach and looked at him. "I don't want you to," she said. He could see that she meant the words, but he heard little passion behind them. She had some idea what he was feeling, and she knew positively what Lorene was feeling. She wanted to hold on to him, but she had already resigned herself to his going.

"There are no other men," he said unnecessarily.

"Will you come back?"

"Yes!" he said at once. Then more tentatively, "Shall I?"

"Yes!" she said matching his tone. She put her hand to her stomach. "This is your child too!"

She did not know how much he wanted to be a father to it. He had been afraid she would do what she could to make that difficult.

"We need men for Lorene and Gwyn," she said.

He nodded. He was glad she had said it. She would share the responsibility this time when they infected two more men. He had known all along what had to be done. He had not thought the women were ready to hear it until now. The other deaths had seemed too fresh in their minds. Without meaning to, he had enjoyed the harem feeling the three women gave him. When he realized how much he enjoyed it, he wanted to look for other men at once. He found any feeling that would have been repugnant before his illness, but that was now attractive, to be suspect. He would not give the organism another fragment of himself, of his humanity. He would not let it make him a stud with three mares. He would make a colony, an enclave on the ranch. A human gathering, not a herd. A gathering headed where, God knew, but wherever they were headed, since they were not going to die, they had to grow.

Present 14

Lupe and Ingraham shared Rane with a newcomer introduced as Stephen Kaneshiro. No one explained what he was doing there. He offered to help with the wall painting when Lupe and Ingraham got out the paint and brushes—real brushes—but Rane did not get the impression he lived with them. He touched her from time to time as Lupe and Ingraham did. After a couple of hours of this, she stopped cringing and trying to avoid their fingers. They were not hurting her. There was no more scratching. They were endurable.

Eventually the reason for Stephen's presence became clear to her.

The painting had been going on for a while when Lupe asked her if she wanted to help. She shook her head. She knew the request might really be a command, but she decided to wait and see. Lupe simply shrugged and turned back to the wall she was working on. The two men were on their way to work on the outside of the house. Stephen stopped, looked at her, then at Lupe. "Do you suppose she'll be this lazy when she has her own house?" he asked.

Lupe smiled. "That one isn't lazy. She's sitting there cooking up an escape plan."

Startled, Rane turned to look at her. Lupe laughed, but Stephen seemed concerned. He put down a can of paint and came over to Rane. He was a small, brown man, so heavily tanned that he and Rane were about the same color. He was clean-shaven and long-haired, his black hair pulled back and loosely bound with a rubber band. Under different circumstances, she would have welcomed attention from him, even been a little overwhelmed. He was as thin as everyone else on the ranch, but he was also one of the best-looking men Rane had ever seen. Somehow, his thinness did not detract from his good looks. Yet he had the disease. She braced herself against the renewed offense of his touch.

But this time he did not touch her. He clearly wanted to, but he held back.

"If you'll come with me," he said, "I won't touch you."

"Do I have a choice?" she asked.

"Yes, but I'd like you to come. I want to talk to you."

Rane glanced at Lupe, saw that she was paying no attention.
Stephen did not seem fearsome. He was her size and not afflicted
with any twitches or trembling. She sensed none of Ingraham's
quick temper behind the quiet, black eyes. More important, she
was learning absolutely nothing sitting in Lupe's living room and
being stroked like an animal whenever someone thought of her.
She needed to look around, find a way out of this place.

She stood up, looked at Stephen, waiting for him to lead the
way.

"We're going outside," he said. "I'll show you around while we
talk. Don't run, though. If you run, I'll have to hurt you—and that's
the last thing I'd want to do."

There was no special warmth in his voice when he said these last
words, but Rane was suddenly suspicious.

Breaking his word, Stephen took her arm and led her out. She
did not mind, really. At least this time he had a reason to touch her.

He took her to a corral where two cows and a half-grown heifer
were eating hay. Far off to one side, there was another corral from
which a bull stared at the cows.

"This place is full of babies and pregnant women," he said. "We
need plenty of milk." The heifer came over to them and he rubbed
its broad face.

"You can get a disease from drinking raw milk," Rane said.

"We know that. We're careful—although we're not sure we have
to be. We don't seem to get other diseases once we have this one."

"It's not worth it!"

He looked surprised at her vehemence. "Rane, you'll be all right.
Young women don't have anything to worry about. It's older women
and all men who take the risk."

"So I've heard. That means my father could die. And, young or
not, my sister will probably die sooner than she would have without you people. And me. What do I do if I live? Give birth to one
little animal after another?"

He turned her around so that she faced him. "Our children are
not animals!" he said. "We are not interested in hearing them called
animals."

She pulled free of him, not at all surprised that he let her. "I never
cared much for the idea of aborting children," she said, "but if

·I thought for a moment that I was carrying another Jacob, I'd be willing to abort it with an old wire coat hanger!"

She had managed to horrify him—which was what she had intended. She was completely serious, and he, of all people, had to know it.

"You know they planned to give you to me," he said softly.

"I suspected. So I wanted you to know how I felt."

"Your feelings will change. Ours did. The disease changes you."

"Makes you like having four-legged kids?"

"Makes you like having kids. Makes you need to have them. And when they come, you love them. I wonder... What's the chemical composition of love? Human babies are ugly even when they're normal, but·we love them. If we didn't the species would die. Our babies here—well, if we didn't love them, if we weren't damned protective of them, the *Clay's Ark* organism on Earth would die. It isn't intelligent, but, God, is it ever built to survive."

"I won't change," Rane said.

He smiled and shook his head. "You're a strong girl, but you don't know what you're talking about." He paused. "You don't have to come to me until you want to. We're not rapists here. And you... Well, you're interesting right now, but not as interesting as you will be."

"What are you talking about?"

He put his arm around her. She was surprised that the gesture did not offend her. "You'll find out eventually. For now, it doesn't matter."

They walked away from the heifer and she mooed after them.

"Cows don't seem to get the disease," he commented. "Dogs get it and it kills them. It kills all the types of cold-blooded things that have bitten us—snakes, scorpions, insects... There may not be anything on Earth that can penetrate our flesh and come away unchanged. Except our own kind, of course. I can't prove it, but I'll bet those cows are carriers."

"The scope attachment of my father's bag could probably tell you that," Rane said. "Though he may not be in any mood to use it."

"I can use it," he said.

She looked at his face, lineless in spite of his thinness. He was the youngest person she had seen so far—in his early twenties, perhaps, or his late teens. "You were in school before, weren't you," she guessed.

He nodded. "College. Music major. I got a little sidetracked taking biology and chemistry classes, though."

"What were you going to be?"

"A concert violinist. I've been playing since I was four."

"And now you're willing to give it all up and move back to the twentieth century?"

He stopped at a large wooden bin, opened it, and watched as a couple of dozen chickens came running and gathered around, clucking. He opened one of the six large metal barrels, took out a handful of cracked corn, and threw it to them. This was clearly what they were waiting for. They began pecking up the corn quickly before the newcomers who came in from every direction could take it from them. Stephen threw a little more of the corn, then closed the bin.

"It's almost sunset," he said. "You'd think they'd be too busy deciding where they were going to roost to watch the bin."

"Don't you care that you're never going to be a musician?" she demanded.

He looked down at his hands, rubbed them together. "Yes."

His voice had dropped low into his own private pain. She stood silent, feeling awkward, for once not knowing what to say. Then he looked up at her, smiled faintly. "It was an old passion," he said. "I haven't touched a violin for months. I didn't know what that would be like."

"What is it like?" she asked.

He began to walk so that she almost missed his answer. "An amputation," he whispered.

She walked with him, let him lead her out to the garden, passing the Wagoneer on the way. The sight of it jarred her, reminded her that she should be watching for a way of escape.

"Did you ever see food growing?" he asked, bending to turn a deep green watermelon over and look at its yellow bottom. "Ripe," he commented. "You wouldn't believe how sweet they are." He was distracting. He moved from one subject to another, drawing her with him, keeping her emotionally involved in whatever he chose.

"I don't care about food growing," she said. "Listen, Stephen, my father is a good doctor. Let him examine you—maybe the disease can be cured. If he can't help you himself, he'll know who can."

"We don't leave the ranch," he said, "except to bring in supplies and converts."

"You'll never be a violinist here!"

"I'll never be a violinist," he said. "Don't you think I know that?" He never raised his voice. His expression changed only slightly. But she felt as though he had shouted at her. She watched him with fascination.

"Why?" she asked. "What's holding you here?"

"I belong here. These are my people now."

"Why? Because they gave you a disease?"

"Yes."

"That doesn't make sense!" she said angrily.

"It will."

His apparent passivity infuriated her. "You were probably nothing as a violinist. You probably didn't have anything to lose. That's why you don't care!"

His face froze over. "If you want to get rid of me," he said, "go on saying things like that."

In that moment, she realized she did not want to get rid of him. He seemed human and the others did not. Just a few minutes with him had made her want to cling to him and avoid the stick people and animal children who were her alternative. But she would *not* cling to him. She would not cling to anyone.

"I don't care what you do," she said. "I don't understand why anyone would want to stay here, and you haven't said anything to help me understand."

"Nothing I say would really help." He sighed. "When your symptoms start, you'll understand. That's all. But try this. I was married. My wife played the piano—played it maybe better than I played the violin. We had a son who was only a year old when I saw him last. If I stay here, my wife can go on playing the piano. The world will go on being a place where people have time for music and beauty. My son can grow up and do whatever he wants to. My parents have some money. They'll see that he has his chance. But if I try to turn myself in, I know I'll lose control and spread the disease. I would begin the process of turning the world into a place with no time for anything but survival. In the end, Jacob and his kind would inherit everything. My son... might never live to be a man."

She was silent for several seconds when he finished. She found herself wanting to say something comforting, and that was insane. "You've sacrificed my family to spare yours," she said bitterly.

He pulled an ear of corn from its stalk, husked it, and began eating it raw. He tore at it like an animal, not looking at her.

"Someone sacrificed you, too," she said finally. "I know that. But Jesus, isn't it time to break the chain? You and I could get away together. We could get help."

"You haven't heard me," he said. "I knew you wouldn't. Listen! We're infectious for as much as two weeks before we start to show symptoms—except for people like you who won't have two weeks between infection and symptoms. How many people do you think the average person could infect in two weeks of city life? How many could his victims infect?—and with an extraterrestrial organism. There's no cure, Rane, and by the time one is found—if one can be found—it will probably be too late. It isn't only my family I'm protecting. It's everyone. It's the future. As Eli told me, the organism is a damned efficient invader."

"I don't believe you!"

"I know. Nobody believes it at first. I didn't."

Rane walked away from him as he picked a tomato and began to eat. He never washed anything. Ate them as they grew out of the dirt. Rane had never seen food growing this way before, but it did not impress her. She wondered whether they fertilized it with the contents of the outhouse and the animal pens. It was just the sort of filthy anachronistic thing they might do.

She climbed some rocks—huge, rough rounded mounds of granite—and stood on top, staring down. To her surprise, she saw the road winding below. Then Stephen was beside her. She started violently to find him there in a space that had been empty a second before. He must have leaped up, almost the way Jacob would leap.

"We can all jump," he said. "We can run pretty fast, too. You should remember that."

"I wasn't trying to get away."

"Not yet. But remember anyway." He paused. "Do you know how they caught me seven months ago?"

"You've only been here seven months?"

"I drove right into their settlement," he said. "I'd gone to see my folks in Albuquerque and on my way home, I decided to do some exploring. I discovered a mountain road that wasn't on my maps, and thought I'd find out where it led. I found out."

"Why were you driving?" Rane asked. "You should have flown."

"I loved to drive. It was a kind of hobby. I'll bet your father has the same affliction."

"Yeah. He has a Porsche and a Mercedes at home. He won't even drive them outside the enclave."

"A Porsche? You're kidding. What year?"

She looked at him, saw excitement on his face for the first time and laughed. Something familiar at last. Car craziness. "1982 Porsche 930 Turbo. My mother used to call it his other wife. My sister and I figured it was his other kid."

He laughed, too, then sobered. "It's getting dark, Rane. We should go in."

She did not want to go in—back to Lupe and Ingraham. Back to hands that made her cringe. Stephen's hands did not make her cringe any longer.

"I don't have a house, yet," he said. "I have a room in Meda's house."

She could not look at him now. She had never slept with a man. The thought of doing so now with a stranger—even a likable stranger—confused and frightened her. The thought of conceiving a child in this place—if you could call them children—terrified her.

"Back to Lupe, then," he said. He put his arm around her, and startled her by snatching her up and jumping off the rocks. They landed safe and unhurt amid stalks of corn. She thought she weighed at least as much as he did, but her weight did not seem to bother him.

"You're not a screamer," he said. "Good." He set her on her feet.

"Am I like your wife?" she asked timidly as they walked back.

"No," he answered.

"But... do you like me?"

"Yes."

She looked at him uncertainly, wondering if he were laughing at her. "I wish you talked more," she said.

Later that night, Lupe tied Rane to a bed.

"We don't have bars yet," Ingraham said. "You should have gone with Stephen."

"Shut up," Lupe told him. "Tying people up is no joke. Neither is trying to send a kid to bed with a guy she doesn't even know. We gotta find a better way. I'm sick of this."

Ingraham said nothing more.

Rane found no comfort in Lupe's sentiment. Tied as she was, she had to ask even to go to the bathroom. And she could not sleep on her side as was her custom. She lay miserable and sleepless, twisting her wrists in the hope of freeing at least one. The twisting hurt enough to make her stop after a while. Then she tried to reach one of her wrists with her teeth. And failed.

By then she was crying tears of frustration and anger. She was totally unprepared for the sudden weight across her stomach that knocked the breath out of her. This time she would have screamed if she had been able to.

She caught her breath, feeling as though she had been punched, then saw Jacob dim and shadowy in the darkness above her.

"You can't bite the rope," he said. "Your teeth are too dull."

"What are you doing here?" she demanded.

"Nothing." He stared down at her from the pose of a seated cat. "I came in the window."

Rane sighed, closed her eyes. "I think I'm glad you're here," she whispered. "Even you."

"Why don't you like me?" he demanded.

She shook her head, answered honestly because she was too tired to humor him. "Because you look different. Because I'm afraid of you."

"You are? Of me?" He sounded pleased. He also sounded closer. She opened her eyes and saw that he had stretched out beside her. She tried to draw away, but could not.

"You *are* afraid of me," he said gleefully. "I'm going to sleep here."

She could have called Lupe. She made a conscious decision not to. The boy was harmless in spite of his appearance, and he did not understand that what she feared was not him personally, but what he represented. Most important, she did not think she could stand to be alone again.

Sometime after midnight, when she had developed a headache from lack of sleep, he awoke and with unchildlike alertness, asked if her arms hurt.

"They hurt," she said. "And I can't sleep and I'm cold."

To her surprise, he pulled her blankets up to her chin. "Bikers put a rope on me," he said. "They pulled me and said, 'Heel, heel!' "

Rane shook her head in disgust. Jacob could not help what he was. He did not deserve such treatment.

"Daddy hit some of them and they died."

"Good for him," Rane muttered. Then she realized she was talking about Eli, who might even now be raping Keira. Confusion, frustration, and weariness set in heavily, and she could not stop the tears. She made no sound, but somehow, the child knew. He touched her face with one of his hard little hands, and when she turned her head away angrily, he turned his attention to her right wrist.

"What are you doing?" she demanded.

As though in answer, she found her wrist suddenly free.

"My teeth are sharp," Jacob announced. He climbed over her and started on her left wrist. In seconds, it too was free.

"Oh God," she said, hugging herself with aching arms and numb hands. She made herself reach out to the child. "Thank you, Jacob."

"You taste good," he said. "I thought you would. You smell like food."

She drew her hand back quickly, heard his gleeful laugh. Let him laugh. He had freed her. How the hell a four year old could have teeth that cut rope was beyond her, but she didn't care. If he had been a little less strange, she would have hugged him.

"Something is happening outside," he said.

"What?"

"People moving around and talking." He bounded off the bed and to the window. "They're your people," he said. He leaped silently to the high window sill, then down the other side.

Then even she heard the noise outside—a car starting, people running. There was shouting, and finally what must be happening penetrated her weary mind. Her people—her father and sister...

She got out of bed, taking time only to slip into her shoes and grab her pants and shirt. She threw both on over the thin gown Lupe had brought her from her luggage and she went through the window. She would have climbed through it naked if she had had to.

She got out in time to see the Wagoneer disappearing down the mountain road, stick people in hot pursuit. Her father had left her!

She took a few useless steps after them, then turned without conscious thought and ran in the opposite direction—toward the rocks she and Stephen Kaneshiro had stood on. Toward the road below where her father would almost certainly be passing soon. It occurred to her as she headed for the steep incline that she could be killed. The thought did not slow her. Either way, the stick people would not tie her down again.

PART 3

Manna

Past 15

Now Eli would become an active criminal as well as the carrier of a disease. Now, with the help of Lorene and Meda, he would abduct a man. He would take Meda's father's Ford and go to what was left of old U.S. 95. Meda knew 95 from State Highway 62 to Interstate 40. It was desolate country, she said. No towns, almost no private haulers on the road. Just a few daredevil sightseers, taking their chances among the bike packs and car families, and a few well-armed, individualistic ranchers.

Eli worried about taking Meda along. She was four months pregnant, and he worried about both her and the child. She was not an easy woman to become attached to, but the attachment had happened. Now he could not lose her. *He could not lose her.*

Meda had always been physically strong, had taken pride in being able to match her brothers at hard work and hard play. Now the disease had made her even stronger, and her new strength had made her overconfident.

She would not, she told Eli, sit at home, trembling and wondering whether her child's father had survived. She intended to see that he survived—and, he thought, maybe get herself killed in the process.

Eli swung from anger to amusement to secret gratitude for her concern. There were still bad times with her—times when she cursed him and mourned her family. But these times came less frequently. Both the disease organism and the child inside her were driving her toward him. Perhaps she had even begun to forgive him a little.

Now she helped him plan.

"We can hide here," she said, using an old paper auto club map. "There's a junction. A dirt road runs into Ninety-five. There are some hills."

All four of them sat clustered at one end of the large dining room table. Lorene, who was to have the new man if he lived; Gwyn, who was already pregnant again and in less immediate need of a man of her own; Meda; and Eli.

Covertly, Eli watched Gwyn, saw that she seemed at ease, uninterested in the map. A few weeks before, she would have torn the yellowed paper in her eagerness to take part and get a man for herself. Now, pregnant by Eli, she was content. The organism had turned them all into breeding animals.

"What do you think?" Meda asked him.

He looked at the map. "Damn lonely stretch of road," he said. "Anyone working here?" He pointed to a quarry that should have been nearby.

Meda shook her head. "Too dangerous. What this highway really is at that point is a sewer. From what I've heard about city sewers, the only reason they're worse is because they have more sewer rats. But the gangs here are just as dangerous, and the haulers... body-parts dealers, arms smugglers—that kind. The few holdout ranchers are dangerous too. If they don't know you, they shoot on sight."

"Dangerous," Eli said. "And close. Too close to us here. I used to see lights from Ninety-five when I went out at night." When he went out to kill and eat chickens to supplement Meda's mother's idea of three good meals. "I think I saw lights from State Highway Sixty-two, too. If we accidentally catch anyone important, I don't want search parties coming right to us."

Meda gave a short, bitter laugh. "People disappear out here all the time, Eli. It's expected. And nobody's important enough these days to search this country for."

Eli glanced up from the map and smiled. "I am. Or I would be if anyone knew I was alive."

"Come on," she said, irritated, "you know what I mean."

"Yeah. I hear bike gangs and car families can be damned vindictive, though, if they think you've hurt one of theirs. Let's go up to I-Forty. If things are bad there, we could even go on to I-Fifteen."

"That far?" Meda said. "Fuel, Eli."

"No problem. We'll take the Ford. With its twin tanks it can go just about anywhere within reason and come back without a fill-up."

"And there are more people on Forty and Fifteen," Lorene said. "Real people, not just sewer rats. I could get an honest hauler or a farmer or a city man." She sounded like an eager child listing Christmas possibilities. In a moment, Eli would have to make her hear herself. Left on her own, she could do a lot of harm before she realized what was happening to her.

"The Ford's been to Victorville and back without fuel problems," Gwyn said lazily. She was from Victorville, Eli knew. Christian had met her there, where she had worked with her brothers at their mother's roadside station. She shrugged. "I don't think we'll have a fuel problem."

Meda looked at her strangely, probably because of her lazy tone, then spoke to Eli. "I assume you want to use Ninety-five for going and coming."

"We can use it for going," he said. "If you think it's worth the detour."

She shook her head. "Car families set up roadblocks. Armored tour buses and private haulers just bull their way through, but cars get caught. Especially one car alone."

"We'll use this network of dirt roads, then. I like them better anyway. You know the best ones?"

She nodded. "In good weather, some of them are smoother than Ninety-five, anyway."

"And the dirt roads will give captives the idea they're more isolated than they are. They won't be able to prowl around and find out the truth the way I did until they've made it through the crisis period. After that, they won't care."

"Are you sure they won't?" Meda asked. "I mean... this is our home, but some stranger..."

"This will be his home."

Lorene giggled. "I'll make him feel at home. You just catch him."

Eli turned to look at her.

"You know," she said, still laughing, "this is the kind of thing you always read about men doing to women—kidnapping them, then the women getting to like the idea. I think I'm going to enjoy reversing things."

Silence. Meda and Gwyn sat staring at Lorene, clearly repelled.

"We won't touch him," Eli told Lorene. "We'll leave it to you to give him the disease."

Lorene's smile vanished. She looked from Meda and Gwyn to Eli.

"He might die on you," Eli continued. "If he does, we'll get you another one."

She frowned as though she did not understand.

"We'll get you as many as necessary," he said.

"You don't have any right to make me feel guilty!" she whispered. Her voice rose abruptly. "This is all your fault! My husband—"

"Remember him!" Eli said. "Remember how it felt to lose him. Chances are, you'll be taking someone else's husband soon."

"You have no right—"

"No, I don't," he said. "But then, there isn't anyone else to say these things to you. And you have to hear them. You have to understand what you are—why you feel what you feel."

"It's because you killed—"

"No. Listen, Lori. It's because you're the host, the vehicle of an extraterrestrial organism. It's because that organism needs new hosts, new vehicles. You need to infect a man and have children and you won't get any peace until you do. I understand that. God knows I understand it. The organism is a damned efficient invader. Five people died because I couldn't fight it. Now, it's possible that at least one person will die because you can't fight it."

"No," Lorene whispered, shaking her head.

"It's something we can't forget or ignore," Eli continued. "We've lost part of our humanity. We can lose more without even realizing it. All we have to do is forget what we carry, and what it needs." He paused. She had turned away, and he waited until she faced him again. "So we'll get you a man," he said. "And we'll turn him over to you. You'll give him the disease and you'll care for him. If he dies, you'll bury him."

Lorene got up and stumbled out of the room.

Present 16

When Blake and Meda had gone, when Ingraham had led Rane away, Eli and Keira sat alone at the large dining room table. Keira looked across at Eli bleakly.

"My sister," she whispered. Rane had looked so frozen when Ingraham led her out, so terrified.

"She'll be all right," Eli said. "She's tough."

Keira shook her head. "People think that. She needs to have them think that."

He smiled. "I know. I should have said she's strong. Maybe stronger than even she knows."

A woman carrying a crying child of about three years came into the house. The child, Keira could see, was a little girl wearing only underpants. She had a beautiful face and a dark, shaggy head of hair. There was something wrong with the way she sat on the woman's arm, though—something Keira could not help noticing, yet could not quite identify.

The woman smiled wearily at Eli. "Red room," she said.

He nodded.

The woman stared at Keira for a moment. Keira thought she stared hungrily. When she had gone into a room off the living room and shut the long, sliding door, Keira faced Eli.

"What's going on?" she said. "Tell me."

He looked at her hungrily, too, but then leaned back in his chair and told her. No more hints, no more delays. When he finished, she asked questions and he answered them. At one point, the woman and child came out of the red room and Eli called them to him.

"Lorene, bring Zera over. I want you both to meet Kerry."

The woman, blond and thin, came over with her hungry eyes and her strange child. She looked at Keira, then at Eli. "Why is there still a table between you two?" she asked. "I'll bet there's no table between that guy and Meda."

"Is that what I called you over here for?" he asked, annoyed. "Don't you want to brag about your kid a little?"

Lorene faced Keira almost hostilely.

Keira and the child had been staring at each other. Keira roused herself, met Lorene's suspicious eyes. "I'd like to see her."

"You see her," Lorene said. "She's no freak. She's supposed to be this way. They're all this way."

"I know," Keira said. "Eli has told me. She's beautiful."

Lorene put her daughter on the table and the child immediately sat down, catlike, arms braced against the floor.

"Stand up," Lorene said, pushing at the little girl's hindquarters. "Let the lady see you."

"No!" Zera said firmly. To Keira, that proved something about her was normal. Before Keira's illness, she had been called on to take care of little toddler cousins who sometimes seemed not to know any other word.

Then Zera did get up, and in a single fluid motion, she launched herself at Eli. He seemed to pluck her out of the air, laughing as he caught her.

"Little girl, I'm going to miss some day. You're getting faster."

"What would happen if you did miss?" Keira asked. "She wouldn't hurt herself, would she?"

"No, she'd be okay. Lands on her feet like a cat. Lorene does miss sometimes."

"I never miss," Lorene said, offended. "I just step aside sometimes. I'm not always in the mood to be jumped on."

Eli put Zera back on the table and this time, she walked a few steps, leaped off the table, and stood beside Lorene.

Keira smiled, enjoying the child's smooth, catlike way of moving. Then she frowned. "A kid that age should be kind of clumsy and weak. How can she be so coordinated?"

"We've talked about that," Eli said. "They do go through a clumsy period, of course. Last year, Zee fell down all the time. But if you think she's agile now, you should see Jacob. He's four."

"What will they be like when they're adults?"

"We don't know," Lorene said softly. "Maybe they peak early—or maybe they're going to be as fast as cheetahs some day. Sometimes we're afraid for them."

Keira nodded, looked at the child. She was perfect. A perfect, lean, little four-legged thing with shaggy uncombed hair and a beautiful little face. "A baby sphinx," Keira said, smiling.

"Think you could handle having one like this someday?"

Keira glanced at her, smiled sadly, then turned back to Zera. "I think I could handle it," she said.

Zera took a few steps toward her. Keira knew that if the child scratched or bit her, she would get the disease. Yet she could not bring herself to be afraid. The child was as strange a being as Keira had ever seen, but she was a child. Keira reached out to her, but Zera drew back.

"Hey," Keira said softly. "What do you have to be afraid of?" She smiled. "Come here."

The little girl mirrored the smile tentatively, edged toward Keira again. She was a little cat not sure it should trust the strange hand. She even sniffed without getting quite close enough to touch.

"Do I smell good?" Keira asked.

"Meat!" the child said loudly.

Startled, Keira drew back. She expected to be scratched or bitten eventually, but she did not want to have to shake Zera off her fingers. Anything as sleek and catlike as this child probably had sharp teeth.

"Zee!" Lorene said. "Don't bite!"

Zera looked back at her and grinned, then faced Keira. "I don't bite."

The teeth did look sharp, but Keira decided to trust her. She started to reach out again, this time to lift the child into her lap, but Eli spoke up.

"Kerry!"

She looked across the table at him.

"No."

His voice made her think of a warning rattle. She drew back, not frightened, but wondering what was wrong with him.

Lorene seemed angry. She picked up Zera and faced Eli. "What kind of game are you playing?" she demanded. "What's the kid here for? Decoration?"

Eli looked up at her.

"Don't give me that look. Go do what you're supposed to do. Then you can take care of her! And if she doesn't make it, you can—"

Eli was on his feet, inches from her, looming over her. Keira held her breath, certain he would hit the woman and perhaps by accident, hurt the child.

Lorene stood her ground. "You're soaking wet," she said calmly. "You're putting yourself through hell. Why?"

He seemed to sag. He touched Lorene's face, then Zera's shaggy head. "You two get the hell out of here, will you?"

"What is it!" Lorene insisted.

"Leukemia," Eli said.

There was silence for a moment. Then Lorene sighed. "Oh." She shook her head. "Oh shit." She turned and walked away.

When she had gone through the front door, Keira spoke to Eli. "What are you going to do?" she asked.

He said nothing.

"If you touch me," she said, "how soon will I die?"

"It isn't touch."

"I know. I mean—"

"You might live."

"You don't think so."

More silence.

"I'm not afraid," she said. "I don't know why I'm not, but... You should have let me play with Zera. She wouldn't have known and Lorene wouldn't have cared."

"Don't tell me what I ought to do."

She could not fear him—not even when he wanted her to. "Is Zera your daughter?"

"No. She calls me Daddy, though. Her father's dead."

"You have kids?"

"Oh yes."

"I always thought someday I'd like to."

"You've prepared yourself to die, haven't you?"

She shrugged. "Can anyone, really?"

"I can't. To me, talking about it is like talking about the reality of elves and gnomes." He smiled wryly. "If the organism were intelligent, I'd say it didn't believe in death."

"But it will kill me."

He got up, pushing his chair away angrily. "Come on!"

He led her into the hall and to a large bedroom. "I'm going to lock you in," he said. "The windows are locked, but I guess even you could kick them out if you wanted to. If you do, don't expect any consideration from the people you meet outside."

She only looked at him.

Abruptly, he turned and left the room, slamming the door behind him.

Keira lay down on the bed feeling listless, not quite in pain, but unable to worry about Eli, his guilt, the compulsion that would surely overcome him soon. Her body was warning her. If she did not get her medication soon, she would feel worse. She closed her eyes, hoping to fall asleep. She had the beginnings of a headache, or what felt like the beginnings of one. Sometimes the dull, threatening discomfort could go on for hours without really turning into a headache. She rolled over, away from the wet place her sweating body had made. *Clay's Ark* victims were not the only people who could sweat profusely without heat. Her joints hurt her when she moved.

She had decided she was to be left alone for the night when Eli came in. She could see him vaguely outlined in the moonlight. Apparently, he could see her much better.

"Fool," he said. "Why didn't you tell me you felt bad? You've got medicine in the car, haven't you?"

Not caring whether he could see or not, she nodded.

"I thought so. Get up. Come show me where it is."

She did not feel like moving at all, but she got up and followed him out. In the dining room, she watched him pull on a pair of black, cloth-lined, plastic gloves.

"Town gloves," he said. "People take us for bikers in stores sometimes. I had a guy serve me once with a shotgun next to him. Damn fool. I could have had the gun anytime I wanted it. And all the while I was protecting him from the disease."

Why are you protecting me? she thought, but she said nothing. She followed him out to the car, which had been moved farther from the house. There, she showed him the compartment that contained her medicine. She had left it on the seat once, not thinking, and someone had nearly managed to smash into the car to get it, no doubt hoping for drugs. They would have been disappointed. They might have gotten into her chemotherapy medicines and made themselves thoroughly sick.

"Where's your father's bag?" Eli asked.

She was startled, but she hid her surprise. "Why do you want it?"

"He wants it. Meda says she's going to let him examine her."

"Why?"

"He wants to. It gives him the feeling he's doing something significant, something familiar that he can control. Knowing Meda, I suspect he needs something like that right now."

"Can I see him?"

"Later, maybe. Where's the bag?"

This time, she couldn't help glancing toward the bag's compartment. It was only a tiny glance. She did not think he had seen it. But he went straight to the compartment, located the hidden keyhole, stared at it for a moment, then selected the right key on the first try.

"You never turn on any lights," Keira said. "Does the disease help you see in the dark?"

"Yes." He took the bag from its compartment. "Take your medicine to your room. All of it."

"The bag won't work for you," she said. "It's coded. Only my father can use it."

He just smiled.

She had to suppress an impulse to touch him. The feeling surprised her and she stood looking at him until he turned abruptly and strode away. She watched him, realizing he may have felt as bad as she did. His smile had dissolved into a pinched, half-starved look before he turned away.

She stood where she was, first looking after him, then looking up at the clear black sky with its vast spray of stars. The desert sky at night was fascinating and calming to her. She knew she should follow Eli, but she stayed, wondering which of the countless stars was Proxima Centauri—or rather, which was Alpha Centauri. She knew that Proxima could not be seen separately by the unaided eye. A red star whose light a little girl born on Earth longed for.

"Hi," a child's voice said from somewhere nearby.

Keira jumped, then looked around. At her feet stood a sphinxlike boy somewhat larger than Zera.

"Daddy said you have to come in," the boy said.

"Is Eli your daddy?"

"Yes. I'm Jacob."

"Does anyone call you Jake?"

"No."

"Lucky boy. I'm Keira—no matter what you hear anyone else say. Okay?"

"Okay. You have to come in."

"I'm coming."

The boy walked beside her companionably. "You're nicer than the other one," he said.

"Other one?"

"Like you, but not as brown."

"Rane? My sister?"

"Is she your sister?"

"Where is she? Where did you see her?"

"She didn't like me."

"Jacob, where did you see her?"

"Do you like me?"

"At the moment, no." She stopped and stooped to bring herself closer to eye level with him. Her joints did not care much for the gesture. "Jacob, tell me where my sister is."

"You do like me," he said. "But I think Daddy will get mad at me if I tell you."

"Damn right, he will," Eli's voice said.

Keira looked up, saw him, and stood up, wondering how anyone could move so silently in sand that crunched underfoot. The boy moved that way, too.

"Eli, why can't I know where my sister is?" she asked. "What's happening to her?"

Eli seemed to ignore her, spoke to his son. "Hey, little boy, come on up here."

He did not bend at all, but Jacob leaped into his arms. Then the boy turned to look down at Keira.

"You tell Kerry what her sister was doing last time you saw her," Eli said.

The boy frowned. "Keira?"

"Yes. Tell her."

"You should call her Keira. That's what she likes."

"Do you?" Eli asked her.

"Yes! Now will you please tell me about Rane?"

"She was with Stephen," Jacob said. "They looked at the cows and fed the chickens and Stephen ate some stuff in the garden. Stephen jumped with her and she didn't like it."

"Jumped?" Keira said.

"From some rocks. She liked him."

Keira looked at Eli, questioning.

"Stephen Kaneshiro is our bachelor," Eli said, heading for the house again. Keira followed automatically. "He saw the two of you and asked about you. I aimed him at Rane."

"And she likes him."

"I'd say so. This little kid reads people pretty clearly."

"Is she with him?"

"She could have been. Stephen said it was too soon for her, so she's alone. Kerry, she's all right, I promise you. Beyond infecting her, no one wants to hurt her."

"Keira," Jacob said into Eli's ear.

Eli laughed. "Yeah," he said. He looked at the boy. "You know it's time for you to go to bed. Past time."

"Mom already put me to bed."

"I figured she had. What'll it take to get you to stay there?"

Jacob grinned and said nothing.

"The kids are more nocturnal than we are," Eli said. "We try to adjust them more to our hours for their own protection. They don't realize the danger they're in when they roam around at night."

He held the door open for her and she went in. "There are bob-cats in these mountains, aren't there?" she asked. "And coyotes?"

"Jacob's in no danger from animals," Eli said. "His senses are keener than those of the big animals and he's fast. He's literally poi-son to most of the smaller ones—especially those that are supposed to be poison to him. No, it's the stray humans out there that I worry about." He stopped, looked at his son who was listening somberly. "Keira, you take your medicine, then go back to your room. There are some books in there if you want to read. I'm going to put this one to bed."

She obeyed, never thinking there might be anything else she could do. She caught herself feeling grateful to him for not hurting her, not even forcing the disease on her, though she didn't know how long that could last. Then she realized she was feeling gratitude to a man who had kidnapped her family. Her problem was she liked him. She wondered who Jacob's mother was. Meda? If so, why was Meda trying so hard, so obviously to get Blake Maslin into her bed? Perhaps he was there now. No, Jacob's mother must be someone else. She sat staring at the cover of a battered old book—something from the 1960s—written even before the birth of her father: *Ishi, Last of His Tribe.* She had intended to read, but she had no concentration. Finally, Eli appeared again to take her to her father.

That meeting was terrible. It forced her to remember that her liking for Eli could not matter. The fact that she was not afraid for herself could not matter. She had a duty to help her father and Rane to escape—and that terrified her. She did not underestimate the capacity of Eli's people to do harm. Her escape, her family's escape would endanger their families. They would kill to prevent that. Or perhaps they would only injure her badly and keep her with them in agony. She had had enough of pain.

But she had a duty.

"I shouldn't have let you see him," Eli said.

She jumped. She had been walking slowly back to her room, forgetting he was behind her. "I wish you hadn't," she whispered. Then she realized what she had said, and she was too ashamed to do anything but go into her room and try to shut the door.

He would not let the door shut.

"I thought it would be a kindness," he said, "to both of you." And as though to explain. "I liked the way you got along with Jacob and Zera. They're good kids, but the reactions they get sometimes from new people..."

She knew about ugly reactions. Probably Jacob knew more, or would learn more, but walking down a city street between her mother and her father had taught her quite a bit.

She reached out and took Eli's hands. She had been wanting to do that for so long. The hands first pulled back from her, but did not pull away. They were callused, hard, very warm. How insane to expose herself to the disease now that she knew she must at least try to escape. Yet she almost certainly already had it. Eli and her father had deluded themselves into believing otherwise, but she knew her own particular therapy-induced sensitivity to infection. Her father knew it too, whether or not he chose to admit it.

The hands closed on her hands, giving in finally, and in spite of everything, she smiled.

Past 17

Ironically, Eli, Meda and Lorene interrupted someone else's attempted abduction. Off Interstate 40, they found a car family or a fragment of a car family raiding a roadside station. There were few stations in the open desert these days. They offered water, food, fuels from hydrogen to fast-charge for electric cars, vehicle repairs, and even a few rooms for tourists.

"Stations help everyone," Meda said as they watched the fighting. "Even the rat packs usually leave them alone."

"Not this time," Eli said. "Hell, this isn't our fight. Let's see if I can get us out of here."

He could not. The Ford had apparently been spotted. Now, as Eli swung it around, the car people began to shoot at it. The Ford's light armor and bulletproof windows were hit several times, harmlessly. The bullet that hit the left front tire should have been equally harmless. Instead, the tire exploded. At the same moment, a high-suspension, tough Tien Shan pickup came across the sand from the station to cut the Ford off. They could not get back to the highway.

Eli stopped the Ford, and grabbed Gabriel Boyd's old AR-15 semiautomatic rifle. It wasn't the newest of old Boyd's collection of antiques, but Eli liked it. He slipped off the safety, and looked the Tien Shan over. Its too-large, crudely cut gunports presented the best targets. He aimed through one of the Ford's own custom crafted gunports. The Tien Shan's big openings were bull's-eyes. The barrel that emerged from one of them seemed to move in slow motion.

Eli fired. The rifle barrel in the Tien Shan jerked. Eli fired twice more, rapidly. The barrel in the Tien Shan slid backward, stopped, then remained still, pointed upward. Eli held back his last two rounds, waiting to see what would happen.

The Tien Shan sat silent. An instant later, Meda fired her rifle. Eli looked around, saw a man fall only a few feet from the Ford. On the opposite side of the car, Lorene fired her husband's rifle at a nearby rise. At first, it seemed she had done nothing more than kick up a puff of dust. Then a woman staggered from concealment, arms raised, one hand clutching her rifle by its barrel. As they watched, she fell face down into the sand.

Meda, who had probably been the best shot of the three of them before the disease, took aim at one of the other cars. She fired.

Again, nothing seemed to happen, but Eli swung the Ford around and charged the two cars. He had literally seen the bullet go through a window that was slightly open. And he could see through the tinted glass of that window well enough to know that Meda had made another kill. Others in the car had apparently had enough. The car turned and fled into the desert, followed by the third, unscathed vehicle.

"Amateurs!" Meda muttered, watching them go. "Why'd they have to come to us to get themself killed?"

Eli glanced at her, saw that she was actually angry at the car family for forcing her to kill. She was almost crying.

"Idiots!" she said. "Big holes cut for shooting! Open windows! Kids!"

"Probably," Eli said, reaching for her hand. She avoided him, would not look at him. "What they were doesn't matter," he said. "They meant to kill us. We stopped them."

"You should be glad they were amateurs," Lorene told her. "If they were more experienced and better equipped, they would have killed us."

Eli shook his head. "I doubt it. We don't die that easily. And did you notice not one of them got off a shot at us after they blew our tire?"

"Yeah," Meda said. "Amateurs!"

"More than that," Eli told her. "We scared the hell out of them. We moved so fast we seemed to be anticipating them. If they're amateurs, they must have thought we were pros." He sighed. "Whoever's in the station might think that, too, so I don't think we'd better hang around here to change that tire."

"A stationmaster, Eli," Lorene said hungrily. "A station man."

He glanced at her. "Maybe it's a station woman or a family like Gwyn's."

"We could see."

"No, Meda's right about these places. They help everyone. We might need them more than most people eventually. No sense closing this one down."

To their surprise, the stationmaster ended their argument for them by poking his head out the station door, then stepping out and making a perfect target of himself.

"I don't believe this," Meda said.

"He's crazy," Eli said. "He doesn't know what we might be—and he doesn't know whether there's anyone left alive in the Tien Shan."

Meda shook her head. "Well, he'll find out for us."

The man drew no fire. He went to the Tien Shan and looked into the cab. He smiled at what he saw there—which must have taken a strong stomach and strong hatred.

"I don't think he's the stationmaster," Eli said. "Stationmasters can be tough and solitary, but they're usually not suicidal."

"And not stupid," Meda said. "He could have held out in that station and yelled for help that would have wiped us and the car people out. This area is still patrolled."

Lorene got out of the car. Meda realized too late what she meant to do, reached out to stop her, but Lorene was too quick. She had shut the door and was exposed to the stranger. Eli and Meda moved in unspoken agreement to cover her. Later, if she survived, they could tell her what an ass she had been.

The man and anyone still inside the station could see both Lorene and her protectors. For the moment, this was another kind of stand-off.

"Can you believe she would risk her life for an ordinary little guy like that?" Meda asked.

Eli took a good look at the man. He was shorter than average, young—mid-twenties, perhaps—overweight, though not grossly fat. His hair was a dull black with no hint of any other color even in the bright sunlight.

"She could have done worse," Eli said. "He hasn't got anything wrong with him. And that extra fat is a good thing, believe me." Her leaner brothers could have used it. "And for her, he's doubly attractive—uninfected and male. Hell, I hope she likes him once she has him."

Meda glanced at Eli. "She will. She won't be able to help herself."

"Is that so bad?" he asked.

She shrugged, said with bitter amusement, "How would I know? I'm as crazy as she is." She rested her hand on his shoulder, finally.

He kept the hand comfortably captive as he watched the man and Lorene. The man was clearly afraid—not of Lorene, but of the two rifle barrels he could see protruding from the Ford. But he was also determined. Either he would live or he would die, but he would not do any more hiding.

"She's got him," Meda said.

Eli had seen. Lorene, clearly unarmed, had offered to shake the man's hand. With a look of uncertainty and dawning relief, the man had given his hand, then jumped as she scratched him. He jerked his hand away, but let her catch it again as she apologized. To Meda's visible disgust, Lorene kissed the hand. Thin as she was now, Lorene was still pretty. The black-haired man was obviously impressed with her—and confused and still suspicious.

"I think it's okay," Eli said. "I'm going over there."

"She doesn't need your help," Meda protested.

He ignored her, got out of the car, opened her door, and waited for her to get out. "Come on," he said. "Seeing an old pregnant woman like you will help keep him calm. Maybe we won't have to hurt him."

For a moment, she looked as though she might punch him, but he grinned at her. She sighed and shook her head, then walked with him to Lorene and her stranger.

"It's okay," Lorene said. "His name is Andrew Zeriam. He was a prisoner. That Tien's his truck."

"Is it?" Eli wanted to see the man's face when he answered. He did not trust Lorene's quick acceptance. The organism and her glands were doing too much of her thinking for her just now. "The car family kept you alive?" he asked Zeriam.

The man stared at him hostilely. "They did," he said. "And the truck's mine." He looked ready to fight if he had to. Not eager, but ready. "They would have killed me soon," he said. "They were planning to."

He was soft and plump and young. One of the car people had probably taken a liking to him. They might not have killed him at all if he had cooperated. His voice, his face, his posture said he had not. He was not a homosexual, then—fortunately for Lorene. And if no one dug too deeply into what had been done to him during his captivity, Lorene might be able to convince him to come with her willingly.

"I'm going to get that sewage out of my truck and get out of here," he said suddenly.

"No!" Lorene said quickly.

Zeriam looked at her. There was no softness in his eyes. He looked from her to Eli, questioning.

Eli shrugged. "She likes you."

"Who are you people?"

"Not another car family, man, don't worry. Shit, we just pulled in here to pick up some auto supplies. Tried to get out when we saw what was going on, but those fools wouldn't let us."

"I saw. I hate to say it, but I'm glad they wouldn't. You probably saved my life." He hesitated. "Listen... can I help you fix that tire?"

"Thanks," Eli said. "What happened to the stationmaster?"

Zeriam turned away. "God, I managed to forget about her for a couple of minutes. One of the women from the car family decoyed her out. The car rat limped in all alone, pretended to be having car trouble. She had to go through a half hour of pretending to try to fix the car and crying and giving a performance that should have been on TV before the stationmaster would come out to help. This is strictly a self-service station, you know. Stick in your cash or card and push the button. But the stationmaster took pity, came out, and the gang came in and grabbed her. While they were busy with her, I made it into the station."

"Did they kill her?" Eli asked.

"No. They get more fun out of killing people slowly."

"You don't look like they've done much to you," Lorene said.

Zeriam turned without looking at her and walked away toward his truck.

"Look," Eli told Lorene, "you lay off that one subject and show him how much you like him and we won't have to use force. You'll have him willing now as well as later."

"But why—"

"Lori," Meda said with more understanding than Eli would have expected. "That's not asking much. Don't you want him enough to do that?"

Lorene wet her lips and went after Zeriam.

Meda came to stand beside Eli. "The guy's nothing to look at," she said, "but there may be more to him than I thought."

"Yeah."

"Want me to help change that tire?"

"Hell no. What do you want to do? Have the kid early? Why don't you go in the station and see what's there that we can use. Without the stationmaster, this place is finished, anyway."

"There should be a Highway Patrol copter out here sooner or later," she said. "The stationmaster probably had a check-in schedule with them that she won't be keeping now."

"So we'll hurry."

Still she hesitated. "Eli, what do you think of that guy, really?"

Eli shrugged. "I think he's okay. And I think he might not want to go home right now. I think he might start to see Lorene as just what he needs."

She nodded. "That was the impression I got." She went into the station, finally. That was when Zeriam came over without Lorene to talk to Eli.

"You know she's trying to get me to join you," he said bluntly.

"I know," Eli told him.

"What the hell would I be joining?"

Eli smiled. "A little nineteenth-century ranch in mountains you can't even see from here. Chickens, hogs, rabbits... The place will work your ass off. So will she, I expect."

The man did not smile. "How many others?"

"One other. A woman."

"Three women? How the hell did you wind up with three women?"

Eli's smile vanished. "Accidentally," he said. "The way you wound up here accidentally."

They stared at each other for several seconds, Zeriam clearly not liking Eli's evasion, but not quite as willing to probe it as he had been. "So you live on a ranch with your harem. What do you need me for?"

"Nothing," Eli said. He jerked a thumb toward Lorene who waited beside the Tien Shan. "She needs you."

"What about you?"'

"I don't care. You're welcome as long as you'll share the work."

"What about Lorene?"

"What about her?"

Silence.

Eli gave a short laugh. "I don't own anybody, man. People do what they want to. If she likes you, she likes you."

Zeriam spent several seconds squinting at him in the sun. "Why do I believe you?" he said finally. "After that shit with the car gang, why should I believe anybody?"

"You dump your garbage?" Eli asked.

"The body? Yeah. Good shooting."

"Why don't you fuel up then. The ranch is a long way from here over a lot of lonely dirt roads."

They stared at each other for a moment longer, then Zeriam looked over at Lorene. She stood where she had been, waiting beside his truck, watching intently, and, though Zeriam did not realize it, listening.

Finally Zeriam went to her. She got into the truck with him and they drove around to the fuel lot.

Present 18

Keira knew what she wanted.

She was afraid Eli would leave without giving it to her because she was young and ill. She was afraid touching would be enough for him. But he showed no signs of wanting to leave.

"Why?" he asked her, rubbing her bare arms beneath the caftan's loose sleeves. "I never tried so hard to spare someone. Why did you do it?"

She liked the way his hands felt. Not bruising or scratching. Just rubbing gently. If everything he'd told her was true, he was enjoying it more than she was. She closed her eyes for a moment, wondering whether he really wanted his question answered. She did not think he did.

"I didn't want to be alone," she said. That was true, as far as it went. "And you. Why didn't you aim that guy Kaneshiro at me when he asked about me?"

His expression hardened and his hands closed around her arms. She smiled. "I think I want to answer your question honestly," she said. "I think I can say it to you."

She hugged him, then backed away, escaping his hands. The hands twitched and he took a step toward her.

"Wait," she said. "Only for a moment. Bear it for a moment while I tell you."

He stood still.

She took a deep breath, met his eyes. "I think..." she began, "I *know* part of the reason I want you is that I'm... dying. But it is you I want. Not just a warm body. Before you I didn't want anyone. There were some guys who wanted me, even after I got sick, but I never... I thought I would never..." She floundered helplessly, unable to finish, wishing she had not begun. At least he did not laugh at her.

"You might die," he said. There was no conviction in his voice. "Stephen Kaneshiro needs a woman whose chances are better. And you... I wanted you with me."

She let out a breath she had not known she was holding and tried to go back to him.

"Wait a minute," he said, holding her at arm's length. "Maybe I have a couple of things to say to you, too. I want you to know me. God knows why. It's always been to my advantage not to have people know me that well at first."

"You know why," she said quietly.

He could not keep his hands off her so he settled for holding one of her hands.

"You have a son," she said. "Who's his mother?"

"Meda."

"Meda?"

"She and I have two sons."

"You're married then?"

He smiled. "Not formally. Besides, I have four more kids by other women."

She stared at him, first in surprise, then imagining what her mother would have said about him. "I've heard about... men who do that," she said.

He smiled grimly. "Your mama told you to keep the hell away from sewer rats like that, didn't she?"

"At least." She wondered why she did not pull her hand away from him. Six children by five different women. Good God. "Why?" she demanded.

"Young women survive," he said. "Right now, we have the best balance we've ever had between men and women. Kaneshiro is the only extra man we've ever had. Now he's not extra any longer."

"But I am."

"You and your father, because you're related."

"So when women are extra, you get them."

"That's exactly right. And when men are found for them, I give them up. We began that way out of biological necessity. I was alone with three women. The organism doesn't permit celibacy for any reason other than isolation."

"But... What about Meda?"

"What about her?"

"Why do you have two kids with her?"

"She's as close to a wife as I'm ever likely to get." He looked a little wistful. "We always get back together."

"But... right now, she's with my father."

"Yes."

"You don't care?"

"I care—though not as much as I would if she weren't already a couple of months pregnant. She's taking care of your father and I'm taking care of you."

And Rane was alone, Keira thought. At least Eli had said she was. Keira wondered why she tended to believe him so easily. She wondered why the things he was telling her were not more disturbing. He was everything her mother had warned her against and more. And she did not doubt that her mother had been right.

Yet all she regretted was that she would not be able to keep him. Her own feelings were so irrational, they frightened her.

"If I told you I didn't want to be part of your harem," she said, "would you go away?"

She felt the hand that held hers stiffen. "I don't think so," he said. "I don't think I could."

She thought if she were ever going to be afraid of him, now would be the time. "Let go of me," she whispered.

His grip on her tightened, became painful, then was suddenly released. His hands were shaking. He looked at them with amazement. "I didn't even think I could do that." He swallowed. "I can't keep doing it."

"That's okay," she said. She took his hand again and felt the shaking stop. He gave her a slow smile that she had not seen before. It confused her, warmed her. She gave him her other hand, but felt utterly foolish because she could no longer look directly at him.

Because he did nothing for a while, apparently felt no need to hurry, she regained her composure. "You like what you are, don't you," she said.

"I didn't care much for it today."

"Because of me." She managed to look at him again. "But you like what you are most of the time. You think you shouldn't like being a majority of one, but you do like it."

He held her by the shoulders. "Girl, if you convert okay and get even more perceptive, you're going to be spooky."

She laughed, then looked at his hands. "Don't you have to scratch me or something?"

"I would if I weren't so sure I didn't have to."

"What?"

He drew her to him, kissed her until she drifted from surprise at the thrust of his tongue to pleasure at the way he warmed her with his hands.

"You see," he said. "Who the hell needs biting and scratching?"

She laughed and let him lift her onto the bed.

She expected to be hurt. She had read enough and heard enough not to expect the first time to be romantic and beautiful. And there was her illness to make things worse. She had never known it to make anything better. At least her medicine was still working.

Somehow, he managed not to hurt her much. He handled her like a fragile doll. She did not think she could have stood that from anyone else, but from him, it was a gift she readily accepted. She had some idea what it cost him.

Eventually, pleased and tired, they both slept.

It was ten to two when Keira awoke. She stumbled off to the bathroom, her mind barely awake until she saw the clock on the bookcase. Ten to two. Two. Oh God.

Eli himself had given her reason to go. If she stayed and somehow lived, he would pass her on to some other man. She did not want to be passed on.

And she did not want her father to leave without her—or try to leave and be killed because she could have helped and had not.

By the time she came out of the bathroom, she had made up her mind. But how to get away from Eli? The door was locked. She had no idea where the key was. In his clothing, perhaps.

But if she went searching through his clothing, then unlocking the door, he would awaken, stop her, and she would not get another chance.

She would have to hurt him.

She cringed from the thought. He had gone to some trouble to avoid hurting her. He was not exactly a good man, but she liked him, could have loved him, she thought, under other circumstances.

Yet for her father, she had to hurt him. After all, he had not only the key to the room door, but the keys to the Wagoneer. Without the car keys, her father might have to spend too much time getting into the car and getting it started. He would be caught before he drove a foot.

There was the clock—a nondigital antique with a luminous dial. It ticked loudly and needed neither batteries nor electricity. If she hit Eli with it, he could probably be hurt, but would he be knocked unconscious or would he wake up and knock her unconscious? The clock was heavy, but awkward and big. The elephant bookend would be better. She had noticed it when she put away the book she had tried to read. The space between the elephant's trunk and its body offered a good handhold. The base was flat and would do less damage, less gouging and cutting when she hit him. It was unpainted cast iron, dull gray, heavy, and already just above Eli's head on the headboard bookshelf.

She went back to the bed, climbed in.

"Hey," Eli said sleepily. He reached for her. The gentleness of his hands told her he probably wanted to make love again. She would have given a great deal to stay there with him.

Instead, she reached for the elephant, gripped its trunk, and brought it down with all her strength on his head.

He gave a cry not much different from the one he had given at orgasm. Frightened, she hit him again. He went limp.

She had hurt her own hands and arms with the force of her blows. She knew she was weak, had feared at first that she could not really hurt him at all. Now she feared she had killed him.

She checked quickly to see that he was still breathing, still had a strong pulse. She found blood on his head, but not much of it. He was probably all right.

She got off the bed, pulled on her caftan, and stepped into her shoes, then she tore into his scattered clothing. She found the car keys at once, but could not find the one for the room. The door was definitely locked, though she could not remember him stopping to lock it. And there was no key.

She went to one of the larger of the four windows. It was not locked with a key, but it was closed so tightly she could not budge it. She could break it, of course, but that would bring any number of people running.

On the bed, Eli made a whining sound, and she tore at the window. It opened inward rather than upward, but it had apparently been painted shut.

She tried the other large window and found the same thing. Finally she tried the two smaller center windows. When one of them opened, she dragged a chair to it, thankful for the rug that muffled the sound. She spent long desperate seconds trying to get the screen open.

In the end, she broke the catch, pushed the screen out, and jumped.

PART 4

Reunion

Past 19

I feel like hell," Andrew Zeriam whispered. "Everything stinks. Food tastes like shit. Light hurts my eyes..." He groaned.

"You want me to go away?" Eli asked. He spoke very softly. Zeriam sat in a darkened room—he had refused to lie down—and held his ears in this silent desert place, trying to shut out sounds he had not noticed before. What, Eli wondered, would happen if the disease spread to the cities? How would newly sensitive ears endure the assault of noise?

"Hell no, I don't want you to go away," Zeriam whispered. "I asked you to come in, didn't I?"

Silence.

"Can you see me, Eli? I can see you, and that's some trick."

"I can see you."

"It's pitch dark in here. It must be. It's night. The windows are shut. The lights are out. *It's dark!*"

"Yeah."

"Talk to me, Eli. Tell me what the hell is going on."

"You know what's going on. Lorene told you yesterday."

More silence. Then: "What are you that you can sit there and admit what she said is true?"

"I'm what you are, Andy—host to millions, or more likely billions, of extraterrestrials."

Zeriam lunged at him, swinging. Zeriam was faster and better coordinated than he had been, but he was not yet significantly stronger. Eli caught him, held him easily.

"Andy, if you don't sit your ass down or lie down, you're going to make me hurt you."

Zeriam stared at him, then burst into bitter laughter. "Hurt me? Man, you've killed me. You've killed... Shit, you may have killed everybody. Who knows how far this plague of yours will spread."

"I don't think I've killed you," Eli said. "I think you're going to live."

That stopped Zeriam's words and his struggles. "Live?"

"Your symptoms are like mine—weird, nerve-wracking, but not devastating. People who don't make it can't even stand up when they're as far along as you are. Hell, you're not even shaky."

"But... people die of this. Lorene's husband, Gwyn's..."

"Yeah. Some people do. The women didn't. I didn't. You probably won't."

"But you did this to me. You, ultimately, because you did it to Lorene. You're worse than a goddamn Typhoid Mary!"

"A what?" Eli asked. Zeriam had just become a history teacher a few months before his capture by the car family. Eli was used to either questioning or ignoring his historical allusions.

"A carrier," Zeriam said. "A disease carrier so irresponsible she had to be locked up to keep her from spreading her disease."

"It's not irresponsibility," Eli told him. "It's compulsion. You don't know anything about it yet—though you will. If I brought you an uninfected person now, you wouldn't be able to prevent yourself from infecting him. If you were without a mate the way Lorene was, nothing short of death could stop you from infecting a woman."

"I don't believe you!"

"You believe every word. You feel it. And you can't hide your feelings from us."

Zeriam turned away, paced across the room, then back. He glared at Eli. He looked around like a trapped animal.

"Andy?"

Zeriam did not answer.

"Andy, there's something you haven't noticed yet. Something that might help you realize you can have a life here."

"What?"

"Lorene is pregnant."

"She's what? Already? I've only been here three weeks."

"You two didn't waste any time."

"I don't believe you. You can't be sure."

"You're the one who can't be sure. I noticed the change because I've seen it before."

"What change in only three weeks?"

"She smells different," Eli said.

"You're crazy. She smells fine. She—"

"I didn't say she smells bad. Just different. It's a difference you'll learn to recognize."

"Hell, I ought to tell you how you smell."

"I know how I smell, Andy—especially to you. I've been through all this before. And you should keep in mind that you're beginning to smell as threatening, as wrong to me as I do to you. Later, we'll have to get used to each other all over again. The organism seems to pull women together and push men apart—at least at first." Eli sighed. "Now we can be men and work this out, work the ranch with the women and keep the disease to ourselves as much as possible, or we can let the organism make animals of us and we can kill each other—for nothing."

"We get a choice? It's not another compulsion?"

"No, just a strong inclination. But it will rule you if you let it. Lay back, and it will drive you like a car."

"So what are you doing? Holding it all at bay by sheer willpower? You're so full of shit, Eli!"

He was giving in to the organism, letting the smell of a "rival" male enrage him. No doubt it was easy. Anger was so much more satisfying than the uncertainty he had been feeling. He did not yet understand how easily his anger could get out of hand.

Eli stood up. "I'll send Lorene in," he said as he moved toward the door. Zeriam was bright. He would learn to handle inappropriate passions eventually. Meanwhile, Eli decided it was his responsibility to avoid dominance fights Zeriam could lose so easily and so finally.

Eli did not quite make it to the door. Zeriam grabbed his arm. "Why should you send her in here?" he demanded. "Keep her! You had her before. For all I know, it's your kid she's carrying!"

He was not saying what he believed. He had given himself over to the organism for the first time. There was no thought behind his words—nor behind his swing a moment later.

Eli caught his hand in mid-swing, held it, hit him open-handed before Zeriam could swing again. Eli struck twice more. He was in control because he knew Zeriam could not hurt him. If he had let the organism control him, if he had acted as though he were truly threatened, he would have killed Zeriam, and perhaps not even realized it until later, when he regained control.

As it was, Zeriam was not seriously hurt. He would have fallen, but Eli caught him and put him in a chair. There, he sat, nursing a split lip and coming out of a rage that had probably surprised even him.

"Eli," he said after a while, "how much of what you do is what you really want to do—or at least, what you've decided on your own to do." He paused. "How much of *you* is left?"

"You're asking how much of you will be left," Eli said.

"Yeah."

"A lot. Most of the time, a lot."

"And sometimes... insanity."

"Not insanity, Andy. Now is the most irrational time you'll have to face. Get through this, and you'll be able to deal with the rest."

Zeriam stared at him, then looked away. He was frightened, but he said nothing.

Later that night, he sat at the kitchen table and wrote Lorene a long, surprisingly loving letter. There was no bitterness in it, no anger. He wrote a longer letter to his unborn child. He had convinced himself it would be a son. He talked about the impossibility of spending his life as the carrier of a deadly disease. He talked about his fear of losing himself, becoming someone or something else. He talked about courage and cowardice and confusion. Finally, he put the letters aside and cheated the microbe of the final few days it needed to tighten its hold on him. He took one of Meda's sharp butcher knives and cut his throat.

Present 20

Blake worried about having to use lights to stay on the poorly marked dirt trail. He had night glasses—glasses that utilized ambient light—but he was afraid to trust them in this dangerous, unfamiliar place. Yet he knew he was giving Eli's people a beacon to follow—and he had no doubt they were following.

"I saw something," Rane said, right on cue. She had climbed into the back because the seats in front were intended for only two. "Dad, they're coming. Three or four of them. You can see them when the mountains aren't directly behind them. They're running without lights."

"They can see in the dark," Keira said.

"So they say," Rane answered contemptuously. "Anyway, unless their cars are as different as they are, I don't see how they can catch us."

"Keep your head down," Blake told her. "They could have guns with night scopes. If they do, they can see in the dark all right. And they know these roads."

"Where will we go?" Keira asked.

Blake thought about that, glanced at his dashboard compass. They were heading due north. To reach the mountaintop ranch, they had traveled southeast, then south. "Kerry, take a look at the map," he said. "Use I-Forty as your northernmost point and the Colorado River bed as your easternmost. Give it fifty miles west of the river bed and south of the highway. Look for towns and a real road. We'll probably have to go all the way back to Needles, but at least there should be a road."

"I wouldn't be surprised," Kerry said as she turned on the map and keyed in the area he had specified. He glanced over, saw Needles in the upper right hand corner of the screen and nodded.

"I didn't think any place could be as isolated as that ranch seemed to be," Keira said. "U.S. Ninety-five runs north to Needles. The problem is, I don't know where we are—how far we are from it. It might be to our advantage to stay on this road until we reach I-Forty."

Blake glanced at the map again. "Since we didn't cross Ninety-five on the way to the ranch, it has to be east of us."

Keira nodded. "Yes, maybe six or seven miles east, and maybe a lot more."

"Damn!" Blake grunted as the car bounced into and out of a hole. "I'm going to turn off as soon as I get the chance."

"We could wind up going twice as far as necessary," Rane said.

"Take another look behind you," Blake told her.

Both girls looked. Keira gasped when she saw how much closer the pursuers were.

"Watch for a turnoff," Blake said. "Any turnoff. I need a road I can see."

Keira leaned back in her seat, eyes closed. "Dad, Ninety-five has 'travel at your own risk' signs all over it."

He glanced at her. She knew what she was saying could not matter, but she had had to say it.

" 'High crime area,' " Rane read over Keira's shoulder. "It's a sewer! I didn't know they existed in the desert."

Blake said nothing. He had treated patients from city sewers—people so mutilated they no longer looked human, would never look human again in spite of twenty-first-century medicine. What the rat packs did to each other and to unprotected city-dwellers was not something he wanted to expose his daughters to. They knew about it, of course. The small armies of police who guarded enclaves kept out intruders, but they could not keep out information. Still, for sixteen years, he had managed to shield his daughters from the contents of sewers and cesspools. Now he was taking them into a sewer.

The turnoff they had been hoping for materialized suddenly out of the night, marked only by a dead Joshua tree. Blake turned. The new road was better—smooth, graded, straight. He increased his speed, slowly pulling away from the pursuers. The Wagoneer could travel. With its modified engine it was much faster now than it had been when it was made—as long as it was not running a half-seen obstacle course.

Just over six miles later, the second dirt road ran into a paved highway—U.S. 95. They had gone from north to northeast. Now they were headed north again on a road that would take them to Needles—to safety.

Abruptly there were headlights directly in front of them—two cars coming toward them on the wrong side of the highway. Two cars that clearly did not intend to let him pass.

Reacting without thinking, Blake swung right. To his amazement, he discovered he was turning onto a road he had not noticed— another paved surface that headed him back almost in the direction from which he had come. Back toward the ranch.

He was being herded, Blake realized. They were on the eastern side, the wrong side of 95 now, but it had not taken much to force him to turn the first time. He could be turned again, made to recross the highway. All his effort so far could be for nothing.

How had Eli's people gotten ahead of him?

He switched out the lights and turned off the road onto a dry wash. At almost the same moment, Keira shut off the glowing screen of the map. Now, let Eli's people prove how well they could see in the dark. Nothing, *nothing* would force Blake back to the ranch—force him out of the profession of healing and into a life of spreading disease. *Nothing!*

Lights.

A dirt road, smooth and level, cut across the wash just ahead. And along that road came a car. Only one. It could be a coincidence— some rancher going home, some hermit, a fragment of a car family, even lost tourists. But Blake was in no mood to take chances with anyone.

He turned onto the dirt road toward the oncoming car. Abruptly, he switched on his lights and accelerated.

The other car braked, skidded through the dust, swerved off the road into a thick, ancient creosote bush.

Blake sped on, knowing the dirt road must lead back to 95. He switched out his lights again, praying.

"That was a van," Rane said. "Eli's people have cars and trucks, but I didn't see any vans."

"You think they let us see everything?" Keira asked.

"I don't think that van was one of Eli's."

"I don't care whose it was," Blake said tightly. "I'm not stopping until I reach either a hospital or the police. We're not giving this damned disease to anyone else!"

"When Eli comes," Keira said softly, "it will be to kill us, recapture us, or die trying. He won't be frightened into a ditch by lights."

Blake glanced at her. He could hear certainty and fear in her voice. For once, he realized, he agreed with her. Eli and his people would do absolutely anything to prevent the destruction of their way of life. He could understand that. The life they had at their nearly self-sufficient desert enclave was better than what most people had these days. But there was the disease—no, call it what it was, the invasion. And that had to be stopped at any cost.

He remembered the thing running alongside his car on all fours. Running like an animal, a cat. Jacob. It was possible if this insanity spread, *it was possible* that he could have grandchildren who looked like Jacob. Things. Christ!

The highway was ahead, down a slope. It looked empty and safe. Blake felt if he could reach it, he would have a chance.

He accelerated, swung onto the highway, headed north again.

"We've made it!" Rane shouted.

Keira looked around. "Someone's back there. I can see them."

"Sewage. I don't see any—"

Lights again. Lights behind them, then abruptly, lights in front.

Blake was not aware of making the choice not to slow down. Apparently that choice had been made before, once and for all. He thought he saw a human shape leap from one of the cars, but the car kept coming. At the last instant, Blake tried to swerve up the slope and around. He did not quite make it. The front left corner of the Wagoneer hit the other car and Blake's head hit the steering wheel.

There was nothing else.

Past 21

Zeriam made it.

He almost failed, almost survived. He had done a thorough job on his neck, but it was half-healed when Meda found him dead. The front of his throat was gaping, but the sides were merely bloody and scarred.

Meda brought Eli to him. When Eli was able to think past shock, past sadness, past the terrible knowledge that Zeriam would eventually have to be replaced, he examined the man's neck.

"I wouldn't have made it," he said.

"Made what?" Meda asked.

"I wouldn't have died—even if I had managed to cut my throat. I'd heal all the way."

"From a cut throat without a doctor? I don't believe you."

"I was in a couple of dominance fights aboard ship." He paused, remembering, shuddered inwardly. "The first time, I was stabbed through the heart twice. I healed. The second time, I was beaten literally to a pulp with a chunk of metal. I healed. Barely a scar. It takes a lot to kill us."

She helped him clean up the blood. It was she who found the letters. They were sealed in envelopes and marked *"To Lorene"* and *"To my son."*

Meda stared at them for several seconds, then looked toward the bedrooms. "I'm going to wake Lorene," she said.

He caught her shoulder. "I'll do it."

She looked down and away from Zeriam. He felt her tremble and knew she was crying. She never liked him to see her when she cried. She thought it made her look ugly and weak. He thought it made her look humanly vulnerable. She reminded him that they were still humanly vulnerable in some ways.

For once, she let him hold her, comfort her. He took her out of the kitchen, back to their room and stayed with her for a few minutes.

"Go," she said finally. "Talk to Lorene. God, how is she going to stand this a second time?"

He did not know, did not really want to find out, but he got up to go.

"Eli?"

He looked back at her, almost went back to her; she looked so uncharacteristically childlike, so frightened. He did not understand why she was afraid.

"No, go," she said. "But... take care of yourself. I mean... no matter how strong you think this thing has made you, no matter what's happened to you... before, don't do anything careless or dumb. Don't..."

Don't die, she meant. She rubbed her stomach, looked at him. *Don't die.*

Present 22

Blake regained consciousness in darkness.

He lay still, realizing that he was no longer in his car. He was lying on something flat and hard—a carpeted floor, he thought after a moment. His head ached—seemed to pulsate with pain. And he was cold.

His discomfort kept him from realizing immediately that his hands and feet were bound. Even when he tried to rub his head and discovered he had to move both arms, he did not understand why at once. He thought there was something more wrong with his body. When, finally, he understood, he struggled, tried to free himself, tried to stand up. He managed only to writhe around and sit up.

"Is anyone here?" he said.

There was no answer.

He squinted, trying to penetrate the darkness, fearing that he might be blind. He remembered hitting his head as he sheared into the oncoming car. He probably had a concussion. And what else?

Finally, dizzily, he managed to turn around, see dim light outlining draperies. He could still see, then.

"Thank God," he muttered.

"Dad?"

He started. "Rane?" he said. "Is that you?"

"It's me." She sounded half awake. "Are you okay?"

"Fine," he lied. "Where the hell are we?"

"A ranch house. Another ranch house."

"Another...?"

"It wasn't Eli's people, Dad. I mean, they were chasing us, too, but they didn't catch us. A car gang caught us."

That took a moment to sink in. "Oh God."

"They think they can get a ransom for us. I made them look at your identification. Meanwhile, they've been exposed to the disease."

"If there was no break in their skins—"

"There was. I scratched one myself. He tore my shirt open and I tore some skin off his arm."

That shook Blake from one kind of misery to another. "Are you all right?"

"Yeah. A few bruises, that's all. Before anyone could rape me, they decided I might be worth more... intact."

"And Keira?"

"They let her alone too. She's right here. She was awake for a while—said she felt awful. Said she'd left all her medicine at Eli's."

"Is she tied?"

"We both are."

He tried to see them, thought he could see Rane sitting up.

"Shall I wake Keira?"

"Let her sleep. That's the only medicine she has left now. How long was I unconscious?"

"Since last night. But you weren't always unconscious. Every now and then you'd mumble and move around. And you threw up. They made me clean it with my hands still tied."

Concussion. And he had lost a day. He had also lost his freedom again. Worst of all, he had spread the disease. He had failed at all he had attempted. All. . . .

"There's going to be an epidemic," Rane whispered.

Blake inched over toward her, groped for her.

"What are you doing?"

"Give me your hands."

"Dad, we're not tied with ropes. That's probably why I can still feel my hands and feet. We're wearing cuffs—choke-cuffs."

Blake lay down again heavily. "Shit," he muttered. Everything the car family did to hold them sealed its doom and increased the likelihood of an epidemic. He tested the cuffs, doing what he could first to slip them, then to pull their bands apart. They were plastic, but felt surprisingly soft and comfortable as long as he did not try to get rid of them. Once he began to struggle, however, they tightened until he thought they would cut off his hands.

Pain stopped him. And the moment he relaxed, the cuffs eased their grip. People could be left hobbled as he was indefinitely. Choke-cuffs were called humane restraints. Blake had heard that in prisons—inevitably overcrowded—order was sometimes maintained by the threat of hobbling with such humane restraints. Hobbled prisoners were not isolated. They were left in with the general prison population—fair game. They frequently did not survive.

Lying on his back, helpless, eaten alive with frustration and fear, Blake knew how they must have felt.

Would it be possible to talk to the car family? Would there be even one member intelligent enough to understand the danger? And if there were one, what evidence could Blake show him? The bag was gone. Neither he nor the girls had symptoms yet. If Meda was right, there would be symptoms in a few days, but how far could a car family spread the disease in a few days?

"Is this their base?" he asked Rane. A true car family had no base, he knew, except their vehicles.

"This place isn't theirs," Rane said. "They took it. They killed the men and raped the women. I think they're still keeping some of the women alive somewhere else in the house."

Blake shook his head. "God, this is a sewer. There's only one source of help that I can think of—and I don't want to think of it."

"What? Who?"

"Eli."

"Dad... Oh no. His kind... they aren't people anymore."

"Neither are these, honey."

"But, please, I gave these all the information they needed to convince Grandmother and Granddad Maslin that we're prisoners. They'll ransom us."

"What makes you think people as degenerate as these will let us go after they get what they want?"

"But they said... I mean, they haven't hurt us." She groped for reassurance. "Let's face it. Grandmother and Granddad would ransom us if we were alive at all—no matter what had been done to us, but the car people haven't done anything."

Blake sat up, tried to see her in the darkness. "Rane, don't say that again. Not to anyone." If only she thought before she opened her mouth. If only she hadn't opened her mouth at all. *If only no other listener had heard!*

Unexpectedly, Keira spoke into the silence. "Dad? Are you there?"

Blake shifted from anger at Rane to concern for Keira. "We're both here. How do you feel?"

"Okay. No, lousy, really, but it doesn't matter. We were worried about you. You took so long to regain consciousness. But now that you're awake, and it's night... what would you think about one of us hopping over to one of those windows and signaling Eli's people?"

Silence.

"Rane wouldn't let me do it," Keira added.

Blake touched Rane. "So you had thought of it."

"Not me. I would never have thought of that. Keira did. Dad, please. Eli's people... I couldn't stand to go back to them. I'd rather stay here."

"Why?" Blake asked. He thought he knew the answer, and he did not really want to hear her say it, but it needed to be said. She surprised him.

"I can't stand them," she said. "They're not human. Their children don't even look human.... Yet they're seductive. They could have pulled me in. That guy, Kaneshiro..."

"Did he hurt you?"

"You mean did he rape me? No! There'd be nothing seductive in that. Nobody raped me. But in a little while, a few days, he wouldn't have had to. I'm afraid of those people. I'm scared shitless of them."

"That's the way I feel about these car people!" Keira said. "Rane... so what if you were sort of... seduced by Eli's people. I was, too. All it meant to me was that they weren't really bad people—not the way rat packs are bad. They're different and dangerous, but I'd rather be with them than here."

Blake began to inch across the room, making as little noise as possible. Hopping would have been too noisy.

"Dad, don't!" Rane begged.

He ignored her. If any of Eli's people were outside, he wanted them to know where he was. It was possible, of course, that they would simply shoot him, but he did not believe they would—they could have done that long ago. The Clay's Ark people wanted their captives—their converts—back. Perhaps by now they also wanted any salvageable members of the car gang and the ranch family. Mainly, they wanted to keep the disease from spreading, keep it from destroying their way of life. They had been totally unrealistic to think they could go on hiding indefinitely, but at the moment Blake was on their side.

He reached the window, managed to stand up, almost pulling down the drapes in the process. The leg restraints tightened as he stood.

The moon was waning, but still bright in the clear desert air. It was possible that someone outside might be able to see him in the moon and starlight, but he hoped Eli's people had told the truth when they claimed to be able to see in the dark. He pushed the draperies to one side and stood in plain view of anything outside. He could see hills not far distant. Before them was a shadowy jumble of huge rocks—as though there had been a slide—or perhaps merely weathering away of soil. The rocks could provide excellent cover for anyone out there.

Off to one side was a building that might have been a barn. From the barn extended a corral. The barn looked spare and modern. The people of this ranch had not lived in the nineteenth century. It was possible that even the cuffs had been theirs. A car family would not care whether restraints were humane or not.

Scanning as carefully as he could, Blake could see no sign of anyone. Still, he stood there, at one point holding up his hands to show that they were bound. He felt foolish, but he did not sit down until he felt he had given even an intermittent watcher a chance to see him.

Finally, he hopped away from the window and let himself down quietly so that he could roll back to where the girls were. He had not quite made it when the door opened and someone switched on a light. He found himself squinting upward into the face of a squat, burly man in an ill-fitting, new shirt and pants that were almost rags.

"Looks like you're going to live," he said to Blake.

Blake rolled onto his back and sat up. "I'd say so."

"Your people want you. Big surprise."

"I'm sure most of your victims have people who want them."

The man frowned at Blake as though he thought Blake might be making fun of him. Then he gave a loud, braying laugh. "Most of you walled-in types don't give a piss for each other, Doc. You don't know family like we do. But the hell with that. What I want to know is who else wants you?"

Blake sat up straighter, staring at the man. "What do you mean?"

The man pushed Blake over gently with his foot. "Those your own teeth, Doc?"

Blake writhed back into a sitting position. "Look, I'll tell you what I know. I just wanted to find out what's happened since I've been unconscious."

"Nothing. Now who else wants you?"

Blake wove a fantasy about Eli's people, made them just another rat pack with ideas no loftier than this one's. Ransom. He said nothing about the disease. There was nothing he could say to a man like this, he realized. Nothing that would not get his teeth kicked in. Or if the man believed him, he might shoot Blake and both girls, then run—on the theory that if he got away fast enough, he could escape the disease. Blake had known men like him before; confronting them with unfamiliar ideas was dangerous even in controlled, hospital surroundings.

He got absolutely no response from the man until he mentioned the mountaintop ranch. The moment he said it, he knew he was talking too much.

"Those people!" the burly man muttered. "I been planning for a long time to bury them. Maybe not bother to kill them first. Bony, stripped-down models. Shit, you're a doctor. What's the matter with those guys?"

"They never gave me a chance to find out," Blake lied. "I think they're taking something." Drugs. That was something a sewer rat could understand.

"I *know* they're taking something," the man said. "One time I saw a couple of them running down jack rabbits and eating them. I mean like a coyote or a bobcat, tearing into them before they were all the way dead."

Blake blinked, repelled and amazed. "You *saw* them do *that?*"

"I said I did, didn't I? What have they got, Doc, and what do you think it's worth?"

"I tell you, I don't know. We were prisoners. They didn't tell us anything."

"You got eyes. What did you see?"

"Dangerous, bone-thin people, faster than average, stronger than average, and close."

"What close?"

"They give a piss for each other. Listen, who are you, anyway?"

"Badger. I head this family."

He looked the part. "Well, Badger, I didn't get the impression these people knew how to forgive and forget. They probably see us as their property. They probably want us back—or maybe they'll settle for a share of our ransom."

"Share? You've got too much sun, man. Or they have. What are they doing, growing something?"

"*I don't know!*"

"I gotta know. I gotta find out! Shit, it must be good stuff."

"They look like a strong wind would blow them away, and you think they have good stuff?"

Badger kicked Blake again, this time less gently. Blake fell over. "You're a doctor," Badger said. "You ought to know! What the hell is it?" Another hard kick.

Through a haze of pain, Blake heard one of the girls scream, heard Badger say, "Get away from me, cunt!" heard a slap, another scream.

"Listen!" Blake gasped, sitting up. "Listen, they have a garden!" His head and his side throbbed. What if his ribs were broken? Meda had said broken bones would be fatal to him now. "Those people have a big garden," he said. "They never really let us see what they grew there. Maybe if you could—"

He was cut off by the crack of a shot. The sound echoed several times into a world that had otherwise gone silent. Another shot. It hit the window near them, somewhere near ceiling level, then ricocheted with an odd whine. More bulletproof glass. A house located where this one was was probably hardened as much as possible against any form of attack.

Someone outside had perhaps seen or heard Blake. Someone outside was either a bad shot trying to kill him or a good shot trying to protect him.

"Shit!" Badger muttered. He turned and ran from the room, slamming the door behind him.

"If we could break the windows," Keira said when he was gone, "Eli's people might come in and get us."

And Rane: "If bullets couldn't break them, we sure can't with our bare hands."

"But we've got to get out! That guy Badger is crazy. If he kicks Dad's ribs in, Dad will die!"

Blake lay listening to them, thinking he should say something reassuring, but now that the danger was less immediate, he could not make the effort. His side and head were competing with each other to see which could hurt more. He lay still, eyes closed, trying to breathe shallowly. He was desperately afraid one or more ribs were already broken, but he could do nothing. He felt consciousness slipping away again.

"I'm going to try something," he heard Keira say.

"There's nothing to try," Rane told her.

"Shut up. Let me do something for a change." She paused, then spoke in an ordinary voice. "Eli or whoever's out there, if you can hear me, fire three more times."

There was nothing.

"What did you expect?" Rane demanded. "All that stupid talk about seeing in the dark and being able to hear better than other people—"

"Will you shut up?" Keira tried again. "Eli," she said, "maybe we can distract them. We can help you get them. You'll want them now that they've been exposed to the disease. Help us and we can help you."

More silence.

Keira spoke again softly. "I'm sorry I had to hit you." She hesitated. "But I did have to. You told me I couldn't have you, then you made me choose between the little I could have and my father and sister. What would you have done?"

For a long while, there was no sound at all. Then it seemed to Blake in his pain, in his confusion at what he had heard his daughter say, he heard three evenly timed shots.

PART 5

Jacob

Past 23

Meda wanted a girl.

Eli merely wanted Meda to survive and be well. When that was certain, he would concern himself with the child.

He worried about her in spite of his confidence in the organism's ability to keep its hosts alive. This was something new, after all. None of the *Ark*'s crew had been able to have children during the mission. Their anticonception implants had been timed to protect them and had worked in spite of the organism since no doctor had survived to remove them.

Before the *Ark* left, there had been discussion of the unlikely possibility (emphasized by the media and de-emphasized by everyone connected with the program) that the crew might find itself stranded and playing Adams and Eves on some alien world. Thus, the effectiveness of the implants was intended to last only through the time allotted to the mission and the quarantine period scheduled to follow it. In spite of everything, Eli had been pleased to discover that his had worn off right on time.

Another fear played up by the media and down by everyone in the program was the possibility that faster-than-light travel might have some negative effect on conception, pregnancy, and childbirth. The Dana Drive that powered the *Ark* involved an exotic combination of particle physics and psionics. Parapsychological mumbo jumbo, it had been called when Clay Dana presented it. Even when he was able to prove everything he said, even when others were able to duplicate his work and his results, there were outspoken skeptics. After years of tedious, uncertain observation of so-called psychic phenomena, after years of trickery by "psychic" charlatans, some scientists in particular found their prejudices too strong to overcome.

But the majority were more flexible. They accepted Dana's work as proof of the psionic potential—specifically, the psychokinetic potential—of just about everyone. Some saw this potential in military terms—the beginnings of a weapons delivery system as close to teleportation as humanity was likely to come. Others, including Clay Dana himself, saw it as a way to the stars. Clay Dana and his supporters demanded the stars. They had clearly feared turn-of-the-century irrationality—religious overzealousness on one side, destructive hedonism on the other, with both heated by ideological intolerance and corporate greed. The Dana faction feared humanity would extinguish itself on Earth, the only world in the solar system that could support human life. There were always hints that the Dana people knew more than they were saying about this possibility. But what they said in Congress, in the White House, to the people by way of the media, turned out to be enough—to the amazement of their opposition. The Dana faction won. The *Ark* program was begun. The first true astronauts—star voyagers—began their training.

Because of the psychokinetic element, a human crew was essential. The Dana drive amplified and directed human psychokinetic ability. Surprisingly, some people had too much psychokinetic potential. These could not be trusted with the drive. They overcontrolled it, affected it when they did not intend to, made prototypes of the *Clay's Ark* "dance" off course. Only strange, old Clay Dana tested out as having too much ability, yet was able to control his drive with a psionic feather touch. Both Eli and Disa had been able to pilot the prototypes and later the *Ark* itself. This meant they were psionically ordinary. And for some reason, old Dana had taken a liking to them, though Disa admitted to being a little afraid of him. And what she felt about Dana, was what a lot of people watching their TV walls felt about the *Ark* crew and backup crew. People were curious, but a little afraid—and envious. Earth was becoming less and less a comfortable place to live. Thus it was necessary that the crew have weaknesses and face serious dangers. People knew children had been born on the moon and in space safely, but the gossip networks with their videophone-in shows and their instant polls, their interviews and popular education classes, jacked up their ratings with hours of discussion of whether or not faster-than-light travel could be dangerous to pregnant women and their children. There was even a retrogressive women's protection movement intended to keep women off the *Ark*.

Eli and Disa were too busy to pay much attention to TV nonsense, as they thought of it, but they went along when the implants were proposed. And Eli left frozen sperm behind—just in case—and Disa left several mature eggs.

Now, Eli wished somehow that his frozen sperm could have been used to impregnate Meda. He knew this was not a reasonable wish, under the circumstances, but he was not feeling very reasonable. He watched Lorene walk Meda back and forth across the room. Meda did not want to walk, but she had tried both sitting and lying down. These, she said, made her feel worse. Lorene walked her slowly, said it would not do her any harm. Lorene had had some nursing experience at a birth center before she married. She had trained to be a midwife to women too poor to go to the better hospitals and too frightened to go to the others.

Meda stopped for a moment beside Eli's chair, rested her hand heavily on his shoulder. "What are you doing?" she asked. "Feeling guilty and helpless?"

He only looked at her.

She patted his shoulder. "Men are supposed to feel that way. They do in the books I've read."

He could not help himself. He laughed, stood up, kissed her wet forehead, then walked with her a little until she wanted to sit down in the big armchair. He was surprised she did not want to lie down, but Lorene did not seem surprised so he said nothing. He pulled another chair over and sat beside her, holding her hand and listening as she panted and sometimes made low noises in her throat as the contractions came and went. He was terrified for her, but he sat still, trying to show strength and steadiness. She was doing all the work, after all, pushing, enduring the pain and risk, giving birth to their child without the medical help she might need. If she could do that and hold together, he could hold together, too.

She never screamed or used any of the profanity she had picked up from him. In fact, she seemed surprised that the birth happened so easily. The baby, when it came, looked like a gray, hairless monkey, Eli thought. By the time Lorene had tied and cut the cord and cleaned the baby up, it was not gray any longer, but a healthy brown. Lorene wrapped it in a blanket and handed it to Meda, still in her chair. Meda examined it minutely, touching and looking, crying a little and smiling. Finally, she handed the child to Eli. He took it eagerly, needing to hold it and look at it and understand that this was his son.

The baby never cried, but it was clearly breathing well. Its eyes were calm and surprisingly lively. Its arms were long and slender—without the baby pudgyness Eli had expected, but he had no real idea how a newborn should look. Maybe they grew pudgy later, or maybe *Clay's Ark* babies never grew pudgy. It was enough that this baby seemed healthy and alert. Its legs were doubled against its body, but freed of the blanket, they straightened a little and kicked in the air. They were as long and slender as the arms. And the feet were long and narrow. Eli looked at the little face and the child seemed to look back curiously. He wondered how much it could see. It had a full head of thick, curly black hair and large ears. When it yawned, Eli saw that it already had several teeth. That could make nursing hard on Meda.

Eli reached for a tiny, thin hand and the boy grasped his finger surprisingly tightly. After a moment, Eli grinned.

The child startled him by smiling back at him. Somehow, it did not seem to be mirroring his grin. Its smile seemed almost sly—the unbabylike gesture of one who knew something he was not telling.

Present 24

Somehow, Blake lost track of time. He was aware of sporadic shoot-ing, aware that the house was under siege, that Rane and Keira were first with him, then gone. He worried about them when he realized they were gone, wondered where they were. He worried about his own helplessness and confusion.

Once the man called Badger came in to see him, bringing several other people along. The group shouted and stank and made Blake feel sicker than ever—all but one woman. She was no cleaner than the others, but her scent was different, compelling. She was just another car rat, but he found himself reaching out to her, groping for her with his cuffed hands. He heard shouts of laughter, then her voice, low and mocking.

"Hey there," she said, taking his hands. "You're not going to die on us, are you? Nobody'll buy you back dead." She had a deep, throaty voice that would have been sexy had it not been so empty of caring. He knew she was laughing at him—at his pain, at his help-lessness, even at his interest in her. He knew, but all he could think about was that he wanted her. He could not help himself. Her scent drew him irresistibly. He tried to pull her down beside him. She laughed and pulled away.

"Maybe later, wallie," she whispered. At least she had the kindness to whisper, not shout like the others. He was confused for a moment by her calling him "wallie." She knew his name. They all did. Then, murkily, he realized she was referring to the fact that he lived in a walled enclave. He wondered whether he would ever see it again.

The woman nudged him with her foot. "How about that?" she said. "Want me to come back when you're feeling better?"

Her friends brayed out their laughter.

But she did come back that night. And this time she only pre-tended to mock him as she unbound his hands and feet. "Don't do anything dumb now. You hurt me or get outside this room, Badger will cut your head off."

He opened his eyes and saw that she was nude, kneeling down beside him on the rug of his bare room. She fumbled with his belt. "Let's see what you've got, wallie. Big old rifle or little handgun."

For a moment, he thought she was Meda, but her hair, now free of the scarf she had worn before, was a startling white. She was a tall, sun-browned woman, plump, but not really fat. Her scent was incredible. It so controlled him, he could not focus on whether she was pretty or not. It did not matter.

He could not have thought he had the strength to hold her as he did with his newly freed hands and make love to her once and again and again. In the end, the woman seemed surprised herself, and pleased, willing to drop some of her carrat emotional armor. Without being asked, she got him a blanket from somewhere. He remembered Rane and Keira trying to beg one for him, and being refused. When he asked the woman for food, she brought him a cold beer and a plate of bread and roast beef left over from the car gang's dinner. The gang, sealed in as it was, had been living off the ranch family's large pantry and freezer.

The meat was too well-done and too highly seasoned for Blake's newly sensitive taste, but he ate it anyway. The gang fed him as well as they ate themselves, but it was not enough. It was never enough. He consumed the extra meal ravenously.

"You eat like a damn coyote," the woman complained. "You want some more?"

He nodded, his mouth full.

She got him more and watched while he ate. He wondered why she stayed, but he did not mind. He did not want to be alone. The food made him feel much better—less totally focused on his discomfort. "Who the hell are you, anyway?" he asked.

"Smoke," she said, touching her hair.

"Smoke," he muttered. "First Badger, now Smoke."

"Those are our family names," she said. "We don't keep the same names once we're adopted into a family. My name before was Petra."

He smiled. "I like that better. Thank you, Petra."

To his surprise, she blushed.

"Are my daughters all right?" he asked.

She looked surprised. "They're okay. They say you screamed at them to get out. Hell, we heard you screaming. And with what you were calling them, we didn't figure they were your blood daughters. We thought you might hurt them."

Screaming? He did not remember. Screaming at Rane and Keira? Why?

Fragments of what seemed to be a dream began to drift back to him. But it was a dream of Jorah, his wife, not of the girls. Jorah, smooth and dark as bittersweet chocolate, soft and gentle, or so people thought when they saw her or heard her voice. Later they discovered the steel the softness disguised.

The dream recaptured him slowly, and he could see her as she had been with the cesspool kids she taught. The kids liked her or at least respected her. They knew she cared about them. The bigger, more troublesome ones knew she had a gun. She was too idealistic for her own good, but she was not suicidal.

He saw her as she had been when he met her at UCLA. He was going to fight diseases of the body and she, diseases of a society that seemed to her too shortsighted and indifferent to survive. She preached at him about old-fashioned, long-lost causes—human rights, the elderly, the ecology, throwaway children, corporate government, the vast rich-poor gap and the shrinking middle class.... She should have been born twenty or thirty years earlier. He could not get particularly involved in her causes. He did not believe there was anything he could do to keep the country, the world from flushing itself down the toilet. He meant to take care of his own and do what he could for the others, but he had few illusions.

Still, he could not keep away from her. She was an earlier, happier compulsion. He let her preach at him because he was afraid if he did not, she would find someone else with open ears. He knew her family did not like her interest in him. They were people who had worked themselves out of one of the worst cesspools in the southland. They had nurtured Jorah's social conscience too long to let it fall victim to a white man who had never suffered a day in his life and who thought social causes were passé.

He married her anyway, had two daughters with her, even acquired something of a social conscience through her. Eventually, he began putting in time at one of the cesspool hospitals. It was like trying to empty the Pacific with a spoon, but he kept at it—as she kept at her teaching until a young sewer slug blew away most of the back of her head with a new submachine gun. The slug was thirteen years old. He did not know Jorah. He had just stolen the gun and wanted to try it out. Jorah was handy.

Why had Blake dreamed of her, then recalled her so vividly? And what did she have to do with his driving Rane and Keira away?

"Are they really your kids?"

He jumped, looked around, was surprised to see that Petra was still there.

"The two girls. Are they your kids?"

"Of course."

"Shit, I felt sorry for them. You were calling them sluts and whores and slugs and sewage—everything you could think of. One of them was crying."

"But... why would I do that?"

"You asking me? Hell, who knows? You hit your head pretty hard against the steering wheel. Maybe you just went crazy for a while."

"But..." But why had he dreamed of Jorah? Such a realistic dream—as though she were with him again. As though the utterly senseless killing had never happened. As though he could touch her, love her again.

Keira.

His mind flinched away from thinking of her. She was a too-thin, too-frail, younger version of Jorah. She had that same incredible skin. And she had, Blake knew, more of her mother's steel than most people realized.

Christ, had he tried to rape Keira?

Had he?

The girl was so weak. Could he have tried and failed? "Jesus," he whispered.

"You okay?" Petra asked.

He looked at her, realized she was only a few years older than Rane and Keira. A young girl, still able to drop the carrat identity and take pleasure in doing so.

"I'm all right," he lied. "Listen, now that you've told me about the girls, I have to see them. One of them, at least. I have to apologize."

She looked away. "I don't know if I can bring them."

He understood her, and wished he had not. The girls might not be alone. "Try," he said, "please."

"Okay." But she stopped to kiss him and he was caught up again in the scent and feel of her. She giggled like a delighted child and lay down with him again.

By the time she went away and came back with Keira, he was badly frightened. He was no longer in control of himself. Tiny microbes controlled him, had forced him to have sex with a young girl when an instant before, sex had been the farthest thing from his mind. What had they made him do to his daughter?

Keira came into the room much as she had come into another room—how many days ago? Eli had released her then for a few painful minutes. Who had released her this time? God, what would Jorah think of the way he was taking care of their children?

"Dad?"

She had a bruise on the side of her face. It was swollen and puffy. She could not conceal the fact that she did not want to get near him. And, heaven help him, her scent was as good as Petra's had been.

"Did I hit you?" he asked, looking at her swollen face.

She shook her head. "Rane did."

"Why?"

She stared at him for several seconds. "You don't remember, do you?" She took a step farther back from him. "Jesus, I wish I didn't."

He said nothing, could not make himself speak.

She went to the window, pushed the drape aside, and seemed to examine the frame. "This house won't burn," she said. "Light it and it will smolder a little, then go out. Eli's people have tried lighting it a few times. I think one of them was shot in the attempt."

"They tried to burn the house with us in it?"

"Badger called for help on his radio. They heard him. Or if they didn't hear him, they heard me when I repeated what he said next to the kitchen window." She turned to face him. "I can hear them sometimes, Dad. When the car people aren't making too much noise, I can hear them talking. I heard Eli."

"Saying what?"

"That if everything goes okay, the car people will go over to him when their symptoms begin. If it doesn't, if the help Badger called for actually comes, Eli might have to sacrifice us."

"Sacrifice...?"

"They have some explosives already planted. They don't want to do it, but... well, they can't let anyone in the house leave."

"Kerry, did I rape you?" He had said the words. And somehow, they had not choked him.

She swallowed, went to the door and stood beside it. "Almost."

"Oh God. Oh God, I'm sorry."

"I know."

"Rane stopped me?"

"Yes." She hesitated. "Rane stopped us. I... I wasn't exactly fighting."

He frowned, repelled and uncomprehending.

"Don't look at me like that," Keira said. "I know how I smell to you—and how you smell to me. I had to see you to be sure you were okay. But... I'm afraid of you—and of myself. It's so crazy. Rane hit me mostly to get my attention so I'd stop fighting her when she tried to pull me away. She said when she hit you, you didn't seem to feel it." Keira rubbed her face. "I sure felt it."

Blake moved away from her because he wanted to move toward her so badly. "Were you hurt otherwise?"

"No."

"How do you feel?"

She stared past him, surprising him with the beginnings of a smile. "Hungry," she said. "Hungry again."

Keira believed she was going to live. She felt stronger and hungry. Her hearing was startlingly keen. That was enough for her. The fact that she was still a captive, still the carrier of a dangerous disease, still caught between warring gangs had almost ceased to matter to her. Those things could not cease to matter to Blake.

When Petra had taken Keira away, he went over the bare room as he could not have with bound hands and feet. He peeled back the rug, looking for loose flooring. He examined the walls, even the ceiling. Finally, he examined the closet-like bathroom—a toilet, a sink, and a tiny window that did not open. None of the windows opened. The air conditioning was good. The air stayed fresh and probably would until Eli decided to foul it, but the air-conditioning ducts were too small to be of use to Blake.

Because he was desperate, Blake tried pushing at the glass—or the plastic—in the window. It was only one small pane. It might be breakable.

It did not break. But the frame gave a little. Blake took off his shirt, wrapped his right hand in it, and as quietly as he could, began trying to pound the entire window out. Even if he knocked it loose, the hole would be almost too small to crawl through. But he felt stronger now, and anything would be better than sitting around like a caged animal, waiting for someone else to decide his fate.

When his right hand tired, he continued the pounding with his left. The muffled sound was loud to him, but no one else seemed to notice. He realized now that he could not trust his hearing to tell him what sounds might be reaching normal people.

Finally, the window fell out onto the ground. The noise that it made when it hit and bumped against the house was loud. Blake heard someone call out, then heard the sound of approaching motors. Frightened, he hesitated. Keira had said Badger had called for reinforcements. What if he escaped from one group into the hands of another? On the other hand, if he stayed where he was, the window would be discovered and he would be shackled again. They would take no more chances with him.

As the sounds of approaching motors grew louder, he made up his mind. He was at the rear of the house. He could not see the road or the approaching cars or cycles so he was certain the newcomers would not be able to see him. Eli's people might see him, but he did not think they would shoot. He hoped he could escape them too and get real help. Medical help, finally. Meanwhile, he prayed they would rescue the girls and keep them safe—since he could no longer trust himself near them.

He feared that if he reached a town, a hospital, his chances of seeing the girls again would be slim. They would be going into Eli's world, going underground, becoming whatever the organism would make of them. He would be beginning a war against the organism.

He managed to squeeze out of the window, leaving a little skin behind, and drop quietly to the ground. He ran toward the rocks, expecting at every moment to be shot in the back or accosted from the rocks by Eli's people. But in front of the house, the approaching cars had arrived and the shooting had begun. All the hostilities were there.

Blake ran on. From the rocks, he could climb into the hills and get a look around. He could find out where the road was, figure out which way was north. He could head for Needles—on foot this time. He could do the necessary things—give his warnings, get the research started.

He moved quickly, but with no feeling of triumph this time. He wondered whether Rane and Keira would understand his leaving them. He wondered whether they would forgive him. He knew better than to suppose he would forgive himself.

A jack rabbit leaped into his path, and without thinking, he leaped after it, caught it, snapped its neck. Before he could reflect on what he had done, he heard human footsteps. And before he could take cover in the rocks, someone shot him.

He felt a burning in his left side. Terrified, he dropped the dead rabbit and fled to the shelter among the rocks. Moments later, frightened and hurting, he stopped. Someone was following him noisily, perhaps trying to get another clear shot. He concealed himself behind a jagged wedge of rock and waited.

Past 25

By the time it was certain that Jacob Boyd Doyle was not normal, there were two more babies with the same abnormalities.

Jacob never crawled. At six months, he humped along like a big inchworm. Two months later, he began to toddle on all fours, looking disturbingly like a clumsy puppy or kitten. He walked on his hands and feet rather than crawling on hands and knees. With the help of an adult, he could sit up like a dog or cat begging for food. As time passed, he grew strong enough to do this alone. He learned to sit back on his haunches comfortably while using his hands.

He was a beautiful, precocious child, but he was a quadruped. His senses were even keener than those of his parents and his strength would have made him a real problem for parents of only normal strength. And he was a carrier. Eli and Meda did not learn this for certain until later, but they suspected it from the first.

Most important, though, the boy was not human.

Eli could not accept this. Again and again, he tried to teach Jacob to walk upright. A human child walked upright. A boy, a man, walked upright. No son of Eli's would run on all fours like a dog.

Day after day, he kept at Jacob until the little boy sprawled on his stomach and screamed in rebellion.

"Baby, he's too young," Meda said not for the first time. "He doesn't have the balance. His legs aren't strong enough yet."

Chances were, they never would be, and she knew it. She tried to protect the boy from Eli. That shamed and angered Eli so that he could not talk to her about it.

She tried to protect his son from him!

And perhaps Jacob needed her protection. There were times when Eli could not even look at the boy. What in hell was going to happen to a kid who ran around on all fours? A freak who could not hide his strangeness. What kind of life could he have? Even in this isolated section of desert, he might be mistaken for an animal and shot. And what in heaven's name would be done with him if he were captured instead of killed? Would he be sent off to a hospital for "study" or caged and restricted like even the best of the various apes able to communicate through sign language? Or would he simply be stared at, harassed, tormented by normal people? If he spread the disease, it would quickly be traced to him. He would definitely be caged or killed then.

Eli loved the boy desperately, longed to give him the gift of humanity that children everywhere else on earth took for granted. Sometimes Eli sat and watched the boy as he played. At first, Jacob would come over to him and demand attention, even try, Eli believed, to comfort his father or understand his bleakness. Then the boy stopped coming near him. Eli had never turned him away, had even ceased trying to get him to walk upright. In fact, Eli was finally accepting the idea that Jacob would never walk on his hind legs with any more ease or grace than a dog doing tricks. Yet the boy began to avoid him.

Eli was slow in noticing. Not until he called Jacob and saw that the boy cringed away from him did he realize that it had been many days since Jacob had touched him voluntarily.

Many days. How many? Eli thought back.

A week, perhaps. The boy had ceased to come near him or touch him exactly when he began wondering if it were not a cruelty to leave such a hopeless child alive.

Present 26

Rane sat frightened and alone among members of the car family. They had put her on the floor against a wall in what had been the living room of the ranch house. She was still shackled, feeling miserable and tired. Her arms, legs, and back ached with wanting to change position. Once she had inched away from the wall and lain down. The instant she closed her eyes, there was a hand on her left breast and another on her right thigh.

She had sat up quickly and squirmed away from the hands. The car rats had only laughed. They could have raped her. She thought they might eventually. At that moment, they were preoccupied with the ranch women—a mother and her thirteen-year-old daughter. There was also a twelve-year-old son. Rane had heard some of the car rats had raped him, too. She didn't doubt it. They had placed her opposite an open hall door that was directly across from the door of the bedroom-cell of what was left of the ranch family. She could not help seeing occasional car rats going in or out, zipping or unzipping their pants. She could not help hearing moaning, pleading, praying, weeping, screaming whenever the room door was opened. The ranch house was solidly built. Sounds did not carry well unless doors were open. Rane suspected the car rats had put her where she was so that she could see and hear what was in store for her.

They were watching a movie from the ranch family's library—a 1998 classic about the Second Coming of Christ. There had been a whole genre of such films just before the turn of the century. Some were religious, some antireligious, some merely exploitive—Sodom-and-Gomorrah films. Some were cause-oriented—God arrives as a woman or a dolphin or a throwaway kid. And some were science fiction. God arrives from Eighty-two Eridani Seven.

Well, maybe God had arrived a few years later from Proxima Centauri Two. God in the form of a deadly little microbe that for its own procreation made a father try to rape his dying daughter—and made the daughter not mind.

Rane squeezed her eyes shut, willing the tears not to come again, failing. What was worse? Being raped by three or four car rats before she was ransomed or submitting to Eli's people and microbe? Or were the two the same now that the car gang was infected? No, she would probably have been safer back with Stephen Kaneshiro, who could have hurt her but had not, who had tried to share part of himself with her even though she had not understood.

But there was Jacob to think of. All the Jacobs. Stephen Kaneshiro could not give her a human child. It did not matter what the car gang gave her. They would free her as soon as they had the ransom money. Then she could have a doctor take care of the disease and any possible pregnancy. If only the car family did not kill her before the ransom was paid.

Somehow, in spite of the noise from across the hall, in spite of its effect on her, she fell asleep sitting up. If there were more hands, she did not feel them.

When she awoke, she was intensely hungry. The movie was over, and the car rats were shooting and shouting and stinking with sweat so foul she could almost taste it. Her first impulse was to try to drag herself away from them, but her hunger was too intense. Even her head throbbed with it.

She begged the nearest car rat for food, but he shoved her aside with one foot and kept reloading guns as they were passed to him. Most were not passed to him. Their users reloaded them themselves in a couple of seconds. Others were older, slower, more likely to jam. These the reloader handled.

Helplessly, automatically, Rane inched toward the kitchen. She knew where it was. She and Keira had been left in it when they were rescued from their father.

Rane shook her aching head, not wanting to think about that. She did not know where Keira was or what was happening to her. She cared, but she did not want to think about it now. She was not even sure where her father was. She worried about him because he was obviously sick. He might hurt himself and not even know it.

The car rats might hurt him because he could not respond to their orders. But as worried as she was about him, she could not keep her mind on him. She was so weak, so sick with hunger, and the kitchen seemed so far away.

She was not sure how far she had gone across the vast room when someone stopped her.

"Where the hell do you think you're going, sis? What's the matter with you?"

"I'm hungry," she gasped.

"Hungry? Shit, you're sick. You're soaking wet."

Rane managed to look up, see that it was a deep-voiced woman who had stopped her, not a man as she had thought. Of course. She smelled like a woman. Rane shook her head, trying to remember whether men and women had always smelled noticeably different. But she could not keep her mind on the question.

"Please," she begged, "just give me some food."

"You're probably not even strong enough to eat."

"Please," Rane wept. She had done more crying in the past few days than she had in the past several years. What would happen if the woman prevented her from reaching food? She was already in more pain than she thought could result from hunger.

"You get back to your place and keep from underfoot," the woman said. She was large and blocky. Rane at her best could not have gotten past her. Now, all but helpless, Rane felt herself dragged back to her place at the wall.

"Stay put!" the woman said, then stomped away in her heavy boots. Immediately, Rane began crawling toward the kitchen again. She could not help herself.

She had her hand stepped on once, painfully, and someone shouted at her and cursed her, but no one stopped her again. She reached the kitchen, noticed peripherally that someone had found a gunport there alongside the sink. A bald, shirtless man stood before it, firing mechanically. The man had enough hair on his body to cover several heads.

A gorilla, Rane thought. No more human than the things he was firing at. Jesus, was anyone negotiating with her grandparents or were they all here trying to kill Eli's people? How long had the siege gone on? Two days? Three? More? She could not remember.

She managed to drag herself upright by using the handles of the large refrigerator, then stand while she pulled one of the doors open. There was little food to be found. A few fresh vegetables—tomatoes, a limp carrot, two cucumbers, green onions, green beans.

She ate everything she could find. By the time the shooting let up and the hairy man on the other side of the kitchen had time to pay attention to her, she had opened the other side of the refrigerator and found several steaks probably intended for the night's dinner. The steaks were raw, some of them still icy. There was some cooked meat, too—what was left of a pair of large roasts scraped together onto one platter.

Without thinking, Rane chose the raw meat. Its coldness disturbed her but the fact that it was raw did not even penetrate her consciousness until she had cleaned the bone of the first steak and was beginning the second. Raw smelled better than cooked, that was all.

Finally she began to feel stronger, aware enough for her bloody hands and the bloody meat she held to startle her. She had never liked her meat even medium rare, had always eaten it well-done or, as Keira said, burned. But this meat, except for its coldness, was the best thing she had ever tasted.

Now the car rat saw what she was doing, and, amazed, came to take the second steak from her. She did her best to bite off one of his fingers. If her bound hands and feet had not restricted her movement, she would have succeeded. As it was, her unexpected swiftness and ferocity drove the car rat back.

"Goddamn," he said staring at her as she tore off a piece of steak. "Goddamn, you and your whole family are crazy."

He was an ape. Heavy brow ridges, flattened, broken nose, body hair no one would believe. But now that she had eaten, now that she felt stronger, she realized he smelled interesting.

She finished her steak while he watched, repelled and fascinated. Then she wiped her mouth and smiled. "I won't hurt you," she said, knowing he would laugh.

He laughed humorlessly. "Damn right you won't, sis."

"I was hungry."

"You were crazy—*are* crazy."

He liked her. She could see it as clearly as though that wary face of his were leering.

"So?" she said, shrugging. "Who the hell isn't crazy these days?" One of her father's patients had said that to her—a young thief with skin as smooth as Keira's except where acid had scarred him. He had been brought to the enclave hospital for special treatment and had laughed at her when she tried to talk him out of leaving the hospital and going back to his gang. He could not get even with the acid thrower, he said, until he was with his own again. This in spite of the fact that his own had run away and left him writhing on the ground.

"You're crazy!" she had screamed at him.

"So who isn't crazy these days?" he had demanded.

"I'm not," she had said. "And I never will be. Go ahead and flush yourself down the toilet if you want to!"

Her father had only just begun letting her volunteer at the hospital. The boy's self-destructive stubbornness had upset her, but she had comforted herself with the knowledge that she was stronger than he was. He could have healed completely and gotten work in one of the enclaves. She had told him she would talk her father into helping him. But he had chosen the sewers. She was stronger and smarter.

Or was she merely untested?

She knew the disease organisms were pushing her toward this repulsive man. And she was yielding to them mindlessly. Stephen Kaneshiro had resisted, had not raped her. She could resist, too.

Deliberately, she took another steak. She was not very hungry now, but the meat still smelled good. It was not hard for her to tear into it as messily as possible. She let blood run down her chin and arms, chewed with her mouth open, occasionally smacking her lips. Eventually, she heard the ape make a sound of disgust and stomp away.

The shooting had stopped. Rane was alone in the kitchen—happy to be alone. She thought she might be able to get out the back door if she could get free of the cuffs. Very likely, nothing in the house would cut them. The plastic only looked flimsy. But she thought if she did not fight them, she might be able to slip them. She had seen her father try to do this and fail. But it seemed to her he had not used his muscles effectively, and he had had no fat to help him. She had to try. Anything was better than just sitting and waiting to see what her captors or the disease organism would do to her next.

Several minutes later, as she was freeing one hand through flexibility and control that amazed even her, a young white-haired woman caught her.

If Rane had had time to free her feet, she might have been able to silence the woman before the woman shouted an alarm. As it was, all Rane could do was hop toward her, only to be stopped by the ape who came running to see what was wrong.

The ape grasped her wrists and held them. "Son of a bitch," he said, grinning. "That's the first time I've seen anybody get out of the jail cuffs. Shit, I've tried to get out of a few pair myself. What'd you do, sis?"

He was too close to her. *Too close!* He smelled almost edible. Irresistible. She pressed herself against him.

"Jesus," the white-haired woman said. "What is it with these people?"

"You tell me," the ape said, holding Rane. She rubbed herself against his hairy body, smiling outside and screaming inside. It was as though she were two people. One wanted, needed, was utterly compelled to have this man—perhaps any man. Her hands fumbled with his belt.

Yet some part of her was still *her*. That part screamed, soundlessly weeping, and clawed with imaginary fingers at the ape's ugly, stupid face.

Her true fingers quivered, hesitated for a moment at his belt. Then the organism controlled her completely. Her body moved only under its compulsion and her feelings were abruptly reconciled with her actions. Part of her seemed to die.

"Let her alone," the white-haired woman said. "You can see she's running on empty. Who knows what crazy thing she might do? Besides, we've got to keep her in good shape for the ransom."

And the ape growled, "You worry about yours, Smokey. The buyers for this one will just have to take her back a little used." The ape lifted Rane off her bound feet. "At least this kid is young. What the hell do you want with that sick old man you've got?" He laughed as he carried Rane away into another room.

The new room was not empty. There were people there, writhing together, moaning, making other sounds that Rane paid no attention to. The ape threw her onto an empty bed. There seemed to be several beds in the room. The ape freed her feet, then casually tore her clothing off. Finally, he climbed onto her and hurt her so badly she screamed aloud. But even as she screamed, she knew that what she was doing was *necessary*. She could have hurt him back. He did not realize how vulnerable he was, hunching between her thighs; she could kill him. There was a time, she recalled dimly, when she would have used her advantage. But that time was past. His throat, his eyes, his groin were safe from her. She bore the pain somehow, and when he finished, she lay bleeding, uncaring as he shackled her again. This time he bound her, spread-eagle, to the bed.

Sometime later, there was another man. She did not know him, did not recall having seen him before. He did not hurt her as much. Before he touched her, her body felt almost healed. She did not mind what he did, did not mind the man who came after him. By then, she was aware of her body repairing itself. The organism was taking care of her.

She lost track of time, of the men. Once when she began to feel hungry, she asked the man who was with her for food. He laughed at her, but later he brought her food—raw meat and raw vegetables. He unshackled her and watched in amazement and disgust as she ate. Several people had come to watch. They smelled unwashed and wary, but since they did not bother her, she ignored them.

When someone tried to shackle her again, she resisted. There was, it seemed to her now, too much danger in being tied to a bed—or tied at all. She was stronger now, more aware of what was going on around her.

In one corner, a young boy, naked, covered with blood, lay like discarded trash. He did not move. He had clearly been tortured, mutilated. His hands were still shackled. She was certain he was dead, had probably bled to death. His ears and his penis had been cut off.

The woman on the bed near her had been crying hoarsely. Now, filthy, bound spread-eagle across a small bed, she was unconscious. Rane could see and hear her breathing shallowly.

A young girl, tied across another bed, lay watching what happened to Rane. The girl's wrist and ankles were bleeding in spite of the relative gentleness of the security cuffs. Her body was bruised and bloody and there was something wrong about her eyes.

Abruptly, the girl gave a long, shrill scream. No one was touching her or paying any attention to her, but she continued to scream until one of the men went over and slapped her. Then she was abruptly, completely silent.

"I don't want to be tied," Rane said gravely to the man who was struggling to hold her arms. She realized that she was having no trouble avoiding the cuffs. The man seemed weaker than the others who had handled her—though he did not look weaker. Perhaps she was stronger.

Other people laughed when she spoke, but the man trying to tie her did not. "Help me," he said. "She's as strong as a goddamn truck! She's playing with me!"

She was not playing. Abruptly, as a second man seized her, she thrust both away and got up. She was still naked, as dirty and bloody as the young girl. But she was beginning to understand that she was stronger. Perhaps she was not as strong as she would be. She thought not. But she was stronger than anyone would expect her to be—strong enough to escape. Even getting away naked would be better than staying here, having her organisms keep her alive while the car rats thought up new things to do to her.

A black woman with red hair leveled one of the newer automatic rifles at her as she fought off a second attacker. When she saw the gun, she thought she was dead. But at that moment, she heard shouts through the open door.

"Hey, Badger," someone yelled, "the old man is gone. He kicked out his window!"

"Huh!" the red-haired woman said. "Nobody could kick out one of these windows alone. He'd have to kick out half the wall. Somebody must have helped him!" And as an afterthought, "Where's Smoke?"

Her father was gone.

He had escaped! He had used his new strength and gotten away! And what about Keira? Perhaps she had gotten away, too. People tended not to pay much attention to her because she looked too frail to try anything. But maybe...

Rane lunged at the redhead. The woman's attention had been drawn away from Rane. Now, she seemed to react in slow motion as Rane moved.

Rane seized the gun, swatted the woman on the side of her head with the stock, then swung the gun around on the other car rats. Two-hundred-round magazine, fully loaded, set on automatic. A couple of seconds passed, then someone laughed. Maybe a naked girl holding a rifle looked funny. Let them laugh.

Someone made a grab for the barrel. That was a degree of stupidity Rane had not expected. She fired, managed to shoot only the man whose hand had brought the gun to bear on his own belly. She resisted the urge to spray the whole group.

The wounded man screamed, doubled over, fell to the floor. Rane stepped back from him quickly, looking to see whether anyone else was feeling suicidal. As it happened, no one else was armed. People did not come to this room with their guns.

Nobody moved.

"Get your clothes off," Rane told one of the smaller women.

The woman understood. She stripped quickly, threw her clothing to Rane, glanced sideways at the rat bleeding and groaning on the floor. The red-haired woman had knelt beside him, trying to stop the bleeding with direct pressure.

"Get the hell out of here," Rane said. "All of you, out!"

They spilled through the doorway ahead of her and she followed close behind, hoping her speed would give her an edge over their numbers and organization. She barely paused to snatch up the discarded clothing. She could dress when she was safe, when she had joined her father and they were on their way to Needles again.

She darted out the door, across the hall, across the large living room. She could see reaction around her, but it was so slow, she knew how fast she must be moving.

But there was noise outside. Motors, vehicles approaching, people shouting. This was what she had distracted attention from. New car people arriving. New car rats on the outside where she had to go. They were already shooting, fighting with Eli's people. More crossfire for her to be caught in.

She put her back against the wall near the front door and aimed her gun at one of the car rats.

"Open this door," she said.

"I can't," he lied. "It needs a special key." It could not have been more obvious to her that he was lying if he had worn a sign.

She fired a short burst, and he fell. Now the screaming inside her returned. She was shooting people, killing people. She was going to be a doctor someday. Doctors did not kill people; they helped people heal. Her father had carried a gun for years and never shot anyone. He had escaped without shooting anyone.

But she could not.

The instant she showed indecision, weakness, mercy, these people would cut her to pieces. In this room several were as formidably armed as she was. All she had going for her was terrifying speed and perhaps their belief that they would soon be rid of her one way or another without anyone playing hero. Nothing she had ever heard about rat packs gave any indication they were heroic. At best, they mistook ruthlessness for heroism.

"Open the door," she said to a second man.

He stumbled quickly to obey.

"You!" she chose a third. "Help him!"

"He doesn't need any hel—No!"

She had come within a hair of shooting him. He scurried to the first man, then stood by while the first opened the door.

Of course, the instant the door moved, Eli's people opened fire at it. Someone—one of the new group of car rats, perhaps—managed to run onto the porch, but did not quite make it to the door.

Rane heard all this as she ran from the room. She had never intended to step into the battle at the front of the house. She would never have headed for the front if she had known what was going on there. Once there, however, she had to create a diversion so that she could get to the back door.

Someone shot at her as she ran, but she was too quick. In the kitchen, she stopped, turned, fired a short burst at the door she had just run through. That should stop any pursuit. She hesitated, saw a flash of color at the door, sprayed the doorway again. Then she went to the back door. If it required a key, she might be trapped. That depended on how thoroughly bulletproof the house was.

Her hand flew over the various locks that did not require keys. She had to shoot the last one off, though at least it came off. As she fired, however, someone else fired at her, hit her in the lower back.

She fell to her knees, tried to swing around, but was shot again. This time, the impact of the bullet spun her around. She held on to her rifle somehow and managed to spray the other side of the room. She heard screaming, knew she had hit something.

She released the trigger only when, briefly, through a haze, she thought she saw her sister staring at her over a counter, through a doorway. Then, because she was propped up against the door, unable to move her legs—unable even to feel her legs, she sprayed the last of her bullets into the car rats as they showed themselves. She had the satisfaction of seeing the ape fall before someone shot her again.

The disease organism was merciless. It kept her alive even when she knew she must be almost cut in half. It kept her conscious and aware of everything up through the moment someone stood over her, shouting, then seized her by the hair and held her head up as he began to saw slowly at her throat with something dull.

Past 27

The women had become frightened of Eli—frightened for their children. Gwyn's daughter by Eli was beginning to toddle around on all fours and Lorene's daughter by Zeriam clearly had the same physical abnormalities. She would be another quadruped, another precocious, strong, beautiful, little nonhuman. Eli could see that. He watched the children in grim silence.

The women sat Eli down and talked to him. Gwyn spoke for them all for a change while Meda sat withdrawn and silent.

"We don't like being afraid of you," Gwyn said, leaning forward against the dining table around which they had gathered. "We need you." She glanced sideways at Meda. "And we love you. But we're afraid."

"Afraid of what?" he demanded harshly. He did not care what the women had to say. His own misery over the children consumed him.

"You know of what," Gwyn said. "Even the kids know. They don't understand, but they're scared to death of you."

He stared at her in bitter anger. She had brought the others together against him. They had never united against him before. He was father or foster father to all three kids—all three hopelessly nonhuman kids. No one had the right to tell him how he should feel about them.

"Eli, you love them," Meda whispered finally. "You love them all. You'd have to go against your deepest feelings to hurt them."

"We won't let you hurt them," Lorene said.

"We can't change them," Gwyn said. "And no matter how you feel... if you try to hurt them, we'll kill you."

Eli stared at her, amazed. She was the gentlest of the three women, the one most likely to need reassurance and want protection.

"*We will kill you,*" she repeated very softly. She did not flinch from his gaze. He looked at Meda and Lorene and saw Gwyn's feelings mirrored in their faces.

He reached across the table, took Gwyn's hands. "I can't help what I feel," he said. "I know it hurts you. It hurts *me.* But—"

"It scares us!"

"I know." He paused. "What in this world is going to happen to kids with human minds and four legs? Think about it!"

"Who says they have human minds?" Meda asked.

Eli glared at her.

"They're obviously bright," she said, "but their minds may be as different as their bodies. We can teach them, but we can't know ahead of time what they'll become."

"No," he said. "We can't. But we know the world they'll have to spend their lives in. And I know what their lives will be like if they can't fit in—and, of course, there's no way they can fit in. You think sewers and cesspools are bad? Try a cage. Bars, you know. Locks."

"Nobody would—"

"Shit! They're not going to be cute little kids forever. To other people, they wouldn't look like cute little kids now. And we're not going to live forever to protect them."

The women stared at him bleakly.

"I'll tell you something else," he said. "These kids are only the first. You *know* there'll be more. If anything happened to me, you'd go out and find yourselves another man or two. Hell, you'll do that even if nothing happens to me. We'll probably bring in more women, too. Our organism won't let us ignore all those uninfected people out there completely."

No one contradicted him. The women could feel the truth of what he was saying as intensely as he could.

"What are we doing?" Lorene whispered. "What are we creating?"

Eli leaned back, eyes closed. "That's what I've been asking myself," he said. "I've got an answer now."

They all faced him, waiting. He realized then that he loved them. He wondered when he had begun to love them—three plain women with calluses on their hands. Answering them would not be an act of love, but it was necessary. If anyone deserved to know what he thought, they did. "We're the future," he said simply. "We're the sporangia of the dominant life form of Proxi Two—the receptacles that produce the spores of that life form. If we survive, *if our children survive*, it will be because we fulfill our purpose—because we spread the organism."

"Spread the disease?" Lorene asked.

"Yes."

"Deliberately? I mean ... to everybody? After you said—"

"I didn't say we should spread it deliberately. I didn't say we *should* spread it at all. I said we won't survive, and the kids won't survive, if we don't. But I'll tell you, I don't think they or we are in any real danger. Once we knew what to look for on Proxi Two, we found the organisms in almost every animal species alive there. Some were immune—herbivores tended to be immune—and though I can't prove it, I suspect a lot of species had been driven into extinction."

"Some would be here," Lorene said. "Dogs."

Eli nodded. "Dogs, yes, maybe coyotes, wolves, any canine. I wouldn't give much for the chances of cats either, and some snakes—maybe all snakes, rats, most rodents. Heaven knows what else."

"What about the people?" Lorene whispered. "They'll die, too. Four out of seven died here. Five, if you count Gwyn's baby. Ten out of fourteen in your crew died. And what about Andy? How many more Andy Zeriams, Eli?" She had begun to cry. "How goddamn many?"

He got up and went to her. She pushed him away angrily at first, but then reached out and pulled him to her.

"What about the people?" she repeated against him.

After a moment, he put her aside and sat down next to Meda.

"What do you want to do?" Meda asked.

He shook his head. "Nothing. Just go on as we have."

"But—"

"What else? You're right about the kids. They are what they are. I'm right too. They can't make it in the world as it is. But I'm not going to make a move to spread the disease beyond the ranch, here. Not even for them. We'll have to bring people here now and then, but that's all."

"You're talking about leaving everything to chance," Meda said.

"No," he told her, "not quite. I'm talking about stifling chance, doing every damn thing I can to keep the disease right here. Everything. And I'll need all three of you with me."

"But the kids," Meda said.

"Yeah." He sighed. "I couldn't hurt them. Even without the three of you ganging up on me, I couldn't have. But... in this one way, I can't help them, either. Can you?" He looked from one of them to the other. No one answered. "What happens happens," Eli continued. "I won't make it happen. Dead people, dead animals, no more cities because we'd go crazy in cities. No more of a lot of things I probably haven't even thought of." He stared at the table for several seconds.

"It will happen, though," he said. "Sooner or later, somehow, it will happen. And ultimately, I'll be responsible."

Present 28

Keira had just eaten a large meal—overcooked, overseasoned, but filling. She was feeling well until the white-haired girl came to take her to her father. She was feeling *well!* She could not remember how long it had been since she had last felt truly well.

The car family had locked her in a walk-in hall closet. She had been in pain and Badger had demanded to know why. When she told him she had leukemia, he had shrugged.

"So?" he had said. "There's a cure for that—some kind of medicine that makes the bad cells turn back to normal."

"I've had that," she told him. "It didn't work."

"What do you mean, it didn't work? It works. It worked on my mother. She had the same shit you do."

"It didn't work on me."

So he had locked her in the closet. Some of his people, ignorant and fearful, could not quite believe her illness was not contagious. Badger locked her away from them for her own safety. She had seen for herself how eager they were to get her out of their sight. She wondered what they would do if they knew what she and her family had really given them—what they were really doomed to. They would begin to find out soon enough. That was what Eli was waiting for. That was why he was keeping them boxed in. He did not have to do anything more than that to win. She had heard him talking about explosives, but then the car family had begun showing a noisy movie and the faint voices from outside were drowned.

Yet there were explosives. Eli would do anything necessary to stop the car people if they threatened to break free before they were ready to join him. He certainly would not let the friends they had called reach them. Keira did not know what would happen to her, but somehow she was not afraid. She sat on the closet floor with bound hands and feet, reading from cardboard boxes of old magazines. The lavish use of paper fascinated her. A one-hundred-and-twenty-page magazine for only five or six dollars. A collector's item. Computer libraries like her father's made more sense, occupied less space, could be more easily updated, but somehow, weren't as much fun to look at.

The light in the closet was dim, but Keira preferred it dim. She thought she might not be able to tolerate it if it were normally bright. She was looking through an old *National Geographic* when the white-haired girl opened the door.

"Your father wants to see you," the girl said in her low, throaty voice.

Keira looked up from her magazine, stared at the girl, wondered what it might be like to be her—dirty, knowing, tough, headed nowhere, but still young and not bad-looking. The girl's dark-tanned skin contrasted oddly with her white hair.

"He might want to see my sister," Keira said, "but I don't think he wants to see me."

"You the one he had the fight with?" the girl asked.

Keira did not hesitate. "Yes."

"Doesn't matter. He just wants to see one of you to make sure we haven't shot you. Come on." She unfastened Keira's hand and leg restraints.

Keira started to refuse. She did not think the girl would force her. Then she realized that in spite of what had happened between them, she wanted to see her father—probably for the same reason he wanted to see her. Just to be sure he was all right. He had seemed so weak and sick when she saw him last. The organism seemed to be making her strong and him weak. That was all that had permitted her to get away from him when Rane made her realize what was happening.

It occurred to her that as things stood now, each time she saw him might be the last. The thought frightened her and she tried to reject it, but it had taken hold.

"All right," she said, standing up.

The girl watched her intently. "Is he really your father?"

"Yes."

"Is he part black, then, or is it just your mother?"

"My mother was black. He's white."

The girl nodded. "My mother was from Sweden. God knows why she came here. Got raped her first week here. That's where I came from."

Shocked, Keira spoke the first words that occurred to her. "But why didn't she have an—" Keira stopped, glanced downward. There was something wrong with asking someone why she had not been aborted. She wondered why the girl would tell her such a secret, shameful thing.

"She couldn't make up her mind," the girl said unperturbed. "She wanted to get rid of me, then she didn't, then she wasn't sure, then I was born and it was too late. She kept me 'til I was fourteen, though. Then she went nuts and when they took her away to cure her, I left." The girl sighed. "After that, life was shit until I got adopted into the family. How old are you?"

"Sixteen," Keira told her.

"Really? How old is he?"

Keira looked at her sharply. The girl looked away. For a moment, Keira hated her, wanted to get away from her. Her rage surprised her, then shamed her because she could not help understanding its cause: jealousy. The girl had slept with Blake—as Keira herself almost had. His scent was on her like a signature. For a moment Keira wondered how she could distinguish such a thing. His scent... Yet there was no doubt in her mind, and she was almost stiff with jealous rage.

Then came the shame.

"Forty-four," she said slowly. "He's forty-four." Neither she nor the girl said anything more. The girl let Keira in to see her father, then minutes later, let her out again. Only then could she look at the girl and realize her father needed an ally among the car people. The girl liked him and she could be useful to him in ways Keira certainly could not.

"Forty-four isn't old," Keira said as the girl took her back to the closet.

The girl glanced at her. "What'd you do? Decide it was okay for me to fuck him?"

Keira jumped. Not for the first time, she was grateful she was not as light-skinned as Rane. Nothing made Rane blush. Everything would have made Keira blush.

"I just thought you liked him," Keira muttered.

"What if I do? He's your father, not the other way around."

Keira tried once more. "Did you bring him the blanket?" she asked. "And food?" She had seen an empty plate on the floor near him.

"Yeah, so what?"

"Thank you," Keira said sincerely. She went back into the closet, waited to see whether the girl would put the cuffs back on her. But the girl only looked at her, then closed the door. Keira waited for the soft click of the lock, but did not hear it. Moments later, she heard the girl's footsteps going away.

Keira was almost free. With her enhanced senses, she might be able to slip out of the house, escape.

Alone.

But the white-haired girl had given her a choice she did not want—to challenge the car family by attempting to escape, to desert her own family, or to remain in dangerous captivity. Here, she certainly could not help her family. At any time, Badger might decide to kill his captives, rape them, use them as shields, anything. He had kicked her father almost into unconsciousness for no reason at all. He and his people were unpredictable, ruthless, and, worst of all, cornered. What would happen when they began to realize they were sick as well?

And whatever they decided to do, how would her staying affect them? Would it stop them from doing harm? Of course not.

But if she escaped, the gang might take their anger and frustration out on her father and Rane. She hooked her arms around her knees, pulled her knees up close to her chest. There she sat miserably as though she were still bound, still locked in.

Each time she thought of her father, her mind flinched away, then fastened onto him again, forcing her into memories of the thing that had almost happened—into confusion, fear, shame, loss, desire. . . .

Then she would remember the way Eli had looked at her, the feel of his body along the length of her own and inside her, hurtful, but good somehow. That would not happen again. Meda would be there and Keira's father would not. Eli would steer her toward someone else; he had warned her. That hurt, but it could not matter.

She listened intently for several seconds, heard the movie end, heard the shooting flare up and die down. Down the hall, people were making love—or the ranch women were being raped. She had heard a little of that before and did not want to hear more. There were people wandering around, talking, firing occasionally at targets they probably could not see. Someone was talking about eating raw meat.

The words made her mouth water. Her hunger was not painful yet, but it would be soon. Nothing else was hurting her body now, but hunger could change that quickly. If she waited much longer, let herself be locked in again, she could starve. The car gang would not understand. It might ignore her. This closet could become her tomb.

She grasped the knob, turned it slowly, noiselessly. She heard nothing nearby—not even breathing.

Yet the instant she opened the door, something small, silent, and incredibly quick leaped into the closet with her. Only her speeded-up reaction time saved her. Her moment of confusion and terror passed so quickly, she was able to keep herself from screaming. Instead, she shut the closet door quickly, quietly, and turned to face Jacob.

He was naked and trembling. Before she realized what he meant to do, he leaped again, this time at her.

To her amazement, she caught him. He was heavy, but she had no trouble holding him. A few days before, she did not think she could have lifted him from the ground, let alone caught him in midair. He clung to her, utterly silent, but clearly terrified.

"What are you *doing* here?" she whispered, hugging him and rubbing his trembling shoulders. She was surprised to realize how glad she was to see him—and how frightened she was for him in this deadly place. "Jacob, you could get hurt! You could get—" She stopped. "You have to get away!"

"You do, too," he said. "Nobody knew where you were in the house so I came to find you. Everybody from home is outside."

"Do your parents know you're inside?"

"No!" He drew back from her a little, his trembling quieted. "Don't tell them. Okay?"

"I won't tell them a thing. Just let's get out of here. How did you get in?"

"There's a room with a hole instead of window glass. You were in there before. It smells like you—and like other people."

"A room with a hole?"

Distantly, Keira heard shooting and running feet. It sounded like fighting within the house. Car people fighting among themselves.

Jacob glanced toward the door. "They were hurting her," he said. "She's got a gun and shot one of them. Now she's shooting more."

"Who?"

"Your sister. She's getting away."

"Is she? My God, let's go!"

"Your father's gone, too, I think. I smelled the room where he was back at home. His same smell was in the room with the hole."

God, while she had sat worrying about leaving them, they were leaving her. She opened the door, crept out of the closet, still holding the boy.

"I'll show you where the hole is," he said. He squirmed against her, leaped soundlessly to the floor, sped down the hall toward her father's room. Of course the hole would be there. But how had her father broken out the glass?

And Rane. Was she all right? Could she make it alone? Keira turned, crept back up the hall to the family room. This room adjoined the kitchen and the dining room. From the hall door of the family room, Keira could see car people crouched behind the counter, occasionally looking around or over it into the kitchen. Keira could see over the counter and into the kitchen, could see Rane sitting at the back door, cradling an automatic rifle. For an instant, Rane's eyes met Keira's. Then Jacob was tugging at Keira's dress.

"Go!" Keira whispered. "Get out!"

"You come too," the boy pleaded. "The whole house smells like blood. People are dying."

Rane began firing again, and people did die. Keira saw one of them raise his head at the wrong time and get the top of it blown off.

Terrified and repelled, Keira snatched up Jacob and fled. Doctor's daughter that she was, sick as she had been, she had never seen anyone die before. She ran almost in panic, reached her father's bare room and looked around wildly.

"There!" The boy pointed to another door. The bathroom—no bigger than the closet she had been shut in, but it had a window.

She ran into the bathroom, shut the door and locked it, then lifted the boy to the windowsill. He was over it and down in an instant. She pulled herself up after him, no longer marveling at the return of her strength, no longer marveling at anything. She had to get out of the house, get back to Eli and safety. Her father was probably already safe, and Rane soon would be.

She dropped to the ground and ran.

Keira ran through the rocks, hoping they would conceal and protect her as she circled around the house. She was halfway around and already aware of the distinctive scent of Eli's people when she recognized another familiar scent. The new scent confused her for a moment because of its clarity. She was so utterly certain it was her father's that for a moment she thought she had actually seen him.

The wind favored her. It blew toward her from Eli's people and across the path of her father. She looked down the slope through the rocks. Her nose told her this was the way her father had gone—away from the house and Eli's people, toward the highway.

Of course.

Her enhanced sense of smell led her to spots of his blood, some of them still wet on the rocks. In one place near a brown wedge of rock, blood had actually pooled—an alarming amount of blood. Before finding this, she had thought she would go on to Eli and say nothing about her father. Jacob, running ahead and back to her like an eager puppy, might notice the scent and he might not. If he spoke of it, she would have to admit what she knew, but perhaps by then her father would have made good his escape. She would have let him escape, even knowing what that would mean to Eli and his people. This was all she could do for her father. And in his way, he was not wrong. He was taking the long view, trying to prevent a future epidemic. Eli and his people were trying to live from one day to the next, trying to raise their strange children in peace, trying to control their deadly compulsion. Eventually, inevitably, they would fail. They must have known it. If not for the blood, Keira would have deliberately permitted that failure to happen now.

But the blood was there, slowly drying in a natural depression in the rock. Her father had been hurt, needed help. Eli had the medical bag, maybe even had it with him here to treat his own people. He should not be able to use it, but Keira suspected he could—and her father might die before he could reach other help.

She turned aside to follow the blood trail. The next time Jacob raced back to her, approaching in utter silence, and concealed except for his scent until the last instant, she stopped him.

"Come on," he said. "I'll take you to where Daddy is."

"You go," she said. "Tell him my father's hurt and I have to find him. Tell him to send someone after me with my father's bag. Okay?"

"Yes."

"Good. Now go. And be careful."

The boy bounded away, leaping among the rocks as though they presented no obstacle at all. Her children would do that someday. They would have four legs and be able to bound like cats, and they would be beautiful. Perhaps she was already pregnant.

Somehow, when she found her father, when Eli helped him, he had to be convinced to stay and be quiet. *He had to be!* Living day to day, free on the desert was better than being a quarantined guinea pig in some hospital or lab, better than watching Jacob and Zera treated like little animals, better than perhaps being sterilized so that no more children like them could be born. Better than vanishing.

She ran down the rocky slope with new speed and agility she hardly noticed. It seemed she could always see a place for her feet, always find a handhold when one was necessary. She felt as secure as a mountain goat. Once she stopped to examine the body of a red-bearded, balding man. He was not one of Eli's people, not one of Badger's. Most likely, he was one of the new group Badger had called. He was newly dead of a broken neck. Her father's scent was especially strong near him, and she realized her father had probably killed this man. It was even possible that this was the man who had wounded her father—though she saw no gun. Perhaps her father had taken it. That would mean she had to be careful. If he were wounded and armed, he might be panicky enough to shoot without waiting to see who he was shooting at.

She continued down the slope with greater care. She did not have Eli's or Jacob's ability to move in complete silence, but she moved as quietly as she could, missing the rock and sand she could have knocked loose, avoiding the dry plants that would crackle underfoot, quieting her own panting.

She paused briefly to listen. The wind, now blowing toward her from her father, brought her the sound of his uneven footsteps. He was limping slightly. His breathing, though, was even, not labored. She marveled for a moment that she could actually hear his breathing over such a distance. The organism had given her a great deal. It must have given him something too. How else could he survive being shot and losing so much blood? How else could he keep going? If only something could be done to stop it from killing so many people while it helped others.

She became aware of a low rumble behind her. Looking back, she saw a truck—a big private hauler—probably carrying something illegal if it were daring to use a map-identified sewer. She dove for cover as the truck came over a rise. Perhaps the driver was in his living quarters and would not see her or her father. Perhaps. But what driver would leave his rig on automatic in a sewer? He would be at the wheel. And his truck would be armed and armored to fight off gangs and the police.

The truck rumbled past her, not even slowing in spite of the fact that the rock she had crouched behind was not large enough to conceal her completely. Unmoving as she was, perhaps the driver had seen her as just another lump of rock.

But up ahead, beyond the hill that now concealed her father, the truck slowed and stopped. Frightened, she walked toward the truck, then ran toward it. People traveling legitimately did not stop to pick up strays, did not dare. Her father had told her of a time when a person could stand with his thumb held in a certain position, and cars and trucks would stop and offer rides. But Keira could not remember such a time. All her life, she had heard stories of strays being decoys for car families and bike gangs. Real strays were people with car trouble and without working phones or people thrown out of cars by friends who suddenly became less friendly. People who picked them up might be only dangerously naïve or they might be thieves, murderers, traffickers in prostitutes, or, most frighteningly, body parts dealers—though according to her father, involuntary transplant donors were more likely to come from certain of the privately run, cesspool hospitals. But for a freelancer, strays were fair game.

Keira ran, not knowing what she would do when she reached her father and the hauler, not thinking about it. All she could think was that her father might be shot with a tranquilizer gun and loaded onto a meat truck.

Suddenly, as she ran, there was an explosion, then several explosions. For a moment, she stopped, confused, and the ground shook under her feet.

The ranch house. Eli had done what she had feared he would do: triggered his explosives, blown up the car people—even the white-haired one who had been kind.

And Rane? Had she gotten out? Was that why Eli had decided to settle things? Or was it because Keira and her father had escaped so easily? Eli almost certainly did not have enough people to surround the house *and* fight the new gang. Were two escapees all he was willing to risk?

Black smoke and dust boiled up over the hills. Keira stared at it, frightened, wondering. Then she heard the hauler start and saw it begin to pull away.

Again, she ran toward her father, pushing herself, fearing to find nothing where he had been. Instead, she found her father half-crushed by the wheels of the truck. His legs, the whole lower half of him looked stuck to the broken pavement with blood and ruined flesh. He could not possibly be alive with such massive injuries.

Her father groaned. Keira dropped down beside him, sickened, revolted. She could barely look at him, yet he was alive.

"God," he whispered. "My God!"

Weeping, Keira took his hand. It was wet with blood and she touched it carefully, but it was uninjured. Clutched in it was a piece of blue cloth—a bloody sleeve, not his own.

"I did it," he moaned. "Oh Jesus, I did it."

"Daddy?" She wanted to put his head on her lap, but she was afraid she would hurt him more.

"Kerry, is that you?" He seemed to be looking right at her.

"It's me."

"I did it. Jesus!"

"Did what?" She could not think. She could hardly talk through her tears.

"He was looking for my wallet... or something to steal. He hit me deliberately... had to swerve to hit me. Just wanted to steal."

She shook her head in disbelief. She had never heard of haulers running people down to rob them. Car families were more likely to do that. But in a sewer, anything could happen.

"I grabbed him," her father said. "I couldn't help it, couldn't control it. He smelled so... I couldn't help it. God, I tore at him like an animal."

So like the blue sleeve, the blood on his hand was not his.

He had spread the disease.

"Please," he pleaded. "Go after him. Stop him."

"Stop who?" Eli asked.

She had not heard him coming. Enhanced senses or not, she stood up, startled. Then she saw her father's bag in his hand. She knew how utterly useless it would be and she broke down.

Crying, she permitted Eli to take her by the shoulders and move her aside. He knelt where she had been. When she was able to see clearly again, she saw that he was holding her father's bloody hand.

She felt something happened between them, a moment of nonverbal communication.

Then, with a long, slow sigh, her father closed his eyes. Eventually he opened them again widely. His chest ceased to move with his breathing. His body was still. Eli reached up and closed the eyes a final time.

Keira knelt beside her father, beside Eli. She looked at Eli, not able to speak to him, not wanting to hear him speak, though she knew he would.

"He's dead," Eli said. "I'm sorry."

She knew. She had seen. She bent forward, crying, all but screaming in anguished protest. With her eyes closed, she could not imagine her father dead. She did not know how to deal with such an unimaginable thing.

Eli took off his shirt and covered the most damaged parts of her father's body. Blood soaked through at once, but at least the horrible injuries were hidden.

Eli stood up, took her hands, and drew her to her feet. Her hands tingled, almost burned where he touched her. Confused, she tried to pull away, but somehow her desire to pull away did not reach her hands. They did not move.

"Be still," he said. "I just went through this with your father. His organisms 'knew' something mine want to know. So do yours."

That made no sense to her, but she did not care. She was not being hurt. She did not think she would have noticed if he had hurt her. She was still trying to understand that her father was dead. Eli kept talking. Eventually, she found herself listening to him.

"When we've changed," he said, "when the organism 'decides' whether or not we're going to live, it shares the differences it's found in us with others who have changed. At least that's what we've decided it's doing. We had a woman who had had herself sterilized before we got her—had her tubes cauterized. Her organisms communicated with Meda's and her tubes opened up. She's pregnant now. We had a guy regrow three fingers he'd lost years ago. You... There's no precedent for it, but I think you may be getting rid of your leukemia. Or maybe the organism's even found a way to use leukemia to its advantage—and yours. You're going to live."

"I should die," she whispered. "Dad was strong and he died."

"You're not going to die. You look healthier than you did when
I met you."

"I *should* die!"

"Jesus, I'm glad you're not going to. That makes up for a lot."

She said nothing.

"Kerry?"

"*Don't call me that!*" she screamed.

"I'm sorry." He put his arm around her as soon as he could free
his hands from hers—as soon as the organisms had finished their
communication. How the hell could microorganisms communicate anyway, she wondered obscurely.

Eli answered as though she had asked the question aloud. Perhaps she had. "We exchanged something," he said. "Maybe chemical signals of some kind. That's the only answer I can come up with.
We've talked about it at home and nobody has any other ideas."

She did not understand why he was talking on and on about the
organism. Did he think she cared? Out of the corner of her eye, she
saw the column of smoke from the ranch house and she thought of
something she did care about.

"Eli?"

"Yeah?"

"What about Rane?"

Silence.

"Eli? Did she get out?"

More silence.

"You blew up the house with her inside!"

"No."

"You did! You killed my sister!"

"Keira!" He turned her, made her face him. "I didn't. We didn't."

She believed him. She did not understand why she believed so
quickly, why watching him speak the words made her know he was
telling the truth. She resented believing him.

"What happened to her?" she demanded. "Where is she?"

Eli hesitated. "She's dead."

Another one. Another death. Everyone was dead. She was alone.

"The car people killed her," Eli said.

"How could you know that?"

"Keira, I know. And you know I'm not lying to you."

"How could you know she was dead?"

He sighed. "Baby..." He drew another breath. "They cut her head off, and they threw it out the front door."

She broke away from him, stumbled a few steps down the road.

"I'm sorry," he said for the third time. "We tried to save all of you. We... we work hard not to lose people in the middle of their conversions."

"You're like our children at that stage," another voice said.

She looked up, saw that a young oriental man had come over the hill behind her.

The man spoke to Eli. "I came to see if you needed help. I guess not."

Eli shrugged. "Take her back to the camp. I'll bring her father."

The man took Keira's arm. "I knew your sister," he said softly. "She was a strong girl."

Not strong enough, Keira thought. Not against the car family. Not against the disease. Not strong at all.

She started to follow the new man back to the ranch house, then stopped. She had forgotten something—something important. It must have been important if it could bother her now. Then she remembered.

"Eli?" she said.

He was bending over her father. He straightened when she spoke.

"Eli, someone got away. The hauler who hit my father. He was headed north."

"It was a private hauler?"

"Yes. He got out and tried to rob my father. My father scratched him."

"Oh, Jesus," Eli whispered. He sounded almost the way her father had at the end. Then he turned and spoke to the other man. "Steve, tell Ingraham. He's our best driver. Give him some grenades. Tell him no holds barred."

The man called Steve went leaping up the slope as agilely as Jacob could have.

"Jesus," Eli repeated. Somehow, he managed to lift her father and carry him back as though he were merely wounded, not half-crushed. He had fashioned a kind of sack of his shirt. Keira walked beside him, hardly noticing when a car sped by down on the highway.

Up the hill, Steve—Stephen Kaneshiro, he told her—joined her again. He brought her food and she ate ravenously, guiltily. Apparently nothing would disturb her appetite.

Stephen kept her away from the ruin of the house. He stayed with her, silent but somehow comforting. He found an empty car and sat with her in it. Eli's people had apparently driven away or killed all of the second, uncontaminated group of car people. Now they were cleaning up. Some were digging a mass grave. Others were loading their newly appropriated cars and trucks with whatever they thought their enclave could use.

"Take a couple of radios," Stephen told a woman who passed near them. "I think for a change we'll be needing them."

The woman nodded and went away.

Jacob found Stephen and Keira sitting together in the car. Without a word, he climbed into Keira's lap and fell asleep. She stroked his hair, accepting his presence and his youth and thinking nothing. It was possible to endure if she thought nothing at all.

Sometime later, Ingraham returned. He had driven all the way to the edge of Needles, but found no private hauler. Everyone had gathered near him to hear about his chase. When they had heard, they all looked at Eli.

Eli closed his eyes, rubbed a hand over his face. "All right." He spoke so softly, Keira would not have heard him without her newly enhanced hearing. "All right, we knew it would happen sooner or later."

"But a private hauler," Stephen said. "They go all over the country, all over the continent. And they deal with people who go all over the world."

Eli nodded bleakly. He looked years older and agonizingly weary.

"What are we going to do?" Ingraham asked.

Meda answered him. "What do you think we're going to do? We're going home!"

Eli put his arm around her. "That's right," he said. "In a few months we'll be one of the few sane enclaves left in the country—maybe in the world." He shook his head. "Use your imagination. Think of what it will be like in the cities and towns." He paused, reached down and picked up Zera, who had sat at his feet and was leaning sideways against his right leg. "Remember the kids," he said softly. "They'll need us more than ever now. Whatever you do, remember the kids."

Epilogue

Stephen Kaneshiro waited until he began to hear radio reports of the new illness. Then he put on his gloves and drove with Ingraham into Barstow. From there, by phone, he tried to locate his wife and son. He had been with Keira until then, had seemed content with her, but he felt he had a duty to bring his wife and son to relative safety, though they must have given him up for dead long ago.

Eli warned him that no one knew what effect the disease might have on a young child. Stephen understood, but he wanted to give his family what he felt might be their only chance.

He could not. It took him two days of anonymous, sound-only phoning to discover that his wife had gone back to her parents and recently had returned with them to Japan.

He came back to the mountaintop ranch and Keira. Her hair was growing in thick and dark. She was pregnant—perhaps by Stephen, perhaps from her one night with Eli. Stephen did not seem to care which any more than she did.

"Will you stay with me?" she asked him. He was a good man. He had helped her through the terrible time after the deaths of her father and sister. He did not excite her as Eli had. She had not known how much she cared for him, how much she needed him until he went away. When he came back, all she could think was: *No wife! Thank God!* Then she was ashamed. Sometime later she asked the question.

"Will you stay with me?"

They sat in their room next to the nursery. Their room in Meda's house. He sat on the bed and she on the desk chair where she could not touch him. She could not bear to touch him until she knew he did not plan to leave her.

"We'll have to cut ourselves off even more than we have so far," he said. "I brought new weapons, ammunition, and foods we can't raise. I think we're going to have to be self-sufficient for a while. Maybe a long while. You and I couldn't even have a house. Not enough wood."

"It doesn't matter," she said.

"San Francisco is burning," he continued. "I bought a lot of news printouts in town. We haven't been getting enough by radio. Fires are being set everywhere. Maybe uninfected people are sterilizing the city in the only way they can think of. Or maybe it's infected people crazy with their symptoms and the noise and smells and lights. L.A. is beginning to burn, too, and San Diego. In Phoenix, someone is blowing up houses and buildings. Three oil refineries went up in Texas. In Louisiana there's a group that has decided the disease was brought in by foreigners—so they're shooting anyone who seems a little odd to them. Mostly Asians, blacks, and browns."

She stared at him. He stared back expressionlessly.

"In New York, Seattle, Hong Kong, and Tokyo, doctors and nurses have been caught spreading the disease. The compulsion is at work already."

She thought of her father, then shook her head, not wanting to think of him. He had been so right, so wrong, and so utterly helpless.

"Everything will be chaos soon," Stephen said. "There have been outbreaks in Germany, England, France, Turkey, India, Korea, Nigeria, the Soviet Union.... It will be chaos. Then a new order. Hell, a new species. Jacob will win, you know. We'll help him. And Jacob thinks uninfected people smell like food."

"We'll have to help him to help ourselves," she said.

"We'll be obsolete, you and me."

"They'll be our children."

He lowered his eyes, looked at her belly where her pregnancy was beginning to show. "They'll be all we have," he said, "the two of us." There was a long pause. "I've lost everyone, too. Will you stay with me?"

She nodded solemnly and went to him. They held each other until they could no longer tell which of them was trembling.

PATTERNMASTER

Prologue

Rayal had his lead wife, Jansee, with him on that last night. He lay beside her in his huge bed, secure, lulled by the peacefulness of the Pattern as it flowed to him. The Pattern had been peaceful for over a year now. A year without a major Clayark attack on any sector of Patternist Territory. A luxury. Rayal had known enough years of fighting to be glad to relax and enjoy the respite. Only Jansee could still find reason for discontent. Her children, as usual.

"I think tomorrow I'll send a mute to check on our sons," she said.

Rayal yawned. He found her too much like a mute herself in her concern for her young. The two boys, aged twelve and two, were at school in Redhill Sector, 480 kilometers away. She would have gone against custom and kept them near her at the school in Forsyth, their birth sector, if he had let her. "Why bother?" he said. "You're linked with them. If there was anything wrong with them, you would be the first to realize it. Why send a mute to find out what you already know?"

"Because I'll be able to see them through the mute's memory when he comes back. I haven't seen either of them for over two years. Not since the youngest was born."

Rayal shook his head. "Why do you want to see them?"

"I don't know. There's something... not wrong, but... I don't know." He could feel her uneasiness influencing the Pattern, rippling its vast interwoven surface. "Will you let me send a mute?"

"Send an outsider. He'll be better able to defend himself if the Clayarks notice him." Then he smiled. "You should have more children. Perhaps then you would be less concerned for these two." She was used to his mocking. He had said such things to her before. But this time she seemed to take him seriously. He could feel her attention on him, focused, aware even of his smile, though she could not see him in the darkness.

"You want me to have children by one of your outsiders?" she asked.

He looked toward her in surprise, his mind tracing the solemnity of her expression. She was calling his bluff. She should have known better. "By a journeyman, perhaps."

"What?"

"Have them by a journeyman, or at least an apprentice. Not an outsider."

"And which... journeyman or apprentice did you have in mind?"

He turned away from her in annoyance. She was continuing this nonsense to goad him. No other woman in his House would dare to bait him so. Perhaps, for a change, she should not be allowed to get away with it either.

"Michael will do," he said quietly.

"Mich... Rayal!" He enjoyed the indignation in her voice. Michael was a young apprentice just out of school and about ten years Jansee's junior.

"You asked me to choose someone for you. I've chosen Michael."

She thought about that for a while, then retreated. But her pride did not allow her to retreat far. "Someday when you promote Michael to journeyman and he can hear me without embarrassment, I'm going to tell him about this." She laid a hand alongside his face. "Then, husband, if you still insist that you will give me no more children, I will accept your choice."

This was, he realized, as much a promise as a threat. She meant it. He reached for her, pulled her closer to him. "It's for your own good that I refuse you. You're really too much the mute-mother to have more children. You care too much what happens to them."

"I care."

"And they're going to kill each other. You're so strong that even your child by a weaker man might be able to compete with our two sons."

"They wouldn't *have* to kill each other."

He gave a mental shrug. "Didn't I have to kill two brothers and a sister to get where I am? Won't at least some of my children and yours be as eager to inherit power as I was?" He felt her try to pull away from him and knew that he had won a point. He held her where she was. "Two brothers and a sister," he repeated. "And it could easily have been two sisters if my strongest sister had not been wise enough to ally herself with me and become my lead wife."

Now he let her go, but she lay still where she was. The Pattern rippled with her sorrow. It reflected her emotions almost as readily as it did his own. But unless he cooperated, it would not respond to her control. He spoke again to her gently.

"Even our sons will compete with each other. That will be difficult enough for you to watch, if it happens during your lifetime."

"But what about your other children," she said. "You have so many by other wives."

"And I'll have more. I don't have your sensitivity. Those of my children who don't compete to succeed me will live to contribute to the people's strength."

She was silent for a long while, her awareness focused on his face. "Would you really have tried to kill me if I had opposed you or refused you?"

"Of course. On your own, you might have become a threat to me."

There was more silence, then, "Do you know why I allied with you instead of contesting?"

"Yes. Now I do."

She went on as though she had not heard him. "I hate killing. We have to kill Clayarks just to survive. I can do that. But we don't have to kill each other."

Rayal jerked the Pattern sharply and Jansee jumped, gasping at the sudden disturbance. It was comparable physically to a painless but startling slap in the face.

"You see?" he said. "I've just awakened several thousand Patternists by exerting no more effort than another person might use to snap his fingers. Sister-wife, that is power worth killing for."

Jansee radiated sudden anger. She thought of her sons fighting and her mind filled with bitter things to say about his power. But the pointlessness of verbalizing them to him, of all people, undermined her anger. "Not to me," she said sadly, "and I hope not to my sons. Let them save their savagery, their power, for the Clayarks." She paused. "Have you noticed the group of mutes outside in front of the House?"

This was not the change of subject that it seemed to be. He knew what she was leading up to but he let her go. "Yes."

"They've come a long way," she said.

"You can let them in if you like."

"I will, later, when they've finished their prayers." She shook her head. "Hajji mutes. Poor fools."

"Jansee..."

"They've come here because they think you're a god, and you won't even bother to let them in out of the cold."

"They get exactly what they expect from me, Jansee. The assurance of good health, long life, and protection from abuse by their Masters. Making a religion of their gratitude was their own idea."

"Not that you mind," she said softly. "Power. In fact, since you hold the Pattern, you're even a kind of god to the Patternists, aren't you? Shall I worship you, too, husband?"

"Not that you would." He smiled. "But it doesn't matter. There are times when I need someone around me who isn't afraid of me."

"Lest your own conceit destroy you," she said bitterly.

The Clayarks chose that moment to end the year of peace. With an ancient gun of huge proportions, they stood on a hill just within sight of the lights of Rayal's House. They had found the gun far south in territory that was exclusively their own. With rare patience and forethought, they had worked hard with it, cleaning it, coming to understand how it was supposed to work, repairing it, practicing with it. Then they dragged it to the House of the Patternmaster, their greatest enemy. It was unlikely that they would be able to use it more than once. Thus it would be effective only if they could use it against Rayal.

Rayal's sentries noticed them, but, lulled by the peace and unaware of the cannon, they paid no attention to Clayarks so far away. Thus the Clayarks had all the time their clumsy fingers needed to load their huge weapon, aim it, and fire.

Their aim was good and they were very lucky. The first shot smashed through the wall of the Patternmaster's private apartment, beheading the Patternmaster's lead wife and injuring the Patternmaster himself so severely about the head and shoulders that he was totally occupied for long important minutes with saving his own life. For all his power, he lay helpless. The people of his House were surprised enough, disoriented enough, to give the Clayarks time to fire again. But the destruction had excited the Clayarks. They abandoned the cannon to swarm down and finish the House in a more satisfying, personal way.

Chapter One

The sun had not been up long enough to burn off the cold dampness of morning when Teray and Iray left their dormitory room at Redhill School for the last time.

Iray was all eagerness and apprehension and her emotions were contagious. Teray had resigned himself to being caught up in them. The act of leaving the school together not only reinforced their status as adults, but made them husband and wife. Teray had waited four wearisome years for the chance to leave safely and begin working toward his dream of founding his own House.

Now, with Iray, he walked toward the main gate. There was no ceremony—not for their leaving school, nor for their marriage. Only two people paid any attention to their going. Teray sensed them both inside one of the dormitories, a Patternist girl who had been Iray's friend and a middle-aged mute woman. They stood together at a dormitory window, looking down at Iray. The friend kept her feelings to herself, but the mute radiated such a mixture of sadness and excitement that Teray knew she and Iray must have been close.

Iray was too full of her own emotions to be aware of the pair. Teray flashed her a brief mental image and she reached back, contrite, to say her good-byes.

He sent back no parting thoughts of his own. He had had nothing to do with mutes for years. His maturing mental strength had made him too dangerous to them. For their sakes, he maintained only an impersonal master-servant relationship with them. And he had made few friends among his teachers and fellow students. They too were wary of his strength. He had been a power at the school, but except for Iray he had been much alone.

Outside the main gate, he and Iray met the two men who had been waiting for them. The older man was of medium height and hard, square build, a man of obvious physical strength. The younger man was built more like Teray—tall and lean. He was probably no older than Teray.

Joachim! Teray's thought went out to the older man. *I didn't expect you to come yourself.*

The man smiled faintly and spoke aloud: "It isn't often that I take on such a promising apprentice. I wouldn't want anything to happen to you on your way to my House."

Teray transmitted surprise: *There's been trouble, then? Who was raided?*

"Coransee. And vocalize. I'm spreading my perception as widely as I can just in case the raiders are still in the area."

"Coransee?" said Teray obediently. "So close inside the sector?"

"And the most powerful one of us." The man with Joachim spoke for the first time. "The raiders killed two of his outsiders and kidnaped a mute."

"I hope to heaven they killed the mute too," said Joachim. "Killed him quickly, I mean."

Teray nodded, sharing the hope. Mutes who were not tortured to death and who did not die of the Clayark disease became the worst of their former-masters' enemies. "You think there are still Clayarks inside the sector?" he asked Joachim.

"Yes. That's why I brought Jer along." Joachim gestured toward his companion. "He's one of my strongest outsiders."

Teray glanced at Jer with interest, wondering how the man's strength measured up against his own. Through the Pattern, Teray had already sensed that Jer was strong. But how strong? It was not possible to make a definite determination guided only by the Pattern. No doubt Joachim knew, though. He had probably tested Jer as thoroughly as he had tested Teray. And after the testing, he had made Jer an outsider and accepted Teray as an apprentice.

Iray's voice brought Teray out of his thoughts. "But, Joachim, with both you and Jer here, won't your House be in danger?"

Joachim glanced at her, his grim expression softening. "Not likely. The Clayarks know my reputation. We're all linked in my House.

My lead wife can draw strength from everyone in the House for defense. If the Clayarks attack one of my people, the rest know, and they all respond. The Clayarks wouldn't risk attacking them with less than an army, and I don't think they've managed to smuggle an army into the sector."

"We'd have more dead than the larger Houses," said Jer, "because we don't have their strength. But their people fight as individuals, and we fight as one. Their people always miss some Clayarks and let them escape. We kill them all."

Teray noticed the pride in the man's voice and wondered how Joachim could inspire pride even in an outsider. But then, Teray's attitude toward outsider status was, he knew, colored by his desire never to occupy it. It was a permanently inferior servant position. The best that an outsider could hope for was to find a Housemaster like Joachim whom he could respect and serve with some semblance of pride. The worst he could get was slavery.

The horses waited for them a few steps away in a grove of trees, and Teray noticed that Iray walked the distance beside Joachim. She, who only a few moments before had been so excited about leaving the school with Teray. True, she had known Joachim before she met Teray. The Housemaster had been her second when she made the difficult transition from childhood to adulthood and membership in the Pattern. She would probably have gone into his House as one of his wives if she had not met Teray. Now Teray watched them together with suspicion. He would spend at least two years with Joachim, learning, preparing to begin his own House. If only he did not lose his wife in the process.

He came up beside Iray as they reached the horses. He touched her mind lightly with a one-word reminder carefully screened from Joachim and Jer: *Wife!*

His caution was lost on her. She seized his thought carelessly like a happy child and magnified it to a mental shout. To it, she added enthusiastically, *Husband!*

A proclamation. Joachim and Jer could hardly have missed it. He could feel their amusement as keenly as he could feel his own embarrassment. But at least she had told him what he wanted to know. And, fortunately, she had completely missed his meaning. Of course there was a bond between Iray and Joachim. But it was no more than the bond between any man and a woman he had seconded. Affection. No more.

He cast around for a way to end the silence and focus Joachim's and Jer's attention elsewhere. It was then that he noticed the horse that Joachim had mounted. It was a show horse, of course, as were the three others. They were all as carefully bred and trained as most mutes. They were part of a project that Joachim had undertaken more for enjoyment than profit. But the one Joachim rode was something special.

"Joachim, your horse..."

The Housemaster smiled. "I wondered when Iray would let you notice."

Teray let his curiosity be felt partly because he was actually curious, and partly in relief that Joachim too was ignorant of his foolish jealousy. But the horse... "You have no mental controls on it at all?"

"None," said Joachim.

Gingerly, Teray felt the stallion out. Gingerly because animals, like mutes, were easily injured, easily killed. And too, uncontrolled animals unconsciously hit intruding Patternist minds with any emotions they felt. Especially violent emotions. But Teray received only calm from the horse. Unusual calm.

"An experiment of mine," said Joachim. "This horse doesn't need to be controlled any more than the average mute. In fact, you program it like a mute. And once it's programmed, the Clayarks could fire a cannon next to it and the programming would hold. You wouldn't have to waste time controlling the horse when you should be giving all your attention to the Clayarks." Joachim grinned. "I'll tell you more about it when we get home."

Teray nodded. Home. Joachim could not know how good that word sounded. The school had been Teray's home for far too long. He had made his transition to adulthood nearly four years before. Even then, there had been little more that the teachers could teach him. But he had stayed, learning what he could about his abilities on his own, getting occasional help from a visiting Housemaster, waiting and hoping for a Housemaster who would accept him as an apprentice.

Several had offered to take him on as an outsider. If he had not still been under the protection of the school, some of them might have been tempted to take him by force. Doubtless that would be possible now, while he was still young and unskilled. And if they took him now, they could prevent him from learning the skills that might make him a danger to them. But no one wanted to risk accepting him as an apprentice. An outsider was a permanent inferior. An apprentice was a potential superior. An apprentice was the young colt hanging around the edges of the herd, biding his time until he could kill off the old herd stallion and take over. Or at least that was the way the Housemasters he had met seemed to feel.

It was much to Joachim's credit that he had not been afraid. In fact, when Iray had introduced Teray to Joachim, the Housemaster had mentioned the possibility of an apprenticeship before Teray even thought it wise to bring up the matter. It took a confident, powerful Housemaster to accept an apprentice with Teray's potential. But Joachim had had the necessary confidence and power, and now, finally, Teray was going home.

Joachim had taken a lead position with Jer. Now he called back, "We're going to have to stop at Coransee's House first. He wants to see me—probably to get me to help him with his Clayark problem."

Iray caught her breath sharply. "To visit Coransee! Joachim, is he your friend? So powerful a lord." She was a child about half the time.

There was a pause before Joachim answered, then, "I know him." He sounded almost bitter. "We're not friends, but I know him."

As the strongest Housemaster in the sector, Coransee was a kind of unofficial local leader. That made him a celebrity to people like Iray. Teray had heard him spoken of with admiration and envy, but never with bitterness. But then, Teray had been shut away in the school and people were careful what they said before schoolchildren. Well, he was out of school now. It would be best for him to know something more about the Housemaster he was about to visit. "Joachim?" he called.

Joachim dropped back to ride beside Teray, leaving Jer to lead. *You'd better make it "Lord Joachim," Teray. For the rest of the day. And definitely "Lord Coransee." He values formality.*

Teray accepted this with interest. It was the first nonvocal communication he had had with Joachim this morning, and it was nonvocal only to emphasize its seriousness. It was an order, and a warning.

Joachim went on and Teray realized that he was reaching Iray too. *Be introduced to him with Jer and me, then drift away among his women and outsiders.*

"Joachim, what is it?" Iray asked.

Joachim looked at her silently, until she corrected herself.

"Lord Joachim."

"Sector politics," Joachim said aloud. "Nothing more." And he again took his place beside Jer.

Teray watched him, wondering at his sudden reticence. Now Teray had more questions than ever. But Joachim's silence was a closed one. It did not invite questions.

By midday they had reached Coransee's House. It was a four-story mansion, columned, ancient, ornate, surrounded by well-landscaped grounds and flanked by outbuildings. It had been built on a hill and was visible for miles. Teray could see why it was the envy of many lesser lords, and why Coransee had risked fighting a duel for it several years before. To get it, he had had to kill a powerful woman who had held it for over two decades. In school, Teray had seen pictures of ancient palaces that were probably smaller. Teray gazed out over Coransee's land, seeing the side pastures and the grazing horses and cattle. Coransee supplied the sector with most of its meat and its riding animals. The small herd that Joachim kept had never been more than a hobby.

Two mutes hurried from one of the outbuildings to greet the four newcomers politely and take their horses. As Joachim led the way to the House, he warned Teray and Iray once more:

"Both of you remember what I told you. Take up with a woman, an outsider, even a mute, and get out of the way fast. I'll make it as easy as I can for you."

Teray nodded and Joachim led them inside.

There were several women and outsiders seated and standing near the fireplace of the huge common room in which Teray found himself. Before Teray could decide what they were doing, one of them sent the informing thought, *He knows you're here. He's coming.*

Joachim acknowledged with thanks and sat down. The others followed his example. Their wait was not long.

The atmosphere of the room changed, grew tense as Coransee entered. The Housemaster radiated power in the way of a man not only confident but arrogant. A man who meant for people to stand in awe of him. A man Teray disliked instantly. The Pattern told Teray that he and Coransee were temperamentally incompatible. They could be said to be far apart in the Pattern. The reason for the distance might have been great temperamental dissimilarity, or dangerous similarity—similar inclinations toward dishonesty or greed, for instance. Whatever it was, it separated Teray and Coransee definitely, thoroughly.

The four visitors stood up as the Housemaster entered. Coransee was a big man, tall, well-muscled, but without the heavy, stocky look of Joachim. Teray found himself staring at Coransee's long cold face with a feeling that disturbed him because it was gone before he could recognize it. It took him a moment to realize that Coransee was looking at him in the same way. But Coransee was slower to cover his reaction. Teray had time to wonder whether what he had seen in the Housemaster's eyes, and for an instant in his thoughts, was recognition. But whatever it was, it faded quickly into puzzlement. Then Coransee's shield snapped into place and Teray got nothing more. Reflexively, Teray shielded his own thoughts but behind his shield he continued to wonder.

Suddenly, as though in attack, Coransee drove his massive mental strength hard against Teray's shield. He meant to break through it. There was no doubt of that. He had apparently seen something in Teray's thoughts that caught his attention. He wanted another look, he did not get it; Teray's shield held firm. Before Teray could respond to the unprovoked attack. Joachim spoke up angrily.

"Coransee! My apprentice is a guest in your House. He's given you no offense. What's the matter with you?"

For a moment Coransee stared at him in cold anger, stared at him as though he was an unwelcome intruder breaking into a private conversation. "Nothing is the matter," he said finally. "Your apprentice is a very able young man. I think I may have seen him before—perhaps in one of my visits to the school."

Joachim gave Teray no time to deny this. "You may have," he said. "Although I can't see why that would be reason for you to attack him now." Joachim took a deep breath, calmed himself. "His name is Teray. This is his wife Iray, and my outsider Jer."

Coransee nodded, acknowledging all three introductions at once. But his attention had fastened on Teray.

"Teray," he repeated, drawing the word out thoughtfully. "How did you happen to choose a name ending in 'ray,' boy?"

The "boy" rankled, but Teray pretended to ignore it. "I'm told that I'm one of the sons of Patternmaster Rayal," he answered. His name had attracted attention before but he had fought for it and won the right to keep it while still in school.

"Rayal?" Coransee raised an eyebrow. "Rayal's children must number in the hundreds by now. But you're the first I've found who thought himself worthy to take his father's name."

Teray shrugged. "An adult is free to take any name. I chose to share my father's."

"And cause your wife to share it too, I see."

"No, Lord. She came to me freely and chose her own name."

"Did she." Coransee's attention seemed to wander. He had relaxed slightly, thinning his total shield down to a more comfortable heavy screen. For a moment, something flickered so close to the surface of his thoughts that Teray almost had it. He could have had it if he had dared to be obvious about his probing. But he let it pass. Abruptly, Coransee changed the subject.

"Joachim, I have an artist for you."

The sudden switch obviously surprised Joachim as much as it did Teray. But Joachim was cautiously enthusiastic. "An artist? I've been around the sector looking for a good one to work with some of my outsiders."

"I know." For the first time, Coransee smiled. "And this one is special. Sensitive. Fantastically sensitive."

Joachim began to draw in even his cautious enthusiasm. "They're usually more than a little crazy when they're too sensitive. They don't have enough control of their ability to receive selectively."

"Oh, this boy has all the control he needs. Picks up latent images from anybody—Patternists, mutes, animals, even Clayarks. How many artists do you know who can lay their hands on a boulder that a Clayark has leaned against and read you the story of that Clayark's life?"

"Clayarks?"

"Test him."

"I've never had an artist who could pick up Clayark images. Call him."

Coransee turned toward the group of women and outsiders near the fireplace and called, "Laro!"

One of the outsiders in the group got up at once and came over to Coransee. He was a young man, probably only a few years older than Teray. Short and small-boned, he moved with quick, fluid grace. The Pattern betrayed him as a man of little mental strength. However competent he was at his art, he could never be anything more than an outsider. If he was lucky, his talent would buy him a comfortable place in someone else's House, and he would be troubled by none of the competitive spirit that sent stronger people out to found Houses of their own. If he was unlucky and did have such spirit, it would soon get him killed.

Coransee introduced the artist. "Laro, this is Lord Joachim and some members of his House. His people are artists and craftsmen."

Laro lowered his head and spoke respectfully. "My Lord." He was close to Joachim in the Pattern, Teray realized. That meant Joachim would probably buy him. Joachim's people were able to form themselves into the deadly fighting machine that Clayarks avoided only because Joachim chose them so carefully. He chose them not only for their skill and strength, but for their compatibility within the Pattern. The Pattern was a vast network of mental links that joined every Patternist with the Patternmaster. Its first purpose was supposed to be to give the Patternmaster the strength he needed— strength drawn through the links from the Patternists—to combat large-scale Clayark attacks. Actually, though, the Pattern was more often used as Joachim used it, as Teray was using it now. To judge, roughly, the mental strength of other Patternists, and to judge, more precisely, their compatibility.

Teray brought his attention back to the two Housemasters and realized that Coransee was listing the artist's accomplishments— doubtless to make the young man look as attractive as possible before they began talking about a price. Neither Housemaster was paying any attention to Teray, and Teray had no interest in the bargaining to come. He touched Iray lightly and started to go over to the group that Laro had left. Iray, evidently remembering Joachim's instructions, started to follow. Coransee stopped them.

"Teray, Iray, wait." He smiled again. He had an open, friendly smile that Teray would have trusted on anyone else. "View Laro's work with us." A command disguised as an invitation.

Caught, Teray and Iray came back slowly and sat down. Teray watched as the artist went past him and crossed the huge room to the group of women and outsiders that he had just left. From them he took three ceramic figurines and a small painting. Teray realized now why the group had seemed so absorbed. The artist had been entertaining them. Now Joachim's party was to sample his work.

Laro handed the painting to Joachim. The figurines went to Teray, Iray, and Jer. Teray first thought his was a wild animal. Not until he held it did he realize that the well-muscled four-legged body was human-headed. The thing was a Clayark.

Teray stared at it with interest. He had seen pictures of Clayarks at the school, but nothing as lifelike as this. His hands could almost feel warmth and a texture of flesh.

He folded his hands around the figurine, closed his eyes, and opened his mind to whatever experience awaited him. He expected a jolt. He had prepared himself for it—but not nearly enough.

Abruptly, shockingly, Teray was the Clayark. There was no time for anticipation, no disorientation. He felt himself seized and possessed by the artist-implanted "consciousness" of the figurine. Fortunately, by the time Teray recovered enough to struggle, he had also recovered enough to know that he should not struggle. He was still the Clayark.

He was within a torch-lit cave in the mountains far to the east of Redhill. He could see the rough gray-rock walls and the fire of the torches. He was a member of a munitions clan. His people made the rifles with which other Clayarks hunted food and fought Patternists. Now, though, his mind was not on gun-making. Now he had been challenged.

The sleek young female who stood apart from other onlookers, watching and holding her head so high—she was his. She was the daughter of his mother's brother, and long promised to him. Only he had a right to her. Not this other, this dog with his long jowly muzzle of a face. The other, the challenger, was big both with fat and with muscle. Years of handling heavy metal weights had given him great strength. And years of stuffing his belly like a pig had made him slow and clumsy. Savagely, the Clayark who was Teray lunged at him.

As the Clayark, Teray bit and punched with heavily calloused hands—or forefeet. He seized and tore and gouged, all the while leaping about with speed and agility that his opponent could not match. All his opponent's power was in his massive arms. Or forelegs. As long as the Clayark Teray could avoid those arms, he was safe.

Then the Clayark Teray stumbled, and almost fell over a loose rock as he dodged one of his opponent's clumsy swipes. His hand closed around the rock as he leaped away.

He wheeled and charged again. This time he reared back on hind legs, which were more catlike than human. As his opponent reared eagerly to meet him and finally lay hands on him, Teray smashed the rock against the side of the creature's head. Then he stood back in triumph and watched while his opponent died.

Teray opened his eyes and stared at the small figurine in his hands. He could see its beauty, its perfection, even more clearly now. What was it the Clayarks called themselves? Sphinxes. Creatures out of ancient mythology, lion-bodied, human-headed. The description was not really accurate. The Clayarks were furless and tailless, and they did possess hands. But they were much more sphinxes—creatures who were at least partly human—than they were the animals Teray had always considered them.

And outsiders were not necessarily the inferior people Teray had considered them. The artist Laro had done something that Rayal himself could not have done. No Patternist could read the mind of a Clayark directly. The disease the Clayarks carried gave them at least that much protection from their Patternist enemies. And only the most sensitive artist could lift latent impressions of Clayarks from objects the Clayarks had touched. Laro not only lifted those impressions, he refined them, amplified them, and implanted them in his figurines and paintings. Teray caught the artist's attention and sent him silent appreciation. Laro smiled.

Jer and Iray had finished their experiences as Teray had. All three waited now as Joachim gazed silently at the painting. No sign of what he was experiencing appeared on his face, but they all could see that he was completely absorbed in the painting. Finally, Joachim's show was over and he looked up.

He put down the painting and turned to Coransee, his eagerness barely veiled. "What do you want for him?"

Moments later, in Coransee's office, Teray, Joachim, Laro, and Coransee himself were seated, waiting for Coransee to name his price. Joachim had tried to send Teray to entertain himself with more of Laro's work, but Coransee had insisted on his sitting in on the bargaining.

"He's an apprentice," the Housemaster had said. "He might as well start learning right now." Then, about the trade:

"Joachim, I had to trade with another sector to get Laro. He's a rare find, and I had intended to keep him. He's not close to me or many of my people in the Pattern, but that's not as important to me as it is to you. I'll trade him to you, though, if he agrees to the trade."

At once, Laro spoke up. "I do agree, Lord. I've been content here. I mean no disrespect. But Lord Joachim and his people seem much closer to me in the Pattern."

Coransee nodded. "That's what I thought. We trade then, Joachim."

Joachim leaned back in his chair. "As I asked before, what do you want for him?"

"I trade for strength, as always," Coransee said. "The success of the last Clayark raid makes it obvious that I don't have enough."

"If you were trading with anyone else, I'd advise you to trade for compatibility within the Pattern," said Joachim. "With more compatibility, you wouldn't have any of the Clayarks who attacked you still alive and dangerous. But you're trading with me and I don't have anyone even close to you in the Pattern."

"Would you be willing to trade Jer, the outsider you brought with you?" Coransee asked. Teray frowned. It seemed to him that the Housemaster was less serious than he should have been. Teray got the feeling that he had no interest at all in Jer.

"Jer's young," said Joachim, going along with him. "Only two years past transition. But he has the strength you're looking for."

"You would trade Jer?" asked Coransee softly.

"If you wanted him."

"I don't, of course."

"No."

"I just wondered. You're sentimental about your people some-times. But you want this artist. I can see that. You'd trade anyone short of your lead wife for him."

Joachim looked uncomfortable. Coransee was playing with him. Dangling the artist temptingly before him, but refusing to name a price. And doing it all in a mildly insulting way.

"Coransee, for the third time, will you tell me what you're trad-ing for?"

"Of course," said Coransee. "Of course. I offer you Laro for Teray."

The words were said so casually that it seemed to take Joachim a moment to digest them. More likely, though, Joachim used his moment of "surprised silence" to think of a negative answer that would not close the trading.

Teray looked from one man to the other. He had known what Coransee was going to say just an instant before he said it. Joachim had probably known too. Coransee had been a little too eager, had not concealed his thoughts as carefully as he might have. In his carelessness, he had permitted Teray to learn one other thing—a thing that was somehow part of the reason why the Housemaster wanted Teray badly enough to trade a tal-ent like Laro's. A talent that had surely cost him several of his people.

But perhaps it would not matter. Already Joachim was turning down the offer.

"Coransee, I've told you this man is an apprentice, not an out-sider. He's not my property. In fact, as an apprentice he's still under the protection of the school. I can't legally trade him."

"And you wouldn't if you could." Coransee spoke lazily, as though he had gotten the answer he expected and was merely play-ing another game. "Let's be realistic, Joachim. You want my artist, I need your apprentice. Laro is much closer to you in the Pattern than Teray is. And law or no law, Teray would have no power to object if you traded him."

Surprisingly, Joachim seemed to reconsider for a moment. Teray, watching him, felt the beginnings of fear. He had waited so long to avoid being taken as an outsider. If now, on his first day out of the school, all his waiting was to prove in vain...

"You were talking about strength," Joachim was saying. "Now that the Clayarks have found a way to get into the sector undetected, I'll be needing Teray's strength myself."

"For what? That miniature Pattern of yours would wipe out any Clayarks who haven't heard what a waste of time and lives it is to attack you."

"Even a miniature Pattern can always use additional strength."

"I protect the school," said Coransee. "I need the strongest outsiders I can get for the good of the school."

Joachim made a sound of disgust. "You don't even expect me to believe that. What is it really, Coransee? Why do you want my apprentice so badly?"

"Perhaps because he's another son of Patternmaster Rayal?" Teray spoke for the first time. "One of my many brothers?" His questions were not really questions but he looked toward Coransee as though expecting him to answer.

Coransee stared at him blankly for a moment. Then he smiled without humor and spoke to Joachim. "You see? Already he proves his usefulness to me. I was careless about maintaining my shield, and immediately he reminded me." And to Teray, "What else did you pick up... brother?"

By now Teray knew that he had made a mistake. He should have kept his findings—and the strength and stealth of his probe—to himself. But it was too late now. No lie would get past an alerted Coransee.

"Only your determination to make me your outsider, Lord."

"And how do you feel about that determination?"

Perhaps it was the condescending man-to-child tone of Coransee's voice that made Teray shut out the urgent warnings Joachim was sending and answer in his own way.

"Slavery has never appealed to me, Lord."

Something hardened in Coransee's voice. "You consider outsiders slaves then. And, of course, you would never voluntarily become a slave, would you?"

Teray! Joachim finally managed to make his thought felt. *Stay out of this! You don't know what you're doing. The more you antagonize him, the less chance we have.*

I won't become his outsider, Joachim. Teray screened heavily, protecting the thought from Coransee's interception.

You will if you don't stop talking and let me handle it. I've got the rest of the day to talk him out of it.

He won't be talked out of it. He's made up his mind. I'm going to have to face him sooner or later, no matter what.

If you're foolish enough to attack him, Teray, I'll help him against you myself. Now be quiet and fade into the background with Laro!

The intensity of Joachim's anger burned into Teray. He had no doubt that that Housemaster was completely serious. The dialogue had taken place in only a few seconds, so there had been no more of a pause in his conversation with Coransee than Coransee's last questions deserved. Now he still had to answer that question and do it in a way that would not lead to his deeper involvement. Somehow. He was about to speak when Joachim took the matter out of his hands.

"Are you trading with me, Coransee, or with my apprentice?" he asked angrily.

Coransee turned slowly to look at Joachim. Teray was startled at the relief he felt to have the man's eyes off him.

"Don't you think the boy should have something to say about this?" asked Coransee.

"You said it yourself." Joachim ran the words on both the vocal and mental level for emphasis. "What we decide, he will have to accept. He shouldn't even be here. Neither should the artist."

"All right," Coransee agreed. Teray wondered, under his renewed fear, how it felt to Joachim to have his most serious words answered with no more than mild amusement. "But the boy is right, you know. Sooner or later he will have to face me."

Teray said nothing, sent no parting thought as he left the office. Coransee's casual undetected eavesdropping into his conversation with Joachim was no more than payment for his own earlier snooping. But it angered him. No one should have been able to bypass his screens so easily without being noticed. He had been careless himself. It would not happen again.

He located Iray as quickly as he could, then managed to find a private corner where he could tell her what had happened.

She heard him, her eyes widening with disbelief as he spoke. Then before she could respond, a mute interrupted them with an offer of cool drinks and food. . . . It was the first time he could recall her being harsh with a mute.

"Get away from us! Leave us alone!" *Teray, what are you saying?*

"Speak aloud," he ordered. "And screen. This will be all over the house soon enough."

But Joachim wouldn't . . .

"Iray!"

She switched in mid-sentence. ". . . trade you. He wouldn't. He needs you. You're the strongest man he's ever been able to fit into his House."

"I didn't say he was going to trade me. I said Coransee wants him to."

"But why?"

"I don't know." Teray frowned. "He's found that he's my brother—half-brother, probably. It has something to do with that."

"What difference could that make?"

"I tell you, I don't know."

"It must be something else. Maybe he really does need your strength now that the Clayarks are raiding him."

"He can use my strength. But he doesn't really need it. He didn't even expect us to believe him when he said that."

"Maybe he just wants to do something to Joachim—get even with him for something." She shook her head angrily, bitterly. "Maybe he just likes being a son of a Clayark bitch!" She stood leaning against him, radiating her anger. "Joachim won't let it happen," she said. "He must have expected some kind of trouble, the way he kept warning us. But we can depend on him."

"I hope so. But there was something. . . at the last, when he made me leave, he threatened to help Coransee against me if I attacked."

"He was angry. He didn't mean it."

"He was angry, all right. But he meant it. He would have done it."

She opened her mouth to protest again, to defend Joachim. Then she closed it and lowered her head. "It can't happen, Teray." She seemed to surrender to the fear that she had been holding at bay with her anger. She pressed herself against him, trembling. "Don't you see what it would mean?" she whispered. "The outsider restrictions."

He said nothing, only looked at her. He knew which restriction she had in mind. There were several: outsiders were not free to father children as they wished, and of course they had little or no say in where they lived or how long they lived there. They were property. But the restriction Iray had in mind was the one that said outsiders could not marry. They were free enough to have all the sex they wanted with any woman in the House who would have them—as long as they were careful to father no unauthorized offspring. But if, as in Teray's case, a man was married before he lost his freedom, his wife took her place among the women of the House, the House-master's wives. And she became the only woman in the House permanently forbidden to her former husband.

The laws were old, made in harsher times. Perhaps it was reasonable, as the old records said, to forbid weak men to sire potentially weak children. But what reason could there be for denying a man access to his chosen one, his first, while permitting him so many others? What reason but to remind him constantly that he was a slave?

Teray drew a ragged breath. No matter why the laws had been made, they were still in effect, being used every day. Now, if Joachim failed him, they would be used against him.

No, he had chosen Joachim as well as been chosen by him. He knew the man. Iray was right. Joachim would not make the trade.

When they had talked for a while longer, Teray assuring Iray, reassuring himself, another mute approached them to say that Joachim had decided to stay the night. They had been assigned a room. If they wished to go there now...

They had dinner in their room that night, served by a young mute girl who knew enough to go about her work without bothering them. The girl was on her way out when, finally, Joachim came to see them. The mute girl smiled at him and continued out of the room. Joachim watched silently until she closed the door behind her. Then he crossed the room to them, still silent. Teray stood up.

Joachim faced him, met his eyes. "I'm sorry, Teray."

"Sorry?" Teray repeated the word mechanically, then explosively: "Sorry! You mean you did it? You traded me?"

"Yes."

"Joachim, no!" Iray almost screamed the words. Then she was on her feet too, and beside Teray. "You've betrayed us." She radiated more anger than fear. "After I introduced you to Teray."

"How could you do it?" Teray demanded. "Why would you do it?"

Joachim turned away, went to stand beside a window. "You heard him. He wanted you. I couldn't stop him."

"Then why didn't you let me try?"

"You can try if you want to." Joachim shook his head wearily. "You probably will, sooner or later, because he wants you to. He wants to know just how strong you are. And he wants you to know his strength. He wants to put you in your place."

"You're so sure that I have no chance against him?"

"No chance at all. In a few years, maybe, when you've had more training, more experience, when you learn more control. But now... he'll humiliate you before the rest of his House, before Iray." He looked at Iray. "And that will be that."

"That's already that as far as you're concerned," said Iray.

Joachim said nothing.

"After all, you've sold us, and you've been paid." Her voice was harder than Teray had ever heard it. "You're sorry! What do you want? Our forgiveness?"

Joachim answered softly, "I tried. I did everything I could to make him change his mind."

"I don't believe that. Either you wanted the artist and you did what was necessary to get him, or you let Coransee frighten you into making the trade." She looked at him closely. "You are afraid of him, aren't you?"

Startled, Teray looked at Joachim. The Housemaster looked tired, looked almost sick. But he did not look frightened.

"I'm afraid for Teray," said Joachim softly, "and for you."

"Then help us," demanded Teray. "We need your help, not your fear!"

"I can't help you."

"You mean you won't help us. No one outsider is worth the trouble you could give him for taking me. You wouldn't even have to fight."

"Teray, it doesn't have to be as bad as you think, being an outsider." There was desperation in Joachim's voice. "If you can just accept it, stop fighting Coransee, he can teach you more than I ever could. And he's not as far from you in the Pattern as you think."

"And what about me, My Lord?" If there had been any of Iray's childishness left, it was gone now. "Will it also be 'not as bad as I think' with my husband forbidden to me, and his slaver my owner!"

Joachim shook his head, his pain clear in his expression. He reached out to her, but she was closed to him. He took her by the shoulders and held her when she tried to turn away. "If I could help, do you think you would even have to ask me?"

Teray watched him silently for a moment, then, "Tell us why you can't help, Joachim." He thought he knew why. Joachim's anguish was real enough. But he still showed no signs of the fear that Iray had thought she had seen.

Joachim released Iray and turned to look at Teray. "You know, don't you?" he asked softly. "You're too good. You see too much. It got you into trouble this afternoon. Finished any hope I might have had of talking Coransee out of the trade. Too good."

"Tell us why you can't help," Teray repeated. He did know now, but he wanted to hear Joachim say it.

"I wonder how long it will take him to make an outsider of you," Joachim said.

Teray waited.

"All right!" Joachim seemed to have to force himself to go on. "I'm conditioned... controlled! That special horse of mine has more freedom than I have when it comes to dealing with Coransee."

Iray looked at him with disgust. "Controlled? Like a mute? Like an animal?"

"Iray!" Teray wondered why he bothered to stop her. Did Joachim still have pride to save? Did it matter? He was alone. Joachim was useless. What was he going to do?

"Do you know why I allowed him to plant his controls, Teray?"

Teray did not know. Or care. He said nothing.

"Because I wasn't as patient as you were. Because I left the school too soon. And I left alone except for my wife. Coransee picked me up, forced me into his House as an outsider." Joachim hesitated. "So you see, I know what you're both going through. I had been with him seven years when he offered me a chance for freedom. I had to cooperate with him, let him plant his controls in my mind. It's delicate work—the planting. Not like just linking with someone.

As strong as he is, even he couldn't have done it if I had resisted. So I didn't resist. By then, I would have done anything to get free. Anything."

"You call what you have now freedom?" Teray's own contempt was coming through.

"Yes!" said Joachim vehemently. "So will you after a few years of captivity." Then his tone changed, became what it had been earlier—saddened, hopeless. "No. I've been 'free' for years now and Coransee's controls have been in place every minute. He doesn't need my cooperation to hold them. I think I'll wear them for the rest of my life." He shrugged. "He doesn't use them often. But when he does, there's nothing I can do."

A contrite Joachim was no more helpful than an angry one. Teray wanted to ask him to leave. But then he would be alone with Iray, and she would ask him the questions that he was already asking himself. He had no answers even for himself. What could he do?

Joachim talked on, but he had changed his tone again. Now he spoke quietly with anger. "Teray, you were wise enough to stay under the protection of the school until you were accepted for apprenticeship. You were careful. You did everything right. Yet through my weakness and Coransee's dishonesty, you've lost your wife and your freedom. All while you were supposed to be under my protection. No matter what hold Coransee has on me, I can't just go away and forget about you."

"What will you do?" Teray asked resignedly. He already knew the answer.

"I can't do anything directly. You know that. But indirectly, I'll do everything I can, including an appeal to Rayal if necessary." Joachim was moving toward the door and Teray was relieved to see him going.

Parting words: "Teray, believe me, I'll get you away from him."

Teray did not believe him. Nor did he bother to pretend. He went to the door and opened it. "Good-bye, Joachim."

Joachim looked at him a moment longer as though trying to instill belief in his good intentions. As though he would have reached out to Teray if he had not feared finding Teray closed to him. Then he was gone.

Teray turned to Iray and saw that she was trembling.

"What are you going to do?" she whispered.

"I don't know." He ran a hand over his brow and was not surprised to have it come away wet. "I don't know. Maybe tomorrow..."

She was shaking her head. "Now, Teray. Don't you feel it? Coransee is coming now."

Chapter Two

As Iray spoke, both she and Teray received Coransee's wordless announcement of his presence, a mental image of the Housemaster standing outside Teray's door.

With mechanical politeness, Teray returned an image of Coransee inside the room. Not that he wanted Coransee inside. He was not ready for a confrontation. He had had no time to gather his thoughts, decide what battle strategy might give him the best chance. If he had a chance at all. Joachim had left him all but drained of confidence, of hope. Yet he had to fight.

But did he have to fight now?

As Coransee entered, Teray glanced back to Iray. She was watching him, her expression frightened, questioning, her eyes bright with unshed tears. Yes. He had to fight now. A duel, one to one, unless he wanted to give Coransee an excuse to call in members of his huge Household.

Coransee came into the room and stood near the door, looking from one of them to the other. He gave his head a weary half shake and sighed. "Now, eh, brother?"

Teray glared at him.

"Bad timing," continued Coransee. "You're tired and emotionally drained. You should have chosen to wait. I would have let you spend the night here with Iray like a guest, and you could have fought me in the morning when you were rested."

He spoke as though humoring an irrational person—as though chiding a child. Hot with shame and anger, Teray struck.

He meant to kill as quickly as he could. He knew he had no chance against a man of Coransee's strength and experience unless he could get through Coransee's shielding and bludgeon him to death at once. Given time, Coransee could outmaneuver him, kill him with tricks instead of strength.

But Coransee's mental shielding seemed to absorb the blow without damage. Coransee slammed back with crushing force. Perhaps he too wished to end the fighting quickly. He struck again and again with almost-physical impact. Teray stumbled back against the bed, his shield withstanding the assault but his senses reeling. Blows were openings, were pathways to be traced back to their source. No Patternist could strike a blow through his own solid shield. To strike was to open one's own shield, however slightly, however briefly, and make oneself vulnerable, it was part of Teray's strength that he could strike with mind-blurring speed through a pinhole of an opening. It was part of Coransee's strength and experience that he could strike Teray repeatedly without Teray being able to get a fix on one of his blows and trace it back before Coransee's shield became solid again.

Teray knew at once that he had met his match. Coransee was at least as fast and as strong as he was. At least.

He hammered at Teray's shield with a ferocity that left Teray able to do nothing more than maintain that shield and endure.

Still, it was a standoff. Teray was enduring and Coransee was probably wearing himself out. Teray waited, shaken, jolted, but not really hurt—waited for his chance.

But because Coransee was hammering at Teray's shield so continuously, Teray was only half aware of what was happening to his body. He realized that someone had grasped his wrist but it took him longer to realize that the someone was Coransee.

Contact! Coransee was so occupied with keeping Teray subdued that he wanted physical contact to help him focus a second kind of attack, and do physical harm. The realization came too late. It came after Teray realized that something had happened to his heart.

Teray found himself clutching his chest in pain. He was suddenly not breathing properly, gasping, coughing. The pain seemed to spread and worsen. Teray tore his wrist away from Coransee, but the Housemaster had already done his work. The pain continued, grew.

He could have stopped it, but if he gave his attention to his body, Coransee would be free to break down the defenses of his mind.

But his heart. He was dying.

Somehow, he began again to strike at Coransee, to throw all his strength into a new attack. If he lived, he could repair his body later. If he died, he meant to take his brother with him.

Suddenly Coransee ceased his own battering attack, and withdrew behind a total shield. Perhaps he was tiring. Desperately, Teray hit harder. But his body hampered him. He was slowing, faltering.

Teray became aware of Coransee tracing a blow back through Teray's shield. And even aware of him, Teray was too slow to shut him out.

Coransee had his foothold. He slashed at the rest of Teray's shielding, his mind a machete. Teray felt his shielding being stripped away. He tried to hold it, struggling to remain conscious. Coransee grasped him, held him, blasted him into oblivion.

To Teray's utter surprise, he regained consciousness on the bed of the guest room, with Iray looking down at him. He had not expected to regain consciousness at all.

He moaned and closed his eyes again. He felt weak but he was in no pain. Apparently, Coransee or Iray had already made whatever repairs his body needed. He felt hungry the way people did after being healed, but it was a bearable hunger. He had only recently eaten part of his dinner. Iray had been sitting up. Now she lay down beside him. He put his arm around her and drew her closer so that her head rested on his shoulder. How to say it? How to tell her he was sorry?

"Iray..."

She put a hand over his mouth. "Didn't I see? Don't you think I know what you feel?"

He shook his head silently, his body suddenly trembling with shame and fury. He made a ragged sound of anguish and twisted away from her. He wanted to go down and take Coransee on again—make him finish the job this time. He wanted to kill, or to die. He had lost everything. Everything! Why hadn't Coransee killed him?

Iray tried to turn his head, make him face her. He caught hold of her hands and looked at her. He had lost her. What was she even doing there?

"I'll get us out of this," he said. "I swear..."

"Teray..."

"I won't stop trying until—"

"Teray, listen! There's a way out."

He broke off, staring at her. "What?"

"Listen. Coransee said you were to report to him tomorrow... tomorrow morning. He said he might make you his apprentice. You're stronger than he thought. He said you'd make a better ally than servant. Teray, he said I might... we might be able to stay together."

"Might?"

"He wants to talk to you. I don't know why. And he said he had to find out something from the school. But we have a chance, Teray. At least a chance."

"Maybe. But what is there to talk about—or find out? Either I'm an apprentice or I'm not."

"You could learn more from him than from Joachim. Much more. And maybe you'd be able to have your own House sooner."

Teray shook his head wearily. "Love, don't put so much of your trust in him. I don't know what he has in mind, but..."

"Teray, whatever it is, go along with him." She was leaning over him, looking down into his eyes. "Please. Go along with him. I don't want to be a *thing* won in a fight. I want to be your wife. Please."

He drew a ragged breath. "Do you think I'd miss a chance—any real chance—to get what we both want?"

She seemed to relax. She kissed him and brought him to stronger awareness of her body softly against him. She was what he needed now. He slipped his arms around her. She would always be what he needed.

Early the next morning, as the rest of the House awoke and began the day's work. Teray announced himself outside Coransee's private quarters. He stood in the great common room that he had entered the day before with Joachim. He had not realized then how big the room was. The fireplace seemed a long way off at the other end of the room. Right now there were two mutes in it, cleaning it. There were couches, chairs, and low tables scattered around the room, and the walls were lined with cases of books, learning stones, game boards, small figurines, and more. Yet the room was not cluttered. In fact, at this hour, it seemed far too empty. There were only a few mutes cleaning, and a Patternist who had chosen for some reason to come down the front stairs and walk around to the huge dining room.

Abruptly, Teray received Coransee's invitation to enter. Teray followed the invitation and found himself not in the Housemaster's office but in a comfortable-looking carpeted sitting room. There, Coransee, wearing only a black robe of some glossy material, was having breakfast, served to him by a blond mute woman. The woman had set two places.

Coransee glanced at Teray and waved him into the empty chair at the small window table. Just as though they hadn't been trying to kill each other only hours before, Teray thought. He sat down, was served steak and eggs from the mute's cart, and, like Coransee, ate silently until the mute left. Then Coransee spoke.

"Have you ever seen our father, Teray?" His tone was surprisingly friendly.

"No."

"I thought not. You look like him, though—much more than I do. That's what caught my attention about you yesterday."

Teray was interested in spite of himself. Rayal did almost no traveling. Probably only a small fraction of the Patternists had actually seen him. He was the Pattern. He was strength, unity, power. Every adult Patternist was linked to him, but the link did not involve tracing out his features. Most Patternists neither knew nor cared what he looked like.

"You and I are full brothers, you know," said Coransee. Same father *and* mother. I awakened the Schoolmistress last night to find that out, though I already suspected it."

Teray shrugged. He knew nothing of his mother. Rayal had many wives.

"Our mother was Jansee, Rayal's sister and lead wife."

Teray froze, a forkful of steak halfway to his mouth. He put down the fork and looked at Coransee. "So that's it."

"That's it."

"Are you going to kill me?"

"If I was, you would have died last night."

Teray turned his attention back to his food, not wanting to be reminded of his defeat. The informality of the scene suddenly

seemed incongruous to him. He had expected to stand before
Coransee's desk like an errant schoolboy and listen to the House-
master's sarcasm. Yet here he was having breakfast with Coransee.
And not once had he called the Housemaster "Lord." Nor would he,
Teray decided. He might as well find out now just how far he could
go. What could Coransee possibly want?

"As it is," said Coransee, "we both might live. It would be best if
we did, now that our father is dying."

"Dying? Now?"

"He's been cheating death for twenty years," said Coransee. "Even
at the school, you must have learned that."

"That he has the Clayark disease, yes. But I thought you meant he
was really about to die from it."

"He is."

Teray ate silently, refusing to ask more questions.

"He's let me know that he can last perhaps a year longer," said
Coransee. He lowered his voice slightly. "Do you want the Pattern,
brother?"

"You're asking me if I want you to kill me."

"I mean to succeed Rayal."

"I can see that."

"So you're right. If you contest, I will have to kill you."

"Others will contest. You won't just step into Rayal's place."

"I'll worry about them when they reveal themselves. Now, you
are my only concern."

Teray said nothing for a long moment. He had never really
thought that he had a chance to succeed Rayal. The Patternmaster
simply had too many children, a number of them not only older
but, like Coransee, already Masters of their own Houses. Clearly,
though, Coransee thought Teray had a chance—and was now
demanding that he give up that chance. Teray had no doubt that
Coransee could and would kill him if he refused. If the Housemaster was not actually stronger—and that was still in doubt—he was
more versatile, more experienced. And if it was possible for Teray to
live the kind of life he had planned for himself without fighting, he
would rather not challenge his brother again.

"I won't contest," he said quietly. The words were surprisingly
difficult to say. To be Master of the Pattern, to hold such power...

"I let you live thinking that you wouldn't." Coransee looked across at him calculatingly. "Shall I accept you as my apprentice?"

Teray tried to conceal his sudden excitement. He met Coransee's eyes with simulated calm. Was it going to be this easy? "I would willingly become your apprentice."

Coransee nodded. "What I'm trying to do," he said, "is use you to avoid making the mistake our father made."

"Mistake?"

"When our mother allied herself with him, he let her live. He wanted someone as powerful, or nearly as powerful, as he was to be ready to take the Pattern if anything happened to him. Someone he could trust not to try to snatch it away from him ahead of time. But he kept Jansee with him. Made her his wife instead of permitting her to set up a House of her own in some other sector. That meant that when trouble came to him, she was vulnerable to it too. And as it happened, it killed her instead of leaving her to take over for him.

"Now, to prevent that from happening again, I want to leave you here at Redhill. When the time comes, I'll have to move to Forsyth, to the House of the Patternmaster."

Teray frowned, not daring to understand what Coransee seemed to be saying. "Brother...?"

"You've understood me, I see. When the Pattern is mine, this House will be yours. I'll take from it only the closest of my wives, and a few outsiders. The rest I will leave to you."

Teray shook his head, fearing to believe. It was too much, and far too easy. "You offer me all this at no cost? You give it to me?"

"What price could you pay me?"

"None. You're right. I have nothing."

"Then you have nothing to lose." He paused. "I do ask something. But it's not what you would call a price."

Teray looked at him with sudden suspicion, but Coransee went on without seeming to notice.

"It's more like a guarantee. Brother, I have to know that when you're older and more experienced you won't decide that you gave up the Pattern too easily. I have to be certain that you'll be content as a Housemaster and not decide to try for Patternmaster."

"I've said it," said Teray. "I'll open to you, let you see for yourself that I mean it."

"I already know you mean it. I know you aren't lying to me. But a man can change. What you believe now might not be worth anything five or ten years from now."

"But you'd hold the Pattern by then. You could stop me from any attempt to usurp..."

"Perhaps I could—and perhaps not. But I'm not about to wait and find out tne hard way."

Teray knew the price now. He found himself thinking of Joachim. Controlled. But he recalled Joachim's words. Coransee needed the cooperation of his victim if he was to plant his controls, he could not do it unless Teray let him.

"I want you alive for the sake of the people," said Coransee. "We've got Clayarks chewing at the borders of every sector from the desert to the northern islands. They know Rayal has been too much concerned with keeping himself alive to give proper attention to raiders. When he finally gives up the power and dies, I mean for the people to have security again. But I won't permit you to be a threat to my security."

"I'm not a threat," said Teray stubbornly.

"You know what assurance I want, brother. Your words aren't worth anything to me."

"You're asking me to step from physical slavery into mental slavery!"

"I'm offering you everything you claim to want. Are you getting ambitious already? My controls would do nothing other than make certain you kept your word."

"Joachim told me how you use your controls."

"Joachim!" Coransee did not bother to hide his contempt. "Believe me, brother, Joachim needs the controls I keep on him. Without them, he would never have succeeded in taking a House of his own."

"How could he, as your outsider?"

"He became my outsider through his own bad judgment. Just as he accepted you for apprenticeship through bad judgment."

"You mean because he wasn't as suspicious of me as you are? Because he believed me when I let him see that I wasn't after his House?"

"Teray, the moment he realized that you are stronger than he is— you are, by the way, and he knew it—he should have dropped you.

That's common sense. When you're Master of your own House, see how you feel about accepting an underling who just might learn enough from you to snatch your House away."

"Did you help Joachim win his House from its previous Master?"

"Indirectly. I gave him some special training."

"But why? And why keep control of him?"

Coransee gave him a long, calculating look. "Sector politics," he said finally. "I wanted to be certain of a majority vote on the Redhill Council of Masters. Joachim's predecessor opposed me very loudly, very stupidly."

The warning was unmistakable. Teray sighed. "I don't oppose you," he said. "How can I? But I can't pay your price either. I can't bargain away my mental freedom, sentence myself to a lifetime of mental slavery."

"How free do you think you are now?"

"Free at least to think what I want to."

"I see. Well, since you put so much stock in promises, I'd be willing to give you my word that I won't interfere with your thinking except to stop you from usurping power."

Teray glared at him.

After a moment, Coransee laughed aloud. "I see you're less naïve than you pretend to be. Thank heavens for that. But listen, brother, noble lies aside, just how much control over you do you think I want? You'd live your everyday life as free mentally as you are now. Why not? I haven't the time nor the inclination to meddle into the petty details of someone else's life. The only thing you won't be free to do is oppose me. All my controls would do is put you at the same level as everyone else, once I'm Patternmaster. You'll be different only in that your strength makes it necessary for me to have an extra hold on you—a hold beyond the Pattern. You have no more reason to object to my controls than you have to object to your link with the Pattern."

"The Pattern is different. It doesn't control anyone's thinking." Teray drew a deep breath and said bluntly, "Even if I thought I could trust you—even if you were Joachim, whom I did trust—I couldn't accept the leash, the brand that you want to put on me."

"Not even to save your life?" Coransee's voice remained quiet, conversational.

Teray opened his mouth to give him a defiant "No!" but somehow it was not that easy to say the word that could condemn him. He closed his mouth and stared down at his plate. Finally he found his voice. "I can't." The two words were so shamefully much weaker than the one would have been that he felt compelled to say more, to redeem himself. "What's the point of buying my life with the one thing I still have that makes it worth living? Go ahead and kill me."

Coransee leaned back and shook his head. "I wish I had read you less correctly, brother. I thought that was what you would say. I will give you as much time as our father has left to change your mind."

Again Teray betrayed himself. He wanted to insist, as he believed, that he would never change his mind. But that would be like asking to be struck down now. He said nothing.

"I can only accept you as an apprentice on my terms," said Coransee. "Until you accept those terms, you remain an outsider, subject to all the outsider restrictions and observing all the formalities." He paused. "You understand."

"I . . . yes, Lord." As long as he was still alive, he had a chance. Or did he think that only because he wanted so badly to live? No, there was a chance. One could escape physical slavery. The physical leash was not as far-reaching or as permanent as the mental leash.

"As for your work," Coransee said, "one of my muteherds is due a promotion. He's in charge of the mutes who maintain the House and grounds. You will replace him."

"A muteherd?" Teray could not keep his dismay out of his voice. Caring for mutes was not only the job of an outsider, but, for the sake of the mutes, a weak outsider.

"That's right," said Coransee. "And you start today. Jackman, the man you're replacing, is waiting for you now."

"But, Lord, mutes . . ."

"Mutes! Damage them with your strength, and when you recover from the beating I'll surely give you, you'll find yourself herding cattle."

Jackman waited just outside the door to Coransee's private quarters. He was a tall, bony man with straw-colored hair and mental strength so slight that he could easily have been a teacher at the school. Teachers, even more than muteherds, dealt with mentally defenseless people, and were required to be relatively harmless themselves. Jackman was harmless enough. He could not quite hide his shock when he met Teray and, through the Pattern, recognized Teray's greater strength.

"Son of a bitch," he muttered. "If you're not even-tempered, you're going to kill every mute in the House."

At that moment Teray was feeling far less than even-tempered, but he realized that Jackman was right. He pushed aside his anger at Coransee and followed Jackman up to the fourth-floor mute quarters, where his new room would be.

A pair of mutes were already moving Jackman's things out. One of them, the woman, was weeping silently as she worked. Teray looked at her, then looked at Jackman.

"I'm taking her with me, if you don't mind," Jackman said.

"Your business," said Teray.

"And yours." There was a note of disapproval in Jackman's voice. "Every mute in the House is your business now."

It was not a responsibility Teray wanted to think about. "You care about the mutes, don't you?" he asked Jackman. "I mean really care. It wasn't just a job to you."

"I care. Right now I'm downright worried about them. I'm afraid you're going to wind up killing some of them out of sheer ignorance before you find out how to handle them."

"Frankly, so am I." Teray was getting an idea.

Jackman frowned. "Look, they're people, man. Powerless and without mental voices, but still people. So for God's sake try to be careful. To me, killing one of them is worse than killing one of us, because they can't do a damn thing to defend themselves."

"Will you show me what you know about them—how you handled them?"

Jackman's expression became suspicious. "I'll teach you what I can, sure."

"That isn't what I meant."

"I didn't think it was. What the hell gives you the idea you're entitled to anything more?"

"I'm not entitled. I just thought you might be willing to do the one thing you could do to safeguard your mutes."

"*Your* mutes! My mental privacy doesn't have a goddamn thing to do with it. Nobody but Coransee can make me do what you're asking."

"And I wouldn't ask it if other people's lives weren't involved. But I honestly don't want to kill any of these mutes. And without your help, I will."

"You're asking for my memories," said Jackman. "And you know as well as I do that you're going to wind up with a lot more than just my memories of muteherding."

"There's no other method of teaching that's fast enough to keep me from doing some damage."

"Nosing into my life isn't teaching."

Teray sat on the edge of the bed and stared at the floor. He had thought it would be easy, that a man so clearly attached to the mutes would be willing to sacrifice a little of his mental privacy for their good. He glanced at the two mutes still in the room. "You two leave us alone for a few minutes."

Irritatingly, the mutes looked at Jackman and received his nod before they obeyed.

"Don't hold it against them," Jackman said when they were gone. "They've looked to me for orders for five years. It's habit."

"Jackman, open to me voluntarily. I don't want to have to force you."

"You've got no right!" He tried to reach out to alert Coransee, but to do that he had to open his already-inadequate shield. Instantly, Teray was through the shield. He held Jackman trapped, isolated from contact with the rest of the House. He had the foolish urge to apologize to Jackman for what he was doing as he tapped and absorbed the man's memories of the previous five years. He wasn't doing to Jackman quite what Coransee wanted to do to him, but he was invading Jackman's mental privacy. He was throwing his weight around, acting like a lesser version of the Housemaster. And he wasn't even doing it solely for the good of the mutes. They were important, of course, but Teray was also avoiding a promised beating and a cattleherding assignment. Things were bad enough.

When Teray let Jackman go, he knew everything the older man did about keeping mutes. He also knew Jackman with great thoroughness. For instance, he knew what the muteherd was afraid of, knew what he could do to help him, and perhaps to some degree, make up for invading his privacy.

"Jackman," he said, "I'm Coransee's brother—full brother. I might be second to him in strength here, but I don't think I'm second to anyone else. Now I know you're worried about having a rough time when you move to the third floor, and you're right to be. You're almost as weak as one of your mutes, and you're going to be everyone's pawn. If you want to, you can keep a link with me. After a couple of people try me out, no one will bother either of us."

"After what you just did, you think I'd hide behind you?"

Teray said nothing. He knew the man well enough now to realize that he had already said enough.

"You're trying to bribe me to keep my mouth shut about what you did," said Jackman. "Coransee'd make you think you were being skinned alive if I went to him."

This was a bluff. Teray knew from Jackman's own mind that Coransee generally let his outsiders find their own level within his House. He was not especially concerned about the strong bullying the weak, as long as the weak were not left with serious injuries— and as long as both strong and weak obeyed him when he spoke. Teray watched Jackman calmly.

Jackman glared back at him, livid with rage. Then, slowly, the rage dissolved into weary submission. "If there was any way for me to kill you, boy, I'd do it gladly. And slowly."

"I've linked us," said Teray. "If you get into trouble, I'll know. If I find that you caused the trouble to make trouble for me, I'll let you be torn apart. But if you didn't cause it, and you want my help, I'll help you. Nothing else. The link isn't a control or a snoop. Just an alarm."

"Like the kind some Patternist mothers keep on their kids to be sure the kids are okay, right?"

Teray winced. He would never have said such a thing. Why did Jackman go out of his way to humiliate himself?

"May as well call a thing what it is," said Jackman.

"The minute you decide you don't want the link, you can dissolve it. Right now if you like." Teray kept his attention on the link, making certain that Jackman was aware of it and that he saw that it was under his control, that he could indeed destroy it.

But Jackman made no move to destroy the link. He gave Teray an unreadable look. "You're not really doing this to bribe me to be quiet, are you?"

"It doesn't matter," said Teray.

Jackman grinned unpleasantly. "You're doing it to soothe your conscience, aren't you? Doing it to blot out the 'bad thing' you did before. You never really left the goddamn school, did you, kid?"

Teray struck Jackman in the carefully restrained way he had just learned to strike a mute. He hit Jackman a little harder than he would have hit a mute, because the muteherd did have some defenses to get through. But on a physical parallel it was too much like slapping a child.

Jackman reeled back against the wall as though he had been hit physically. For a moment he stood still, bent slightly from the waist, his head down, cursing.

Teray reached out to find the two mutes. He located them easily, knowing their minds from Jackman's memories. With careful gentleness, he called them back into the room to finish moving Jackman's things. He used exactly the same amount of power that Jackman would have used. The most important thing he had gotten from Jackman was a thorough knowledge of how much mental force mutes could tolerate without harm.

Jackman straightened the moment the two mutes came in. They looked at him curiously, then gathered up armloads of clothing and other possessions.

Jackman spoke to Teray once more as he and the mutes were leaving the room. "Conscience or not," he said quietly, "you're his brother all right." And strangely, it seemed that he said it with admiration.

Chapter Three

Teray searched for Iray using only his eyes. Had he used his mind, he could have found her in a moment. But he was not in that much of a hurry. He searched for her not knowing what he would say to her when he found her. Was it only the night before that he had promised her he would accept any chance he could get for freedom?

The thought reminded him painfully of Joachim.

He stopped, suddenly recalling Joachim's intention to spend the night at Coransee's house. Had he done it? Was he still there?

Teray reached out, swept his perception through the House, and found Joachim as quickly and easily as he could have found Iray. The Housemaster had a guest room in Coransee's quarters. And now that Teray had found him, he wondered whether he really wanted to see him. Why should he want to see him? Did he need advice from Joachim? Hadn't Joachim already told him that in a few years he too would view Coransee's mental controls as a small price to pay for freedom? For limited freedom. For the illusion of freedom.

But Teray was to have only one year, or less, to make that decision—if he made it at all.

Breaking away from his thoughts angrily, Teray reached out again and located Iray. She was in the courtyard, a large garden area three-quarters surrounded by the walls of the House.

He went to her and found her sitting alone on one of the concrete benches placed at intervals around the rectangular pathway. Teray stood still for a moment, looking around the garden. There was a fountain at its center, pleasantly breaking the morning quiet with the sound of falling water.

There were paths leading to the fountain and flowers between the paths. Outside the rectangle of the main path there were shrubs, some of them flowering, and trees. All this, Teray realized, was tended by his mutes. Thank heaven they already knew their work. Teray knew almost nothing about gardening—nor had Jackman known, Teray realized, examining the memories he had taken from the man. Jackman had never bothered to learn. He had simply let the mutes go on tending the garden as they had before he took charge of them.

Teray realized that he was still putting off speaking to Iray.

He went over and sat down beside her, felt her expectant waiting.

"I've failed you," he said quietly. "Again. I couldn't pay the price Coransee asked."

She was abruptly closed to him, shut behind a full shield, alone with herself. Physically, her reaction was mild. She sighed, and looked down at the hard-packed sandy reddish soil of the pathway. "Tell me what happened. Tell me all of it."

He told her. She had a right to know. And knowing, she had a right to hate him. He had sacrificed her freedom as well as his own. As he had trusted Joachim, she had trusted him. She was beautiful and strong in her own right. Not strong enough to establish a House of her own, but strong enough to make a secure place for herself in any existing House she chose. Other men had wanted her—established Housemasters. She had turned them down to stay with Teray. And now...

Teray finished his story, and drew a deep breath.

She turned and looked at him—looked at him for a long time. He grew uncomfortable under her gaze but he could think of nothing more to say.

"Are you going to let him kill you?"

Her words seemed to bring him to life. "Of course not! I wouldn't *let* anyone kill me!"

"What are you going to do?"

"Fight... again. If it comes to that. I'm not going to waste the time he's given me. I'm going to learn whatever I can. Maybe learn enough to..." He could not finish the sentence, the lie. No outsider would be watched more closely than he. No one would be more shielded from knowledge that might help him win his freedom. Yet he could not accept the final defeat. He could not do what Joachim had done.

Iray laid a hand on his shoulder, then raised it to his face. "I'm not going to change my name," she said.

He set his teeth, not wanting to say what he knew he had to say. "You're going to do whatever is necessary. You have to make a place for yourself here."

"Teray..."

"I can't protect you. You... aren't my wife anymore. Perhaps you will be again. I'll fight for that. If I break free, I won't leave you here. But for now... we both know what you have to do."

"I'd like to help you kill him!"

"You know better. You hate him for what he's done to me! You can't afford to do that. Think of yourself. You're beautiful, and strong enough to rise high in any House. Please him, Iray. Please him!"

She sat silent, staring at the ground. After a while she got up and went back into the House.

* * *

The House mutes knew their jobs. They were well programmed and hardly needed Teray to direct them. For days he simply moved among them, permitting them to get used to him. It annoyed him to realize that they missed Jackman. They did not dislike Teray. Their programming did not permit them to dislike any Patternist. They simply preferred Jackman, whom they knew—and who had treated them kindly. Teray did not treat them in any way at all.

He could not focus his thoughts on them, could not really make himself care about them. His own problems held his attention, weighed on him. And it did not help him to see Coransee and Iray together around the House. Coransee had moved quickly. Sometimes in the morning Teray would see them coming out of Coransee's quarters together and going out on some business of Coransee's. Several of Coransee's wives had begun to look at Iray with open jealousy. Clearly, she was becoming one of Coransee's favorites. And how did she feel about that?

She seemed subdued at first. Quiet, withdrawn, resisting emotionally what she could not resist physically. She was no actress. She had never been able to hide her feelings from Teray. Even when she closed her mind to him, her face and her mannerisms betrayed her. Teray watched her, concerned that she would anger Coransee with her stubbornness; though Teray took secret pride in that stubbornness. Then Iray began to smile, and Teray watched her with another kind of concern. Was she finally learning to act, or was her stubbornness beginning to melt?

Coransee was a handsome, powerful man. He could be charming. Several of his wives made no secret of the fact that they were in love with him. And Iray was young—just out of school. It was one thing for her to resist the attentions of wealthy lords who came to the school, where they would flaunt little of their wealth or power before her. Where they were just other men. But here on Coransee's vast estate... How much difference did it make?

Teray watched, sickened by the way Iray was beginning to look at Coransee. And Iray would no longer meet Teray's eyes at all.

And time was passing. And Teray was learning nothing, as he had feared. And Joachim, who had submitted, was at his home with his outsiders and wives and mutes—with the wealth and power that he controlled at least when Coransee left him alone.

Teray was solitary and morose. His mutes feared him. They knew, as he did, that it would be nothing new for an angry Patternist to take out his frustrations on the nearest mute. Of course, abusing mutes was illegal, was punished painfully when it was discovered. But the mute-herd, guardian as well as supervisor of the mutes, could make certain that his violence went undiscovered. Years before, Rayal had swept the sectors regularly, seeking out and punishing instances of mute abuse and other lawbreaking. But there had been no such sweeps for some time. Rayal did nothing now except keep himself alive and in power. Thus, the mutes of Coransee's House watched Teray warily and leaped to obey when he spoke. It would never have occurred to him to abuse a person as helpless as a mute. Yet he could not summon the initiative to reassure them, ease their fear. He could not make himself really care. Not until the morning a frightened mute awoke him before dawn to tell that there had been an accident in the kitchen.

Teray got up silently, radiating annoyance that the mute could not feel, and followed the mute down to the huge kitchen. A cook had dropped a pan of hot cooking grease on his foot. The foot was badly burned.

Teray bent at once to examine the foot. He could read the man's pain on his face but he was careful not to read it in his mind. Like all Patternists, Teray had been taught as much as he could learn of healing before he left the school. The healing ability had little to do with mental strength it was a different sort of power. Most Houses kept at least one woman or outsider who specialized in healing. One who could do massive work like regenerating limbs or ridding a body of some poison or deadly disease. A good healer could handle anything short of the Clayark disease. But Teray was not a good healer. Carefully, he doused the man's agony. That was simple enough, but the healing...

He considered calling Coransee to find out who the healer of the House was. He should have found out long ago, he knew. And he knew that Coransee would tell him as much in no uncertain language. Then he remembered the large, only partially digested lump of his Jackman memories. He reached into them, and found the healer's name and the emergency mental call that she responded to. Knowing eased his mind, gave him confidence. If the healer was there and ready to answer quickly, then he could risk not bothering her. He could risk healing the mute himself.

He found it easiest to act as though the mute's body were his own, as though Teray were regenerating his own flesh. Much cooked, dead flesh had to be sloughed off. The mute's pain could not be allowed to return. Teray closed his eyes in concentration. He did not open them until he was finished. The mute's foot was whole again, and he sat gazing, fascinated, at the new pink flesh.

"It will be tender for a while," Teray told him. "But it's all right. Have a good breakfast and take the day off."

The mute smiled. "Thank you."

And Teray went back to bed feeling pleased with himself for the first time since he had become a muteherd. He had performed the healing slowly but properly. He would have had the House healer check the mute, but he felt certain that the man was completely well. Teray had not done such a thing for anyone other than himself since he had learned how to do it, years before.

Slowly he began to take an interest in the mutes. He had made no friends among the outsiders or the women of the House. And he had taken no woman to replace Iray, though he had noticed a few of the women looking at him with interest. A couple of them had even spoken to him, openly offering, but he had turned them down as gently as he could. It might be easier if he did not see Iray around the House nearly every day. It might be easier if he had more to do. His mutes still seemed too efficient. Except for an occasional healing, they did not need him. Or so he thought until a small red-haired mute woman named Suliana collapsed at his door one night.

Teray turned his attention from the history stone that he had been absorbing to the noise outside his door. Instantly he was overwhelmed by a wave of agony.

He gave a choked cry, screened himself from the pain, and hurried to the door. Suliana lay on the floor, half propped up by the door. Teray opened his mind a little more, still screening out the woman's pain. He became aware of the exact position of her body, then he opened the door carefully, catching her so that she would not fall and hit her head on the floor. She whimpered at his touch and he realized that most of her body was cut and bruised. And she had internal injuries. He lifted her gently, centering his total awareness on her body. She had two broken ribs, and if he handled her carelessly one of them would puncture her left lung. He put her on his bed and took away her pain. Then, knowing that he was out of his depth, he called the healer.

The healer's name was Amber. She was a golden-brown woman with hair that was a round cap of small, tight black curls. And she had a temper.

She took one look at Suliana lying silent on Teray's bed and attacked Teray.

"What the hell is wrong with you, letting this sort of thing go on! I thought you were a little better than Jackman—or at least stronger. I thought I'd repaired this poor girl for the last time when you took over."

"Hold on," said Teray, stepping away from her in surprise. "I don't know what you're talking about. Why don't you take care of Suliana, then tell me?"

"You don't know!" It was an accusation.

"No, I don't. Now let's wait until you've finished before we argue about whether or not I should. Take care of the mute."

She glared at him, radiating resentment, and he found himself recalling what he had learned at school—that even Housemasters were careful how they antagonized healers. A good healer was also a terrifyingly efficient killer. A good healer could destroy the vital parts of a person's body quickly enough and thoroughly enough to kill even a strong Patternist before he could repair himself. But Teray stood his ground. He had already angered her, apparently. He was not going to back down out of fear of her.

After a moment she turned from him with a sound of disgust and began working on Suliana. She gave the mute woman sleep, then silently worked over her for nearly an hour. Meanwhile, Teray reached down to the kitchen and ordered a large meal for Suliana. The healed usually needed food as soon as possible after their healing, since healers drew on the energy and nutrients of their patients' bodies to heal them. The food came as Amber was finishing, and the mute who brought it looked at Suliana sadly and murmured, "Again?"

As he left the room, Teray delved into his thoughts. It was time he found out what everyone else apparently already knew.

Suliana, he learned, was kept as the private property of an outsider named Jason. Two years before, Coransee had forced Jason into his House when Jason left the school with his wife. Later, Coransee had traded the wife to another House. Unfortunately for Suliana, she looked very much like Jason's wife. Thus, he had taken possession of her. Even more unfortunately for Suliana, she was not Jason's wife. Thus, periodically, in perverted anger and frustration, Jason beat the mute woman almost to death.

"Did you get it all?" asked Amber.

Teray realized that she had finished and was looking at him. "I got what that kitchen mute knew, anyway."

"And you didn't know anything about it?"

"Not consciously. I see now that I have knowledge of it from Jackman, though. And I see that it's been going on because Jackman was too frightened of Jason to go to Coransee about it."

"Your name is Teray, isn't it?"

"Yes."

"Teray, what the goddamn hell have you been doing for the past few weeks?"

Somehow, Teray held on to his temper. "You've made your point," he said quietly. "Now drop it."

"Why?" Her voice was dryly mocking. "Are you ashamed? Good. If you can feel ashamed, I guess there's some hope for you. What are you going to do?"

He took a deep breath. No doubt he deserved her sarcasm. Or someone's. "I'll see that Jason never gets his hands on her again—or on any other mute. And I'll warn Coransee in case Jason finds a Patternist woman weak enough for him to abuse."

"All right. What else?"

Teray sat down and looked up at her. "I'm going to listen while you tell me about the other cases of this sort of thing that you've had to treat. Then when I've heard them all, I'm going to take a chance and pass the word that anyone who abuses my mutes will have me to deal with."

Amber frowned. "That's not taking a chance. That's your job. The only reason Jackman didn't do it was because he didn't have the strength to enforce it—or, as you said, the courage to go to Coransee."

"For me, it's taking a chance. You'll have to take my word for that."

She lifted an eyebrow. "In trouble with Coransee already, eh? I see. Well, I can't help there, but if you find that you need help with any of the others, you can call on me. I know you're strong, but you take away their fun, and they might not come at you one at a time."

She was abrupt and confusing. Teray couldn't decide whether to like her, tolerate her, or hate her. He was startled to realize that it was still possible for him to like her. He shook his head and smiled briefly. "Amber, why the hell haven't you gone out and started your own House?"

"I will, sooner or later," she said. "I just let Coransee sidetrack me for a while."

He hadn't asked the question seriously, hadn't expected an answer. But the answer she had given intrigued him.

"Are you an apprentice?"

"No."

"But you sounded serious—as though you intend to just walk away from Coransee's House someday."

"I walked in."

"Voluntarily?"

"Yes. He didn't have a healer and I didn't have a place to stay while I healed myself of some serious wounds the Clayarks had given me. I had just come down from Karston Sector. Then Coransee and I realized how well we got along, and I've been here ever since. But I'm not one of his wives, Teray, I'm an independent."

He had heard of such people—Houseless wanderers, usually possessing some valued skill that made them welcome at the various sectors. And possessing strength enough to make holding on to them not worth Housemasters' trouble.

"I didn't know there were any more independents. As bad as the Clayarks are now..."

"We're still around. We just stay in one place longer than we used to. We're still free people, though."

"I hope I'm around the day you try to leave Coransee."

"You probably will be. That time's coming fast. You know, we're supposed to be talking about mutes."

Teray let himself be shifted back. "All right. Tell what you know about mute abuse here in the House."

She turned and looked at Suliana. The mute woman seemed to be sleeping peacefully. Apparently Amber felt it more important that she rest than that she eat at once.

"Open," said Amber. "I'll give it to you all at once."

He was not completely comfortable opening to her. After all, if she had chosen to stay with Coransee, she must have felt some loyalty to him. But then, what could she pick up from Teray that Coransee did not already know? What difference did it make? He opened.

What she handed him made him feel as though he had suddenly been dropped into a cesspool. He digested the list of atrocities weakly, revising his thinking. He had thought Jason an animal for what he had done to Suliana. Now he knew that alongside some others, Jason could qualify as the House humanitarian. No one actually killed mutes, but certain of the outsiders and women made a grotesque game of coming as close to killing them as they could. Having two mutes fight each other, for instance, until one of them was so mutilated and broken that he could no longer control his body enough to fight on. Privileges and possessions were wagered on these fights. And there was a certain Patternist woman who had made an art form of controlling and changing the development of unborn mute children. Already she had created several misshapen monstrosities that had to be destroyed. She got away with what she did because infants and even older children, Patternist or mute, were considered expendable. Those who were defective in some irreparable way were routinely destroyed.

There was an outsider who had researched ancient methods of torture and made a hobby of trying them on mutes. Another outsider took sexual pleasure in stabbing a mute with a kitchen knife several times. And there was a woman who...

Teray shielded wearily and shook his head. "Amber, has this been going on while I've been here?"

"Not much of it. People know you're strong, and they're cautious. And too, most people repair the damage after they've done it—or they call me. But Jason had apparently decided that you're not going to be any more of a problem than Jackman was."

"How can Coransee let all this go on? He must know about some of it at least."

Amber looked away. "He knows. I've told him often enough myself. He won't let me do anything about it unless I give up my independence and settle here. I don't think he'll stop me, though, if all I do is help his muteherd avoid getting killed."

"But doesn't he care that his mutes are being tortured?"

"There's only one thing he cares about right now. And even though I understand his problem, it's driving me away from him."

"What are you talking about?"

"You ought to know better than I do." She looked at him curiously. "You're his brother. Jackman told everybody that. Full brother. I wouldn't be surprised to find you just like him—sitting around waiting for Rayal to die so you can try to win the Pattern."

Startled and suspicious, Teray spoke carefully. "I'm not after the Pattern," he said. "As I told Coransee, I want my freedom and a chance to establish a House of my own. That's all."

She looked at him for a long moment, one eyebrow lifted. "I think you're telling the truth. Which is surprising. Coransee wants the Pattern the way you and I want to go on breathing. It's just about that basic. If somebody stopped me from healing, I might be the way he is now—climbing the walls."

"He didn't seem that way to me."

"He can't afford to *seem* that way. But if you were a healer, you'd know. Or just if you'd known him longer. He does things to people now, or lets things be done, that he would never have tolerated two years ago when I met him."

"All because he wants the Pattern so badly."

"More than wants—*needs*. Holding the Pattern is what he was born to do, and it needs doing. He was all right when Rayal was doing an adequate job of holding it. Now... Rayal has all he can do to keep himself alive, and it might be better for the people if he didn't even do that. The people need a new Patternmaster, and believe me, it's a need Coransee can feel. But he doesn't dare do anything about it until Rayal lets go."

"You think you know a lot about it."

"I'm a good healer. I can't help knowing."

"If you're right, it seems to me there's not much more wrong with Coransee than there is with Jason and probably a lot of other people in this House. They're confined here together with people they're far from in the Pattern, and denied the right to do work that would have meaning to them—and denied a few other important things."

She nodded. "And you see what it's doing to them, what it's driving them to do. Think of the damage Coransee could do if he really gave way to his frustration."

"Don't think he isn't giving way to it just because you see him."

"You're still alive."

He jumped, and stared at her, wondering how much she knew. "All right. But if he can neglect his House the way he obviously has and allow the kind of perversion that goes on here, I'm afraid to even think of what he'll do if he takes on the larger responsibility of holding the Pattern."

"No need to be. Once he has the Pattern, once desire for it isn't eating him alive, then he'll be able to settle down and attend to the details of protecting and leading the people. The way he protected and led his House before Rayal's health got so bad."

"You're biased," he said. "You care about him. You can make excuses for him."

She shrugged. "Anything else I can tell you to help with your mutes?" She was getting up to go.

"No. I guess I'll get this one back to her room." He looked at Suliana, then at the meal he had ordered. "Shouldn't she eat?"

"When she wakes up. Why don't you keep her here? She's well enough."

"Mind your own business."

She laughed, then sobered. "Just keep her away from Jason. That will be plenty for me." She went out the door, leaving Teray staring after her, frowning. She was next to him in the Pattern. So close that he could have had a free, effortless, almost-involuntary communication with her. In fact, Teray had had to make a conscious effort to avoid such communication once he had accepted information from her mentally. Best to keep away from her. If he did manage to learn something that would help him against Coransee, he didn't want to inadvertently give it to her just because they communicated so easily.

He glanced once more at Suliana, then cast around the House for Jason. The man was in his room, sleeping peacefully. Teray headed toward his room.

Three minutes later, Jason was wide awake and protesting indignantly from the floor where Teray had thrown him after he'd dragged him out of bed. Jason was not hurt, not afraid. He was angry. Angry enough to lash out hard at Teray without first noticing what the Pattern could have told him about Teray's strength. He was strong himself, according to the Pattern; nevertheless, it would have been prudent for him to find out what he could about his opponent before he attacked.

But Teray had not wanted him to be prudent.

Teray absorbed the first wild blow and instantly traced it back to its source, through Jason's shield. Jason was strong all right, but he had no speed. Now Teray held him, left him no more control over what happened to him than he had left Suliana. Teray extended his own screening and enveloped Jason in it so that he could not call for help. Then, quietly, methodically, Teray held the man conscious and beat him. Beat him until he begged Teray to stop, and on until he no longer had the strength to beg.

Finally, Teray gave him a parting thought and let him lose consciousness. *Touch another of my mutes,* he sent, *and you'll find out just how gentle I've been with you.*

Jason passed out without replying. There was nothing permanently wrong with him, no physical injury at all. But Teray had made certain that he suffered at least as much as he had caused Suliana to suffer.

Back in Teray's room, Suliana was awake and eating ravenously. She looked up, frightened, as he came in, and he smiled to reassure her.

"I thought I was going to have to carry you back to your room," he told her.

"I don't have to go back to Jason?" Her voice was soft, tentative.

"You don't have to go back to Jason. Ever."

"I don't belong to him anymore?"

"That's right."

She sighed. "Jackman said that once."

"I'm not Jackman. And after the ... discussion I just had with Jason, I don't think he'll bother you again."

She looked at him uncertainly, as though she still did not know whether to believe him. He could have set her mind at ease immediately, simply by directing her to believe, directing her even to forget Jason. That was the way mutes were usually handled. Teray preferred to let her find out for herself. He found himself unwilling to tamper with the mutes' minds any more than he absolutely had to. They were intelligent. They could think for themselves if anyone ever gave them the chance.

"If I don't have to go back to Jason," said Suliana, "why can't I stay here?"

Teray looked at her in surprise, then took a good look at her. She was small and thin—too thin, really. But she had an appealing, almost childlike kind of prettiness. And there had still been no one since Iray.

"You can stay if you want to," he said.

She stayed.

He worried at first that he might forget himself and hurt her, but he programmed himself by his Jackman memories, made the restrictions of his self-programming automatic. Suliana enjoyed the small amount of mental stimulation that she could tolerate, and Teray enjoyed her pleasure as well as his own. He had not made love to a mute since before his transition. He found now that mentally and physically he had been missing a great deal.

The next day Suliana moved her few belongings to his room. Amber wandered up to check on her, saw that she was comfortably situated with Teray, and grinned broadly.

"Just what you need," she told Teray. "I thought you might take my advice."

"I wish you'd take mine and mind your own business," said Teray.

"I am. I'm a healer, remember?"

"I don't need healing."

She folded her hands tightly together and held them before her. "I hardly know you," she said. "But as you damned well know, we're like this in the Pattern"—she gave her folded hands a shake—"so when you lie to me, don't expect me to believe you."

She checked Suliana over briefly and went back downstairs without another word to Teray.

And as the weeks passed, Teray, in his enjoyment of Suliana and his new interest in his work, began to come alive again. Grudgingly, he admitted to himself that Amber had been right. In a way he had needed a kind of healing.

Now, healed, he began to think of leaving Redhill Sector. He would run away, escape to a sector where Coransee had less influence. He was not certain how much good that would do if and when Coransee succeeded Rayal. In fact, it might not do any good period, since Housemasters had a tradition of returning one another's runaways. And there was the even greater question of whether it was possible at all.

For as long as Teray could remember, travel between sectors had been too dangerous for a person to hazard alone. People moved in groups outside sector boundaries—groups of ten, fifteen, as many as they could. Even Amber, if she managed to get away from Coransee, would probably join one of the caravans of travelers that sometimes passed through the sector. But Teray would not be welcome in such a caravan. No one who knew Coransee would deliberately help a runaway from his House to escape.

Before the Clayarks gave their disease to Rayal, people had traveled freely, safely, from one end of Patternist Territory to the other. Even mutes had traveled alone, carrying merchandise between sectors and making their pilgrimages to the House of the Pattern. But now ... In leaving Redhill, Teray might easily be committing suicide. But staying was surely suicide. Coransee might get tired of waiting and decide to kill him ahead of time if he stayed.

If he left, though, if he went to Forsyth, for instance ... The idea seemed to fall into place as though there had never been any other possible destination for him.

Forsyth, birthplace of the Pattern, home of the Patternmaster. There was no way for Coransee to take Teray back from Rayal if Rayal could be persuaded to give Teray sanctuary. Surely the Patternmaster would resent Coransee competing for the Pattern while its present Master was still alive. In fact, Teray could even recall some kind of law forbidding such premature competition. If Teray could just get to Forsyth to plead his case. And at Rayal's House he could gain the knowledge Coransee was keeping from him. He could get training enough to make the outcome of his next battle with Coransee less predictable. If Rayal himself could not give the training, perhaps his journeymen would. Even they were highly capable people.

Teray began handling learning stones that told of travel, that revealed the terrain between Redhill and Forsyth. He memorized whatever he could find—memorized routes, memorized sectors that he would have to skirt. He could not memorize the locations of Clayark settlements because the Clayarks inside Patternist Territory had no permanent settlements. They were nomadic, roaming in great tribes, settling only long enough to strip an area clean of food. They had been known to eat Patternists, in fact. But a Patternist was an expensive meal costing many Clayark lives. The eating was ritualistic anyway, done for quasireligious reasons rather than out of hunger. Clayarks consumed Patternist flesh to show, symbolically, how they meant someday to consume the entire race of Patternists.

Chapter Four

A few days after Teray had decided to run away, he saw the Clayark. It was like a sign, a warning. Teray had taken several learning stones out far from the House to study in the privacy and solitude of a grove of trees. He had been so involved with the stones that he had neglected his personal security. There had been no trouble with the Clayarks within the sector since the day he left school, but still there was no excuse for his carelessness. To let a Clayark almost walk upon him unnoticed...

Normally, any Patternist wandering away from the buildings of his Housemaster's estate spread his awareness like a canopy around him. The moment that canopy—perhaps a hundred meters around—touched a human-sized creature, the Patternist was warned. Fortunately, Clayarks possessed none of the Patternists' mental abilities and had to depend entirely on their physical senses. Unfortunately, the Clayark disease, which so mutated human genes that it caused once-normal mutes to produce children in the familiar sphinx shape, also placed the minds of those children beyond Patternist reach. Only Clayark bodies were vulnerable. As Patternist bodies were vulnerable to Clayarks. Teray drew back farther behind the tree that had thus far concealed him from the Clayark.

The creature was a male, now standing on three legs and eating something with the fourth. Teray found himself watching, fascinated, comparing the creature to Laro's figurine. He had never had such a close look at a live Clayark before. And now that he was aware of the creature, aware that it was alone, it could not possibly act quickly enough to hurt him. But it was armed. It had the usual rifle slung across its back, the butt protruding over one shoulder so that it could easily be seized.

The creature threw something away, and Teray saw that it was an orange peel. Doubtless the Clayark had been stealing in the groves of Bryant, a neighbor of Coransee who raised fruit. The Clayark also had something that looked like saddlebags strapped across its back. The bags were bulging, probably with stolen fruit.

The Clayark was like a life-size version of Laro's figurine—well-muscled, tanned, lean, human-headed, and almost lion-bodied. It moved with the easy grace of a cat and wore a flaring red-gold headdress to make up for its lack of a mane. Being furless, it also wore clothing—the skin of some animal fixed about its loins, and another skin wrapped about the torso, probably to ease the strapped-on load.

But most unlikely were those forefeet that served also as hands. For Clayarks who bothered to wear running gloves of the kind that this one was now putting on, the hands remained supple and humanly soft. Clayarks who did not wear gloves developed the heavy callouses that caused the legendary clumsiness of the species.

Suddenly intensely curious, Teray checked the area once more, making certain that the Clayark was alone, then rose and stepped clear of his hiding place. A moment later, the creature saw him. It froze, stared at him.

"Kill?" The voice was deep and harsh, but undeniably human.

"Not unless you make me kill you," said Teray.

"Not kill?" The Clayark sat back on its haunches like a cat. "Why?"

"I don't know," said Teray.

"Boy? Schoolboy?"

Teray smiled grimly, reached out, and contracted the muscles of the Clayark's right foreleg. The Clayark gasped at the sudden pain of the cramp, half collapsed, righted itself, and glared at Teray in silent hatred.

"Man," said Teray. "So don't do anything foolish."

"You want?"

"Nothing. Only to hear you speak."

The creature looked doubtful. "Your language... not much."

"But you understand."

"To live."

"If you want to live, you'd better stop stealing in Redhill. The Masters here are already after your people."

The Clayark shrugged. On it, the gesture seemed strange.

"Why do you raid us? We wouldn't kill you if you left us alone." He knew the answer, but he wondered whether the Clayark knew it.

"Enemies," the creature said. "Not people."

"You know we're people."

"Enemies. Land. Food."

It did know, then, indirectly at least. Clayarks always needed more land and food. They bred themselves out of whatever they acquired almost as quickly as they acquired it.

"You had better go," said Teray. "Before another Patternist finds you and kills you."

The creature stood up and stared at Teray for several seconds. "Rayal?"

For once, Teray did not understand. He frowned. "What?"

"You... your father. Rayal?"

Teray had the presence of mind not to answer. "Go, I said."

Catlike, the creature bounded off toward the southwest boundary of the sector.

Teray stood where he was, wondering how a Clayark had managed to recognize him as Rayal's son. Well, Coransee had said Teray looked like Rayal, and the Clayarks had gotten a good look at Rayal once years before. Some of them had even lived to tell about it. Perhaps one of them had lived to draw a picture.

Disease carriers that they were, they had deliberately mutilated Rayal, bitten him to give him the one disease that no Patternist healer could cure—the Clayark disease. Were they now seeking out his children, his possible heirs, to do the same to them? Was that why they had come raiding at Coransee's House to begin with?

Teray reached out, searching the direction in which the Clayark had gone. He swept the area, seeking, searching, but the Clayark was gone. That was one of the difficulties Patternists had—not being able to reach Clayarks' minds. They could locate Clayarks only if those Clayarks were physically close to them—close enough to be touched by a spread canopy of awareness. Teray's canopy was much wider than usual because Teray was strong. The Clayark must have strained even its agile muscles to get out of range so fast. Teray wished he had killed it when he'd had the chance.

Hours later when Teray wandered home, he sensed something different about the atmosphere of the House. There were a number of strangers in the common room with the usual clusters of mutes, outsiders, and women. His first thought was that there had been some trouble with the Clayarks and Coransee had called for help. But things were too relaxed for that. The strangers were sprawled about, lazily, resting, being entertained by a stone or a figurine, or trying to seduce members of Coransee's House.

Teray looked around the room and spotted Amber deeply immersed in the contents of a learning stone. He went over to her and touched her wrist lightly to make her aware of him.

She jumped, and looked around like a person just waking up. Then she saw him and put the stone aside. "I think you may have come home just in time," she said.

"Why? What's going on?"

"Your friend Joachim. He's brought one of Rayal's journeymen here. I don't think it was a very bright thing for him to do, but I think he did it for you."

He frowned at her. "Why would you think that?"

"You mean how do I know anything about it?"

"Yes!"

She hesitated, "Well, you might as well know. Remember that heart attack Coransee gave you on your first night here?"

He said nothing, stared at her in comprehension and humiliation.

"It's so much easier to hurt or kill than it is to heal," she said. "Especially to heal someone other than yourself. Coransee had to call me to save your life. I didn't ask any questions then, but I did later—after Suliana. And Coransee answered them."

Teray turned away from her in disgust. She caught his arm before he could leave, and held on just a moment longer than necessary. Communication flared between them, wordless, startlingly easy. No information was exchanged. There was only the unexpected unity, closer than Teray had ever experienced, and certainly closer than he wanted.

Amber took her hand from his arm, and the unity ended. It did not halt abruptly, but seemed to ebb away slowly until Teray was alone with himself again.

"I didn't ask him out of idle curiosity," she said.

It took him a second or two to remember what she was talking about. By then, he did not care. "Listen," he said, stepping back from her, rubbing his arm. "Listen, don't do that again. Ever."

"All right," she said.

She agreed too quickly. He did not trust her. But before he could reinforce his words, he received a call from Coransee. He turned without a word and walked away from Amber.

As he went, he tried to shake himself free of the shared unity. He should have remembered his own resolution to keep away from Amber unless he needed her as a healer. What if she accidentally— or not-so-accidentally—picked up his plan to escape? But no, as he had gotten nothing from her, she had learned nothing from him. She hadn't been trying to snoop through his thoughts. He would have shielded against that automatically. She had been trying a little seduction of her own. He wondered whether she had heard his "no."

In Coransee's office, the Housemaster himself waited with Joachim and another man, who was built along the same solid lines as Joachim but who was several years older.

"This is Michael, Teray." Coransee gestured toward the stranger. "He's a journeyman in Rayal's House."

Still standing, Teray looked at the man, sensed in him solid strength, surprising nearness to Teray within the Pattern, and quiet maturity. The man could have been a very competent Housemaster on his own, Teray guessed. But apprentices in the Patternmaster's House often opted to stay on as journeymen and never try for Houses of their own. Apparently, they found prestige enough in being Rayal's officials. And Rayal, as powerful as he was, still needed powerful, impressive servants. Michael was easily both.

"Teray," Michael greeted quietly. "I have some questions to ask you. First, though, I want you to know what's happened. Joachim, who was your Housemaster for a short period, has accused Coransee first of illegally forcing you into his House while you were still under the protection of the school—thus, of trading in schoolchildren."

Teray winced inwardly.

"And second, of competing for the Pattern now, before the legal beginning of the competition—while Patternmaster Rayal is still alive."

"It's true," said Teray. "I was Joachim's apprentice—technically still in school. Coransee forced me into his House as an outsider so that he could keep me from competing with him for the Pattern."

"Why do you say he forced you into his House for that reason?"

"He told me that's why he was doing it."

Even Joachim looked surprised at that. "It's clear then," he said. "Coransee was competing for the Pattern ahead of time."

Michael looked at Coransee. "I could look into the boy's thoughts for verification, but I would rather not have to."

Coransee shrugged, almost lazily. "If you expect me to confirm all that, you're going to have to. It's true up to a point, of course. I did take Teray from Joachim. And Joachim accepted payment for him. He accepted a very good young artist I had just acquired. I claim that to be a legal trade."

"Legal, hell!" said Joachim. "There is no legal way to trade an apprentice."

"Why did you trade him then—if he was an apprentice?" It occurred to Teray that Coransee was at his most dangerous when he seemed most relaxed. That was when he had a surprise waiting.

"You forced me to trade him," said Joachim. "I've told Journeyman Michael about the hold you have on me. It shames me, but it's a fact. I won't sacrifice Teray's freedom by pretending it doesn't exist."

"You sacrificed Teray's so-called freedom months ago, Joachim. You sacrificed it to your own greed."

"I will open to Journeyman Michael to prove that you forced me to make that trade!"

"Open. Journeyman Michael will see that I forced you to give up Teray—as I did. But I did absolutely nothing to force you to take payment for him. You could easily have given him up as I demanded, without taking payment, and then gone to Rayal to complain if you felt you had been forced to do something wrong. Instead, you made a profitable trade for a valuable artist. Now you come back trying to cheat me out of the price you paid for that artist."

Joachim stared at him incredulously, understanding dawning in his eyes. He rose to his feet. "You lying son of a bitch. You son of a whelping Clayark bit..."

Coransee went on as though uninterrupted. "Of course, only outsiders can be traded legally. And, Joachim, clearly, you did trade Teray. You accepted payment for him. How could you have done that if you honestly considered Teray an apprentice?"

Helplessly, almost pitifully, Joachim turned to Michael. "Journeyman, he hides his crime behind technicalities. Read my memories. See what actually happened."

Coransee looked at Joachim with something very like amusement. Then he looked at Michael. "Journeyman, what is the penalty for the crime I'm charged with? Trading children, I mean."

"The loss of... your House." Michael glanced at Joachim.

Coransee nodded. "A Housemaster who trades an apprentice—or accepts one in trade—loses his House. But, of course, a Housemaster can trade as many outsiders as he wants to." Now he looked at Joachim. "And certainly, any posttransition youngster a Housemaster picks up outside the gates of the school can be classified as an outsider."

Joachim leaned back and rested his head against one hand. "God, I don't believe this."

Michael's mouth was a straight thin line. "Lord Joachim, you made the charge. Is there any part of it that you want now to retract?"

Joachim gave a wild kind of laugh. "You're going along with him. You want him to get away with this."

Michael looked pained. "Lord, did you receive an artist in trade for this boy Teray?"

"I never would have taken him if... Oh hell. Yes, I took the artist. But look, I'll give him back if you'll just..."

"That's between you and Coransee if the trade was legal, Lord Joachim. Are you saying now that it was legal, that Coransee did not force you to take the artist?"

"Shit," muttered Joachim. "I withdraw the charge. That part of it anyway." He glanced covertly at Teray.

Teray realized at once that now was the time he could have revenge on Joachim if he wanted it. His own memories would prove that Joachim had traded away a man he had acknowledged as an apprentice. Whether Joachim had Coransee opened or not, Teray's memories would be enough. He could cause Joachim to lose his House. Not only that, but such an act might win Teray's freedom. Joachim would lose his House, Teray might go free, and Coransee...? Certainly Coransee deserved far more than Joachim to lose his House. He might actually lose it for the less-than-one-year period that Rayal had left to live. Of course, within that period Teray would have the freedom to learn. He would be able to travel safely to Forsyth and study at Rayal's House. But for that possible freedom he would have to sacrifice Joachim. There was no way around that.

And somehow, in spite of his severely lowered opinion of Joachim, he could not quite bring himself to destroy the man.

He realized that Michael and Coransee as well as Joachim were looking at him as though awaiting his decision. He met their eyes for a moment, then went to a chair at one side of Coransee's desk and sat down. "What about the other charge?" he said disgustedly.

Joachim seemed to sag, eyes closed in relief. Michael was impassive, and Coransee seemed almost bored. He toyed listlessly with a smooth cube of stone—probably a blank stone with nothing yet recorded into it. Perhaps he was even recording into it now.

"The other charge," said Michael wearily. "Competing for the Pattern before the competition is open."

"I deny it," said Coransee simply.

Michael frowned. "You deny that you took Teray into your House in order to keep him from competing with you for the Pattern?"

"Yes."

Teray sat up very straight, wanting to dispute, wanting to damn Coransee for the liar he was, but Joachim's fate had made him cautious. He waited to see how Michael would handle it.

"Teray," the journeyman said, "you say Coransee told you he meant to keep you from competing?"

"Yes, Journeyman."

"And how did he plan to stop you?"

"Either by controlling me as Joachim is controlled, or by killing me—if I refused to be controlled."

Michael turned slightly in his chair so that he faced Teray squarely. "Are you controlled, then?"

"No. I refused control. He's given me time to change my mind." Immediately Teray wished he had left off the last sentence.

"How much time, Teray?" It was Coransee who asked the question.

Michael looked at him in surprise. "Lord, are you admitting that you used such intimidation?"

"Yes. Though not for the reason Teray gives. But even if I had threatened Teray as he says... answer my question, Teray. How much time did I give you?"

There was no point in telling anything but the truth. It was in his memory—and he was not as good at twisting it as Coransee was.

"Teray?"

"You gave me as much time as Rayal has left, Lord."

"As much time as Rayal has left. And of course when Rayal dies, the competition for the Pattern opens."

Teray fumed silently, seeing the look of defeat come to Michael's face. The second charge had died even more quickly than the first. Teray let his mind go back over that morning, that breakfast with Coransee, trying to find some truth he could tell or twist. There was nothing. He himself could think of arguments to kill any arguments he might make.

Teray glanced at Joachim. "Thanks for trying," he said quietly.

"He's a hell of a talker," said Joachim. "Among other things."

Michael shifted in his chair, and said to Coransee, "Unless anyone has memories to the contrary, Lord, the charge against you is disproved. But there is something I would like to know for myself. Is Teray still under sentence of death?"

"He is."

"Why?"

"For the same reason Patternmaster Rayal killed the strongest of his brothers and his sister. Even if I win the Pattern, Teray uncontrolled could become a danger to me. He will submit to my controls, or he will die."

"I see." Michael lowered his head for a moment, then looked at Teray. "You don't have to answer me if you don't want to, Teray, but I'm wondering whether you think you might eventually be able to accept the mind controls."

"Not even if he was going to kill me right now," said Teray. "Especially not after this chance to see him in action." That was reckless. Teray wondered why he was bothering to talk recklessly while he was still in Coransee's House. Maybe the Housemaster's lies had angered him more than they should have. After all, lies were what he should have expected from Coransee in such a situation. But Coransee had prepared for his lies long before he had to tell them. Coransee spoke quietly:

"Journeyman, if you're finished with my outsider, I'd like to speak with you privately."

And that simply, it was over. Teray and Joachim were dismissed so that Michael and Coransee could discuss more important matters.

In the common room, Joachim said to Teray, "I owe you thanks, too."

Teray shrugged.

"The trouble I went to to get that Michael here!" Joachim continued. "And then all the lot of us did was give Coransee a few moments of amusement."

"It doesn't matter."

Joachim looked at him strangely. "I'm more upset about this than you are."

Teray said nothing, his face carefully expressionless. He did not want to lie to Joachim but he could not confide in him. Joachim was Coransee's man, whether he liked it or not.

Joachim must have understood. He changed the subject: "What has Coransee promised you if you submit to his controls?"

"This House."

"This!" Joachim only breathed the word. He looked around the huge room. "He must be certain of winning the Pattern."

"I think he is."

"If you can resist this..."

"I can. I am."

"Teray... most of the time, the controls aren't that bad. And when he has the entire Pattern to keep him busy, he'll have even less time to concern himself with you."

Teray ignored him, and looked around the room to see whether Amber was still there. She had gone. Good. "Joachim, do you know a woman named Amber?"

"Teray, listen! You wouldn't be giving up as much as I did when I submitted. He's made me a kind of political puppet. But when he's Patternmaster he won't have to do such things with you. You'll be almost independent. And you'll be alive."

Teray shook his head slowly, eyes closed for a moment. "I can't do it, Joachim. I wouldn't be able to live with myself. A long leash is still a leash. And Coransee will still be at the other end of it, holding on. Now, do you know Amber?"

"All right, change the subject. Kill yourself. Yes, I know Amber. What do you want to know about her?"

Teray frowned. "Anything you know about her that isn't personal. She says she's an independent."

"She is. Strange woman. She's only four or five years out of school, but she managed to kill a man, a Housemaster, before she even made her transition. You ought to ask her about it. Interesting."

"No doubt," muttered Teray. "But look, how likely is she to go running to Coransee with anything unusual she hears?"

Joachim shook his head slowly. "Not likely at all. She likes Coransee, but she doesn't make any special effort to impress him. She does her healing and otherwise keeps out of House business."

Silently, Teray hoped he was right. It would be too easy for the woman to pick up something. No matter what happened, he was going to have to leave soon.

He found himself wishing he could speak privately to Michael, but he knew it would do no good. Even if the journeyman sympathized with him, the law really was on Coransee's side. Michael could not change that.

* * *

Journeyman Michael stayed two days more, then headed farther north on more of Rayal's business. North. Forsyth was 480 kilometers south. Teray could not even hope to catch up with Michael and try to attach himself to the journeyman's party. That might not have been a good idea anyway, though, since it would have meant asking Michael to risk his own life by defying Coransee. After all, if things went as Coransee expected, Michael would soon be under Coransee's direct control.

Teray would have to go alone. He realized that he was putting off leaving for just that reason—because the journey looked more and more like suicide to him. And what should he do about Iray?

That was something he did not want to think about. He was afraid to talk to Iray—afraid she might not want to leave Coransee, afraid her apparent interest in Coransee might be real. But even if it was not—she had kept her word, after all, she had not changed her name—how could he ask her to risk herself with him again? How could he take her out and perhaps get her killed? Then, strangely, it was Amber who gave him hope.

She was waiting for him in his room the night after Michael left. He walked in and found her staring out his window.

"Good," she said as she turned and saw him. "I've got to talk to you."

"You came all the way up here to talk to me?"

"Necessary. I have a message for you from Michael." And suddenly he was listening.

"Why would Michael give you a message for me?"

"Because I offered to carry it. He and I are old friends, so he trusted me. He couldn't very well give it to you directly."

"Why not?"

"God, you must really be preoccupied with something. Don't you have any idea how closely Coransee has watched you and Michael for the past two days?"

Teray went to his bed, sat down, and took off his shoes. "I didn't notice. It's probably a good thing that I didn't."

"Michael didn't think you would have lived long if he had shown any particular interest in you. There would be some kind of accident. You know."

Teray shuddered. He hadn't known. He hadn't even thought about such a possibility. It was true enough, though, that personal attention from Michael could lead to personal attention from Rayal. And surely Coransee would not want Rayal to have the chance to pay attention to another potentially powerful son.

"What's the message?" he asked Amber.

"That there's sanctuary for you at Forsyth if you can get there on your own."

In the moment of utter surprise that followed her words, he did the thing he had feared he might do: He betrayed himself to her. His screen slipped—not far, and only for an instant. Coransee would have been hard put to read anything in so short a time. But Amber, it seemed, knew how to use her closeness to him. She read everything.

"Well," she smiled at him, "it looks like I've brought you better news than I thought I had. Just the news you need, in fact."

Teray dropped all pretense. Now, either she would report him or she would not. And Michael had seen fit to trust her. "What I really need," he said, "is a few good fighters to go along with me. I counted twelve women and outsiders traveling with Michael."

"Fifteen," she corrected. "Are you taking Iray?"

"I don't know yet. It seems to me—" He broke off and looked at Amber. She was still barely an acquaintance. Someone to sleep with, perhaps, but not someone to talk over his personal problems with. But on the other hand, why not? It was so easy. And who else was there? "It seems to me that I've done enough to Iray."

"I don't think you've done anything to her. Joachim has, and certainly Coransee has. But you're only about to."

"By leaving her—or by taking her?"

"By deciding for her."

"I don't want to get her killed."

Amber shrugged. "If it were me, I'd want to make up my own mind."

"I told her once that I wouldn't leave her here."

"Well, it's between you and her."

"Just out of curiosity, what are you trying to build between you and me?"

She smiled a little. "Something good, I hope."

"What about Coransee?"

"Yes." She took a deep breath. "Point to you," she said.

"What?"

"You remember telling me you hoped you'd be around the day I tried to leave Coransee?"

"You tried?"

"No. But I should have—some time ago. Now I've become a kind of challenge to him. Now I'm going to settle here as one of his wives whether I like it or not. He says. Which shows that he hasn't gotten to know me very well in two years."

"What are you going to do?"

"The same thing you're going to do. We'll live longer if we do it together."

He took several seconds to digest this. His main emotion was relief. "Two, or perhaps three, traveling together. That's better than one—though not much better."

"You're going to ask Iray, then?"

"Yes."

"Good. We'll need her."

" 'We.' " Teray smiled. "I wish you were just a little harder to accept."

"I'll wish that myself when the time comes for me to leave you. But I don't wish it now."

"You're staying the night."

"What about Suliana?"

"I just reached her. She's going to sleep in her old room—or wherever else she wants to."

"I'm staying, then."

She was a lighter golden color beneath her clothing. Honey-colored. The cap of black hair was softer than it looked and the woman was harder than she felt. He would have to keep that last in mind, if he could.

Chapter Five

Early the next morning, Teray left Amber asleep in his bed and went down to the dining room, where he had sensed Iray. He would assume that Iray had not changed. He would know nothing that she did not tell him. He would not prejudge her. She was eating with another woman and a man at the end of one of the long tables in the nearly empty room. Most of the House was not awake yet.

"I have to talk to you," he told her.

She glanced at him hesitantly, almost reluctantly. Then she took a last bite of pancake, swallowed some orange juice, and excused herself to her friends. She followed him out to the privacy of the completely empty courtyard where they had last talked. Since then, they had looked at each other, and they had refused to look at each other, but they had hardly spoken at all.

They sat down on one of the benches and Iray stared at her clenched hands.

"I'm sorry," began Teray, "but I have to ask you.... Is there any way... through you, that Coransee will hear what I say?"

"No," she said softly. "I'm linked with him, but only so he can be sure that you and I... that we don't make love."

"The link is just an alarm, then?"

She nodded. "And I won't tell him anything you don't want him to know."

She was offering him the same loyalty that she had always offered, but somehow, something was wrong. Was it only her link with Coransee that had started her twisting her hands, that made her willing to look at him only in quick glances?

"Will you open to me?" he asked.

"You don't trust me," she said. There was neither surprise nor anger in her voice.

"I trust you... trust who you were. I want to trust you now."

"You can. I won't open to you, but I won't betray you either."

"Has he hurt you? Has he done something you don't want me to...?"

"No, Teray. Why should he hurt me?"

"Then what's happened?"

"I took your advice."

There it was. All his fears wrapped in four words. He could not pretend to misunderstand her any longer.

"I started out playing a role," she said. "A hard role. Then..." She faced him, finally, wearily. "Then it got easier. Now it's not a role anymore."

Teray said nothing, could think of nothing to say.

"He's not what I thought," she said. "I thought his power had made him cruel and brutal, but instead..."

"Iray!" He could not sit still and listen to another woman inventing good qualities for Coransee. Especially not Iray.

She looked at him solemnly, her shielded mind not quite hiding the fact that she did not want to be there with him. She had stilled her twisting hands, but her very stillness bespoke tension, withdrawal.

"Iray... what if there was a way out? For us, I mean. What if you didn't have to stay with him?"

"Is there?"

"Yes!" He had to trust her. How could he expect her to believe him if he did not tell her what there was to believe? He had failed her once. Twice. She had reason to be hesitant. He outlined his plan quickly, giving her the assurance that Michael had passed on to him through Amber without mentioning Amber herself. Now was not the time to cloud things further.

Iray took a deep breath and shook her head. "Clayarks," she said. "All the way to Forsyth. Hundreds of kilometers of Clayarks."

"Not that bad," he said. "We could make it. We could...."

"No."

He was silent for a long moment. He could look at her and see that she meant it. Instead, he looked at the ground, at a wall of the House. "All right. I can't really blame you. I almost didn't ask you because I didn't think I had the right to risk your life as well as my own. And I don't have that right, of course. But I said I wouldn't desert you. I had to ask you if you wanted to take the risk."

"I'd take it. If I wanted to be with you the way I did once, I'd go."

He said nothing, only stared at her.

"You couldn't accept his controls," she said. "Even though your own freedom wasn't all that was involved, you couldn't accept them."

"Would you have wanted me controlled—like Joachim?"

"No! No, I understand what you did. That's why I never blamed you, never tried to make you change your mind. I knew you'd rather be dead than controlled. You did what you had to do. Then you told me what I had to do. And you were right both times. Well, now I've done what I had to do. And it was good, and I'm home. I'm going to stay here."

There was nothing he could say to her that would not twist back and indict him, too. Even his anger was more at his own helplessness, and at Coransee, than at her. He had thought of her with Coransee, even thought of her coming to prefer Coransee. But he had never really believed she would. In spite of all Coransee's power and apparent attractiveness to women, he had never let himself believe it.

She touched his arm and he savored her touch for a moment, then moved his arm away. She was still shielding him out and her touch brought her no closer to him. He could have taken more pleasure in Suliana's touch—the touch of a mute.

Or Amber's.

"Teray," she said softly, "I have to tell you—" She broke off suddenly as he looked at her. "I'm sorry," she said. "That can't mean much to you now, but I am sorry."

He stood up and started toward the common-room door.

"Wait!" She caught his arm again, this time in a grip that he would have had to hurt her to loosen. He stood still, looking down at her, waiting for her to let him go.

"Leave soon, Teray, if you're still going. Soon. I said I wouldn't betray you, and I won't—not deliberately. But accidentally... Well, I'm with him a lot now, and sometimes he hears things I don't mean for him to hear."

After a moment he nodded and she let him go. But he stayed where he was, watching her, not wanting her to see the pain in his eyes but not able to turn away again. He raised his hand to her face.

She drew back from him sharply, then turned away and hurried past him into the House.

Teray stood still for several seconds longer. Finally he shook his head. He reached out to one of his kitchen mutes. The man whose foot he had healed. Silently, with careful gentleness, Teray gave the man orders. Then he reached a stable mute—a mute who was not one of his charges, but who, of course, was obliged to obey any Patternist. He gave orders to the stable mute, then went back up to his room.

Amber was dressed and having breakfast. Teray realized that he had eaten nothing, and at the same time realized that he had no appetite.

"When you get through with that, go get your things together," he told her. "We're leaving today. I don't want to spend another day in this place."

She looked surprised, but nodded slowly. "All right."

"And take as little as possible. Put some more clothes on over those or something. We can't go out of here looking like we're running away."

"I know."

"I'm having a supply of food packed for us and horses readied. And... there'll only be two of us."

She said nothing to that. She went on eating.

They traveled southwest toward the coast and toward the nearest borders of the sector. Teray had decided to take the coast trail south, if he could. The inland route was easier, less likely to be washed out or blocked, but it was also the most-often-traveled route. It was where Patternist caravans passed and where Clayarks lay in wait for them. The inland route was a little shorter, too, because it did not follow the eccentricities of the coast. But it did go straight through the middle of twenty-one Patternist sectors. The little-traveled coast route went through three.

There were some Clayarks along the coast route. But then there were Clayarks everywhere, breeding like rabbits, warring among themselves, and attacking Patternists. Teray hoped to find them only in small family groups along the coast.

Michael, he recalled, had traveled part of his way north along the coast route. Teray had asked a pair of his outsiders about their trip, prying as casually as he could. With his large party, Michael had had little trouble, but he had sensed at least one large tribe. He had gone into a Patternist sector to escape it. And that was something Teray could not do. He had a better chance against the Clayarks than he would have against a group of his own people who decided to earn Coransee's gratitude by capturing him. Until he reached Rayal's House, the only Patternist he could trust was Amber.

She rode along beside him, strangely accepting of his surly mood. But then, she knew the reason for it. He wished she didn't. She said quietly, "I think we should link, Teray."

"What?"

"I know it will make us closer than it would make most people, and maybe you don't want me that close to you right now. But we'd be safer linked. If I sense Clayarks, I want you to know immediately—even if you're sound asleep at the time. If we don't work together, we don't have a chance."

"Oh hell," he muttered.

She said nothing else.

They rode for several minutes in silence. Finally, without speaking, he opened, reached out to her. Linking was like clasping hands—and did not require even that much effort. Now her alarm, her fear, almost any strong emotion of hers, would alert him. And his emotions would alert her. But beyond that, as he had feared, he was too much aware of the link—aware of a strong, ongoing sense of oneness with her. Normally, a link, once established, became part of the mental background, not to be noticed again until one of the linked people did whatever the link was sensitized to respond to.

But any kind of contact with Amber had to be different, had to be too close. There was nothing for him to do but accept it—and surprisingly, it was not that hard to accept. He felt himself relaxing almost against his will. Felt the anger and the hurt that Iray had caused him ebbing, not vanishing completely but retreating, shrinking so that it no longer occupied his whole mind. And Amber was not doing it, was not reaching him through the link to offer unasked-for healing. It was her mental presence alone that he was responding to. Her presence was eclipsing emotion that he would normally have taken much longer to get over, and he was enjoying it. He should have felt resentful at even this small invasion. Instead he only felt curious.

"Amber?"

She looked at him.

"What does the link feel like to you?"

She grinned. "Smooth. How else could it feel between people as close in the Pattern as we are?"

"And you don't mind?"

"No. And neither do you."

He considered that, and shrugged. He was too comfortable for her presumptions to bother him. He indulged his curiosity further. "All along you've known more about me than I have about you. Now I'd like to know something about you."

There was something guarded, almost frightened, in the way she looked at him. "What do you want to know?"

Her manner confused him. Apparently she had something to hide. But then, who didn't? "I heard you managed to kill a House-master even before your mental abilities matured. You could tell me how you managed that."

She sighed, and then kept silent for so long that he thought she was not going to answer. "It was an accident," she said finally. "The result of being a pre-Pattern youngster with no control over what was done to me. Who told you about it?"

"Joachim. He didn't tell me about it, he told me to ask you about it."

She seemed to relax. "At least. Well, the Housemaster was my sec-ond and he shouldn't have been. From the beginning, we didn't get along. And because I was too close to transition to stand mental abuse, he used physical abuse—beat the hell out of me whenever he wanted to until one day I managed to push him so that he fell against the sharp corner of a low concrete wall. He hit it with his head. Died before anybody could contact a healer. Of course, my abilities weren't mature, so I couldn't help him."

"But none of that makes sense," said Teray. "Why didn't you tell the Schoolmaster that you didn't get along with your second? You could have gotten a new—"

"No, I couldn't. Like I said, pre-Pattern children can't con-trol what's done to them. Leal—the Schoolmaster—knew he had given me the worst possible second. He did it deliberately because he knew I had already chosen my own second. And he did not approve." She gave a bitter laugh. "He would have seconded me himself if he could have—if he had been strong enough. He wanted to. He wanted a lot of things that a teacher can't have."

"You, for instance."

"Oh, he had me, for a while. For my last six months at school. I didn't mind. But we both knew he was going to have to give me up once I reached my transition. There was no way that I was going to be a teacher. Not with my ancestry. Leal could accept that, but he couldn't accept Kai, the second I had chosen. The second whose House I would have gone into. Although he might even have been able to stand that if I had been able to hide the fact that I was already in love with Kai. We met when she came to the school on some other business and Leal was the—"

"Wait a minute." Teray turned to stare at her. "She?"

"That's a good approximation of Leal's tone when he realized what was happening," said Amber. "I hope you're not going to react as badly as he did."

"I haven't decided yet," Teray answered. "Tell me the rest of it."

She stopped her horse, causing Teray to stop, then spoke very softly. "You'd better decide before we get into Clayark Territory," she said. "Leal's reaction almost got me executed. I'm not going to risk my life with anybody else who's that hostile."

The link betrayed her hurt. She had taken Teray seriously and was waiting for rejection.

"Do you feel any hostility in me, Amber?"

She looked at him mistrustfully, then read the message the link held for her—his lack of any emotion beyond surprise and curiosity.

She relaxed and they started forward again. "I'm touchy," she said. "Leal taught me to be touchy."

"Why did you tell me that part of it?"

"Because you would have found out anyway. Piece by piece. I would be thinking about it and off guard, and you would pick it up. We're going to pay a price in mental privacy for our closeness."

Teray nodded. "Well, Leal had reason to react with jealousy, but I ..."

"Jealousy, anger, humiliation. How dare I put him aside for a woman? Poor teacher. He had trouble enough trying to compete with men for the women he wanted."

"I don't see why. He was the Schoolmaster. He should have been able to attract plenty of women."

"Yes, but not the ones he wanted. He could attract women teachers, but he considered them beneath his notice. He could and did attract older girl students, but they always had to either leave him or become teachers. He had the idea that women from outside the school were better. He tried to attract them—and usually failed. But until I met Kai, he had never lost one of his student girlfriends to one of them. It was too much."

"And Kai even had her own House."

"Leal wouldn't have hated her for that if she had gone to him instead of to me. Prestige. But since she didn't, her House just became more fuel for his jealousy. He had always wanted a House of his own anyway, and he knew he'd never have one. He was almost too strong to be a teacher, but not nearly strong enough to be a Housemaster."

"A stronger man would have reacted more reasonably." Teray shrugged. "After all, you're not that unusual."

"Coransee didn't react too well."

He looked at her, startled. "What difference did it make to Coransee? It happened before you met him, and it didn't keep you from staying for two years with him."

"But it made a difference. I didn't tell him. He found out by snooping through my thoughts just a few weeks ago. That was when he decided that I was more of a challenge than he had thought. That was when he told me he intended to keep me in his House—deny my independence. Most people don't try things like that with a healer."

"Could he have succeeded?"

"Maybe, with his strength. Frankly, I'm afraid of him. That's why I'd rather run away from him than fight him."

Teray shook his head ruefully. "He has a habit of trying to domesticate people."

"What about you?"

"I'm still curious. I want to know how a pre-Pattern child managed not to be executed for killing a person as important as a Housemaster. I'm surprised that his friends didn't have you declared defective so that you would be destroyed before you gained your adult rights. And I'm curious about you and Kai. But all of that is your business. I don't want you to tell me because you're afraid I'll ferret it out anyway. I won't."

"I don't mind telling you, but that isn't what I meant."

No. He knew what she meant. "Last night I asked you what you wanted between us, and you said 'something good.' I think there was also the implication of 'something temporary.' That's all right for a start, but I might turn out to be as bad as Coransee. I might try for more, too."

She laughed. She had a nice laugh. "Don't do it. One Coransee was enough. Now I'll tell you the rest of my story. By the way, are you checking wide for Clayarks? I've seen them in these hills."

"Checking as widely as I can." They were just getting into the low grassy hills that they had to cross to reach the ocean.

"All right. I wasn't executed because Kai talked, bullied, and bribed some of the Housemasters of the sector council into voting to spare me. She didn't tell them anything they didn't already know—just that the killing was an accident, that I was only days away from my transition and my full rights as an adult, that the man I killed should never have been assigned to me anyway. They knew all that, of course, but they were so outraged, and, I think, so ashamed, that I, technically still a child, had managed to kill one of them... well they were more after vengeance than justice. The lead wife of the man I killed was there to goad them on. Leal was there telling as little of the truth as he could because he knew he was really to blame for the man's death.

"Kai got me off, but she couldn't get me all the way off. Instead of killing me, they exiled me from the sector. They meant for the Clayarks to do their killing for them. Kai was supposed to take me to the sector border and leave me there. Instead, she took me to her House. She induced transition—just a few days early, but early nevertheless."

Amber drew a ragged breath, remembering. "I swear I'd rather let the Clayarks get me than go through anything like that again. I kept trying to just die and let it be over, and she kept bringing me back. Did I mention that she was a healer too? Lucky thing. Although I didn't think so then. She dragged me through all of it—stripped away my childhood shield before I was ready to shed it. Left me mentally naked to absorb all the free-floating mental garbage within miles of me. I got other people's agony, violent emotions, everything, until I could manage to form the voluntary shield that I wasn't really ready to form yet. I almost killed her while she was trying to save me. I didn't know what I was doing. And I turned out to be stronger than she was.

"She pulled me through. But that wasn't enough. She had to prepare me to leave the sector—to use the abilities I barely knew I had. There wasn't time to teach me or time to do anything but print me with her memories. She gave me her fifteen years of leading her House. She made me assimilate all of it, not just let it sit the way you did with most of your Jackman memories. It was like becoming part of her—getting a whole new past that was only a few years shorter than my real past.

"She made me eat and took away my weariness and healed the bruises and sprains I had gotten thrashing around during my transition. Then she gave me supplies, put me on a horse, and told me to run. I got out just ahead of the group of Housemasters that had finally—twelve hours too late—realized what was happening."

Amber stopped talking and they rode along in silence for a while, urging the horses faster as they came to a stretch of level ground, then slowing to climb another hill.

"She loved you," said Teray finally.

"It was mutual. She almost lost her House because of me."

"Only almost?"

"She would have if it hadn't been for Michael. That's where I knew him from. She had called for help from Forsyth when I was first charged. Michael was in our area on other business but he had Clayark trouble on his way to us.

"He arrived and looked at my memories—I was allowed to come back into the sector to be heard. He looked at the truths the Housemasters had ignored, then decided in Kai's favor. He didn't make them take me back, but at least he made them leave her alone."

"It was too late anyway. You couldn't have gone back to her then."

"I know."

"With you stronger than she is and possessing so much of her knowledge and experience ... I don't think she would have dared to take you back."

"I'm glad she didn't have to decide."

Teray changed the subject abruptly. "I think I've spotted some Clayarks." He hadn't had to say it. She was already looking off in the direction of the Clayarks. They were not visible, but there was definitely a group of them ahead, moving toward Teray and Amber. They were just beyond the next hill.

"Only a small group," said Amber. "About twenty. They might go around the hill and pass us by."

"Yes, and then they might notice our trail and follow us while one of them goes for reinforcements. Best to kill them."

"All right. You take it."

She opened to him as no one had since school, giving him access to and control over her mental strength. It was the way people who were close in the Pattern fought best. The way Joachim's House fought, the way everyone fought in war when Rayal used the power that he held. But only Rayal could pull all the people together, funnel all their strength through his own mind, focus it on Clayarks anywhere from Forsyth itself to the northernmost Patternist sector. Lesser people grouped when they could with whomever they could—with whomever they trusted not to try to make the control permanent.

Inexpertly, Teray channeled Amber's strength into his own. Then, almost doubly powerful, he reached out to the Clayarks.

The new strength was exhilarating, intoxicating. He almost had to hold himself back as he reached the Clayarks. Within one of them he located a large artery that led directly from the heart. He memorized its position so that he could find it quickly in the other Clayarks, then he ruptured the artery. The Clayark stumbled to the ground, clawing its chest.

Instantly the other Clayarks fled, scattering in all directions, but Amber, otherwise inactive, kept track of them, focusing and refocusing Teray on them until all were dead or dying.

Several minutes later they began riding past bodies. Amber was closed again—as closed as she could be while they were linked—and Teray had returned to her control over her mental strength. That strength was temporarily lessened, of course, as was Teray's, but the lessening was slight. One of the dangers of lending mental strength to another person was that the other person might use too much of it, might drain the lender to exhaustion and death. But neither Teray nor Amber was anywhere near death.

Teray stared at the bodies sprawled over the hillside, saw the expressions of agony on many of the Clayark faces, and did not know whether to feel sick or triumphant. Not one Clayark had had time to fire a shot or even get a look at the enemy who killed him. Still, Clayarks too were known to do their killing from hiding. It was strange fighting, repelling somehow.

"You've never done that before, have you?" asked Amber.

"No." Teray rode past a Clayark female, dead, with arms outstretched toward a smaller, completely naked version of herself. A relative perhaps. A daughter? Clayarks kept their children with them to be raised by the natural parents. Teray looked away from the pair, frowning. They were Clayarks. They would have killed him if they could have. They were carriers of the Clayark disease.

"I wanted you to handle it because I thought you hadn't done it before."

He turned to look at Amber almost angrily.

"I wanted to see you fight in a situation where there was no immediate danger," she said.

"Did you think I hadn't learned what to do back in school?"

"No, I was afraid you had. And unfortunately, you have."

"The Clayarks are dead, aren't they?" He was letting his disgust over what he had had to do spill over onto her and he didn't care. What was she complaining about, anyway?

"The last couple of them almost got away."

"Almost, hell! They're dead."

"If there had been just one or two more of them, we would have missed them. They would have been out of range before you could kill them. And sometime tonight or tomorrow, they would be back with all their friends."

"You're saying..."

"I'm saying you're too slow. Way too slow. A big party of Clayarks would swallow us before you could do anything about it."

"You could have done better?" Cold anger washed over him but his tone was mild, quiet.

"Teray, I'd be a little more diplomatic if it weren't for the chance of our meeting an army of Clayarks over the next hill. But to put it bluntly, school methods just aren't good enough out here. Will you let me teach you some others?"

"You want to teach me others?" he said in mock surprise. "Not handle the fighting yourself from now on?"

"Yes. You ought to have a chance to survive this trip even if something happens to me, or if we separate."

"And I won't without your teaching?"

"That's right."

"The hell with your teaching."

She sighed. "All right then, you owe me this much. The next Clayarks we meet, let me handle them."

"So you can show me how good you are at it. And I can change my mind."

"No, Teray, so I can be sure of us living at least that much longer." She spoke wearily, her words reaching him both through his ears and his mind. She was open again. And with his mind, he could not help but be aware of her absolute belief in what she was saying. In spite of her manner, she was not boasting. She was afraid. Afraid for him.

He felt the anger drain out of him to be replaced by something else. Something he could not quite name but that was far less comfortable than even the anger had been.

"Could you make it, Amber? Alone, I mean, from here to Forsyth."

"I think so." She was closed to him again.

"You know so."

She said nothing.

"You've done it before."

She shrugged. "I told you I was an independent. We travel."

"Why didn't you tell me?"

"Why should I have? The fact that I've done it before doesn't insure that we're going to make it now."

"Especially not with me acting as a brake."

Again she said nothing.

"We're about the same age," he said. "I'm the son of the two strongest Patternists of their generation, and I'm strong enough myself to succeed the Patternmaster. Yet here you are with your fifteen years of someone else's memories and your four or five years of wandering...."

"Would you rather travel with somebody who was deadweight?"

"I just don't like feeling that I'm deadweight myself."

"Don't worry. With your strength, you aren't. I would never have invited myself along with you if I had thought you would be."

He looked at her sharply.

"No, that's not the only reason," she said, smiling. "You've got a few other good points."

He sighed, and gave up without quite realizing that he was giving up.

"Like your tractable nature," she said. "Open and let me show you how to kill Clayarks quickly."

He obeyed, watching her with the same mistrust that she had shown for him earlier.

Chapter Six

You see," Amber was explaining, "we can't afford to waste our time and strength punching holes in the Clayarks. That's what they're trying to do to us with their guns. Fight them on their own terms and sooner or later they'll get you. There are just too many of them. In a large attack you'd have some of them blasting you apart while you were trying to punch holes in others."

Teray only half listened. His ears were full of the unfamiliar sound of the surf. He had spent all his life no more than a day's ride from the beach, yet he had never seen the ocean through his own eyes. He had seen it through the eyes of others in the learning stones he had studied, but that was not the same. Now, as he and Amber rode down toward the oceanside trail, he gazed out, fascinated, at the seemingly endless water.

He could see tiny rocky islands off shore. Nearer, the waves broke against sand and rocks with a noisy vigor that sometimes drowned out what Amber was saying. But that did not matter. She was only emphasizing the information she had already given him mentally. Mental communication detracted from their awareness of the land—and possibly the Clayarks—around them. Thus she was repeating, summarizing aloud.

"I can do it," he told her.

"Try it as soon as possible."

"The next time we meet Clayarks." But he was not eager to try her method of killing, or any method of killing, again soon. In his mind's eye, he could still see the Clayarks he had already killed. Maybe it would be easier if they were not human-headed or if he had not had a conversation with one. But she was right. He would not only have to get used to killing them, but he would have to kill more efficiently, in the way that she had shown him, if the two of them were to survive. He recalled the memory that she had given him of herself on foot, alone, running for the safety of Redhill two years before. She had been wounded but she had kept going. Her healer's skill had kept her alive and conscious. And she was still killing, limiting the area of her perception to a long narrow wedge, sweeping that wedge around her like a hand of a clock. The Clayarks she touched in the deadly sweep convulsed and died. By the time they were dead, she had swept over six or seven more. They had managed to shoot her by firing from beyond the range of her sweep. But such long-range shooting required marksmanship that not all of them—not enough of them—possessed.

Her sweeps turned the Clayarks' own brains against them. She used their own energy to stimulate sudden, massive disruptions of their neural activities. The breathing centers in their brains were paralyzed. Their hearts ceased to beat and their blood circulation stopped. They died, almost literally, as though they had been struck by lightning. Or as though...

Teray frowned. "You know," he said after a while, "your way of killing Clayarks isn't that different from the way we Patternists kill one another."

"It's not different at all," she said. "You just focus differently to kill Clayarks. You focus directly on the Clayark's body—his brain—instead of focusing on his thoughts."

"But... Then why do they teach us in school that you can't kill a Clayark the same way you kill a Patternist?"

She shrugged. "Probably because they don't know any better. Most Patternist nonhealers don't have any idea why other Patternists die when they hit them in a certain way. And they don't care, as long as it works." She frowned, and thought for a moment. "The focus is everything, Teray. Of course, we can't lock in on Clayarks the way we can on each other. We can't read their thoughts or even sense that they have thoughts, so we can't go after one of them the way we'd go after one of our own."

"What happens if you try—if you focus on a Clayark by sight, or you sense his physical presence and then hit him as though you were hitting a Patternist?"

"What would you be hitting?"

"His head, of course."

"I wouldn't," she said. "You might give the Clayark time to put a bullet through your head. The only people we can hope to kill by just mindlessly throwing our strength at them are mutes and other Patternists. With Clayarks, you have to know exactly what you're doing, and do it just right, or you'll get killed."

"A Clayark wouldn't be harmed at all if you hit him?"

"If *you* hit him—his head—with all your strength, he might have a seizure. But for most people, nothing."

Teray frowned, not understanding but not wanting to question further.

"Feel the wind?" she said.

"What?"

"The wind. There's a pretty good breeze blowing in from the ocean. There's a lot of power in the wind—even in a breeze like this. Ask Joachim. His House uses windmills. It doesn't usually seem like much power, though. Not until you find specific ways to use it, ways to make it work for you."

"I understand," he muttered.

"If I hit a Clayark as though he were a Patternist, he'd notice it about as much as you noticed the wind before I mentioned it."

"I said I understood."

"All right."

It was the disease again, blocking the way. A disease that protected its carriers and killed their enemies. The disease of *Clay's Ark*, brought back hundreds of years before, so the old records said, by the only starship ever to leave Earth and then return. A starship. A mute contrivance that had supposedly ended the reign of the mutes over the Earth they had sought to leave. That part of history had always held a grim fascination for Teray. His own race had been small then, scattered, disunited, a mere offshoot of the mutes. His people had been carefully bred for mental strength—bred by one of their own kind who happened to have been born with as much mental strength as he needed. One whose specialty had not been healing, teaching, creating art, or any of the ordinary talents. The Founder's specialty had been living. He had lived for thousands of years, breeding, building the people who were to become Patternists. Finally, he had been killed by one of his own daughters—she who first created and held a Pattern.

And meanwhile, mutes had been building a society more intricate, more mechanized, than anything that had existed since their downfall. Some Patternists refused to believe this segment of history. They said it was like believing that horses and cattle once had mechanized societies. But in Coransee's House, Teray had seen for himself that mutes were more mechanically inclined than most Patternists. And mutes were intelligent. So much so that Teray would have enjoyed challenging them—letting them have more freedom, encouraging them to use their minds and their hands for more than drudgery. Then he could find out for himself whether the inventive ability that had once made them great still existed. After all, even now it was the mutes who handled what little machinery there was in Patternist Territory. And the Clayarks, who were only physically mutated mutes, were said to use simple machinery in their settlements beyond the eastern mountains. On the western side of the mountains, however, Clayarks produced nothing but weapons and warriors. At least, that was all Patternists had ever known them to produce. Yet Teray found himself thinking about the Clayark he had talked to. The creature had known Teray's language, at least enough to communicate. But Teray, like most Patternists, knew nothing of the language the Clayarks spoke among themselves. Patternists almost never let Clayarks get close enough to them to hear them talk. Patternists and Clayarks stared at each other across a gulf of disease and physical difference and comfortably told themselves the same lie about each other. The lie that Teray's Clayark had tried to get away with: "Not people."

That night another group of Clayarks drifted near them. Teray and Amber were camped on the beach, back against a hill. Amber had checked the horses over very carefully in what was to become a nightly ritual. She healed any injuries she found before they became serious, seeing to it, as she said, that they did not wind up on foot, and Clayark bait. They saved their rations and ate quail that Teray had mentally lured from one of the canyons in the hills. The Clayarks came into range behind them while they were eating.

Amber, aware of the danger the moment Teray sensed it, opened to offer him her strength. He accepted it, and used it to extend his range.

At once, he could sense the entire group of Clayarks walking toward them, moving through the hills rather than along the trail. Very shortly, those in the lead would see the two Patternists' fire.

Swiftly Teray reviewed the technique he had learned from Amber, then he swept over them like an ocean wave. A wave of destructive power, killing.

The Clayarks had almost no time even to scatter. The group was slightly larger than the one they had met earlier. But Teray handled it in a fraction of the time he had needed to handle the first group. He handled it using less energy, since he was not required to puncture or tear anything. And since he handled it so quickly, he did not need Amber to spot potential escapees for him. There were no potential escapees.

Since he would never see them physically, he swept over them once more to see that they all were dead. There was no movement at all.

He turned to look at Amber. "Satisfied?"

She nodded gravely. "I'll sleep better."

"You ought to pass your methods on to the schools—the one in Redhill, anyway. Save some Patternist lives."

"Healers usually stumble across it on their own. Most nonhealers can't learn it even with teaching. They have to either rip or puncture something, or they have to hit as though at a Patternist. My way is somewhere in between. I was afraid you wouldn't be able to do it."

"You didn't act as though you were afraid."

"Of course not. I didn't want you to try it with the idea that you couldn't really expect to succeed."

He looked at her, shook his head, and smiled slightly.

"Has anyone ever tried to make a healer of you?" she asked.

"They taught me what they could in school. I don't have much of an aptitude for it, though."

"So a lot of nonhealers told you."

"I don't, really. I don't have the fine perception for it. I miss symptoms unless they're really obvious. Pain, profuse bleeding, no one could miss those. But little things, especially things that are caused by disease instead of injury—I can't sense them."

She nodded. "Coransee has that problem, too, but you might not be as bad as he is. If you want to, when we get to Forsyth I'll try teaching you a little more. I think you're underrating yourself."

"All right." He hoped she was right. It would be reassuring to be able to do something better than Coransee could.

Travel grew more difficult the next day. They reached the higher mountains and found that the trail lost itself among them, "washed out, as usual," Amber said. The sectors nearest the coast were supposed to keep it clear, but during Rayal's long illness such work had become too dangerous. Teray and Amber walked and led their horses more than they rode.

On the third day they did no riding at all. There was no longer a beach. The waves broke against rocks and the rocky base of the mountains. They knew the canyons and highlands that they had to travel. These they had memorized. There was no chance of their getting lost. But they were losing time. Walking, scrambling over rock and brush, wondering themselves where they and the horses were finding footholds. The trek was physically wearing, but at least they encountered few Clayarks.

There were deer and quail for hunting, and there were cattle that they left alone. The cattle belonged to coastal sectors whose attention they did not want to attract. On the fourth day they traveled within the boundaries of one of these sectors. They passed through as quickly and carefully as they could. They were farther inland than they wanted to be. At one point they found themselves looking down on a large House comfortably surrounded by its outbuildings, which lay below them in a small valley. They hurried on.

It was while they were passing through this sector that they became aware of a great tribe of Clayarks. They were well out of sight of the House, riding easily now since the people of the sector took care of their part of the trail. But they didn't take care of themselves very well if they let themselves be invaded by so many Clayarks.

The Clayarks were resting—or at least they were not moving. Teray and Amber, their strength united, tried to find out how large the tribe was. They could find no end to it. It extended beyond their double range. Hundreds and hundreds of Clayarks; surely death to any but a large, strong party of Patternists. Teray and Amber detoured widely to avoid any possible contact with them. The Clayarks seemed not to notice, but neither Teray nor Amber could relax again for some hours.

Midway through the journey—on the ninth day rather than on the fifth, as it should have been—they had to leave the trail entirely even though it was well kept and smooth now. Here, it left the coast and ran through the middle of a large sector. It had only gone through an edge of the sector in which they had found the Clayarks. Now, though, the coast jutted out in a large peninsula while the trail continued on due south. Teray and Amber decided to lose a little more time and stay near the coast. They would not follow it as closely as they had, but they would stay well away from the Houses of the sector. As careful as they were, though, early the next day they suddenly became aware of Patternists approaching them on horseback. Seven Patternists.

By now Teray and Amber worked together almost instinctively, worked together as though they had been a team for months instead of days. And they both were strong. It was possible that together they could take on seven Patternists and have a chance of winning—if none of those Patternists was Coransee. Amber spoke as though on cue.

"I don't think any of them is Coransee. I only got a flash of them before I shielded, but I think I would have sensed him if he had been with them."

"People from this sector, perhaps," said Teray.

"No matter who they are, we're fair game."

The two groups met in a grove of trees, Teray and Amber on one side, and the seven strangers—four men and three women—on the other. Teray and Amber sat still, tense, shielded from the strangers, joined to each other only by the link. They waited.

"It would be best for you," said a small, white-haired woman in the center of the seven, "if you came with us without fighting."

The woman's hair was naturally white, not graying with age, yet Teray knew she was old. He could not have explained how he knew. Her age did not show in any definable way. Either she or her healer had stopped all physical signs of its progress, to leave her looking about thirty-five. Yet Teray had no doubt that the woman had lived more than twice her apparent thirty-five years. Which was unusual for a Housemaster—as this woman seemed by her manner to be. Most Housemasters were killed for their Houses long before they reached this woman's age.

"There are seventeen of us," the woman said quietly. "Ten that I don't think you've noticed yet. We're all linked. Attack one of us, and you attack us all."

Immediately Teray and Amber became aware of the ten others approaching from the opposite direction, only now coming within range of the quick scan that they dared to make. Teray looked at Amber. Amber shrugged, then relaxed into a posture of apparent submission. What could they do against seventeen linked Patternists?

"What do you want of us?" asked Teray.

"To pay a debt," said the woman.

Teray frowned. "A debt to whom?"

"Unfortunately for you, young one, to your brother. To Coransee."

"You mean to hold us for him?"

"Yes."

Teray relaxed as Amber had, aware of the tension in the link between them. It was not the tension of a thing on the verge of breaking, but of a thing held in check, ready to spring into action.

"No," said Teray quietly.

The ten approaching Patternists came into view from among the trees. Teray ignored them, and felt Amber turn her attention to them, as he had expected her to. She was fast enough to sense any attack from their direction before it could do damage. Teray spoke again.

"If Coransee catches me, he'll kill me. So I don't have anything to lose in defying you."

"You have the life of your woman to lose. I can see that you and she are linked."

And Amber spoke up: "I'm not eager to have Coransee catch me either. And I'm my own woman, Lady Darah. Now as before."

For the first time, the woman took her eyes off Teray. "I was afraid you might be. Hello, Amber."

Amber lowered her head slightly in greeting. "You're right, Lady. We are linked. We're going to stay linked. And you should be able to guess where we're going to direct all our power the moment you attack us."

Teray picked it up at once, suppressing his surprise that Amber knew the woman. "You know Coransee is my brother, Lady. That should give you some idea of my strength. Unless you're willing to sacrifice your own life as well as the lives of several of your people, let us go."

"I know you're strong," she said. "But I don't believe you could kill me. Not linked as I am with so many. If you think about it, you won't believe it either." She signaled the ten riders now waiting a short distance behind Amber and Teray. The ten began to move forward, clearly intending to herd Teray and Amber before them.

But neither Amber nor Teray moved. Through the link, Teray felt Amber's slight expenditure of strength an instant before he realized what she had done. Then he understood.

Six of the horses approaching them—the six closest—collapsed. Shouting with surprise, some of the riders jumped clear. Some fell. All seventeen Patternists had been expecting an attack on themselves, or at least on Darah. This attack on their horses caught them completely by surprise. Amber finished it quickly, giving them no chance to take advantage of the momentary opening in her shield. Teray was instantly on guard to stop any who tried.

But there was no movement other than that of the fallen riders and their horses picking themselves up from the ground. None of them seemed to be hurt. And as the Patternists remounted, none of them seemed eager to close with Teray and Amber again.

"Lady," said Amber softly, "you may have forgotten my skill, but I haven't. I can kill you here and now, no matter who you're linked with. I can kill you as easily as I'd kill a Clayark. I'm fast enough to do it to at least one person before anyone reaches me."

The woman held Amber's gaze steadily. "You'd die for it. My people would kill you."

"No doubt. But what good would that do you?"

"You're not under any death sentence from Coransee."

"No."

"And ... in view of the favor you once did me, I might be willing to let you go. If you go alone."

"Might you?"

"Do you want to die, Amber?" The woman's voice had become hard.

"No, Lady."

"Then go!"

"No ... Lady."

"I don't believe you're willing to sacrifice your life for him."

Amber smiled. "Yes, you do."

"And," the woman continued over Amber's words, speaking to Teray again, "I don't believe you're the kind to let someone else do your fighting for you."

"Do you think I'd be foolish enough to refuse her help against you and sixteen other people?"

"I just wanted to give you a chance to save her life—since you can't save your own."

"Lady, you choose any three of your people. Keep linked with them and sever with the others. I'll take the four of you on alone. That's the kind of chance I'd like."

The woman stared at him, then laughed aloud. "Boasting in a situation like this. You're his brother all right."

She didn't think he was boasting. In fact, Teray thought, in a way she was boasting—assuring him that he was doomed, yet not attacking. Trying to separate Amber from him.

"Are you ready to die now, Lady?" he asked.

She said nothing but her people looked more alert.

He nodded. "I thought not. I have no more time for you." He whipped his horse forward suddenly, sending it straight into Darah and her companions. He was aware of Amber moving beside him but he kept his attention on Darah and her people. Their horses reacted, leaping aside, startled, half rearing before their riders tightened controls on them, calmed them.

At a canter, Teray and Amber continued on, Teray now focusing his awareness ahead while Amber focused hers behind on Darah and her people. But Darah was not following.

Teray wanted to urge his horse into a headlong gallop, get away before the woman changed her mind. But he knew better. There was no "away" within his immediate reach. Darah could catch him if she wanted to as long as he was anywhere near her home sector. She had allies, no doubt—other Housemasters who would be willing to help her. And she had other members of her own House whom she could command to help her. It was all a matter of how much she was willing to lose to repay her debt to Coransee. He had no doubt that she was willing to sacrifice a few of her people. But apparently her own life was another matter. Now if only she did not find someone else more courageous—or foolhardy—to lead another attack in her place.

They rode on, no longer following their roundabout route, but traveling due south across the peninsula. It seemed better to take the chance of riding through more of the sector now than to take the time to ride around it. If Coransee wanted Teray held, then he was coming after him. He was probably already on his way, and possibly not far behind.

Teray and Amber had not spoken since their escape, but through the link, Teray could feel Amber's anxiety. She was as eager to put the sector behind them as he was. She was grimly alert, her awareness now mingling shieldless with his. Together they covered an area nearly twice the size that either of them could have managed alone.

With only brief rest stops, they rode on through the evening and into the night, not stopping until they had to, until both they and the horses were too weary to go on.

Then they camped in the hills, in a depression too small to be called a valley. It was surrounded by low grassy hills, so that while a Patternist passing nearby might sense them, no one who failed to sense them would see them and have reason to be curious. They lit no fire, ate a cold meal from the rations they had been conserving. Biscuits made that morning, water, jerked beef, and raisins. And for the first time they felt like the fugitives they were.

The night passed uneventfully. They slept as usual since the canopy of their awareness guarded them, once set, whether they were awake or asleep. The next morning they ate a quick skimpy breakfast and rode on early. They were no longer within Darah's sector but they were still close enough to it to be nervous.

A little of their urgency was gone, though. They reassured each other, calmed each other, without intending to. They had hardly spoken since escaping from Darah—had hardly communicated in any way beyond sensing each other's feelings. That had been enough until now. Now Teray was in a more talkative mood. And now he had something to say—perhaps.

"Amber?"

She glanced at him.

"Where did you know Darah from?"

"Here," she said. "The last time I came through, Darah didn't have a decent healer and she looked twenty years older than she does now. Of course forty years older would be more accurate. Anyway, I helped her. I had thought of her as an old friend. Until now."

"An old lover, you mean?"

She raised an eyebrow. "No. All her lovers are men."

He looked at her for several seconds, studying her. Golden-skinned, small-breasted, slender, strong. Sometimes she looked more like a boy than a woman. But when they lay together at night their minds and their bodies attuned, enmeshed, there was no mistaking her for anything but a woman. Yet...

"Which do you prefer, Amber, really?"

She did not pretend to misunderstand him. "I'll tell you," she said softly. "But you won't like it."

He looked away from her. "I asked for the truth. Whether I like it or not, I have to know."

"Already?" she whispered.

He pretended not to hear.

"When I meet a woman who attracts me, I prefer women," she said. "And when I meet a man who attracts me, I prefer men."

"You mean you haven't made up your mind yet."

"I mean exactly what I said. I told you you wouldn't like it. Most people who ask want me definitely on one side or the other."

He thought about that. "No, if that's the way you are, I don't mind."

"Thanks a lot."

"You know I didn't mean any offense."

She sighed. "I know."

"And I wasn't asking just out of curiosity."

"No."

"You risked your life for me with Darah."

"Not really. I know her. She's managed to live as long as she has by gathering a solidly united House, and by avoiding situations that could kill her. She talks a good fight."

"She believed you were ready to die with me."

Amber was silent for a moment. Then she smiled ruefully. "I was. She's not only good at bluffing, but at seeing through a bluff, so I had to be."

"No, you didn't."

She said nothing.

"Stay with me, Amber. Be my wife—lead wife, once I have my House."

She shook her head. "No. I warned you. I love you—I guess we're too close not to get to love each other sooner or later. But no."

"Why?"

"Because I want the same thing you want. My House. Mine."

"Ours..."

"No." The word was a stone. "I want what I want. I could have given my life for you back there if we had had to fight. But I could never give my life *to* you."

"I'm not asking for your life," he said angrily. "As my lead wife, you'd have authority, freedom...."

"How interested would you be in becoming my lead husband?"

"Be reasonable, Amber!"

"I am. After all, I'm going to need a lead husband."

He glared at her, thoroughly angry, yet still searching for the words that would change her mind. "Why the hell did you stay two years with Coransee if you wanted your own House?"

"To enjoy the man, and to learn from him. I learned a lot."

"You needed that on top of what you already had from Kai?"

"I needed it. I didn't want to be just a copy of Kai, running on her memories. Clayarks. Teray."

Her tone did not change as she gave the warning, but through the link he was instantly aware of her alarm. She had reason to be alarmed. She had sensed the edge of a vast horde of Clayarks—perhaps the same tribe that they had noticed days before. They were behind Teray and Amber, approaching from the direction of Darah's sector. It was possible that they had attacked one of the Houses there.

Teray and Amber had come through the hills to finally meet the old coastal trail, but the Clayarks were still in the hills. By the way they were moving, they meant to stay in the hills. There was game in the hills, and there were edible plants. The Clayarks were moving on a course that roughly paralleled the coastal trail. It was possible, even likely, that they would pass the two Patternists without ever seeing them. Unless they changed course. Or unless they spread out more widely. Or unless they had already seen Teray and Amber—spotted them from their higher vantage point before they blundered into the Patternists' range.

That last was a real possibility. Clayarks knew that two Patternists alone would not dare to attack a tribe.

"If they don't go any faster," said Teray, "we can keep ahead of them."

"I'm not so sure I wouldn't rather be behind them. I don't like the idea of their driving us."

"There are supposed to be some mute-era ruins not far ahead of us. Maybe the Clayarks will settle there for a while."

"I don't think so. I've been through those ruins. There's not enough left standing to give shelter to a family of Clayarks, let alone a tribe."

"That's not what one of the stones I studied said."

"Then that stone was out of date. I think people from Darah's sector tore the ruins down because they attracted Clayarks."

That was reasonable. That was why most of the ancient mute ruins had been leveled over the centuries, at least in Patternist Territory. But he was in no mood to be agreeable.

"Maybe they'll stop there out of habit," said Teray. "Whether they do or not, we'd better keep ahead of them."

"Or find some cover and let them pass."

"No. If they get ahead of us and stop, they'll spread out. We'll have to detour back through the hills to get around them."

"Fine. At least we'll be alive to make the detour. If we stay ahead of them, and they decide to come out of the hills, we'll have nowhere to go."

She was at least partly right, Teray knew. She was always right. He was getting tired of it. "Listen," he said, "if you want to stay here and let them pass you, go ahead."

"Teray..."

He looked at her angrily.

"We can't afford this. Only people safe and secure in Houses can afford to let their emotions get in the way of their judgment."

"Do you want to stay behind?"

"Yes. But I won't. I'll stay with you unless the Clayark's start to veer in our direction. If that happens and you still haven't cooled off, I'll stay back and watch you go to meet them."

And that, he thought bitterly, was probably the closest thing to a victory that he would ever have with her. Surely she had done him a favor by refusing to become his wife.

The Clayarks picked up speed a little and more of them came into range. Without thinking about it, Teray and Amber also moved faster. Then the Clayarks began to catch up again.

At that moment Teray realized that he and Amber were being pursued—or driven. Abruptly, there was no longer any question of what they should do. They had to find cover, a place from which they could make a stand. They could not outrun the Clayarks if the Clayarks were aware of them and intent on catching them.

Teray looked around quickly for a place where they could take shelter. Even as he looked, the Clayarks increased their speed again and turned toward the two Patternists.

Clayarks were, if nothing else, magnificent physical specimens. Running without restraint on level ground, they could reach speeds of one hundred kilometers per hour. Of course, they were running on hilly ground now—but they were running.

They were in a kind of flying wedge formation, and they were holding back, not running even as fast as the hilly terrain would allow. Even at their present speed, though, they could run down a horse. Left alone, they could race past the horses, stop more quickly than anything moving that fast should be able to stop, turn, and fire at the passing horse and rider. They had been known to do such things to mutes. More-daring ones had even been known to attack the horse and rider directly, leaping onto the horse's back or neck. They seemed totally oblivious to the risk to their own lives if they saw a chance to kill their enemies.

At a full gallop, Teray and Amber passed a grove of trees, ignoring them because they did not offer enough protection. There were rocks ahead, jutting up from the sand and continuing at irregular intervals out into the surf. Teray could see one place where they seemed to be high enough and wide enough to give shelter even to the horses. He directed Amber's attention toward it and left it to her to see that they got there. He turned his own attention back to the Clayarks.

With shock, he realized they were in sight. He looked back to verify the impression and saw them first as a line, then as a wave coming over the crest of a hill, far too close behind the fleeing horses.

He began to kill.

The first ones died easily, their legs collapsing under them. Their bodies, impelled by their speed, rolled over and over, tripping those behind them who did not see them in time, causing some to dodge or leap over the sudden tangle of bodies.

There was a sound like a baying of hounds, and the formation broke. Hundreds of howling Clayarks scattered, put distance between one another, some speeding up, some slowing, many keeping to the other side of the hill where they could not be seen, where most could not even be sensed. A few rushed completely out of the hills, speeding toward the two Patternists until Teray cut them down.

The shooting began.

The horses, sides heaving, reached the rocks, outran them slightly, and twisted back as more shots rang out. Teray's horse stumbled and almost fell. He did not realize until he had jumped off that it had been hit. Even then, his attention remained on the scattering Clayarks. He was only peripherally aware of Amber beside it, cursing and apparently healing. It was a Clayark habit to shoot Patternists' horses since shooting Patternists themselves was not as immediately effective. A Patternist on foot was at least a slower-moving target.

Amber controlled the horses totally for a moment, made them lie down in the shelter of the rocks, then pushed them into unconsciousness. That was safest. It eliminated the possibility of their being frightened, or their bolting and being lost. Teray was aware of Amber shifting her attention, turning to help him. Then abruptly her attention was elsewhere.

He needed her strength to extend his range, to reach the Clayarks who had fled back into the hills and who were now trying to approach them, shoot at them from a better angle. They were managing to stay just out of his range. He looked at her angrily.

She was gazing off into space, her mind closed to him except for the link, and she was making no use of the link. He realized suddenly that she was in communication with someone. Another Patternist. Through the link, he received shadowy impressions of her fear, desperation, and hopelessness. Only one person could excite such emotions in her. Coransee.

He turned furiously and swept for Clayarks. He found only a few within his range, and those he killed instantly. Then he snapped back to Amber.

"How far away is he?" He did not want to reach out himself and touch his brother. That would come soon enough. That would come when for the second time he tried to kill Coransee.

"Not far. He'll be here in a few minutes." Amber's voice was soft, faraway. She was still in communication with Coransee. Teray seized her by the shoulders and shook her.

"Cut him off!"

Her eyes refocused on him sharply. She sat still, glaring at him until he let her go.

"If he's almost here, surely you can wait to talk to him."

Her gaze softened. She sighed. "I was trying to bargain with him."

He swept once more for Clayarks, and found none, but was now aware of the larger shapes of several approaching horses and riders. The Clayarks were leaving. Coransee had a party of about ten—ten, yes—of his people with him. Apparently that was more Patternists than the Clayarks thought they could pin down and kill. The shooting had stopped entirely.

Teray sighed and turned his attention again to Amber. "I assume you failed—in your bargaining."

"I think so."

He put an arm around her. "I could have told you you would. But thanks anyway."

"He wants to take you back alive."

"He won't."

She winced. "If we weren't so close, you and I, I'd try to get you to change your mind."

"No."

"I know. We're alike that way. Stubborn beyond any reasoning."

He looked at her for a long moment, then drew her to him. "Look, I want you to stay out of it when he gets here."

"No."

He pushed her away in alarm. "Amber, I mean it. He isn't Darah, to be frightened off. He'll kill you."

"Maybe. But he'll surely kill you alone."

He severed the link with her and almost gasped at the sudden terrible solitude. Solitude had never seemed terrible before. He had come to depend on the link more than he had realized.

"Teray," she pleaded, "please. This isn't an ordinary confrontation. He made you his outsider illegally. You haven't challenged him. You don't want anything he has. He's dead wrong, but he's still going to kill you. Your only possible chance is for me to help."

"I said no. He'll face me alone, without any of his people backing him. That's the way I'll have to face him."

She looked up at the riders now in sight, coming down the trail. "The hell with your stupid pride," she said. "You've forgotten that I don't want to go back to Redhill any more than you do. You'd better link up with me again, because when he hits you, I'm going to hit him. If we aren't linked, one of us is liable to get killed, without doing the other any good at all."

"Amber, no...!"

"Link. Now!"

He linked, furious with her, half hating her, feeling no gratitude at all. Pride. He was trying to save her life.

He stood up to meet Coransee and his people. Amber stood next to him, close enough to make Coransee aware that his arrival had not caused her to change sides. She was the one Coransee spoke to as he dismounted. He came up to them, but his people stayed back, still mounted, apparently watching for Clayarks.

"I don't suppose you persuaded him to submit."

"I didn't try."

"And you're staying with him. I thought you were brighter than that."

"No, you thought I was more frightened of you than that. You were mistaken."

He turned away from her with a sound of annoyance. "Teray... do you really want to die here?"

"I'll either die here or I'll go on to Forsyth. Nothing is going to get me to go back to Redhill with you."

Coransee frowned. "What did you expect to find in Forsyth, anyway?"

"Sanctuary." Coransee would find out sooner or later anyway.

"Sanctuary? For how long?"

"Even if it was only a few months, at least I'd spend them in freedom."

"You'd spend them learning everything you could to defeat me."

"Only because you've left me no choice."

"I left you one very simple choice and you..." Coransee stopped and took a deep breath. "There's no point in arguing that with you again. Whether you believe it or not, though, I really don't want to kill you. Look... I'll give you one more choice."

"What choice?" asked Teray suspiciously.

"Not much of one, maybe. It's just that even with our ancestry, I find myself wondering more and more how much of a threat you could become."

Teray ignored the implied insult in Coransee's words. "Left alone I'd be no threat to you at all. I've already told you that."

"And it still doesn't mean a thing. It's not your promises I'm interested in, it's your potential, and that's something I can only guess at. Rayal would be able to do more than guess."

"You want Rayal to evaluate me?"

"Yes."

"What would happen if he found out that I... that I didn't have the potential to interfere with you?" It was a humiliating question to have to ask. No matter what words he used, he was really saying, "What will you do with me if I turn out to be too weak ever to stand against you?"

"What do you want to happen?"

"I want my freedom!"

"No more?"

"Freedom from you will be enough."

Coransee smiled. "You wouldn't ask me for more, no matter how much you wanted it, would you, brother?"

Teray said nothing.

"No matter. Are you willing to be judged by Rayal?"

"Yes."

"We'll go on to Forsyth, then. We're nearly there and I want to see Rayal anyway. But there is one more thing. Only Rayal's findings can free you. You go to Forsyth as my outsider."

Teray shrugged.

"My property."

"You've captured me."

"Say the words."

Teray stared at him in silent hatred.

"I've wasted enough time with you, Teray. Say the words or face me now."

Say the words and give up any right to sanctuary in Forsyth, should Rayal's decision leave him still in need of sanctuary. Say the words that could later be picked from his own memory and used to damn him. Or refuse to say them, and die.

"I am your outsider," said Teray quietly. "Your property."

Chapter Seven

Time seemed suspended. The thirteen riders rode two abreast with Coransee alone in the lead. Teray and Amber rode directly behind him, still linked, but resting, no longer watching for Clayarks. There were eleven others who could watch. Teray felt his own weariness shadowily echoed by Amber's. They had not let themselves realize how draining the constant vigilance had been, especially during the past twenty-four hours. And to have that vigilance end in capture by the very person they had endured it to escape.

Teray looked at Amber, and read not only weariness but bitterness in her face. He realized abruptly that the bargain that he and

Coransee had made in no way included her. She had fled from Red-hill because Coransee had denied her independence, tried to hold her against her will. And now she was his again. At least Teray had a chance for freedom, but she was caught—unless she wanted to try against Coransee her healer's talent for swift murder. And she had already admitted that she was afraid of him.

Abruptly Teray urged his horse forward to pull alongside Coransee. He could not abandon the woman, could not let her be drawn back into captivity without even trying to help her. She had helped him. The shot rang out just as Teray moved.

Teray felt the bullet's impact so strongly that he slumped to one side, almost falling from his horse. He held on somehow, aware of pain now, growing, but oddly dulled. It was then that he realized that it was not he who had been shot, but Amber.

The link, fulfilling its function too well, had given him so great a share of her experience that if they had been alone he could have been shot too while he was recovering. But he was not alone.

He realized from the alert, intense expressions of the outsiders and women that they were already seeking the Clayark sniper. The party had come to a stop. Teray left the hunt to them, dismounted, and went to help Amber.

She had not fallen. She sat hunched over, coughing blood, fight-ing desperately to keep herself alive. She had taken a bullet through the throat. As Teray lifted her down she seemed to pass out. He felt the limp, dead weight of her and only the link reassured him that she was still alive.

He carried her onto the soft sand of the beach, put her down, and knelt beside her for a moment, wondering whether it would be dangerous to disturb her with an offer of help. Did she need help? A wound like that probably would have killed a nonhealer before anyone could do anything about it. She was not only alive but working to heal herself. Teray felt a hand on his shoulder. He looked up, startled, as Coransee knelt beside him.

"You looked as though you were just about to reach out to her," the Housemaster said.

"To help her. She might need it."

"No. I've seen her badly hurt before. She manages better if she's left alone."

Teray looked at him doubtfully, wondering whether he knew what he was talking about. But the link was no longer transmitting distress. Amber had gotten rid of her pain and she was no longer bleeding either from her neck wound or from her mouth. She seemed in control. Teray decided to leave her alone unless she seemed in trouble again. He got up, went to his horse, and got a clean handkerchief. He wet it from his canteen and brought it back to wipe the blood from her face and neck. Coransee watched him silently for a moment, then said, "Were you speeding up a little just before she was shot?"

"Yes, to talk to you. To talk about her, in fact."

"That's interesting. From what Lias said—she was riding just behind Amber—if you hadn't moved when you did, the bullet would have hit you."

Teray thought about that, and nodded slowly.

"It was probably you they were aiming at. You were lucky."

"Where was the Clayark?"

Coransee pointed inland toward the hills. "He was high and far back, but he waited until you and Amber were almost directly in front of him. I hope they don't have many rifles or riflemen who can make that kind of shot."

"Well, at least now they have one less."

"No. We lost him."

Teray stared at him incredulously. "All of you? You couldn't catch one Clayark?"

Coransee lifted an eyebrow. "That's what I said, brother."

Teray heard the warning in his voice and ignored it. "I don't see how you could possibly have missed him. So many of you..." He thought of something suddenly. "Lord, are you linked with anyone?"

"I'm not, but the others are linked in pairs."

And the range of a linked pair of them would be little better than Coransee's range alone. What good did it do Coransee to have ten people with him if he didn't use them sensibly? Teray found himself glaring at the Housemaster in open accusation.

"Blame?" said Coransee calmly. "What are we doing out here between sectors with the Clayarks, Teray? Why are we here?"

Teray made a sound of disgust. "All right, make it my fault if you want to. But you know as well as I do that you should link up with at least some of your people. You could stand it with a couple of them even though they're not close to you. Hell, you're the one who wants the Pattern. That will link you with everyone." He could see that Coransee was getting angry, but he did not care.

"You know," said Coransee quietly, "I would have stopped you some words back if I didn't realize you were speaking out of your feelings for the woman. But even for that, you've said enough."

Teray looked at Amber and saw that she was breathing normally now. For a while she had hardly seemed to be breathing at all. But she was pulling out of it. The wound was closed already. She was going to be all right. And this wouldn't happen again, because weary or not, he and Amber wouldn't depend on the protection, the watchfulness, of others. They would look out for themselves as before, working together, their combined, extended awareness missing nothing. For days they had traveled safely alone. Now, amid a group of strong Patternists, the Clayarks had reached them. Coransee could not even be trusted to give protection to the people he claimed as his own.

Teray touched Amber's arm and knew that she was aware of him, that she took comfort in his presence. He looked at her silently for several seconds, then spoke to Coransee.

"You're right, Lord, I did speak out of love for her. I... do you intend to keep her?"

"Yes."

"I was afraid you did. If Rayal's findings free me, will you let me buy her?"

"Buy her with what?"

"With service, brother, work. I had planned never to see Redhill again if I was freed. But I'll go back and work at whatever you say if my service will buy her."

But Coransee was already shaking his head. "You're welcome to come back to Redhill, to my House, if you're freed. But she's not for sale." Coransee smiled slightly. "You'd never be able to hold her anyway."

"I wouldn't try to hold her against her will. I want her as my wife, not as my prisoner."

"You won't have her as either. At least not until I'm tired of her. But you'll have the same access to her as any other outsider if you return with me."

Amber opened her eyes and looked at Teray, then at Coransee. She did not speak. Perhaps she could not, yet.

"Of course," said Coransee to Teray, "you can have it all if you decide to stop fighting me. Amber will be the least of what you'll get."

Amber sat up, closed her eyes again for a few seconds, then opened them and stood up. Still without speaking, she walked over to her horse, took down her canteen, then went off several steps to a large rock. She leaned against the rock, kicked aside some sand, and vomited into the depression she had made. When she was finished, she rinsed her mouth, then took a long drink of water. She kicked sand into the depression, turned, and came toward them, eating something that Teray had not seen her take from her horse. Her eyes were on Coransee.

"I'm an independent, Lord." She spoke with slight hoarseness. "I'm an independent because most people realize how much trouble I can cause them if they try to hold me."

"You think I don't, after two years?"

"I think you haven't thought about it enough."

"That sounds like a warning."

"Good. At least you know me well enough to understand that much."

He hit her just as she was turning away. She shielded too late to escape the force of the blow. She fell to one knee, and stared her hatred at him.

"I've taken you into my House," he said. "You belong to me. You don't give me warnings."

"I'll give you this one!" Her voice was a harsh whisper. "Hit me again and you won't have an undamaged organ left in your body!"

Teray came between them. He stepped between them physically, and emphasized the link mentally so that Coransee understood the situation.

"This is none of your business, Teray," said the Housemaster.

"Lord, she's just recovering from a wound that would have killed anyone else. Can't you at least wait until she's rested before you start on her?"

Amber came up beside Teray and said quietly, "Stay out of it, Teray. You've made your deal."

"Keep quiet." He didn't bother to look at her. Both she and Coransee ought to be grateful to him. He was giving them a way out. A way to avoid a potentially suicidal confrontation. Or, at the very worst, he was joining the confrontation and thus making it less certainly suicidal for Amber. "We're one," he told Coransee. "She and I are one. Attacking her is the same as attacking me."

Coransee looked at Teray with mild surprise. "She's worth your life to you?"

"She is." Not that he expected to pay with his life for siding with her. The moment of greatest tension had passed. Now Coransee would find a face-saving way out.

"Has she already agreed to stay with you?" the Housemaster asked. Had Teray succeeded where Coransee had failed?

"No, Lord. In fact, she refused."

Coransee laughed aloud. "Then you're a bigger fool than I thought."

Teray said nothing, stayed where he was. Coransee said to Amber, "Would you let him throw away his foolish life for you, girl? You know I'd kill him."

Amber did not answer.

"You might even have some chance against me since I'm no healer. He'd have none at all." He sounded like Darah.

"Do you really want my life now?" Amber asked softly. "Are you trying to move him out of your way so you can kill me?"

He smiled. "I doubt that that would be necessary. Believe it or not, what I'm trying very hard to do is keep both of you alive."

"Then what do you want from me?"

"For now, a link. I want you to open and let me see what slowly lethal thing you may already have done to my body. Then I want a link that will let me know if you try to do it again. Only that in place of the beating you deserve."

"I'm linked with Teray."

"That's your problem—and his. To keep you from murdering me, I need a link with you. You warned me, after all. Refuse, and I'll have to kill you here and now."

She stared at him for several seconds, then looked at Teray helplessly.

"If you decide to fight, I'll stand with you," he said.

"No."

"We have a chance. Your strength coupled with mine..."

"No, Teray." She coughed and then was still for a moment, as though making some inner adjustment. "Not now. Not unless I have to, and especially not with you. I'm too tired, drained. I might fail you." She hesitated. "Shall I break our link?"

"Break it? No, of course not."

"But you'll be joined with him through me."

"Only incidentally. He won't be able to read me any more than he already does. He and I are too far apart."

"But... he'll be more aware of you. You won't be able to..."

"Take him by surprise? I probably couldn't anyway. Besides, if you want our link broken, you don't have to ask. You can just break it."

"I don't want to. I should, for your sake, but I don't want to. I want you with me."

He only looked at her, loving her, wanting her, knowing that somehow he had to take her from Coransee. As he had to have his own freedom, he had to have her.

She turned away from the intensity of his gaze and he felt a flickering of fear in her. Fear of him?

A moment later she opened to Coransee. Teray had no awareness of the exact communication that passed between them. That they held private. Only through the link could he feel her fear suddenly expand, grow momentarily to terror, then lessen just as he was about to interfere. It lessened to anger, humiliation, hatred.

Then, as her emotions settled, Teray became aware of Coransee as a part of the link. The Housemaster was an intruder, unwelcome, bringing discomfort to the link for the first time. Teray tried to rid himself of the sensation of being mentally invaded. He knew that Coransee could not reach his thoughts unless he opened. Yet the feeling would not go away.

Teray ran his hand through his hair, wondering how he could ever learn to live with such a sensation. The constant feeling of being watched, spied on, by a hostile presence.

Amber, jaws clenched, caught his hand and held it. Teray realized how much more aware of the sensation she must be. She was linked directly. He was only receiving through her. Through his link, he offered her sustaining strength. After a moment of hesitation she accepted it.

With a start, he realized that she was near collapse. Healing such a serious wound when she was already so tired had weakened her greatly. And despite whatever she had eaten, she was ravenously hungry. He put his arm around her.

"Can we rest here for a while?" he asked Coransee. "You can probably feel how far gone she is."

"Is she?" Coransee glanced at Amber. "Tell him what you were going to do to me."

"What difference does it make? I can't do it now without alerting you ahead of time."

"I said tell him!"

She glanced at Teray, then looked down at the sand. "I was going to try to kill him tonight while he slept. The way we kill Clayarks. It might have worked if I could have caught him completely off guard."

Coransee nodded grimly. "Anytime you want to try your luck, healer, you can face me. But it will be face to face, with both of us wide awake."

She said nothing.

"Now, are you ready to go on or are you too tired?"

"I'm tired, Lord, but I can go on."

Teray started to protest, but the look Amber gave him kept him silent.

"Get to your horses, then," said Coransee. He went away, shouting to the others to mount up.

"At this point," said Amber softly, "I think he would have killed me regardless of the damage I'd do him before I died. Killed me and left me here. He's angry enough to take the risk. He still has the nerve to be outraged when he finds someone else trying to take unfair advantage."

"Would you really have done it?"

"Of course I would have done it. That's why he's so angry—and that's why he's more than a little worried. He's starting to think. He's thinking about how far he is from the nearest healer—other than me. God, I wish I didn't feel so weak!"

"I should have attacked him the moment I saw him."

"You haven't given up, have you?"

He looked at her, startled. "Of course not."

"Good. Because I think he's planning something for you. I got something from him while he was snooping through my thoughts. Not much, but it was hostile, and it was against you."

"That's not surprising."

"But... I don't know. It feels as though he's lied to you about something."

"About what? Letting me go on to Forsyth, or...?"

"I don't know. I have to think about it more. I'll tell you as soon as I think I've figured it out. Hopefully, I'll tell you before I have to tell him."

Teray glanced back toward Coransee. "You think you'll have to open to him again?"

She smiled tiredly. "If you were him, Teray, would you trust me?"

They traveled for the rest of the day, Teray offering Amber as much of his own strength as she needed. She accepted only until she found in her rations enough readily edible food to steady herself. She refused Teray's offer of his rations.

"If that sniper is still around, you might wind up needing them yourself," she told him.

Teray's awareness of Coransee's link had dulled, was nothing more than an annoyance now. It kept Teray tense, made him do more looking over his shoulder than necessary, but that was just as well. The canopy of his awareness, spread as he had vowed it would be, covered even less of the area around him than it normally would have covered unassisted. This was not only because he had given part of his strength to help Amber, but because he was tired himself. He was worried about the Clayark sniper. If the creature fired again from as far away as he had when he hit Amber, Teray would have no chance of sensing him.

Then there was the possibility that Teray had not had time to think about. The possibility that Coransee had been more right than he knew when he suspected that the Clayark had been aiming at Teray.

They made camp that night against a long rocky ledge. They had not heard or sensed anything more from the Clayarks, but one of Coransee's women had sensed a doe back in the hills and lured it out. After everyone had eaten, Teray called Coransee aside.

The Housemaster had apparently gotten over his anger—or he remained angry only at Amber. He followed Teray away from the group far enough along the rock ledge to be out of earshot. There he told Coransee of the Clayark he had talked to before leaving Redhill.

"Lord, it recognized me," he finished. "It knew me as a son of Rayal."

"So you think the sniper today really was shooting at you specifically, rather than at the handiest Patternist."

"I think it's possible. And I think it might happen again—to either of us. After all, they've captured at least one of your mutes, so they probably know you're a son of Rayal too. They might even know just how near death Rayal is."

Coransee frowned, thinking. "They've captured more than one of my mutes over the years, but that last one... you're right. He would have had quite a bit to tell them. But as for the Clayark who identified you, you did kill it, didn't you?"

"No."

Coransee raised an eyebrow.

"I should have, but I didn't. No excuse."

Coransee looked away, exasperated. "You know, those four extra years in school didn't do a damn thing for you."

Without a word, Teray turned away to go back to the fire. He had delivered his message. Only hours before, Coransee had made a mistake that had almost cost Amber her life. A mistake that the Housemaster not only did not want to be told about, but that he had not yet bothered to correct. He had certainly not linked with Amber to widen the range of his awareness.

"Brother!"

Teray looked around at him.

"Back," said Coransee simply. As though he were calling an animal, Teray thought. Or a mute.

"Brother!"

Teray trudged back.

Coransee leaned against the ledge, relaxed. "You will send the woman to me."

Teray stared at him, speechless, for a moment. "Amber?"

"Of course Amber. You will send her to me."

It was his right since he had claimed Amber. No woman of his House had the right to refuse him. His women could refuse any other man if they wished, but not him. "If you want her," said Teray, "call her yourself." Coransee could have called her without moving from where he was or saying a word aloud. But he preferred to humiliate Teray.

Coransee smiled. "She's less likely to do anything foolish if you send her to me."

"You're the one who's doing something foolish. You're pushing her even though you know that if she attacks you out here, miles from anywhere, you might kill her, but not before she's mortally injured you."

"I'm pushing her all right. I'm pushing you, too, brother."

Teray glared at him, hearing the challenge, ignoring it.

"You stood beside her today and tried to talk her into attacking me. You offered to help her. Do you expect me to thank you for that? If you were anyone else, you'd already be dead. Now go and convince the woman to come to me quietly—unless you want to find out just how badly I can hurt her without being hurt myself."

Teray completely surprised both himself and Coransee. He smashed his fist hard into the Housemaster's face.

Caught off guard, Coransee stumbled and fell to the ground.

Teray turned and, without hurrying, walked back to the group. He was tensed and ready to defend himself if Coransee attacked, but surprisingly the Housemaster let him go.

Amber was not beside the fire. He looked around and saw her preparing their pallet a short distance away from the others against the ledge. He went over to her and she turned to look at him apprehensively.

"I couldn't help feeling some of that through the link," she said. "From the emotions on both sides, I thought you two were going to have it out now."

"He wants you," said Teray tonelessly.

She was on her knees on the blankets, looking up at him. Now, after a moment of surprise, she rose and walked a few steps away and stood with her back to him. The contained fury he sensed in her alarmed him. He went to her and put his hands on her shoulders. She turned and was in his arms.

"I'd like to break his legs and leave him here alive for the Clayarks," she muttered. "I'm sorry, Teray."

"Sorry for what?"

"Sorry to be of use to him against you." Her voice grew bitter. "He doesn't give a damn about me now except to break me. He's doing this to humiliate you."

"I know."

"And that's not all he's doing. I finally realize how he was lying to you. I should nave seen it from the first."

"Yes?"

"He's not taking you to Forsyth to be judged by Rayal. He's already judged you himself. He's taking you to Forsyth to kill you. He's as wary of you as he is of me, and he wants someone around to heal any damage you might do to him. Meanwhile, he'll make do with just humiliating you."

"You interpret the little you got from his mind to mean all that?"

"Yes. And it fell right into place. I know him, Teray. I know how he lies. You should, too, by now."

"But he could have killed me back at Redhill."

"Why should he have? You were still being a good, respectful outsider. Still doing as you were told. There was always the chance that you might come to your senses and submit. But then you had to go and run away—to Forsyth, yet, and with me." She took a deep breath, slowed down. "Well, think about it. I admit it's guesswork, but I couldn't be more positive that I'm right. If you decide you agree with me, you'd better start thinking about what you're going to do."

She bent to pick up a blanket. He caught her arm. They straightened, facing each other.

"You haven't said it all," he told her. "There's enough anxiety coming through the link to tell me you've left out something important."

Without speaking she severed the link.

Solitude came to him jarringly. "Why did you do that? What's the matter with you?"

"You want me to stay linked to you while I'm with him?"

Understanding, Teray grimaced. For the second time that day, their extreme closeness made the link a handicap. "All right," he said. "You had reason to break the link. But you didn't break it soon enough. I know something else is bothering you."

"It's personal," she said. "My business."

From anyone else, that would have been enough to stop him. But he knew her better than he had ever known anyone else. He did not believe she really wanted him to stop.

"Tell me," he said quietly. He was still holding her arm and she wrenched away from him.

"You're as big a fool as I am," she said. "Looking for more trouble when you've already got plenty."

"What have you done that you consider foolish?"

She gave a short, mirthless laugh. "It's only my timing that's foolish, Teray. I decided that I wanted a child by you. And since I didn't know how long we'd be together, I didn't want to wait."

For a moment Teray's surprise left him without words. Finally, "You mean you're pregnant now?"

"Oh yes. And believe me, I wouldn't have told you if Coransee hadn't already found out. He realized it when he made me open."

"But you've opened to me and I haven't seen..."

"You don't snoop the way he does. It's practically an art with him. Open to him and he lifts your whole life."

"He's the last person who should know." Teray frowned. "Hell, he has the right to kill it if he wants to—since he claims us and he hasn't given us permission to have a child."

"It's barely a child yet. It's only a few days old—just a ball of cells growing."

"You should have told me. I can't understand why he hasn't killed it already."

"I haven't let him," she said. "Because the way things are going, I wasn't sure you'd be around to replace it."

Teray winced. "That's encouraging."

"Just don't let him get you to Forsyth."

"How did you keep him from killing the baby?"

"I let him see how determined I was to have it. He decided to let me wait until we get to Forsyth, too."

"He told you he would kill it in Forsyth?"

"No, he withdrew without comment. He withdrew in that special way of his that means, 'Later.'" She sighed. "I think he only wants to kill it out of vindictiveness—because I refused to have a child for him."

Teray frowned. "I should let you know that I'm not ignoring the warnings you're giving me about Forsyth."

"I didn't think you were. You don't have to say anything more about it."

"Good. And I want you to know that I consider protecting an unborn child a responsibility for two. If Coransee reads that in your thoughts, fine."

"I'd feel the same way," she said softly, "if you and I had talked about it ahead of time. If we had both decided that it was a reasonable responsibility to assume at a time like this—which it isn't."

"No, it isn't." He hugged her and suddenly found himself smiling. "And I wouldn't have asked it of you until we were a lot more secure. But I'm glad you did it. Why did you refuse to have his child?"

"He waited too long to ask me. He waited until I had gotten to know him."

Teray laughed softly. She had given him a kind of victory. Not a large victory, but one he could savor. One that Coransee's humiliations could not destroy. And the child would be a living link between them even if Teray was unable to convince her to stay with him. Or it would be a part of him that survived even if Coransee succeeded in killing him. But he did not want to think about that last. Living suddenly seemed more important than ever. Living and keeping Amber and the child alive.

"Teray?"

He looked at her, knowing that she was about to leave him.

"What did you do to Coransee a while ago? I felt him almost lose consciousness."

He told her.

She smiled a very small smile, kissed him, gathered up a blanket, and went to Coransee.

Chapter Eight

Amber returned to Teray before breakfast the next morning. She was quiet and withdrawn. She seemed to relax a little when he asked her to link up again. But through the re-established link he could feel her smoldering anger.

"Did he make you open again?"

"Yes." The anger flared for a moment.

"Are you all right?"

She did not answer.

"Is the child all right?"

"We're both all right... for now. I have to go back to him tonight."

Now Teray felt anger of his own. "If he's alive tonight."

"God!" she whispered. "Don't tell me anything."

"I don't know anything to tell you. I'm just waiting for my chance. He has to know that much already."

"He does. He knows everything I told you last night. He wasn't even surprised when he read it—and he didn't deny any of it. Look at him."

Teray looked toward the main group and saw Coransee standing encircled by his people. He was talking to them, and though Teray could not hear what he was saying, Teray felt suddenly apprehensive.

"We now have eleven enemies instead of just one," said Amber.

"Is he linking with them?"

"No. That's our edge. It wouldn't do him any good to link with them. He can't use a link for anything but an alarm. He's just ordering them to watch us. If one of us attacks him they're supposed to sit on the other one. That way, we can be almost sure that whichever one of us takes him on alone will be committing suicide. He'll be sure of taking someone with him even if he gets killed."

Teray nodded. "I can't blame him. That's what I'd do."

"*You* wouldn't hold free people prisoner and put yourself in the position of having to do it."

"Why can't he use a link with them—at least some of them—to borrow strength? I know they're not close to him, and it wouldn't be very pleasant, but he should be able to stand it. I could."

"If I had to," said Amber, "I might be able to take a few of them myself. But Coransee can't. He's too close to succeeding Rayal."

"What does that have to do with it?"

"He can't take strength from anybody until he can take it from everybody. I was with him the last time he tried, and I can't tell you in words how close he came to losing control. He almost made a grab for the Pattern."

"Almost provoked Rayal into killing him, you mean. Rayal isn't going to give up his power a day sooner than he has to."

"That's just it. When Coransee and I were on better terms, he told me he would try to snatch the Pattern from Rayal if he weren't so sure of having it handed to him soon. But to get killed trying to snatch it away now would be worse than stupid."

"All right, so he can't use his people in the way they'd be most effective. All that means is that I'll have to fight him in the way I intended to from the first. Alone."

"Either you will or I will."

"I will, if for no other reason than that there are two of you."

"It doesn't matter much," she said.

He frowned at her, surprised. He had expected an argument.

"If you kill him, well and good," she said. "But I can feel that even you don't think much of your chances. And if he kills you, he'll still claim me. He'll kill our child and then he'll have to kill me. I'd rather be dead than be his property anyway."

She wasn't just angry, he realized. She was bitter and resigned. Her last sentence reminded Teray of what he had said when Michael asked him whether he could ever accept Coransee's controls.

"Listen," he said softly, "if I can't kill him, I'll cripple him. I'll hurt him as badly as I can. I'm not as quick as you are at that kind of thing, but I'll do what I can to soften him up for you. If you're able to break free of his people... you'll have an advantage." He wondered what the chances were of her breaking free of ten Patternists. They had to be far worse than his chances of killing Coransee. "I'm sorry," he said.

"Sorry for what?"

He did not answer. Their eyes met in understanding.

"He'll be watching you," she said. "Be careful."

As it happened, though, Coransee, like everyone else, was kept busy enough watching for Clayarks. The Clayarks were apparently closing in for the kill.

At least one sniper was with the Patternists constantly—sometimes more than one. The creatures kept out of sight, traveling through the hills. And they kept out of range—just out of Teray and Amber's combined range. It had occurred to Teray that one of the reasons Coransee still permitted him to link with Amber was the unusually wide range of their awareness. That and the knowledge that no other linked pair was as anxious about Clayarks, after what had happened the day before.

The group had come a short distance inland, crossing a small peninsula. In the clear air, they could see the ocean in the distance as they rode over a slight rise. There were Clayarks in the hills alongside them, firing uselessly. The Patternists had become used to them. But as the Patternists reached the top of the rise and looked down at the land and the vast expanse of ocean, a single deeper, louder shot thundered out.

One shot. Teray knew nothing more than that the sound seemed to have come from ahead of them, and that neither he nor Amber had been hit. He snatched more strength from her, reached, stretched, extending their combined perception as far as he could ahead of them, sweeping a wide area, finding and killing a single Clayark. There was only one in range.

Teray shifted his attention back to the Patternists and realized that they had stopped. Coransee had dismounted or fallen from his horse. He was kneeling on the ground, Amber approaching him, others dismounted, going toward him.

Teray swung down from his horse quickly and strode over to the Housemaster.

"I'm all right," Coransee was saying to Amber. "I'm fine. Even I'm healer enough to handle this." He turned sharply as Teray approached. For a moment they stared at each other. Teray assessing the damage with his eyes alone. His mind was suddenly tightly shielded. Coransee said softly, "Try it, brother, and the Clayarks will make a meal of you."

Teray relaxed slightly, cautiously. Coransee's wound was not serious. The bullet had only torn through the flesh of his shoulder. He was not incapacitated mentally, not forced to give large amounts of his attention to keeping himself alive. He was no more vulnerable for his wound.

"You would have done it," said Coransee with surprise. "If you had come up and found me fighting for my life, you would have finished me off."

"As you would have finished me in the same situation, brother," said Teray softly. "I learn from you. And you have no idea what a good teacher you are."

Teray met Coransee's eyes levelly, but he was shaking inside with reaction to what he had almost done. And he was shaking with anger—anger at himself. He had been too obvious, in too much of a hurry. If Coransee had not turned and spoken, Teray might have made a fatal error. Inexperience. Never in Teray's life had he stooped to attacking a wounded person. He was surprised now at how ready he had been to do it. Coransee had indeed been a good teacher. But Teray found himself a little ashamed of having learned this particular lesson. He would do it again if he had the opportunity. But he wouldn't learn to like it.

Coransee seemed to read his emotion. The Housemaster smiled. "I see you surprised yourself too," he said. "You're shedding your school morality quicker than I thought. I'll keep that in mind." Coransee turned from him and began healing his wound.

Teray glanced at Amber and saw that she had been quietly surrounded by Coransee's people—just in case. Frustrated and angry, Teray went back to his horse and remounted.

"Where do you think you're going?" Coransee asked, looking up again.

"I killed the Clayark who shot you. I want a look at the gun he was using."

"Stay here."

Somehow, Teray controlled his temper. "Brother, by the sound of that gun, it wasn't the kind that the Clayarks usually use against us. It was something special, and if we leave it where it is we'll be hearing from it again." As Teray spoke, Amber went back to her horse, watched but not stopped by Coransee's people.

"You too, girl," said Coransee. "All this concern over a Clayark rifle."

"No, Lord," said Amber. "Actually, I just want to get away from you for a while."

Coransee stared at her coldly. "Go with him then. Be my alarm in case the gun gives him foolish ideas. Be my alarm and my eyes." He looked at Teray. "But don't even think about trying to get away again."

Without answering, the two urged their horses forward, away from the group.

"I should have followed through," said Teray. "Even though he was ready for me. It has to happen soon anyway."

Amber said nothing.

"It will be harder than ever now." He looked at her. Her face was too carefully expressionless. "Whatever it is, say it."

"Just something you should be aware of."

"Yes?"

"You made a good kill just now, but you went after the wrong animal."

Teray frowned and turned to stare at her with sudden realization.

"I've never known you to move faster than you moved just now," she said. "You took strength from me, you hit the Clayark—nobody even knew what you had done until a couple of seconds after you'd done it. Now if you had forgotten about the Clayark and hit Coransee..."

Teray shook his head miserably. "I was responding to the Clayark," he said. "Not thinking, just responding. I don't think I could have moved as quickly if I had thought about it."

"I know. And he's not going to give us the chance to try it again, you can depend on that. The minute we get back to him, he's going to break us up. No more link."

"If he does, the Clayarks are liable to finish him for us. None of his people can handle Clayarks as well as we can."

"Maybe. Or the Clayarks might kill one of us. We're only two days from Forsyth now. If I were him, I'd take my chances with the Clayarks."

They came upon the Clayark sprawled on the side of a low hill, his rifle lay beside him. They did not touch the weapon. Patternists had learned through bitter experience that Clayarks often booby-trapped their rifles just before using them—set them to inject a little recently taken saliva into the fingers of unwary Patternists. This could be done with nothing more than a few well-placed wood or metal splinters. Kept warm and moist, the Clayark disease organism could live for a few moments outside a human body.

Teray and Amber only observed that the rifle was not the usual Clayark weapon, as Teray had thought. It was heavier, and doubtless more powerful. Neither Teray nor Amber had seen one like it before. Mounted atop it was a telescopic sight that had already proven its usefulness. In the past, Clayarks had rarely used such things. But then, in the past, Clayarks had not shot Patternists from nearly a kilometer away with rifles.

Either the long period of Rayal's illness had given them time to improve their weaponry or they were simply bringing out their best guns—and their best marksmen—to kill two of Rayal's sons. Probably both.

"What shall we do with the gun?" said Amber. "Burn it?"

"Scorch it, you mean." Teray stared at the polished wood of the rifle's stock. "There's not much more than grass around here to start a fire with. Mostly green grass."

"The gun has three bullets left in it."

Teray probed at the rifle where it lay, and sensed the three remaining bullets. He nodded. Then as Amber covered it with the driest grass she could find, Teray reached down to Coransee. He did not want contact with the Housemaster, but it was necessary. He found Coransee waiting for them, apparently finished healing his shoulder.

You're going to hear shots, Teray sent. *It will be us destroying the gun. Warn the others.* He was carefully open enough so that Coransee could see that he was telling the truth—that open, and no more.

Coransee returned wordless agreement.

Teray brought his attention back to Amber and saw that she was ready. She lit the grass, then both she and Teray took cover down the opposite slope of the hill.

There, while Teray kept watch for Clayarks, Amber saw that the tiny fire did its work. As the fire heated the metal of the gun's receiver, Amber extended her perception into the metal itself and observed minutely the reaction of the metal to the fire—how it changed as it heated. She claimed later that she had never examined an inanimate object so closely before. But she seemed to have no difficulty doing it. She observed the quickening motion of the molecules of the metal. And once she had observed it, understood it, she could control it. She could intensify the heat of the metal to a point beyond the ability of the tiny dying fire. For a moment she sweated, concentrated on doing the unfamiliar thing. Then the three cartridges exploded almost simultaneously.

The rifle leaped into the air with a roar. If fell to the earth in two pieces, receiver blown open, stock and barrel completely separated. The pieces landed heavily on the body of their Clayark owner.

Teray and Amber went down the hill to where they had left their horses and found that Coransee and the others had ridden forward to meet them. Immediately Coransee gestured Teray up beside him. He spoke as they rode.

"You know you're going to have to pay for what you did, don't you?"

"Almost did."

"Oh, you did enough. However clumsily."

"What do you want?"

"The woman has told you what I want. I saw it in your mind when you called to me a few minutes ago."

Teray looked away from him in silent defeat and desperation. As careful as he had been, Coransee had read him—had read him as easily as he had that first time months before on the day Teray left school.

"Break the link, brother."

After a moment, Teray obeyed and dropped back silently to his place beside Amber. Everything Coransee did made Teray more aware of how little chance he had of surviving a fight with the Housemaster. He had let himself hope, let himself forget. Coransee might make even quicker work of him this time, because this time the Housemaster would be out to kill instead of only to subdue.

Teray would die. Then Coransee would turn his attention to Amber. Eventually she would die. The embryo growing within her would die. Painfully, Teray considered giving in, submitting to Coransee's control. It was not something he would do to save himself. Could he do it for Amber's sake? He had not done it for Iray's, and Iray had been his wife. He thought about it, head down, perception indrawn, not caring at this point whether the Clayarks shot him or not.

No. No, that was stupid. Dying by a Clayark bullet would be the same as dying in combat with Coransee. Amber would still be left to the Housemaster. In fact, even if Teray submitted to Coransee's controls, Coransee would still be free to kill Amber. Teray would be of no more help to her than Joachim had been to Teray. Submitting would solve nothing even if he could have done it. And he couldn't have. He couldn't.

Amber.

What could he do to help her, beyond trying to cripple Coransee? And with ten Patternists restraining her, how could she get to Coransee if Teray did manage to cripple him?

He looked at her, then looked away. She was watching him. She was beside him, watching him, yet he had never felt so cut off from her. He could not link with her or speak openly to her. And tonight, against her will and his, she would again share Coransee's pallet.

Teray turned his thoughts away from that quickly. In that direction lay fury, recklessness, death. And he realized now more than ever that to be of any help at all to Amber, he had to find a way to keep himself alive. If there was a way.

Teray found himself thinking about Rayal. Journeyman Michael had promised Teray sanctuary if Teray managed to reach Forsyth on his own. How much of a difference would it make to Rayal if Teray reached Forsyth not on his own, but in tow, the acknowledged outsider of Coransee? Not a successful runaway, but an outsider. How much did Rayal care about either of his two strongest sons? He was the one man who could surely take Teray from Coransee if he wanted to. But would he want to? Apparently he had all but openly designated Coransee his heir. That was contrary to the law of succession, but who was going to force Rayal to obey the law? And if Rayal had chosen Coransee, why would he now oppose Coransee over Teray? But then, why should Rayal have offered Teray sanctuary at all? Would it be worth Teray's while to trust Rayal, go on to Forsyth, giving up hope of leaving a crippled Coransee for Amber to kill? If only he could reach Rayal and find out before he arrived at Forsyth. But he did not know Rayal. He had never had any communication with him, and never recorded within his memory the knowledge of anyone who had. That meant that he could not call Rayal as, for instance, he could call Coransee or Amber. It was possible that Amber had met the Patternmaster on her last trip to Forsyth and could share her knowledge of him with Teray. But Teray did not dare to ask her. Thus, there was only one way for him to reach Rayal. One illegal way.

Through the Pattern.

Since the Pattern connected each individual Patternist with Rayal, in theory, any Patternist, however lowly, could use it to contact Rayal. In fact, though, the use of the Pattern for communication was restricted to Housemasters, Schoolmasters, Rayal's journeymen, and Rayal himself. Rayal, of course, could use it whenever he chose, but Housemasters, Schoolmasters, and journeymen were permitted to use it only to report a Clayark emergency. Lately Rayal had chosen to ignore their emergencies. It was possible that he would also ignore Teray's. He might even punish Teray for misusing the Pattern. But Teray had to take that risk. Had to take it soon—that night. Forsyth was getting closer.

That night when everyone was bedding down, Amber stole a few moments from Coransee and came to sit on Teray's pallet. She said little. She simply took Teray's hand and held it. The sensation was much like being linked with her again. Teray could feel her begin to relax. He could feel himself relaxing. He had not realized how tense he was.

Then a woman named Rain came over with a message for Amber. "He wants you."

Amber winced, got up, and left. Rain stayed a little longer.

"I was who he spent most of his nights with before we caught up with you," she told Teray. "You don't look any happier about being alone than I am."

Teray looked up at her and forced himself to smile. It wasn't hard. She was a beautiful woman, well-shaped, smooth-skinned, with a long mane of black hair hanging loose down her back. Another time, under other circumstances..."I don't like it," he said. "But it's best. I'm too surly now to be anything but alone."

"Are you that tied to her?" Rain smiled and sat down where Amber had been. "Give her a few minutes and she won't be thinking about anything but him."

"Rain." Teray held on to the shreds of his temper.

"So it seems only fair that you should have someone else to think about too."

"Rain!"

She jumped, and looked at him.

"Get away from me."

She was not accustomed to being refused. She flushed deeply and muttered something that was probably insulting, though Teray hardly heard. Then she stalked away angrily. Beyond being glad that she had gone, Teray did not care. Without moving, he closed his eyes and focused his awareness on the Pattern.

He had been lying on his back, looking up at the stars. Focusing on the Pattern now was like shifting to view another night sky within his own head. A mental universe. Other Patternists were seen as points of light constantly changing in shape, color, and size, reacting as individual Patternists changed their thoughts, their emotions, their actions. When a Patternist died, a point of light blinked out.

Teray, seemingly bodiless, only a point of light himself in this mental universe, discovered that he could change his point of view without seeming to move. He was suddenly able to see the members of the Pattern not as starlike points of light but as luminescent threads. He could see where the threads wound together into slender cords, into ropes, into great cables. He could see where the cables joined, where they coiled and twisted together to form a vast sphere of brilliance, a core of light that was like a sun formed of many suns. That core where all the people came together was Rayal.

Because Teray was doing something he had never done before, he first had difficulty understanding that the sphere of light was not a thing that he had to travel to, but a thing that he was a part of. He could not travel along the thread of himself. He was that thread. Or at best, that thread was a kind of mental limb, a mental hand that Teray discovered possessed a strong instinctive ability to grasp and hold. Teray grasped.

And instantly, he was grasped.

He struggled reflexively, uselessly, for a moment, then forced himself calm. He was not being hurt or even roughly handled. He was simply held in a grip that he knew he could not break. Something was done to him. He was disoriented for a moment, then he lost his focus on the Pattern and found himself channeled through to Rayal as though to a friend—as though he had simply reached out to the

Patternmaster. And he was no longer held. He could break the contact if he wished.

The Pattern was again clear for emergency calls. Teray waited, giving Rayal access to his thoughts so that the Patternmaster could see and understand the situation quickly. It seemed to Teray that Rayal examined his thoughts longer than necessary, but there was nothing he could do about it. He was in no position to rush the old man. Finally, though, he became aware of Rayal sending.

Things have gone too far, young one.

Too far?

You're going to have to face him.

You mean you won't give me sanctuary? Not even for... Teray caught himself, stopped the thought. But Rayal guessed what his words would have been anyway.

Not even for the time I have left? That's right, young one, I won't give you sanctuary for even that long. It wouldn't do you any good.

It would keep me alive! Me, Amber, our child. I'd have time to learn the kind of fighting that they don't teach in school.

You've had time.

In Coransee's House! Do you think anyone there would dare teach me what I need to know?

Rayal gave a mental shrug. *You've learned enough.*

I've learned nothing! You offered me sanctuary through your journeyman. Why are you turning your back on me now that I've almost reached you?

You know why. I offered you sanctuary if you could make it here on your own. Obviously, you couldn't; you were caught.

That doesn't have to mean anything to you if you want to help me.

It means a great deal. Especially since if you hadn't been caught, you would probably have been killed by Clayarks. Don't you think I had a reason for making your sanctuary conditional—for making it a thing you had to earn?

Teray was beginning to understand. He had been tested, and as far as Rayal was concerned, had been found wanting. That apparently made him not worth bothering about.

Can you... will you help Amber? he asked. *I'll let myself be brought into Forsyth, fight him there, if you'll give her sanctuary.*

No.

The thought was like a stone. There was nothing more to be said. Teray could feel the old man's absolute inflexibility. Teray shot him a wordless obscenity and broke contact.

Rayal was old and sick and useless. He had not fulfilled his responsibilities to the people for years. Teray was not really surprised to find him unwilling to go a little out of his way to help only one person. Especially when he might be helping that one to defeat Coransee. Teray still could not see why Rayal had bothered to offer sanctuary at all. Why even waste time testing Teray when he had already chosen Coransee to succeed him?

Teray sighed, opened his eyes, and looked around the camp. Apparently no one had detected his communication with Rayal. The camp was as it had been before Teray closed his eyes. He closed his eyes again, resolving to sleep one more night, live at least part of one more day before he challenged Coransee. He would not ride into Forsyth with the Housemaster. He would not give his life away. Tomorrow perhaps the Clayarks would give him another chance at Coransee. If they did, he would make good use of it this time. But whether they did or not, no matter what it cost him, he would do his best to spare the people the burden of Coransee's leadership.

Chapter Nine

The next day Clayark snipers harassed the Patternists from the moment the Patternists broke camp. The snipers kept well out of the Patternists' range and fired their rifles more to keep the Patternists on edge than to kill. It was possible that Teray's kill the day before had made them cautious. Which was just as well since Teray could never make such a long-distance kill now, alone.

Only once did the Clayarks become careless. A trio of them lying in wait let the Patternists get too close. Coransee spotted them first. He killed all three almost before Teray was aware of them— certainly before Teray could take advantage of Coransee's momentarily diverted attention.

Or rather, Coransee injured all three Clayarks.

Surprisingly, he fought Clayarks in the way Teray had before he'd learned Amber's way. He killed by imitating the action of a bullet and damaging Clayarks' vital organs. But he did it with blinding speed. He jumped from one mortally wounded Clayark to another, working as quickly in his way as Teray or Amber could have in theirs. Coransee's Clayarks took several seconds or even several minutes to die. But once he wounded them, they were helpless. His method denied the merciful quick death of Amber's, but it was just as effective.

The Clayarks apparently took Coransee's kill as a warning. No more of them came into range. They stayed well back and made noise. There seemed to be more of them now, shooting their guns at odd moments, sometimes singly, and sometimes in such large numbers that they sounded like a battle in progress all by themselves.

The Patternists' horses were skittish and had to be controlled more closely than usual. The Patternists themselves were skittish, first wearing themselves out seeking what was beyond their reach, then resolving to be content with what they could reach and assume that they were safe. But of course they were not safe. They could not know when the next Clayark with a special rifle would announce himself by killing someone.

The land around Forsyth had once contained a huge population of mutes. Mutes who had lived packed together in great cities. Clusters of the buildings left over from those cities still stood, in spite of centuries of Patternist demolition efforts. Nowadays, as Rayal conserved his power and kept himself alive, Clayarks did not just frequent these ruins. They gave up their wandering and lived in them full time. The Clayarks who had been harassing Coransee's party picked up local support. A young outsider named Goran—who happened to be riding directly behind Teray—had his horse shot from under him. Another special rifle. The sniper got away.

Amber could have saved the horse, but Coransee ordered it abandoned. He was in a hurry. He ordered Goran to ride with Lias, the woman with whom Goran usually paired.

As the group rode on, Teray saw Amber turn and look back. He realized that she had reached back and killed the wounded horse. He found himself wondering whether Coransee would have abandoned a wounded Patternist as easily as he had abandoned the horse. Why not?

The thought bothered Teray enough so that amid a nerve-shattering but otherwise ineffective volley of shots, he rode close to Amber and spoke to her.

"Keep your eyes open. I have a feeling we're going to have to take shelter sooner or later. And we're not going to have time to look around for it when we need it."

She nodded. "You think they're going to try to pin us down, then?"

"I'm sure they are. They know by now that we're not a linked group. We can't just reach out and send all of them to the hell they believe in. They want Coransee and me." He had told her about his talk with the Clayark. "And they know they're numerous enough now to take us—along with any other Patternists they can reach, of course."

"If you're right, they must have an ambush planned somewhere ahead."

"Either that or they're just trying to work up enough nerve to come and get us. It won't be easy for them even though we aren't linked. An awful lot of them will die whether they get us or not."

She said nothing for a long moment. Then finally, "There are some ruined buildings ahead. Just around the bend. No Clayarks inside—no sign of their having been inside recently."

Teray probed ahead and found the ruins. "Good. That's the kind of thing we'll need. I'll look too. It might be better to use your eyes, though. You'll need all the rest of your awareness for the Clayarks."

"I can manage both."

He glanced at her. She probably could with her healer's propensity for poking around inside and outside of things. Fine.

A moment later, as they rounded a bend, they came within sight of the ruins Amber had spotted. These were just the shells of a cluster of buildings. They were ahead of the Patternists and farther inland, away from the trail. Roofless and half demolished as they were, they could provide shelter.

The shooting had died down a little now. Most of it seemed to come from behind them, where there were hills and trees for cover. Most of the land before them now was flat and empty, covered only by tall, slowly dying grass and an occasional tree. The territory around Forsyth was semiarid. Redhill was lush and green all year, but now, in late spring, this land was turning brown.

A few yards away from the Patternists on one side was a sheer drop of about five meters. Beyond that was a slender ribbon of sand, and the ocean. The Clayarks could not shoot from that direction. In front of the Patternists and to their other side there was little cover beyond the dying grass—and the buildings, of course. But they were definitely empty. It looked as though the Clayarks would have to wait until the Patternists turned inland toward Forsyth. Not until then would there be more hills—the low hills that surrounded the sector itself. Teray could feel a general relaxation in the group.

The shot caught everyone off guard. Coransee's horse stumbled and went down. Amber's horse reared, out of control for a second, and the next shot went through Amber's left hand. Teray, fearful that she would be shot again, ignored the fallen Coransee and whipped out in search of the sniper. He could not find the creature, but he did discover the place from which the Clayark probably had fired. It was a dark round hole in the ground. Teray traced it down with his perception and discovered beneath the ground a network of tunnels. Doubtless they were ancient mute structures, dangerous now, even partially collapsed. But obviously the Clayarks had found them usable.

Coransee's horse was dead, a bullet lodged in its brain. The Housemaster took Amber's horse and ordered Amber to ride with Teray. They rode only the short distance to the ruins, though. It was time for a rest stop, and Amber needed a protected place to repair her shattered hand. Teray needed a protected place too—to do what it was certainly time for him to do.

He sat down beside Amber on the grassy floor of the building shell. She had chosen a spot as far as she could get from the others and began to repair her hand. Her injury bothered him because healing it would leave her weakened. She had to be strong if she was to have any chance of finishing Coransee—if he left Coransee in need of finishing. On the other hand, he could not tell her to get ready, that he was about to attack. Not while there was still the possibility, however slim, of surprising Coransee. If she had been still linked with him, she would already know, and her emotional reaction would alert Coransee—and the fighting might already be over.

"I came over here to avoid spoiling anybody's lunch," she told him. "You won't like this either, but stay anyway."

"Won't like what?"

She opened her mouth as though to answer, but instead made a kind of wordless exclamation. "There," she said.

Teray's eyes were drawn automatically to her wounded hand where it lay in her lap, covered by her other hand. He looked at it, then back up at her quickly, in surprise.

"What did you do?" It was a foolish question. He could see what she had done. Her left wrist now ended in a smooth pale cap of new flesh. The thing that had been her left hand lay shriveled, detached in her lap.

"It was ruined," she said. "I had it doubled into a fist when the Clayark fired, and the bullet hit at just the right angle to destroy it." She held up the severed hand. It was literally nothing more than dried skin and bone—a claw. A misshapen claw with at least three of the fingers held on only by shreds of dried flesh.

"Looks like something mummified," said Teray.

"I took everything I could use from it before I shed it. I'll have another fully regenerated in about a month. If..." She shrugged.

If she lived another month. He was grateful to her for not finishing. "So long?" he asked quietly.

"It won't be that long. Not when you consider that it's not the only thing I'm growing." She smiled slightly.

He did not return her smile. He found himself staring at the smooth, new cap of skin. It was easier to try to figure out how she had done such a thing than it was to think about the things she kept saying. "I'll get you something to eat when it's ready," he told her. He wanted her to eat and be as strong as she could. Coransee's people had located and lured in several wild rabbits. They were preparing now to roast them.

"That's all right," she said. "I'm not very hungry. In effect, I just ate my hand."

He grimaced, both repelled and pleased. However she had managed it, she had kept her strength. She could fight.

She looked at him silently for several seconds, then looked away. "You have an edge," she said quietly. "You're a latent healer. I'm sure of that now. Your teachers were either completely incompetent or too far from you in the Pattern to be able to work effectively with you. Or maybe they were just afraid of all that raw new strength that you could have accidentally killed them with."

"Wait a minute," he said. "What are you talking—"

"I don't have time to say it slowly, Teray. You're untrained so I don't know how much good your talent will do you. But he has almost no healing ability. You saw how he killed the Clayarks?"

"Yes, but..."

"What you learned easily, he can't learn at all. He's tried."

"Amber..."

"I'm sorry. I couldn't help realizing that you were about to go after him. And of course, he knew the moment I did. He's coming now."

Her last words echoed Iray's months before, when he had fought Coransee for the first time. He looked around, concealing sudden fear, and saw Coransee striding toward him. He spoke to Amber quietly. "All right, it doesn't matter. But you get out of here. Wait your turn."

"I don't want a turn."

He touched her face. "I'll try to see to it."

She left, glaring at Coransee as she passed him. She was with her ten guards before they realized that they were on duty.

"I thought you'd be ready sometime today," Coransee told Teray.

Teray considered getting up to face him, then rejected the idea. If he stood, he would have to waste part of his attention keeping his feet. He leaned back against the building wall. He was tightly shielded, as ready as he could be.

"Did you really expect Rayal to help you?" asked Coransee softly.

Teray held his face expressionless. He was almost used to Coransee invading his mental privacy by now. "If you knew I had called him, why didn't you attack?"

"Why should I have? Only someone who had spent all but the last few months of his life in school would believe he could get help by calling on Rayal."

Teray hit him.

The blow, not one of Teray's hardest, bounced off Coransee's shield. Teray struck again, testing the strength of the shield. It was

like pounding with his fists against a stone wall. He remembered
with longing the muteherd Jackman's eggshell shield.

Coransee hit back, rammed Teray's shield, not testing but trying
at once to demolish. Teray's shield withstood the blow.

Teray realized already that neither he nor Coransee would be
pounded into defeat in the usual way. Something more was needed.

Teray swept his perception through Coransee's brain as though
through the brain of a Clayark.

For an instant, Coransee frowned, seemed disoriented. But he
was recovering himself even as Teray swept again. Somehow he
deflected Teray's second sweep. Then abruptly he struck back.

As quick as Teray's sweep had been, the Housemaster almost
caught him unshielded. And that deflection...

Safely shielded, Teray tried to understand what had happened.
It was as though he had tried to land a physical blow and had had
the blow blocked by his opponent's arm. It was not like running
against the solid wall of a shield. No Patternist could lay a mind
shield around his physical body. But apparently a strong Patternist
could strike out with part of his strength to deflect attacks against
his body. An attack that could be sensed could at the same time
be deflected. Teray thought he understood. A second later Coransee
tested his understanding.

Coransee struck at Teray's head. For a confused instant, Teray
thought he perceived a physical object flying at him. A fraction
later, he knew what it was, and used his new knowledge with fear-
inspired accuracy.

Without understanding quite how he knew, Teray realized that he
had just avoided—or at least postponed—a cerebral hemorrhage.
Coransee was unwittingly teaching him to defend himself. If only
he could learn fast enough.

Teray contracted the muscles of Coransee's legs savagely.

Before Coransee could stop himself, he fell screaming to the
ground. He had been too busy guarding the vital parts of his body.
He had not realized what agony his legs could give him.

And before he could shut that agony out, Teray hit him again—
hit at what had to be a weakened, unattended shield.

And smashed through! He had a foothold.

Instantly Coransee forgot his legs and slashed at Teray.

Teray hit back hard, hit again and again. He was a man in armor battering a naked man. He had won. Surely he had....

Coransee slammed him back, hammered at him as no shield-less Patternist should have been able to. Teray fought with savage desperation, unable to believe what was happening. The naked man was beating him into semiconsciousness.

Finally, Coransee tore Teray loose from his hard-won foothold. Tore him loose, held him, and continued to batter him. There was no longer any question. Coransee was stronger.

The Housemaster broke through what was left of Teray's shield and began beating Teray in earnest. Now Teray was the naked man.

Pain.

Teray could not think. He was ablaze with agony. He lashed out blindly. The old way of killing Clayarks—Coransee's way: the large artery just where it emerged from the heart.

Coransee had been foolish enough to relax his defenses. After all, he was winning.

For all his speed, he could not reestablish them in time. Teray ruptured the great blood vessel.

Coransee's attack collapsed. But even as he lay on the ground clutching his chest, trying to prevent himself from bleeding to death, he took his revenge.

Teray found himself suddenly disoriented. His head hurt. His head was exploding. He tried to reach up, clutching it between his hands. One of his arms would not work. He was going to be sick. He managed to turn his head so that he did not vomit over his own inert body. His mind was still working, still aware. In spite of the broken blood vessel in his brain, he was still conscious. He could still fight.

With his last strength, Teray swept through the struggling House-master's brain. Coransee had no defense now. He was completely occupied with his injury. Teray swept over him again and again, leaving himself no strength to keep his own body alive. He was kill-ing both Coransee and himself, but his awareness had deteriorated to such a degree that he did not realize it. He realized only that he could not hold on to consciousness much longer. That he must do as much damage as he could while he could.

He did not know when Coransee's body went into violent convulsions. He did not know when Coransee's muscles contracted so violently that they snapped one of the Housemaster's legs. He did not know when Coransee bit off a large piece of his own tongue. He knew nothing until just before he lost consciousness completely. Only then did he realize that he had won. Coransee was dead.

Teray opened his eyes to a vast expanse of clear blue sky. It took him a moment to see the ragged walls of the ruin and realize where he was. He was weak and tired and ravenously hungry. He tried to remember what had happened.

Then it came back to him and he sat up abruptly. Too abruptly. He would have fallen back had Amber not been there to help him. She had come from nowhere, kneeling beside him, steadying him.

"It's over. You're all right. Eat."

There was food. Roast meat from somewhere. He stared at it. "What...?"

"Rabbit, remember? We are as encircled by wild rabbits as we are by Clayarks."

He had been out for a while, then. They had had time to cook. That was to be expected. Coransee had all but killed him. He flexed his right arm—the one that hadn't worked the last time he had tried to use it—and moved his right leg. Both moved easily. Satisfied, he settled down to eating roast rabbit and fresh biscuits and drinking a great deal of water. He ate in silence for several minutes, concentrating only on the food. Finally, he spoke. "He is dead, isn't he?"

"Of course."

"He earned it."

She said nothing.

"I should be dead too. You saved me."

"Healed you."

"Did the others give you any trouble?"

"Not after they saw that he was dead. Two or three of them wanted to stop me from helping you but I convinced them not to."

He raised an eyebrow questioningly.

"They're still alive. They're probably going to give you trouble."

"I can handle them now that Coransee is dead." He looked around for Coransee's body. She read his glance and pointed past the clusters of waiting outsiders and women. Just beyond a ragged edge of wall, he could see two outsiders working at something, digging a hole, a grave.

"No," he said quietly.

Amber looked at him.

"The Clayarks will be at the grave the moment we leave. He's freshly killed. They'll gut him and eat him the way we did those rabbits. I'm not going to give any Patternist to them."

"What, then?"

"Burn him. Burn him to ashes." He looked at her. "Can you see that it's done thoroughly? Are you strong enough after your hand?"

She nodded.

The Patternists had gotten wood for their cooking fire from a pair of ancient dead trees behind the ruin. Now they took more of the wood, and made a funeral pyre for the fallen Housemaster.

The woman, Rain, had washed smeared blood from Coransee's face and closed his eyes. She had straightened his body on its pyre and wept over him. Now, as he burned, as Amber saw to it that he was completely incinerated, others wept too. Teray watched them impassively for a few moments, then walked away. There was something missing. He had hated Coransee. He had never been more pleased at another person's death. Yet...

The mutes would have made a ceremony, a funeral. Mutes were ceremony-making creatures. Patternists had left such things to them for so long that there were almost no Patternist ceremonies left. For a funeral, ancient words would have been said, and the body consigned to the earth with quiet dignity. Even Patternists who thought no more of mutes than they did of draft animals attended such ceremonies with respect. They had become the due of any Patternist or mute who died—a time for friends, husbands, and wives to pay last respects. The ten who had belonged to Coransee, who now belonged to Teray, would have appreciated it.

Amber came to stand beside Teray. "It's done."

"All right."

"What are you going to do?"

"Get us out of here as soon as they've buried the ashes."

"While you were unconscious, they asked me which of us would lead them—you or me."

Teray turned to look at her, his expression cautious, questioning.

She smiled. "Would I have saved you if I wanted them that badly? You know they're yours. His whole House is yours."

"Did you ... did you want it at all?"

"A House like that? If you had been anyone else, Teray, you and Coransee would have burned together."

He shuddered, knowing she meant it, knowing that he was alive only because she loved him. Not for the first time, he realized what a really dangerous woman she could be. If he could not make her his wife, he would be wise to make her at least an ally.

"I'd give you that House if it weren't so far from Forsyth," he said.

She raised an eyebrow.

"I don't want you that far away from me if I succeed Rayal."

"I think you will succeed him, but..."

"If I do, it will probably be in spite of whatever Rayal can do to stop me. But look, if it happens, I'll try to find a Housemaster in Forsyth who's willing to make a trade—move to Redhill. If I can't, I'll give you any help you need to establish a new House in Forsyth."

"You've decided I'm going to settle in Forsyth."

"At the very least, you're going to stay in Forsyth. After all, I'm offering you a bribe."

She laughed, as he had intended her to, but did not give him an answer, exactly. "Do you realize we're linked again?" she asked.

That startled him. He could see at once that it was true, but he had not been aware of linking with her. He could not recall when it had happened.

"I was healing you," she said. "I wasn't shielded, of course, and you just caught hold."

"I don't remember."

"You didn't know what you were doing. You were just returning to a familiar position. I didn't mind. Frankly, I was glad to have you back. If you wind up in Forsyth, one way or another, I'll get a House there."

He kissed her. She had put him in just the right frame of mind for the other thing he had to do. He went over to the cluster of outsiders and women who stood watching as Coransee's ashes were covered with earth. When that was done, he spoke to them.

"Come back into the building and sit down," he told them. "We have one more thing to do before we go on."

They obeyed silently. Some of them, Rain in particular, clearly resented him, but they had seen him kill their Housemaster in a fair fight. Custom said they should lower their heads and accept him as their new Housemaster, unless one of them wanted to challenge.

"We're surrounded by Clayarks," he said. "If we go on through them the way we have, someone will be killed. Instead, I intend to kill the Clayarks. All of them. Now." The ten Patternists understood him. They began to look apprehensive. "I need your strength as well as my own for this," he continued. "I want all of you to open and link with me."

Immediately there was protest.

"You don't have any right to ask that of us," said a man named Isaac. "Even if we could be sure you knew what you were doing, that would be too much."

Teray said nothing, just looked at the man.

"We hardly know you, and you're asking us to trust you with our lives."

"Your lives will be safe with me."

"You say. Even Coransee never asked this of us."

"I'm not asking it either."

Isaac glared at him for a moment, then glanced out to where the ashes of Coransee were buried. Finally he lowered his head.

"Lord." It was Goran who spoke. There was no hostility in his voice. "Lord, we are all far apart in the Pattern. Are you certain that anyone other than Rayal *can* bring us all together?"

"I can." He was surprised to realize that he actually was as confident as he sounded. He had never gathered such a widespread group before, yet he had no doubt that he could do it, or that he should do it. "Open to me," he said. "It will be easier on you if..."

"You don't know what you're talking about!" Rain. Teray had expected to have trouble with her. "You think you can do what he could because you're his brother? You think you're as good as he was?" She was standing up now, and shouting. Teray spoke to her quietly.

"Sit down, Rain, and be quiet."

"You're nothing compared to him, and you never will..."

She was much stronger than Jackman, but getting through her shield was not too difficult. Very carefully, he pushed her into unconsciousness—that to prevent her from wasting her strength fighting him. He formed a link with her. The unity was not pleasant even while she was unconscious, but he would get used to it.

"I understand her problem," he told the others. "I realize that some of the rest of you feel the same way. That's why I've been patient. But now I'm through being patient. Those of you who refuse to open, I will force—not necessarily as gently as I forced Rain. Goran?" He had chosen Goran because he knew the young outsider would not refuse.

Goran opened. Beside him, taking her cue from him, Lias also opened. That got things started. It was not necessary for Teray to force anyone else.

Within seconds, he controlled the combined strength of ten Patternists. He had linked, then taken from all ten at once. The exhilaration he felt was something totally new to him. The canopy of his awareness first seemed almost as broad as the sky itself.

Feeling like some huge bird, he projected his awareness over the territory. He could see, could sense, the lightly wooded land dotted with ruined buildings. He could see the distant ranges of hills, was aware of the even-more-distant mountains. The mountains were far beyond his striking range. In fact, they were near Forsyth, still over a day's journey away, but he could see them. He swooped about, letting his extended awareness range free through the hills and valleys. Then, finally, he settled down, and focused his awareness on the Clayarks who formed a wide half-circle around his party. He swept down on them, killing.

Before, with Amber, he had killed dozens of Clayarks. Now he killed hundreds, perhaps thousands. He killed until he could find no more Clayarks over all his wide range. He even checked the system of underground tunnels. When he was finished, he was certain that there were no more Clayarks anywhere near enough to affect him or his party.

Then suddenly Rayal was with him.

You've done well, young one. Very well. But be careful when you let your people go. Release only their strength. Keep your links with them.

What am I being careful of? he asked coldly. *You or my people?* He would never forgive the old man for refusing him help when he needed it so desperately. Rayal picked up his thought.

I don't care whether or not you forgive me, young one. But keep in mind what you told Coransee's people a few minutes ago. I suspect I'm even less patient than you are.

Teray took the hint. *What do you want of me?*

Let the woman know that you'll be unconscious for a while once you let go of your people's strength. Tell her not to try to help you—just to keep your people off you. She did it once. She'll have to do it again. It's a good thing you hadn't taken from her too.

He had not taken strength from Amber because she had obviously been tired. She had done her share for the day, he had thought. Now, obediently, he relayed Rayal's thought to her. Rayal continued before she could reply.

Now let them go. All at once, the way you took them. If you try it one at a time, you might kill the last ones by giving back too much to the first one.

Teray obeyed, let the strength of the ten Patternists snap away from him like a released spring.

The breath seemed to go out of his body. There seemed to be nothing left of him. He sagged, the strength of his muscles gone. The strength of his mind kept him alive, but it did nothing more. He could still understand Rayal's mental voice speaking inside him, but it would be a while before he could respond.

It's never easy, sent the old man. *But the first time is always the worst. Ten or ten thousand, it doesn't make any difference if they aren't compatible with you. You pay for the power you take from them. You pay whether you take it through a few temporary links or through the Pattern itself.*

Can you tell whether the others are all right? Teray could not project the thought. He had no strength for that. But he hoped Rayal would pick it up.

They're fine. Even the one you had to knock out is still all right. They wonder what's the matter with you.

They aren't the only ones.

Rayal projected amusement. *You're fine. Recovering faster than I expected. You'd better be fine. I've stayed alive fifteen damnable years longer than I wanted to, waiting for you.*

In his surprise, Teray could not form a coherent thought.

Surprised, young one? It doesn't matter. As long as you're good enough to succeed me, nothing else matters.

But why would you wait for me? You had chosen Coransee.

Coransee had chosen himself.

But he said . . .

That's right. He said. Of course, he could have succeeded me. No doubt he would have if you hadn't killed him.

But you didn't want him to?

He wasn't good enough, young one.

He was stronger than I am.

That's not surprising. He was stronger than I would be alone—though I never let him know it. But the strength was all he had. That healing ability that your Amber found in you was all but missing in him. She's not the only healer who's tried to teach him.

But why would healing ability be that important to a Patternmaster?

The healing part of it isn't. It's the way a healer can kill. The way Amber taught you. Without that method just now, you would have killed at least three of the people you just took power from. Three out of ten. You would have been punching holes in Clayarks, wasting strength that wasn't yours to waste. Imagine killing thirty per cent of the Patternists in even an average-size House.

Teray winced away from the idea. *Why didn't you tell me? Why didn't you tell him? If he understood, he might not have had to die.*

I wouldn't have sacrificed one of Jansee's sons if he hadn't had to die. Do you really think anyone could have talked him out of wanting the Pattern?

You could have, perhaps.

Young one, me least of all. Think! The only thing that kept him from attacking me outright to take the Pattern was the belief that it would come to him without a struggle if he waited a little longer.

Could he have taken it?

Very possibly.

Teray sighed, feeling the strength flowing back into his body. He could have opened his eyes if he had wanted to and seen Amber next to him waiting.

I will never gather the strength of the Pattern in my mind again, sent Rayal. *It would kill me. When the need arises next, young one, the Pattern will be yours. That will kill me, too, but at least I'll die alone—not take thousands of people with me.*

But you can't just give it to me. Others will contest....

I will give it to you. You'd win it anyway if there was anyone better than you around, I wouldn't have chosen you. And once you have it, with your health and strength, those who contest will be no more to you than that girl Rain. Remember that and treat them gently. Your only real opponent is dead.

But another healer ... a better healer....

You've got a better healer sitting next to you. And she'll always be a better healer. You won't ever surpass her in healing skill. And she won't ever surpass you in strength. There are plenty of better healers, but no stronger healers. And no weaker healer could survive what you just survived. You have the right combination of abilities.

Teray sighed, opened his eyes, and sat up. He looked at Amber and she nodded slightly.

"I'm receiving too," she said. "He wants me to know."

Teray addressed Rayal. *You couldn't have kept Coransee from killing me, could you?*

No. Not unless I fought him. He had already made up his mind about you—and from his point of view, he was right. You were definitely a danger to him even though at first you didn't want to be. I didn't dare fight him. There was too much chance of his winning. So it was all up to you.

And you couldn't very well tell me without taking the chance of also telling him. Teray shook his head. *You've been bluffing everyone for a long time, Lord.*

Only for the past couple of years. Only since I've become so weak and sick that taking strength from any but the most compatible of my people would have killed me.

Still a long time to bluff people who might have read any slip in your thoughts.

A long, wearying time, the old man agreed. *Hurry and get here. You have no idea how tired I am.*

About the Author

Octavia E. Butler (1947–2006) was the first black woman to come to international prominence as a science fiction writer. Incorporating powerful, spare language and rich, well-developed characters, her work tackled race, gender, religion, poverty, power, politics, and science in a way that touched readers of all backgrounds. Butler was a towering figure in life and in her art and the world noticed. A critical force, she received numerous awards, including a MacArthur "genius grant," both the Hugo and Nebula awards, the Langston Hughes Medal, and a PEN Lifetime Achievement award.

About herself, Octavia E. Butler once wrote: "I am a fifty-three-year-old writer who can remember being a ten-year-old writer and who expects someday to be an eighty-year-old writer. I'm also comfortably asocial—a hermit in the middle of Seattle—a pessimist if I'm not careful, a feminist, a black, a former Baptist, an oil-and-water combination of ambition, laziness, insecurity, certainty, and drive."

Wild Seed, Mind of My Mind, Clay's Ark, Patternmaster
The Classic Series in One Volume
SEED TO HARVEST

Acclaim for the Novels of *Seed to Harvest* and
Octavia E. Butler

"Moving, frightening, fun, and eerily beautiful."
—*Washington Post Book World*

"One of the finest voices in . . . science fiction." —*Denver Post*

"Marvelous . . . Butler's own strength is the individual portrait meticulously painted . . . Butler's books are exceptional . . . The hard edge of cruelty, violence, and domination is described in stark detail . . . real women caught in impossible situations."
—*Village Voice*

"Her books are disturbing, unsettling . . . Her visions are strange, hypnotic distortions of our own uncomfortable world . . . Butler's African-American feminist perspective is unique and uniquely suited to reshape the boundaries of the genre." —*LA Style*

"Superb . . . challenging and visionary."
—*Seattle Times/Post-Intelligencer*

"Well-written, thoughtful." —*St. Louis Post-Dispatch*

"She is one of those rare authors who pay serious attention to the way human beings actually work together and against each other, and she does so with extraordinary plausibility." —*Locus*

more . . .